Heart
IN THE
Field

Heart IN THE Field

Jillian Dagg

Black Lyon Publishing, LLC

HEART IN THE FIELD
Copyright © 2015 by Jillian Dagg

Our books may be ordered through your local bookstore or by
visiting the publisher:

BlackLyonPublishing.com

Black Lyon Publishing, LLC
PO Box 567
Baker City, OR 97814

This is a work of fiction. All of the characters, names, events,
organizations and conversations in this novel are either the products
of the author's vivid imagination or are used in a fictitious way for the
purposes of this story.

ISBN-10:   1-934912-71-9
ISBN-13: 978-1-934912-71-3
Library of Congress Control Number: 2015904556

Published and printed in
the United States of America.

Black Lyon Contemporary Romance

For Pauline and Don – 50 years.

Chapter One

That's him! The man who sparked the idea for her new TV show.

Memories of a girlfriend's brother had provided Serena Brown with a story idea for *Neon Nights.* And this was him! Or at least someone who resembled the guitarist standing on the sidewalk. His thick black hair straggled to his shoulders from beneath a straw hat and he swayed his body to the rhythm of the music.

"It's a hot September afternoon in Toronto. Hot. Hot—"

Serena punched the radio off. The last thing she needed, while trapped in traffic with dazzling sunshine beating down on the roof of her black Porsche, was a motor mouth deejay informing her that it was hot. She knew it was hot. She switched the air-conditioning to high and felt icy waves of air ruffle her hair and penetrate her navy blue linen suit.

The man moved on, walking through the crowds with a slow gait. Serena had done a lot of research on the homeless for her new show. The first segment, beginning the following week, was *City Streets.* Excitement formed in the pit of her stomach. She couldn't wait for the new show to begin. It was a huge career move for her.

Before she drove forward a few feet to the bus in front of her, she looked at the man again. He stopped to beg money from the people rushing from the subway entrance, and she felt guilty sitting here in her expensive air-conditioned car.

Her cell phone secured on the car's dash board rang. Recognizing the number of the caller, she connected the call. "Hi, Don."

"Where are you?" Don Steel asked.

Serena tapped her fingers against the steering wheel. "Stuck in traffic half way between the new school addition mother just opened and the rear of a bus that happens to have your grinning mug on it."

"The new *Steel Yourself for our News* ad?"

Don might be well into his fifties but he was such a kid. "Yes. The 'Steel Yourself' ad. You, wearing jeans and a yellow shirt covered in green elephants. Instead of silver, your hair is blond."

"That agency never gets it right. But does it look good?"

Serena smiled. Don always said the same thing but he never changed ad agencies, his brother-in-law owned the one he used. The ad also made him appear younger than he was. "It looks fantastic."

"Great. Now, look. The reason I called you, Serena, did you hear the news?"

"You know I never actually listen to the news."

"This time you will. It's about you. Well, really it's about John Duncan. But it affects you."

Serena's stomach tightened and she tasted the salmon sandwich she'd eaten after the school opening ceremony. "What's he done?"

"You know he hasn't been feeling good. It seems he's got some sort of a syndrome. A fatigue thing."

"Poor John."

"I agree. Poor John. But *Neon Nights* starts next week and he has to rest and take it easy for at least six months."

"You mean he won't be doing the show?" Serena heard the alarm in her voice. No show. No job.

"You've got it."

"Hell! Damn!"

"To put it mildly. But don't panic yet. I have a plan. Have you ever heard of Nick Fraser?"

Serena pictured a dark-haired man possessing a precise broadcasting accent. It was the accent she remembered the most because it made him sound like her famous journalist father, Stuart Redding Brown. "Yes. I've heard of him. I've seen a few of his news reports."

"Good. He came to me in April wondering if there was something for him at Steel this September. There was nothing for him then, but this might be his ticket. He's a strong journalist who likes to get his teeth into controversial stories. So I called him in London, and wouldn't you know it? He's flying in today. Can you get here by six o'clock to meet him?"

"I suppose I can." Serena wasn't at all certain she wanted Nick Fraser as a co-host. "Are you sure he's the one?"

"No. But he's a start. We don't have much time. If we think he's going to work out, all we have to do is superimpose Nick over John in some of those promo spots. What do you think?"

"I think field journalists like to stay in the field. Studio work bores the pants off them." Serena spoke from experience with her father.

"Nick doesn't want to be in the field. He wants to be here. I'll see you in Studio Three at six."

She heard Don hang up. He never argued once he'd made up his mind about something. She disconnected her own phone. The bus moved forward about three feet. She moved her car with it, figuring, at this rate, she might or might not make the appointment with Nick Fraser.

•

With his black leather jacket hooked over his shoulder, Nick strolled to the Steel TV Tower. The hot weather had brought out the shorts and T-shirt crowd, the skateboarders, and opened the patio restaurants. All this provided a holiday atmosphere in the city. And, even though Nick knew jet lag would catch up with him, right now he felt buoyant. He'd been expecting to return home to search for work and now he didn't have to do any searching. He had a job.

Nick spotted the mirrored windows of the Steel TV building and crossed at the next lights. He remembered when the tower had been built by Don's father, Robert Steel, who'd started one of the first news radio stations in Toronto. When Bob had died, Don had taken over Steel and ventured into news television.

Nick entered through the swing doors. The high ceiling in the foyer was painted sky-blue and reflected down on to a white marble floor. The woman with cropped black hair and deep brown eyes at the reception desk asked him to fill out a temporary pass that Don had arranged for him. *If all the women who work here look like her, this might be fun,* Nick thought, pushing the elevator button. The light didn't come on.

"You have to jam your finger on the button," a woman said.

Nick did as she told him and the light popped on. "Thank you."

"You're welcome. This building is getting old, so is the equipment. The elevators are always sticking."

"Warning taken." Nick stood aside to let her enter the elevator. He pushed three and then glanced at her to find out what floor she wanted.

"Five. Please."

He selected the floor and took a more thorough look at her. She was, what a British friend of his would have called, his cup of tea. Golden hair, swept back from her forehead to fall in a smooth bell to her shoulders, emphasized high cheekbones and a delectable mouth. The navy blue suit with the short skirt and thin-heeled navy sandals made her appear model-slim.

The elevator crunched and jerked to a halt. "I see what you mean," he said.

"Scary, isn't it?"

He grinned. "Yes. Have a safe trip."

Nick walked down the long corridor to Studio Three. Before he pushed open the door he thought about the woman in the elevator.

Very nice.

The few technicians lounging around the bank of equipment and screens turned to look at him when he entered. Don Steel was there as well, noticeable in an oversized black and pink shirt he wore with jeans.

Don flashed his bright, toothy grin and came over with his rather springy walk to pump Nick's hand with enthusiasm. "Hi, Nick. Thought you might have been Serena."

Nick tossed his jacket over the back of a chair. "Serena being …?"

Don lifted one of his thick dark eyebrows, a dramatic contrast to his silver hair. "Your co-host, Serena Brown. Didn't I tell you?"

Nick shook his head. "You didn't tell me much at all, past the salary."

Don smiled. "That was the main lure. Serena might be the second."

"I didn't realize I was getting a co-host."

Don's smile faded. "It won't change our arrangement?"

"No. It won't change anything like that. It just hadn't occurred to me that I might be, let's say, sharing the limelight."

"You will be sharing with the best co-host I can provide. She's Stuart Redding Brown's daughter. You know who Redding Brown was?"

"Yes. I do. You're not kidding about this?"

"No way. Redding Brown was her father. And her mother is Reeva Brown-Carstairs, a city councilor." Don rubbed his hand around the back of his neck. "She doesn't admit publicly to being his daughter. So don't mention anything to her. She prefers to go on her own merit, of which she has plenty."

"I won't say a word. All I want is a good vehicle for my work." Nick prided himself on his own distinct, below-the-belt type of journalism. Short, clipped, entertainment news turned him off. He began to feel apprehensive about his new appointment at Steel. He'd free-lanced for the past few years and he was used to being number one. He envisioned there might be a battle on his hands with Don and Serena to remain number one.

Don seemed to sense Nick's indecision. "I promise you'll get whatever you want. Don't worry."

Nick shrugged. Maybe his anxiety was unnecessary. What did it matter if he had to share the fame or fight for his principles? He was home, where he needed to be. That was all that mattered.

Don gave the door an impatient glance. "Where the hell is she? I told her six."

Nick eyed his gold watch. "She still has ten minutes."

"If she doesn't get here soon I'll call her again. She was stuck in traffic the last time I talked to her."

With obvious time to spare Nick let his glance wander around the studio to a set with all black and white props. Nick presumed this was the set for *Neon Nights*, and imagined himself sitting on the black leather sofa with a woman who was Redding Brown's daughter. He realized that he might be putting himself into a situation that tapped into his own insecurity and nervousness. Redding Brown had been one of his journalistic idols. Before his death, Brown had published a book about his life as a war correspondent. Nick trusted *Heart in the Field* was still on his apartment bookshelf, because he knew he would want to read it again after he'd met Serena.

In his more avid, learning-how-to-be-a-foreign-correspondent days, he'd had a brief affair with a seasoned female journalist who'd given Nick the book as a birthday gift. Brown had died when Nick was a kid, but the book had become a bible among the media crowd. Nick had understood why when he'd read it. Brown's philosophy was close to what he wanted to be his own.

Nick remembered a chapter of Redding Brown's book on how he'd felt about leaving home. Nick had been surprised at his own reaction to the writing because it had filled him with unexpected emotion. After he'd finished the book he hadn't forgotten those few paragraphs. He'd made a pact with himself never to put himself in the same painful position as the older journalist. No wife and family. No problems. It was easy enough to accomplish. He'd been trained not to feel much since the day his father had taken him to his first private boys' school and left him alone with a mere handshake. Stephen Fraser had never returned until the year ended. Summer vacation had seen Nick go to a camp. His parents had driven him to a bus and left him with a horde of other abandoned children.

"It's all for your own good," his mother had told him. "You need to be with young people."

But behind closed doors he'd heard his mother complain once to his father: "I was too old to have that baby."

Don stood over him. "What do you think of the set, Nick?"

Nick forced his mind back to the less painful present. "Great."

"Yes indeed. Black and white. The programs will be in color. Should be powerful."

Power, Nick decided, was what he'd given himself by leaving home and forging a career for himself. Was he going to lose some of that power here at Steel, where Don seemed to have complete control and his co-host was to be the daughter of a famous journalist? Had he made the right decision to leave the field? Time would tell, he supposed. Besides, he was only here for one season, six to eight months, long enough to deal with his personal situation. After that he could return overseas and continue to pursue a career dear to his heart, which was the same way Redding Brown had felt.

•

Serena pushed open the studio door, turning her wrist to see that her watch read six o'clock. She had made it on time.

Don waved at her. "Hey. That suit looks good. Nice short skirt. Nice long legs."

Serena grimaced. "Stop it. We're selling news, not sex."

"Sex sells news."

"Sex sells anything," an amused voice added.

Serena's gaze moved to Don's companion. It was the man from the elevator. As she'd gone upstairs to freshen up, she hadn't stopped thinking about him. He'd added a tension in the elevator ride that she wasn't used to feeling with most of the men she knew and worked with.

"This is Nick Fraser," Don said. "Nick, Serena Brown."

She should have known who he was, she thought as she reached for a smile out of the heavy feeling of trepidation she'd been experiencing ever since Don's phone call. "Hi, Nick. I'm pleased to meet you."

His hand clasped hers. "Serena."

The way he spoke her name was like a spring breeze after a long winter. Even so, Nick's voice retained the broadcast smoothness off the screen, a clue to his identity that she'd missed earlier. She now took a good look at him. With his black, vibrant thick straight hair and a distinctive masculine angled face, Nick was almost more handsome than she could bear. Even the faint lesion climbing his cheekbone added a heroic battle scar. He wore not the required black suit, white shirt and black tie John would have worn, but a pair of scuffed sneakers, faded jeans and a burgundy flannel shirt. The clothes fitted his body to show off a taut, physical power without outlining his muscles in a vulgar way. Not only was his voice like her father's, but his eyes were also the same shade of steel-gray that showed little emotion or expression.

Don twisted with a brisk squeal of his rubber soles. "Try the couch on the set with Serena, Nick. Let's see how you work out."

Serena withdrew her hand from Nick's hoping he didn't work out. After all, Nick was what her father would have called a true blue journalist from the trenches. Why would he subject himself to tedious, controlled studio work?

Nick said, "Go ahead."

Serena sat on the couch, her palm sliding against the puckered leather. Then Nick lowered his body beside her, his hip nudging hers. The line of his muscular thigh was inches from her own, his encased in faded denim, hers in sheer hose. She wanted to fidget, but TV didn't allow for fidgeting. Instead, she turned to look at Nick with a smile pasted on her face. He also smiled, and their eyes locked for a second. Tension rose inside her. Sexual tension? She hoped not.

Don had hijacked a camera and was peering through the lens. He waved his arm. "Shift a little to your left, Serena. Turn your head toward Nick a little more. I like that smile. Nick, angle to your right. Acknowledge Serena. Great. Serena, tuck your legs aside. Wow, I'll say it again, I'll say it forever, you've got great pins."

"Cut the crap," Serena mouthed, still smiling, and she heard Nick chuckle. Their eyes met for longer this time, Nick displaying a grin that could disarm anyone who wasn't strong. She realized that she didn't feel very strong this evening. Rather like a lone tall flower in a gale.

"Okay." Don came over to them. "There is an introductory lead-in on the monitor. Let's have a run through to see how it looks."

Don returned the camera to the orphaned cameraman. He talked to the technicians, instructing them on what he wanted. A young girl with fluffy blond hair, wearing jeans and a blue denim shirt, added makeup and clipped on their microphones. Serena noticed that Nick's casual pleasant manner made the girl's face flush a solid red. So he flustered all women the same way, Serena thought. Good. That meant she would soon get over this strained awkwardness with him.

Or would she? Serena felt the glow from the studio lights sprinkle perspiration on to her brow. Nick's subtle aftershave or cologne drifted on the air. He showed no nervousness. Serena's stomach muscles tensed even more. She had to remind herself of her overabundance of studio experience compared to his, although Nick seemed as much at home here as he would in a news report from the middle of a desert.

Nick shifted his body beside her. "Relax."

"I am."

She ignored his raised eyebrow, gritted her teeth, and responded to the floor direction. A bearded technician cued them up. "Three, two, one. On air."

Serena spoke her lines, smiled, and tossed the cue to Nick, who also knew how to act. He was expert behind the camera.

Afterward they watched themselves.

"You are excellent together," Don said. "We'll put together a commercial with the two of you on Friday afternoon and begin running it in every spot we can to bring the viewers in for next Thursday. It'll be a rush, but we can't help it. We might go with the series you worked up with John, Serena. But see what Nick thinks of it first. You guys should meet as soon as possible. He might want to change some things. It's also a plus that neither of you are married nor involved with anyone, because it'll give the show a sizzle to present you as a couple. That doesn't mean you have to go and climb into bed together." He grinned. "But I'd like to see some intimacy radiate from the screen."

Serena was furious. Nick was a given as her co-host, a done deal. There was no seeing how he worked out about this one way or another. Adrenaline pumped through her veins. She knew she had to escape before she exploded at Don in front of everyone. She didn't want Nick as her co-host. He was too much like her father to make her comfortable. He was also too sexy, one of those men who made women lose all of their self-control. She'd spent years perfecting her self-control, on and off the camera. She'd been excited about the debut of *Neon Nights*, and now all she felt was apprehension.

She ignored Nick and said to Don, "I think I'll call it a night."

Don placed one of his big hands on her shoulder. "Hang on. Make sure Nick comes to my soirée on Saturday evening, Serena. Are you free for a party on Saturday, Nick? I throw a bash every year to begin the new season."

"Sure," Nick said. "I have to plunge back into life here. I might as well do it in style."

Serena tried to squirm from Don's grip. "We'll make the arrangements later. Meanwhile, I've got some things to do."

"All right." Don released her shoulder.

Serena stalked to the door. She didn't look back, but she let the door bang shut.

•

Nick heard the door close with more purpose than was necessary and wondered what had happened in the last few minutes to cause Serena's anger.

Don glanced at Nick. "So, what did you think?"

He thought she was the most beautiful woman he'd ever met. He didn't want Don to know that though. "She's very interesting. I'm going to follow her right now to set up our meeting before she leaves." He wanted to make sure Serena's anger hadn't been channeled toward him.

"She's on the fifth floor. The office with the white door down at the end of the corridor."

Nick picked up his jacket. "She has her own office?"

"All my stars have offices. You'll get one, don't worry."

"I'm not worrying. I've got a feeling *Neon Nights* will be a blast."

In more ways than one. Nick was pretty sure Serena was going to cause an abundance of sparks.

Chapter Two

Serena hung her navy suit in the closet of her personal powder room and slammed the closet door. She tugged on khaki cotton pants, a white top, a pair of socks and sneakers, patted off the extra set makeup, then glared at her reflection in the mirror. With rapid angry arm-strokes she brushed her hair. Don had pulled a number on her today.

Okay, so John was ill and they were in a tight spot but Don had intimated that this evening would be a test for Nick. A mere pairing on a sofa for a ten minute clip didn't mean he would work out. She'd had no say in the matter. That's what infuriated her the most. And if she'd had a say in the matter, she would have said no. She didn't want Nick Fraser as her co-host, even if it was for a few months.

A rap at the door made her body stiffen. Still holding her hair-brush, she walked into her office.

Nick Fraser popped his head around the corner. "Located you. This building is a maze."

"Yes. It can be. They supply a map down at Reception."

"That's the truth?"

She made her lips smile. "Absolutely. Steel only occupies a few of the floors. The third floor. The News Room is here, on five. There are more offices on seven. And Don's on ten. He has the entire floor."

"Good for him. So who fills the rest of the space?"

"Advertising agencies and other media-related organizations." She kept the smile for a moment longer. "Don's lawyer is on nine."

Nick strolled closer. "Now that's handy."

He stood in a ray of sunlight, holding his black leather jacket over his right shoulder, and observing her with those metal eyes like her father's, making her feel as if she were under a microscope. As his skin showed no trace of the light film of powder the woman had whisked over his face on the set, it was obvious that he'd popped into the men's room on the way up.

Serena walked back into her powder room, tossed her hairbrush down on the vanity counter and returned to her office. She supposed she had to deal with him.

Nick had hung his jacket over the back of one of her chairs, and was prowling around with his hands stuffed into his back pockets.

Serena sat down behind her desk, which was full of file folders containing all of her previous anchor work. When she'd handed over the spot to Juliette Marshall, correspondence had begun to pour in about the loss of Serena. She'd hoped her popularity would steer the viewers over to *Neon Nights.* Now she thought it might be Nick Fraser who would bring in viewers.

"What's going on?" Nick asked. "You seem angry."

She glared at him. "I am angry. It was a done deal with Don, wasn't it?"

He frowned. "You didn't know that Don negotiated it with me on the phone this morning?"

"I knew he talked to you, but he told me he'd see if we worked out."

"I thought we did."

"We sat on a couch with a fake introduction to read. That's all."

"And we did well. For your information, just so it's fair all around, Don didn't tell me I was to have a co-host until I arrived at the studio."

Whether Don had done that on purpose Serena didn't know. "Would you have turned down the offer if you'd known?"

"No."

"Well, then. What are you upset about?"

"I'm not the one upset. You are."

Was she upset about Nick being on the show, or Nick being who he was, a man who resembled her father? Serena pushed back her hair with both hands. "I'm not upset. I think I'm more in shock. That John's sick, and the show begins next Thursday, and now I'm not prepared like I thought I was. It takes away the excitement."

Nick moved closer to her desk. "I understand that. But I'm here to help and make sure we will be prepared. If you have the first month's programs ready to go, there's no problem. Who's our producer?"

"Cameron Steel, Don's younger brother. He's not as strong-willed as Don. In fact, he's pretty loose when it comes to letting us do our own thing. But he's a good detail man. He's away on vacation until Monday. I doubt if he knows about John yet."

"I'll look forward to meeting him. But he sounds like a plus. I like as much journalistic control as I can get."

She'd never have guessed.

Nick withdrew his hands from his pockets, leaned his hips against her desk and crossed his arms. "Come on. Brighten up. We've got to be positive. This is a great opportunity for both of us. What do you think of Don's vision for the show?"

"I like it."

"So do I, so we're even on that score." He fastened his gaze to hers. "Is this about the intimacy Don wants?"

"He's not getting it."

"Maybe not in reality but we can act. It will draw in viewers."

Serena pounded the desk with her fist. He was frustrating. This entire situation was frustrating. "I'm going to be working, not having an affair."

Nick raised an eyebrow. "Calm down. No one mentioned anything about having an affair." He chuckled.

Serena felt her face grow hot. "I just meant that nothing was going to go on. Nothing."

"You're not going to treat any aspect of this show as fun, are you?"

"You might think this studio stuff is mere fooling around compared to field journalism, but it's not. It's hard work."

"I know it's hard work. But we don't want it to become a grind. We have a new show. We've got a chance at stardom. We have to play to that."

"Then you're just like Don. He plays with TV."

"Successful play?"

"Indeed. But he manipulates careers. His ideas count. He's very forceful. We have to be equally forceful in return."

"I've already figured that out. It means we'll have to make certain we put our own personal stamp on *Neon Nights*. To make it a success we can't leave any holes. We have to come up with material so tight he can't fault it. In other words, we have to take ourselves to the edge. And we have to be side by side on this. If we both have an identical view for the show it will work better. I'm not saying we should agree on everything. But we shouldn't accept any inferior content just because we can't come up with anything better. No hoops for Don to dance through. Okay?"

Nick made John seem like mush. But she had to admit she agreed with him. If Don couldn't fault their presentations, then Don lost control of *Neon Nights* and it was all theirs. "I understand. You have my commitment to the show. I've given up my day job, as it were."

"Which was?"

"I was the afternoon news anchor." She knew for him that was likely considered a very lowly news job.

But he didn't show any disdain. "This will be much more challenging."

"Exactly. That's why I jumped at the chance, even if it is rather like diving into the deep end without knowing what's underneath." She wasn't sure why she was exposing her vulnerability.

"Then we'll have to make sure there are no rocks at the bottom."

His grin was friendly, reassuring. The adrenaline and anger were now gone and her body felt limp and devoid of any energy. She opened her right-hand desk drawer, drew out her purse, and stood up. To reach the stainless steel coat rack she walked around the desk to where Nick was standing. She unhooked a khaki bomber jacket that matched her pants and tucked the jacket over her arm. "I'd better be getting home. It's been a long day."

Nick blocked her vision. Tall and lean, with a hint of a shadow on his hard jaw. "I've come to meet you, to chat about our new show. You can't go home yet. Let's go for a drink. You look like you need something strong."

His eyes were so much like her father's it was uncanny.

"How do you know what I need?"

"Because you might need the same as what I want, a way of calming down from the day. Let's continue this somewhere else." He plucked his jacket from the back of the chair and shrugged his broad shoulders into it.

Serena turned away from him and she heard the rustle of leather.

"Are we going?" he said.

"Yes. My keys." She opened her purse and dug around for her keys.

Nick walked outside and waited while she locked her office door. It was a long walk up the corridor to the elevator, and Serena had to hurry to keep up with Nick's stride. He pushed the button hard, the way she'd shown him, to make the light come on. Serena knew she was going to have to get used to this scene. She and Nick together. In a few months, with *Neon Nights* well underway, she would laugh at her initial jittery attitude. She might even laugh over it one day with Nick. But not tonight.

One thing, he was polite, Serena thought as he let her walk into the elevator first.

"This time I know who you are."

"Yes. You do." But Serena still wanted to run away from him. No way was she going for a drink.

In the foyer they checked out with Joseph, who was the elderly evening security guard. The swing doors opened into a humid, fragrant evening. People strolled around them on the sidewalk, probably reminding themselves that winter in Toronto kept one cooped up inside, and a beautiful calm night in September was a luxury.

"Where's a good place for a drink?" Nick asked.

Serena waved her hand. "You'll find a pub called The Bear's Pause right up the street, across the next block. Everyone goes there."

"Show me."

"It's just up the street. You won't miss it."

He sighed. "Look, we have to spend a great deal of time together. Part of our job is getting to know one another so we can work together. If we don't begin tonight we're going to have problems. Time's too short."

He was right, of course. If she didn't go with him tonight, then she was only putting aside the inevitable. Besides, she wouldn't mind some relaxation before she drove home, even if it was with Nick Fraser. Possibly, as she got to know him, she would discover he was nothing like her father. He might have any number of differences in his personality. He might not even attract her.

"Are you coming with me?" He sounded impatient now.

"Yes."

As Nick strolled beside her, Serena realized how pleasant it was to be walking with a man in the evening. Except Nick wasn't a man she should get interested in. She couldn't handle short affairs, or even long affairs for that matter. She began with good intentions, but she ended up erecting protective barriers that pushed men away. She'd lost someone very dear to her when she was still a child. Her mother had lost a husband she'd loved passionately. And her brother had never known his father. The silent grief in the household had been palpable for years. Stuart Redding Brown's presence had been powerful in their lives. While Serena believed her mother was now healed, she knew her own scars were a mere shell, covering all the anguish. Deep down she still felt a great deal of pain.

Nick stopped beside a pub with outdoor tables surrounded by a white picket fence and pots of flowers. "Is this the place?"

"Yes. It is."

Nick stepped back to let her go in first. Serena walked through the door, feeling as if she were beginning a journey that she might never return from. And the unknown frightened her so much that her insides balled into a knot. Her body froze.

Nick jammed up against her and his hand went to her waist. "You do want to go inside, don't you?"

She turned and he was right there, the leather jacket against her arm, the muscle of his body warm and solid, his fingers splaying over her hip. "Of course."

"Then move, sweetie. There are about half a dozen people behind me, trying to get through the same door."

He couldn't be feeling any of the same sensations she was. What was she doing anyway? He was her co-host. This was a business supper, not a date. Straightening her shoulders, Serena moved ahead of him and forced herself to become the person she was seen to be on TV, a cool, beautiful woman. Not some fumbling, swooning fool.

♦

The pub was decorated with traditional beams across the ceiling and dark paneled walls hung with country landscape photographs and horse brasses. The appealing aromas of the food mixed with malt ale whetted Nick's appetite, making him realize he was hungry. He caught the eye of a pretty waitress and wheedled a booth from her. Soon another young woman was clearing the table and setting it up with fresh placemats and cutlery. A waitress stopped by their table to place menus in front of them. He saw Serena glance at hers and place it down on the corner of the table. "I'll have a salad," she said.

Nick noticed she sat with her body erect. Nervous? No. She didn't look nervous. More like unyielding. Or reluctant. That was it. She seemed reluctant to be with him.

Silence stretched between them as the waitress served their drinks. Beer for Nick, coffee for Serena. She came back a little later to take their food order. He ordered fish and chips and Serena ordered her salad.

Nick drank some beer and looked straight into her unusual dark blue eyes. "I know it's difficult for you, with your co-host changing before the show has even begun. However, this is the way it is. I'm here to stay, for a while. So be reasonable. Help me."

She slipped a lock of her wonderful silky hair back over her shoulder. "I was under the impression I was helping you."

"No. You're not. You're being awkward. We're going to be alone together like this a lot during the weeks to come, so get used to it."

"We won't be alone much. As well as Cam, and others, we have Paul Kryker on our team."

Added apprehension slithered down Nick's spine. "Paul's at Steel?"

"Yes. He's been with us about a year. Do you know him?"

"I've met him."

She raised her eyebrows. "You don't like him?"

"Let's be honest. I'm ambivalent about him. I know he considers himself a high-class photo-journalist, and he is. But in a danger zone he can go to pieces."

"I doubt if *Neon Nights* will put Paul in any danger."

"Exactly. So he might work out just fine."

"But you still sound apprehensive about him." She leaned her arms on the table. "I understand where you're coming from. I called him a videographer when he first came to Steel, and he shot me down. He's a photo-journalist. Not even a cameraman."

Nick grinned. "That sounds just like Paul."

"But he's good. I've been quite impressed. You can't judge him by his past work. He must have learned a few new tricks by now. As we all have in our time."

"If you think he'll work out, then that's okay."

"If he doesn't, Don will soon replace him. Paul knows what he's up against with Don. Don's a perfectionist."

"And so am I. What about you?"

"I like everything in order."

"Which is why you are resenting my intrusion?"

"Truthfully. Yes. I had everything in order. At least I thought it was when I got up this morning. Now the future is cloudy."

He saw her cheeks flush as she spoke and he smiled. "I like honesty. It's good of you to admit that. It's my belief that we have to come down to a certain level with one another to be able to work well together. I'd say we have to form a friendship."

"Friendship is fine with me."

"Good." A friend he would be, but she was still the most beautiful woman he'd ever met.

His meal arrived. He was starving hungry. He doctored his fish with vinegar and lemon, and shook ketchup on to the plate to one side of his chips. He offered the chips to Serena. "Help yourself."

She snagged a chip from the side of his plate. He watched her perfect white teeth nibble the French fry. The action was sexy.

"Have some more."

He turned his plate so that the chips were on her side, and while Serena ate one or two and finished her salad, he polished off the fish. When the plate was empty he pushed it aside. The familiarity of eating together from the same plate seemed to have diluted the combative atmosphere between them. Feeling calmer inside now he'd eaten, he said, "I suppose we should schedule that meeting for tomorrow?"

Serena nodded. "Fine. We can meet in my office at eleven, if you like."

"Great." He finished his beer and summoned the waitress for his check. He added a tip, signed his credit slip, and slipped his card back into his wallet. He wouldn't put this meal in for expenses. He felt that the time they'd spent here in the pub had been significant on a personal level rather than on a business level. This shouldn't be. He wasn't about to make a move on her and give her something else that may turn her against him.

Chapter Three

Serena strolled along the sidewalk beside Nick, her jacket resting over her arm creating a barrier between them.

Nick slung his own jacket over his shoulder. "Sorry I can't offer you a lift anywhere, but my car's still in storage."

Serena couldn't even imagine the heightened intimacy of sitting beside him in a car, especially on a hot, sultry night such as this one. "Oh, it doesn't matter. I have my own car parked in the Steel lot."

"Then I'll walk with you. I have to go home that way."

As it was obvious she wasn't going to get rid of him, she decided that finding out everything about him until he became ordinary might be the antidote for her tension. "Where do you live? Or are you in a hotel for the time being?"

He turned to look at her and she was forced to meet his gaze. "No hotel. I own an apartment I rented out while I was away. Luckily the renter bought a house a few months ago, so it's free for me to move back into. What about you? Where do you live?"

Serena hadn't intended to discuss herself. Although, he would probably find out soon enough where she lived. "I live in West Vale. It's about forty miles north of the city."

"I don't think I've ever been there."

He made his statement sound as if he wanted to go there one day. And he would this weekend. Don lived out that way as well. "It's a very small place. Barely on the map."

"Don't you find it awkward living out of the city?"

"It was a bit tight with the daily afternoon news. Some days if the weather wasn't good, I'd stay in the city. But it should be easier with a once-a-week evening slot." Serena bounced the conversational ball back to him. "How long were you away?"

"Ten years."

"That's a long time. I bet your family are pleased you're home for a while."

Serena noticed a defined hesitation before Nick shrugged his shoulders. "Possibly."

Now she was curious. "You don't know?"

"I only arrived home today. I haven't seen them yet. It's a small family. Most of the aunts and uncles don't live in this part of Canada, so it comes down to mother and father. They live here in Toronto."

"No brothers or sisters?"

"No."

"I have a brother."

Nick stopped walking. "You have a brother?"

She laughed. "Is there a problem with that? He has a recent music degree and a band that's doing quite well. They've just put together an album and are having success with a single download."

"Good for him."

They'd reached the Steel parking lot behind the building and Serena headed for her car. At the car, Nick's lean fingers caressed the smooth surface of the black Porsche in the same way Serena sensed he might caress a woman's skin and wondered what it would be like to be touched by him.

"Very nice. Leased or owned?"

"Owned." She opened her door, tossed her purse and jacket on the passenger seat and slid behind the steering wheel. She inserted the key, strapped on the seatbelt, started the engine and wished she didn't have to roll down the window to talk to him again. She wanted to take off in a spray of gravel and leave him standing there. But she had pledged friendship for the next six months. So she did roll down the window.

Nick squatted to her level and placed his fingers over the top of her door.

"How are you getting home?" she asked.

"I'll walk or take a cab."

"Do you want a lift?" She inquired to be polite, not because she wanted him slouched in the low seat beside her.

Nick straightened. "No. It's fine." He patted the top of the window. "Drive with care."

"I always do," she said. "Good night. Thanks for the salad and the coffee." She waved and drove to the gate.

•

Nick watched the taillights flicker and disappear. He would prefer to be beside her in the car. For a crazy moment he'd wanted to invite her to his place and kiss her until they found themselves naked on his bed. Because he hadn't been with a woman for a long time, or because she really did attract him? A bit of both, he supposed.

It didn't take Nick long to walk back to his apartment. As soon as he was indoors, he tossed his jacket aside and hunted his bookshelves. The book was still there on his shelf, and Nick slipped it out from between the others. He turned it over in his hands and Stuart Redding Brown looked at him.

The cover photo had been taken when the man was young. Brown had wavy hair with sideburns, and wore a beige safari jacket over a black Rolling Stones T-shirt. He'd been a good-looking guy and it was obvious from where Serena had inherited her distinct cheekbones and stubborn chin. She also had the same intense, but sometimes vulnerable mouth. It was the eyes that were different. Redding Brown's were a flat gray, not conveying much emotion. Serena's midnight-blue eyes were like flames that flashed and danced to her moods.

Nick sat down in an armchair with the book and leafed his way through to the photo album section. The only photo of Serena was when she was a baby held in her smiling mother's arms. Mother and Child was written underneath it, probably in Redding Brown's own handwriting. There was no mention of a boy. So was the brother Redding Brown's, or had her mother re-married? Don had told her the name of Serena's mother, but he couldn't remember what it was.

Nick flipped the pages, looking for the section where Brown had mentioned his family and the toll that his career had taken on his personal life. The section was well thumbed, and Nick didn't have any difficulty locating the paragraphs. It was almost as if the book fell open at that point. When Nick read the words he felt the same jerk of emotion as he had so long ago, except now he was picturing Serena. Redding Brown didn't mention his wife and daughter's names, but he'd obviously missed them both, to the point of hitting the bottle and smoking pot, and had, at one time, in what Brown called a 'Mary Jane haze of unbearable pain', considered calling it quits. And he hadn't meant his career and going home. Nick wondered if at the time he was killed the journalist hadn't been quite so dedicated to the conflict he was reporting. He might even have been thinking about his wife and daughter, hadn't watched his back quite so diligently and had made a mistake.

Or he could have been blotto from substance over-indulgence. Or his death wish might have been so strong that he'd found an easy, heroic way for suicide. Whatever Brown's reason, Nick wouldn't mind investigating the death to discover what the exact circumstances had been. Of course Serena might even know. He could merely ask her, and she would supply the information.

Dream on, he told himself, closing the book and putting it aside on the table for further reading. If she hadn't bragged about her father's identity tonight, then she certainly wouldn't be forthcoming about his demise. But he'd love to know more. Not only about the death circumstances, but about Brown's entire life.

Still not feeling tired, even though he should be after traveling most of the day, Nick walked into the bedroom, where he'd dumped his luggage earlier. He got out his laptop computer and set it up in the living room on the desk. Beside the computer he put his tattered notebook. Then, after unbuttoning his shirt and making a cup of instant coffee, which was all he had for the time being, until he was able to grocery shop, he sat down and opened a new folder on his computer. He called the folder SRBROWN. Then he opened a new document. The first words he keyed on to the page were: Daughter—Serena.

•

Serena turned right at the West Vale corner store, and into a side road. She drove up the narrow, tree-lined lane. Feeling relieved to be home, she parked the Porsche in the driveway of her house in front of the garage.

She patted the car on the way to the front door, and murmured, "Nick Fraser was impressed with you." But she didn't think he was very impressed with her. She hadn't acted friendly, even though she'd agreed friendship was what they needed to work well together.

Feeling guilty, and exposed, for this lapse in her personality, she pushed her key into the lock. The people who had built the split-level house on a ravine lot had been transferred to California on business and needed to sell it fast. Serena had fallen in love with the rose-covered trellises, the wooden deck walk-out from a sunroom, and the garden full of perennials. Inside the house there were three bedrooms, three bathrooms, and a finished basement with more comfortable rooms and plenty of storage space. The kitchen, dining room and living room were spacious enough for entertaining.

Serena's next-door neighbor, Ginny Friedrich, had been a great help as Serena settled in. Ginny's husband traveled with a communications company and she was alone a great deal, which was why she had six cats. One of the cats had just had a litter when Serena arrived, and Serena had been forced, by a set of gold eyes and reaching silver-gray paws, to choose a kitten for herself.

Pascal greeted her now by trying to sidle his furry body by her legs as she pushed her way in through the door. She turned on a light and he pattered behind her down the hallway and the two steps to the apple-green and pine kitchen. Serena dumped her purse down on the table, hung her jacket over the back of a chair and squatted down to take him into her arms. He was her baby and she cuddled him to her, thinking Pascal helped her through all sorts of bad times these days. And today had been bad.

When he wriggled away, she fed him, all the time talking to him.

"A terrible thing happened today, Pascal. John Duncan got sick and I've been stuck with a new co-host. His name's Nick Fraser. Oh, Pascal, I'm not sure about this move to nighttime TV. Especially with Nick. You'd like him Pasc, I'm sure. He's good-looking, like you. Very sleek. He sort of stays with a person. Know what I mean? But he's not John. He won't be easy."

Pascal began the serious task of eating his dinner.

"And I felt this intense attraction to him. And I can't have that. It'll wreck my job. So I wasn't exactly pleasant to him. But he's like my father. His heart is in the field. This is just some temporary respite, for whatever reason. He's not for me. Not that he'd want me. So why am I getting all up in the air about him?"

Pascal showed disinterest. Serena smiled and let him be. She would like nothing more than to take a shower and slip into bed, but she knew she couldn't do that yet. She had the meeting with Nick to prepare for in the morning.

Serena poured iced tea and carried the tall glass rattling with ice cubes, to the corner of the sunroom where her computer was set up on a desk. The deck and the lush garden outside the curved windows were in darkness, and therefore weren't a lure, so she turned her attention to the monitor as she opened up her word processing program.

While she waited for the file containing *Neon Nights* notes and script to appear, she remembered when she'd first gone into journalism and how idealistic she'd been then. She had her career planned. She would always report the stories with the happy endings, not the sad ones. She certainly wouldn't go into the field and expose herself to war or horror the way her father had. Although at times she thought she should have gone into the field and seen with her own eyes what had drawn her father there, discovered what drew guys like Nick Fraser there.

Her college professors laughed at her expectations. Happy endings weren't news. Therefore, she'd had no choice but to go with the flow. After a stint at freelancing, Serena landed her first job on a local TV station that wanted the sensational, the fires, the murders, the muggings, the fatal highway crashes. She rode a news van for the station, wearing jeans and toting a video camera. Sometimes she experienced the excitement of the story, the thrill carried her along. But she longed to be in the studio, where she could report the news from a distance.

When Serena saw no chance for advancement in her first position, and when Steel opened its doors from radio to TV, she was accepted into the Steel fold. Steel TV was a news and information station, with an intelligent worldwide slant. Serena had found her slot. Presenting mostly international news didn't give her happy endings, but the events weren't happening in her city, they were happening across the other side of the world, thus there was even more of a distance. Sometimes she even interviewed a visiting dignitary or an entertainment figure to add more human highlights to her programs. She'd become quite a local personality, even though she felt this might be due to her mother's political prominence in the community, and felt her career had gone well.

She hoped everything would continue to go well. This new show was, in Don's words when he first asked her to do it, 'a coup.' She had to remember that. Even if Nick Fraser did mess with her head.

Meeting Nick had scrambled her brain so much that she didn't fall asleep right away, and she was awake for the storm that began after midnight. She watched lightning flash on her wall, then cringed while waiting for the crash of thunder. When it was still again she heard other noises that weren't in this house.

Slamming doors. Raised voices. Giggling laughter. Lusty moans. Her mother crying, "Don't go this time, Stu." The weeping that never stopped.

Some images stood out from childhood. And that was one of them. Those times when her father was home. Nick reminded her so much of her father that she couldn't stop thinking about either one of them.

When the rage of the storm ended, all that was left was the gentle patter of the rain on her wooden deck, but she couldn't go to sleep again. She was out of bed early, feeding Pascal and slipping into jeans and a white Steel T-shirt. As she braided her hair she knew she was keeping herself busy to stop herself from thinking about the list of things she didn't care to think about. That list now had an addition: Nick Fraser.

By nine-thirty Serena had stuffed her briefcase into the car and was on her way to Toronto. She pulled up in the Steel Tower parking lot at ten thirty-seven, hopefully at least thirty minutes before Nick. She wanted to see Don before she met Nick again.

She took the elevator straight to the tenth floor. Don's red-haired assistant, Patty-Jane Barker, sat in the middle of a huge foyer and she called through to Don to let him know Serena wanted to see him.

Serena tapped on the door and entered the office. Even Don could appear small in the luxurious gold and burgundy surroundings.

He gave her a huge grin. "Hi. How's it going?"

Serena pushed her hands deep into her rain jacket pockets.

"Thanks to you, I have a co-host I don't particularly want."

"Ah, but he's good, Serena. You have to see his merit. Come here, with me." Don beckoned her over to his computer. He tapped a few keys. "Look at this. I got the rights to the film clip to show it in the commercials."

Nick's face appeared on the screen and he was relaying a news report. "Pro-government troops." there was a slight lurch of the picture, but Nick continued with his story. Blood dribbled from a wound on his face.

Serena remembered the scar that made Nick appear heroic. She also remembered seeing her father reporting similar stories, with conflict raging around him.

Don paused the video. "Battle scars. Nick won't cave in."

Serena clenched her fists inside her pockets. "You're comparing him to John?"

"No." Don looked sheepish. "But he has got an advantage."

"It's not John's fault that he's ill."

"I know that. But he is, so we have to do what we can to replace him, and Nick's an excellent replacement."

"I hope you're right."

"I'm always right."

Serena laughed and went down to her own office to meet Nick. He was outside her door, hands jammed into the leather jacket pockets, faded jeans hugging his long legs. A large paper cup of coffee stood on the carpeted floor.

He leaned down to pick up the coffee. "You're almost late."

"I went to see Don."

"To yell at him about me, I suppose."

"No. He showed me a video."

Nick chuckled. "Sounds like fun."

She held her key ready to open her office door. "It starred you."

"Yeah?"

She glanced at his scar. "It was a How-to video. Keeping a story going with a bullet wound. Don's got the rights."

He touched the scar. "The main thing was we got the story and the world saw it."

"What about you? Afterward?"

He sipped from the big cup. "I passed out. My team panicked when they saw all the blood, and their clumsy efforts were enough to revive me. But after getting patched up I spent the night re-living the what-might-have-beens. And I have to admit I've relived them quite often."

She thought of her recurring dream about her father when she relived the pain. Did Nick do the same? "Has it made you less brave?"

"I don't think I am brave, but I wanted that story. I believe adrenaline kept me going."

She eyed the big cup. "Or too much caffeine."

He chuckled. "This is my antidote for jet lag. Are we going inside, or shall we conduct our meeting out here in the hallway?"

Serena opened her door and they walked into her office. She placed her briefcase down on her desk and hung up her jacket. Nick put his cup on her desk, also hung his jacket on the coat stand, and rolled up the sleeves of a dark green flannel shirt. Serena forced her eyes away from Nick's strong arms. Obviously colored shirts, jeans and the black leather jacket were his favorite gear. "I've got the script for the first series." She opened her briefcase.

Nick chose a deep leather chair, pulled it closer to her desk and sat down. Behind Serena, heavy rain pounded against the window. She felt stifled in her office with Nick, as if they were the only two people on the entire earth. To make sure that they had a disturbance, she reached for the phone to call Jen, her assistant, to order coffee. Then stopped.

"I can't order more coffee. I don't have an assistant anymore."

Nick sank deeper into the chair. "That's okay. You were right. I'm on a caffeine high anyway."

Serena watched the spread of his muscular legs, the tug of denim on his thighs, and knew why she didn't want him for a co-host. He was far too attractive. She shoved the pages forward. "Have a look at this."

Nick reached forward and lifted the pages. He didn't bother reading much of the first pages. He leafed through them. Serena shifted uneasily in her chair, feeling rather like a kid handing in her first essay to a teacher.

Finally he flung the pages on to her desk. "How far have you gone with this, other than a pretty good title, *City Streets*?"

"We interviewed a number of street people and some politicians. I figure we have enough for three weeks."

Nick shook his head. "It's not powerful enough for the first show. Maybe we can slot it in later in the season, when we've pulled the viewers. But not to begin with. We need something much more exciting. What else did you have on tap?"

"That was it for now."

"You weren't very well prepared, were you?"

He did annoy her no end. She felt her insides prickle. "John wasn't very lively for the past few months. I guess he was ill. I didn't know."

"But surely you have some ideas? You weren't leaving it up to John?"

She thought about the guitarist on the street the other day. She did have that idea. "There's something I came up with, but I hadn't discussed it with anyone."

Nick shifted his feet. "All right. Let's hear it."

Serena leaned her elbows on the desk. "I went to university with a woman whose brother went to prison. When she visited him she met another inmate who was alleged to be in for murder. She fell in love with him and this intrigued me. How could a woman love a man who might have committed murder? I'm interested in why women would love men who are so obviously wrong for them, and I think it could work because it's a dark subject, and Don wants dark subjects, hence the title *Neon Nights*. What do you think?" She held her breath.

His mouth thinned. "Sounds feasible. How does Don work with proposals? And what about Cam? Where does he fit in when it comes to story ideas?"

Nick hadn't really answered her question about whether he liked or disliked her idea. She wished she hadn't pushed it forward. The idea was precious to her and she didn't want it wasted.

"How does Steel TV work?"

"Don doesn't run a huge staff. We have to get our hands dirty, which means we can write our own material. But for this program Don wants us to pitch our new ideas to him. If he approves, then Cam will take over the production process. Cam has no input in the actual ideas."

"Did Don like the homeless thing *City Streets*?"

Homeless thing. Serena felt she should stay loyal to John. "He went for it because John's quite canny, and in some ways his work appears flatter on paper than when actually presented."

"So it's a go?"

"Well, we haven't got much time for anything else, have we? Unless there is some world shattering event. Did Don mention that we have to be ready any time to go on air with breaking international or national news stories when they happen?"

"I'm not sure he did mention that. Therefore, what it amounts to is that we have a schedule of programs we can shift aside and reschedule for news breaking stories?"

"Exactly."

"Great. So why not the first week present an introduction to the program? We should give the viewers an indication of what they might expect. Maybe we can go out on to the streets and interview people and ask them what they want to see. Then we can lead in the following week with your murder/love piece. That would give us another week to work on it. I agree with the overall idea that the stories need to be darker to correspond with the title."

I agree.

"Have you discussed any of this with Don yet?"

"No. I just thought about it last night and came up with how I would like the show to feel."

I would like.

"How about my view on this?"

"You've given me your view in your idea about a woman who loved a murderer. Very dark, very heavy. It's excellent."

Even if he'd taken his time before telling her of his reaction, Serena couldn't stop the flush of pleasure from heating her face. "Thank you."

For a second he didn't say anything, just stared at her flushed features, then he smiled. "You don't need my approval. You know you're good, don't you?"

"I don't know. I haven't done a show like this before. And I don't think I have as much confidence as you do."

"I'm not confident. I haven't done anything like this before either. But fear helps us do it better. Don't you agree?"

Nick admitting that he was frightened made him more human and kept him down at her own level. "Yes. Probably."

"Believe me. It does. So we'll meet on Monday to give Don our ideas on the first few programs. Is that okay?"

"Sounds fine to me." At least Nick didn't waste time. Serena liked that. John had been so laid back, full of too many maybes. Nick was positive, and the energy was there in every word and action. She'd just need to keep herself aware of what was going on around her.

Nick stood up and stuffed his hands into the back pockets of his jeans. "Do you want to take off?"

His abrupt departure from the subject stunned her. "What do you mean?"

"We don't have to meet Don until tomorrow for the commercial. Why don't we go out for a while? Clear our minds."

"We're supposed to be having a meeting, Nick."

"We'll continue our meeting somewhere else."

"Why? All we need to know is what's going to happen next Thursday evening when we're on air."

"We discussed it. We'll take the team out on Monday and do whatever. Hit the streets, turn up the volume on some loud alternative music group and pitch our wares to everyone."

Serena laughed. "Sounds like fun news. Not your style?"

"It won't be fun news. But the draw into the program will feel like fun. It'll be hard work, so let's take a break today."

"No, Nick. I can't. We have to work together, not take off together."

"We'll need to eat lunch."

That was true. Serena didn't know what to do. She didn't want to go to another restaurant and sit opposite him and wonder what to say to a man she felt so uptight with. Walking in the fresh air with him might be okay, she supposed. She couldn't dismiss him when they had so much left to discuss between them about the show.

"All right," she said, and tugged her rain jacket from the hook.

•

The rain had stopped, the air clean-smelling, unlike other more squalid cities Nick had been in over the past few years. Did he really prefer ducking snipers to being home? Or was he getting old enough to appreciate home? Would he actually have made this change to his life if he hadn't distantly yearned for it? Of course he still had his parents to visit. They were the main reason he was home in the first place. So far he'd put his job before them, but later he'd have to face the music.

"You're a restless type, aren't you?" Serena said.

He glanced at her. Her features were like the landscape after rain. Clear. Sparkling. Yet there were depths in her that hinted of her father. Nick thought she was pretty lucky to have a father as prestigious as Redding Brown, even though she didn't seem to think so. She hadn't mentioned a word about him. Nick wasn't going to mention a word either. He found it quite a fascinating little game to see how long she would hold out, and how the facts would eventually present themselves when she finally did let him know. He eased his fists into his jacket pockets. "Yes. I'm the restless type. I'm also the hungry type. I denied myself the monster squishy donut that came with that coffee on a special this morning."

"I ate a good breakfast. Grapefruit, a boiled egg and toast."

"My, aren't we the picture of health. All I had was some dried-up cereal as I haven't had a chance to get any groceries in yet. And my instant coffee is down to sort of a lump of brown stuff."

She chuckled. "Poor you. You should have given yourself a couple of days to get adjusted back home. You didn't have to fortify yourself with coffee and meet me this morning."

"Oh, yes I did. We're in a bind. Remember?"

"How could I forget? But don't worry too much, Nick. I've been at Steel for nearly six years. I have learned to wing it so Don doesn't even notice."

"I know how to wing it. But you'll have to teach me how to hide the gaffs from Don."

"Just watch me."

Oh, he would. He knew then he couldn't sit in a public restaurant with her. He just wanted to be completely alone with her. "How about we pick up some groceries and eat lunch at my place? I don't feel like a restaurant. Probably because I've been on the road a lot lately."

"Okay," she said. "I should know where you live, I guess."

"Absolutely." He led the way to his home.

Chapter Four

Serena had expected Nick's apartment to be no more than a sterile place for Nick to hang his hat if he ever got home to Toronto during his time in the field. Instead, the street was up-scale residential, with lots of big trees and flower gardens. His apartment, he told her, urging her with a hand on her shoulder to look upwards, was the penthouse perched above an ancient, well-preserved six story brick block. "But first we'll go to the store," he said.

On the corner was a variety store that catered to people like Nick, who purchased his needs on the spur of the moment. There was even an in-store bakery.

Nick gathered four pots of chrysanthemums from the display tumbling across the sidewalk and added them to a crusty loaf of olive bread, cheese, eggs, milk, fruit and plenty of packages of coffee.

Carrying the bags of food and the flowers, they rode the elevator together. When Nick smiled at her Serena felt his smile move through her body in a rather sensual way and wondered if she'd been wise to come here with him. Not that she expected him to pounce on her. However, she was very attracted. If he did make a move she might succumb.

There was only one door in the sixth floor hallway. Balancing the groceries and flowers in one arm, Nick inserted the key and pushed the door open with his back.

"Go in."

She walked in first and liked what she saw at once. A spacious room with a high ceiling and wood flooring displayed Nick's sleekly designed furniture. He closed the front door and led the way to a black and silver kitchen. They stood the groceries and the flowers on a small round table.

"There are some pots outside on the roof garden where we can plant the flowers," he said.

Serena thought they should keep this time together light. "So that's why you invited me here. You wanted me to be your gardener."

"Ah." He beckoned her to the living room, where he began unbolting a single glass door. He opened the door. "Come and see the view."

She passed him in the narrow doorway. But as soon as her body brushed his, she felt a pounding in her chest. Nick's hand touched her hip to urge her forward and she almost stumbled onto the roof garden. She walked to the iron railing and made herself stare at the view. Some taller buildings obscured Lake Ontario, although she glimpsed a patch of water between the walls.

Nick came to stand beside her. "I've lost some of my view."

She glanced down to the street. "It's still neat."

"Yeah. I forgot how much I liked it." He turned his head slightly and she was forced to face him.

"Do you want some lunch?"

She had to stop herself from moving to make their arms touch. "Sure. That bread looked delicious."

He left her to fetch the meal. The sun was shining and pouring a lot of heat down on the roof. Serena removed her jacket and hung it over one of the green iron chairs. She wondered if she should go in to help Nick. Maybe not. She might not be able to bear being that close to him in the kitchen. She tucked her arms along the top of the railing and looked at the view once more. Sex-starved her girlfriend Rita often said she felt, when the attractive redhead found a man she wanted. Serena had always felt she was above such crude sentiments. But right now she felt sex-starved. She wanted Nick with a lusty intensity.

Nick returned. This time without his jacket and carrying a tray. He put the tray down on the iron table and looked at her. "I have one bottle of beer. Do you want to share it? I'm not even sure how old it is. I could put on coffee if you'd rather."

He seemed bigger out here on the roof. Maybe she hadn't realized before how well-proportioned his body was. He wore his jeans and shirt with such easiness. And his hair was sleek like a raven's wing in the sunshine.

"Beer is fine," she said.

They sat down on the chairs opposite one another. Nick had placed bread, cheese, grapes and slices of apple on each plate. He poured the beer into the two glasses.

He lifted his glass. "Cheers."

Serena lifted her glass. "Cheers."

Nick began tucking into his food, so Serena did the same. They didn't say much, but they looked at one another often. Occasionally they would smile across the table. On the street below sometimes a horn would honk or voices would be heard.

"Aren't we supposed to be discussing the show?" Serena asked.

Nick laughed. "Yeah, I suppose, but the sun is making me kind of sleepy."

"You must be feeling the time change?"

"I must be."

He looked lazy and handsome, sprawled in his chair and holding the glass with the remains of his beer. Serena pushed aside her plate. "What about your flowers? Are you going to put them in those pots?"

"Yes. Do you want to help?"

"Of course. I love gardening."

It didn't take them long to plant the flowers in the big clay pots. The floral display made the roof garden look bright and inviting. Serena washed her hands at the kitchen sink while Nick went through the refrigerator contents. She used a piece of paper towel to dry her fingers.

"I definitely need some more beer," Nick said. "I'm going to run out and get some. Okay?"

"I don't need any more. I think I should go now."

He closed the fridge door. "You're rushing off. That's no way to establish a friendship."

She crumpled the towel she'd dried her hands on and disposed of it in a corner wastebasket. "We will, in time."

"Why not start today?"

She wondered then if he was talking about plain friendship or something more. So what if they did make love? Would it cool her attraction for him? Or would she want more? Would she become like her mother with her father? Reeva used to pace the floor waiting for her husband to appear, and when he did they were in bed as soon as they could put Serena down for the night. Serena used to hear them. She couldn't bear to be a woman with such basic needs and wants. She couldn't live that way.

She glanced through the kitchen window. This view was completely obliterated by another building, with concrete walls and many windows glinting in the fresh sunlight. "We can't."

"Can't what?"

She turned around and knew she was looking at a man with similar traits to her father. A man who reveled in war and disaster. A man who could love a woman one night and then walk away with the same coldness he displayed in his work. "Can't be too good of friends."

"I don't get that. Why not?"

"Because we have to work together. Don't we? So we have to be friends with conditions attached."

"What kind of conditions?"

"We have to retain a distance."

"Are you telling me not to make a pass at you?"

Had he guessed how she felt and what she was really saying? "No. I'm not even thinking that." *Liar.* "What I mean is that if we get too close, too friendly, then if we have a disagreement over work we might not be able to keep the discussion business like enough."

Feeling she'd made her point clear, Serena returned to the roof garden. She lifted her coat off the chair and carried it back to the kitchen. She picked up her purse from the table. "Thank you very much for the lunch." She walked into the living room. Nick followed her. "Besides, I need to get back to the office to work on my story. The one about women who fall for the wrong men."

He pushed his fingers into his front pockets. "That says it all about you, Serena. You want to know why women love the wrong men?"

He seemed to be able to nail down her insecurities. "And what's wrong with that? It's true. Most women fall for the wrong men."

"And a lot of men fall for the wrong women."

She wouldn't mind discovering if he'd ever fallen for the wrong woman. She'd like to know if he'd ever been in love. That was why she had to escape. She wanted to know far too much about him. "Possibly that's true as well."

"Of course it is. None of us are immune. Let's go then."

He came downstairs with her. When they were on the street he said, "Until tomorrow afternoon for the commercial."

"Yes. I'm not sure of the time."

"I think Don mentioned two-thirty."

"I'll double check. If it's different I'll let you know."

He raised an eyebrow. "You don't have to. You're not my assistant, you're my equal."

His attitude was the opposite of what she'd thought it might be. She was rather surprised. She'd thought Nick would want to control their working situation. "I know, but we have to coordinate with one another."

"I suppose. Do you have my phone number?"

"No. I guess not."

Nick lifted his wallet from his pocket and handed her one of Don's business cards. Nick's own phone number was scrawled on the back. "I'll get a new cell phone as soon as I get settled," he said.

"That's okay." Serena took the card and slipped it into the front pocket of her jeans. She saw Nick's eyes watching her fingers slide into her pocket and she felt her face flush.

Nick grinned. "You read my thoughts."

"I don't know." She felt flustered. He was too darn sexy for his own good.

He tapped her shoulder with his fingertips. "Till tomorrow. Keep cool."

Serena walked away from him without a backward glance. When she was around the corner, despite the heat, she began to run.

◆

Nick watched her disappear with disappointment in his heart. He'd wanted her to stay longer because he felt a deep attraction to her. If she came into his arms and pleaded for sex, he wouldn't say no, but that hadn't been his prime motive for wanting her with him.

He went back to his apartment. She was still here, her perfume like a floral bouquet. Nick raked his fingers through his hair. He hadn't expected to come home and meet a woman he wanted so much, so soon. He had too much to do while he was at home, too much of his past life to sort out.

Instead of thinking about Serena, he would go out and buy his beer and fill up the fridge with decent food. He'd also buy some wine. If there was a next time to her being here, he'd offer her wine.

Also, while he was shopping, a new TV might be in order, plus a full size computer and the phone. Yes. He had lots to deal with. And he still had his parents to visit. *Well, hell, Nick you're going to be buzzing with so much activity you won't even have time to think about Serena.*

•

Serena's jeans and T-shirt were clinging to her by the time she reached her office, and her braid had come apart. She brushed her hair loose, at the same time letting her body cool down to the air-conditioned room temperature. She wondered what she was actually running from. Nick or her own feelings? Both, she decided, sitting down at her desk. She didn't want to be involved with Nick Fraser. She had to work with him. Period. That should be all that mattered.

Someone knocked at her office door and Serena rose to her feet. It was Juliette Marshall, her news-hour replacement, all five foot ten of her in white shorts and a gray Steel T-shirt, her flowing brunette hair in a perky tail. Behind her a young man with shaggy blond hair carried a heavy box.

Juliette said, "You can put the box beside the desk, Rick. Thanks. Then go get another one." She grinned at Serena. "Don did tell you I'm moving in today, didn't he?"

Juliette looked so freshly washed and all together without a problem in her life that Serena felt like a slob at this moment. She was also stunned by Juliette's announcement. She stared at the box. "No. Don didn't tell me. Are you taking over my office?"

"'Fraid so. You're getting the suite of offices on seven, so you'll have more room for *Neon Nights* meetings." Juliette placed her carefully manicured fingers on her hips. "Are you sure Don didn't tell you?"

"No. He didn't." Serena was getting more and more peeved at Don by the day. But she knew he was going behind her back so she wouldn't cause any aggravation.

"Well, I don't think he intended on moving you in the first place, but since Nick Fraser is taking over from John, he figured things should be bigger and better."

Serena frowned. "You mean John didn't deserve the suite, but Nick does?"

"Something like that." Juliette flicked her ponytail. "Nick Fraser is a bit of a star, you know."

"I suppose." Serena wasn't sure if she'd actually thought of him as a star. She'd been more worried about the matching personality likeness to her father, and the way he affected her physically and emotionally.

Juliette gave Serena a probing look. "What did you think of him when you met him?"

"Nick?"

Juliette bared her white teeth. "Naturally, Nick."

"He's okay."

"That's not what I've heard. I've heard he's darn sexy in person and deserves his reputation with women. Broken hearts strewn all over Europe and beyond."

For some reason Serena wasn't surprised to hear this. "Maybe so. But he didn't affect me."

"Then he's not so great in person?"

"Not so great." She didn't want Juliette starting any gossip. Avoiding gossip was all the more reason to be very circumspect in her relationship with Nick.

"Then going by your take on things, he sounds quite unimpressive. By the way, Rick will move your stuff for you if you pack it into boxes. We can empty mine and fill them with your things." Juliette glanced around. "This is a nice office. I'll like it here."

Serena was suddenly aware of what she had to do. Moving all her belongings could take hours, well into the night. She had to get started. What she really felt like doing was going to Don and arguing about the change, but she knew that type of action didn't work on Don. He usually let you rant and rave, and then he laughed, like he had this morning. Besides, Nick was a given now, and it made sense to have the co-hosts of *Neon Nights* together in one place. "I'll go and take a look at the suite," she said.

"Only another three floors until you're up with Don," Juliette told her.

Serena made a face this time. "*Neon Nights* has to really take off for that."

"Do you have reservations about it?"

Realizing she was giving Juliette the impression she was dissatisfied, Serena shook her head. "No. None at all."

Serena walked the two flights of stairs to the seventh floor, thinking that Juliette might secretly hope *Neon Nights* would flop. The woman was ambitious. If Serena's show didn't make it, an opening would be made for The Juliette Marshall News Show, or whatever.

Don was in the suite, talking to Paul Kryker. Paul was fair-haired and tall, and muscular enough in his old jeans and shirt not to be dwarfed by Don. His blue eyes twinkled at Serena. "Hi. How're you doing, Serena?"

"Fine, Paul. How are you?" His handshake certainly didn't unnerve her, the way Nick's did.

"I'm great. Are you looking forward to the show?"

"Yes. I am." Then she glanced at Don, unable to resist a poke at his manipulative strategy. "Thanks for the warning about the office change."

Don's expression was a little sheepish. "I knew you'd understand."

"I understand when I'm being railroaded"

"But you won't take it personally?"

"No. I'm not taking it personally when I believe it's all to do with accommodating Nick Fraser."

Don sighed. "Not necessarily, Serena. We might have moved up here with John."

"Might."

"Nick has to be accommodated. He won't work for us if things don't go his way. He believes he wouldn't have landed a job when he came back on the off-chance, but that's not true. I know three places that would have welcomed him with open arms. Which is why we want to keep him. So where is he?"

"He's home, but he'll be here for the commercial tomorrow."

"Did you have a meeting yet?"

Serena nodded. "Yes. We met this morning and discussed the direction of the show." She let out a short breath. "He didn't particularly jump up and down in delight over the planned programming."

Don shook his head. "Naturally he wouldn't. It's garbage."

"I thought you were agreeable."

"For John Duncan, but not for Nick. It's not for you either. Did you come up with anything?"

"We will by Monday."

"Good. We'll schedule a meeting in this board room for everyone at ten-thirty Monday morning." He waved his arm. "So, what do you think of this set-up?"

Surrounding a comfortable coffee meeting area were three offices and a boardroom with an oblong oak table. Serena was pleased to see all the offices had their own connecting clothes closets and washrooms. She wasn't giving up those privileges. "It looks good."

"She says cautiously," Don said. "Realizing she has to give in to Don's bright idea that they needed more office space."

She grinned at him. He was one of the most maddening yet easy to get along with men she'd ever met.

Still, it was annoying she had to move. It was as if she were giving up everything to Juliette, including her afternoon news stardom. The new show was a gamble. It could be dead at the end of this season. And it might have been with John. But with Nick there was a chance for a second run, and John could ride on Nick's coattails for that season. After that? Well, that was two years down the road. She couldn't worry about the future when the present was looming in on her.

Serena returned to the fifth floor. By now Juliette had boxes covering the carpet.

Juliette straightened for a moment, hands rubbing her silken thighs. "Some are empty for you to use. Maybe you could unload your desk first, so I get sorted out. Pat McHaney is doing the news today to allow me time to do this."

Serena agreed to clean out her desk, even if she did feel as if she'd been tossed into a life of mayhem. When she was ready, she commandeered Rick to carry a couple of boxes. Paul was alone in the suite when she got there.

He jumped up from a sofa, agile for such a big man. "Do you need help?"

"It's not one of your duties."

He grinned. "I'm not sure it should be one of yours either. But, hey, I can't stand all this sitting around. Tell me where you want everything and I'll oblige."

Even with Paul's help, for which she was grateful, when it came to reassembling some shelves, it took all afternoon to move upstairs. She had the front desk call out for pizza at six. As they ate she chatted to Paul about the direction of the new show. On the surface he seemed full of enthusiasm and raring to go, but she sensed a little hesitancy when it came to Nick.

"You've known Nick a while, haven't you?" she said as they packed the pizza box into the wastepaper basket.

"We met once. Are you getting along with him?"

Serena smiled at him. "Shouldn't I?"

"Sure you should. But beware of him." Paul's expression turned grim for the first time today. "My sister, Lise is a journalist. She fell for him like a ton of bricks a few years back. When he dumped her she took it hard."

This seemed to confirm Juliette's comment about Nick's reputation with women. "Well, if that's a warning, consider me asbestos hide. I'm not in the market for any man like Nick."

"Neither was Lise. But Nick got to her."

"That's unfortunate." Serena saw that Paul was still looking agitated. "It won't make any difference to you working with Nick, will it?" The last thing she felt she needed was added tension in her life.

"Other than I'd like to smash his face in for hurting my sister."

"Paul, I didn't think you were the violent type."

"I'm not usually, but Lise is my little sister, and I feel protective."

"I understand, but these things happen between men and women. Especially in the line of work your sister and Nick are in."

Paul's big shoulders relaxed slightly. "Yeah, I guess. I've probably left a trail of broken hearts as well, when I've had to move on. Which is why I've been staying put. I'm getting married."

"Congratulations." Serena was pleased to change the subject. "Who's the lucky woman?"

"Her name's Elaine and I'll be bringing her to the soirée on Saturday evening. So I'll introduce you to her."

"That's great, Paul. I'll look forward to meeting her."

After Paul left, Serena fished the card Nick had given her out of her front pocket. She remembered his eyes watching her put the card there in the first place. Wondering how it would feel to have

Nick's hand slide to that secret place on her body, she felt the now familiar warm sensations flood her veins.

Oh, dear, will I survive this? Serena thought as she punched out the scrawled number on the back of the card on to the phone key pad. Nick's phone rang four times before it was picked up. She thought she heard a stifled yawn as she said, "Hi. It's Serena."

"Hey." He sounded sleepy.

"Did I get you up?"

He chuckled. "I was just dozing away my jet lag."

"Are you feeling better?"

"Now that you've phoned, yes. So what's up?"

"I just wanted to say that my office has been moved to the seventh floor. And you're next door to me."

"I have my own office?"

"Yes."

"Great. Now we can get down to business."

"Yes. We can."

"Thanks for letting me know. See you tomorrow."

Serena hung up the phone and closed her eyes for a moment. She had to get over this breathless reaction she had to Nick.

Chapter Five

Nick couldn't relax again after Serena's call, so he put on cotton shorts, and poured himself a large glass of orange juice from his new supplies. He'd spent the afternoon shopping. A new TV, computer, printer, mobile phone, all the goodies. He hadn't been to visit his parents yet. Though he did call to say he was home and promised he would be there tomorrow after work. He knew he was putting off something that would be disagreeable to him. No. More than disagreeable. Downright painful.

After he'd set up the TV and computer he picked up the book *Heart in the Field,* sat down and opened the cover. Like the first time, he couldn't stop reading Stuart Redding Brown's story, but behind all the words now were visions of Serena.

The Brown family were still very much with him the next day when, dressed in a black suit, he took a cab to the Steel Tower. He found the door to the seventh floor suite open and Paul Kryker lounging on one of the sofas in the central meeting area. Paul returned a magazine to the round coffee table and stood up.

"Hi, Nick," Paul said.

As the two men shook hands Nick felt the tension in the other man's handshake. He knew it was because of his sister. They'd only dated a few times, but Lise had taken the dates more seriously than he had. When Nick had moved on to another assignment, Lise had spread the word that he'd treated her badly. Someone had warned him Paul was furious at him.

Nick pushed his hands into his pockets. "So how's it going, Paul? Given up on the rest of the world and come home for a bit?"

"I've been home for nearly two years. I'm getting married."

"Congratulations. Anyone I know?"

Wrong thing to say, Nick decided, as Paul frowned.

"No one you know. You'll meet her at the party on Saturday, if you're going."

"I'll look forward to it." Nick nearly asked how Lise was, then thought better of it. He glanced around him. "Not a bad space."

"It's great. You and Serena have the end two offices." Paul indicated the location of the offices with a head movement. "Then there's a boardroom. Don mentioned I could use the third office when I need one. Cam's staying put on five."

Paul was forcing friendliness. To ease the tense atmosphere, Nick walked around the suite. He saw one office was full of belongings that he recognized as Serena's. The office next door to hers had a computer, phone and a phone directory on the desk.

"This mine?" he asked Paul.

Paul nodded. "Yep. Serena's next door. I helped her move in yesterday. I'm only here for a few minutes. I came in hoping to see her again to make sure everything was fine. Now you're here you can help her if you have to. I have to run."

"Don't both of you run," a female voice said from the door.

Dressed in a short-skirted mauve suit, the woman held the doorpost with one hand. Her hair was a lush, deep brown, and eyes of the same color settled on Nick. "I know who you are, Nick Fraser. I'm Juliette Marshall. Serena's replacement on the afternoon news."

Juliette strolled forward, shook Nick's hand, and turned to Paul. "Hi, Paul."

"Hi, Juliette," Paul said. "But I really do have to run. I have to meet someone." He picked up his large leather camera bag and made himself scarce.

Juliette had a mouthful of perfect teeth and flipped her hair from her face with a practiced shake of her head. "I've heard so much about you, Nick. I knew Cara quite well when she was freelancing here in the city."

Cara had been the woman who'd given him Redding Brown's book. "Where is she now?"

Juliette fluttered her hand. "Last I heard she was married and was living in Mexico. Writing, I believe."

"That's great. Any writing from her will benefit society."

Juliette smiled. "Anyway, I must be off. I just stopped to say hi. Welcome to Steel. I'm on air in ten minutes. Have a good day."

She swung around and Nick watched her mauve hips and long legs glide from view. She was sexy but that was about all. She didn't hit his gut hard the way Serena did.

He knew exactly why this should be when Serena came into the office a few minutes later wearing pants and jacket in a light oatmeal with nothing but a coffee silk and lace chemise peeking from beneath the wide satin lapels. The outfit made her look very tall and slim. She was stunning, Nick thought.

She tossed briefcase and handbag on to a leather couch. "Hi. I just saw Juliette, so I presume you've met her."

"Yes. She flew in to tell me she knew who I was."

To Nick's astonishment, Serena laughed with real humor. "She eats men for lunch and spits them out for dinner."

"I figured that."

"Your type?"

"Could be."

She put her head to one side and her sleek hair fell in a smooth wing. "Well, then, you're in luck. She's very free. Hates the thought of being tied down. Likes hot, flaming affairs that burn but leave no scars."

"No more to be said. Absolutely my type." But even as he spoke Nick felt his words were mere rhetoric. Serena was his type, and he couldn't see beyond her at the moment.

•

Serena had met Juliette in the corridor. "Nick's here," Juliette had told her. "Be prepared."

Juliette didn't stay around to say what she should be prepared for, but as soon as Serena saw Nick she thought it might be that Nick looked so broad-shouldered and gorgeous in his black suit, crisp white shirt and black tie. His hair was sleek, his skin smooth and tan, his smile so white. Instead of being speechless Serena had found herself being smart, and she'd learned a few truths in the process that made all the gossip about Nick true. The Juliette Marshalls of the world were his type of women.

"Have you seen your office?" she asked.

"Yep. But I haven't been in it yet. I'll try the chair."

Serena thought he seemed cautious of her as he walked into the office and sat down behind the desk. He swung around in the chair, tilted the back, and then moved forward to turn on the computer.

Serena stood at the door. "I think everything's set up. We have a guy named Mark who works on the computers. He's a whiz. All you'll need is a password at the prompt. There's a spot to register." She glanced around at the empty bookshelves. "You'll be able to make this place feel like yours with some personal stuff."

"I'll be fine, Serena."

She was savoring the way he said her name when his phone rang in his pocket. They both jumped in surprise.

Nick took the phone out. "Nick Fraser."

Unable to keep her eyes off him Serena watched him listen for a moment. "Yeah, it's a problem." He sounded annoyed, but listened some more. "I understand. Okay. Monday's fine. Let me know." He disconnected and looked at her. "My car is a Jaguar. It's been in storage and it needs some parts. It won't be ready until Monday."

"Ah." She thought about the party. "I guess you'll be walking for the weekend." She knew she sounded flippant and uncaring.

"I don't think I can walk to Don's place, can I?"

Trying to avoid his gaze, she ran one neatly manicured fingernail up the doorpost. What was he asking? She had no wish to be in a car with him. She didn't want to go to the soirée with him. But she had to be truthful. "No. It's out my way."

"Which you told me was quite a distance."

She nodded. "Yes."

He shrugged his shoulders. "I guess I'll rent a car, then."

"That sounds reasonable." Perfect. She wouldn't have to worry about him. She could briefly show her face at the party and leave before the do got going. Don's parties usually ended up going on most if not all of the night. Affairs between staff members had begun at some of Don's parties. For that very reason Serena never stayed very long.

"I'd better get moving on renting a car, then."

Serena picked up her briefcase and purse from the sofa and took them into her office. There was half an hour before the commercial taping, so she began to fix up this office the same way she'd fixed up the other one. She hated her life disorganized. Nick was disorganizing her life.

He came in a few moments later when she was in the midst of

sliding a book on to one of the shelves. Her gaze wandered from his sharp black leather shoes all the way to his handsome face. All the heat she'd ever felt for him over the past hours blasted her body, and she experienced a moment of sheer weakness and anxiety that she wasn't going to hold up against his magnetism for an entire season. "Did you get a car?"

"Yes. I got one. I'll go and pick it up later." He put his hand out toward her. "Should we go down to the studio now?"

Serena removed her fingers from the now sticky book cover and pushed the book on to the shelf. "I guess we should."

She would get used to all this: The elevator rides, the brush of his arm against hers, the aroma of his aftershave, the heat in her veins from his hand on her elbow. She would get used to working beside him, seeing their legs almost touching, his smile. She would. Oh, yes, she would. Even when they watched the unedited commercial he was far too close. The scent of his aftershave gave her visions of sub-tropical islands where there was nothing to do but make mad, passionate love.

"The show will need more besides clever cutting," Nick said. "It needs music."

"You're right," Don told him. "Any suggestions?"

"How about a local group we could give some exposure to."

Don glanced at Serena. "What about Seth?"

"Possibly." She thought this might be a great chance for her brother's band, Lite, even if their music was anything but light. It would certainly give the band some solid exposure, and urge people to buy their music. "Although," She had to be truthful. "They are pretty way out. They're what you would call alternative with a capital A."

"That's my type of music. I'd like to hear them," Nick told her.

"All right. I'll talk to him. When do you want to run this commercial Don?"

"ASAP. Can you bring him in this evening?"

"I'll try."

"Phone him," Nick urged.

Serena felt as if she were being shoved into a corner. What if Seth didn't want to do this? He walked his own path. Drummed to his own beat. He rarely appeared at family gatherings. She very rarely saw him. He was another man who reminded her of her father. Naturally he would. He was her father's son. "They might have a gig."

Nick's gaze penetrated hers. "Check anyway. We're running out of time."

She didn't have much choice. She had two powerful men pushing their instructions down her throat. Of course, if she went against their ideas she might be doing her brother out of a great deal of publicity. Her reluctance to call her brother was because of her own insecurities, not because she didn't want him to succeed.

Nick moved closer to her. "Are you okay?"

"I'm fine. Why?"

"You look a bit dazed. I was wondering if you were feeling well. Because if you are, sweetie, phone your brother. We're short of time, and it would save a lot of hassles if we could use him."

Nick affected the same type of tone that he had in the pub on Wednesday evening, when she'd stopped suddenly in the doorway. It was a condescending tone, and it told her that all he wanted was to get this show on the road.

"I think I have his number." She picked up her purse, knowing full well that his number was on her cell phone.

Feeling the two men watching her, Serena went to the other side of the studio. She opened her purse and found her phone. After placing her purse-strap over her shoulder, she punched Seth's number. Her breath was on hold while the phone rang. Seth's voice, sounding like her father's, came on to the answering machine. After clearing her throat at the beep, she left a message for him to call her back on her phone. She added what the call was about to spark his interest. She then called her mother at her city hall office to find out if she knew Seth's whereabouts. Her mother was closeted in meetings for the rest of the afternoon.

When Don knew the score he said, "Why don't we split? We'll get this thing edited and you guys can come back tonight. Hopefully with your brother, Serena."

"I'll do my best." If Seth didn't feel it was the right venue for his sound she would have to add persuasion.

Serena decided to go and visit Seth's apartment. He might be home by the time she reached there. She'd rather talk to him in person than on the phone.

◆

Nick took a cab to the rental agency to pick up his car. It was a fully loaded new Buick, a comfortable car. The car gave him a chance to drive to his father's jewelry store.

Fraser's Precious Gems was still open each day, even if his father didn't have much faith in the younger man who came in to work for him. Stephen Fraser couldn't manage even a few hours a day himself now. The store was running at a loss. Nick wanted to talk to his father about selling it. Then his parents could move from the apartment above the shop into a more modern place and live off the proceeds from the real estate. He hadn't put the plan to his parents yet. It was something he'd decided between seeing their situation in April and now. He was always aware of how much of a stranger he was to them, as they were strangers to him.

Nick parked the car behind the store in the overgrown back lane. He opened the wooden gate, walked up a paved pathway, climbed the iron stairs at a run and knocked on the door. The action reminded him of when he was a kid, coming home from school. Only then he didn't have to knock and he always received a scolding for running.

"Break your neck doing that," his mother always told him.

His mother, Maria, didn't say that this time. She wore a pair of light blue slacks and a white top, her gray hair tied in a sleek knot away from her now wrinkled features. Once her hair had been raven-black, the same color as Nick's. She'd had a few small illnesses over the past year that had sapped her strength, but she still managed to look handsome and in command.

"Nick." Her manner was vague, as if she needed time to remember who he was.

She raised a hand full of rings. Beautiful rings, some merely engraved bands, some bursting with different stones, all crafted for her by his father over the years. It made Nick realize how full of talent and what a wonderful craftsman his father was, and it made him sad that Stephen had never taught him his craft.

Nick took hold of his mother's hand, wondering why she'd never offered a hand when he was a kid. Now he had to hold withered, cool fingers, and they would be his only memory of his mother. Swallowing back a lump of emotion, he said, "My car's still being fixed so I rented one."

His mother was the first to drop her hand. "That's good. Are you working now?"

His mother had never thought that working in the field was actual work. One had to go somewhere to work, a store, a factory, an office. "Yes. I got my new office this morning. Dad in?"

"Yes. He's in the front room. He went down to help in the store this morning."

Sniffing a slightly musty lemon oil, Nick walked through the narrow hallway of the dark apartment. He wasn't sure why the rooms always seemed dark. The paintwork was light cream and the floors a light wood. Possibly the darkness was caused by the lack of windows, or the highly polished towering pieces of antique furniture. He definitely saw his parents in something more modern and brighter, without the stair-climb.

Stephen Fraser was sitting upright on a leather armchair in the living room. Despite his most recent heart attack, Stephen was still a big man with an authoritative presence. His suits were always an immaculate dark navy blue. He wore a red kerchief in the breast pocket. Nick remembered his mother ironing the selection of different colored silk handkerchiefs.

From his position by the window Stephen could look down to the sidewalk and see who entered his store. Rarely did anyone enter the store these days. Nick had discovered the advertisements his father used to run in the local newspapers had stopped a year ago.

"Look who's visiting," Nick's mother said, and went over to her husband. She touched the high back of the chair and his father smiled at his wife. Nick was surprised that he still felt completely left out. They'd been a twosome when he was born, and they'd always wanted to stay that way. Possibly one night of unbridled passion had made Maria pregnant with Nick.

Nick chose a chintz armchair and sat down opposite his father. Nick met his father's pale blue eyes. "How are you, Dad?"

Stephen patted his chest. "No pains any more. Your mother takes care of me."

Nick forced a smile. "She sure does."

Maria sat down on a footstool near his father so the two of them faced him, appearing like a portrait. The left-out feeling persisted.

He was an intruder here, always had been. But they needed him now. He wasn't sure if he was using the excuse of help to hide his own deeper feelings. Did he want to show them he was worthwhile having after all, even if it was for help in their old age? Or to make them realize that they loved him after all? Maybe they did love him in their way. Who knew? In some ways he wished they'd died long ago, so he didn't have to face this uncertainty.

"I want to take care of you as well." Their silence made his words ring out into the room and sound as if he were begging to do something for them. Which he was. He wanted their acceptance. He wanted to know that they thought he'd done well in life. He wanted to be thought important to them. And he wanted to help them. He really did. It was more than duty it was something he needed to do.

"We appreciate that," his father said after a while.

The pause had been long enough for Nick to make the decision. He was going to plunge right in and tell them about the changes he felt they should make to their lives to improve the quality, financially and physically. "I was thinking that maybe you should sell the store and move somewhere else. Somewhere more convenient, maybe with a bit of a flower garden to sit outside in. I can help with the money, so you don't have to worry about that."

They both stared at him.

"I'm not selling the store," Stephen said. "It's doing well today."

Nick knew that was his father's pride talking. "That's not true, Dad. Last time I was here I saw the books, and it's doing abysmally. There isn't the foot traffic along this street there used to be, and you let the advertising slip. Besides, you lose out to big specialty stores these days. If you were in a different area it might be of some help, but trendy tourist traffic areas are expensive and, well, frankly, it's not worth a move at your age." He held his breath, but nothing was said about his reference to age. They knew where they were in their lives.

Maria moved forward. "Your father can't sell the store, Nick. It's his life."

"I'm talking about his life, Mom. You two deserve to have a good life in the next few years, and I can help out with that. There's a hell of a lot of money tied up in real estate here. This place is too much for both of you to cope with now. I'm not saying you have to make a decision right away, but I'm here to stay over the next few months and I want you to give some consideration to what I've said about moving to somewhere easier to handle. In the meantime, I'll look into hiring someone to come in and clean and help with the meals."

Stephen pounded the arm of the chair with his fist. "I don't want anyone in here fiddling around with my personal things. I only eat your mother's meals."

Nick got up and walked to the window. The sun shone hard and bright onto the road and glinted off the windshields of the cars parked at the curb. A truck backed up to a grocery store across the road. He could hear the beep of the alarm even inside these solid brick walls. He'd spent little of his childhood here, but he remembered it enough that the place depressed him. He'd never been allowed to bring friends here, or make a mess with his toys. Not that he'd had many toys. His parents had given him books, which he always read voraciously. All the solitude and all the books were likely why he'd found himself writing by the time he was a teenager. He knew if he'd had more inner peace with his home situation he might have become a writer instead of careening around the world in search of adventure.

Maria rose to put the kettle on. Nick settled back in the armchair opposite his father to partake in the tea ceremony. He left about half an hour later, feeling he hadn't accomplished anything. But at least he'd planted the idea.

•

Seth's apartment was in a converted warehouse area. Serena parked her car and hurried into the brick building. The stairs and the wooden hallway between the loft apartments felt like a fire trap. But she knew that inside the vast spaces were either artists' studios or luxury living quarters and the fire regulations had been taken care of.

She'd only been to her brother's apartment once since he'd moved in about a year ago. She knew all her reasons why. As well as Seth being extremely like her father, she didn't really like the area, and she was also somewhat in awe of her brother, even if he was younger. He was a bit like Nick Fraser. A cool, handsome man, who didn't have to make a move to set women's hearts fluttering madly in their breasts. My lean, mean brother, she'd called him once, when he was sixteen and she felt he might have broken a girl's heart. All he'd done was smile, shrug, and say, "Whatever."

Seth answered the door, his six-foot frame covered in black jeans and a black T-shirt with his band's name, Lite on the front in silver letters. His wavy brown hair was long and he'd grown sideburns. He looked so much like her father that Serena didn't say a word for a moment as he raised an eyebrow over his silver-gray eyes.

"Well, Sis." He spoke in his rather sarcastic eloquent tones that were similar to Nick Fraser's. "I got your message, so I'm not surprised you're here."

"Can I come in?"

"Sure." He opened the door and she walked in.

He'd done quite a bit to his living quarters since her last visit. The wood floors were polished. The furniture was sparse but expensive, each piece chosen individually and not because it matched anything else. One good thing her father had done for his family, he'd left them well enough off not to have to worry about finances. She put her purse down on a red and white striped sofa.

Seth watched her. "Do you want a beer, wine, something?"

"I'm driving. Do you have any coffee?"

"Sure. I'll put some on." The all-white kitchen was in a corner alcove of the apartment. Seth prepared coffee in a white coffee maker. He took out two white mugs and put them on the counter. "Do you take anything in your coffee?"

"No. I drink it black."

"Good." He smiled slightly. "'Cause I don't have anything to put in it."

When the coffee was ready, Serena sat down on the couch and Seth perched on a red leather footstool. "So what is the new show about?" he asked.

"It's a weekly program, consisting of documentaries and news commentary." Serena sipped her coffee. "For the first week we're going to hit the streets and ask the people what they would like to see. And we thought some good music would be in order to add some drama to the piece."

"We?"

"Me and my co-host. It's not John Duncan anymore. He's sick, and I have another co-host."

"Who?"

"His name is Nick Fraser." Serena felt herself fill up with emotion when she spoke Nick's name.

Seth's look implied he guessed how she felt about Nick. "I do believe I might have seen him on TV."

"Possibly. He just came back from overseas."

Seth shook his head. "I wondered what it was. He's a field journalist."

"Yes." Serena felt she spoke the word far too succinctly. But then why bother hiding what Seth already knew?

"Aren't things going too well?"

"He's a strong personality."

"So are you. That shouldn't be a problem."

"It's just that I hadn't really got a handle on this show ahead of his coming in to take over. John was so loose, and I realize now that was probably because he was ill."

"Will me supplying the music help?"

Serena met his intent gaze. "Let's put it this way. If I don't get you, then I might feel that Nick thinks I'm pretty useless."

Seth frowned. "Is that how he makes you feel?"

"I feel like I need to overachieve with him. You might not understand that because you're a man."

"No. I understand. It's the same way we both feel with mother."

Serena nodded. "Yes. In some ways. So please, Seth, I'd appreciate the favor. If you're not playing a gig."

"Happens we're free tonight, but—you know we're not everyone's choice."

Serena looked into his face. He was so like her father now he was older that she felt a heavy sensation in the pit of her stomach. But she also wanted to reach out to touch her brother and hug him. "It might give you wonderful exposure, and it would put the show in a central spot for us. We need to carve a place in the market. Right now it's hanging out there unproven."

"We'll come down and see what it's about."

He surprised her with his capitulation. "You mean that?"

"I always mean what I say. I'm willing to help you out. I also want to meet Nick."

"Why?"

Seth grinned. "Because he's got you in a flap. Is he like Dad?"

Serena cupped her mug. "Actually, he is. Very much like my father."

"My father as well. Even if I never knew him. Even if he was never mentioned in the family. I read his book, by the way."

Seth had always been bitter about the absence of his father from his life. He knew he was dead before he was born, of course, but he hated the way Serena and her mother never mentioned him or acknowledged him. "Did you learn anything?"

"I learned a great deal. I wish I'd known him."

"Even if he hadn't died you'd never have known him. He was never darn well here." She placed the mug down on the floor, as there were no tables, and stood up. She picked up her purse. "Well, if it's okay with you, I'll see you at Steel tonight. I'll meet you in the foyer at six-thirty. You can't get in without a pass."

"Why won't you ever talk about him? Why don't you tell me something about him?"

"I don't know much. He came, he went. He."

"He what?"

"He's not my idol, not by a long-shot. He hurt us all. He came home and made mother pregnant, then went away and got himself blown up. What kind of guy would do that?"

"Someone dedicated to his work."

"Is that what you've learned from his book?"

"Yes, it is." He stood up to join her. "I wish you and mother would talk about him, that's all. I wish she'd tell me things."

"Well, she won't. He hurt her. He hurt me. It's too deep. The wounds are still there."

"I can see that, with you anyway, and I find it damned annoying. I think mother's over it. She's just too bloody busy all the time."

Serena heard bitterness. "I thought you liked getting on with your own life."

"To some extent I do. But it would be kind of nice to have a family get-together once in a while. A little acknowledgment that I do exist."

Serena hadn't known he felt neglected. "I'm sorry."

"You can be sorry." He touched her shoulder. "I'll see you at six-thirty in the foyer with the other guys. All right?"

Serena reached up and touched his hand. "All right. Thanks for the coffee."

Seth walked her to the door. He surprised her. He put his hand on her hip and leaned down and kissed her cheek. "From Dad."

"What do you mean?"

"Read his book and you'll find out."

"I don't think I'm ready."

"What has to happen to make you ready?"

"I don't know, Seth. I just know that I can't open the wound."

He patted her hip. "Ah, Serena. You know what you should do?"

"What?"

"Go get yourself a man of your own, and then you'll relegate Dad to where he's supposed to be, a memory. You can't keep running from pain, you know. You have to face up to it."

"How do you know this? You're younger than me."

"I was born old." He grinned. "Now go. I'll see you later."

Impulsively Serena kissed her brother's cheek. "Thanks."

In her car Serena sat for a moment before starting the engine. Seth had been wonderful today. She realized how much she liked him, how good he was. She was definitely going to have to talk to her mother about this new insight into Seth's feelings. She would certainly try to see her brother more often. Staying away because he reminded her of Stuart Redding Brown was a silly reason. If she faced Seth long and hard enough then she might even get over her father's desertion. In turn that would mean she wouldn't be so hung up over men like Nick Fraser. She might even begin to appreciate men like Nick. Maybe, as Seth suggested, even have a love affair.

As she drove back to the Steel Tower, Serena couldn't believe how good the decision to take positive action actually felt.

Chapter Six

When Serena introduced him to her brother, Nick thought, *He's his father's double.* There was no doubt of Seth Brown's heritage. As they shook hands he almost told the young man that he admired his father, but he wasn't sure what Seth's position was on Redding Brown.

Nick glanced at Serena, who was chatting to one of Seth's band members. She wore her khaki pants tonight, with a sweater the creamy color of French Vanilla ice cream. Her hair was loose, less sleek and more ruffled than usual. She looked delightful, sexy and confident. Rob, the drummer she was talking to, was very good looking with a mane of golden brown hair. He was obviously smitten with her and Nick felt a dark sensation he recognized as plain old jealousy.

He hid his feelings by rounding up the band to play their music. He stood next to Serena while they listened to Lite, inhaling her perfume and trying to concentrate on the job at hand.

Luckily the band was good enough to sway his mind to their music, and Nick heard just the sound he was looking for. He specifically liked a cut called *The Darkest Hour* and thought it would be a perfect musical accompaniment to their show.

He whispered to Serena. "They're great."

"I didn't realize they were so good." Her eyes were shining in a way he hadn't seen them shine since he'd met her on Wednesday evening. He realized then that there was a great deal of pain down deep inside Serena. Pain he would like to bring to the surface and erase. With her eyes shining with pride for her brother she was so beautiful she made his heart ache.

He moved his shoulder closer to hers. "Haven't you ever heard them?"

"No. I don't see Seth very often." Then she stood up and walked over to the band. "You guys are excellent."

Nick went with her, making sure he stayed by her side. "I thought so as well," he said.

"You've got a gig," Don told Seth. "Do you want to come up to my office and we'll discuss finances?"

Nick thought for a moment Seth seemed to hesitate, and he understood why. The man had messages in his song-writing that could possibly be diluted, even overshadowed, by a TV show.

Nick said, "Why don't you give him the weekend to think about it, Don?"

But the other band members were enthusiastic. After glances all around, which proved they were close to one another as friends and artists, Seth agreed to go to Don's office.

"I think it's a great opportunity for Seth," Serena said to Nick as they walked out of the building together later.

"Certainly a talented man."

"I always knew it, I guess, but I'd never had it confirmed."

They reached her Porsche. Nick had parked the rental car a few vehicles down.

"See you at Don's," he said.

She stood with her hand on her car door handle. "Do you know where it is?"

"Don gave me an invitation with a map, but I've no idea how to get there."

"It's not far from my place."

"Then why don't I pick you up?" He wanted to be with her. "Save you driving. You can show me the way."

She tugged on the door handle and opened the car. "It's not necessary."

"No. But it might look good for Don to see us as a united front."

"Well …"

Nick's heart actually lurched with excitement as he saw her succumbing to his plan.

"All right. It will save taking two cars, and it means I can have a glass of wine or two." She smiled.

"Absolutely." Nick wished he didn't feel quite so thrilled about the thought of an actual sort of date on Saturday evening. Excitement meant more than casual involvement. Dates were for kids falling in love. But then so was jealousy and wanting to erase her pain. All these feelings were new to him, new and exciting. "Tell me where you live."

She explained where in West Vale she lived then he watched the Porsche leaving the parking lot before he turned to his own car. He looked forward, with a soulful yearning, to tomorrow evening when he would see Serena once more.

•

Her mother had phoned four times and left messages on the answering machine. Reeva never used cell phones. While she slipped out of her clothes, Serena pushed the automatic dial on her cordless phone and listened to the phone ring at the other end. Gerry answered. She asked Gerry for her mother. She'd never been very close to her mother's latest husband. Or any of her mother's men for that matter. She was just pleased that her mother had seemed to settle at last for one man. Gerry Carstairs adored Reeva.

"Serena, where have you been? You left me a message, so I called Steel and they said you were in the studio. And also that you have moved offices." Reeva possessed a beautiful accent. She enunciated every word. She was a very popular local politician and had been elected in two terms in a row. Serena was never quite sure of her mother's platform. Sometimes it seemed geared for the ordinary Joe or Jane, other times for the upwardly mobile couples.

"Yes. I moved offices for my new show, *Neon Nights*."

"Did you have to move far? Up or down?"

Serena smiled as she wriggled into a cotton night shirt. "Up, naturally. This show is a step up, Mom."

"As long as it is up. Never go down, baby."

Serena spoke the words her mother would want to hear. "If I go down, I quit."

"A positive attitude. That is what I like. I will be seeing you soon anyway, sweetie. Don Steel sent us an invitation to his soirée tomorrow evening and Gerry thought it might be a good idea for us to drop by your place and have a little drink with you. We'll drive over in the Lincoln, which will save you driving yourself."

Serena pulled the shirt down around her thighs. Why did life have to suddenly become so complex? "I'm not driving myself."

"You mean you have a date?"

"Not really. But Nick Fraser, my co-host, has never been to Don's before because he's just joined Steel. He's coming by to pick me up."

"That's fine. No problem. We can all have a drink and easily squeeze into the Lincoln."

Serena knew she had no choice. The Lincoln was large enough to accommodate them all. Besides, her mother ruled. "I suppose Nick won't mind."

"Of course he won't mind. We'll all go together. It'll be fun."

Fun, Serena thought, as she hung up the phone. How was she going to have fun stuck between her bossy mother, meek Gerry and sexy Nick? She wondered if she should call Nick to inform him about the change of plans, then decided against the call. He'd find out when he arrived what the plans were, and he'd also discover you didn't argue with Reeva Brown-Carstairs.

Her mother hadn't always been that way. The mega-strength had evolved from the mishaps and tragedies in her life. In some ways Reeva and Serena had grown up together, and her mother had excelled in adulthood beyond the boundaries.

Not wanting to think about all that tonight, Serena walked moodily around her house. The weather was humid and sticky, not at all as one would expect in September, and her body felt entirely unhappy burdened with the emotions circulating through her in the past few days.

She stopped in the kitchen and poured herself a big glass of cranberry juice from the container in the refrigerator. Pascal hovered around her legs. She drank, put down the glass and squatted to pat him.

"What am I going to do, Pascal? I've never really been in love. Yet sometimes I wish I could fall in love. Just for the hell of it."

Pascal flopped on to the floor and Serena settled beside him for his nightly rub down. She began with his ears and he purred loudly. "Like that? You do, yes. I wouldn't mind someone rubbing me this way tonight." Nick Fraser's face came into her mind, and for a second she let herself feel his touch. Her imagination left her hot and trembling, proving that it was definitely Nick who'd placed all this uneasiness inside her.

Pascal eventually got bored. Serena rose to her feet and began the routine of locking up the house for the night. This predicament was all her own fault. She should have let herself fall in love years ago. But she'd never met anyone she felt she could trust with her inner self. She ran like a frightened rabbit whenever she'd felt herself falling in love with a man. Now she was hung up with dissecting every relationship that came along. Even the thought of falling in love brought on a mini-anxiety attack. She knew all about the hurt and pain love brought with it. She'd lived with her mother's suffering.

Serena finished the lock-up and walked into her bedroom to find Pascal already settling down in the middle of the floral green and pink duvet. He was licking himself expansively.

She laughed and tucked herself into bed beside him. "What guy would put up with you every night on the bed?"

But even having Pascal with her tonight didn't stop her feeling lonely and full of longing. She rolled over on to her stomach and pressed her face desperately into the pillow. Tomorrow evening she would see Nick Fraser in a social situation. Maybe he'd get drunk, or obnoxious, like a lot of men she knew. Anything so she wouldn't fall in love with him.

•

Nick missed the corner store landmark the first time, and then wasn't sure which road he was to take, so he went into the store to ask the way. When he saw the bunches of pink and white asters, he purchased a bouquet for Serena to accompany the bottle of wine he'd slipped into the car on the way out of Toronto. He made himself feel like a guy on a first date, when in reality this wasn't a date at all.

He took the flowers to the counter. "Do you know where Serena Brown lives?" he asked the woman.

She began wrapping the flowers. "Yes. Just down the road. She's famous around here. I took one of her courses once, on television journalism. She doesn't teach them anymore, but when she first came here, three years ago, she taught two evenings a week at the West Vale High School." She handed Nick the bouquet and gave him his change. "Have a nice evening."

"You too," he said. He thought it interesting that Serena should teach journalism. It was really even more interesting that she'd followed her father's career. But then he was discovering that anything about Serena interested him.

Nick found the narrow laneway he'd missed the first time and located Serena's house. A broad white Lincoln in the driveway was parked in front of a double garage. As the luxury car stood in the center blocking both doors, he had no choice but to pull in behind it. He felt disappointed that he might not be alone with Serena, unless she also drove a Lincoln.

Carrying the wine and the flowers, he tried to decide whether he should approach the front door or go around the side of the house. When he heard voices from the back, he ducked beneath the wooden trellis and walked around the brick house to where there was a low octagonal wooden deck that led out from one of those sunrooms with curved windows. Upon the deck was a pine table shaded by a dark green umbrella and some matching pine chairs with seat cushions in green and purple. Two people sat talking and drinking. The man in trendy white cottons wore glasses, and was slim with smooth, dark brown hair. The woman, in a flowing exotic print dress was blond, stunning. Both were probably in their early sixties.

Nick walked up the steps and the woman rose like a butterfly unfolding. She was an older version of the woman in Stuart Redding Brown's photo album. Nick saw her beautiful eyes assess his ivory slacks and black silk shirt before she said, "You must be Nick. Serena's just indoors, getting ready. I'm Reeva Brown-Carstairs. Serena's mother." Actually, she was assessing more than his clothes as she put out her hand for Nick. He had to juggle the wine and flowers to shake her hand, and when they parted fingers he felt thoroughly dissected.

Reeva raised her arm dripping with the multi-colored material. "This is Gerry Carstairs, my husband."

The man rose, smiling. "Pleased to meet you, Nick." He came forward to shake Nick's hand.

"Let's put those on the table." Reeva relieved him of the bottle and flowers. "Sit down. Do you want a drink?"

"No, thanks." Nick saw Reeva give him another long look while he pulled forward one of the chairs. Reeva and Gerry were either here to babysit the house for the evening or they were accompanying Serena to the party. He hoped it was the babysitting duty, but as they were so dressed up he presumed they were also going to the party.

Reeva floated through a glass door into the plant-filled sunroom. "I'll go and tell Serena you're here."

Gerry settled back into his seat, cradling his beer. "Ladies always have to get gussied up for parties."

Nick sat down, nodded and smiled, although he didn't feel like smiling. He felt irritated at the possibility that he might not be alone with Serena this evening. He felt annoyed he wasn't alone with her now. He was even more frustrated when Serena appeared, looking beautiful in a pair of flowing cream silk pants and a snug top with a narrow gold belt at her waist. On her feet were pale gold leather sandals and her hair was upswept. Long gold earrings with a diamond in each flashed money. He wanted her all to himself.

"Hi, Nick." She smiled her TV smile. "Sorry about the commotion. Mom and Gerry were invited tonight, so they decided to come by and we'll all go together. All right?"

It wasn't, but he couldn't very well demur in front of her mother and stepfather. He rose and indicated that the flowers and the wine were for her.

"You shouldn't have bothered." She peeked at the flowers and gave him a smile that was less TV. "But they're pretty. Really pretty. I'll go and find a vase to put them in. Do you want to come inside and see the house, Nick? Mom make sure Gerry has another beer from the cooler."

Serena carried the flowers. Nick carried the wine. She ushered him inside the sunroom and closed the door. He followed her lithe, slim, sexy scurrying figure from the sunroom into a bright, pretty kitchen.

"Put the wine on the table," she directed, and began opening doors to look inside cupboards until she eventually drew out a crystal vase. She turned on the tap at the sink.

She held the vase under the running water. "I'm sorry about the extras for this evening. But Mom called last night to give instructions. That's what my mother does, gives instructions."

Nick's eyes were on her fluid body beneath the silky outfit. "And you don't?"

Her eyes were huge tonight. "Don't what?"

"Give instructions. Like, 'Put the wine on the table.'"

She touched her forehead with the back of her wrist. "Sorry. It's just that when mother visits she likes everything just so, and I feel I have to please her all the time. This is me pleasing."

"Don't you ever tell her no?"

Serena stood the vase of water on the counter, opened the paper and spread the flowers beside the vase. Nick saw her hands were shaking, and he realized just how fragile she was. He felt enormous warmth and sympathy for her as she began to slide each flower into the vase in a floral arrangement that seemed to come instinctively to her. "I used to once, but since she's become Reeva Brown-Carstairs, Councilor, I let her have her way. It's easier."

Nick pushed his hands into his pockets. "I can see why that would be. She's quite a powerhouse. What was she like once, when you could say no?"

"Oh." Serena popped a white daisy into the vase beside a pink one. "It's a long story."

Nick figured everything about Serena was a long story, but the possibility of problems didn't dim his attraction to her. He was even aware that his attraction wasn't completely sexual. It was everything. And that worried him. This was no chick he could seduce for great sex. This was a woman who might crawl into his heart. But he still wanted to seduce her. The need to have her was becoming quite painful.

She stood away from the flower arrangement, touched a loose tendril of hair on her neck and glanced at him. "How's that?"

"Very professional."

"I worked for a florist when I was a teenager."

"Before you decided on journalism?"

She nodded. "Yep." She walked forward to adjust one of the ferns. "I'll put the flowers on the table." She carried the vase to the table. Then she picked up the wine bottle and held it up to read the label. "Sauvignon Blanc. My favorite. Thank you. Do you want a glass?"

Nick wished things were different. Yes. He'd like a glass, or even two, but with her, alone. Not with other people outside awaiting them. Not with a party to go to, where he'd likely drink more than his share anyway. He didn't even want to go to the party. He'd like to stay here with Serena and get down to something hot and heavy. She made his body burn like a furnace.

He pushed his hands deeper into his pockets. "Let's save it for later."

"Okay." She glanced at the microwave clock. "We have to get going anyway. I guess we'll have some shuffling of cars in the driveway. Gerry's a drive-up-and-just-park-anywhere type of driver. Did you park behind him?"

"I did. What does he do for a living?" Nick wanted to get away from his scalding thoughts of what he would rather to do tonight.

"He consults, mostly in property deals. Makes a bundle. Mother's not badly off. She sold her string of successful florist shops when she decided to go into politics."

Nick shouldn't be surprised at anything Serena told him. "So flowers are in your blood as well as journalism?" He knew after the words were formed that he'd said the wrong thing.

Her wide forehead creased. "What do you mean?"

Nick shrugged. "You know what I mean."

"Did you just know, or did Don tell you? Because if Don told you, I've got some bones to pick with that man."

Nick prepared himself for a rocky road. "Don told me, but I think I would have figured it out, especially after meeting your brother. You see, I have your father's book at home with his face on the cover, and your brother is the spitting image of him."

She nodded. "He is, isn't he? Just lately, since he's got older and become a man."

Nick heard her voice quiver and knew he was treading extremely delicate ground. "Don did mention that you didn't associate your work with your father. That's fine. It doesn't make any difference to me one way or the other."

She posed her head to one side. "Oh? It does to most journalists. I mean, he was sort of a pioneer of modern TV journalism. He's an idol." Her voice broke and she tried to cover her confusion by fiddling with the flowers once more. A pink one here, a white one there. She gave up with a piece of fern she couldn't jam down between them and began to wrap it around her fingers.

Nick moved closer to her. He could smell her expensive perfume. Beneath the creamy silk her body rippled with all sorts of feminine delights. But it wasn't sex she was rippling with. It was grief. Tears flooded her eyes.

She looked at him. "Why did you have to say anything?"

"It just came out. I didn't mean to."

"But you knew all this time." She flung the fern down on the table. "Damn Don. He shouldn't have said a word. He knows I like to go on my own merit. Now you'll be comparing me, thinking, 'Oh, her journalism is weak compared to her father's. Where does she get off?'"

"Is that why you don't acknowledge him?"

"Partly, I guess. It's not important."

He raised an eyebrow. "No?"

"No."

She wasn't telling the truth. Her father's memory bothered her to no end, otherwise she would acknowledge him. Knowing everything about family dysfunction and how it hurt, he moved closer to her, wanting to comfort her.

She moistened her lips with her tongue and put her head to one side so that her diamond earrings flashed in the light. "We'd better go."

"No. You're too upset." He put his arms around her, hoping to soothe, but instead she turned her head so that her mouth came close to his. He couldn't stop himself from kissing her.

Nick expected to be pushed away, but instead she ground her hips against him and he felt himself losing part of his sanity as his tongue delved between her teeth and she parted her lips to let him inside. His hands desperately massaged her hips, and their mouths hungrily locked together.

The sunroom door opened and Reeva called through the house. "Serena. Are we leaving yet?"

Serena suddenly seemed to realize what she was doing, and she thrust Nick away and stumbled from him to hang on to the kitchen counter. She held her head high and straightened her shoulders, calling out, "We'll be there in five minutes, Mom."

Nick heard the door close again.

"That's been coming since we met," Nick said. Then he raked his fingers through his hair, knowing there was a high flush of color on his cheekbones, knowing he couldn't hide how aroused she made him. He'd never been affected by a woman so quickly, so mindlessly in his life.

●

Serena didn't know where the anger came from. It welled from inside her and she thought as she lashed out at Nick that she might be actually lashing out at herself. "It wasn't coming from me. I don't know what ideas you've got into your head. We work together, Nick. That's it. Nothing else."

"I didn't start that. You wanted me."

"You caught me unawares."

"I was going to comfort you."

Serena touched her lips with her fingers and she could still feel his mouth there. She had been far too aggressive. "My lipstick. I have to fix my lipstick. Go and tell the others I'll be with them in seconds. I'll lock up the house. We have to go."

"Okay. Ignore what's going on. What the hell do I care? You're trouble anyway."

"What do you mean, trouble?"

His eyes were narrowed, so she couldn't see his expression. "You know what I mean. You're hung up about your father for some reason. Lord knows why. He was famous. You should revel in his fame. He did great things for journalism."

She realized that Nick Fraser was getting right down into the core of her. "Maybe for journalism. But he didn't do great things for anyone else in his life."

"So that's it? It's not his professional life that you're running from, it's his personal affiliations."

Serena felt like she'd been wound up with a key inside. Hell, she'd felt like she'd been wound up ever since she had heard Nick Fraser's name over her cell phone the other day. "Personal affiliations. That's a cute way of saying that my father's family interaction stank."

"Is that what it is?"

"Yes, that's what it is." Serena placed her hands on her hips. She had to cool down if she were to be in any shape for the party. "I don't want to discuss this tonight, Nick."

"But we will discuss it?"

"Why do we need to discuss it?"

"Because it upsets you so much. I think you need to talk about it with someone who understands. I was thinking of doing a documentary on your father. I need your permission. Well, I'll need your family's permission. But it would give you a chance to think about him, to talk about him."

Serena couldn't believe he was so brazen. Kissing her one minute, the next standing there saying he wanted to do a documentary on her father. "That's all you want from me, is it?"

Nick stepped forward, looking as if he wanted to hold her in his arms again. "Serena."

She backed away from him. "Don't touch me again. And I want you to shut up about him and don't bring up his name in my presence."

Nick raised an eyebrow. "I don't think we even mentioned his name."

Pascal, who had slid unnoticed into the kitchen, jumped on the table between them, startling them. He poked his black leathery nose into the flowers and promptly sneezed.

Serena scooped him off the table, uncaring she was wearing silk and his claws could do damage. She was just pleased for the interruption. "Pascal, this is Nick."

Nick extended his finger to Pascal, who rubbed his cheek on his hand. "This is your housemaster, I presume."

"Yes. He is."

Nick patted the shiny gray head between the upright ears. "Extremely pleased to meet you, Pascal."

Pascal also seemed very pleased to meet Nick, and Serena had to actually move closer because Pascal wanted to sniff his hand in more detail.

Serena watched Nick's big capable hand gently rubbing Pascal. "He seems to have taken to you."

"I think we've all taken to each other. Whatever you think. Now, I'll go and see Gerry about switching cars."

Serena noticed some of her lipstick had been transferred on to Nick's mouth. She let Pascal wriggle away and went to the counter to tug a tissue from the box there. She returned to Nick. "Let me wipe my lipstick from your mouth first."

He stood still as she wiped his firm lips. Her mark on his mouth, proving they had been about to lose it temporarily. If she was ever going to lose it with any man, it would be Nick. She knew that now. Her body still pulsed from the pressure of his.

She was about to remove her hand when he caught her fingers

with his own. Kisses flew across her fingertips, reigniting the fire. Breathlessly, she tugged her fingers from his, seeing their hands parting in reluctant slow motion.

"Serena." Her mother again, calling from the door. "Gerry can't get out with Nick's car parked there."

"Go."

He went, and for a second she didn't know what to do with herself. Then she tossed the tissue into the garbage bin under the sink and decided she might have lost it temporarily but she wasn't going to lose it forever. From now on Nick Fraser was going to be kept exactly where she wanted him, at a great distance.

Pascal was back on the table, sniffing around the flowers, and Serena decided she was going to have to put the flowers in a higher spot if she didn't want to find them on the floor when she arrived home. She carried the vase into the living room and placed it on the mantel. She didn't think Pascal ever jumped up there.

Her mother walked in on her as Serena turned around.

"The flowers are pretty," Reeva said. "He's an interesting man."

"Nick?"

"Naturally, Nick. All I'm going to say, Serena, is watch him. He has the same look in his eye as your father, and he was entirely unreliable. You want a man you can dominate, not a man who dominates and controls your life until you can't operate without him. All I'm saying is, don't fall in love with him."

Serena touched one of her earrings. Could her mother see her lipstick was worn off by a man's mouth? "Heaven's, no. I'm working with the man. And I have to admit I've already noted the similarity."

"It's pretty obvious. He's a handsome devil, with that hard shell exterior." Reeva swished forward and adjusted a couple of flowers in Serena's arrangement.

Serena wanted to go over and return the flowers to their former position, but she knew she couldn't do that in front of her mother. Actually, she didn't have the guts or the inclination for a fight tonight. Her mother was so damn strong and manipulative. She couldn't believe she was the same crumpled woman who had been used and manipulated by Stuart Redding Brown.

"Still, it doesn't matter that you are working with the man. You can still fall for him. Beware. That's all I'm saying. Now I just want to pay a visit to the little girls' room. Is your cat supposed to be on the furniture, sweetie?"

Serena lifted Pascal off the back of the high sofa that was closest to the mantel and carried him outside. She closed the living room door. Pascal was up to tricks. And so was Nick. He thought she was eager for him, and she'd given him that impression. Or had his kisses merely been a way of trying to soften her up, so he could persuade her to give him permission to do a documentary on her father's life? If he'd read her father's book, then he was probably a fan. That he wanted to do the documentary proved his interest. Trying to get closer to her than necessary, like taking her for supper the other night and lunch at his apartment might be triggered by his desire for the documentary. If that was his motive, then she really was going to have to watch herself. No more slip-ups like the one tonight. As soon as she'd been in his arms she'd lost all coherent thought and wanted only him.

Serena popped into her bedroom and swiped some more lipstick across her lips.

"I'm ready now," her mother said from the doorway. "Are you ready?"

Serena picked up her gold leather handbag. "Yes. I'm ready." But she knew she wasn't.

Chapter Seven

Don's house was a stone mansion set in a few acres of land that had once been part of a farm. Barbara Steel greeted them as soon as they left the Lincoln. For some reason Nick had expected Don to be linked with a younger woman, but, like her husband, Barbara was in her fifties. Her hair, a brown and gray mixture, was loose around her bony shoulders and the long, gold cotton dress and flat gold sandals made her appear very thin.

As they were escorted by Barbara to the back of the house Reeva whispered to everyone, "She looks like a street person."

Suppressing a twitch of humor, Nick noticed Serena raise her eyes heavenwards as if praying for her mother not to say anything like that to Don.

"She's an artist," he heard Serena say softly. "And you, of all people, shouldn't be so politically incorrect."

"It's not being politically incorrect. It's being truthful. I don't know what Don sees in her."

"Mother. Cut it out. They've been married for thirty years and have three grown children. So something must have fused."

"I still think she looks wrong for him."

Nick wasn't so sure about that. Barbara might not have Reeva's sophisticated style but she appeared to live by the strength of her convictions. That type of strength always impressed him.

Barbara beckoned them across a lawn that took up half of the naturalized garden. The rest of the vast property was a surrounding forest of trees. It made for a perfectly private setting for a party. Nick moved up beside Serena so that Gerry could walk in front of them with Reeva. "What are your mother's politics, by the way?"

"She's all over the place. I never quite know what wavelength she's on."

He could see Serena was annoyed with her mother. She was still annoyed with him as well. She'd sat far apart in the back of the car on the way over here and hadn't joined in with the conversation. He'd been pretty stupid to mention doing a documentary on her father after discovering how wrought up she was about Stuart Redding Brown. What he'd really meant was that maybe doing a documentary on her father might help her combat her pain. She hadn't got that message though.

Barbara's entourage came to a stop at Don. Don placed his arm around his wife's shoulders and tugged her close to his hip. The possessive gesture reminded Nick of his parents' way with each other. Which in turn reminded him of why he was connected to Steel TV. He was here for his parents' welfare, not to get enmeshed in an affair, or even more, with Serena.

Don, wearing jeans and a more subdued blue shirt tonight, beamed at them all. "Good to see you again, Reeva and Gerry. There's a great deal to celebrate this evening, with Serena's and Nick's upcoming show." He acknowledged Nick with a grin and gave Serena rather a sly glance. "I'm going to leave it to Serena to introduce you to everyone, Nick. She's been with Steel longer than most."

Don moved on to greet his next guests. Reeva and Gerry disappeared to make their presence known. Nick was left with Serena.

"Are you going to introduce me?"

"Naturally I will. I can't leave you standing on your own."

He made his expression one of mock sadness, hoping to lighten the atmosphere between them. "No. You definitely can't." Then he caught hold of her hand. "Forgive me for what happened in the kitchen."

He felt her trying to remove her fingers from his and he had to let them go without a struggle.

"Nick. Forget it."

He wanted to explain what he'd meant about her father, but he didn't want to upset her again. "All right. Forget it. Let's enjoy the party."

She glanced around with a twist of her slim body. "I see some of the floor crew over there. They're fun."

Nick was introduced to Gene Rowson, a videographer with a round, boyish face, Dick Lane, who said he had been in Canada ten years from England but he still retained a British accent, and Margie Dawes from Makeup, short, plump and dark-haired.

"Anyone heard how John is?" Serena asked the group.

"He'll be having a damn good rest if he's smart," Dick said. "I suggested he pull a bird and shack up for the next few months."

"You would," she said. "That's all you think about."

Dick had a wicked glint in his green eyes. "Sex is the only free entertainment these days."

"Don't believe it," Gene told him. "The last woman I went out with ditched me for a guy with a Mercedes."

Margie nudged his arm. "Your old Ford not good enough, Gene?"

"It's still going." Gene defended his car.

"Like you," Dick retorted. "It limps along. Maybe it was the limp she didn't go for, Gene, old boy."

Gene grinned. "Limp is not my problem, old boy."

Serena laughed and Nick enjoyed seeing her loosen up.

"You guys going to work with us on *Neon Nights*?" Serena asked.

Dick gave her a deep look. "If you want us honeybunch."

"Can't live without the Dick and Gene show?" Margie asked.

"Oh, maybe I can. I need to be more serious on *Neon Nights*." She turned to include Nick. "My co-host, here, is a serious news man."

Nick felt her dig. He also saw the other employees give him a look that said he was a little bit of an intruder. Well, maybe he was. Don had hired him on a large salary to bail out a show. He was here for a short time and he didn't have to become involved with any of the staff on a personal level. They knew all that.

Serena began talking to Margie, and Nick found himself parted from her. Hell, this was a party, he decided. He should mix. Except he didn't know anyone. For a second he felt out of his element, rather like the day he arrived off the bus at camp with a bunch of strange boys. Then someone came up to him and touched his arm. It was Juliette, wearing a silver mini-dress with spaghetti straps and black shoes with high silver heels.

"You look lost, Nick."

He was relieved to see her. "Not anymore. Do you want to go and get a drink?"

"I'd love that. Thanks."

•

Serena didn't realize Nick had left until Margie said, "Look at that. Juliette's getting her claws into Nick Fraser right away. Poor Pat."

Serena looked in the direction Margie indicated. Nick and Juliette stood close together. They seemed to have a lot to say to one another and it appeared as if Nick couldn't keep his eyes off Juliette's plunging cleavage. "Why poor Pat?"

"Didn't you know she and Pat were a big item once?"

"No. I didn't."

"Well, Pat's pretty circumspect. But we all knew, even if he didn't think so. He began dating Juliette and he got serious. Slithery Juliette doesn't want serious. No way."

"I've heard from Juliette herself that Nick is a love 'em and leave 'em type, so they'll make a good couple."

Margie nodded. "Could be. They do look good together."

The couple was at the beer cooler. Nick extracted two bottles from the crushed ice, de-capped them, and handed one to Juliette. Leaning back a little, she let the condensation from the bottle drip against her breasts, to cool herself down, and Nick looked at her as if he wanted to bend over and lick the droplets of iced water from her flesh. Serena wondered if Juliette could possibly have told Serena those stories about Nick to warn Serena off a man she wanted for herself. Well, Juliette didn't have to worry. Serena wasn't going to fall into bed with Nick. But it was going to be darn hard trying not to.

"Anyway, Serena," Margie said. "I'm gonna go see Gene again. One day I'll get that guy to notice me."

"Good luck." Margie had been crazy about Gene since she started at Steel.

Someone put cool hands on Serena's shoulders. "Guess?"

She knew the voice. "Pat."

"You're good." Patrick McHaney smiled. He hosted *This is Science* on Steel. He was a very tall, rugged man in jeans and a checked shirt. Tonight his brown hair had taken a daring leap into a ponytail. Pat rarely shaved right down to his skin, and his jaw bore a shadow of a beard. "Having fun?"

Knowing about his affair with Juliette now put Pat in a different light for her. "I don't know yet. We haven't been here very long."

"You came with Nick Fraser?"

"Not really. He didn't know the way, so we met at my house first, seeing I only live around the corner." She found herself glancing across the pool, and saw no sign of a woman in a silver dress and a man in ivory trousers and a black shirt. Serena's heart sank like a stone down into her stomach until her body felt shaky.

"So you're not here together?"

"No. We're not."

"Great." Pat sounded angry. And before Serena had time to answer him he took hold of her hand. "I want to go and find them."

Serena found herself being dragged over the lawn. "Who?"

"Fraser and Juliette. I saw them together. And he's not having her."

Serena had never seen Pat emotional. His show was succinct and professional. But right now he was in a state. Margie had been right about him. He was crazy about Juliette.

Pulling Serena along at a quick pace, he said, "We'll just take a walk around the property and check out their whereabouts."

"A walk? This is a run. Slow down."

"Sorry." He slowed his pace.

"Oh, Pat. You might get hurt." Not to mention how she would feel if she came across the couple in a compromising embrace.

"I'm already hurt. I've got nowhere else to go."

"I didn't even know you went around with her."

"Well, I did and it was hot and heavy for about three months. But she's her own person, know what I mean? She likes living in her elegant penthouse and racing around in her white Mustang. She likes being single."

"Don't you?" Serena knew that Pat also had a fancy apartment and a fast car. She'd heard the twin exhausts rumbling in the parking lot many times.

"I'd trade everything tomorrow for a two-story house and a mini-van load of kids. I was adopted into a wonderful family and I'd like to return the favors bestowed on me for my own kids, and for others if I can adopt. But it can get too late to adopt."

Serena was always amazed at what came out of the people you least expected it to come out of. "You think Juliette is that type of mother?"

"I think she could be."

"I'm not so sure about that." Serena felt worried. Pat seemed to be going after the wrong woman. "Her parents are well heeled. She had a private education. I can't see her driving a mini-van full of kids to hockey practice."

"I love her. She loves me. I'm sure of it. She merely got cold feet when I asked her to marry me."

They were on the other side of the rectangular swimming pool now. Nick and Juliette were still nowhere to be seen. Serena tried not to imagine Juliette being the recipient of one of Nick's hot, urgent kisses.

"Serena," a voice said behind her, and she turned around to see Paul Kryker. On his arm was a thin, angular woman with upswept brown hair. She was dressed in a print suit and conservative stubby heels, the sort of clothes that made her look as if she'd recently stepped out of a downtown office block.

Paul introduced her as Elaine Marcotti, his fiancé, and Serena wondered why everyone seemed so mismatched. Don and Barbara. Juliette and Pat. Now Paul and Elaine.

Elaine put out her hand in slow motion, as if she were in awe of Serena. "I've seen you on TV. I was really excited when Paul told me who he was going to work with."

Serena shook the woman's limp hand. "That's wonderful." Then she introduced Pat, who Elaine had also seen on TV. Serena could tell Pat was only interested in finding Juliette, and this introduction was a mere irritation.

"I'm finding this so thrilling," Elaine told Serena. "What's it like starring on TV?"

"It's a job." Serena wondered what Paul had got himself into. This woman was weird. "What do you do, Elaine?"

"I work in a bank. It's soooooo boring. But since I met Paul I've been really fortunate in being able to live more of an exciting life."

Pat spotted Nick and Juliette. "Come on, Serena. Nice meeting you Elaine. Paul. See you around."

Serena didn't want to interrupt Nick with Juliette. "I'm going to rest for a while," she told Pat. "You go see her by yourself."

Serena walked across the lawn, wondering what she could do next. She'd just about talked to everyone she wanted to talk to.

Nick and Juliette were surrounded by a crowd now, and Pat was on the prowl around the outskirts of the group. Well, good luck to him.

She sat down on a bench that circled a tree, drained the rest of her wine and put the empty glass on the seat beside her. She felt like plunging her head into her hands in despair. Some part of her wanted to cry.

If she had any guts she'd go up to Nick, grab his hand and drag him away from Juliette. She'd take him to an empty room and she'd tell him she wanted what she had shown him she wanted in the kitchen. If she did that she might get her sexual frustration over and then she'd feel fine again. She was sure that was the answer. But she didn't have the guts. She couldn't face the fact that she would have to interact with his body and his mind. Relationships, she decided, picking up her empty glass, were far too complex. What she needed was a lot more wine. Then she could cope with the rest of what was already a long evening.

Serena met her mother at the bar.

"There you are," Reeva said. "We were just talking about choosing a table to sit at for dinner. Doesn't the barbecue smell good?"

Serena had been so twisted into her own thoughts that she hadn't noticed the food was almost ready to be served. "Yes. It does smell good. Shall I sit with you?"

"Of course. Gerry's found a spot."

The spot was a redwood picnic table.

"Shall we dump our purses and go and get something to eat?" Reeva said.

Serena agreed and followed Gerry and Reeva to the barbecue. Don's oldest son, Len, who was already a giant like his father, and was sometimes seen around Steel TV doing odd jobs, had cooked lean chicken breasts and hamburgers to complement the table full of vegetables and salads. As they filled their plates she felt Nick beside her.

"Hi," he said. "Do you have a family table?"

"Yes. We do."

"Mind if I join you?"

"What about Juliette?"

"She's been snagged by a guy named Patrick McHaney, who seems to have the hots for her."

"So you might as well slum it with Serena?" She shouldn't sound so jealous but she was.

He grinned. "Believe me, you are not slumming it. And you don't have to get so upset. I'll be with you this evening, if you want me to be."

"I didn't mean that."

"Yes. You did."

Serena wished he wouldn't keep prodding her for the truth. "Come with me. I'll lead you to the table."

"Nick. How nice." Reeva waved when she saw him. "Let's cozy up and eat. What do you think of the party so far? Meeting lots of interesting people?"

Serena had to admit that Nick had a certain charm. Reeva usually did all the talking, but with Nick she actually stopped and listened for once. Even Gerry seemed amused by this.

When they'd finished their first course Gerry and Nick went to get coffee and dessert, and a maid served glasses of after-dinner brandy.

"I saw Seth yesterday," Serena told her mother, thinking she should fill Reeva in on Seth's career. "Don's agreed to use his group as the music for my new show."

"What an opportunity for him. That's wonderful. How is he?"

"He looked good."

"He looks like your father, doesn't he? More and more." Reeva shook her head.

Serena nodded. "Yes. He does look like him. Mom, he said something to me that I felt bad about. He said he felt that we neglect him. He seems to want to have some family get-togethers."

Reeva looked surprised. "He said that?"

"Yes. He seems hurt that we don't see him more often."

"I always thought he wanted to be left alone to pursue his career. He left home young enough. He was a moody young man."

"Well, he's not so young any more, and I think he wants more of a family connection. I wouldn't mind seeing more of him either. I'm not going to have much spare time in the next few weeks, but there is Thanksgiving. We could all go out to dinner."

"Now that's a great idea. Gerry and I will arrange something. I'll call Seth and invite him. Let's hope he's not on a gig."

"Even if he can't come at least he'll have been invited."

"That's true. I've always felt so out of my depth with him. He needed a father. It's such a pity he died."

"He didn't have to do what he did."

Reeva pleated her wide sleeve. "Oh, yes, he did. Your father wouldn't have been happy any other way. You can't stop people doing what they want to do. If he'd stayed, it would have had to have been his choice."

"That's the point, Mom. He chose to be away from us."

Reeva sighed. "I know. That's what hurt. I wasn't important enough, I suppose." Her glance moved to Gerry who was walking toward them with Nick. Both men were carrying trays. "But I am important to Gerry. Your father was probably just the wrong man." As Nick would be the wrong man for her.

Serena didn't really taste much of the delicious vanilla and blueberry cheesecake. Neither did the coffee taste of much more than bitter water. She really just wished this evening would be over, and she gulped down the brandy so fast it made her brain spin.

Someone turned the music up, and she saw that couples were dancing. Margie had snared Gene, and had pushed herself really close to him. If Gene would see sense, then Serena did see a well-matched couple in the two of them.

Reeva and Gerry rose from the table. "Are you two going to dance?" Reeva asked.

Nick moved closer to Serena. "Interested?"

Serena shifted away from the V formed by his spread thighs. He was like fire, closing in on a block of ice. Ice he'd almost melted once tonight. "I'd like my food to be digested before I begin jumping around."

Reeva had her arm looped through her husband's. "All right. Come on Ger."

When they were alone Nick smiled. "Fine by me. I'm not much of a dancer."

They sat for a while in silence, the music throbbing over them. Nick shifted closer. He wasn't actually touching her but his breath fluttered the wisps of hair on her cheek line. He made a mock attempt to bite her earring, and she ducked her head.

"Nick, please don't do that." Serena picked up her glass and finished off the brandy.

"Want mine as well?" Nick pushed his glass toward her.

"Don't you like brandy?"

"I don't drink spirits. It's sort of—" He shrugged his shoulders. "Something I don't do."

That made him different from her father, she thought, remembering the empty whiskey bottles on the kitchen counter when he was around.

"I don't really like it much either."

"But tonight you need a little extra courage?"

"I'm not really a party person."

He chuckled. "That's because you can't let go of your inhibitions. Like you did in your kitchen with me. Now that really disturbs you, doesn't it?"

"Didn't we say we were going to forget it?"

"Yep. But I can't."

The vibrant emotion in his voice rocked through her. It was emotion she would never have expected from Nick. She turned her face and his mouth was close to hers. His lips touched her lips for a moment.

Nick's scar appeared vulnerable at close range, and she remembered the video she had viewed in Don's office. She reached up and traced the scar with her forefinger. He kept his gaze on her. She felt the pressure of one of his thighs against her lower back. She was enveloped by his lean, hard body, and she knew how it would feel naked in the dark. Deep needs trembled up through her to make her throat ache and her head throb. She knew he could feel her trembling.

He swept back a wisp of her hair with his fingers, very gently, but she could feel every moment, every movement. "You don't like people close, do you?"

Feeling as if all her muscles and tendons were about to snap, she shook her head. "No."

"I don't like people in my face either, but for some strange reason I don't mind you. And I love it when you touch me like that."

She withdrew her fingers from his face.

He stroked her lower back. "Want to tell me why you're so jumpy about being close? Is it me in particular? Because it seems that way. You seemed to have something against me when I met you on Wednesday evening. And we'd never met before."

Nick kissed her mouth again. He was stealing kisses when she least expected them. She was becoming breathless from his seduction. His next kiss was a definite kiss that made him confident. She gave in, and, longing to touch him, her hand moved across the space between them. Closing her eyes, she let her fingers massage the taut muscle of his thigh. Then she realized what she was doing and moved her hand, knuckles brushing his groin.

He ended the kiss then, and he was smiling and breathing hard at the same time. "Stop that." He lifted his finger and traced it over her lips. "You're hot beneath that cool exterior. I like it. What is your reason for being difficult?"

What could she tell him to make him understand? The truth? "You remind me of my father. That's one reason."

"Ah." He looked surprised. "I must say I'm flattered."

"You shouldn't be."

"Oh, but I am. But now we've got him out in the open it might do you good to talk about him. You must have read his book."

"No. I haven't."

"I'll lend it to you if you haven't got a copy. I'm sure you would find things in it that would help you."

"Help me with what?"

He caressed her spine. "Help you to get a grip on what type of man he was."

"I know what type of man he was. Now let me go."

"I might have to. There isn't time for hang-ups in the short time I have home."

Thank goodness he understood. And thank goodness he'd reminded her that he was only here indefinitely. Serena smiled with relief. "Well, then. That's it. We've come to a decision. No hanky-panky between us."

He chuckled. "What you want is safety, isn't it? You want to stay in your little cage and be secure. You're the last little patch of snow that the sun can't melt because you remain in the shade. You know, affairs are fun, Serena. You don't have to involve your heart. You just get together, go on a few dates and have great sex."

"Is that your philosophy?"

"Yes. That's my philosophy. That's what I offer up front. A good time. Would you go for that? That way you remain in your safe little nest."

"It wouldn't be that way, Nick. Every experience changes a person. Leaving any nest is difficult."

"To some extent, maybe, but if you go into the experience with a certain frame of mind, you can remain sane when you leave it. Believe me. I've done it many times."

Serena thought for a moment she saw a little boy in front of her, stubbornly thrusting out his jaw in an effort to be brave. Then she saw him grin. "You're so tense, Serena. I could help. Great sex."

"Shut up about your great sex." She struggled away from him, but in the end there was no struggle because he moved away. Now she missed his warm body and the possibility of feeling his mouth upon hers again. How perverse?

Nick rose from the seat. "So that's my offer. No strings. You'd be perfectly safe. So if you ever feel the need I'll be willing. You really turn me on Serena Brown."

He walked away from her with the air of a man who was completely confident in who he was, who had no cares in the world, who lived by his beliefs. And yet Serena felt haunted by that brief vision of a small boy stubbornly being brave.

Chapter Eight

Serena picked up Nick's untouched brandy and sipped the fiery liquid. Anything to calm her down, she thought.

Pat slouched onto the opposite bench seat. "You let Fraser loose and Juliette's snagged him again."

That news made her feel worse, but it was her own fault. She could have had Nick. "What's the time?"

Pat checked his watch. "Ten past midnight. Can't you tell? Everyone's hammered. Don's already assigning beds and sleeping bags."

"Are you staying?"

"No. I like to go to my own place." Pat placed his arms on the table and leaned forward. "I know she's not with me at this moment, but I can tell Juliette still likes me. There's something there. Would you mind keeping Fraser occupied over these next few months? I'd like a chance to work on her."

Serena didn't need this. "Pat. If occupied means what I think it means, I can't do it."

"All you have to do is keep him working hard so he hasn't got time for play."

"He'd find time for play. He's only been back since Wednesday and he's on the hunt."

"That's why I'm worried. Juliette's an ideal short term toy for him."

"I can't stop Juliette." Serena felt very strung out. She finished Nick's brandy and lined up the two bowled glasses beside one another.

"But you can hinder the progress of an affair between them. It would hurt me greatly if they became a couple, even for the short duration that Fraser is here. I couldn't stand it, Serena."

His last words were like an aching cry, and Serena realized how very much Pat did love Juliette. It would also hurt her greatly if Nick had one of his affairs with Juliette, although she wasn't going to admit that. So she nodded. "All right. I'll keep him busy. But not the way you mean."

"That's fine. You don't have to go to bed with him, but you can keep him interested. He's already interested. I can see that. So keep him chasing you."

"What if he catches me though, Pat?" That scenario was a very distinct possibility. How much strength of will did she actually possess?

"You won't allow it to go that far. You're known as the Ice Maiden."

Serena gazed at Pat in shock. "I am?"

Pat shrugged. "Yes. Some guys even think you prefer women."

"This is my reputation?" She poked her chest with her finger.

"Yes. It's not discussed at great length, but guys have said things when I've been around."

"What do you think?"

Pat shook his head in a way that said he wished he'd never begun this topic. "If I didn't care about Juliette so much I'd go for you. How's that?"

"Not good enough. The gossip has to be stopped. It's not true."

"Then keep Nick Fraser interested and away from Juliette. That will disprove the rumors."

How was she ever going to do that? Serena saw Nick and Juliette dancing together. Juliette sort of plunged her body against men when she danced with them. Nick was probably aroused at this moment, and, having been turned down for great sex by Serena, was contemplating where he was going to take Juliette in the next five minutes.

Feeling as unhappy as Pat was looking, she wondered if she did have it in her to give Nick a chase? He didn't have to catch her. She could keep him happy with a few crazy kisses like the one in the kitchen. She knew how to keep herself distant from emotions. She'd kept distant from her father all of her life. She'd just have to use the same tactics when she dealt with Nick. Actually, when she thought of him in comparison to her father, she didn't care for him much anyway. It might be easy, and it would give Pat a clear field to

Juliette and, in the process, banish her own strange reputation.

However, she couldn't begin tonight. No way could she walk up to the couple dancing on the grass and demand a dance with Nick. No way could she loll up against Nick's body the way Juliette was doing, especially in front of her colleagues. She might think she could do this for Pat and her reputation, but she might not be able to put the action into practice. Although she had sat at this very picnic table and kissed Nick. Had anyone seen that? Could they tell where her hand had strayed? So what? If her reputation was the way Pat intimated then maybe her interlude with Nick, if it had been observed, might stop the rumors.

Feeling utterly confused, Serena excused herself from Pat and walked to the house. She needed some time away from the throbbing sound and the sight of Nick and Juliette laughing into one another's eyes.

Don intercepted her on the way. "Haven't seen you all evening, Serena. Where have you been hiding?"

He slurred his words and his breath smelled strongly of beer. Serena averted her face. "I haven't been hiding anywhere."

"Well, let's say, then, that you haven't been conspicuous. Everyone has the idea that Fraser and Marshall are the hot couple of the moment, not you and Fraser." He tried to focus his eyes upon her.

Serena wished that all this Nick and Juliette stuff would disappear into thin air and leave her alone. She longed to return to the other day, before the phone call in her car from Don. She'd been ecstatic at the school opening ceremony, with the prospect of her new show ready to start with John.

"I can't help who Nick likes."

Don put his arm around her shoulders and turned her into a huddle. "Except I want him to like you. Now I would have been happy with John Duncan. I could have lived with him. But we haven't got him anymore. Nick Fraser makes John look like a dink. Let's face it. John's a pretty face without much between his ears. Nick Fraser, and I hate to say this, is like your father. He's got it all."

Serena disliked it when men got drunk and got serious at the same time. And why was everyone suddenly bringing up her father? It was as if Nick Fraser had stepped into the picture and, bingo, Stuart Redding Brown had been brought to life. "That's another thing, Don. My father. You told Nick who my father was."

"He would have guessed anyway."

"Maybe. But I go on my own merit. You know that."

Don crowded her even more. "I also know that your dad was a great news guy. Like Fraser."

She couldn't dispute that remark. She knew that Don had worked for her father once, when he was younger in the field himself. "Okay. I admit he was a great news guy. But all this has nothing to do with you manipulating Nick Fraser into being my co-host."

"I did that because I know my stuff. He's the best one for the job. It's like it's meant to be. John Duncan gets sick. Nick Fraser hops on his plane and gets here to save the day."

"A real superman."

Don smiled. "Yep. So make the most of this. It could set you up for an even bigger career."

"I could also be overshadowed by the great Nick Fraser."

"Don't even think it. You each possess your own qualities. Together you will sizzle. Believe me."

Serena did believe him. She believed him because she had already felt the sizzle with Nick. She continued on to the house to escape this madness.

The simplicity of the stone walls on the exterior of the Steel home deceived the viewer into believing the interior would be just as simple. Not so, Serena knew. The interior was cluttered, cluttered with Barbara's paintings and the original advertising art for Don's shirts, cluttered with Don's penchant for strange sculpture, cluttered with magazines, books and large screen TVs on the walls of every room. Serena knew the kitchen was an absolute delight, with an island counter that contained an extra oven and a vegetable cleaning sink. But it was also cluttered with copper pots and pans and rows of china and canned goods. Barbara was a very do-it-herself woman.

The small powder room Serena headed for was occupied. She remembered there was another downstairs bathroom. As she passed through a room she found Barbara sitting quietly on a scarlet velvet sofa, bathed in the glow from a shaded lamp and sipping from a mug.

"Hot chocolate," Barbara said. "Do you want one?"

She couldn't imagine downing hot chocolate on top of the brandy she'd rather stupidly consumed. "No. I'm fine. Thanks. Your small powder room was busy so I was going through to your other bathroom."

Barbara smiled and Serena thought that her mother was wrong. Barbara had classic features that needed little decoration.

"It's been busy all evening. I really hate these parties, you know, but Don's father began the soirée and Don has continued the custom. It's good for morale I suppose, but I find my head begins to buzz from all the noise and the activity."

"I agree with you. Nothing against the party, but I was hoping to drop in and leave early. Then I ended up coming here with my mother, who likes to socialize."

"Socializing is the nature of her business, isn't it? She's a very successful woman. I'm just a more introverted person who doesn't mind being alone. You also came with Nick Fraser, didn't you? I'd never met him in person before."

Serena perched on a footstool that was covered in the same thick red velvet as the sofa. "What did you think of him?"

Barbara took a sip from her mug. "What do you think of him?"

"Intelligent. Good-looking. Smooth."

"Not that smooth. I think he has some rough edges. I only talked to him for a few moments but I've been watching him. He's sure of himself, but he's cultivated that. He has an emotional depth that he tries not to show. But it comes out in his news reports because he's emotionally involved with his job. He loves it."

"You've obviously watched his news reports."

"I started to when Nick came to Don about work. Don brought some videos of Nick's news reports home with him. I found I was fascinated by the man. Not only is he good at his work but he's also easy on the eye."

Serena wasn't surprised by Barb's observations of Nick. She had been to a number of Barbara's art shows, and when her work contained people they always showed a great deal of characterization detail. She studied people. "You're right. Although I haven't really had the chance to work with him yet. All we've had is one meeting, which was really an introduction to one another."

Barb nodded. "Did you like the introduction?"

Serena ran the scarlet velvet nap backward with her fingers. "I haven't come to any conclusion."

"He must have confused you then. He's quite a mixture of cool and emotion. But I believe that's because he's nurtured the cool side. He's either achieved the result to become excellent for the medium of TV, or something happened along the way to hurt him and caused him to build a shell around himself. Does he have a family?"

"He told me that his mother and father live in Toronto and that's about it." Discussing Nick this way made Selena think about the way she had hardened her own emotions against pain because of her father. Was Barbara right? Had Nick had something happen to him that had produced the same result? She recalled the stubborn, little-boy look she'd glimpsed in him this evening. Had it been real or her imagination?

"He's never been married though. Has he?" Barbara asked.

"No. Not as far as I know."

"I'm sure you'll find him fascinating to work with."

"From what I've experienced so far, I'm positive I will."

Barbara laughed. "You sound as if he's giving you a hard time."

Serena was sure Barbara knew exactly what type of hard time Nick was giving her. Wanting to leave the subject of Nick, she glanced around her. "It's soothing here in the house."

"Isn't it? Some peace for me while Don plays his party animal role. Len's like Don, and will follow in his footsteps. He's starting full time at Steel as soon as he's finished college."

Serena hadn't known this. "Will Don slow down with Len's help?"

"I doubt it. He'll make Len start at the bottom, like his father did to him. Besides, he's on to a lot of new projects. Like your show, for one. I'm looking forward to it."

Serena raised an eyebrow. "To see me or Nick?"

"To see both of you. Don has high hopes for you out of this."

This comment made Serena curious. "Has he said much about the show?"

"No. He just told me that John wasn't well and he'd had to replace him with Nick, and that he'd been crossing his fingers for the show when John was going to do it, even though he was pretty sure you could carry it. But now, with Nick, he feels much more confident."

"I understand that. Nick's strong."

Barbara made a face. "But he's still human. One day someone, and it'll be a woman, will come along and hit him in the gut and he'll learn what being strong is."

"You really do think he's hiding something, don't you?"

"Not exactly hiding, but I think he has unresolved differences with himself." They heard some people walk into the house. "I think you'd better go find that bathroom before that lot find it."

"I suppose I should." Serena rose to her feet. "Nice talking to you, Barb."

"A pleasure. Have fun on the show."

Serena locked herself in the bathroom and glanced at her flushed features in the mirror. She looked disheveled so she set about fixing her hair and makeup. Fun. That was something she hadn't had much of in her life. Mainly because she tried so hard to keep herself intact. Nick had been right about that tonight. And was that the image she gave the other employees, which had brought about her ice maiden reputation? If she let loose with Nick, as he suggested, would all that change? Or would she find herself involved with a man who also had a lot of pain in his life? Could she cope with someone else's baggage as well as her own? She stuffed her comb and makeup back into her purse and snapped the clasp. Wasn't this confusion the reason she didn't get involved with men? *Exactly*, she told herself in the mirror. *So don't.*

•

Nick was trying to disentangle himself from Juliette so he could search for Serena. For a long while he'd kept her in his vision, now she had completely disappeared.

Juliette lifted two bottles from the beer cooler, popped the tops and handed him one. She dripped the condensation down her breasts and Nick wished she wouldn't do it. She'd done it once. He'd responded. Now he wouldn't give a damn if she stripped and jumped naked into the pool. Well, he might give a damn. He was a man, after all. But he'd rather be with Serena. He looked at his watch. It was almost one and he was tired. He could feel the pressure around his eyes that told him his jet lag had definitely caught up with him.

Juliette patted his wrist and covered his watch. "The night is young."

"Maybe. But I'm still working on a five-hour jet lag."

"Then why don't we go find a bed and lie down?" She wriggled her hips. "You'll soon have more to think about than being tired."

"I'm not planning on staying here the night. But if you are, go ahead."

"I wasn't planning on staying the night if you're not."

"Well, then, that settles that. I'm not. You're not." He drank from his bottle then looked around. Reeva and Gerry were still soaring from one group to another. He had the impression they might be saying their farewells. In that case they'd be leaving soon.

Juliette moved impatiently. "Nick. What are we going to do?"

Serena could be in the house.

Juliette tapped his shoulder. "Nick?"

"We're not doing anything."

"Great. Then I'll say goodnight. It's been fun. See you around."

Nick watched Juliette stumble away from him. She'd had too much to drink. There was something about the woman that bothered him. She was far too brittle.

Pleased to be alone, Nick dumped his beer bottle down on a table and walked toward the house, where he hoped to find Serena.

He expected an elegant interior, instead he'd never seen such clutter in his life. There was so much furniture and so many TV sets that it was difficult to actually get a picture of the house layout. Nick was sure it was a great place. But for someone like him who liked simplicity of design, Don's house was like walking into chaos.

He found the downstairs powder room, and as he washed his hands he thought he looked tired and even haggard. He had a serious mission to accomplish on his time home. Well, two serious missions, one, his parents' welfare, two, his job, which he needed to help pay for his parents' welfare. He shouldn't be torturing himself with a woman he might be wasting all his energy on. Did he really want to get hooked up with a woman who was hung up over her dead father? Who thought he reminded her of her dead father? Even though it flattered him to be compared to Stuart Redding Brown, there was also something creepy about Serena's thinking he was like her father.

Confused by all that had happened since last Wednesday, he ambled around the house, looking at some of the paintings and sculpture. He was particularly interested in the original paintings that had become some of Don's trademark shirt designs. He was surprised to run into Barbara Steel in one of the rooms. Despite Reeva's reaction to Barbara, he actually rather liked her. She had an acute mind with a deep intelligence. He'd noticed her summing him up, and he was under the impression she'd liked what she saw.

Although he did wonder what she'd seen.

"Hi, Nick." She smiled.

He returned her smile. "Are you getting away from it all?"

"You'd better believe it. Although I'm gathering a crowd. Serena's just passed this way. Now you."

He tried to say casually, "Is she still around?"

"She hasn't come back from the bathroom yet."

Relief that Serena was nearby breezed into his body and cheered him up no end.

"Have many people left?" Barbara asked.

"The crowd did seem to have thinned a little."

"Good. It's probably down to the hard core now. The ones without children and babysitters." Barbara rose from her seat. "I suppose I'd better go and check on what's happening. See you again, Nick."

Nick nodded. "If I don't get to see you before I leave, thanks for a great party, Barbara."

"You'll always be welcome." She disappeared from the room.

Nick took it from her words that she liked him. And he liked her. Barbara was the type of person he could actually sit down and talk to without anything else getting between them. Like a mother would be. That was his problem. He'd never had a mother who cared. Therefore, he had gone through his life treating all women as potential sex partners. Even the women he had intellectually connected with he had screwed, for lack of a better word.

Serena entered the room and looked around.

He said, from his position in the dark, "Barbara went back out to the party."

Hand to her slim throat, Serena twirled around, making the diamond earrings flash. "Nick. Don't scare me like that."

"Sorry. Didn't mean to." He pushed his hands into his trouser pockets so he wouldn't be tempted to touch her. He knew he needed some distance from Serena. But he also knew he wanted to be with her on an intellectual and physical plane. Except there wasn't time. A few short months. He couldn't promise anything. He had nothing to promise but distance between them. He was just like her father. All Stuart Redding Brown had offered her was a life without him.

"Where's Juliette?" she asked.

So she'd noticed he'd spent some time with the other woman. But he decided to go for honesty instead of trying to make her jealous. "We got tired of one another. I was looking for you to see about calling it a night. Reeva and Gerry seemed to be saying goodbyes."

She tucked her slim gold purse-strap over her shoulder. "Great. Do you want to go and find them with me? I'd love to leave now. I'm tired."

Keeping his hands deep in his pockets he gazed at her tidy up-swept hair and glossed lips. "You don't look tired. You look as fresh as you did at the beginning of the evening."

She gave him a critical look. "I can't say that about you. You do look a little weary."

"I am. So let's go find your mom."

He didn't take her hand, but he wanted to. As they walked across the now damp lawn to where Reeva and Gerald stood alone, he could feel eyes upon them. They were, he believed, Steel's new star couple. The position should be capitalized on. But he wasn't going to be able to capitalize upon it by antagonizing Serena. He was going to have to be very gentle in the way he treated her, mentally gentle. Unlike most of the women he'd been with. They'd been hard cases to begin with, field journalists, war correspondents. They'd succeeded in a predominantly male career and they weren't about to give up anything of themselves. They'd made life easy for him. He could keep intact. Those that seemed different, like Lise Kryker, who might have become a drag on him, he'd soon dismissed. Then why couldn't he dismiss Serena?

Reeva smiled when she saw them. "Gerry and I were just talking about calling this a night."

Serena said, "Nick and I were just saying the same thing."

Nick and I. He rather liked that.

Gerry said, "I'll go get the car started and meet you all out the front." He loped off.

Reeva tucked her arm through Nick's on one side and her daughter's on the other. "Let's not keep him waiting."

The Lincoln was purring in the front driveway. Nick helped Reeva into the front seat, then opened the back door and ushered Serena inside. He didn't squeeze against her on the plush velvety upholstery, but he didn't leave any room between them. This action wasn't because he'd made up his mind about anything he'd thought about.

He just couldn't handle not being close to her. His imagination kept returning to her kitchen, and the way she'd responded to him. He wanted her in his arms again, giving him that hip-grinding response. He wanted her opening her mouth to his. He wanted to be inside her. He'd wanted it since the moment he'd seen her in the elevator, before he'd known who she was. He couldn't stop wanting it.

Yet he knew he might never have what he wanted. And that would equal the pain level when he actually discovered that his parents couldn't care less about him. So why was he torturing himself? Answer: because, whatever his sane mind told him, he couldn't stop himself.

Serena lifted her hips and shifted imperceptibly away from him. She was staring straight ahead, and he noticed a few stray hairs she had missed pinning up whispering against her neck. He wanted to place his lips there and sip the nectar of her. The way he had on the picnic table bench. Remembering that interlude was anguish, because he knew how she could respond. He had never felt this way about a woman before, and he restlessly slid across the seat and lounged into a corner. He'd thought it once, he must think it again: a moment of lust with this woman could sabotage him and his career.

Chapter Nine

Serena was relieved when the Lincoln slid into her driveway. She had stayed up too late. Her last drink, the brandy, tasted stale in her mouth. Her stomach didn't feel particularly stable. And her feelings toward Nick were entwined inside her like a ball of wool that had been tangled by a kitten.

Also, there was everything else that had happened this evening. Had she really almost seduced Nick in the kitchen then later told him that he reminded her of her father? And had she actually heard Pat tell her that the employees of Steel referred to her as the Ice Maiden? Had she really promised Pat that she would give Nick a chase and thus veer him away from Juliette? She now didn't think this action would be necessary, judging by Nick's earlier non-enthusiasm for Juliette.

Gerry turned off the engine and Reeva said, "Now we've trapped Nick's car into the driveway. Serena, maybe it would be wiser if he stayed the night anyway. We'd never forgive ourselves if anything happened to him."

"That's up to Nick." Serena was sick of all the ups and downs her emotions had been through since she had first heard Nick Fraser's name the other afternoon. The thought of him sleeping in her other spare bedroom put the seal on the most desperation she would ever feel. She felt like clawing her way through the roof of the car and running away.

"Nick is pretty tired and he wouldn't mind staying," Nick said.

She glanced at him through the haze made by her outside light. For most of the evening his expression had been pretty open, as if he'd pulled aside a curtain to expose a part of himself for the party. Now he looked more enigmatic. She began to suspect that Barbara was right, and there was more to Nick than a handsome face.

She actually felt a pang of sympathy for him and conceded to her mother's suggestion. "I have another spare room. You're welcome."

"Thanks." His smile was perfunctory. "I did kind of belt back the beer at the beginning of the party."

"Then stay. We wouldn't want you to get pulled over. Especially when you've been out with a city politician for the evening."

"Also it would be bad publicity for your new show," Reeva added.

With that settled, everyone went inside the house to congregate in the kitchen. Serena held Pascal in her arms, feeling a letdown restless sensation throughout her entire body. She hadn't wanted to stay at the party, but she didn't feel ready for bed either. She was almost relieved when Reeva discovered the bottle of wine that Nick had brought her this evening.

"It's not very cold," Reeva said. "But let's add ice. Serena do you have any glasses?"

Serena let Pascal go and retrieved the glasses from the cupboard. Nick opened the bottle. Gerry found the ice cubes in the freezer. Nick poured four glasses.

Reeva perched on a kitchen chair, holding the glass. "Ah, this is nice. So cheers, everyone. To Serena and Nick's new show. We hope it goes splendidly. Don't we, Gerry?"

"We sure do." Gerry smiled. "You make such a great couple. Cheers and good luck."

They polished off the bottle of wine, dissected the party, and Barbara and Don's home, and then Reeva and Gerald retired to their room.

Her head reeling from the late hour and the wine, Serena watched herself rinse the glasses. They were expensive crystal with a gold rim, and too good for the dishwasher, so she would wash them properly in the morning. She stood them carefully in a row and the gold shimmered before her eyes. She touched her forehead to stop the dizziness.

"All right?" Nick asked.

When she turned from the sink he was right in front of her. "I feel dizzy."

He smiled. "You're looped. That's why."

She shook her head. "Am I? How about you?

"I'm feeling fine. And I want to feel yours."

She laughed, and he placed his hands on the edge of the counter until she was trapped by him. Her fingers caressed his waist and his head dipped to claim her mouth. This is what she had wanted. Serena closed her eyes as his kiss lulled her into a mist of desire. The only sounds she could hear was their breathing. All she wanted was him.

She ran her fingers down his thighs to discover he felt as muscular as he looked. His tongue, hot and seeking, was inside her mouth now. She battled him with her own tongue. The part of her that wasn't involved in his embrace wondered what she was doing.

His hand slid upward, between her top and her skin, and she sank lower into him. He began to move his hips in a thrusting movement, into her. She felt his fingers explore her nipples and she was going to explode with feelings. She wanted to wrap her legs around him, but he removed his mouth and his body, leaving her sagging against the counter.

"I want you sober the first time." Nick had a definite shake to his voice as he adjusted his belt and raked his fingers through his hair. He rubbed the side of his jaw, as if feeling for the stubble collecting there. "I want to be sober as well."

"I didn't think there was going to be a first time."

"There has to be if we continue like this."

She reached up to her hair and found that it had loosened and was straggling down her neck. Her veins were beating beneath her skin. She felt open and vulnerable. "Didn't we talk about this earlier?"

"Talking isn't helping what we feel for one another."

He sounded so desperate. She must affect him the same way as he affected her. What was between them was like a physical explosion. She shuddered. "I want you as well."

He seemed more calm now. "Thank you for admitting that."

She ran her finger along the curved edge of the counter. "I have a reputation at Steel? Have you heard?"

He shook his head.

"Apparently I'm an ice maiden."

"I don't believe that."

"Well, it's true." Serena smoothed the silk down her hips. She felt more composed now. "I'm not ready yet, Nick."

"Me neither. If I'm honest."

"Good Because it's better if we don't. Working together. Like I said before."

"Yeah." He glanced at the microwave clock. "It's pretty late. We should get some sleep."

"I have to lock up."

"I'll help you."

Serena went to locate Pascal who, with the living room out of bounds, and the kitchen too noisy and occupied by strangers, had been sleeping on the cushions on the wicker sofa in the sunroom. He managed a yawning stretch to greet her, and rolled up into a ball once more. All the time Nick followed her, pattering behind her like a puppy she knew he wasn't. He was a tiger, dangerous and raw. She felt his presence in every one of her bones and all through her veins. When he was around her she experienced a sensation like being connected to him physically. She didn't like it. She had always been a loner, like her father.

That sudden realization hit her like a vehicle ramming against a brick wall. If she was like her father then she was like Nick. Was that why she was so attracted to him on one hand and skittish on the other? Did she see herself in him? Did she see a person who actually preferred to be alone because it was safer for the psyche, a person who had a low threshold for pain? And yet she wanted passion. At least her body wanted passion.

Serena tapped open the door to her other spare room and flipped the ceiling-light switch. "This is your room. You can use the bathroom across the hall."

As Nick passed by her into the room she caught in a breath while he was close, and barely let it out again as he looked around.

"It's great." He gave her a serious look. "You must think you're running a B&B tonight."

"I do, rather. But it is safer that you stay than drive home all that way. It's only for a few hours anyway. It's pretty late." That was the way she'd reconciled his reasons for staying at her house.

"It's early morning, to be exact." He sat down on the edge of the bed and tested it. "Nice and soft. Great."

"Good." She was agitated with their relationship. She felt like screaming and tearing out her hair.

He patted the top of the black and pink duvet. Then he stood up again and began unbuttoning his shirt. "I'm going to have a few hours sleep."

Serena's throat ached. She could close the door, cross the room, press her fingers to his smooth, golden chest, lift the shirt from his shoulders, unbuckle his belt, feel how hard he was and take that hardness inside her own softness. She wanted him to plunge and plunge inside her until she was taken completely out of herself and out of her mind.

He slipped out of the shirt and touched his belt buckle. "Goodnight, Serena."

Mutely she stepped back. "I'll leave towels on the rack in the bathroom for you."

"Thanks." He smiled his clean white TV smile. The smile reminded her of who he was and what she was actually contemplating, a relationship with no conclusion. But it was a smile that hid his true feelings. And she was the same way.

"Then I'll leave you." She backed out of the door and closed it.

By now Pascal had wandered into the hallway. Serena scooped him up and carried him to the kitchen, where she poured herself a glass of water. Carrying cat and water, she went to her own room. While Pascal settled down for the night, Serena stood under a steaming shower, disregarding the fact that it was gone three in the morning. She just knew that she was wide awake and in a terrible situation. To put it simply, she had to work with a man she wanted to sleep with.

When she eventually stopped thinking about Nick she began to worry about the new show and wondered how she was ever going to cope with the volume of work. With that anxiety attack under control, it was five thirty, and Pascal was clawing her rug letting her know he was impatient for his breakfast. She fed him and slumped back into bed and fell asleep. The next time she woke up she could smell strong coffee, and she heard voices in her house.

•

Nick liked Reeva. The same way he liked Barbara. And although he received messages from Reeva that she might think things about him that were different from her exterior platitudes, he still found her entertaining. Poor Gerry barely got a word in edgeways, but he didn't seem to mind. If his expression was anything to go by, he adored Reeva, and was just pleased to be her husband.

Luckily Nick had thought to put his battery shaver, a change of briefs, shirt and a pair of jeans into his car before he'd left yesterday. Not that he'd expected to stay at Serena's house, but just in case he might have stayed anywhere, be it at Don's or at a highway motel. That it was Serena's had made the night just a trifle more restless. He'd spent most of the time aroused and trying to dismiss that she could become a serious problem. Which is why he made an effort to keep cool now, when she walked into the kitchen where he was sharing coffee with Reeva and Gerald.

Serena wore a robe of midnight-blue silk to match her eyes. The material rippled in the sunlight streaming through her kitchen window. Her hair, ruffled from sleep, was like strands of gold, and her features, without make-up, totally alluring. She carried Pascal snuggled against her breasts.

She let Pascal out of the back door, bending over to do it with the silk shimmering down her thighs. "Morning all."

Reeva scooted over to her daughter and pecked her on the cheek. "Good Morning, darling. What can I get you?"

"I'll have some orange juice. Please." She glanced around the kitchen table. "I see you've all been taken care of."

"We're fine, Serena," Gerry said. "Only a tiny bit groggy from the late night."

She pushed back her hair with a gesture that was becoming familiar to Nick. "You okay, Nick?"

He never would be okay as long as she was around. "Yeah, I'm fine." Then he made up his mind over his next move. "I'm not staying much longer. If Gerry doesn't mind moving the car?"

Reeva handed Serena a glass of orange juice. "You must have some brunch. It's almost noon. Come on, Serena, let's cook up some pancakes."

Serena stood against the fridge door. "If Nick wants to leave then let him leave."

He'd got the message. Serena didn't want him here. He also had his own agenda about her that he had to sort out. He should do that alone. He couldn't think straight this morning.

He stood up from his chair and held the back while he pushed it beneath the table. "Coffee's fine. I'll grab something on the way home. Thanks."

"Well—" he heard Reeva say as he walked out of the kitchen and down to the room he'd used for the night.

Wishing he could have heard Reeva's opinion of him, he made the bed and collected together his shaver and his clothes from the evening before. *Get out of here before you break down, ass. She's admitted she hated her father, and you remind her of the man. Reeva's likely got the same hang-ups. And they're right. You are the same type as her father. You know that. You felt the affinity in the opening pages of his book. You almost got up and cheered because you knew for the first time in your life you weren't alone in the world. But you were alone, because Stuart Redding Brown was already dead by then.*

"Nick?"

She stood at his door. "What?"

"You could stay for breakfast."

"I'm not hungry."

He picked up the hanger with his clothes, grabbed the keys to the rental car from the dresser, and walked to the door to where she was standing. She smelled of soap and herself, and he felt his entire body respond to her warmth. She would be coming home for him, the coming home he had always dreamed of as a kid, hot soup and crackers on a crisp, cold day. But that coming home dream had diminished with time. His place was in the field. Their show was his temporary means to be here to help his parents. He had to remember those terms.

And yet. He bent to kiss her cheek and rested his lips against her soft skin for a moment. "Thanks for the hospitality. The bed was more than comfortable."

"You're welcome." She moved into the hallway.

She followed him to the kitchen, where he bid goodbye to her mother. Gerry was out moving the Lincoln. Then Serena showed him to the front door.

"See you tomorrow," she said.

He forced a smile. "Right on."

He walked to the car, unlocked it and slung his things into the back seat. He backed the car out to the road and Gerry drove back in. Feeling he should say goodbye to him, he drove into the driveway again and got out to shake Gerry's hand.

"It's been a pleasure meeting you, Nick. Sorry you have to leave without the pancakes."

"I've got work to do anyway." Nick told the truth. From now on, his life would be such a hustle that he wouldn't have time to think about what might have been with Serena.

•

"Well, if that's not like your father, no one is," Reeva said.

Serena pushed the lifter underneath a pancake on the griddle and saw the pancake disintegrate. She swore under her breath and scooped up the mess. "I'm no good with pancakes."

Reeva ushered her out of the way. "Let me, then."

Serena surrendered the brunch to her mother's capable hands and poured herself a big mug of coffee. She drank half the mug, hoping that the caffeine might set her brain straight. "What did Dad offer you when you met him?"

Reeva tossed a pancake and it landed perfectly. Round, smooth, golden brown. "Love everlasting. What has Nick offered you?"

"Why would he offer me anything?"

Reeva chuckled. "Because he wants you. It's obvious. He's a man in heat. Love them, but they are dangerous animals."

"You should know. You had enough men."

Reeva turned to raise an eyebrow at Serena while still managing a symmetrical pancake. "That's unfair. But it is true, I suppose. Or it looked that way to you. After your father I was demoralized. I needed men to tell me I was worthy. Then I decided to use all that money your father left and put it to good use. I opened the first florist shop and I began to feel my own power. I haven't needed men for that reason again."

"Your experience put me off men, though."

The pile of pancakes on the plate grew higher. "Until Nick?"

"You have to admit he's attractive, Mom."

Reeva smiled. "Gorgeous. But beware. Go for it, if you want, but don't have expectations. That's all I'm saying."

Serena nodded. It was exactly what her heart was also saying.

•

Rain pounded on to the Steel parking lot on Monday morning and sat in puddles in the low ground. Serena tucked the hood of her rain jacket over her hair and zigzagged around the pools of water. Her insides felt as jumbled as the inclement weather. Her mother and Gerry had stayed for most of Sunday. They'd had a pleasant time, Serena supposed, but having company had rattled whatever calm she'd still possessed after the party. She hadn't even had a moment to prepare for the meeting today. She'd have to wing it, the way she'd winged newscasts to eliminate dead air when they ended before the required time.

She was also unprepared for seeing Nick. She was unsure of how they had actually parted on Sunday. Had they been friendly or had they been antagonistic? Had they solved anything between them? Or were things still volatile?

In the foyer she felt like a melting block of ice with the rain cascading from her jacket. She didn't even have her private office to fix herself up in any more, before facing the others, so she had to go to the powder room on the main floor. She shook out her jacket, rubbed mud from her black leather ankle boots and straightened her jeans and black *Steel yourself for our News* sweatshirt. Luckily her hair was merely damp and a comb through made it presentable. But she didn't feel like her usual sleek self. She might never feel that way again since meeting Nick Fraser.

Carrying her jacket, she rode the elevator to the suite. Don, his brother Cam, who looked nothing like him with a beard and a stocky physique, and Nick were already sitting around the table in the boardroom, with coffee in white cups on saucers in front of them. A coffee maker stood on a side table, along with a selection of muffins and fruit.

She said a broad, "Hi," to the men and went to hang her jacket in her office. She left her purse in a desk drawer and took her notes from her briefcase. One deep breath and she entered the boardroom.

A young woman with long dark hair, wearing black slacks and a tight, white lace shirt introduced herself as Melissa Franklin, the new assistant for the show. She insisted Serena sit down, and she placed a coffee cup and saucer on the polished surface of the table before her.

Serena smiled her thanks. Don didn't overdo the number of staff at Steel, and she knew that Melissa would end up running errands, compiling scripts, taking minutes and whatever else there was left to do for each weekly show.

She took her first sip of coffee and smiled at Cam. "Did you have a good vacation?"

"Great. Thanks, Serena. Sorry I missed the party, though. And I was sorry to hear about John."

She looked across at Nick, who wore his familiar jeans with a blue shirt today. "We have an eminent replacement, though, don't we?" She figured the only way to conquer Nick was to face him head on. Be cool, the way he was. She thought his features appeared hard, and she wondered what he actually felt inside. Did he get mixed up the way she did or was his mind logical?

Nick glanced at Cam, then Serena. "We've already decided we're going to work well together. Also, Seth was here, but he's gone to pick up some demos he recently recorded."

Don leaned his arms on the table. "We like his recorded work and will use it, but we need a musical theme."

Serena nodded. "That's a good idea. I hope he can come up with something."

"We'll make sure he does. He's good. We want him," Nick said.

She liked Nick's faith in her brother. "What about Paul? Where is he?"

"He'll be in later."

She pushed aside her cup. "Then what do we do? Wait?"

"No." Don touched a few sheets of paper in front of him. "Let's go over these proposals. Cam needs to be filled in. Melissa, could you take some notes?"

Melissa sat down at the table with a laptop in front of her.

Work begins in earnest, Serena thought. *No more playtime.* Her first decision was that she wasn't going to be overshadowed by Nick. But as the discussions went around the table she realized that he wasn't intending to overshadow her. He let her voice her views without interrupting anything she said. Mostly he agreed with her. He made the two of them seem like the tight team he'd suggested they should be at their Friday meeting.

However, she couldn't let down her guard. Especially when Cam asked about her proposed program. She gave him the same spiel as she'd given Nick on Friday.

Don interrupted, "Do you have a name for this program?"

"No."

Nick suggested, "Bad men, Good Women."

"I like that," Cam said. "However, this Thursday's show is our immediate priority."

She knew that.

Serena had expected them all to climb into a news van and immediately hit the streets, but Nick decided they would meet at eleven PM and do the street scenes and interviews when the neon lit the city. This meant that Serena would have to find somewhere to stay in the city for the night. Luckily she always kept a packed overnight bag for emergencies such as this. She sometimes stayed with her mother or at a hotel.

Seth's appearance broke up the boardroom meeting because they needed to go down to the studio to hear his music. Serena was proud of Seth, and felt a great deal of guilt for not acknowledging that he was a man in his own right, a passionate, intense human being.

Lunch was brought in by Melissa, Swiss cheese and ham with salad on crusty buns, bottled juice and some fries for Nick, who shared them all around. By mid-afternoon they had an edited commercial accompanied by Seth's new musical theme for the show. When the editing of the composition pleased them all, Don immediately arranged for the advertisement to bombard the airwaves.

Session one was over.

Seth rose from his chair and stretched his long arms. "I hear you're going out late tonight. You can stay at my place, if you want."

She thought this might be her opportunity for a closer relationship with her brother. "Thanks. I didn't expect to actually go out late at night."

Seth smiled. "I don't think Nick does anything that anyone expects."

Serena glanced over to where Nick was talking to Fred Dexter, the sound man who would go with them tonight. "You might be right. What do you think of him?"

"I like him. And I know exactly what you're thinking. I'm not comparing them. There's a huge generation gap. I know because I've read Dad's book."

"Possibly that's true."

"It is true." He reached in his pocket for a set of keys. He pressed his spare loft key into her palm. "I'll see you later. Take care."

Serena watched him go, feeling good about having her brother in her life once again. It reminded her of when he was a little boy and she'd often been asked to care for him when Reeva was busy.

She tucked the key into her purse and went upstairs to her office to call Ginny to ask her to look in on Pascal, to feed him that evening and in the morning. When her personal affairs had been taken care of, she logged on to her computer, checked her e-mail, answered a few messages, and then made some notes to herself about the meeting. *Bad Men, Good Women.* She thought the title had a resonance, and it sort of gave her idea a solid base. So she would have to get moving on it.

She leafed through her old address book. When she'd been in university she'd shared an apartment with two other women, Rita Mason and Angela Turner. Angela's addresses had all been stroked out, which was unfortunate as Angela was the woman who had fallen in love with the prisoner, and thus the friend Serena needed to contact. However, she knew Rita was a broker with a local real estate office. She put through a call to Rita and was told Rita would be paged with the message to call Serena back. Rita would likely be surprised to hear from Serena after a number of years of silence.

As she hung up the phone she heard the outer door click and Nick glanced into her office.

"Hi."

"Hi." She closed her address book. "Everything went well, didn't it?"

"Yes." He dug his fingers into his back pockets. "Don didn't have much choice but to go along with want we want. We're his way out of a sticky patch. He's put a lot of resources into this show. We have to perform. And Cam seems amenable enough."

"That's all true. I thought Seth did well."

"Absolutely. He's talented up to his eyeballs. You're quite the family."

"Want to do documentaries on all of us, then?" Serena regretted the question as soon as the words emerged from her mouth.

His gaze rested on her. "If we do the one on your father then you'll get a mention."

"No way."

"That you don't want a mention?"

"No way are we doing a documentary on my father. I'm not giving permission."

"What if your mother and brother give permission?"

"They won't. Mother can't have her dirty laundry aired because she's in politics, and Seth doesn't want a black cloud at the launch of his career."

Nick withdrew one hand from one pocket and touched the doorpost. His brow furrowed. "Did he beat the family or something?"

Serena gasped. "No. Don't even think it. I'm talking about mental anguish. Someone you love being away from you all the time."

"That's what I thought it was. You felt neglected by him. I understand."

"No. You don't. You're the same type as Dad, Nick. The only crime you haven't committed that he did is saddle yourself with a family. How selfish to have a wife and child at home and never be there for them."

"I read in his book that your father's parents died when he was a teenager. He could have needed the stability of the home in his mind."

"Don't excuse him. When he was an adult he should have seen the damage he was doing. Instead he ignored it. He came home each time with a suitcase full of beautiful gifts from all the countries he'd visited. It felt like the way Christmas feels when you're a kid."

"I wouldn't know."

Serena stopped ranting from her pain and looked at him. "You weren't excited when you were a kid?"

"I wanted to be, but I couldn't be because there was nothing for me to be excited about."

"Didn't your parents have Christmas for you?"

His knuckles were now taut around the doorpost. "I have a lot of pain in my past as well, Serena. I understand where you are coming from. Never think I don't."

"But you have two parents, don't you?"

He released his hand from the post and returned it to the back pocket of his jeans. He let out a breath. "Yes. I do."

"Then you don't understand, Nick. You can't."

"Have it your own way. I'm going to do some work for a while."

Serena nodded. She felt shaken because she had bared some of her soul to Nick, shaken because Nick had almost told her something about himself. Something she wanted to know more about.

The click of Nick's keyboard was constant. He didn't seem to need time to contemplate his work the way she did. Were ideas flowing that fast? Didn't their heated conversation bother him? It was as if each time they got together they exposed one more section of their minds and lives to one another. It wasn't only physical, it was also mental. That invisible cord connection was pulling her closer to him in short tugs.

Her phone rang and she picked up the receiver. As soon as she heard Rita's voice she was in control again. This was work.

"It's great to hear from you," Rita said. "Want to do lunch?"

"Yes. I'll do lunch. Also, I want a favor. Do you have Angela's address or phone number?"

"Nope. I've now lost track of her. But I know where her brother, Max is because I saw him the other day."

"Then you do have something." Serena prodded her friend, who always said she didn't know anything before she brought up her trump card. "Where did you see him?"

"On the street."

On the street? Serena recalled the man with the black hair who had reminded her of Angela. "Did you talk to him?"

"No way."

"Why not if it was Max?"

"I gave him some money, Serena. He's been in and out of prison all his life. It's a shame. He's a good looking guy and he plays a mean guitar on Yonge Street near College."

So the man she'd seen that day had been Max. "Did he recognize you?"

"No. I don't think so."

"But you recognized him?"

"Yes. He looks like Angela, with long black hair. Anyway, he's obviously dropped out of society. While I always give street people money, I wish something could be done about them on a larger more political scale."

"Don't we all." Serena decided that their conversation sounded far too trivial for the serious nature of the plight of poverty. "We were going to do a series called *City Streets* for my new show *Neon Nights*, but it got vetoed."

"That's too bad. Things need to be said. Anyway, I have a client coming in. So how about lunch?"

Serena checked her calendar on her cell phone even though she knew everything she would be doing over the next few days. Thursday evening was looming. "How about Friday lunch at The Bear's Pause?" By then Thursday would be over. She'd be either a success or a failure.

"Perfect. I'll meet you at the entrance at one."

"I'll be there." Serena hung up the phone and pushed her fist into the air. She had a lead.

If only she'd paid more attention that day when she'd sat in her car and watched the man who could possibly be Angela's brother. Now she needed to see him. Did she have time for a walk down Yonge Street? She looked out of the window. The rain had stopped and the sun was trying to shine. She could do with some fresh air. Quickly she put on her jacket. When she passed Nick's office, she noticed the door was closed. At least he didn't see her leave. But then why should he care if she left? He might be her co-host but he wasn't her keeper. This was her life. Her job. Her story.

A man was wrapped in a bundle of cloth, snuggled close to a building, another man sold magazines, but there was no Max.

Serena walked back through dogged crowds to the Steel Tower, feeling let down. She had to speak to him. Otherwise she'd never find Angela. Unless she phoned all the Turners in the Toronto phone book. She might have to resort to that.

When she arrived back, she saw Nick had left his office. Well, it was lunchtime. She hung up her coat and sat down at her desk. She opened an old file on her computer and began to read some notes she'd written on Angela. She thought she had her lover's name somewhere. Not that it would help. Angela must have moved on from that event in her life. However, Serena thought that by looking at the name once more it might revive her own memories and help her with her approach to the story. She came to the end of the document. At the bottom she found the name she wanted: Lawson Thomson.

Chapter Ten

With her research notes strewn around her desk, Serena began her script for *Bad Men, Good Women.*

She realized she was a bit rusty at this type of journalism. She'd always been a fairly fluent writer, but, after having read the news for the past six years, she wasn't exactly in touch with her creative side. No wonder she had left most of the story ideas to John. She wasn't doing a good job with this one. She needed more focus. And that focus should be Angela, because Angela was the one woman who interested her the most.

She heard Nick's keyboard still going. What did he find to write? How did he let the mundane studio skills go so his mind wandered into a story? Because that's what she needed to learn how to do. It was a skill she'd lost, somewhere between her news van days and her news anchor hours. It was a skill her father had possessed, because she remembered him hunched over a portable typewriter on a tiny desk in a corner. He hadn't even had the ease of a computer. How many books would he have produced by now, if he'd lived?

Damn. She pushed her palm against her forehead. Why did Nick have to come into her life and destroy her peace of mind?

Her mind keenly attuned to the other office, she suddenly heard the keyboard in the adjoining office finally halt. The next thing she knew Nick was on her sofa and was gunning her with his cool gaze. "Want to go for dinner?"

Seth was right. Serena was never sure of what Nick was going to come up with next. She hadn't got over their last heated exchange yet. She needed distance from him. "It's okay. Go ahead. I'll grab something from the staff cafeteria."

He lounged deeper into the sofa. "I didn't know there was a staff cafeteria."

"It's on the fifth floor. They do good hot food as well as sandwiches. Has no one showed you around?"

"No one has shown me much at all. But I think I'd prefer The Bear's Pause again."

He shifted restlessly. Serena couldn't help letting her gaze flow over his taut, sexy body. As usual the sight of him set off sparks inside her and she wanted to reach out and touch him.

"Come to the pub with me. I'm beginning to have a real problem."

"What type of problem?" She knew she was probably playing into some sort of scheme Nick had in mind.

"Culture shock. Europe versus North America. Half my head is still overseas."

"So that's your problem. I wondered why you looked so strange today."

He grinned. "Funny, honey. Just come to the pub with me. Then I need a drive over to the garage to pick up my car."

Serena raised an eyebrow. "Ah, so that's the reason you want me to have a meal with you."

He chuckled. "I also want a ride in your Porsche. Please."

As long as Nick remained friendly, like he was now, she'd be fine with him. She certainly wasn't going to be able to ignore him. She'd go with her old opinion that maybe the better she knew him the less mystery he would hold.

They went to The Bear's Pause and Serena ate fish and chips, the same as Nick. As they ate they discussed the earlier meeting and the way they might structure tonight's show. Serena also surprised herself by coming up with lots of good points. She hoped this was a clue that her creative juices were now stirring.

Afterward they walked to her Porsche in the Steel lot. It was when Nick had strapped on the seatbelt in the low passenger seat that Serena felt the wallop of him against her senses. He was snug beside her in the bulky leather jacket, and she couldn't move to change gear without her own arm brushing his.

"Where do we have to go?" Her voice shuddered with the force of all the feelings. She almost suggested they go to his place and try out his idea for great sex.

He turned sideways, his shoulders broad and hunched. "If you take the next left, and then right at the first lights, it's a little gray building tucked in beside a Greek restaurant."

"You could have walked there."

"No. I wanted to be with you."

"Even after our argument today?"

"That wasn't an argument. That's you and me trying to come to terms with what's happening between us."

She had to agree with him. She bit into her bottom lip.

"Turn here."

She turned the car into a parking lot.

"You can park up the side of the building."

Serena stopped the Porsche outside the glass doors next to a silver Jaguar.

"That's my car."

Even though her car was stopped, and the engine turned off, she kept her hands on the steering wheel. "It's really nice. Are you actually going to drive it through the winter?"

"I doubt if I'll be doing much driving because I live so close to the Steel Tower. And, if I do, I'll try to avoid snowy, slushy days."

"I hope so. I wouldn't want to see a great car like that rust out with all the salt they put on the roads." She wished he'd just leave her car so she could be alone and gather her wits about her once more.

But he seemed in no hurry to leave her. "What do you drive in the winter?"

"I have a four wheel drive Jeep in my garage."

He chuckled. "So you become Rural Woman during the winter?"

Her fingers squeezed the wheel tighter. "Yes. This car gets cleaned up and left alone until spring."

"How long have you had it?"

She looked at him. "This car?"

He was so close that he could kiss her if he wanted to. It reminded her of the moments they had shared on the picnic bench at the soirée.

"Yes. This car. How long?" His eyes were like a flame flaring against a piece of metal.

"Three years or so." She stumbled over the words. This wasn't going to work. Whichever way she decided she was going to act, she seemed to lose ground when she was with him. She felt like she'd gone for a swim and couldn't remember where to put her arms and legs to glide through the water.

Nick moved forward until she was enveloped by his warm body and the fragrant leather. Against her cheek was the roughness of stubble. She closed her eyes and heard only their breathing.

"I can't do it," he said.

"Do what?" Yet she knew, because she didn't know if she could do it either.

His lips kissed her jaw just below her ear. A shiver ran through her and her body trembled. "Keep away from you, be business-like, be whatever and not have any hanky-panky. I still want you."

Then he moved away, opened the door and got out of her car. He leaned back in the door and she thought his expression was full of pain. She saw her hand move through the air, wanting to touch him but of course he wasn't there anymore. But she could still feel the roughness of his jaw against her own soft skin. She felt branded by him.

He reached in and his hand grasped hers. "Thanks for the lift. I'll see you at Steel tonight."

Serena's fingertips tingled with desire. "At eleven?"

"I'll be there all evening."

"I'm going to Seth's place for the night. I'll go there first and come along afterward."

"Great. You have a place to go." He let her hand slip away from his.

Serena saw a mechanic come out of the glass doors and Nick glanced at him. He looked back at Serena. "See you later."

He shut her door and she sat for a moment, getting her breath back. Then she turned her car around in the small lot. She drove out on to the road, looking in her rearview mirror to see Nick talking to the mechanic.

•

Nick barely concentrated on the mechanic's rundown on the car. All he could think about was being with Serena in the Porsche. He was setting himself up to be a bloody target, he thought as he finally got into his own car and he settled back against the red leather seat.

He drove around the city for a while, exploring a place he realized he had missed. There was only one local school he'd ever attended, but he drove by the brick elementary school to see what he recalled of that early time in his life. He remembered being bundled up in a snowsuit and stumbling through the snow on short legs. A rather happy time, he thought. A few years later he'd become more aware of what was going on in his family life. Suddenly he'd suspected that the cool treatment he received wasn't quite normal.

The school was only a block from Fraser's Precious Gems, and he stopped the car on the road near the store. Should he go and visit his parents?

He decided to visit, but found there was no answer at the door, so they must be out. He didn't know where they would be. In April he'd found them without a car because of Stephen's health and his mother's inability to drive. He thought they were in walking distance of the subway, so maybe they'd gone shopping.

The store was open until eight in the evening, so he pushed on the wooden door. When he was a kid the windows had been shiny and open, now they were set with bars and alarms. The interior of the store was dark and full of brown wood. Occasionally a piece of silver or gold jewelry would glitter in any meager stream of light.

The smell was musty.

The man his father had working for him, Tim Masters, was sitting behind the counter repairing a watch. He was a tall, elongated man, with small, oval glasses through which he squinted at his work. He had graduated from college as a jewelry designer, and this job for Nick's father was a part time pursuit in his own pursuit for fame.

"How's it going?" Nick asked when Tim's attention had left the watch and his watery eyes were focused on Nick.

"Fine. Just fine." He poked at the watch innards with a long finger. "We live off watch repairs these days."

"Then it's not fine."

"No. Your father hasn't been able to pay me for three weeks."

Nick wasn't surprised. He found out how much Tim was owed and wrote him a check.

If my father sells this place, I'll make sure you have six months' pay to give you time to get another job or whatever you want to do."

Tim looked pleased with the check, but gave him a skeptical look. "That's kind of you, but do you think he's going to sell?"

"I'm pushing for it. Neither of my parents are healthy."

"You're right. Your mother can barely cope with the hospital visits. I try to help with the groceries, but he likes the store open the full hours." Tim shook his head. "I can't help when there's no business. No money."

"Absolutely."

Tim began to fiddle with the watch parts again.

"See you later." Nick remembered speaking the same words to Serena a while back.

There was no use hanging around. He drove to the Steel Tower. He would need a pass for the parking, he was told by the officious man at the gate, but Nick was let through with a daily fee this time. Nick would get Melissa to handle the pass. She'd told him earlier this morning, before Serena arrived, that she was at his beck and call.

Nick sat down at his desk and called Melissa to put the parking pass into motion. But he soon left his desk again to glance out of the window and stare down to the parking lot. He saw his car parked there. He didn't see Serena's Porsche. He tried to imagine her driving into the city in a Jeep all winter. He rather liked the vision of a female in a masculine vehicle. He also liked the vision of her naked in his arms, her body wrapped around his, her need in a skirmish with his need. It would be more than great sex. It would be everything.

He rammed his fist into his palm. How to love had never been taught to him, so he'd never allowed love to enter into his relationships. But since he'd met Serena he was wondering if he did have the fortitude. If this was love?

Someone tapped at his door. He turned to see Juliette in a short-skirted magenta dress. She meandered into his office on her high heels and glanced around. "Hi," she said, "I had a few moments to spare so I thought I'd see where you landed up."

I've landed up a wreck, he thought, but said instead, "Hi. Take your time."

She smelled of a very strong perfume that wasn't unpleasant but knocked his senses off key. This wasn't the woman for him.

He didn't think he could even date her. Yet he was sure in the days before he had met Serena he would have been able to take her out and home to bed. Or was he right to blame Serena for all his up and down emotions? What about the sensation in Heathrow, that he was in for changes? Hadn't he even precipitated this change by pledging to help his parents in their old age?

Juliette tossed her hair. "I wasn't too keen about what happened on Saturday evening, Nick. I don't like being made a fool of."

He didn't need this. "I wasn't under the impression I made a fool of you."

"We hung around all evening and then, poof." She waved her hand in the air in a swirling motion. "You were gone."

"Because the people I came with were leaving." He had to extricate himself from this right away. He walked away from the window and closer to her. "Look, Juliette. I got off the plane last Wednesday. I haven't had much time to think since. I've got a hot show starting on Thursday and it's taking all my energy. I relaxed a bit on Saturday night, but that's all the relaxation I'm going to get."

She reached out, touched his shoulder, and made sure her eyes were staring into his. "You didn't have to run like a scared rabbit. I wasn't going to snare you."

He withdrew her hand. "I didn't think that at all. I was tired. I wanted to leave. Right?"

He could see her regain her confidence quickly. "I suppose. I must have been under the wrong impression. So see you around."

She left briskly and closed his door behind her. Nick closed his eyes for a moment. He was going to swear off women for good, and he'd begin this evening with Serena. Then he'd stick to business. Otherwise he was going to get hurt.

The Steel News van, driven by Fred Dexter, slid through dark streets that were enveloped in flashing neon. Serena, dressed in a black tailored pant suit and low, thick heels, sat beside Melissa. Nick and Paul were behind the women, and Cam was in the front passenger seat with Fred.

Serena wondered if it would have made more sense to have scheduled *City Streets* after all. They could have beefed up the content to fit their requirements. At least John's work had been solid. This aimless driving seemed fruitless. Or was it that her nerves were on edge from Nick's offhand treatment of her this evening?

She'd arrived at Steel TV feeling quite energetic after sharing a drink with Seth in a bar near his loft. Getting to know Seth was like getting to know a new person. She'd been pleased with herself about the developing relationship with her brother, which had now become part of her program to banish the pain of her past and start afresh. She'd been chipper enough to smile at Nick and be friendly. Her smile had soon faded when he'd greeted her with a very cool attitude. All he'd done was shrug into his leather jacket and tell her Fred was waiting downstairs with the van.

Well, up yours, she'd thought as they rode the elevator with Melissa, who'd been trying to juggle notebooks and an extra camera, and Cam, who'd also been carrying a load of equipment. Nick helped Melissa with the camera, but he hadn't spoken to Serena.

It was Cam who instructed Fred to stop the van, jerking Serena's mind back to present problems. The neighborhood was a shopping street, a lot of the shops still open. As it was a mild night, there were enough people on the streets to stare at the news van coming to a fast halt at the curb. Their expressions were wary when they saw the crew tumble out.

Serena wasn't entirely sure what Nick had in mind, but she realized he must have spoken to Cam about his ideas because Cam seemed to know what was going on. Therefore, over the next two hours the entire team was busy.

Nick stopped people on the street. "I'm Nick Fraser. You're appearing on the debut show of *Neon Nights*. The show will reflect the people, and the real concerns of your city. Tell me about the issues you want covered."

Cam directed the moments for Nick to hand the mike to Serena so she could ask the questions. These were night people. Some were drunk, and ranted and raved. Some were speechless at the sheer magnitude of the thought of appearing on TV. Others at last found their forum to talk, and voiced their concerns, angry tirades, humor, and well-thought-out intelligent monologues. All the time Paul kept the camera trained on Serena or Nick and their subjects.

At last, Fred drove them back to Steel. By now Serena wasn't sure if she was tired from the late hour or annoyed with Nick, who seemed to be in a bad mood despite the seeming success of the evening. He had a sort of tenacious element about him. Almost like he was being driven by something that she hadn't spotted before in his personality.He wanted to go straight into a studio and begin the edit.

"It's two AM," Serena told him. "Can't it wait until the real morning?"

His jaw took on the stubborn thrust she had noticed the first time at the party. "I want to do it now. Tomorrow will be too late. The show airs on Thursday at nine. If what we got tonight was trash, we go out again tomorrow."

"I didn't feel like we got trash tonight."

"It depends on what we can make of it. Studio Three in ten minutes."

No one else appeared to mind working late. Cam looked more animated than Serena had ever seen him. She suspected it was because he worked well with Nick. Nick might be opinionated, but his opinions and ideas were concrete. Cam liked that. And Nick wasn't averse to backing down when Cam's vision seemed more logical.

At last they disbanded. Serena, her head buzzing after such a long day, went up to her office to grab her purse. The Steel Tower felt eerie and silent at night. When Nick came into the office suite behind her, Serena jumped.

"Must you creep?"

"I wasn't creeping intentionally."

She let her gaze focus on his. Had she ever really seen emotion in his eyes? Anyway it was too late to argue with him. "I'm leaving now."

"You're always running out. Did you think things went well tonight?"

"Very well. You seem to get along with Cam."

"He's a good guy. He takes instruction." Nick put on his jacket.

"What do you mean by that?"

"He doesn't screw me around."

"Like me? Is that what you're saying?"

He removed his car keys from the inside pocket. "Could be I'm saying that. Come on, you do look bushed. I'll walk you to your car." In the hallway Nick pressed the elevator button hard. The light came on.

While they waited Serena couldn't help asking, "Okay. What the hell is wrong? You haven't spoken a civil word to me all evening."

He stuffed his hands into his jacket pockets. His gaze was glacial. "Nothing is wrong. I'm merely tired."

"Then why didn't you call it a day when we got back here. Why go to the studio and do the edit?"

"Because I wanted to do the edit while everything was still fresh. And so did Cam."

The elevator arrived. They got on. The doors closed. Serena felt the elevator drop a little and then stop.

"Damn." Nick pressed the alarm button. A shrill buzz rang out through the silent building around them.

Serena panicked. "I knew this would happen to me one day. Everyone gets stuck in here eventually."

"I guess it's our turn." Nick pushed the alarm again and patted down his pockets. "Damn. Left my phone in my suit pocket. Do you have yours?"

She dug in her purse for it. It wasn't there. Damn. She'd left it at Seth's apartment. She remembered taking it out when she repaired her make up. "It's not here. It's at my brother's place. Oh, Nick. I have to get out of here."

"You will. So calm down."

"I can't."

"Breathe easy."

"I can't."

"Think of it being like when you're sitting under the lights waiting for your cue. Take big, calming breaths."

"Is that what you do?" She really couldn't imagine Nick suffering from a case of nerves.

"Sometimes."

Did that make him human? "Press the alarm again."

He did so, and then moved closer to her. "Okay. Stop panicking. I'm here with you." He placed his arm across her shoulders in what Serena termed an affectionate sort of brotherly gesture. Something had definitely changed between them since earlier in her car. She could hardly believe he was the same man who had looked at her with such heat in his eyes and touched her with desire in his fingertips.

She wanted that heat again, a complete contradiction to how she felt they should really behave with one another. She couldn't bear this cold stranger standing with his arm heavily across her shoulders while her body flooded with warmth and longing.

Nick glanced at her. "Aren't you frightened anymore?"

"You're helping me."

His chest heaved, and she heard him let out a breath. "You're not helping me."

"What do you mean?"

"You know, we either go for it or we don't go for it."

"I don't—"

He cut her words off with a kiss. A kiss that forced Serena to accept the pressure of Nick's body against hers and to wrap her arms around his waist inside his open jacket until her palms were clinging to his back and she could feel heat pouring from him the way it was pouring from her own body. When he left her lips aching for more he held her face between his hands and kissed her eyelids and her nose and her cheek and her ear and stroked his thumbs against her jaw.

"Not frightened now?"

Her hands moved down his back to the smooth leather of his belt. "No," she whispered, her eyes locked with his.

"Who's in there?"

Nick raised an eyebrow and let her go. "It's Nick and Serena."

"Well, this is Joseph. We're running again. You should go down to the ground floor now."

Serena could feel the movement in the elevator once again.

She looked at Nick. He shook his head at her, as if he was saying he didn't know what to do about their predicament. Her only suggestion to herself was that she be brave and go for it, knowing full well that he was only for a short time and would be gone in the future. But was she brave enough for that?

Nick walked her to her car.

"All right?" he asked as she opened her car door.

"Not particularly."

He moved closer. "I haven't been right since I met you, Serena. I always thought I had my head together when it came to women, but I'm not sure I do anymore."

"Kiss me again."

She closed her eyes and let his mouth drive her into delirious fantasies: together they were on a bed. They were naked. He was inside her. They were making love like there was never going to be an end. He was filling her emptiness.

She opened her eyes and slid both her arms around his neck. She clung to his kisses, she pressed herself against him, felt his need against her. Then he left her limp against the side of her car.

His features were outlined in the jumpy shadows cast by the interior light from her car. "Go to Seth's. He's expecting you."

Serena drove to Seth's, hardly registering the way. Seth's big van was already parked in one of the two spaces he said were reserved for him. Serena parked in the other one. She went up to Seth's loft and realized, as she was creeping about inside the loft in the dark, that despite his van being there Seth wasn't even home.

She turned on some lights and found a note pinned to his bulletin board: Make yourself comfortable. The sofa pulls out into a bed. There is a comforter and some pillows tucked inside.

She made up the bed, undressed, and tumbled beneath the quilt in her underwear. She lay staring at the high ceiling. She'd known loneliness when she was a child, when she'd waited for her father to come home and when he never did come home any more. But she'd never known such loneliness of the spirit or of the body. She'd never felt such a desperate craving for a man.

She buried her face in the soft pillow. She was really mixed up these days. If work wasn't such a pressure on her life, she'd take off on a holiday. Which was exactly what she'd done when another relationship had threatened her peace of mind a few years ago. She'd run away to the Bahamas for two weeks. When she'd come back she'd been rested and calm, and had made up her mind there was to be no more of this love stuff. She wasn't suited for relationships or being in love. She couldn't take the agony, the pain, the complete disorder a man made of her life.

Chapter Eleven

Kiss me again. Serena's words hurtled from one side of Nick's brain to the other. It was four AM and he was popping a beer cap off a bottle and drinking from the bottle as if hoping the contents would help him drown the ache in his gut. He knew they wouldn't. He'd learned that early in his life. Mornings brought the same pain.

Holding the bottle, he wandered into the living room. He could blame his parents for this predicament even though he'd unfairly blamed them for all of his past predicaments. Even if they were the reason he was now home doing a studio show with a gorgeous co-host who drove him to distraction. He had to stop that blame. He was an adult they'd lost control of years ago. He wouldn't be here if he didn't honestly feel that he needed something more in his life. Was that the basis for the tug of war in his body and his mind? Did he want something more, other than a career that took him around the world and put him in dangerous situations?

Did he want Serena Brown?

Yes. He did.

And that was the core of his internal battle.

Some of these feelings were the beginnings of love.

He dumped the bottle down on a table. *Get some sleep Nick. You'll be a wreck tomorrow, and you can't afford to be a wreck with a new show debuting on Thursday.*

He stripped off his clothes and climbed into bed. But with his hands behind his head on the pillow he stared at the ceiling light above him. What if he never had Serena? What would happen to him then? His stomach spiraled into an abyss and he closed his eyes against the pain that washed over him.

•

When Seth came in, he turned on a small desk lamp and asked if she was still awake.

Serena leaned her elbow on the pillow. "If I wasn't I would be now." She smiled. "What have you been doing?"

He plunged into a chair and stretched out his long legs in black jeans. "Rehearsing in Rob's parents' garage."

"You're too good for garages now. I hope this show really helps you get some exposure."

"I hope so as well. And I hope you and Nick get together."

"Why?"

"Because I think he's the kind of guy you need in your life."

"If I need a guy."

"That's up to you of course."

"Do you have a girlfriend?"

"No one steady."

"You have, though?"

"Oh, I have, though. Have you had many boyfriends?"

"No."

"You have a lot of hang-ups, big sister."

"I do. All connected to one person."

"Not all. Some of them you invent because they provide a cool, mysterious shield to hide behind. I know." He levered himself from the chair. "Because I do it myself. Anyway, I'm tired. See you later this morning. Help yourself to coffee or whatever if I'm still dead to the world."

"Do you always come in this late?"

"It's part of the music game. Strange hours." He yawned. "I'm beat."

Serena snuggled beneath the quilt. "Go and sleep. Be there to-morrow."

"You used to say that when you baby sat me."

"I know. After Dad died I always wanted everybody to be there tomorrow."

"That's understandable." He came over and touched her shoulder. "Sleep tight."

"Thanks. I really appreciate this."

He smiled. "It's quite fun."

It was. The light flicked off and Seth went behind the screen into his sleeping quarters. Serena listened to his movements for a while, then he slipped into his bed. She rolled on to her side, ready for a long night craving Nick. But she must have fallen asleep because she awoke to light coming through the windows and silence. It was obvious that Seth was gone.

She scrambled from the cocoon of the comforter and reached for her watch on the table. It was nearly noon. Darn. She couldn't afford not to be at Steel early this week. She should have asked Seth to wake her. He'd left her some coffee in a carafe and it was still quite warm, so she poured a mug, discovered how to work Seth's shower, and then dressed in the jeans and silk shirt from her overnight bag. This time she made sure her phone was in her purse.

Serena arrived at Steel to find everyone down in Studio Three. She thought Nick looked wasted. His cheeks seemed hollow and his eyes blank. Didn't late nights agree with him? Or was it something to do with her? They had shared passion last night and parted without discussion of that passion. To her it proved that neither one of them wanted a commitment. She wished they could just meld together and have sex without all these initial mental gymnastics.

She glanced at him, to see if he would respond to her with some wry remark or even a look, but he ignored her. Their kisses last night might never have been.

•

Three, two, one. On Air. *Neon Nights* was launched with exhilarating chords from Seth's guitar. Serena was prepared for Nick on the set from all their rehearsal takes. She knew he smiled, he teased, he cajoled. However, the program he was about to present was serious. Even though the content appeared like entertainment, it wasn't. Nick's agenda came through: clean up your act, world. Get the homeless and the drugs off the city streets. None of this should be in our good democratic society. Serena could feel the edge so much it was as if someone was running a high-pitched drill in the studio.

With forty minutes to spare before she was back on air Serena removed her mike and stood up to stretch her limbs. The interviews chosen from Monday night were edited into a fast-paced neon-streaked documentary that voiced, via the people, all Nick's concerns and a lot of her own. She had to admit that Nick and Cam had given her equal air time.

Nick stood beside her and she gave him a glance. The chemistry between them today was all on-air. Off the set Nick acted as if Serena wasn't even there. But immediately they were tucked together on the black sofa, he became a different person. Serena hadn't got a clue what was going on in his complex mind. If it was that complex. She was just relieved when night one of *Neon Nights* was over.

It was late by the time she walked up the steep concrete stairs to her office. She hadn't ridden in the elevator since that night with Nick, and she didn't intend to ride in it again. Getting stuck was not her idea of fun. She also didn't want the memories. She'd obviously done something to displease Nick that night. Had she been too forward? She should never have begged, *Kiss me again*. Maybe guys like Nick needed the upper hand. Which made sense if he didn't want to get his emotions involved. Which was exactly what she wanted. So why was she worrying about him? This way they could remain business like.

She thought she was in good shape for the few flights of stairs, but she was out of breath by the time she reached the suite. All the lights were on. Nick was there, so were Cam and Don.

Don said when he saw her, "We've decided to go with *City Streets* next week."

Serena was so tired that Don's comment didn't register at first, but when it did, anger fired up inside her. Hell, it was bad enough that Nick kissed her one night and ignored her the next morning, but to take away her scheduled program. Oh, she saw his agenda clearly. She really did. Reduce her to mush and then he'd have his way with all the programming. He obviously didn't want to share the fame. But, instead of showing them she was close to losing her cool, she said, "Haven't we scheduled *Bad Men, Good Women* for next week?"

"We did," Cam said, "But we're on a track here. The switchboard is buzzing. This show started a heartbeat. Nick and I figure if we jazz up the footage we already have, we can draw this into a few more weeks and really cause a stir."

Nick looked at her. "You haven't got much ready, have you?"

"I'm working on the script and I have a contact." She needed to sound confident about her story. She'd have to go and look for

Angela's brother again. He was becoming her imperative link to Angela.

"It sounds like you haven't got enough. Which means, now you don't have to rush," Don put in. "If this works, we've got a few weeks programming in the can. Then we can do your story. All right?"

Serena lost it then. "No. It's not all right. You scheduled my show for next week and I was going to produce a product."

"You're tired, Serena," Nick said. "Go home and think about this. In the morning it will make perfect sense. We're only postponing the other show."

She glared at him. "You told me you thought John's idea was garbage."

"It won't be when I've finished with it."

"You bastard." She walked into her own office and slammed the door. She changed into black slacks and a sweater and hung up her pristine white suit. She hated Nick. Hated him for what he was doing to her. She'd been conned. Thoroughly conned. Her mother thought he was unreliable. Well, unreliable was too good a word for Nick Fraser. And Seth thought he'd be a good man for his sister.

Well think again, Seth. He's a bastard.

She sat down in her chair and realized she was shaking so much she felt sick to her stomach. Had she actually considered going to bed with Nick? Had she actually considered she might be falling in love with him?

When there was a rap at the door she didn't acknowledge it. The door opened and Nick was there, reminding her of that first night, which wasn't that long ago, when he walked into her other office. She'd been furious that night as well. She was being deceived right, left and center.

Nick pushed his hands into the back pockets of his jeans. "It's only a postponement."

She avoided his gaze. "It's rotten."

"You hadn't got anything concrete anyway."

"I do. I was going to deal with it tomorrow."

"That's fine. This will give you time to present it well."

She clasped her hands together and stared down at them. "Don't sweet talk me, Nick."

"I'm not. Reality says keep going with what is causing a stir. We have to wing this show. It's new. But let's give the viewers what they want, and they want a chance to explore the questions we laid on them tonight. We might even bring some political changes about because of this."

"Always the journalist."

"Aren't you?"

"No. I have some sense of decency when it comes to other people."

"You don't think I've treated you decently?"

"It's not only you. It's Don as well. I feel like I'm being shoved around."

"I can understand that feeling. But all we're doing is re-scheduling programs. Shuffling them around, in other words, to make sense. There was no sense to *Neon Nights*. It was a concept. Don had some idea in mind but he wasn't sure what it was exactly. Tonight we showed him a direction. Hell, you were up there on the screen doing your thing as well. You asked some pretty tough questions and got some pretty vast answers. You broke the dam on this as well."

She stood up to give herself more power. "If I reschedule my program, I want definite dates for it."

"You'll get them. And it's not your program. It's our program. It's our show. Remember that."

Nick walked out of her office and closed the door behind him. She didn't feel quite so vehement about him now. She could understand his desire to succeed. His career was on the line as well.

◆

"They sizzled," one reviewer wrote in the morning paper. "Black and white, neon color, music, sharp editing, ingredients that make *Neon Nights* work."

One newspaper columnist dropped her usual topic to salute, dissect and discuss *Neon Nights*. "Steel TV has pumped some new life into what is usually old life. Nick and Serena make it happen."

Paul chucked one of the papers down on the boardroom table. "Nothing about me. I thought I shot some pretty hot footage the other night."

"You did," Serena told him. "But it's like the screenplay writing of a movie. It doesn't get any credit. The actors do."

He gave her a lopsided grin. "I should have known that Fraser could overshadow an elephant. I should have signed off as soon as I heard John wasn't available."

Serena leaned her hip against the table. "That's half of it, isn't it? You don't like Nick."

"Ah, I don't really dislike him, but he does have a sort of power over people. And I have to admit I've been set straight by my sister. When I talked to Lise the other night, she said, "Don't be silly, Paul, that's all over. It was an affair in my own mind.""

Serena felt relieved about this. "Really?"

"She said nothing happened but a couple of dates."

"Well, then. You don't have to be mad at Nick anymore. Just ignore him. I try to."

Paul pursed his mouth at her. "He tries to control you, doesn't he?"

"Not exactly, but he's been used to being number one and it shows." She pushed away from the table edge. "We have to be strong, Paul."

He laughed. "Well, I guess I was a bit edgy about him from the beginning. Maybe if I relax things will improve."

She touched his arm. "Good idea. And remember that Nick wants this to succeed. He won't let the show fail."

Nick strode into the boardroom at that moment and gave her hand on Paul's arm a look. "If you're not busy, Serena I thought we should go through *City Streets* and see what we can salvage?"

"I don't have time right now. I have to meet a friend for lunch."

"I'll see you around Serena. Nick." Paul left the boardroom.

"Who are you meeting?"

"A friend of mine."

"A woman?"

"She happens to be, yes." Serena passed Nick and went to her office. She walked behind her desk and pulled her purse out of her drawer. Then she slipped on the burgundy suit jacket over her slacks and pink satin blouse.

Nick had followed her. "Who is this woman?"

She straightened her jacket and blouse collars. "A friend of mine from university."

"Is she linked to your story?"

"She's not the woman who fell in love with the prison inmate, if that's what you mean."

His eyes narrowed. "But she is connected?"

"We were all roommates together."

"So she knows the woman who fell in love with the prisoner?"

"Nick. Please don't interrogate me."

"I'm just trying to figure out why you're being so secretive. Your reaction to having to change time slots for your show tells me you're possessive about this story."

"Naturally, I am. It was my concept."

"And it could be dangerous."

Serena shouldered her purse-strap. "Why could it be dangerous?"

He raised an eyebrow. "Because you're dealing with a story from a woman who loved a criminal."

"Who is probably still behind bars."

"Don't count on it."

"What do you mean now?"

He shrugged his shoulders. "People don't always stay in jail forever. They get out. Women could tell stories on them over the air and they might not be happy about it. Have you looked into him still being in prison?"

"No."

"That's exactly what I mean. Yet you get so damn mad at me. You haven't got this story yet. I think you need help. Therefore, I'm coming to lunch with you."

She went up to him. "That is only because you want complete control of the show."

Their eyes met and locked. "That's from your perspective."

"It's the perspective you're giving me."

"I don't mean to. I want you to put in your fifty percent as well. I'm not leaving you out." He raked his fingers through his hair. "Serena, please don't make waves between us. It's difficult enough keeping Don and Cam off our backs."

"Is that what you're doing?"

"I want it to be our vision on the screen on Thursday evenings. That's what I want. Now, come on. Relax with me and realize I'm on your side."

Serena's shoulders slumped as she thought of her non-creative brain trying to write her script the other day. "All right. I'd like your viewpoint. I'm a bit stumped."

He shook his head at her. "I appreciate that admission. It doesn't diminish you in my eyes one bit. But you have been tied in by studio news reporting for a number of years. It's bound to be a little stifling."

"How do you know that?"

"Because I've done it myself. I did an anchor job for a year once."

Serena couldn't help laughing. "I didn't know that."

"I don't make it public. Now, let's go. We'll keep your friend waiting."

Serena gave up. He was right. They were supposed to be a team. And she did need his help. She was floundering with the story.

Outside the suite, Serena ignored the elevator and headed for the stairs.

Nick followed her down the steep stone steps. "Now what?"

Their footsteps made a hollow echo and the light was harsh. Serena glanced over her shoulder. "After we got stuck, I don't want to use the elevators anymore."

"Are you walking up seven floors all the time?"

"Yep. Keeps me in shape. You can take the elevator. I'll meet you down in the foyer."

"No. This is fine." He moved beside her. "Are you okay after Monday night?"

"I didn't think you remembered it."

"I've got a better memory than that."

"Well, I'm fine. All I'm interested in now, is my story and meeting Rita."

"Point taken."

Serena glanced at him, but he seemed quite in control. Good, she thought. They'd sorted out a few things between them about work and that should be their main focus.

Rita was a tall, slender woman with lots of auburn hair. The black patent high heels she wore with her green tweed suit made her even taller. She had been married twice and divorced twice. Serena thought Rita seemed nervier after each occurrence.

Rita gave Serena a surprised look when she introduced Nick, then shot out her hand and smiled in her best real estate manner. "I'm so pleased to meet you, Nick. I know you're Serena's co-host on her new show. Unfortunately I've only seen the commercials, as

I work most evenings."

Nick shook her hand. "I understand. It's also my pleasure."

They sat in the same booth in the pub that Serena and Nick had shared the first night they were together. Serena could barely believe that night was only about a week ago. So much had happened to her.

Rita nudged her side. "People are staring at us."

Serena glanced around. They were being stared at. But of course they would be. It made sense. Their show had debuted last night. "It's the nature of the business. You recognized Nick."

Rita whispered. "Who wouldn't. You're so lucky."

Was she?

Rita glanced at her watch. "We'd better order. I've got an hour and a half before I have to meet a client."

Nick didn't set out to charm Rita, but Serena saw it happen, as it did with most women. Even Serena enjoyed the conversation, the salads and Cajun-style grilled chicken, and realized she could relax with Nick—sometimes.

Over coffee Nick said, "Rita, I understand you used to room with a woman who had a relationship with a prisoner."

Serena could have thrown her water, ice and all, over his head.

"I did," Rita said, "But we've lost track of her."

Nick looked at Serena with one of his cool, journalistic gazes. "You didn't tell me you'd lost track of her?"

"We haven't really, have we, Rita? We know where her brother is."

Rita glanced at Serena. "I didn't know this was an interview."

"It's not. Nick, stop it. I didn't invite you to lunch. You invited yourself. And Rita really has nothing to do with my story."

"Story?" Rita asked.

"I suggested a program on Angela because she'd been in love with a criminal."

"I thought you just wanted to see her again?"

"I do. But I also wanted to see if she'll be willing to be interviewed."

"About the creep she said she loved?"

"Was he a creep?" Nick asked.

"I never met him, but I was pretty upset with Angela for being involved with him. Although I don't think he was a real hard core case. He was on a manslaughter charge, and there was always some question about the killing being accidental, because it was during a hunting expedition." Rita turned her head to Serena. "You know my thoughts on hunters. My father was one, and I hated him killing animals. I wouldn't eat anything he brought home. So I figure, well, the guy did us a favor by knocking off another hunter."

"Rita, that's a terrible thing to say."

"I know, but that's the way I feel."

So she hasn't changed much, Serena thought. She'd been an activist for just about everything in university. "Then you don't know what happened to the guy?"

"No. When I got married the first time, I lost track of Angela. Then we met one day in a department store. The Bay, I think it was, and we went for a quick coffee. But she didn't say much about anything. In fact, I thought she was very vague."

Serena frowned. "That's strange. Angela was always pretty real."

"You call corresponding with a prisoner real? Personally, I thought it was sick. Anyway, I knew her before you did, so I'm privy to lots of stuff about her you never knew."

"Like what?" Nick asked.

"Oh, we went to high school together. She was always a little rough around the edges, and my mom didn't really like her very much. My mom being from a sort of upper-class background. Angela's dad drank a lot and caused problems at home. Max, her twin brother, was like his father, but all the girls went mad for him. Angela went for guys similar to her brother. I thought university would straighten her out. But it didn't. She fell in love with a prisoner, of all things and that sort of did it for me with Angela."

Rita turned to Serena. "Do you remember his name?"

Serena said, "Lawson Thomson."

"Unusual name," Nick mused. "Distinguished for a criminal. Is it his real name?"

Rita glanced at Serena. "I don't think I even knew his name before."

"I wrote it down because the case interested me."

"She's always been a journalist at heart," Rita told Nick. "She doesn't believe me, but I think it runs in the blood. You have a father like hers and it's bound to be there inside you, isn't it?"

"I believe so," Nick said.

Serena saw that he was amused by Rita's comments, but she wasn't about to bring her father into this. All right, so she did over-compensate for her background. She knew that. She didn't want anyone to think that Stuart Redding Brown's daughter was a wimp. She wished she didn't come from such preeminent journalistic lineage. And sometimes she wished she'd ignored her calling and gone into a different career.

The lunch continued without any more mention of Angela until they were out on the street.

"If you do get to see Angela," Rita said, "say hello for me."

"I will," Serena told her.

"And it's been great meeting you, Nick. I'll watch your series from now on."

"Series?" Nick remarked as they walked away from Rita.

"Well, you know, she's one of the masses." Serena spoke with a hint of sarcasm.

He looked at her. "I don't think that way."

"I thought you might."

"Well, for your information, I don't. And that's hardly the way I'd describe Rita. She's got some fiery activist blood in her veins."

"That's very true."

"Which makes me quite eager to meet Angela. The three of you together must have been quite a trio."

"We got along. Sort of. We had some good discussions, late into the night sometimes. It made university a lot of fun."

"I bet." He grinned. "It gives you another angle."

She liked being with him when they chatted this way. "Is that good?"

"Excellent. I can imagine you getting all het up and excited over an issue and losing your cool."

"I don't lose my cool that often."

He gave her a sideways glance. "You did last night."

"Wouldn't you have?"

"Yes. Anyway, the reason for your concern last night was this story, which gives us a problem. How to find Angela."

"Her brother would be my first contact."

"The twin? Okay. Do you know where he is?"

"Yes. He's on the streets around Yonge and College."

"Homeless?"

She nodded.

"Great friends you have, Serena. Angela could be on the streets as well."

"If she is, then everything will tie in together with *City Streets*."

"True. Okay. Let's go look for the brother."

Serena walked with Nick through the afternoon crowds until they reached the area that Max Turner inhabited. This time Serena saw him. He was wearing the same battered straw hat she'd seen him in the first time.

Serena felt Nick touch her elbow, as if he wanted to prevent her from running over to Max, and the tilt to her stomach at his touch made her realize that she would never be able to lose her reaction to him. He'd always be with her, even if they never made love. "That's him. He looks like his sister. But I never realized they were twins before. It sort of explains a lot."

"Like what," Nick asked.

"Oh, the reason she was so upset when Max went to prison and why she visited him all the time. Twins are close. And her parents had split up, her father remarried or something. Her mother moved away. They were a completely estranged family except for Max and Angela."

Nick let go of her elbow to throw some change into the cardboard box at Max's feet and asked if he was Max Turner.

"Yup." The man didn't move from his position on the sidewalk against the wall. He held his guitar and strummed a few chords. Then he glanced up at Serena and frowned. "Don't I know you?"

"I'm Serena Brown. A friend of Angela's."

The frown deepened. "Yeah?"

"I went to university with her. You and I met a couple of times at parties."

"Okay. I think I remember. Do you want me or Angela?"

"I'd like to get back in touch with Angela."

He shrugged. "She comes here sometimes to see me."

Serena felt excitement rise inside her. She wasn't going to lose this story. She'd show Nick she was as good as any journalist he'd met. "Any particular day?"

He pushed back his hat with his hand so it perched on his dark curls and she saw the good looking man he could be. "No. She just appears sometimes. I don't do days or time."

Serena noticed Nick smile at this. "Where does she live?" she asked.

"Somewhere in the country near Niagara Falls. I can't help you more than that. I've never been there. She's married."

"She got married." Serena's relief that Angela wasn't on the streets was evident in her voice. "That's great, Max." But she also wondered why Angela didn't help out her brother. Surely Angela could have him stay with her to enable him to find a job. She was aware that a fixed address was necessary to find employment.

"Who did she marry?"

He scrunched his forehead. "I don't know his name."

Serena squatted to Max's level. "You don't know who your sister married?"

"Nope."

Serena felt Nick's hand press down on her shoulder. She wasn't quite sure what the pressure meant. "Do you know when she got married?"

Max's dark eyes met hers. "I don't remember. I just know, she said she got married and she moved down to Niagara Falls. She doesn't tell me much. She buys me lunch and gives me money."

"But she doesn't offer for you to go and live with her?"

"No. And I don't want to. I like it here."

Sure you do. "Okay, Max. Thanks." She rose to her feet.

Nick put a twenty in the box this time. "Thanks, Max."

"He does know who she married," Nick said as they walked back to Steel.

Serena had to pace herself at quite a clip to keep up with him. "Not necessarily. He could have forgotten. He's not in great shape. At least I've got an idea where she lives. Except she might have changed her name."

"A lot of women don't these days, so you might be in luck. Anyhow, we can use Max for *City Streets*. There is a lot of desperation in that man's eyes."

Serena stopped suddenly. "I might need Max in my story."

Nick reached for her hand and made her walk beside him once more. "You mentioned yourself we need continuity, and Max will give us a continuing character."

Serena felt as if she were attached to a rope as Nick led her through the rushing late lunch crowds with a firm grip on her hand. "Turn our program into a soap opera, why don't you?"

"You mentioned tying in subject matter with each program."

"Only if Angela was in the same predicament as her brother, which she's not."

"No. She's married and that might be a problem for you. She might not want to talk about an ex-lover."

"I don't think he was a lover. What can you do with a guy who is in prison?"

"He might have got out."

"You're intent on thinking everyone gets out, aren't you?"

"Yes. Because guys do get out. Unless they're really gruesome murderers. From all accounts this man's case sounded a bit iffy."

Serena tried to unclasp her fingers from his but he gripped them firmly. "You don't think I should do this, do you?"

"I'm not saying that. But you're very emotionally attached to the story and you could be disappointed."

"If it doesn't go, it doesn't go. I won't mind."

"I'm not so sure about that. I think you really want to prove something with this story."

She did. She wanted to prove to Nick she was worthy of being Stuart Redding Brown's daughter. But she wasn't going to tell him that.

Nick glanced at her. "Rita's right. You have more of your father in you than you care to admit."

"What's my father got to do with any of this?"

"Your father has everything to do with everything you are. Rita said it all."

"Why are we making this personal?"

"Because this story of yours is personal, and it's making you touchy about it."

They came to a red light and had to stop walking to let the traffic pass. They stood side by side, hand in hand on the curb. Serena was breathing hard. She wanted to lash out at Nick with her hands and words, while at the same time she wanted him to hold her in his arms the way he had last Monday evening after the elevator got stuck.

Chapter Twelve

"We'll go to Studio Three and look at the work you did with John now," Nick said as they walked into the Steel Tower.

Serena groaned. "Can't you leave work for a few hours? I want to go home. I haven't been there all week. Pascal's likely thinking I've deserted him. And I have no more changes of clothes left."

"Okay, go home, but we have to work sometime over the weekend."

"Not tonight, Napoleon. I'm bushed. Sorry."

Nick had to admit she looked tired. Her hair was blown by the wind from their hurried race down Yonge Street, and her features looked a little strained. Was he being too hard on her? "Okay. We'll take the weekend off."

"Thank you very much." She walked to the stair entrance. "I have to get my things, and I'm off."

Nick watched the heavy door close on her. Then, with his hands shoved deeply in his pockets, he left the Steel Tower. He walked briskly to the parking lot, trying to ignore the voice inside him that said he was in love with Serena. He must be if leaving her, even for a couple of days, was agony.

He climbed into his car and drove to his parents' place. But as he sat in the car by the curb he realized he wasn't up to arguing with them today, so he continued on until he was home. He didn't think the car engine sounded too great but he didn't feel like dealing with it right now either. He went up to his apartment, flung himself, still in his jacket, down on the sofa and picked up the remote control for the TV.

He surfed his way through a lot of late afternoon TV programs that meant nothing to him. He'd been away from North America too long to know the programs and he'd never watched afternoon

TV anyway. He clicked around to Steel and caught Juliette in her newscast. She was a sexy lady, he decided, and he should have gone for her. But how could he do that when he was falling in love with Serena? It was Serena he'd wanted from the word go.

He snapped off the TV. Hell, he couldn't spend the weekend messing around like this. He felt like he was wasting his life. He got up, ripped off his jacket, and started his computer. He began to work on his Stuart Redding Brown documentary, but he couldn't stop thinking about Serena. He quit the script and played Spider Solitaire.

Now what was he doing, shuffling a virtual deck of cards? He had loads of work to do at Steel. *So get down there, Nick. Go watch John's footage alone. You don't need Serena. She's only a distraction in the dark anyway.* He walked over to Steel. As he entered the building, he realized that he was getting used to the buzz and activity in the place. And he really wasn't unhappy about being here.

He found Studio Three empty and searched the shelves for the *City Streets* videos. He was part way through one of John's boring interviews when Paul came in.

Paul pulled up a chair and sat backward on it beside him. "I thought you'd vetoed this stuff."

"Nah. We're going to try and improve on it for next week."

"I'm sure we can improve on it. John never liked to rock too many boats."

"Well, I do."

Paul gripped the back of the chair with his hands. "I know you think you've rocked my boat because of your treatment of Lise."

"What treatment? We dated a couple of times. That's all."

"Okay. Calm down. I know that now. She told me the truth. I think because she's getting married soon."

"That's great. Congratulate her for me."

With Lise out of the way between them, Nick was able to work better with Paul. They arranged to go out on Saturday and shoot some more film. Nick was pleased. It kept his weekend busy.

◆

Serena thought she was going to have a peaceful weekend at home, but she ended up pacing around most of the time and feeling pretty sorry for herself. She did do some heavy duty gardening on Sunday afternoon, which made her feel better, but she missed Nick when she wasn't with him. As she dug and hoed the soil she envisioned him dating someone else this weekend.

Monday was a bright, sunny morning and she got to Toronto quickly. She rushed into the tower, ran up the stairs until she was puffing badly, and went into the office suite. The blinds in the boardroom were pulled and Paul, Nick, Cam and Don were watching TV. Serena didn't bother going to her office first. She went to stand behind the men. She noticed that they were watching material that had some resemblance to the original *City Streets*.

Nick glanced at her. "Paul and I worked on this over the weekend."

Serena felt a mixture of relief that he hadn't been with another woman and anger that he'd gone ahead without her. After all he'd said on Friday about working together and helping her. "That's nice." She walked out of the boardroom.

She stormed around in her office. Damn him. If he wasn't trying to get into bed, he was undermining her working ability. She couldn't live like this much longer. She'd go mad.

She heard footsteps and expected it to be Nick who came into her office, but it was Don.

"Why aren't you joining us, Serena?"

"Because he's gone ahead and done our work without me. He keeps saying we're supposed to be a team, but he goes off and does what he wants to do anyway."

"He had time on the weekend. He told me on Sunday that you wanted the weekend off."

"I did."

"Well, then."

"Don't *well then* me, Don. It's your fault we have that guy in the first place." Serena plunged her hands on to her hips. She'd worn a nice blue wool suit today, with a long jacket and chunky-heeled black shoes, and her hair was upswept. She didn't know who she had meant to impress.

To her surprise, Don chuckled. "He's really got to you. I admire him for that."

"What do you mean?"

"You're taking everything personally, which to me says that you have an emotional investment in Nick."

"Emotional investment?"

"You know what I mean, Serena." He chuckled again. "Now come and help us with this. We need another eye. I hope you notice that Nick has preserved all your interviews. They were excellent."

Despite this positive aspect, Serena still spent the day feeling as if someone had wired her up and was pulling on the wires. She had a splitting headache by evening, but she drove home and fell into bed, trusting that by Thursday she'd be in better shape for the second installment of *Neon Nights*.

Serena had to admit that, after Nick's hand had stirred the editing pot, the *City Streets* episode had changed into a visual outpouring of humor and angst. Serena understood the control Nick desired over his programs, but she also noticed that the technicians weren't too happy with his input. They thought they knew their jobs. Well, they did, but Serena had to admit, Nick had an eye for direction, and he had left in all her best work. Cam must have noticed Nick's talent as well, because he didn't interfere, and Thursday evening proved to be another popular show.

When they went out on Friday morning with a crew, to put some finishing touches to another segment of *City Streets*, Serena found it a relief to be going into the weekend knowing next Thursdays' programming was just about ready to go.

After a street shoot with Max Turner, they returned to the news van, and Fred drove back to Steel. Paul, who sat next to Serena in the back, stuffed something into Serena's jacket pocket.

"From Max," he whispered. "You know, the street guitarist?"

Serena slipped her hand into her pocket and pulled out a blank sealed envelope. "I know who." She had the feeling that whatever was inside the envelope was important, and she didn't want to see what it was in the crowded van, especially with Nick in the front seat. Already he had turned his head slightly with curiosity. She pushed the envelope into her purse.

But as soon as she was back in her own office she slit open the envelope. There was a note inside. *Hi, Serena, Max told me you'd been in touch. If you want to come down to visit, Saturday afternoons are good. Love, Angela.*

Angela had written her phone number at the bottom and Serena smiled broadly to herself as she reached for her phone and punched out Angela's number. If she could see Angela this Saturday her story would be underway.

The phone rang twice, and then it was picked up. "Hello."

It was Angela's voice. Serena moistened her dry lips with her tongue. "Angela, Serena. Max gave me your number. I'd love to see you."

"Me too. I know it's short notice but is tomorrow all right?

"Tomorrow is fine. Tell me where you live."

With directions to Angela's house now in her possession, Serena felt excited, and went into Nick's office to brag that she'd got her story. He was wearing black jeans and a white shirt that he wore when they interviewed on the streets and Serena thought his features appeared contained and irritated. Serena was getting tired of the distance he seemed intent on putting between them, so she spoke in a positive upbeat manner. "Max gave me Angela's phone number. I've talked to her and I'm visiting her tomorrow afternoon."

She saw the glimmer of a smile on his face. "That's great. We'll drive down together."

"I thought going alone the first time would be best."

"Why? What did you hope to achieve?"

She pushed her hands into her pockets. "I don't know. Maybe her confidence."

"You'll either get it or you won't. My presence won't make much difference. Besides, we haven't got all year to work on one story. We're under the gun to produce."

"I know. Okay. Pick me up from my house?"

"Fine. Now I'm going home for some rest."

"And I've got some shopping to do." She had planned on shopping today. She hadn't been near a clothes store in months, and her wardrobe was beginning to feel empty.

He unhooked his jacket. "Have fun, then."

"I will." Serena stood in his office until she heard the door of the suite thud shut. Go shopping. Get out of here. Take a break.

Serena purchased a pair of exquisitely soft black leather pants, a bomber jacket to match, and a new white silk blouse. She definitely had Nick in mind as she stared at her blonde and black leather reflection in the changing room mirrors. Would he like this vision of her? She tucked her hair up on her head and affected a sexy pose in the mirror. *Why don't you find out? Take what you want. Now. While you have the chance. You might regret it forever if you don't.*

•

Nick parked the Steel News Van in Serena's driveway. Serena didn't want this interference from him but she was going to get it. He jumped from the van, slammed the door and walked under the trellis. He felt the same excitement he'd experienced the night of Don's party. He'd been so cocky about his achievement of overcoming his childhood traumas and becoming a hard-edged journalist. Serena had brought him down to basics. He was so much in love with her he couldn't think straight.

He saw Pascal first and stopped to greet him. Pascal began to purr when he remembered Nick. The cat's reaction brightened Nick up. If her cat liked him, then eventually she might like him as well.

He rapped on her sunroom door and saw the shadow of her walk through the jungle of plant life to open the door for him.

The sight of her in black leather made his entire insides throb. There was a different attitude about her today as she moistened her lips.

"Hi," she said.

Their eyes met and stayed locked together. "Hi. Did you have to wear that outfit?" She was undoing him.

She glanced down at herself and ran her palms innocently, but with a lure to entice, down her thighs. "This?"

She didn't flirt very often. Her tongue popped from her between her lips for a second and then she twisted around and wriggled. "Do you like them? They're new."

He couldn't help but reach for her. He pulled her into the nest of his thighs. "Yes. I like them."

"They do things to you, don't they?" Her voice quivered.

"They do a great deal to me." His own voice sounded as if he'd been running hard. He tucked his arms around her waist and kissed the back of her neck, then buried his face in her mass of golden hair. "We feel so good together."

She cleared her throat. "We do."

He moved his hands over her stomach, his fingers tracing her feminine shape through the supple leather. She didn't stop him, and he felt the pressure inside him increase.

But she gave a little moan and then tugged out of his embrace. "Nick, why didn't you acknowledge what happened in the elevator?"

He shook his head. "Because it wasn't what I wanted to happen." His voice broke.

"Me neither. But what if I say yes to an affair, then?" She let her arms rise and then fall to her sides. "Damn the consequences."

"I'm not sure now. I thought it would be easy. At first it might have been. But now," He rubbed his jaw. "It's different now. We're involved. We know one another better."

"Which is probably why I feel ready for you."

She's ready for you, fool. Take what she offers.

"Please, Nick. I'm going crazy, Nick. Really crazy. I have to go for it. I really do. If I go another weekend, I'll go around the bend. I really will."

He took her into his arms and he held her. After a while he felt her arms entwine around his neck and her fingers slide into his hair. He knew he couldn't walk away from her offer without hurting her or hurting himself.

His lips remained against her hair. "When?"

"After we've seen Angela. We can go to a hotel."

"All right. We'll do that."

She disentangled herself from him. "I'll go get Pascal in."

Serena passed him, walked out of the sunroom on to the deck and began calling Pascal. After a few moments the cat came to her and she scooped him into her arms. She brought him indoors and closed the door and locked it. Nick thought she seemed to have that fragile, nervy way about her she'd had the night of the soirée. It reminded him that he'd need to be so careful with her. There wasn't going to be any turning back when this was started.

Serena picked up a soft briefcase that Nick suspected held a laptop computer. When she saw the van she said, "Why did you bring a van?"

"My car needed some engine adjustments." She irritated him when she broke the moods between them. "It's not a social visit anyway. It's business. You're a journalist. Be truthful. Go in your right colors. It's better we go as legitimate news people. Why put another face on the visit?"

"Because Angela doesn't know."

"You didn't tell her why you were visiting her?"

"No. I let her think it was social."

Nick sighed. "Then we'll park and walk. Get in." He reached for her briefcase to hold it for her so she could climb into the van.

"You're angry at me?"

"Yes. I am. I believe in professional honesty. I don't believe in pretending I'm something I'm not just for the sake of a story."

"That wasn't my plan. I'm just not very sure how to go about this entire story."

"That's why I'm with you. To help you. All you need is a push in the right direction. You've got what it takes. The way you hounded that politician about municipally funded food banks was admirable. The best part of *City Streets*."

She smiled. "One minute you seem to be brow-beating me, the next complimenting me."

"I'm just wanting you to be the best. Now tuck yourself in."

Nick closed the door and went to sit beside her. He fastened his seatbelt, started the van and drove out of her driveway. He turned on the radio and they moved away from her house amid the haunting strains of a love song that might as well have been written for them. It was all about taking chances.

Serena turned to Nick. "You know, you're right about me. I'm having a hard time making myself realize I have to go after my own stories that they aren't going to be presented to me over the wire to read."

He let out a breath. "I don't want to undermine you, sweetie, but I could see that you weren't quite sure what course to take. You've got a lot of potential you don't always use."

"I know." She laughed and told him about her happy endings.

"We'd all like happy endings, wouldn't we? But happy endings don't work unless there is a great deal of drama leading up to them. Take this story, for instance. If you reported Lawson Thomson going to prison, then that's fine. But now you want to go further. You need Angela's story. You have to scrape the superficial. That's what it's all about, Serena."

Serena heard emotion in Nick's voice and remembered Barbara's words about how his love for his work showed through. That's how Serena wanted to know Nick. She wanted to know all of him.

She wanted to know his thoughts and hear about the parents he barely mentioned. She wanted to know why he'd been away for ten years without returning until last April, and why he would have been here again, with or without Don's offer. Why he was so attached to his work but not to any woman? Why did he need short affairs that didn't touch his heart? If she knew all that she could be the woman to break him down, change him, make him stay. But she knew she might never get that far. She'd go for today, or tonight, or whatever it took.

They left the country roads to take the freeway west that would lead them to the Niagara Peninsula. Serena tried to relax next to Nick, but all she felt beneath the black leather was a burning desire to be with him in bed.

The landscape was flat close to the shores of Lake Erie and against the brilliant blue sky Serena spotted the small single story house with white siding that Angela had described. On one side was a fruit farm, on the other a vineyard.

"That's it," she told Nick. "Don't go any further. Go back to that last bend and park there."

He reversed the van, drove around the bend, and parked off the road on some flat grass. "It's going to be a hike from here," he said. "And the wind is cold."

Serena drew a small leather purse from her briefcase. "I don't care. Whatever your opinion of journalistic honesty, I'm not taking anything with me. No notebooks. No voice recorder. No nothing. If she decides she'll go for it, we come back to the van for everything."

"Fine. We'll do it your way."

At least he was being cooperative, Serena thought as she slipped from the van and Nick came to her side. There might be a definite sexual tension between them, but Nick was no longer distant. They had something secret between them to share later.

Angela was on the front porch waiting for them. Her friend was thinner than Serena remembered. Her jeans and sweater hung on her tall, slim body. However, her black hair was thick and shiny, and her features just as classical as always. Serena thought her friend's smile was guarded. But she stepped forward to hug Serena.

"It's good to see you again." Angela grinned. "Dig the black leather gear. You look great."

"It's good to see you again as well, Angela. This is Nick."

Nick held out his hand. "It's a pleasure, Angela. Serena has told me you were in university together."

"Yes. We were. I'm pleased to meet you. Come on in."

There was no foyer. They walked straight into the living room. The beige sofa and armchairs were brightened with cushions with blue and cream flowers. A TV screen was on the wall opposite the sofa and there was a circular coffee table in the middle scattered with some magazines, as if they'd been placed there for show.

Coffee was also set out on a table.

Serena sat down on the sofa. Angela sat down to one side. Nick on the other armchair. All the chairs were positioned to be tugged around to watch the television set.

"Help yourself to the coffee. I'm not really sure what to say, or why you wanted to see me."

"As a friend, Angela."

"Stop it, Serena. I saw you guys park the van up the road behind the trees. I've seen Nick on the news. You forget I took journalism. It was one of my dreams as well."

"What happened?" Nick asked.

"Financial problems made me drop out and I went to work in an office. Serena is the success story. Although, you mentioned on the phone Rita was doing well."

"She says the real estate market is busy." Hoping to dilute a tense atmosphere, Serena described the way Rita had been last Friday, and they talked about some of the things they used to do when they had roomed together.

Serena noticed that Nick remained silent. Whether his silence was in respect for her past alliance with her friend that he had nothing to do with, or because he was observing Angela, she wasn't sure.

"How long have you been married?" Serena asked.

Angela twisted her thin wedding band. "A year."

"Then you're a newlywed." Nick's voice sounded very husky and male after the patter of higher pitched female chatter.

Angela glanced at him. "Yes. I suppose you could say that, but we knew one another a long time."

"Was it anyone I knew?" Serena asked.

"I married Lawson Thomson when he got out."

Serena put down her coffee cup rather hard. Angela's words were a shock. Yet excitement stirred in her veins. This was more than she'd expected. Or hoped for. Aware of her friend observing her, she cleared her throat. "I didn't know. But Lawson is the reason I'm here. Not because you married him. Nick and I are co-hosts for a new show called *Neon Nights* and I wanted to do a program on you."

Angela shook her head. "I can't, Serena. You see, you don't understand."

"I know I don't. That's why I want to interview you. I want your feelings about your man. I want other people to understand what I don't. Especially now I know you've married him. That makes a happy ending, doesn't it?"

Angela stood up. "I'd like you to go. Please."

Serena didn't move from her seat. "Tell me as a friend?"

She shook her dark head. "No. I don't trust you."

When Nick rose, Serena also stood up. She opened her purse and took out one of her business cards. She was ready to call it quits, but not under Nick's sharp gaze. She could always call Angela later and let her know the request was off. "Call me when you think you can trust me, Angela. Because it hurts me that you think you can't."

Serena felt Nick's hand reach for her waist as they walked away from the house.

"It's a new twist, her being married to the guy," he said.

"That was a shocker. Now I'm not sure if her happy ending will make a good story."

"There's no happy ending. She's hiding a lot. She's cautious as hell. I think we should crack this story."

"Not if Angela doesn't want it, Nick."

"She'll want it. She'll think about it. She's in a trap. She needs to get out. We might be her ticket to freedom."

"You don't know that for certain."

"I sense it in my gut."

Serena sensed it as well. But she wasn't going to agree with him. She wanted to forget about Angela. She didn't want to hurt her friend in any way. Yet, she knew she couldn't turn Angela down if she came to her. She was now committed to this story.

Chapter Thirteen

Nick inserted the key in the van ignition but he didn't start the engine right away. He wasn't sure how being turned down by Angela would affect their plans for today. Serena seemed a trifle pensive.

"Are you okay?" he asked.

Her hair danced in the bright sunlight as she glanced at him. "Maybe a little disappointed, but I'm willing to wait. I've planted the seed of the idea in Angela's mind."

"That's all you can do." He didn't want to rush into anything, but he was eager to be alone with her. "Let's just forget about work for the rest of the day and go find a little restaurant somewhere. How's Niagara-on-the-Lake these days?"

"It great. However, it's a popular place, with the theaters and the nice shops, restaurants and hotels. It does get crowded on weekends."

"We'll take a chance. If it's okay with you?"

She laid her hand on his arm. "I haven't forgotten what we planned. I'd really like some space from Steel TV for a while."

He lifted her hand and kissed her fingers. Their eyes met and the heat was still there between them. He felt relieved. "How do I get there?"

"It's easiest from the freeway."

Even though it was a chilly day Niagara-on-the-Lake bustled with tourists. Car parks were full, roadside parking was jammed, and tour buses challenged the horse and carriage rides. Even after they'd found a place to park the van, the sidewalks were crowded with people enjoying the Victorian charm of the town.

Nick held Serena's hand and they walked along as if they were also tourists. It was great to have some time off. For once they weren't vying for air position or program space. For once they were just Nick and Serena, man and woman. And Nick hoped Serena had the same idea for how she wanted to spend her afternoon as he did. If he didn't make love with her today he wasn't going to survive the months he had left to work with her.

But even though he was eager Nick still felt the need not to hurry. He thought it was because he wanted to stretch out something that ultimately would prove to be beautiful.

He squeezed her fingers. "How are you doing?"

She smiled and rubbed her shoulder against his. "I'm having fun. Aren't you?"

"Yes. I am." He didn't want to be anywhere else at this very moment.

They found a pub in one of the hotels and sat down in tapestry armchairs by the window, where they could watch the street. They both ordered a glass of red wine and a salmon dish that was being offered as the lunch special.

Nick raised his glass. "Cheers to a few hours off."

Serena reached over and touched her glass against his. He thought she looked wild and beautiful. Her golden hair ruffled by the breeze, her luminous eyes gazing at him. She had taken off her leather jacket and she wore a feminine white silk blouse.

He sipped his wine and placed the glass on the polished table top. "Don't slap me, but while we're waiting for our order I'm going to book a room."

"You don't waste time."

"I won't if you don't want me to. We'll go shopping after lunch."

She touched her neck in that way she had. "I've made up my mind about this. Go do it."

He rose from his chair with a similar feeling he had that morning at Heathrow. This was commitment.

•

Serena picked up her wine glass and forced herself to relax in her chair. This is what she'd planned. This is what she needed. She glanced at the crowded tables. Did everyone know what they were going to do this afternoon?

She saw Nick make his way back to her around the tables and felt her heart leap at the way he looked. Tall, good-looking, with a rather soft expression on his face for her as he sat down in his seat.

"Did you get a room?" Her voice was husky.

He patted his inside pocket. "Yep. But you can still back out."

She shook her head. "No. I've given my word. It's just that I might be over thirty but I'm not used to this."

He let out a breath and rested back in his chair. "I'm not used to what is happening between us either. We're both novices."

"It thought you were the experienced one."

He picked up his wine glass and took a drink. "Not that experienced. I think my reputation rises far above my consumption."

She laughed. "You expect me to believe that?"

"I do. Because it's true. Anyway, I've never felt for a woman what I feel for you."

She felt elated by his words. Maybe he could even fall in love with her and never leave her. Then this action today would be much more than a brief liaison. She could let herself go with him and she wouldn't feel quite as if she were floundering in a rough sea. But she didn't want to get her hopes up. She'd live for today first and see what happened.

The waiter came by, with a smile and a flourish of their plates. Serena ate all the food. The salmon was light and fluffy, with a hint of lemon, and the rolls were warm and fresh. She noticed that Nick also drank a second glass of wine. Did they both need courage? Like her, was he venturing into deeper waters than he usually ventured? Did he feel as if he were putting his emotions on the line the way she did?

Nick paid with his credit card and they rose from the table. He helped Serena on with her jacket and squeezed her shoulders. She looked at him and smiled. Now they were actually down to the moment she seemed much more relaxed and certain about her actions than he did about his own.

He placed his hand at her waist on the way out of the pub and he guided her into the hotel section, through a maze of corridors until he located the right room. He inserted the card and pushed open the door. All his movements felt ethereal. Serena moved inside the room in front of him. He walked inside and closed the door. He locked it. The room was dark, because the blinds were pulled against the bright afternoon sunshine, but shafts of light striped the king-size bed and pine furniture in the room. Serena stood with her back against the wall, her hair also catching a bright ray of light. Her eyes were midnight blue, dark.

Nick didn't move into the room or take off his jacket. Instead he returned the swipe card to his inside jacket pocket and he moved forward until his body was in line with hers. Their eyes met, and stayed fastened and she touched him.

At first her fingers were tentative between his thighs, and then, as her interest grew, she caressed with a sure stroke. Reeling from the sensations, Nick touched her and felt her heat and her damp warmth even through the leather. Holding her that way, he leaned and kissed her mouth. Her lips opened, with no hesitation when he let his tongue delve deep. Her hunger as intense as his own.

He moved away from her and saw her hand drop from him in slow motion. He removed his jacket. She slipped off her own jacket. She tossed it on top of his on an armchair. She unbuttoned the top two buttons of her white silk blouse and he saw a glimpse of the white satin that covered her perfect, creamy breasts.

He opened his shirt and tugged the bottom from his jeans. Her fingers trembled over the rest of her buttons and she removed her blouse. She let it drop to the carpet. Then she held the top of the side zipper to her pants.

He unbuckled his belt.

She slid down the zipper.

He unsnapped the button on his jeans.

She slid her hand provocatively between leather and flesh.

"Let me now," he said.

She sat down on the side of the bed for him to remove the rest of her clothes. He kissed her through her white satin panties, kissed her thighs, her knees and her feet, worshiping her. When he rose he found it a struggle to remove the rest of his own clothing. He had lost his head over this woman.

Serena watched Nick come to her. Naked, he was magnificent. She never thought she'd ever think that about a man's body, but it was true. He was muscular, golden and sleek and he wanted her badly, but he held himself in control. Once she was naked with him she opened her thighs to him and took him to the throbbing place deep inside her.

She heard herself cry out with the unfamiliar pressure of his body, but she couldn't stop the pleasure, the sensations that raked her and broke her into a sobbing mass in his arms. And then again: Facing one another, gazing into one another's eyes: The push, the pull, the fantastic healing feeling of being with a man and the joy as they drove to the same heights with the same sounds of ecstasy.

And once again: Serena atop Nick. She flung back her body and his hands rode up her stomach and over her breasts, and she felt the room began to spin and she couldn't get enough of him. She had never known such urgent, physical hunger, but then she had never let herself go with a man this way.

She bent down and cupped his face with her hands. His tongue wet her lips and she wet his lips with her own tongue. She was teetering on the verge of fulfilment. She never wanted this to end. They were in a secret place, nobody knew they were here, and these were stolen, delicious moments.

Nick lost control first, and she felt high on the power of being able to give him such wild satisfaction, a wild satisfaction that became her own only moments later. They finally parted and collapsed on to the damp sheets.

Half awake, half sleepy, Serena listened to the sounds outside: the traffic, people talking, laughing. She chuckled. "I can't believe what we've just done and we're only a step away from the sidewalk." Nick rolled on to his elbow beside her. He slowly stroked her from hip to breast. "I'm pleased you sound happy about it."

"I needed it, didn't I?"

"Me too."

She turned her head to look into his face and she realized with an all-over feeling that came to her like waves crashing on a beach that she was in love with him. *You fool,* she told herself. *You absolute idiot.*

He brushed her hair from her forehead and traced his fingers over the creases. "Why do you frown?"

She lifted herself on her elbow, the way he had. "Was it great for you?"

"You don't have to ask that question. Didn't you feel how I was? I gave you everything."

Not everything. Not nearly everything. Serena sat up on the bed. "I guess we should be moving on."

"No." Nick reached up and tugged her down beside him again. He kissed her eyes, her cheeks, her mouth. He kissed her breasts and her stomach and he kissed between her legs. The hunger was far from satiated. But this time her pleasure was mixed with the knowledge of loving him.

•

Nick left the shower, and after drying himself, returned to the room. Serena was spread out beneath the covers, sleeping. He noticed the rise and fall of her breathing and the soft way her face looked at rest. If he'd done nothing for her, he thought, he'd given her this respite. He'd given her the calming sleep after being well loved.

Except strangely, although his body felt relieved to have finally given itself to Serena, he didn't feel very calm himself. He actually felt pretty guilty. For he was going to be for Serena the same as her father, a missing person from her life.

He sat down on the side of the bed and reached over to touch her hand. She felt the movement and her eyelids flickered, and she smiled, her teeth pressing into her bottom lip. "What's happening?"

"I took a shower. You'd better as well. Then maybe we should have some dinner."

"I don't want to leave here."

"Me neither. Shall we stay the night?"

"I'd like that." She scraped her hair away from her face with her hand. "This has been wonderful. You were right. Great sex is an answer. However, it's all still there waiting afterward. So, if afterward doesn't have to come until Sunday, then that's all the better."

"I understand."

"I'm not sure if you do."

"Well, I do. I was a lonely kid. My parents were old and sent me off to boarding school when I was pretty young. Summers it was camp. They wanted to be by themselves, and I respect that. Except I also believe they took on a responsibility when they had me, and they didn't really acknowledge it. They gave me the physical comforts, but emotionally they left me out." He made a face. "And that's truth time for me."

"Do you get along with your parents?"

"Merely on a superficial level." He wished he hadn't started this conversation, but felt that it was time to tell someone, and that someone was Serena. There was no question she was the right person to tell. He rubbed his hand over his naked thigh. "I was in the way, I was sent away, so I chose a career that kept me away."

"Then why bother coming back?'

"Because they're old, not in very good health, and they need help, and one side of me feels responsible for them. I think I might be hoping to salvage something of the past and bring it into the present, so my memories of them are now, not then." He glanced at her. "Heavy stuff, huh?"

"So that's why you're home?"

"That's why I'm home. Hopefully by the time my contract is up I can persuade my parents they should move to more comfortable digs and I can be satisfied at leaving them." At that time he'd also have to leave Serena. That thought didn't sit well with him at all.

"They don't want to move?"

"No. They're being stubborn."

"Like you," she whispered with a little smile. She reached up to him to caress his jaw. "You get a stubborn, little-boy look sometimes."

Feeling warm inside that she'd noticed that about him, he clasped her fingers with his. "I suppose I inherited that."

"So where do your parents live now?"

"Above my father's jewelry store."

"He still works?"

"No. He's had some heart attacks, so he hires a guy to clean watches, which is his only business now."

She squeezed his fingers. "I would never have guessed your reason for coming home."

"Why? Because you think I'm cold and unfeeling?"

"Yes. To be honest."

"I've had to be that way, Serena. It's kept me sane."

"I know. I'm the same way."

"I figured that." He leaned down to kiss her mouth. Her lips were soft beneath his and he felt a slow moving heat flood his body. This was more than mere sex, it was for everything she gave him. He tucked himself beneath the covers with her. Their mouths fastened together once more and their bodies clamored into an embrace. He went into her with no thought of anything other than she was beginning to feel lovely and familiar. Later, when she knelt before him, melted into a fusion of sexual euphoria, Nick wasn't sure how he was going to feel about all this tomorrow.

•

"What's the time?" Serena whispered through the dark. Her hands reached out to touch Nick and she drew herself closer to him. Outside the street was now quiet in the dense darkness.

She felt him stretch out for his watch. He squinted into the face. "Midnight."

"Appropriate," she whispered. "I was always awake at midnight when I was a child. I never slept very well."

He replaced the watch on the bedside table and lay beside her. "So do you prefer working evenings instead of days?"

"It's okay." She thought he seemed a little withdrawn now. They had finished making love the last time about an hour ago. They'd been sleeping on and off. In between she'd been thinking about how she was going to reconcile this weekend into her life.

She stroked his shoulder. "Are you tired?"

He glanced at her and she saw his teeth flash white. "A little." He eased over beside her and took her into his arms. "Let's try and get some sleep."

Serena supposed she did sleep, because she awoke to the smell of fresh coffee and the clinking of cups.

Nick was wearing unsnapped unbelted jeans and his shirt open overtop. "Room service. Aren't you starving? We forgot to go for dinner."

"We ate a good lunch," she said. It was daylight now. Sunlight flickered behind the blinds.

"Almost a day ago," he said. "Okay. This is the menu. Coffee, fresh squeezed orange juice, warm croissants, butter, marmalade, scrambled eggs, hash browns that look like chips, you know me and chips."

She laughed. "It sounds delicious. I'll get some clothes on."

"No need." He lifted a thick terry robe from the end of the bed. "Complimentary. Slip into this."

She rose from the bed, aware of her nakedness and slight cool air of the room caressing her flesh. Behind her, Nick slipped her into the terry robe and he leaned over her, kissing her nape and tying the belt at the same time. Then he ran his hands down her hips, and she could feel him pressed against her, and she felt the same honey-damp heat invade her that had been her constant companion for the night.

But she moved away from him and teased. "Let's eat first."

They sat in armchairs either side of a small circular table and made short work of the food. They lingered over coffee and when her cup was empty Serena stood up. "I think I'll go for a shower."

Nick also rose. "Not so fast."

She placed her head to one side. "What do you want?"

He came closer. "What do you think I want?"

She made her eyes big. "Not that again?"

"Yes, that again."

She untied the robe and shrugged it from her shoulders. Naked, she walked to the bed and sat down on the edge. "Come here."

He undressed and came to her, aroused. She took him in again, wondering, now that she was wound up, how she would ever wind down?

When she finally went to her shower, she still felt restless with lust.

"One last condom," Nick said, poking his head around the shower curtain where she was standing, lathered beneath the pounding hot shower. He climbed in with her. "Shame to waste it."

•

Holding hands, they strolled through the bright sunlight to the van. Serena felt well loved, and wondered why she had never tried anything like this before. Maybe Nick was right. Maybe she could just go for the moment and leave unscathed at the end. Except, when she looked at him, she felt great surges of love for him. She squeezed his fingers.

He grinned at her. "It was fantastic, Serena. Really fantastic."

She rubbed her arm against his. "Does that mean it was better than great sex?"

He gave her fingers a return squeeze. "Sure does."

"Greater than greater sex?"

"Wondrous sex. Perfect sex."

She left it at that. At least she was with him. If she was lucky, she had six months to look forward to, maybe even eight.

Nick swore and leaned over, pulling a ticket from beneath the windshield wiper. He didn't bother looking at it. "I should have moved the van behind the hotel once we'd checked in."

"It's okay. Steel will pay it. Just put it in with your expenses."

"But it was parked all night. Someone might guess what we were doing." He pocketed the ticket. "I'll pay for it myself."

"Don't tell me you have a sense of decency?"

He gave her a grave look. "Of course I do. Especially with you. You wouldn't have gone to that hotel room with just anyone."

Was it so obvious she was the type of woman who had to be in love with her man to make love with him? She tried to make light of his comment so he wouldn't guess. "Oh, yeah?"

"Don't fool with me, Serena." He patted the pocket containing the ticket. "I don't like this."

She didn't think there was much to worry about but she didn't say any more about it. Nick was holding open the door of the van for her, so she climbed in. He tucked himself in beside her and started the engine. He really did seem annoyed by the ticket, and the atmosphere had changed between them from euphoria to tension.

He grumbled over the slow traffic as they inched their way through the crowded Sunday streets. Once they were on the highway, he drove fast. The miles were soon eaten along The Queen Elizabeth Way through the Niagara Peninsula. Then they were crossing The Burlington Skyway over Lake Ontario, now on their way around the lake and east to Toronto.

Nick's moodiness was in contrast to Serena's body, which was still with his in high ecstasy in the shower. Their love making had been more poignant, less of a hurry, longer and even more stimulating.

She glanced at Nick's profile. She felt she knew it better now. She knew the thick line of his dark hair, the ridge of the scar beneath his flesh, the way his beard grew a little fuzzy from his jaw. His eyes weren't always cold. Sometimes they grew dark and showed his needs.

They were nearing Toronto. She could see the city buildings and the tower behind a faint haze. Across the blue sparkle of Lake

Ontario, that forced a horseshoe out of the surrounding land, was Niagara-on-the-Lake and their hotel room. A nice, secret place for secret doings. A midnight that hadn't been full of hell.

"What do you want to do?" Nick asked as they sped along Lakeshore Drive.

It was a typical sunny Sunday afternoon by the lake, with people jogging, walking, cycling and skating. She wasn't sure what one did after a weekend of love. "I'll go home, I guess."

"Do you want me to take you home now, or do you want to come to my place for a while? We should eat. We can order Chinese."

She didn't really want to go home right away. She would only wander around and make her life miserable. "Chinese sounds good. I'll have to phone Ginny, my neighbor, to make sure she feeds Pascal for another day."

"Did she know you were going to be away last night?"

"I told her I might be late. She knows I sometimes don't make it."

"Okay. Then I'll drive you home later."

"That's fine." She felt anxious now, because he seemed to be slipping away from her, as if she could stretch out her hand and not feel him there anymore.

It was a neat thing to do, to share an impromptu casual meal with Nick. But she could still feel his coolness, even beneath his easy grins and light caresses. Driving her home in the dark, he was silent. He came in for a second, and made sure she was safe, but he didn't ask to stay.

When she hung up the black leather pants in the closet, she blamed them for her lack of control this weekend.

•

When Nick returned to his apartment, it smelled like a Chinese restaurant. He washed the dishes they had used and cleaned up. He took out the parking ticket and sat down at his desk. He wrote a check and sealed the envelope. The parking ticket made him feel stupid. He should have thought of everything when he knew he was going to spend a weekend in a hotel room with Serena. But then when he parked the van he hadn't been intending to spend the entire weekend.

He raked his fingers through his hair. All he'd bargained for was the afternoon after lunch. Then they'd go for dinner in the hotel and drive home. Instead, it was now midnight Sunday, and they had spent hours making love, and even then it had been difficult to leave the hotel. And even more difficult to leave Serena.

What was he going to do? Hang her on until he left? Or let her go now, before he had a chance to hurt her? The thought of letting her go hurt him like hell. He almost had to double over, the pain was so excruciating. He went to bed with no decision made. He couldn't say what was going to happen tomorrow when he saw her again.

Nick didn't see Serena until the afternoon on Monday. By that time he'd read the newspaper gossip column circulating around Steel TV.

Possibly the heat they create on TV isn't all a sham. Where were Serena and Nick while a Steel TV News van sat on a Niagara-on-the-Lake street most of the weekend?

"We went to investigate a story and it took longer than we thought," Nick explained to Don, but he was thinking: I didn't want all this for Serena.

Don put his hands in the air. "I don't care what you do together. Or why? This adds intrigue to the show. I like it."

Serena won't like it, though. And he was right. She followed him into his own office.

Wearing a gray and white pinstriped pantsuit, and brandishing a copy of the newspaper, she said through gritted teeth, "Why the hell did you bring a Steel van on the weekend? We could have gone in one of my vehicles."

"I didn't know what was going to happen between us. Did I?"

"Maybe not, but I don't like my personal life insinuated upon by newspaper columnists. A theater critic down for the Shaw Festival saw us."

"It's unfortunate we were spotted, but, as I said, I wasn't thinking straight. I only had one thing on my mind."

"Sex. That's all you've had on your mind since we met. Well, now you've had it. Satisfied?" She threw the paper down on his desk and flung her purse and briefcase on to his sofa. "Now we'll be gossiped about. Hell! Damn!"

He shouldn't laugh, but he couldn't stop himself. She was a beauty. He couldn't get her out of his mind or her scent from his body. He'd wanted her since he met her, he'd wanted her all weekend, he wanted her now. There was no letting up. Part of him might feel worn out from having her, but it didn't stop that same part of him from being aroused.

"Don't laugh," she said. "We have to put the gossip to rest."

"It'll be forgotten tomorrow." He hoped. "Look. I didn't want this for you, believe me."

Her hair was upswept and neat. She reminded him of the way she'd been the night of the party. Not the way she'd been all weekend, ruffled, hot and desperately hungry.

"Let it be, Serena."

"I didn't want anyone knowing about us."

"Why?"

"Because I don't like stuff like that. I'm a cool chick. On the weekend I lost my head."

"And I lost mine. So what are we going to do about it? Go around headless?"

She caught the ridiculous remark and laughed in a brittle manner. "I'm saying I don't want it to happen again."

He felt sick. "You have to be joking."

"No. I'm not. It's going to be too difficult for me on too many planes to continue." She rubbed the side her cheek. "I had brain failure."

He wasn't even seeing her now. All he could picture was a life without her, and it stretched into a bleak future. "You'll think this over, of course."

"I've thought it over. I was up all last night." She placed her hands on her hips. "I'm sorry, Nick. But affairs aren't me."

He couldn't think of anything else to say, or retort to, or laugh at.

She picked up her purse and briefcase and went into her own office. He felt nauseous now. The phone rang. It was Don.

He went into Serena's office and said, "Don wants us in the studio for a moment." He couldn't even look at her. She was too bright, too painful for him.

She went into the elevator with him.

He didn't ask when she had stopped using the stairs. The memory of that night was also too painful.

Down in the studio, Nick realized that around Steel TV gossip thrived.

Fred Dexter indicated Serena with a nod of his head. "Melted the Ice Maiden, I hear."

Nick said, "I don't know what the hell you're talking about."

Maybe Serena was right. Maybe they should nip their affair in the bud. Or at least give it some space for the gossip to die down.

He left the studio before Serena, to give her that space.

•

Serena watched Nick leave without a word to her. Oh, well, what was she worried about? The less she saw of him, the less the gossip would flourish. By the time she returned to her office and felt the horrible sinking sensation of loss when she found Nick gone even from there, she wasn't so sure she had done the right thing by turning him away. Maybe she had stayed up all night worrying about the consequences of her actions of the weekend, but she had also stayed up thinking about how much she loved him.

Her voice mail light was flashing, so she checked out the message. It was her mother. "It's urgent," Reeva said. She phoned her mother's office and was surprised to get her on the phone right away.

"I was accosted by the media on the way to my office this morning, Serena. I've had at least a dozen phone calls. Is it true?"

Serena slumped into her chair and pressed her fingertips into her now aching forehead. "Is what true?"

"Your affair on the weekend with Nick?"

She never lied to her mother. She wouldn't dare. "Yes. It's true."

"Then you're an item?"

"No. That's it. Just the weekend."

Reeva made a clucking sound in her throat. "What are you thinking of, darling? You can't have that type of reputation. You're more famous in this city than you think you are. *Neon Nights* is watched by a lot of people. They respect you. They look up to you. At least make your affair look as if it's a real love match."

"Well, it isn't. Why lie?"

"Because you want your show to be a success. You've got a hit on your hands. Besides, think of me. Think of Seth's career. We're all on public view. We have to be circumspect. Oh, couldn't you have shacked up at your place for the weekend? Why go to a hotel?"

Serena knew the answer to that. It was because she had wanted to keep her time with Nick separate and secret from her real life. But she hadn't succeeded. She'd brought everything back with her and caused quite an explosion.

"I don't know, Mother. Please, don't make it difficult."

"I'll deal with it, darling. Just take it easy and don't worry."

Don't worry? How could she not worry about a weekend with Nick, when she had discovered she was in love with him.

Chapter Fourteen

Nick had a meeting with Don early on Tuesday morning. He hadn't had much sleep. Thinking about Serena had kept him awake half the night. He entered Don's office to the aroma of fresh coffee. A huge Steel mug of it was given to him by Patty Jane, Don's assistant.

"You look tired," she said with a grin.

So she'd heard also the gossip. Nick went into Don's office. Don was on the phone, and he waved for Nick to come forward to his big desk.

"It's Reeva Brown-Carstairs," Don mouthed. "She's resigning."

Don went on chatting to Reeva about something else. Nick sipped his coffee. It was quite a surprise to hear that Reeva was resigning.

"Nick," Don said. "I'm going to put this on a conference call. Let's talk to Reeva about appearing on *Neon Nights*."

"Nick," Reeva said. "What do you think? I could announce my resignation at the end of the program. I like to go out in style."

"It's not exactly *Neon Nights* type of news. But we are tight on programs near the end of October. Let me think about it."

"All right. Come up for dinner this evening at six, and afterwards we'll attend The Song and Poetry Festival and we can discuss it."

"Sounds good," Nick said. "I'll be there."

Reeva told Nick where she lived, then Don chatted a few more minutes and disconnected the call.

Nick frowned at Don. "She's really not a dark enough subject for *Neon Nights*."

"We can't say no, though. I want her to do a weekly political commentary. We already discussed that at the party."

Nick turned his mug around in his hands. "What do you think

Serena's reaction will be? She might not want to work with her mother."

Don grinned. "You can handle that. She's your woman. I can't believe you got that far with her, Nick. I really can't."

So everyone thought they were still a going concern. Nick took the stairs down to seven, wondering if they should continue their affair for a while, or at least make it appear that they were involved in something genuine. He didn't want people thinking he had dumped Serena after the weekend, as if he'd got what he wanted. Because he hadn't got all he wanted. He wanted more than an affair. He wanted her company in his life. Worrying about hurting her six to eight months from now was kind of a knee-jerk reaction when she might not even care about him enough to last that long. She could be tired of him by Christmas. He would rather make it look as if their affair had petered out, than have her gossiped about because Nick Fraser had given her a dirty deal.

He looked in at her office, but he didn't disturb her as she was dialing her phone. He sat down at his desk to make a note of his appointment with Reeva this evening, acutely aware of Reeva's daughter through the thin dividing wall.

•

Serena had just come from a corridor meeting with Cam, who had asked about the progress of the *Bad Men, Good Women* program. She was beginning to see through Cam's laid-back attitude. She felt it was intentional. When he could, he put the pressure on. He made you feel that if you didn't do as he asked he would be extremely unhappy.

Angela's phone rang four times, and she was surprised by an answering machine. It was a man's voice. Lawson Thomson? His voice was deep and droning, almost hypnotic. Serena didn't bother leaving a message. If Nick's gut instinct was correct, Angela wouldn't want Lawson to know that Serena had been in touch with her. She would just keep trying until Angela answered the phone herself. She wasn't happy with a situation that made her friend mistrust her, but then she was the one who had decided that Angela's story should be told. She was the one who needed to prove something to Nick.

Not wanting to think about Nick right now, Serena decided that she would go shopping and buy herself something to wear tonight that would meet with the approval of her mother. She had a long-standing date this evening to attend the Song and Poetry Festival to see Seth perform. Gerry was out of town for a few days, so she had been invited to dinner and to stay the night.

Dinner at her mother's plush apartment was always an occasion. Because she was so busy, Reeva's meals were catered by one of her favorite chefs who threw together, Manno's own words, wonderful, fluffy concoctions. He was a big man, with a creased, interesting face and delighted in serving Reeva and her guests. He was working in the kitchen when Serena arrived, and greeted her with a huge grin.

"I have poured you both wine in the living room," he said. "Now get out of my kitchen. Tonight is a surprise."

Serena changed clothes in her assigned bedroom and joined her mother in a room with thick peach carpet and massive windows that overlooked the sparkling lights of the city. Serena sat down in one of the plush armchairs.

Her mother nodded to the silver tray on the table that held two crystal glasses of white wine. "Have a glass. You look nice. I like that blue silk. It complements your eyes."

Serena stroked the long, slim skirt over her knees. "I bought it this afternoon." She was pleased she had as Reeva wore a glamorous emerald green suit.

"It's attractive." Reeva sat down in the opposite chair and lifted her glass to her lips. "This is nice. Time like this is rare with you, Serena. Actually, a lot of things are rare since I've been in politics. Although," She paused for effect. "I have decided to call it quits at the end of this term. I'm not running again."

Serena felt so surprised by the sudden announcement her hand swayed and her glass almost spilled. "What will you do?"

"I'll always find something to do, but I'd like to see more of you and more of Seth. There are also Gerry's kids. Carrie is getting married next July, and we'd like to take the trip out to Edmonton for the wedding." Reeva peered at the sparkle of the liquid in her glass. "I just feel that I've put a lot of pressure on myself for most of my life and it's time to relax. Maybe we can get down south for a few months each winter and enjoy ourselves."

"I think that's great. You deserve a good time. Have you made the announcement official yet?"

"No. Not yet. But I was chatting to Don Steel today and he mentioned it might be worthwhile to make a public announcement on Steel TV. He just happened to have Nick in his office and we went on a conference call to suggest you do a documentary on me for *Neon Nights*, then I'll announce my resignation at the end of the program. A grand farewell."

Serena felt the now familiar irritation with Nick and Don for making plans without her. "Did you agree to this?" She knew she sounded quite harsh.

"I agreed. But Nick didn't think a political program on me was really *Neon Nights* material. He said they might need to fill some time later in October, though."

Serena knew what all that was about. Nick was dubious that *Bad Men, Good Women* would be ready. And he was probably right. "So when does this happen?"

"I felt I should discuss it with Nick. So I invited him to dinner and to Seth's concert. He should be here any moment."

Serena was so flabbergasted at her mother's maneuvers that she lashed out at her. "Why didn't you ask me first about this?"

"Because Don wants me to appear in a weekly political commentary spot. We discussed it at the party. I mentioned I might be calling it quits at the end of this term. He thought I should go out in style. You know, Don. He likes to dramatize."

"Yes. I know Don. And Nick. And they both like to manipulate everything. Absolutely everything."

Reeva's eyebrows rose. "Darling. Don't be so upset. This is a chance for you to be seen with Nick to keep the gossip under wraps."

"So you're doing this on purpose?"

"No. I grasped an opportunity that's all. It'll be for the best. Besides, I feel you need a man in your life. You're becoming hard and bitter."

"I didn't even think you liked Nick."

"I like him. All I said was, beware. But as you've gone the whole way with him, you might as well continue, otherwise it would appear to be a pretty shoddy affair. As I said yesterday, that isn't the way you should conduct your public life. Besides, it will do you good to get out of that shell you've built around yourself."

Serena touched her throat where her dress dipped into a V. Her flesh felt hot.

The buzzer sounded into the apartment.

"That must be Nick," Reeva said. "Go along to the dining room, dear. We haven't got much time. The limo is coming at seven fifteen."

Serena walked through to the dining room. A maid was setting up the table with Manno's shrimp delight starters. Serena gulped down the rest of her wine. Nick came in, dressed in one of his black suits with a white shirt and black tie. He looked superb. As usual.

He smiled at Serena. "Surprise."

She acknowledged him with her head. She really had nothing to say. She hadn't spoken to him since Monday morning, when she'd told him it was all over between them. Of course the rest of the world didn't know that.

•

Nick thought Serena looked fantastic in a long-sleeved, ankle-length midnight-blue dress.

Reeva patted his shoulder. "Sit down, Nick. Manno is a wonderful chef. You'll love the meal."

Nick waited until the women were seated, then he sat down with them. The starters did look rather delicious. Everyone began eating, while Manno poured wine. Nick noticed Serena picked at her food. She would turn over a shrimp, stare at it then do the same with another one. He wondered if she felt the same emptiness inside that he felt.

"I've just informed Serena that I'm not going to run a third term," Reeva told Nick.

"You're not going further in politics?" he asked.

"No. At one time I did think I might go on to provincial or federal seats. But I think I'll have to leave that to younger, more energetic people."

Nick chuckled. "Even younger people aren't as energetic as you."

Reeva seemed to like that remark, and patted his white cuffed wrist. "I'm wearing thin, believe me. I'm going to leave time for the family. If the family have time for me." She let her gaze fall on her daughter. "We have plans to go to West Vale next Sunday, to take Serena and Seth out to Thanksgiving dinner." She shifted her eyes to Nick. "You're welcome to join us, Nick. There's a sweet little restaurant near West Vale set in a nineteenth century stone school-house. It overlooks the valley where the autumn leaves will be at their peak of color."

Nick was beginning to see a picture form. Everyone was taking it for granted that, after last weekend, Serena and Nick were a couple. He wondered if he should put Reeva straight, and then caught Serena's glance. She shook her head, so he said, "I'd like that very much. Thank you."

"That's good. And you can bring your parents as well. I'd love to meet them." Reeva put down her cocktail fork. "I don't like gossip in our family, especially the type that got started in the press this week. Even if you two don't go the whole way and get married, at least your relationship, as it stands right now, will be blessed by your families."

Nick was quite surprised that Reeva felt the same way he did on the subject of the gossip. He ignored Serena's deep sigh. "I agree with you. Although I'm not sure my parents will be interested in the invitation. They've never been people to celebrate traditional festivals."

"Serena will invite them, won't you, Serena? They'll come, don't worry."

But he was worrying. What if they did decide to come? How would his parents interact with the Brown family? How would they act with him out in public?

Manno appeared with chicken and vegetables arranged in a de-sign on each plate. He served each plate with a flourish of his arm.

Nick began to think that his parents would be dumbfounded by Reeva and her lifestyle. It might even do them good to get out and see a part of the world they'd missed by being so insular during their lives.

As they ate, Reeva went on, "We'll all be meeting at Serena's and taking off from there next Sunday, Nick."

"Sounds fine to me," he said.

When dinner was being cleared away, and they were waiting for Reeva to fix her makeup, Serena said to him, "This isn't the situation I wanted."

Nick pushed his hands into his trouser pockets. "But it's the situation we seem to be in. If no one knew what happened last weekend we could call it quits, like you want to, but as it happens, we should go along with the ride for the time being. Your mother is very socially conscious."

"She has to be. She's a politician."

"And we're on TV. We have a responsibility to our viewers."

She tucked a wisp of hair behind her ear and stroked her earring. Nick could tell she was full of nerves. "I know."

"Let it go a few weeks. It'll be forgotten."

"I hope so. Now. I have to get ready."

Nick thought he would relax in the theater but he couldn't. If the entertainment had been of a faster pace he might have been able to lose himself in the content, but he couldn't seem to get his mind twisted around some of the complex poetry and classical music. He also couldn't sit still in his seat for very long with Serena by his side. Every once in a while he caught a whiff of her perfume. With her hair upswept and small diamond studs in her ears, she looked elegant. Elegant enough for Reeva to send her daughter an approving glance every once in a while. He realized tonight that Serena must have had a great deal to live up to with Reeva for a mother. Reeva expected brilliant gymnastics in life, and Serena had to excel in her performances.

Nick shifted around in his seat and Reeva patted his hand as if he were recalcitrant child. He grinned. Reeva didn't know that he was hot and throbbing for more loving, while Serena was as cool as a cucumber on ice. Ice Maiden. She was appropriately named by her colleagues. She knew how to perfect a chilling exterior.

Seth's group Lite came on stage. They were rousing, fast-paced and thoughtful in one package. The audience began clapping in time. Some raised their arms in the air in a wave of tribute. Seth put on a fantastic stage performance. He was expert on his guitar, and could improvise until the audience grew wild. Nick watched Seth's boundless energy bring his band to a finale with the theme from *Neon Nights*.

Nick forgot for a moment they had a brick wall erected between them and whispered to Serena, "They've got one hell of a future."

She inclined her head. "I think so as well. They're always so popular. Look at my mother."

Reeva was on her feet, clapping her hands so hard that her palms would sting when the evening was over.

"Aren't they wonderful?" Reeva said, when she at last sat down beside Nick again. "I'm so proud of him. I'm clapping double hard for his father, who would have loved this. If he hadn't been a journalist he would have been a musician."

It was the first time anyone in the Brown family had mentioned Stuart Redding Brown without bitterness and without provocation. Nick nodded. "I would like to have met your husband."

"I'm sure you would have got along famously. You're from the same mold."

So that's what Reeva thought. It was interesting that she had picked up the truth about him.

After the performance they went to find Seth and his band, who were packing up their instruments. Seth glowed with the praise he received.

"We're getting more and more popular," he said to Nick. "Your show has helped my CD and download sales to no end. Why don't you join us at The Bear's Pause? We're going to be performing there all next week, and we're doing an impromptu appearance tonight." Seth raised a dark eyebrow. "We're the introductory offer, you might say, as this is a test to see how entertainment goes over."

Reeva hugged her son. "Sounds wonderful, dear. We'll just come for a little while. We have a limo on hire tonight."

Seth grinned at Nick. "Don't you just adore my mother?"

"She's incredible," Nick said. "So's your sister."

Seth's mouth thinned. "Are you being good to her?"

Nick figured he had been good to Serena. Right now it was Serena who wasn't being good to him. "As far as I know."

"That's great."

Seth turned away, and Nick felt like he'd been warned by the younger man.

•

Later, Serena sat in the back of the limousine with her mother and Nick, thinking ahead to all that was now before her. She had to pretend she was still an item with Nick, at least until after Thanksgiving. She even had the task of going with Nick to meet his parents, and inviting them to dinner in West Vale. She rubbed her forehead. Her mother gave her a headache. It was all very well Seth wanting these family get togethers, but he didn't seem to realize that being left alone by Reeva was to his own advantage as well as Serena's.

Reeva was getting the chauffeur to drive around the long way before he took Nick home, so they could chat about her appearance on *Neon Nights*. It seemed like they had no choice but to run a program on her. Serena could sense Nick wasn't all that enthusiastic about Reeva appearing on their program. And neither was she. She didn't really want to work with her mother in the first place. She also, like Nick, didn't think Reeva was appropriate subject matter.

As they neared Nick's apartment block, he shifted in his seat and his hip pressed against hers. Emotion flared through her body and she felt a wave of relief when the car purred to the curb and stopped.

Nick smiled at the two women. "Thank you, Reeva, for the dinner, and for the evening. We'll be in touch about your interview." Then he placed his hand beneath Serena's chin and pressed his mouth upon hers. "'Night, sweetie."

Her mouth trembling, she found the words. "Goodnight, Nick. See you tomorrow." The chauffeur opened the door and Nick climbed out of the car.

Serena slouched back into the seat.

Her mother said, "Well, that's all taken care of."

Serena wasn't quite sure if Reeva meant that her appearance on *Neon Nights* was scheduled, or that she was prolonging the affair between her daughter and Nick Fraser to allay any more gossip.

Chapter Fifteen

"It's not *Neon Nights*," Nick said. "It's not what the show is all about."

"Nick, calm down," Don said. "Reeva is local interest. She's popular. People will watch her."

"That's not the entire point of the show, Don. So people watch. So what? The show loses its punch."

Don glanced at Serena, who lounged in one of Don's comfortable armchairs in his office. "What do you think? She's your mother?"

Serena crossed her legs and stared at the toes of her neat black leather shoes she wore with a calf-length skirt and a black jacket. "That's a problem right there. But she is popular, and she should be given a decent farewell from the city. But I agree with Nick. It's not *Neon Nights*. Although, Nick, you did tell her that it was a go."

Nick, who stood with his hands jammed into the pockets of a pair of charcoal slacks, glanced her way. "Thank you, Serena. And I know what I told her last night, but I'm regretting it."

Don put his huge feet up on to his desk and clasped his neck with his hands. "Then what do we go with next? *City Streets* will run out of steam, and we have some empty Thursdays later in the month. Serena seems to be getting nowhere with *Bad Men, Good Women*."

Serena shot up from her chair. "I am not nowhere. I'm still very much on top of it."

"But it won't be ready very soon?" Nick said.

She locked eyes with him. "Possibly not. I think Angela is away. I get an answering machine all the time."

"Well, if not, we'll schedule Reeva," Don said. "I've got enough faith in you two to make something out of her. Get her ideas on the homeless or something. She's stepped up on lots of platforms over the years. You'll dig up something."

The last thing Serena needed was Nick digging up stuff on her family. Not that she had much to hide from him now.

The meeting broke up and Serena went down to her office. Nick followed her. "What's happening with that story?"

"If I keep on getting that damn answering service, I might have to scrap it."

"Don't be hasty. I still have a feeling she'll come through. But let's get moving on it. Why don't we begin with Lawson Thomson? We'll get Melissa to do some research."

It heartened her that Nick had a bit of faith left in her story. She did need his help to keep this project going. "All right. I've discovered that sometimes research unearths other ideas."

"Exactly." He smiled. "We might come up with another angle on the story. Maybe it's not Angela alone. We're going to be busy this afternoon, with tomorrow's program, but we could spend all day Friday working on your story and that would give Melissa a couple of days. Would that be okay?"

Serena noticed he'd said your story, and she really did think that they had come a long way in the few weeks they'd been working together. "Fine. I'd appreciate your viewpoint."

"Settled. Now for our other great feat. I mentioned to my parents on the phone that I was going to bring you over to meet them, which will in turn give you the opportunity to invite them for Thanksgiving."

Serena had almost forgotten that duty she had yet to perform. She might as well get it over with. In fact, when Thanksgiving was over, and her mother's interference was out of the way, she could begin to live her life again. Right now she felt as if she were on a fast train ride to the weekend.

After a busy afternoon, Serena went with Nick to visit his parents. She was shown the family jewelry store before Nick drove the Jaguar into the back lane.

"It used to be a nice area," he said. "It's a little run down now."

She got out of the car and stepped over a puddle from recent rainfall. "Is that why you want them to move?"

"No. I think they should move because of these steep stairs, the type of old-fashioned place it is, and the store that my father can no longer attend to. By the way, my mother wanted to know if you liked tea?"

"Yes. I do." She could tell that Nick was uneasy with family foibles. In a way, it was kind of comforting to know he wasn't always the slick journalist.

"That's good. It's the only drink they ever serve to visitors."

Serena held on to the railing on the way up the steep stairs. She could understand why old people would find this climb difficult.

Nick's parents must have been looking out of the window, because the door opened before they reached it. Serena had been expecting two little old people. But Nick's Dad was big. His mother had clearly once been a beauty, and she saw where Nick inherited his good looks. Nick introduced her.

Stephen Fraser ushered her through a narrow foyer into the kitchen of the apartment. "We're delighted to meet you, Serena. You'll have to excuse our humble abode."

"This is fine." It was a neat but old-fashioned kitchen. There were only two small windows and they didn't let in much light.

"Do you like tea?" Maria asked.

Serena smiled because of Nick's earlier comment. "Love it."

"Then we'll go into the living room," Nick's father said. "It's brighter there."

"But not much," Nick whispered into her ear as they followed his father up the narrow hallway.

Stephen pulled out an armchair on castors. "Please sit down. Mother will bring in tea."

Serena sat down and tucked her skirt around her knees. She put her purse on the floor beside the chair. Nick lounged in another armchair.

Maria bustled in with the tea tray. Serena accepted a cup of tea in a bone china cup and homemade cookies that were a very delicious mixture of oats and raisins.

Maria chose to sit on a footstool in front of her husband. Serena saw an expression on Nick's face that was almost resignation. She figured it had always been this way with his parents, that he'd seen their closeness as them against him.

Serena placed her cup on the tray and thought she might as well get down to the reason she was here in the first place. "My family has invited Nick to Thanksgiving dinner on Sunday and we wondered if you would like to accompany us. We're going to a very nice restaurant near West Vale, where I live. Nick would bring you out and drive you home. So there won't be any problem with transportation." She glanced at Nick to include him in the invitation.

Maria glanced at her husband. "What do you think, Stephen?" She looked over at Serena. "We don't get out very often since we sold our car. We used to go for drives near West Vale. It's pretty country."

"It is. Very," she said. "We'd love to have you join us."

Stephen Fraser hadn't said a word yet. While glances were exchanged between Stephen and Maria, Serena felt like tapping her toe with impatience.

"I think we'd like that very much." Stephen said at last.

"Wonderful." She looked over at Nick. "Isn't that great?"

He nodded. "Great."

But she knew he was uneasy with his parents' decision, and when they were back in the car she said, "If they'd said no you would have been upset."

He looked at her, and she saw that his hands were clasping the steering wheel.

"No. It wouldn't matter. And that's the truth. I'm used to being on my own."

"Then why did you accept my mother's invitation?"

"I don't believe I had much choice in the matter. Besides, I believe this entire charade is to protect you and the Brown family from shabby gossip."

He drove out on to a main road and back to the Steel Tower.

Serena's chest felt tight. It had been quite an ordeal going to meet Nick's parents. She wished that she had met them in the true light of being with their son forever. Had she been a fool to cut off their intimacy? Only time would tell, she supposed.

She really didn't have much time to feel too miserable over him as *Neon Nights* took up a lot of hours. Cam produced some more commercials, and she spent all day Friday doing research with Nick. Melissa's efforts had been admirable, and her visits to the library and newspaper offices as well as internet searches, had given them enough material to understand the type of program they wanted to present. The process really brought to light how well Serena worked with Nick.

"Listen to this, Nick." Serena held a newspaper clipping. "This is the writer speaking: 'I felt as if Thomson had two sides to his personality. On the one hand he was charming. On the other very sadistic. I felt he was conning me all along.'"

"He was," Nick said. "His real name is Alan Wayne Thomason, with an A in the middle."

Serena frowned. "I wonder if Angela knows Lawson isn't his given name?"

"She must. She lives with him. She's married to him."

"That's what I mean, though, Nick." Serena felt the excitement that had first brought her to this project. "Women like Angela, who marry and love this type of men, don't always know what they're about. They're conned. Exactly the way that reporter felt he was being conned."

Nick's eyes narrowed. "Angela's pretty astute."

"In some ways, but she's never had much love. If she felt she could get it by not making waves, then Lawson would be her perfect man."

"Then we might be waiting it out in vain. But I don't think so." Nick stood up, yawned and stretched. "Look. Why don't we go with your mother's program? It'll give us a break from extra heavy. Possibly we can get two weeks from her. By then Angela might have made a decision."

Serena watched Nick in the sunlight. He was so handsome she wanted to run to him. But there was a distance between them now.

"Are you still with me?" Nick asked.

"Yes. I just hope you are right and Angela is making a decision."

"If she isn't then my suspicions are wrong about her being in a trapped situation. But I believe if everything was okay she would have come clean right away. From what we've read, her husband is the type who can turn on the charm when he wants to."

"Like you." She regretted the words as soon as they were out.

"Ah, come on, Serena. It's you who is the problem in our relationship. I was up-front. You're the one looking for excuses not to continue with what we started. It's not what I want. It's what you want."

Serena pushed some of the files aside. "Make yourself sound like a martyr."

He shook his head. "I'm not. I'm telling the truth. I've always told you the truth."

"I believe that. But you understand why you're a dead-end street for me?"

"Your father and everything? Yes. I understand." Then he gave a rueful smile. "Anyway, let's clear out of here for the day. We'll decide a day, possibly Monday, to grab your mother and grill her about her politics, especially her position on the city homeless. That way we'll have a focus."

"You're really into this cleaning up the city stuff, aren't you?"

"Because it's damn disgusting, Serena. It's ridiculous in these affluent times."

Serena rose from her chair. "You're right. I feel the same way. Okay. We'll go with my mother."

"Sounds good," Nick agreed. "We'll tidy up this stuff and then I have a dinner date.

Serena began to stack files. "Anyone I know?"

"You sure do. Don and Barbara."

Relief that it wasn't a woman made Serena let out a deep sigh, and Nick grinned. "Gotcha."

When her office was tidy, Nick left and Serena got her personal belongings together to go home. Her relationship with Nick hadn't turned out to be quite as strained as she'd thought it might. He was being amenable. It wasn't what she really wanted but it would do. It was a way of erecting a small fence between them. Then, when he left in the spring, she would be free.

•

Nick picked up his parents at three o'clock on Sunday to drive them to West Vale. They were decked out in their best clothes: His father in a navy suit with a pencil thin pinstripe, his mother in a blue coat over a charcoal wool dress. He felt they looked nice and that he could be proud of them. Despite an invitation to his mother to sit in front with him, his father had insisted she sit in the back with him. This irritated Nick right from the start. He drove out of the city, wearing his suit and sunglasses, feeling as if he were a taxi driver.

He didn't feel great anyway. His body already missed Serena's. It had been a week since they had made love and he wasn't sure if he would ever make love to her again. This situation between them, where they were friendly but not intimate, was becoming a strain on him.

"It's a lovely day, isn't it, Stephen," his mother said. "Such bright sunshine. The leaves will be beautiful this time of year."

Don't talk to me or anything, Nick thought, cursing Reeva for forcing him into this situation. He now understood the strain Serena had been through all her life with her mother.

"This is a very nice car," his father said. "A Jaguar, Nick?"

"Yes."

"Expensive," Stephen murmured. "You must make good money."

"I've told you I do. That's why I've offered to help you."

Silence greeted him. He almost missed a red light and jammed on the brakes. The tires squealed.

His mother gasped. "Ooh. You scared me."

Nick peered at them through the rear view mirror. "This is an unusual situation for us, but we're going to be joining another family for dinner tonight. I want it to go well."

"Your mother only said she was scared by your fast jerky stop," his father said. "You don't have to get upset."

Nick moved through the green light. "I'm not upset. I just want things to go smoothly."

His father coughed. "They will. You can depend on us."

His mother placed a gloved hand on the back of the seat by his shoulder. "Nick. Are you serious with this girl?"

The gossip that worried Reeva wouldn't reach his parents, but they might read something between the lines today, so he decided to enlighten them. "We work together, but we have gone out. All right?"

His mother's fingers worried the upholstery and made his teeth go on edge. "Does that mean you might marry her? I mean, she did come to invite us to meet her family. To me that's serious. I remember when Stephen proposed to me. We went to my parents and he asked permission. Didn't you?"

"That's the way it was done in those days," his father said. "These days they just fall into bed with one another. At least, that's how it seems on TV."

His mother patted the back of the seat. "Serena seemed like a very nice girl."

"She is." Nick let out a breath. What was Serena's expression when things were going crazy? Hell! Damn!

Once on the highway, the powerful car ate the miles. To Nick's relief his parents remained silent. He turned on the radio, realized it was a cutting edge alternative station, and pushed more buttons until he found a classical music station that he was sure was more to their taste. *Relax Nick,* he told himself. *This will be over later this evening. Treat it like a trip to the dentist.*

Gerry's white Lincoln was parked to one side in Serena's driveway this time, so Nick slid the Jag in beside it and helped his parents from the car. Serena, smiling to greet them, glided through the rose trellis. Her hair was loose and tumbled around the shoulders of a black silk dress with long sleeves, a scoop neck and a short skirt. On her feet were very high heeled black suede sandals. Around her throat and in her ears diamonds flashed.

"So pleased you could make it," she said to his mother and father. "Pleased you could make it too, Nick."

She was in a phony mood he didn't like. What he liked was Serena in a passionate mood. He wanted to touch her body through the black silk and feel her flesh respond under his fingertips. They were still together, forced by circumstances, but they'd lost touch. Last weekend was fading into a fantastic memory that might never have been.

Serena kept up ahead with his parents, and introduced them to Gerry and Reeva. Gerry wore a gray suit and Reeva was in winter white. She also flashed diamonds. Nick watched his father look at Reeva's long legs and saw an expression in the old man's eyes he'd never seen. His mother, he noticed, began to fuss as they were all made to sit on the deck for a glass of wine or beer. His mother accepted a small glass of red wine. His father beer. Nick couldn't recall ever seeing his parents drink before. All Nick was ever offered when he visited them was tea.

Stephen raised his glass and smiled at everyone. "I want to thank you for inviting us. We're thoroughly enjoying ourselves."

"I hope you are," Reeva told them. "We needed to meet with our son and daughter going out together."

Wishing things hadn't gone this far, Nick sipped his own beer.

When everyone discovered Nick and Serena were no longer an

item they were going to be disappointed.

They went on to chat about other things, the garden, the leaves, the time of year, the weather. Nick realized that Gerry and Reeva had no hang ups with Stephen and Maria because they knew nothing of their past history. They were Nick's folks and that was that.

He rose to get himself another beer and went into the house. Pascal slid in with him. "Serena," Nick called.

She came from one of the rooms into the sunroom. "How's it going?"

"Fine. I figure if you don't know someone's history you can accept them at face value. Once you know things about them, you have a depth of baggage you have to overcome to see them differently."

She fiddled with an earring. "That's heavy."

He noticed, now he was alone with her, that she didn't look quite as composed as he'd first thought. Her face seemed drawn and there were shadows beneath her eyes. "Are you okay?"

She gave him a dazzling smile. "I'm great, Nick."

He wanted to say something about their relationship, but he didn't want to mess up the day. "Mind if I have another beer?"

"Help yourself."

He went to the fridge and uncapped the beer with the opener on the door. He drank from the bottle.

"Gerry's the designated driver tonight. He'll take us over in the Lincoln."

"Are you saying I'm drinking too much?"

"No. I'm just watching you. And you've guzzled three since you've been here. What happened on the way down?"

"Nothing. It's just that I've never, ever, and that's the bloody truth, been out with them like this since I've been an adult."

"But you did when you were a kid?"

"Sometimes they'd take me over to see my father's brother, either by bus or car. He died and his wife moved to Vancouver."

"What about your mother's family?"

He clenched his fingers around the bottle. "Gone before I came into the picture. She was thirty-nine when she had me, you know."

"I gathered that." She rested her hip against her table. "You know, I never figured you'd have all these hang-ups."

He gave her a narrow glance. He was back to how it had been

that night of Don's soirée, when he had wanted her so much. The fuse had been lit once again. "That should make us compatible."

She rapped the table with her fingers. "I've never said we're not compatible."

"Possibly not. You just want to put me through hell." He hadn't meant to get into this.

"I'm not doing this intentionally. If I'd had my way this weekend would never have been. But Mother does have a point. I'm not the type to spend one weekend with a man and call it quits. Especially—" She walked to the window ledge, where she straightened a couple of pots of flowers.

Nick drained the rest of the bottle and placed it on the table. "Especially a man with a reputation like mine. Is that what you want to say?"

She didn't turn around. He watched the sunlight flicker over her gorgeous golden hair. His gaze roamed her hips and long legs. His breathing quickened. He always felt so aroused with her. He stuffed his hands into his pockets. "I've told you that my reputation isn't quite what you think it is."

She twisted on her heels. "Don't try and make this worse than it already is. I loved last weekend. I needed last weekend. If that stupid critic hadn't been there, I—"

"You'd still be with me, wouldn't you? You're using that as an excuse, Serena, because you haven't got the guts to go beyond two days in bed."

Her features were contorted as she held in her feelings. "I think you're right. If we go on, it'll just be like driving aimlessly without a map."

"What's your idea of a map in a relationship?"

"Two people heading toward the same destination."

"You want to marry me. That's not a question. It's a comment." Nick tried to lighten the atmosphere.

"I don't know. I hadn't thought that far ahead."

"Well, then." He let out a deep sigh. "Serena. You and I will have to talk at length about this, because we've got a lot of time left of the season."

She rubbed her forehead. "Not today."

"No. Not today."

He helped Serena on with a black wool jacket and they went

outside. His parents looked as if they were enjoying themselves. He thought of them cooped up over the shop and he felt angry with himself for not being able to persuade them to move into something more amenable, angry at them for being so damn stubborn. Everyone was damn stubborn. Including Serena. He was sure she still wanted him in the blazing way he still wanted her. He had broken her down once, he could do it again. He just had to take his time and not rush her.

Chapter Sixteen

Beyond the curved windows of the atrium the deep red and orange leaves on the trees cascaded down into the valley and crawled up the rocky gorge. The brilliant sunshine that had greeted Thanksgiving Sunday dimmed into an early evening glow and brought the warmth of the colors into the dining atmosphere of the West Vale Inn. Serena had only dined here a handful of times, though she had always been impressed by the cuisine. She was also impressed by the setting, and it confirmed her reasons for moving out to West Vale in the first place.

If she didn't feel so darned miserable she would be enjoying herself, as everyone else around the table seemed to be doing. Her one highlight was Seth, looking fantastic in black cord slacks and jacket. With Seth's presence, she felt the full circle of her family around her for the first time ever since her father had died. And if she was going out with Nick in the accepted manner, she would have felt great.

Gerry refilled all the glasses and Reeva laughed. "This looks like another night at Serena's."

"I'm sorry," she said. "I have to work tomorrow."

"You are such a downer, sometimes, Serena," her mother told her. "Just because you have to work doesn't mean we can't stay the night."

"I won't be staying," Seth said, a hint of amusement in his tone. "We have to rehearse for our new gig."

"And we definitely wouldn't stay," Nick's mother said. "We wouldn't impose ourselves upon anyone."

Serena smiled. "What about you, Nick? What do you want to do?"

He gave her a tight-lipped stare. "I'll be working with you. We have to set up your mother's interview. We have two more weeks of *City Streets*. Therefore, Reeva, you will be working as well."

Seth glanced at his mother. "You're being interviewed for *Neon Nights*?"

"Yes, dear. I'm quitting politics at the end of this term and we're doing a piece on me."

"You're quitting?"

"Haven't I told you?"

"You never tell me anything. Did Serena know?"

"I only found out on Tuesday."

Seth frowned. "It's Sunday. Quite a few days have passed between then and now."

Serena saw that her brother looked annoyed. This meal was supposed to be for him, to bring him back to his family. Instead, it had been all mixed up with Nick and his family to stop some gossip about her.

He drank some wine. "I'm always the last person to learn anything in this family."

"It wasn't that important." Reeva sounded irritated. "Besides, it's a secret."

"Then why are you telling everyone?" Seth said. "Gad, Ma."

He hadn't used that expression for years. Serena chuckled. "Stop it. This is supposed to be a lovely meal."

"It is lovely," Maria Fraser told her. "Don't worry. Your secret won't go anywhere with us, Reeva."

Serena let out a breath. "Okay. Firstly. Mother's secret isn't going anywhere until she makes the announcement at the end of the program. And secondly. Anyone is welcome to stay at my house if they feel they've had too much to drink."

She saw Nick grin. She'd laid down the law.

They had ordered the Thanksgiving meal, which was a traditional turkey dinner with added vegetables, salads and garnishes. It was excellent. When Gerry brought out his credit card Stephen tried to stop him paying the entire bill, but Reeva flapped Nick's dad's hand away from picking up the bill.

"This is our treat."

And darn your pride, Serena thought.

She was pleased when they were able to go out in the fresh air again. She offered coffee when she got home, and everyone sat in her sunroom to drink it.

Seth was the first to leave in his van. Serena walked him outside.

"That was great, Sis," he said.

"Oh, really?"

"I should be used to mother. It's just that I spoke to her on the phone twice this past week and she never mentioned anything about quitting."

Serena touched his arm. "I know. We don't get together enough, that's the problem. When she has more free time, things might get better."

"Don't bank on it. It's going well with Nick, is it?"

"What do you mean?"

"Well, you two barely spoke to one another today, and I thought all this, with his parents, was because you two had hooked up."

Serena told him about the weekend and the gossip. "So Mother is trying to cover our tracks and at least make us seem respectable."

"For her own good."

"Maybe. I don't know."

Her brother leaned against his van. "I'm not sure I'm getting the point of this. If you spent a weekend with Nick in a hotel room, surely you're serious enough to be going around with him now, a week later."

"I thought we should let the gossip die down."

Seth didn't look convinced. "I think you mean you should leave the fire before you get burnt?"

"Yes. Oh, Seth."

"You love him, don't you?"

"Yes." It was quite a relief to admit that to someone. She wished it could be Nick.

Her brother put his arm around her shoulders and squeezed. "Just take it easy. Play one day at a time. Don't rush yourself into the future. Enjoy the moment."

"It's not easy for me."

"Obviously." He climbed into his van and rolled down the window. "Nick's parents are an odd, uptight couple, though. Doesn't figure."

"He was a late-in-life baby. He hasn't had it easy with them."

"I didn't think so. So what's he doing with Ms. Hang-up-of-all-time?"

"Stop it, Seth. I think I'm becoming quite well rounded in my old age."

"I never denied you didn't have a nice bod."

"Seth. You drive me crazy. Go home."

He grinned and patted her fingers where they gripped the edge of his window. "Come and see me at The Bear's Pause?"

"I will. Don't forget to watch mom on my show."

"Right."

She watched his van take off with a puff of smoke from the exhaust pipe and returned to her house through the sunroom door. If she felt good about anything, it was about her renewed relationship with her brother.

•

Due to a number of breaking news stories, *Reeva: an Exposé* didn't air until much later. During the interview Nick kept to Reeva's political career, and discovered that Reeva was deeper than he had suspected. She had definite views on society that might not be politically correct, but they caused comment. He realized that if he asked the right questions Reeva wasn't quite so in control, and that inconsistency gave the interview an edge that would be in keeping with what had aired so far on *Neon Nights*.

Reeva unclipped her mike. "You know, Nick. I don't mind that I'm connected with Stu Brown."

He'd never heard his idol called Stu Brown before, and it kind of gave him a sense of awareness that this beautiful, sophisticated woman had once slept with the man, had borne his children, had been his wife. "But it's not his story," he said as the floor crew began to deal with the mikes and they were forced to move away from the set.

"That's true. It might be a nice tribute to do his story one day, though."

"I've mentioned it to Serena, but she's not interested."

Reeva glanced to where her daughter was chatting with a couple of the technicians. "Keep on mentioning it. She needs to dump that part of her life and move on."

"I'm going to take that as permission."

"Definitely. But give me my claim to fame first."

Reeva left and he returned to his office, pleased to be alone for a moment to collect his thoughts. Maybe a documentary on Stuart Redding Brown would one day be feasible, but for some reason it didn't seem quite such an urgent project as it had once been. Reeva thought Serena needed to move on and he needed to do the same thing.

Reeva didn't know it, but he'd moved on after spending Thanksgiving with his parents. They had enjoyed themselves, and they kept asking how Serena and her family were. Nick had even taken Serena up to the apartment once more, on their insistence, even though they weren't going out anymore. But they'd pretended they were for the sake of parental peace. Reeva also thought they were holding up that image, and Nick had found himself invited to the same social occasions as Serena.

He rubbed his face with his hands. But he was tired of pretending, even if they did manage to stay friendly and work well together. It wasn't enough. He wanted the real thing. He heard Serena walk into the office suite, and with a sigh, he raked his fingers through his hair.

His phone rang. He had it set up on the speaker, so he left it there. His father's voice came through loud and clear.

"Nick. I am sorry to bother you. It's your father, Stephen Fraser. Your mother slipped on the back steps tonight in the rain. I have her at the hospital, and I'm staying the night with her. I think it might be a good thing if you phoned me here. I am worried about the store and the apartment, which I left in a great hurry. Thank you. Here's the number."

Nick wrote down the number. He was aware of Serena hovering at his office door as he talked to the hospital reception, who put him through to his father.

"Is mother okay, Dad?"

"She twisted her ankle very badly on those darn steps. And she hit her head. Therefore they are holding her here in case of a slight concussion."

Nick held back all the outrage that if they had listened to him in the first place they might not even have had those steps to slip on any more.

"But I'm worried I didn't lock the apartment door, Nick."

Nick cleared his throat to rid himself of his frustration. But his voice still came across with an edge. "That's okay. I'll come to the hospital and you can give me the key to the apartment and I'll check on it."

"I would be obliged if you would do that."

He didn't say, "I'm your son. It's one of my responsibilities." He hung up the phone.

Serena said, "Do you want me to come with you?"

He was already on his feet, shrugging his shoulders into his black trench coat. "It's up to you." He really meant, "Please do come."

She must have sensed his need.

"Let me get my coat," she said.

His father was in a private hospital room with his mother. Serena went straight to the bed and took hold of Maria's hand, something Nick could never do. He saw Maria cling to Serena's fingers and knew then that Maria might have fared better if she'd had a daughter.

"You two look very nice in your TV clothes. Don't they, Stephen?"

Stephen bowed his head in Serena's direction. "I remember once, a long time ago, seeing your father on television."

Nick saw Serena glance at him, but he shook his head. He hadn't mentioned anything about Redding Brown to his father.

"How do you know who my father was?" she asked Stephen.

"Your mother told me. Then I remembered I had his book at home." Stephen looked at his son. "I bought a lot of books by journalists at one time, to try and understand my son's career."

Nick felt his mouth turn dry. He couldn't add anything to this discussion. It was so weird. He'd never thought his father cared a damn about him or his career.

Stephen handed Nick the key to the apartment. "This is your mother's key. Don't lose it."

Nick pocketed the key. "I won't."

Serena smiled one of her white TV smiles before they left. "It was a pleasure to see you again. I hope you're feeling much better soon, Maria."

Nick said, when they were heading toward Fraser's Precious Gems, "You've sure got around them."

"I'm not doing it on purpose, Nick. They're nice old people. After all, you have been away a long time. And your dad just said he has tried to understand your career."

"I'd never heard that one before."

"Well, now you have. Maybe you haven't given them a chance."

Nick drove by the store and everything looked fine. He parked at the back behind the apartment and he told Serena to wait in the car.

"No way. I'm not sitting here alone in the dark."

It had stopped raining now but the air was still damp. So were the steps. Nick took hold of Serena's hand so she wouldn't slip. It seemed ages since he'd held her hand, and he could feel the warmth of her skin create a heat on his own skin.

He had to let go of her hand to unlock the door, and they went inside. No lights had been left on, but a night light glowed in the hallway. Everything was so silent in the apartment that he could hear Serena breathing behind him. She moved up beside him.

"You should feel privileged," he told her.

"Why?" She turned her face to him and her mouth was close enough to kiss.

"Because I was never allowed to bring my friends home. You're the first. And you've been here twice already."

"Do you figure I'm your friend?"

"I feel that you are." And that was the truth.

"Is it easier for friends to part than lovers?"

Her face looked pale in the darkness. He lifted his hands to stroke her hair and tangle his fingers into the golden strands. He heard her breath come from her lips in a shudder. He traced her features with his fingertips. "Are you sure?"

"No."

He wasn't either, but he felt he had her acquiescence. He slipped his arm around her and led her to the room that used to be his when he was a boy. None of his belongings resided here. Everything he'd ever owned here was at his own apartment. It was a small, brown looking room, but in the dark all he saw was glorious white silk, gold hair and soft flesh. He helped her off with her coat and he laid it down over a small chair in front of a desk. Nick undid his tie and opened the top button of his shirt. Then he slid his hands up beneath her skirt and peeled down her hose. She kicked off her shoes and the stockings. All the time she gazed at him. With one hand roaming her thighs and one hand behind the nape of her neck he kissed her, thinking that this was the payoff for never having been allowed to have any toys or bring friends here.

His Serena was the brightest toy he could ever wish for. With her long legs wound around him he took her to the bed and lay her down on the crisp cotton sheet. He undressed and lay with her. She embraced him right away, her hunger as urgent as his own. He held back nothing on the small, creaky mattress because there was nothing to hold back.

Later in the night, when Serena was sleeping, he went along to the living room. On the bookshelves he found the journalism books his father had mentioned. He couldn't believe that Stephen would need to understand him when he'd thought he'd done the best thing possible by getting out of his father's hair.

He glanced down to the street and saw the pavement glimmering from the rain and the street lights. His throat choked up. Damn. Damn. He had been cared for after all and he hadn't known it?

Serena woke up, aware of harsh sheets and prickly blankets covering her instead of her usual soft quilt. A watery light filtered in through a small window hung with beige curtains. She'd slept here all night at Nick's parents' place. Nick had been beside her at one point. After they'd made love all over the narrow bed and once off it. Had she really done all that with Nick? And why had she started their affair again? Or hadn't it really stopped?

The door pushed open and he came in, wearing his black suit pants and his white shirt unbuttoned. "Hi."

She thought he looked tired, with deep lines carved from his nose to the edge of his mouth. She heaved herself up on the hard pillow and drew the covers around her shoulders. "Hi. I didn't expect to stay the night."

"Me neither. But we had a lot to do with one another."

She found she had to force a smile. The atmosphere between them was strange. "Yeah."

He indicated his head in the direction of the hallway. "The bathroom is across the way. I've run the water a long time so it's nice and warm if you want a bath. There's no shower here."

"He said accusingly. So they're old fashioned, Nick. So what?"

She knew it was his parents who were causing Nick to be in this funk. It wasn't their lovemaking. That had been sheer ecstasy.

"It was never just that."

"But part of it. I bet when you were a kid you couldn't stand their old-fashioned ways."

"That's true."

"It's probably why your own furniture is so modern and clean."

He pushed his hands into his trouser pockets. "It's how I like things. Simple, not cluttered."

"That's how you've tried to live your life as well. Simple, no clutter."

His expression was so grim his jaw began to throb. "You're right."

"I know Nick, because it's me as well. That's why I never wanted to go this far with you." She drew herself out of the bed and she saw his eyes alight on her naked form. She saw the grimness turn to lust, and she felt the heat that he generated throughout her body burn into her veins.

He withdrew his hands from his pockets and came to her. "But we have gone this far. We've gone so damn far we're right out in space, hanging on for dear life. We had to do this again. That weekend in the hotel wasn't enough, was it?"

Breathless from his fondling hands, she shook her head. "No."

He returned to bed to set fire to the sterile environment of his boyhood once more.

•

Nick's mother came home from the hospital the following Monday afternoon. Serena went with Nick to help him, and they managed to get Maria up the steep steps into the apartment. Nick was right, Serena decided. The Frasers did need to move into a home that was brighter and more modern, where the heating would work better, with less drafty surroundings and bathroom facilities that were designed for the elderly.

She asked Maria about it when Serena was making Nick's mother tea.

"I think we're going to have to," Maria admitted. "I can't manage those steps like this. I'll talk to Stephen." Serena placed the tea things in front of Maria on the table.

"I've never had anyone do this for me," Maria said.

"You never had a daughter."

"No. I didn't want children."

"But you had Nick?"

The distinguished female head nodded. "Yes. I did. Late in life. I was past having a child by then. You know, if you are going to marry Nick, I wouldn't leave it much longer."

Serena wasn't sure what was going to happen with Nick. She'd begun a sexual relationship with him again, right here in this apartment. His parents would likely be shocked if they knew. "I don't know about that," she said and changed the subject. "Do you want your tea?"

When Serena got home on Friday, she went straight around to Ginny's house. Ginny came out on the steps wearing a pair of slim jeans and a long sweater. She'd had her dark hair cut short.

"Hair looks nice," Serena said.

Ginny placed her palm at the back of her head and posed. "It's a style that makes it easier to handle. Where have you been?"

"Working harder than hard."

Ginny's green eyes twinkled. "Nick Fraser keeping you going?"

"It's a lot of work putting on a heavy weekly news show."

"It shows that you've put in a great deal of effort. It's very good. You've even got me watching Steel TV. Usually I avoid the news like the plague. I loved the interview with your mother this week."

"That's good. We were unsure about that type of program."

"Oh, no. It's great. Nick asked her a few tough questions and you could see her hesitate. Having met your mother, it's quite humorous to watch."

"I don't even want to watch it. I get embarrassed about her politics."

"Ah, don't be. She's fantastic. And beautifully preserved." Ginny opened the screen door. "Why don't you come in for coffee?"

While they drank coffee Ginny filled Serena in on the West Vale gossip, which wasn't much. When Serena was about to leave she offered Ginny money for caring for Pascal, but she wouldn't take it.

"It's enough of a perk that I have someone famous living next door."

"Ginny, that's ridiculous."

"It's true. Now go see that brat of yours. He misses you when you're not here."

When Serena had reacquainted herself with Pascal and her house, she put away the Porsche and drove the Jeep down to the local garage for an overhaul.

"Seen your program," Lester Finch told her as he poked around under the hood of the Jeep. "This looks about as good as it did last spring when I looked at it. Oil change and some anti-freeze should do it."

"All right. Shall I leave it?"

"You can come and get it later. Do you want a ride home?"

"No. I'll walk. Thanks."

The colors of the autumn leaves were now beginning to dull a little, and the air was fragrant with smoke, but there was still a warmth to the air as Serena strode back through the village to her house. She realized she had expanded as a person in the past weeks. It wasn't all Nick. Some of it was her renewed relationship with Seth and the family outings with her mother. But most of it was Nick. He'd taken away the heavy weight of her father's legacy and replaced it with some good times.

These last few nights, after lovemaking, they had talked a lot about their philosophies and the places they had visited in their lives, mentally and physically. They both had hilarious stories of goof-ups while on air, and they related so much on that plane. Serena thought she was as much a tonic for Nick as he was for her.

If he wasn't leaving, she thought as she pushed her key into her front door, then she was sure she would be planning a wedding.

She found Pascal sleeping by her desk. The number one showed up on her answering machine and she pressed play.

"Serena. It's Angela. I called Steel TV but they told me you were at home today. They wouldn't give out your cell phone number, but your home number was written on the card you gave me. I want to make arrangements for that interview. Could you meet me by Max on Wednesday afternoon at two o'clock? If you're not there I'll know that you don't want to do the program anymore. I hope to see you."

"Yes," Serena told Pascal. "Yes. Yes. Yes." And then she let out a loud, "Yahoo!"

Chapter Seventeen

Nick typed in more items about Stuart Redding Brown and then stopped. He really wasn't very interested in the man anymore. He was more interested in the man's family, Serena, Reeva, Seth. Stuart Redding Brown had already documented his own life in his book and in his newscasts. He'd died because he'd been blown up in a country that had been besieged by war in that moment of its history. For some reason Nick had lost something more than his intense interest in Stuart Redding Brown. He didn't quite hold all of his philosophies quite so dear any more.

Leaning back in his chair, Nick stared at the computer monitor. Then he twirled the chair around and stared out of the window instead. What he wanted to do, deep down inside himself, something he'd wanted to do all his life, was write his own books. Not just one book but lots of books. Non-fiction, fiction, whatever. He just wanted to explore some of the themes he'd tried to explore in his teens, before he'd gone on the run to learn more about life.

He picked up his coffee cup and drained the rest of the contents. A day without Serena made him introspective. Or had it been meeting Serena that had made him have more darn feelings about things? He felt as if he'd opened a wound and let it bleed. But it wasn't all uncomfortable. It felt quite good to feel.

The phone rang and he hoped it was Serena, but it was his mother and that surprised him.

"Nick. You don't mind me phoning?"

"Of course not. What's up? How's the ankle?"

"It's very painful. Your father is out at the moment and I wondered if you'd like to come over for a while. I'd like to talk to you."

"Sure." Already he'd turned back to the computer and was using the mouse to save and close his files. "It'll take me about half an hour."

"I'll have the tea on."

"Mom."

"What?"

"I'd rather have a beer if you've got it."

"Yes. We have beer. Of course. You can have one of your father's."

His mother was walking again now. She limped to the door to open it. "I haven't been out yet."

"Do you want me to take you out?"

"No. It's all right. Sit down. I'll get your beer."

"I'll get it."

He went to the refrigerator where he found half a dozen bottles on the top shelf. He rummaged in a drawer for a bottle opener while his mother put a tall glass on the table beside her own tea things. She sat in the chair he held for her. When his mother was comfortable he sat down in the chair next to her. Not across from her. Not at the other end of the table. But next to her. He never would have done that before, but he felt something had changed. He was beginning to suspect it might have been himself who had done the changing.

Maria put her hands on the table. Nick saw she was a little shaky. "I've convinced your father to sell, Nick."

He smiled with his relief that things would go right. "That's great. You won't regret it."

"There's not much time left for regrets, is there? But I can't live here anymore, unfortunately, so we have to move. You said you'd help?"

"Absolutely. We'll find somewhere nice and comfortable for you."

Maria almost reached to Nick's hands on the table. "Your father is a very stubborn man. He hates to admit he's wrong. So he told me to let you know we have to move because of me. It's nothing to do with the store or his heart. He's fine." She smiled. "You understand. Don't say anything to him."

"I understand. I'm just pleased you're giving me the chance to help you. If you don't get moving now I might be gone again by the time you made up your minds."

His mother glanced away at the fridge. "Do you want another bottle of beer?"

Did she not want him to leave again? Or was that his imagination? Nick didn't want to ask in case it was his imagination.

Before he went home, he stopped in at a real estate agent's office close to his parents' store and talked about listing the store and apartment. He had sent the ball rolling.

There was a phone message from Serena at home, but she didn't answer her phone when he called back. He wondered what she wanted. Was she lonely? Did she need him? He was amazed at how anxious he could feel about her when he wasn't with her. He missed her and he was so pleased that they were together again.

He called again later but she still didn't answer her home phone or her cell phone. He was watching Pat McHaney's *This is Science* show on Steel and hoping the phone would ring when the doorbell pealed.

It was Serena in jeans, leather jacket, leather gloves and leather boots. Her hair was in a braid.

"Guess what, Nick?"

He closed the door and leaned against it. He'd never seen her so spontaneous. "I hope you've won the lottery."

She grinned. "It's not better than that, but it's close. Angela's agreed to do the story. I have to meet her on Wednesday with Max."

He was pleased for her. She'd been disappointed about this one. It was a story dear to her heart. "That's great. Really great. What do you think she's going to go for?"

She tugged off her leather gloves and stuffed them into her jacket pockets. "Well, I haven't actually talked to her yet. I get the feeling this is sans Lawson. I don't think he'll know about it." She flipped her braid from her shoulder and perched on the arm of one of his chairs. "As I drove down here, I decided that I want to get right into the gritty emotional reasons for Angela being with this man. I don't care about what he did or why. I want Angela's story."

"I see that, but we'll have to bring in some of Lawson's story."

"Yes. I know, but I'm not sure how yet. I'd like him to unfold with Angela's story."

"That could be the right approach." Nick rose to his feet. "What can I get you to drink?"

"Do you have any wine?"

"White on tap, just for you."

"Thanks."

She removed her jacket to reveal a dark blue ribbed sweater that hugged her breasts and left an inch of flesh between the belt of her jeans. She followed him into the kitchen, saying, "I went to get the Jeep overhauled today, and when I picked it up I just kept driving here. I wasn't sure where you were."

He removed a bottle of wine from the fridge and took two glasses down from the cupboard. "I was here and there. My parents have agreed to move, so I'm putting their property up for sale."

She leaned against the counter near him. "That's wonderful. We've got two things to celebrate."

He poured the wine and handed her a glass. They clinked glasses. "Cheers."

"Cheers."

He didn't know what it was, but he felt she wasn't quite so close to him as usual. And it wasn't the same reaction he'd felt when he first met her, when he'd sensed her withdrawal. There was no withdrawal. She was here, she was bright and she smiled a lot. She was excited that Angela had agreed to do her show. But that wasn't all. She was sure of herself in a way he hadn't seen her quite so sure of herself before. She seemed to have power inside herself.

He knew it when she placed her arm around his shoulders and kissed his mouth. She tasted of cold wine. "I want to go to bed with you, Nick," she whispered.

"Let's drink our wine first."

She put her head to one side. "What now?"

"Nothing now." She irritated him like this. "I just want to drink our wine. I didn't expect you tonight."

"Who did you expect?"

"Nobody." What was wrong with them? Why did he feel her difference made it difficult to relate to her? Did he like being in control so much? Didn't he like it when she tried to show some initiative?

She dropped her arm from him and walked back to the living room. He followed. She was sexy and magnetic in her tight jeans and sweater. But he'd annoyed her. Her features were taut with controlled feeling. Sipping her wine, she strolled around his room for a while. She stopped by his desk and began leafing through his papers by his computer. She pushed a few sheets of paper aside and picked up the book that had been underneath.

She stared at the photograph on the front. She showed the cover to Nick. "That's what he used to look like when he came home. He'd look nice when he walked through the door. But a few days later, after he'd been into the whiskey, he'd get bleary-eyed and his hair would be a mess. He had a pair of jeans with ripped hems and an old T-shirt that he used to flop about in. Sometimes he picked me up from school when he was home. His eyes would glitter. Stoned, you might call it. I didn't know then quite what he was. But I knew as I grew older."

Nick sipped his wine and perched on the arm of a chair. A thin wire might have been stretched between them.

She looked at him. "Did you know he was a druggie?"

"It's in his book."

"Well, he was what you could call an honest journalist. He told the truth."

"If you want to find out, read his book? I think it's about time you did. Do you good."

She kept the book in one hand, her wine in the other. "You keep telling me that. The only thing that does me good and gets rid of my frustration is having sex with you. That's what it's come down to. I'm seeing a man who is like my father, and it's good for me, but it's going to end for me as well. Like he ended." She flung the book on his desk and it skidded to a stop beside his empty coffee cup from the afternoon.

His heart felt heavy for her because he did love her. He just didn't really know what to do with that love. He didn't want to tell her how he felt, only to discover she didn't return his love. For all he knew, she might be on a sexual roll. The same one he was supposed to be on. Luckily, he was well equipped to play act until the end. After that, well, he'd just have to figure out what to do when the time came for them to part.

He shrugged his shoulders to release a lot of tension. "I'm not planning on getting killed."

She looked him in the eye and then stared at his scar. "How do you know that the next bullet might not be lower?"

"That's a risk I take. We wear bullet proof vests." He hated himself for sounding so damn cavalier about safety.

She finished her wine in a couple of gulps, and put down the glass. "I was going to stay tonight but I guess I'm not now."

"What changed your mind?"

"You."

"You're not driving home after that wine.'"

"I'm okay."

She wasn't. He knew one way to stop her leaving. He placed his own untouched glass on a table. She was standing in front of him, breathing hard. He took hold of her hands and found them cold. He rubbed her fingers between his hands to warm her.

"Kiss me."

He wrapped his arms around her and met her mouth with his own. She was desperate for him. Her tongue was inside his mouth before he had a chance to respond. He felt his own desperation rise to meet hers and he began to strip off her clothes. They moved to the floor, and before he went into her he saw her eyes and he couldn't tell what she was thinking.

♦

Wearing Nick's burgundy terry robe, Serena put on coffee in his kitchen the next morning. She leaned against the counter hearing the liquid drip, thinking that her romance with Nick was getting very much like a kitchen sink drama. It was feeling sleazy. It was only sex. No. She crossed her arms across her breasts. It wasn't all sex. Not on her side. She loved him. But she couldn't tell him she loved him. All she could do was show him by giving him her body. A body that couldn't stop wanting him. She'd become what she'd never wanted to become, a woman dependent on a man for her thrills.

She walked into the living room where some weak sun was streaming through the window. She picked up her father's book and turned it in her hands. Should she read it? Would it do her good? She opened the cover and saw the inscription. *Who is Cara? Some other woman who'd once stood in Nick's apartment wondering where to go next with a man who would never love you, who would one day leave you? A man you craved and couldn't get enough of?* Strange that one of his lovers had given him her father's book as a birthday gift.

She closed the book but she didn't drop it. She kept it with her. *Read it, get rid of him for good,* her brain told her. *Do it. And even when Nick does leave you, at least you won't have that burden anymore.*

Nick came into the living room. All he wore was a pair of black briefs, and she liked him half-naked. She held up the book. "I will read it."

He stroked the air with his finger. "One down."

"How many to go though?"

He held the doorpost with his hand. "What happened to you? You were so bright last night?"

She wrinkled her nose. "Too bright. I came down off that high into a pit."

"Well, you'll have to get your act together. We have a lot of work ahead of us."

"I know that."

"It'll be mostly you doing it as well." He grinned. "Come on, Serena. Life isn't that bad. You've got the program you dreamed of at your fingertips, you have a co-host who gives you great loving, and you're going to exorcize your father's memory once and for all."

She lifted the book. "I'll throw this at you."

"No. Keep it."

"Who's Cara?"

"She lives in Mexico and she's married."

"Cara Winsome?"

He nodded. "Yeah."

"She's old enough to be your mother."

"It was mainly a friendship."

"Mainly a friendship? Is that what you'll call our relationship one day? Oh, I mainly had a friendship with Serena Brown. Or is it that I'm my father's daughter and that turns you on?"

He clapped his hand to his forehead. "Get dressed, and we'll have some coffee and get out of here before you can invent more reasons for chucking me over."

"I'd love to chuck you over." But she smiled a little this time. "I tried once, didn't I?"

"I'm not listening." He returned to the bedroom.

Serena figured she might as well go and get dressed as well. She had a heavy day ahead of her, preparing her questions for Angela.

Now she began to worry if her friend would cooperate enough to make the show a success.

Nick insisted on accompanying her to meet Angela, but Serena argued him out of using a Steel News van or a Steel limousine. It had been difficult enough getting Angela to respond to her request for an interview, she didn't want to scare her away now. She even dressed down, in jeans and her leather jacket. She wanted to meet Angela on her own level.

Max was waiting with his sister. Since his appearances on TV, he'd got a place to live, sharing a house with some other homeless men who were trying to get jobs and make a go of living in the mainstream of life again. He looked quite presentable, in a big tweed overcoat, minus the straw hat.

As they approached the couple, Serena kept her smile focused on Angela. She wore a long flowery skirt, black leather combat boots and kept her hands planted in the pockets of a tweed jacket as she returned Serena's greeting.

Serena noticed that Nick stood back and let her have the space beside Angela. "Why don't we just go for coffee," Serena suggested.

"Fine." Angela glanced at her twin brother. "Can Max come? I always buy him lunch when I'm in the city."

"Of course. Max has got lots of experience in TV now. Haven't you, Max?"

Max nodded. "Yeah. I was quite good."

"Very good. I'm pleased you got something out of it." Nick spoke for the first time and he took up the rear with Max, behind Serena and Angela, as they walked along the street.

Serena knew a small restaurant with high-back booths where they wouldn't be disturbed. It was a haunt from her news van days. They all went inside the warm, coffee-fragrant café and managed to squeeze into a booth. Nick suggested they might as well have lunch, but Angela decided coffee was enough for her. While Max and Nick chose their meals, Serena sipped her coffee from a big white mug and looked at Angela.

"I'm planning an interview with you that will let your story unfold, Angela."

Angela stirred her coffee with the spoon, even though she drank it black." That's fine. But I don't want to be shown for the interview. I don't want Lawson's name mentioned. His second name is Wayne. We can call him Wayne."

"Whatever you want." Serena didn't like interviews with disguises. She glanced at Nick and saw his skeptical expression.

"What about my voice?"

"We can fix it. We'll tape the interview ahead, so it can be edited. I'm presuming this is dangerous for you?" She gave Nick a look that said, *Don't say a word.*

"Dangerous? Yes. But it's a story needing to be told."

As they continued to make plans for the interview Serena grew excited. Maybe this is how her father had felt, how Nick probably felt, when they were in a country withholding secrets that the world ought to know about. At last she understood.

Armed with this understanding, Serena read her father's book that evening. She sat curled into an armchair with a quilt wrapped around her and read. She read in her evening bath. She took the book to bed and propped herself up with pillows. She finished it at one in the morning, and when she closed the covers, she didn't know want to think. She felt awash in Stuart Redding Brown's philosophy.

One thing she did know, though. He'd loved her. He hadn't shown it in the way she'd longed for him to show it, by being there for her all of her life, but he had loved her. He'd died loving her and her mother. He would have died loving Seth as well, if he'd known about him.

But he was one mixed-up kid, she decided, still awake by early morning. He'd lived on instinct, booze and drugs. Nick was probably right about Stuart Redding Brown needing a base after her one set of grandparents had died. Unfortunately, his base had been people he had managed to hurt.

She would always resent his absence, but she was more reconciled with his lifestyle now. Nick had helped her to that more peaceful place. She reached for Pascal, who was stirring for the morning, and stroked his soft warm fur. Everything for her came back to Nick these days, and how she loved him more all the time.

•

Nick was startled when Serena tossed her father's book down on his desk the following morning. "I read it."

He looked at her. Her hair was sleek and already coiffured by the studio hairdresser, her makeup and her white suit perfect. "All in one go?"

"Yep. All in one go. Once I got going I just inhaled it. It feels good. You're right. Real good."

He noticed her voice quaver with emotion. "You're not being cynical about that?"

She shook her head. "No. It's the truth. I discovered some things I didn't know. Some things I needed to know. Some things I wish I still didn't know. But that's okay. I'm grown up now. I can take it."

He smiled. "Serena. It upset you?"

"No. Truthfully. I'm fine. I'm over him."

"I'm over him as well."

She frowned. "What do you mean?"

"Well." He sat back in his chair. "I always immersed myself in his story, paralleling it to mine in some ways. But I don't think that's true anymore. In fact, I think I might have moved on from him."

"Exactly, Nick. I'm just going to remember him for what he contributed to journalism, and I'm willing to do a documentary on him if you want."

"Maybe. But we've got quite a bit on our plate right now."

"Fine. However, it's okay with me if you want."

Nick could tell she was being truthful. If he'd done nothing for her, he'd helped her disassociate herself from the pain of her childhood. And she'd done the same for him as well. It would never be over but it was more bearable. "I'll put it on my agenda. In the meantime we have to go interview your mother once more."

"Just before we do," she said. "Would you like to come to my place for the weekend? I feel I need some time at home. I have to do some gardening before the winter."

"You want me to help with your gardening?"

"Isn't that how you got me up to your apartment in the first place?"

"Partly. Sure. I'd love to spend the weekend with you."

"Good." She smiled and turned to leave. "See you downstairs."

The second episode on Reeva aired that evening and she made her public announcement that she was leaving politics. The next day the local papers were full of her. Nick watched Serena go around shaking her head and asking why her mother would want this type of publicity.

"It was entirely your mother's idea," he said. "Admit it. Your whole family enjoys publicity. Otherwise none of you would be in the public eye."

"And you're the same."

He put up his hand. "Count me in."

The rest of Friday Nick spent with the real estate agent at his parents' apartment and he could tell that his mother and father were pleased to let him handle affairs. He even suspected they felt some relief that he was here to do this for them. They were willing to admit that the time had come for them to move. His mother couldn't even negotiate the steps without almost being lifted. Nick arranged for a nurse to go in each day to help her, and his father didn't contradict any of Nick's decisions. He seemed dazed by events. Stephen had experienced a bad shock when his wife had injured herself. Without his wife to run around after him, he had no one.

Nick didn't like to see his parents having to react to this reality of being old. It was sad when he remembered how active they'd been when they were young. But it was reality. And reality was what he was into facing these days. Because behind everything he did over the next few hours he was thinking ahead until the week-end he would be spending with Serena.

•

Serena stayed at his apartment on Friday night. She had the Jeep with her and he was driving it to her house. He was having a hard time believing that Nick the adventurer was looking forward with so much relish to a weekend at home. Home had always been, for him, some place to be avoided.

He drove with the window wound down. The countryside smelled crisp and fruity, the fields at rest awaiting winter snows.

"Not too windy for you, is it?" he asked Serena

"No. It's fine. It's warm for November."

"It's great for November." He was collecting memories of Serena now. Serena the night he'd met her. Serena at work in Studio Three. Serena in the hotel room at Niagara-on-the-Lake. Serena in his parents' apartment.

"What are you thinking about?" she asked.

"I was thinking we're getting serious."

"We're not supposed to be. This is going to end in the spring. So we're taking what we can get. Great Sex. Isn't that what it's all about?" She shrugged. "And a gardener."

He laughed. "You've got your heart set on that?"

"Darn right. It's this weekend or never. It could snow by next weekend."

"Ah, you're right about that. Snow is as inevitable in Canada as sand in the desert."

"Do you miss the desert?"

"No. I don't. I'm not missing anything. You're keeping me quite well occupied."

She turned sideways and slid her hand on to his knee. She massaged his thigh with her fingers. "Then I'm as exciting as the field?"

He grasped hold of her hand and held her fingers with his on the steering wheel. "You're the most exciting thing that has ever happened to me in my life."

"What a line."

He grinned at her. "It's the truth. You've helped me in lots of ways. I'm seeing flaws and problems in my personality that needed attention. I'm actually getting along with my parents and I'm enjoying being home."

"Until the monster restless bug hits."

"I await with bated breath."

"You think it will hit?"

"I don't know." And he didn't know. He might wake up one morning and be over her spell, with the sudden urge to take off in a plane somewhere. He knew what he was really like, at times.

•

Serena couldn't believe that Pascal stood in the middle of the kitchen, hissing at Nick.

"Come on, baby. You know Nick."

Nick removed his jacket and hung it over the back of one of the kitchen chairs. "He liked me at first."

"Just ignore him. He'll come around." Serena laughed and ushered Nick out of the kitchen and down the hall to her bedroom.

She made him put his bag in there. "That's what cats are like. He's protecting me. He thinks you're going to hurt me."

"And I will. And I am. And he's right."

Nick's words cut like a knife through all parts of her body. "Don't. Please. Let's enjoy this weekend."

He swiped his hand across his face in a frustrated gesture. "Okay. But I feel terrible about how this could end for you."

"Look at me." She pointed to her eyes. "They're wide open. I know what can happen. I'm prepared for it."

"But you shouldn't have to be prepared for it."

"That's up to you." She felt irritable with him and left him in the bedroom.

She put on coffee. After a moment she sensed Nick in the room with her.

"I'm sorry."

She turned around and leaned against the counter-top, and it reminded her of the other times she'd been with him in this kitchen. The first time he'd kissed her, the night of Don's soirée, had been her undoing.

That night she'd seen his jaw turn into his stubborn, little-boy look. She'd seen that look quite often since. It was becoming part of him. He looked like that now. She opened up her arms to him and he came for a hug.

I love you, she said in her mind.

Serena took gardening seriously. She wore old jeans, a baggy sweater and rubber boots to divide her perennials. She made Nick follow her to toss compost on all her work. The day had drawn to a dusky, chilly conclusion. Smoke curled through the air from another gardener's leaf bin.

"You should have a fantastic garden next year," he said.

Serena peeled off her grimy gloves. "I hope so. There was quite a bit when I came here, but I've added many types of different shrubs and flowers." She screwed up her nose. "But if it doesn't grow next year, I don't bother fussing. What comes up comes up."

"That's quite a philosophy."

"It's all I have time for. Let's pack up. Do you want to go to the West Vale Inn for dinner?"

"Sure. Why not?"

He's being very amenable, Serena thought as she did her hair in her mirror while Nick took a shower. He probably regretted his first outburst about their relationship not being permanent. Either that or it was a reminder to her to keep her focus. Well, she was focused. She loved him. But hell, she'd be able to give him up when the time came. Sure she would.

Nick had made a last minute reservation for the Inn. It was crowded, being Saturday night. The leaves that had been such a glow of color at Thanksgiving were now pretty well gone, and the gorge was dark and forbidding beyond the atrium windows. Serena wasn't certain how she felt tonight. Gardening this afternoon had been kind of fun. A sort of, show-him-how-she-lived, type of activity. They had showered and changed in her bathroom and bedroom. That had been sort of like a man and wife activity, prior to an evening out. Nick had fondled her a little when she was still in her lace camisole and panties, but it hadn't led to anything. Now they were on that evening out, Nick in a black suit, her in sky-blue wool pants and jacket.

Nick sipped some of the red wine they'd ordered. "Are you okay?"

"Yep. Fine."

"You're not. Why?"

"I don't know why. I feel off-key."

"Maybe you're hungry."

"Maybe I am."

But, even after they'd enjoyed a delicious seafood meal, and were driving home in her Jeep in the dark, she still didn't feel right. She closed down the house and they went to her bedroom. Pascal had taken to sleeping in the sunroom while Nick was here, so she didn't have to kick him off the bed.

"I'm off-key because this is my house," she said.

He took off his tie and unbuttoned his jacket. "That's your problem. I feel fine."

"I know."

Nick walked over to her and he placed his palms on either side of face and lifted her mouth to meet his. Serena closed her eyes and let herself be transported into the spell he always wound around her.

He removed his mouth from hers. "It's what I said earlier, isn't it?"

"Possibly. I've just felt out of step today."

"Maybe we're not meant to be domestic."

"That could be. You're not exactly the daddy type."

He grinned. "Neither are you Ms. Mom. We're professional business people. We have to deal with that and all the misconceptions and expectations people have. You bought this house because you needed something you hadn't had in your childhood. A foundation. I bought my apartment for the same reason. Even though I was thousands of miles from home I had an anchor. But neither purchases need to reflect a desire to go further."

"Are you saying that by inviting you here this weekend, I'm trying to force us into something we're not?"

"Could be that subconsciously you had that in mind."

She poked his stomach. "You know, I think you're right. I'm having an affair, that's all. I'm not prepping you for marriage." She couldn't believe she had mentioned the word, marriage. He'd run a mile if he knew her longings.

"Do you ultimately want marriage?"

Yes. But she wouldn't admit it. "I don't know."

"Then let's not get so heavy. Let's just do what we do best tonight and enjoy ourselves."

He began to unbutton her jacket and bent his head to bury his mouth in the slope of her breasts. Serena touched his thick hair and she felt her fingertips respond to the crispness with a sharp twinge of desire. What she thought she might have lost this evening returned with deep, tremulous feelings that spread to all parts of her body.

When they were naked and clasped together, she said, "I want it to be like it was in that hotel room the first time."

"It will be."

Serena then knew her problem. She had to forget what might happen and concentrate on what was happening. She had to close her eyes and take herself to that place where Nick was never going to leave her.

Chapter Eighteen

A homeless woman died in a city alleyway on the first night of heavy frost, and that became the focus of their next Thursday show. The subject tied in with the rest of their content so far. Nick was pleased with the way the show was picking up on social issues. Reeva's interviews hadn't been junk, and this story was heavy. Angela's interview was set for Saturday.

Nick walked into the studio on Saturday morning and saw Serena. Wearing loose black trousers and a fitted jacket, she leaned against the wall with her arms folded as she talked to Cam. Nick's first instinct, as always, was to go and nuzzle her neck and give her a kiss. But of course he couldn't, with company, so he went over and said, "'Morning all."

"Hi, Nick," Cam said. "We're just discussing the presentation for this program."

"Let's get the interview first, and see if she has a good story."

"I think she's going to have a hell of a good story," Serena told him. "I had to talk to her for about an hour on the phone last night to re-persuade her to even give the interview. I almost lost the show again."

Nick was amused at the way Serena was beginning to understand that she had opened a can of worms and now she had to keep the worms from wriggling away. Her fingers kneaded the material of her jacket.

As the clock ticked away toward the time when Angela was due, Nick began to feel her restlessness enter his own body. Then a call came from the reception desk to tell them that Angela had arrived.

"I've changed my mind," she told Serena and Nick as she was prepped for the interview. "I want to be seen as myself. No disguise."

This is what Nick wanted. He glanced at Serena and saw an answering glitter in her expression. She wanted it too, but she was playing Angela very cautiously.

"Are you really sure?" Serena asked.

Angela nodded. "Very sure. Does it mean I need makeup?"

•

"Tell me what he was like when you first saw him?" Serena asked.

Angela's eyes took on a distant expression. "Even in prison garb, he was gorgeous. His hair was a sort of white blond but it was shaved down and stood up in little spikes. This seemed to show off his brilliant blue eyes that sort of shone out of his face. I found out his name was Wayne."

"Did you know what crime he had committed?"

"Oh, yes. He was in for manslaughter of his best friend on a hunting trip. Although he was appealing the charge. He had witnesses to say it was an accidental death. There was a big thing going on in the papers about him."

"Were the papers proclaiming his innocence?"

"Yes. And I also believed he was innocent. I wrote a letter to him." Angela smiled. "I told him I'd seen him when I visited someone else in the prison, and that I thought he was a hunk."

"Did he reply?"

"Yes. He wrote back right away. He was pleased to be a hunk. He'd like to see me. So I sent him my picture and he wrote and said he'd put it on his wall and looked at it all the time. He loved women with black hair."

"What else did he write about?"

"His loneliness, and how terrible it was for him in jail, because he was innocent. He railed on about the injustice of the authorities and the system."

"Did you think he was sane?"

"Definitely. He was very smart, very intelligent."

"When did you know you were in love with him?"

"I think from the beginning. I know I supported his appeal. And I told him so. We began to discuss what we would do when he got out. I'd had to quit university and I had a job in a store. I worked long evening hours, but I had enough days off that I could visit Wayne. For years, my life revolved around my job at the store and my visits to the prison. As well as a campaign with his friends for his release. I lived for the future. I didn't realize I was fooling around with my present and that I'd never be able to recapture that present when it was past. If you know what I mean."

"Then he got out?" Serena asked.

"About two years ago. He was dazed by the outside. He didn't quite know how to act. In prison, I'd thought him smooth and sophisticated. Out of prison, he was disoriented. But I hoped it wouldn't take him long to get used to the outside. He had me, after all. I'd make sure he'd do well."

"Did you live with him?"

"He had nowhere to go that I knew of, so I took him to my apartment."

"Did he love you?"

"I don't know. I think he did. I know I loved him. But nothing happened."

"What do you mean?"

"Well." Angela touched her face with her fingers. "We didn't go to bed right away."

"He didn't want to make love with you?"

"I don't know what he wanted in those first few weeks. He just stayed around my place watching TV. Then one evening, when I came home, he kind of jumped on me, and that was that. I understood because he'd had nothing for years. He didn't know."

"Did he say he loved you then?"

Angela shook her head. "No."

"After you had consummated your relationship, what happened?"

"He took me to meet his parents, who lived in a house in the country. I didn't even know he had living parents. I was really surprised to meet them, because they were very small old people. They seemed very frightened of their son. They called him by a different name."

"Did you feel something might be wrong?"

"Yes."

"So what happened after this visit?"

"We went back to my apartment. Life stayed about the same. I went out to work. Wayne stayed at home. Then after a few weeks I would come home and he wouldn't be there. Then he told me he'd been offered a job, but he'd have to move to the country."

"Did you want to move?"

"If it would help him. But he didn't invite me along. He was going to leave me. At least I thought he was. It seemed that way."

"What did you do then?"

"I didn't have to do anything. I guess the plan to move out to the country came up because his father got ill. His father died a few weeks later and his mother moved from the house. Wayne wanted to move into their house, but he insisted we get married first."

"Then he must have told you he loved you."

"He did. It was sort of a big switch all of a sudden. He seemed more human, more able to cope in the world. We didn't have a big wedding. He got a minister friend of his mother's to come to the house and do it. His mother was there. He told me he didn't want to live in the house he grew up in without marriage. I liked that about him. Anyway, he got that job, and began to supply money to live on. It was quite a bit of money sometimes, but he said he was doing some truck hauls and that he made a lot that way. It was something he'd done when he was younger, before prison."

Angela sipped from her glass of water. "I'd had to quit my job when I moved to the country, but I managed to get something in a local variety store. I still had my car, so I was mobile enough. I needed to be. Wayne wasn't home very often. He blamed his absence on the truck hauls. I felt he was still trying to adjust to being out of prison. He needed to learn more about pleasing a woman. So I tried to teach him things that would be more pleasurable to me and make him less rough."

"How was he rough?" Serena asked her.

"He just wanted it all for himself. He didn't care about my needs. I know that sounds like a hackneyed cliché, but it's true. He was the roll on, grunt and get off type." Angela grinned.

Serena also smiled. "Did he learn?"

Angela shrugged her shoulders. "He doesn't like people telling him that he's inadequate in any way. He gets very angry. So I stopped doing that."

They took a brief break at that point. Angela drank strong black coffee. Serena's makeup was freshened. She felt as if she were participating in a race. Her heart beat fast, her respiration rate was high. Her blood roiled through her veins. It was like making love with Nick. It was exciting. She was in the midst of an unfolding story.

Serena sat down with Angela again. Nothing Angela had said so far was surprising, but it was Angela's tone, the high-pitched fear behind her words that made Serena feel as if they were climbing a mountain together, and at the top they would tumble over the edge.

"Did you have any social life with other people?"

Angela touched a dark wave of hair that fell over her cheek. "He had some friends, but I didn't like them. They were boisterous and they drank too much. The thing that shocked me the most was that Wayne fitted in. These were his friends, his people. These were the guys he worked with, he told me, but I wasn't so sure that what they did was real honest work. The money coming in was mostly in cash, and in huge amounts."

"Was this the first time you were suspicious?"

"It was the first time since his parents had called him by a different name. It was also strange that I was always the only woman. Wayne would yell at me to get the beer when these guys were around. And he began to be like that when they weren't around. I felt myself begin to crumble. Things weren't the same anymore."

"Did he assault you?"

"No. He didn't hit women. That was one of his good points. Thank goodness."

"What did you do?"

"I quit my job. I couldn't handle the nights with all his friends at the house and my work. I couldn't handle being with the nice people at the store when there weren't any nice people in my life. My only escape was to get in my car and drive into Toronto to see by brother."

"He didn't mind you going?"

"He never knew. I'd go in the times when he was away and always be home by the time he got home."

"But he must have known you used your car?"

"He never said anything so I didn't worry too much. One evening all Wayne's friends were there and they had a haul of drugs. Suddenly I knew how Wayne was making his money. And one of his friends got me in the bedroom and told me to shut my mouth and my eyes and be a good wife to Wayne. I was really scared by now. Wayne had a rifle that he said used to belong to his father. He'd clean it a lot. I wasn't sure if it was loaded, but he used to aim it at me making shooting noises and laugh. I'd get hysterical and run."

"One night he ran after me and we played a game like cat and mouse throughout the house, and he began yelling about when he used to go hunting, and how he'd stalked down his friend this way, and I wasn't safe. There was nowhere I could go that he couldn't get to me."

"Why didn't you just leave then?"

"I did still love him."

"But he killed that man, didn't he? He admitted it to you?"

Angela nodded. "Yes. He admitted it. And I told him, 'You shouldn't be free.' And he just grinned. He was guilty of murder. And I was living with him. And all his friends were criminals. Now that he knew I knew everything, he told me he would kill me if I didn't keep my mouth shut. Next time his friends came over, Wayne locked me in the bedroom."

"Couldn't you escape?"

"I did think of getting in my car and just driving away, but it's not that easy. Besides, he changed after they left. He was all charm. He said he'd got rid of them. He was going straight. He was going to try the marriage thing from the start once more. That I should show him how to act like a real husband, not like an animal. He was a different person."

"We went out to restaurants together. He liked to spend money. He went on fishing trips, real fishing trips. He bought home fish and he cooked it for me. He is quite a good cook. He has a good imagination. He can be very creative when he wants to be. And he was being creative. With me. I knew down in my heart that he was conning me, and that he'd conned me all along. I'd been a way for him to get out of prison, an easy cover for him to live under when he was out." Angela bowed her head. "I feel so damn stupid. So gullible. And I really don't know where to go from now on."

"Do you still love him?"

"I don't know anymore."

The floor director cut them there.

Angela wanted to leave right away. She'd promised Max she would see him.

"Are you sure you are safe?" Nick asked.

"Safer than I was six months ago, because I know the truth now. It gives me a certain power."

"When this is aired, he'll know," Serena told her. "Things will burst open. You'll be in danger."

"I don't think so. He never watches TV. That's why I decided to go on as myself."

"But because you decided to go on as yourself, that means you want something to happen," Serena said.

"I want it to end. I had to get it all off my chest. I've shared it with someone."

"A few million people," Nick said.

She shrugged. "I've done it in style."

She went then, and Nick and Serena returned to the studio to watch the interview. Angela's revelations weren't extraordinary, but behind every word was a scream for help.

Her scream stayed with Serena, and she felt very nervous about airing the show. She wished they could cancel it. She didn't like what she'd started. But Nick seemed excited about Angela's story. He was hoping to get Lawson put back in prison because of it. Serena couldn't very well back down now. What kind of journalist would back down on a good story? One who liked happy endings. Herself.

She was even more nervous on Thursday evening than she'd been throughout her entire career. Her stomach felt tied in knots. She shared dinner with Nick, but she didn't eat any of her chicken. Nick polished it off for her.

They took a cab back to Steel TV. "I have stage fright," she told him.

"To which you are entitled. I'm just hoping this won't put Angela in any danger."

She felt the same way. She knew that this story had come about because she had wanted to stay one step ahead of Nick. She hadn't wanted him to consider her a lousy journalist. She hoped she hadn't been too selfish in her motives for pushing her friend to do the interview.

The program was edited with surreal clips of jail life, using an actor for Angela's husband. It was a decisive interview, and Serena was pleased with the result, so she was surprised the next day when the *Neon Nights* edition made little news. Serena went off to perform a pre-Christmas tea pouring, trusting that the interview would be a catharsis for Angela, nothing more.

•

Nick's parents' were looking through a number of real estate listings. One bungalow was part of a retirement home complex, and Nick was pushing for that. Medical staff were on call, and there was a recreation room. He knew his parents weren't sociable, but they might be forced to be if they had the means at their disposal. After dealing with his parents, Nick drove home in the dark with a touch of snow brushing the windshield. Feeling tired, and knowing he had to stay alert for the slippery streets, he pushed the radio button as he stopped at a traffic light.

"She was interviewed this week by Serena Brown on the public affairs show *Neon Nights*. Serena is the daughter of Reeva Brown-Carstairs, who made her resignation from politics known on the same program. In other news ..."

Nick punched buttons. What the hell was happening? Why was Serena on a news cast? Come on, someone give him the whole story. No wonder he disliked five second, blabbermouth news. You missed the item and it was gone forever. He didn't even have a computer at his disposal.

He heard nothing for the rest of the way home. He parked the car, rushed upstairs and turned on his computer and the TV. Nothing on the internet. On the TV were sitcoms, international news, cop shows, hospital shows. Steel TV. The real news. Evening news anchor Paula Tatchkoff was babbling about something that wasn't what Nick wanted to know. His cell phone rang.

"Yes."

"It's Serena, Nick. I've just arrived at Steel. We have to go down to Niagara. Angela's being held hostage by Lawson. The police think you and I might be able to help. I had a feeling this might happen. It's my fault."

"Cut that crap for a start, sweetie. I'll be right there. Grab a van."

"We've got one. Paul's driving."

◆

The first snow of the season was storming in over the Great Lakes on a weather front from the Ohio Valley. It caused a tie up on the Niagara section of the Queen Elizabeth Way right down to the U.S. border.

Serena sat beside Paul in the front. Nick was in the back, and she knew Nick was restless and would rather be driving. He leaned his arms on the back of her seat and she could feel the tension in him. But Paul was skilled in snow. He detoured the freeway on a back road that was treacherous but absent of heavy traffic.

Because of the insistent snow fall, Angela's road had narrowed to one lane. Paul negotiated the van to where there was a mass of police cars and flashing lights. An ambulance and a fire engine stood waiting to perform any emergency services that might be needed.

Steel TV was already there. Juliette, in a purple leather coat with a big fur collar, was doing the reporting. "To bring you up to date on what is happening. Angela Thomson, the wife of alleged killer Alan Wayne Thomason, who is also known as Lawson Thomson, is being held hostage by her husband. This hostage taking has alleg-edly come about because of last night's interview on *Neon Nights*. Hosts of the show, Serena Brown and Nick Fraser, are on the scene now. It is known that Serena is a personal friend of the victim."

"A great friend I am," Serena murmured as they prepared for a briefing by the police.

A slim man with a moustache, Detective Smith, told them, "He's telling us that he's been victimized by his wife and that she misrepresented him on TV last night. He insists he isn't a murder-er. He wants a public apology from his wife, which she won't give, and he will let her go when, and only when, he's assured he won't be re-arrested. He has to be a free man."

"How can we reassure him of that?" Serena asked. "He's going to be arrested, isn't he?"

"He'll have charges pending for this hostage incident."

"I just want you to get her out of there."

"That's what we're trying to do, Ms. Brown. Don't think we want a dead woman on our hands."

Nick put his hand on her shoulder. "True, Serena."

She glared at him. "This is your fault."

"It was your idea."

"I know. But you pushed me. I wouldn't have bothered to execute it if I hadn't felt I needed to be better than better."

He shook his head. "That's your personality. I can't help that. But right now, we have Angela in that house, in danger."

Detective Smith said, "He's phoning from the house every once in a while. Next time he calls, I want Ms. Brown to talk to him. Tell him that if he brings Angela out then negotiations will be made, but not until his wife is safe."

The snow stopped and the night grew silent, eerie. The flashing lights of the vehicles floated across the sky and the air grew crisp. Serena tightened the scarf around her neck.

Juliette stomped her booted feet beside her.

"Well, it's very quiet in there," Juliette said. "Do you think she's still alive?"

"She better be," Serena snapped.

"Okay. Don't get your back up at me. It wasn't me who interviewed her."

The detective's phone rang. It was Lawson or Alan. The phone was handed to Serena.

"Let her go, Alan. She's only ever tried to help you."

"You don't believe that garbage she spilled on your show, do you?" It was the droning hypnotic voice from the answering machine.

"Alan, let her go and then we will negotiate for your release."

"I don't believe a word you say, you smiley bitch."

The phone went dead. She sighed and handed the detective his phone. "I want to talk to him again."

They waited. Some more press arrived from surrounding cities. A TV crew from Buffalo, New York, grilled the police. Serena wanted to rush in and save Angela, like some super heroine in a movie, but she knew she would only put Angela's life in more danger. She shivered and pushed her hands deep into the pockets of her quilted jacket.

The phone rang again. Serena spoke to Alan once more, but he had the same clear needs. Release, no more prison terms, and he'd let Angela free. They went to sit in the van with the heater blasting. The temperature was sliding down into the night. Serena became fascinated by watching the cold air curl over the area. Lights still flashed. People's breath rose white. She thought it was breath or steam. Then she realized it was smoke coming from the house.

"It's on fire," she said, and leapt from the van. She heard Paul and Nick coming after her. Paul had his camera going.

It was chaos, sirens, people running, fire engines emptying hoses into the burning house. Angela was brought out by a fireman. She was wrapped in a blanket and ushered into an ambulance, which took off as fast as the snow would allow.

Serena waited for Alan Wayne Thomason to appear but he never did.

Chapter Nineteen

There was little snow in Toronto. A few streaky lines of white alongside the curbs and a chill wind. Serena shivered as Paul parked in the Steel lot, and Nick gave her a reassuring pat on the shoulder. She shook her head at him.

"What did I start?"

"A news story."

They went up to the fifth floor news room. The station was staying on air tonight, to keep viewers up-to-date on the hostage taking. All the monitors flashed pictures of the scene they had left at Angela's house. Serena saw Angela being taken to hospital. She pushed up the sleeves of her sweater, prepared to stay for the night, if she had to. "Any news on how she is?"

"Nothing yet," she was told by Melissa. "Do you want coffee or hot chocolate? I'm taking orders."

"Hot chocolate sounds wonderful."

Serena glanced over to where Nick was working with Paul, who had some extra pictures from the incident. Nick was intent on helping Paul and she realized that he loved his work. He loved getting his hands dirty with gritty news. Besides, it was Nick who had been the catalyst for her own changes. Nick who had forced her to face her father's desertion. Nick who had taken away her loneliness and replaced it with joy. Nick who had urged her to stretch herself away from safe news. If nothing ever came of their relationship, she would always remember him. And love him. Deeply.

Melissa returned with the cups of chocolate. Serena perched on a stool and sipped the hot, creamy liquid.

"We're going to run a news break," a man called out.

Juliette was still outside the burned out wreck of the house. Her face was beginning to look very cold and pinched. "We've had a report that Angela Thomson is out of danger. She has been treated for smoke inhalation and a few minor burns to her body. There has been no word on Alan Wayne Thomason also known as Lawson Thomson. There have been reports that someone was seen running from the rear of the house, but that has been unconfirmed. The fire department is going in to sift through the wreckage. To give you more in-depth knowledge of this case we have an interview with Angela's mother, Gwyneth Evans."

"Her mother," Serena said. "Trust her to come on to the scene now. All she wants is fame, I suppose."

Nick perched beside her and peeled off the lid of his own chocolate. "They'll come out of the woodwork now. How do you feel?"

"I want a conclusion. I want to know what the hell has happened to Alan."

"He might be dead."

"Then should I feel guilty because Angela was my friend and now she has no home or husband?"

"It was Angela's choice."

Serena rubbed her forehead. "Yes. I suppose. But she still cared about him on some level. I know you don't know about that type of caring, but I felt that she really did love him."

"Don't blame yourself."

"I'm not, but I'll always feel responsible."

The news became a re-run of the night's events. Angela wasn't speaking until she'd been interviewed by the police.

Nick suggested they go to his apartment for the rest of the night. He could tell Serena was reluctant to leave the television station but she looked worn out and he was beginning to get concerned for her.

◆

Serena used the adjoining bathroom to his bedroom, where she kept some of her things, so Nick went along to the other one. When he returned she was tucked into the bed. He slipped in naked beside her and turned off the lamp. For a few seconds they lay beside one another, and he could hear her light breathing. Then her breathing became more agitated and turned into sobs.

He was surprised to hear her cry. She wasn't a woman to cry

very often. Tears weren't one of her weapons. So when she cried, the hurt must be from deep inside her. He turned to her, and she came to his arms and he felt her tears dampen his bare shoulder.

He stroked her back. "It's okay."

She raised her face to his and he kissed away the tears. When he reached her mouth, her lips clung to his, the way she'd always clung to him since the first kiss in her kitchen on the night of Don's soirée. He couldn't resist her when she was so eager, and he let her move astride his body. He found her beautiful, sad and frustrated with the agony of the night, and his hands rode down over her breasts to her undulating hips. Serena let out strangled sobbing sounds and she took him before he took her. Then he rolled her over and poured his own frustration and a lot of love into her.

When Serena awoke, her head felt as if someone had pounded it with a hammer. Nick wasn't beside her. She flung her arm across his empty pillow and gazed out of the apartment window at the silver sky.

She heard Nick on the phone in the other room. When he came to the bedroom door, his face was unshaven and he was wearing jeans and an old gray sweatshirt. He held the cordless phone in his hand. "Angela's doing fine. Max is with her at the hospital. The police have set up an interview with her later. Steel TV is making a big thing of our ordeal, but everywhere else it's getting a small mention."

Serena sat up in bed and reached for a scarlet flannel shirt of Nick's she used when she stayed with him. She pushed her arms into it and climbed out of bed. "What about Alan?"

"They found his body in the wreckage."

"Oh, poor Angela. Do you think he set the fire?"

"Who knows. Nobody is saying too much until Angela has said her piece."

A hot shower eased Serena's headache. She stood beneath the spray feeling terrible. She was with Nick and she loved him so much, but she knew he wasn't going to last. She was pleased Angela was safe, but she would always remember the terrifying situation she had put her friend into. Angela's husband was dead, the man Angela had loved for a long part of her life. Serena pushed her fists into her eyes and let the tears well behind her fingers. Then she just leaned against the shower wall and cried until there was nothing left.

Nick went into Steel with Serena that afternoon but he didn't feel as if they were together any more. She was very cool and self-contained. He couldn't equate her with the naked, sobbing woman in his arms this morning in bed. He never knew quite how desperate was his love for her until she began to slip away from him.

When they reached the suite Don was there, thrilled with all the publicity the Angela story had brought Steel.

"You can provide the dramatics next time," Serena informed Nick.

He shoved his hands into the back pockets of his jeans. "I hope this doesn't mean you're not going to have any more story ideas."

She touched her neck beneath her upswept hair. "No. But I'll be more careful."

"Careful has no edge."

"I don't like living on the edge. Maybe it's okay for you. You're used to it. But I'm used to having my life under control."

"When did you come up with this? You were losing control last time I saw you." He'd noticed that her makeup had been applied with extra care to hide red swollen eyes.

"I just had to get a few things out of my system. I think I'll go down to five to see what's happening."

Nick let her go. One day, he was going to have to learn how to let her go forever.

•

Angela's interview proved dramatic. Gradually the newscasts pared down her comments to: "He was smoking and he lit his cigarettes with a butane lighter. He put the lighter down when he was on the phone and I grabbed it. Another time he was on the phone I snapped the lighter and threw it at the curtains. He was furious. He began to scream curses at me. But the house was burning, the smoke got too much and I—don't remember much more."

Serena went back to her office and phoned the hospital, where she managed to get through to Angela.

"It's not your fault, Serena," Angela told her. "You just happened to come along at an appropriate time. And I used you as my vehicle to free myself. Even if I am a little sad."

"That's a pretty good rationalization," Serena told her. "So what are you going to do now?"

"Get a place with Max for a while. Then maybe go back into journalism. Maybe I'll end up at Steel."

"That would be great."

"And my mother is back in my life. She came to visit me. She lost touch with me. It's kind of strained, but it might work. Max is quite happy about it. Anyway, I get out of here tomorrow and I start my new life. Thank you."

"Let's keep in touch this time."

"We will. And be good to Nick. I really liked him."

Be good to Nick, Serena thought when she'd hung up. How could she, when she lived a lie with Nick? Everything in her life almost formed a full circle, except for Nick.

She closed up her office, went out to the parking lot and climbed into her Jeep. All she wanted to do was go home. There she would make her decisions.

•

When Nick found Serena gone, he went home. Well, he'd achieved everything he had set out to achieve. He'd set his parent's move into motion. He'd got a hit news show. He'd had great sex with Serena Brown.

He slumped into a chair. But he wasn't satisfied, not nearly satisfied. He'd pretty much told her not to love him, and she didn't. He scrubbed his eyes. Damn. He'd been a fool. He should have just told her to fall in love with him and then they'd both be in love with each other and he could marry her. He knew now that's what he wanted. He wanted to stay home, write a book or two, marry Serena and be with her forever. By not telling Serena that he loved her he was repeating the way he'd reacted to his parents and he was denying himself a loving life.

At their weekly Monday morning meeting he felt like something was closing in on him when he saw Serena. He knew, because she wore one of her pinstriped suits, that something was up. She had a very determined look on her face. After the meeting he went into his office, and wasn't surprised when she followed, closed the door, and stood in front of him.

"I want to break up with you. For good this time. We'll tell our parents, so we won't be manipulated into any more social occasions together." Her words were fast, succinct, as if she'd rehearsed them.

Nick didn't blame her for her decision, but he felt his stomach shrivel even tighter. Everything inside his head throbbed. "Reason?" It was the only word he could get out without letting her hear the emotion gathering in his chest. His fingers clenched inside his pockets.

She wet her lips with her tongue. "You know what the reason is. I can't—" For the first time he heard her voice waver. She cleared her throat. "Why do you need a reason? We were having an affair heading to nowhere, and I don't want it to continue. Isn't that enough of a reason? There's nothing in it for me. No pay off."

"It's only since this Angela thing." He heard his voice sound gruff and unfamiliar.

"Don't blame Angela for us. We were manipulated back together after my last decision to split. So we're over that silly gossip. Now we can break up."

He couldn't argue with her because he couldn't speak without begging, his nails were biting into his palms inside his pockets. He moved past her without seeing anything. He had to get out of Steel, far away from Serena. He was on the way to a major breakdown.

He grabbed his jacket and left the office.

Shrugging the jacket over his shoulders, Nick pushed open the heavy fire door and took the stairs. The stairs reminded him of Serena. He walked to his car but he didn't want to drive anywhere because he didn't feel as if he were capable of driving. So he began to walk.

•

Serena squared her shoulders. She wasn't going to cry. *Be a big brave girl about this, sweetheart. I'll be back.* Her father hadn't come back that time. And neither would Nick.

"You look wiped out," Reeva said when Serena arrived for a scheduled meal that evening. "Do you want a glass of wine?"

"A big one," Serena told her, sitting down in one of the cushiony armchairs and slipping off her shoes so that they lay scattered on the thick pile rug. Her mother seemed to move around in a fog before her eyes.

Reeva handed her a glass of wine. "I imagine you're pretty shaken up after that fiasco on Friday night." Reeva sat down in another armchair. "I hope you stick to interviewing politicians in future. It's much safer."

Serena sipped the drink and smiled. "I agree."

"Anyway, I'm pleased we can have these few hours together. I was thinking about making arrangements for Christmas."

Serena didn't even want to think about Christmas. She had to get over the next few weeks yet. She had to face Nick over and over until she didn't want him anymore. "It's a bit early."

"Not really. We have more people to include this year, with Nick. And Seth wants to join us. I was talking to the Frasers the other day and they would be delighted to share Christmas with us."

Serena couldn't believe her ears. She felt as if she'd woken up from a deep sleep. "You phoned Nick's parents?"

"Of course. I took their number from Maria at Thanksgiving."

"So what does this mean exactly?"

Reeva gave her a sideways look. "We all have Christmas together."

"Mother. Why didn't you check with me first? I've broken up with Nick."

Reeva sighed and shook her head. "Now what happened?"

"Nothing exactly happened, but I can't continue in a dead end relationship."

Reeva raised an eyebrow. "Are you saying that you got back together after Thanksgiving?"

"Yes. I'm saying that."

"That doesn't appear to be a dead end."

"Well, it was. Nick's only committed to this show until next spring. Then he's going back in the field. It's crazy for me to continue any longer. So I called it quits before I can get hurt. We've killed the gossip."

Her mother gave her a thoughtful look. "You're thinking he's going to be like your dad, aren't you?"

"Well?"

"Well, he's not. He might seem like him. But he's not. Your father was much less controlled than Nick. Stu was shattered by his parents' sudden death when he was eighteen. He lived by the seat of his pants and he drank too much and took too many drugs. Nick's thoughtful. Sober. And he makes careful decisions."

Serena had to agree. "Okay. So he's a great guy. But that doesn't mean he's not going to leave me high and dry. In that case, I'm out before he can destroy me. While I'm still in one piece."

Her mother smiled. "I do admire your strength of purpose, I have to say that. But we're still having Nick's Mom and Dad for Christmas. It's arranged. And that means Nick as well. So you're either going to have to make it up with him for the season or get back together."

She couldn't possibly do that. She'd be a wreck. "I can't."

Reeva gazed at her daughter. "I think I once drummed it into you that there is no such word as can't. Go tell him you love him and that you don't want him to go."

"Mother. I couldn't."

Reeva smiled. "You can. But you won't because you have too much pride. What if he loves you?"

"He doesn't."

"You don't know that."

"Mother. If he loved me he wouldn't be leaving."

"He hasn't left yet. He's not leaving for months. He can change his mind."

"You never got Dad to change his mind."

"He was different. Nick has roots here. His parents for one."

"They've never been much to him. They're the reason he left in the first place."

"Do you want to tell me about that."

Serena explained Nick's story.

"All right. But now they are the reason he came back. Before you burn your bridges at least confront Nick with the truth."

"Why me? Why can't he come to me and say he loves me and won't leave?"

"Because I think he might not know how to do that."

Was her mother right? Should she go to Nick and tell him she loved him with all her heart and wanted him forever? What if he laughed in her face, turned her down, told her she was full of it? Could she work with him under those circumstances for another few months? She would be glad to see the back of him if that happened. Even so, maybe she should take her mother's advice and at least let Nick know where he stood with her. Right now he thought she didn't care. At least he would understand her reason for breaking up with him. He didn't want her in love with him, did he?

She spent the entire night in agony with these thoughts.

Nick came into her office the next day and said, "You know what your mother has done?"

She nodded. "Yes. I do."

"Is it okay with you? In the circumstances?"

"No, if you want the honest truth. But we can't disappoint your parents."

She saw his cheek throb. "I don't see why we can't be civilized for one day."

She ran her fingers through her hair and looked at him. "Aren't we being civilized now? I think we've done quite well. We've lasted quite a few weeks, on and off."

He pushed his hands into his pockets, and let out a steamy sounding breath. "Okay. Let's cut to the chase. I've had enough of this. You're acting like a jerk. You had one story that went awry on you because you opened up your creative door and went for it. You had one affair that was going great because you let yourself care. Now you're harnessing yourself, and you're going to become narrow and uptight, the little Ice Maiden you were when I met you."

Serena stood up and glared at him. "That's not true. Number one, I was not the little Ice Maiden when you met me. I was perfectly fine, thank you."

"Except for all your hang ups about your father and your brother."

"I've got rid of those now, thanks to you. I read my father's book. I'm friends with Seth. I'm over all that."

"So I did something right?"

"You push too hard, you know that?"

"I push hard when I really want something."

Serena met his glittering gaze and realized that it wasn't cold and she could see right through him. He was falling apart in front of her. All sorts of feeling showed in his eyes and his strained features. She felt the need to reach out to him, but she couldn't make her arm move forward. They stood staring at one another for a long, tense moment.

Sensing this was the moment, she drew in a breath. "Okay. This is how it is for me. I love you. I can't live without you. I know you hate that scene. Therefore, I'm cutting the cord now, before I get any more involved, while I can still think straight, while my world is still under my control."

She heard him swallow hard. "You mean that?" His voice was hoarse, uncontrolled.

"Yes. I mean it. Because I love you I'm letting you go to be free. That's what you want, isn't it? That's why you let Lise Kryker go, wasn't it?"

"I let Lise Kryker go because I could never love her. Not because she loved me."

Serena raised her arms in the air. "Whatever. That's the situation. I've gone and fallen in love with you, and if it goes on any longer I'm going to be a mess. A huge mess."

"And what about me?" he asked.

"You've had some great sex. It was great sex. For me anyway." Serena could hear her voice breaking. If he didn't leave her soon she would be wailing and sobbing. She gulped down all her emotion and felt it choke her.

Nick took a step forward until he was about a foot away from her. It was like that first night in her other office, when he'd started to invade her space. He'd invaded more than her space. He'd invaded her mind, her senses, her body, her own worth. No. Not her own worth. He'd increased her worth. He'd made her realize her own strengths. He'd also taught her to love a man. Wasn't that incongruous? A man who never wanted to love, teaching a woman to love him. What a crazy world.

He touched her face with his palm. "Serena."

She leaned into his warm hand for a brief moment. She knew the spell he could wrap around her.

"I don't want to break up with you. We have all sorts of good things to go for yet: Christmas, Valentine's Day, your birthday, Easter, my birthday—which is next July."

"You'll be gone by then." A sob escaped with her words.

"No. I won't. I've decided that I want to take a few years off and write some books. Oh, I might do some work here at Steel for Don. I might even get offered next season's *Neon Nights* if John can't come back, but I do want to write. I've always wanted to write. I've just never put myself in one place long enough."

"So you'll just string me along while you do these things you want to do and then you'll leave?"

"I don't think so." He leaned over and touched his mouth against her forehead. "Not feeling the way I do about you. I love you so much."

His words registered. Serena turned her face to look at him and he was very close. She could see the scar, a little more livid against his skin now that his tan was leaving with the cooler weather. Her lips were so dry she had to moisten them with her tongue before she spoke. "Can I trust you on that?"

His eyes locked with hers. "Can I trust you? Isn't that a risk we have to take?"

"It is a risk."

"Then let's take it. Because if you leave me, I'm leaving the show and I'm going and I'm never coming home again. I couldn't go through the rest of the year with you here and not being with you."

"You'd leave the show for me?"

"Darn right I would. I love you. I want to marry you. We'll get engaged at Christmas and plan a June wedding when we've got some time off. We'll do everything right." He put his arms around her and held her as if his life depended on it. "Please?"

Why did she always feel so secure in his arms?

"Hold me," Nick said.

She let her arms crawl around him and hold him close. She could feel his heartbeat close to her own frantic heart. And heard his whisper before they kissed.

"I'll never leave you."

◆ ◆ ◆

Jillian Dagg

Jillian Dagg was born in Surrey, England, and moved to Canada with her parents. She loved reading romance novels so much that she began writing the genre. Her first books were published by Silhouette, Simon & Schuster and a writing career was launched. Jillian lives in Ontario, Canada with her husband and cats.

www.JillianDagg.com

You might also enjoy:

MUSIC TO HER HEART

Her dream man existed only in her songs— until one fateful weekend …

Singer-songwriter and successful restaurant owner Katy Kerr has aspirations of making it big, and dreams of finding the perfect man. But after caring for her dying mother, she realizes both her career and dreams have slipped off the radar. Maybe for good.

Music industry mogul Adam Stevenson is a force in and of himself. A professional maker and breaker of dreams, Adam manages the careers of the elite—to the extent he's forgotten how to manage his own family, his own life.

Now, with Katy's family soon to be tied to Adam's, will their whirlwind romance turn out to be one giant mistake—or the only thing that can bring the music back to life inside their wounded hearts?

Books by John Patrick

Non-Fiction
A Charmed Life: Vince Cobretti
Lowe Down: Tim Lowe
The Best of the Superstars 1990
The Best of the Superstars 1991
The Best of the Superstars 1992
The Best of the Superstars 1993
The Best of the Superstars 1994
The Best of the Superstars 1995
The Best of the Superstars 1996
The Best of the Superstars 1997
The Best of the Superstars 1998
The Best of the Superstars 1999
The Best of the Superstars 2000
The Best of the Superstars 2001
The Best of the Superstars 2002
What Went Wrong?
When Boys Are Bad
& Sex Goes Wrong
Legends: The World's Sexiest
Men, Vols. 1 & 2
Legends (Third Edition)
Tarnished Angels (Ed.)

Fiction
Billy & David: A Deadly Minuet
The Bigger They Are...
The Younger They Are...
The Harder They Are...
Angel: The Complete Trilogy
Angel II: Stacy's Story
Angel: The Complete Quintet
A Natural Beauty (Editor)
The Kid (with Joe Leslie)
HUGE (Editor)
Strip: He Danced Alone
The Boys of Spring
Big Boys/Little Lies (Editor)
Boy Toy

Seduced (Editor)
Insatiable/Unforgettable (Editor)
Heartthrobs
Runaways/Kid Stuff (Editor)
Dangerous Boys/Rent Boys (Editor)
Barely Legal (Editor)
Country Boys/City Boys (Editor)
My Three Boys (Editor)
Mad About the Boys (Editor)
Lover Boys (Editor)
In the BOY ZONE (Editor)
Boys of the Night (Editor)
Secret Passions (Editor)
Beautiful Boys (Editor)
Juniors (Editor)
Come Again (Editor)
Smooth 'N' Sassy (Editor)
Intimate Strangers (Editor)
Naughty By Nature (Editor)
Dreamboys (Editor)
Raw Recruits (Editor)
Play Hard, Score Big (Editor)
Sweet Temptations (Editor)
Pleasures of the Flesh (Editor)
Juniors 2 (Editor)
Fresh 'N' Frisky (Editor)
Taboo! (Editor)
Heatwave (Editor)
Boys on the Prowl (Editor)
Huge 2 (Editor)
Fever! (Editor)
Any Boy Can (Editor)
Virgins No More (Editor)
Seduced 2 (Co-Editor)
Wild 'N' Willing (Co-Editor)

Worldwide Praise for the Erotica of John Patrick and STARbooks!

"John Patrick is a modern master of the genre! ...This writing is what being brave is all about. It brings up the kinds of things that are usually kept so private that you think you're the only one who experiences them."
– Gay Times, London

"'Barely Legal' is a great potpourri ... and the cover boy is gorgeous!"
– Ian Young, Torso magazine

"Collections of stories have become increasingly popular in the past couple of years: leading the way is the prolific and consistently entertaining John Patrick who, under the STARbooks imprint, has edited fifteen or more collections of erotica written another dozen books himself and published several handfuls more by other authors. ... Burly (500-plus pages) anthologies of erotic writing, the perfect bedside companions..."
– Richard Labonte, Q Magazine

"A huge collection of highly erotic, short and steamy one-handed tales. Perfect bedtime reading, though you probably won't get much sleep! Prepare to be shocked! Highly recommended!"
– Vulcan magazine

"Tantalizing tales of porn stars, hustlers, and other lost boys...John Patrick set the pace with 'Angel!'"
– The Weekly News, Miami

"...Some readers may find some of the scenes too explicit; others will enjoy the sudden, graphic sensations each page brings. Each of these romans clef is written with sustained intensity. 'Angel' offers a strange, often poetic vision of sexual obsession. I recommend it to you."
– Nouveau Midwest

"'Angel' is mouthwatering and enticing..."
– Rouge Magazine, London

"'Superstars' is a fast read...if you'd like a nice round of fireworks before the Fourth, read this aloud at your next church picnic..."
– Welcomat, Philadelphia

"Yes, it's another of those bumper collections of steamy tales from STARbooks. The rate at which John Patrick turns out these compilations you'd be forgiven for thinking it's not exactly quality prose. Wrong.

These stories are well-crafted, but not over-written, and have a profound effect in the pants department."
– Vulcan magazine, London

"For those who share Mr. Patrick's appreciation for cute young men, 'Legends' is a delightfully readable book...I am a fan of John Patrick's...His writing is clear and straight-forward and should be better known in the gay community."
– Ian Young, Torso Magazine

"... 'Billy & David' is frank, intelligent, disarming. Few books approach the government's failure to respond to crisis in such a realistic, powerful manner."
– RG Magazine, Montreal, Canada

"...Touching and gallant in its concern for the sexually addicted, 'Angel' becomes a wonderfully seductive investigation of the mysterious disparity between lust and passion, obsession and desire."
– Lambda Book Report

"John Patrick has one of the best jobs a gay male writer could have. In his fiction, he tells tales of rampant sexuality. His non-fiction involves first person explorations of adult male video stars. Talk about choice assignments!"
– Southern Exposure

"The title for 'Boys of Spring' is taken from a poem by Dylan Thomas, so you can count on high caliber imagery throughout."
– Walter Vatter, Editor, A Different Light Review

STARbooks are Available at Fine Booksellers Everywhere

First Edition Published in the U.S. in March, 1999
Library of Congress Card Catalogue No. 98- 98-96829
ISBN No. 1-891855-02-6

SWEET TEMPTATIONS

EDITED BY
JOHN PATRICK

Herndon, VA

Contents

Editor's Note

Most of the stories appearing in this book take place prior to the years of The Plague; the editor and each of the authors represented herein advocate the practice of safe sex at all times. And, because these stories trespass the boundaries of fiction and non-fiction, to respect the privacy of those involved, we've changed all of the names and other identifying details.

"The only way to get rid of a temptation is to yield to it."

– Oscar Wilde

INTRODUCTION:
WHITE-HOT LOVE
John Patrick

Lead us not into temptation, so the commandment goes. Yet those who succumb to temptation tend to gain considerable notoriety for it and live in infamy. Consider the case of the 54-year-old ruler of the Roman Empire, Hadrian, who succumbed to the tempting charms of the 16-year-old Greek boy Antinous. "Their sexual chemistry appears to have been mutual, electric, and immediate," Bela Durnow says in the book Gay Testaments. But, in truth, the debate has gone on for centuries about exactly what their relationship was. Still, it is universally accepted that "Hadrian's own nature, whether or not it was excessively lascivious, was clearly sexually-oriented mainly to boys and young men. His love for Antinous was white-hot," claims Royston Lambert in the book Beloved And God.

Hadrian himself, as recorded in Memoirs of Hadrian by Marguerite Yourcenar, describes the day he first laid eyes on the comely Antinous: "One late afternoon we were reading an abstruse work of Lycophron, whom I enjoy for his daring juxtaposition of sounds, figures and allusions, a complex system of echoes and mirrors. A little apart from the others a young boy was listening to those difficult strophes, half attentive, half in dream; I thought at once of some shepherd, deep in the woods, vaguely aware of a strange bird's cry. He had brought neither tablet nor style. Seated on the edge of the water's basin he trailed a hand idly over the fair, placid surface. His father, I learned, had held a small post in administration of the vast imperial domains; left young to a grandfather's care the boy had been sent to study in Nicomedia, and to reside there with a former guest of his parents, a ship owner and builder of the town who seemed rich to that modest family. I kept him on after the others had gone. He had read little, and knew almost nothing of the world; though childishly trusting, he was also disposed to reflection. I had seen Claudiopolis, his native city, so I led him to speak of his home on the edge of the great pine forests which furnish masts for our ships; of the hilltop temple of Attys, whose strident music he loved; of the superb horses of his country and its strange gods. His voice was low, and his Greek had the accent of Asia. Suddenly aware of my attention, or of my gaze, perhaps, he grew confused, flushed, and fell back into one of those stubborn silences to which I was soon to become accustomed. An intimacy gradually developed. He accompanied

3

me thereafter in all my voyages, and the fabulous years began. Antinous was Greek; I traced the story of this ancient but little-known family back to the time of the first Arcadian settlers along the shores of the Propontis. But Asia had produced its effect upon that rude blood, like the drop of honey which clouds and perfumes a pure wine. I could detect in him mystic superstitions like those of a disciple of Apollonius, and the religious adoration, as well, of an Oriental subject for his monarch. His presence was extraordinarily silent: he followed me like some animal, or a familiar spirit. He had the infinite capacity of a young dog for play and for swift repose, and the same fierceness and trust. This graceful hound, avid both for caresses and commands, took his post at my feet. "I admired his almost haughty indifference for all that was not his delight or his cult; it served him in place of disinterestedness and scruple, and of all virtues painfully acquired. I marveled at his gentleness, which had aspects of hardness, too, and the somber devotion to which he gave his whole being. And yet this submission was not blind; those lids so often lowered in acquiescence or in dream were not always so; the most attentive eyes in the world would sometimes look me straight in the face, and I felt myself judged. But I was judged as is a god by his adorer: my harshness and sudden suspicions (for I had them later on) were patiently and gravely accepted. I have been absolute master but once in my life, and over but one being. If I have said nothing yet of a beauty so apparent it is not merely because of the reticence of a man too completely conquered. But the faces which we try so desperately to recall escape us: it is only for a moment ... I see a head bending under its dark mass of hair, eyes which seemed slanting, so long were the lids, a young face broadly formed, as if for repose. This tender body varied all the time, like a plant, and some of its alterations were those of growth. The boy changed; he grew tall. A week of indolence sufficed to soften him completely; a single afternoon at the hunt made the young athlete firm again, and fleet; an hour's sun would turn him from jasmine to the color of honey. The boyish limbs lengthened out; the face lost its delicate childish round and hollowed slightly under the high cheekbones; the full chest of the young runner took on the smooth, gleaming curves of a Bacchante's breast; the brooding lips bespoke a bitter ardor, a sad satiety. In truth this visage changed as if I had molded it night and day.

"When I think back on these years I seem to return to the Age of Gold. Trouble was no more: past efforts were repaid by an ease which was almost divine. Travel was play, a pleasure well known, controlled, and skillfully planned. Work, though incessant, was only a form of delight. My life, where everything came late, power and happiness, too, now acquired the splendor of high noon, the luminous glow of siesta time when everything, the objects of the room and the figure lying beside one, bathes in golden shade. Passion satisfied has its innocence, almost as fragile as any other: the remainder of human beauty was relegated to the rank of mere spectacle, and ceased to be game for my pursuit. This adventure, begun casually enough, served to enrich but also to simplify my life: the future was matter for slight concern; I ceased to question the oracles; the stars were no longer anything more than admirable patterns upon the vault of heaven. Never before had I noted with such elation the glimmer of dawn on the distant islands, the coolness of caves sacred to nymphs and haunted by birds of passage, the low flight of quail at dusk. I reread the poets; some seemed better to me than before, but most of them worse. I wrote verses myself which appeared less inadequate than usual....

"Love, wisest of gods.... But love had not been to blame for that negligence, for the harshness and indifference mingled with passion like sand with the gold borne along by a stream, for that blind self-content of a man too completely happy, and who is growing old. Could I have been so grossly satisfied? Antinous was dead. Far from loving too much, as doubtless Servianus was proclaiming at that moment in Rome, I had not been loving enough to force the boy to live on. ...The most malicious lies were accurate in their way; they accused me of having sacrificed him and, in a sense, I had done so."

The mystery of the boy's untimely death only adds to the fascination of this love affair. Lambert describes it: "One day in the slanting sunlight of late October in the year 130 A.D. a body was found in the murky receding floodwaters of the river Nile. It was that of a young man, aged between eighteen and twenty, athletic in build, with a massive chest, hair clustered over the brow and down the neck in thick curls and a broad face of such unusual and poignant beauty that it was to haunt the imagination and the conscience of civilized men for nearly two thousand years.

"There were no signs of violence on the body: not a clue why such a vigorous and healthy young man had met so premature and isolated a death: only that he had drowned. The scrawny boatmen of Hir-wer, the miserable little town of mud brick cringing under the stumpy columns and haughty pylons of the ancient temple of Rameses II on the east bank of the river, must have jabbered in wonder as they saw the corpse dragged out of the brown silt and carried over to the lush new grass beneath the palm trees of their plain. Who was he? What had he been in life? How did he die: was it accident, suicide or even murder? Their questions have been repeated and debated ever since. The onlookers and indeed the whole world were soon to learn that this was not just another anonymous corpse cast up by the sullen river to be hastily buried in the nearby desert before it turned green and putrid.

"After his two brief decades of human life, this young man had just attained immortality and, with it, at least another two millennia of posthumous and turbulent notoriety. His name must have been whispered from mouth to mouth with that mixture of avid curiosity and malicious speculation which probably had always been and certainly was ever after to be his lot. All those who gathered to watch the body borne away, the courtiers, scholars and sailors from the flotilla of imperial barges moored nearby, perhaps some of the immaculate linen-clad priests from the sacred city of Hermopolis on the opposite bank, the grimy folk of Hir-wer, would have been amazed if they could have foreseen the extraordinary consequences of that day's event."

Lambert feels that Antinous had either committed suicide out of despair of his difficult relationship with Hadrian or, more sinisterly still, had, on the advice of magicians, sacrificed himself or even been sacrificed to save the Emperor from some hideous fate. "That became the standard view which the ancient historians peddled down to posterity. Hadrian himself felt obliged to issue a curt denial of the last allegation, but the ambiguous brevity of his words provoked only further suspicion and surmise.

"...After his death in 138 there was always a thin stream of pagan criticism of the apotheosis. But it was the Christians who kept the scandal burning, stoking the flames with new explosive ingredients. Timidly under Hadrian himself and his adoptive successors, but boldly for centuries thereafter, they lambasted this most recent spurious man-made divinity and the cheap deceptions of his cult, as a means of attacking the credentials of the whole pagan pantheon. It was they who, obliquely at first and then frontally in a shrill and outraged chorus, raised that other and, for them, ugly and sinful issue: sex. This so-called god Antinous, they asserted, had been nothing more than the depraved and willing object of Hadrian's perverted passion and this consecration of a lust demonstrated the ultimate profanity and worthlessness of the old religion. ...At the end of antiquity, the memory of Antinous might also have been buried forever. Ironically, it was the very scandal which kept it alive."

Yourcenar says, "We are rich in portraits of Antinous; they range in quality from the mediocre to the incomparable. Despite variations due to the skill of the respective sculptors or to the age of the model, or to differences between portraits made from life and those executed to commemorate the youth after death, all are striking and deeply moving because of the incredible realism of the face, always immediately recognizable and nevertheless so diversely interpreted, and because they are examples, unique in classical antiquity, of survival and repetition in stone of a countenance which was neither that of a statesman nor of a philosopher, but simply of one who was loved. Among these portraits the two most beautiful are the least known: they are also the only ones which transmit to us the name of the sculptor. One is the bas-relief signed by Antonianos of Aphrodisias and found some fifty years ago on the property of an agronomic institute, the Fundi Rustici, in the Committee Room of which it is now placed...."

"...But in the thousand years after the end of paganism, it was the writings of those early Fathers or Christian apologists, widely read, copied and circulated, which perpetuated vividly the memory of Antinous and indeed crystallized his character and that of his apotheosis for long to come," Lambert asserts. "There was a perplexing and memorable mixture of praise, blame and pity for him: praise of his beauty, blame for his morals and pity for his fate. Though St. Jerome compares him to a public male concubine, he also declares him 'a boy of uncommonly outstanding beauty'. One minute the violent Tertullian denounces him as a 'bugger', the next he almost pityingly depicts this new boy-god as 'unhappy' and later rapturously asks 'What Ganymede was more fair?' No wonder the memory of Antinous survived. Who would not be struck by Prudentius' scathing image of Antinous nestling in Hadrian's 'purple clad bosom' and being 'robbed of his manhood' or lolling on a couch 'listening to the prayers in the temples with his husband'? Who could not be moved by Clement's profound sorrow at this boy 'of unsurpassed beauty ... blighted by outrage ... in the flower of his youth'? Who would not thrill to the thunderous fulminations of St. Athanasius, vented in about 350 A.D. but extracted here from a free and robust translation of 1713: 'And such a one is the new god Antinous, that was the Emperor Hadrian's minion and the slave of his unlawful pleasures; a wretch, whom those that worshipped in obedience to the Emperor's command, and for fear of his vengeance, knew and confessed to be a man, and not a good or deserving man either, but a sordid and loathsome instrument of his master's lust.

"This shameless and scandalous boy died in Egypt when the court was there; and forthwith his Imperial Majesty issued out an order or edict strictly requiring and commanding his loving subjects to acknowledge his departed page a deity and to pay him his quota of divine reverences and honors as such: a resolution and act which did more effectually publish and testify to the world how entirely the Emperor's unnatural passion survived the foul object of it; and how much his master was devoted to his memory, than it recorded his own crime and condemnation, immortalized his infamy and shame, and bequeathed to mankind a lasting and notorious specimen of the true origin and extraction of all idolatry....' How could anyone ever forget Antinous and Hadrian after reading that?

7

"In those days, it was common for the pages to the court to be separately housed, under the control of a master, usually a freedman, for training. It was as one of these, we can presume, that Antinous started his career. These boys, often from well-to-do backgrounds and, as the graffiti scratched onto the surviving walls vividly tell us, from all over the Greco-Roman world, were being schooled not only to perform domestic duties in the household while young but to graduate into civil servants when older. As such they were highly prized and cared for. In Nero's extravagant days they travelled in special carriages, their delicate complexions protected from the climate by masks of ointment and breadcrumbs, their bodies provocatively clad in tucked-up tunics and adorned by silver rings. In later, more discreet, times they wore gold tunics and purple boots. The school was originally housed on the Palatine Hill in part of the Domus Gelotiana, but by Hadrian's day another had been opened on the Caelian Hill, in the street called Caput Africanae, though some of the rooms in the old one may still have been used, if only for punishment purposes."

Sensuality is the quality most seen in Antinous, yet it is difficult to pinpoint where it resides. Lambert asks, "Is it in the arch of the upper lip, in the liquid protrusion of the lower one, in the fullness of the cheeks, the ambiguous longing of the eyes, the tousled luxuriance of the hair or the voluptuous surface of the skin? There is no gainsaying that Antinous does exert a physical magnetism even from the marble and must have kindled sensual appetites in the flesh. Some authors go much further, basing themselves on the exceptional bust of the Sala Rotonda and the relief of the Villa Albani. Now, it is not just sensuality but 'nauseating satiety,' lasciviousness and vice; not melancholy but sulkiness, not energy but cruelty, not reticence but emptiness, not resignation but impotence. Perhaps these and a few other eccentric images do hint at such extremes: but an Antinous composed of them is surely a caricature. It is difficult to accept that a sensitive and exacting man such as Hadrian would sustain an intense love for someone so difficult, depraved or vapid, still less that other people who knew the boy or his reputation would genuinely adore such a capricious young monster as a god.

"...Even his severest Christian critics readily admitted that 'his beauty was unequalled'. But it was of a novel kind, with distinctive features which pervade all of his images, however varied (including those in the Egyptian mode), and which established a new fashion of male perfection for decades thereafter."

Oh, those Greeks! Antinous was merely living up to a great tradition. Consider Alexander the Great, who ruled most of the known world from 336 to 323 B.C. We know he gave in to many a temptation, but still he remained loyal to Hephaiston, who was the man whom Alexander loved, Robin Lane-Fox says in the book Alexander the Great: "and for the rest of their lives their relationship remained as intimate as it is now irrecoverable: Alexander was only defeated once, the Cynic philosophers said long after his death, and that was by Hephaiston's thighs ... Hephaiston's age is not known and its discovery could put their relationship in an unexpected light; he may even have been the older of the two ... At the age of thirty Alexander was still Hephaiston's lover although most young Greeks have grown out of the fashion by then and an older man would have given up or turned to a younger attraction. Their affair was a strong one. Hephaiston grew to lead Alexander's cavalry most ably and to become his Vizier before dying a divine hero, worthy of posthumous worship.

"'Sex and sleep,' Alexander is said to have remarked, 'alone make me conscious that I am mortal.'"

For us mortals, over the years, yielding to temptation got more and more dangerous. "Tolerance, I believe, to be one of the greatest virtues," Earl Jowitt said in the House of Lords, in 1954, "but a tolerance which is prepared to take no notice of that which is essentially evil and wicked is not at all the sort of tolerance we want ... we are here face to face with a terrible evil and we have to find a solution which is not based on prejudice or on merely a dislike of what is a very evil thing ... it seems to me that the people who are cursed in this way must also resist their temptation. That is the least we can expect of them."

That kind of prevailing attitude in England explains why David Hockney found America so refreshing when he visited New York in 1961. For Hockney, who has said his great inspiration was the Alexandrian Greek poet Constance Cavafy, found America "unbelievably sexy and attractive ... in America you can always find somebody else if it's just sex you're wanting."

And then in 1965, Hockney was in Hollywood when he was tempted by a "ravishingly beautiful blond boy." Hockney says he gave in to temptation and "it was lust on my part, sheer lust, and I thought fantastic." Hockney has said it was the only time he was really promiscuous, and this boy just swept him away. Hockney took the boy to New York, and then to London, where Hockney discovered that the lad was dumb, "really very dumb. He'd no interest in anything at all. Have some sex, and that's it; absolutely no interest; all he was interested in, really, was Hollywood bars. After a week, I said, ' I think you should go back.'"

The go-go boy later died tragically of a drug overdose. "I felt very sad," Hockney said in My Early Years. "He was a sweet boy."

SWEET LIKE CANDY
John Patrick

"I'm coming!" Casey says, his eyes rolling up, his pelvis punching back and forth as Jeremy keeps his fingers moving. Casey locks his thighs, squeezing Jeremy with his thigh muscles, amazed at everything, amazed because everything has happened so fast, amazed he's still wearing his underwear, amazed that a guy who looks like Jeremy, so strong, so studly, would do this. While Casey's cock gushes, Jeremy's face flushes, he groans, removes his fingers, watches the cum fly, and says, "Wow!"

Quickly now, Casey stands, takes everything off.

"God, it's so big," Jeremy says, and Casey smiles and says he isn't that big, but he makes it bounce, just to make Jeremy want it more. Jeremy touches it again; he loves the pleasure of a hard cock in his hand. Especially a new one. No matter how much he likes the stability of his monogamous relationship with Gil, the first touching of a new penis is always wonderful.

Jeremy tears off his clothes, and the fresh contact of their bodies is electric. He goes back to sucking it again. Casey winces. "Does it hurt?" Jeremy asks.

Casey tells him, "Kinda," as he slips a hand down over Jeremy's erection. Jeremy wants his own relief, and whispers, "Oh, yeah. Go on, suck it."

Casey leads Jeremy to the bedroom, makes Jeremy lie back on the bed and open his legs, his knees up, his thighs wide apart to show his full package, the balls, the cock, the anus. Casey takes a long look at everything Jeremy has to offer. Jeremy quivers because it turns him on so much, the lust in Casey's eyes, the hunger for dick, for ass.

Casey licks the cock, smiles. "God, you're sweet, sweet like candy."

Jeremy blushes. Sweet like candy. His cock was sweet like candy? Nobody had ever told him that before. But if it's so sweet, why isn't Casey sucking it? He wants Casey's whole mouth on it. What is he waiting for? Casey is looking at it, tugging the foreskin out as if to see how far it will stretch. Then tickling him lower down, in the crack of his ass. Jeremy squirms, trying to avoid the teasing. But Casey insists, using his middle finger, pushing it inside Jeremy's ass to see how tight he is. Then pulling his finger out, smelling it. "Oh, yeah, sweet like candy," he says. "Whoever you're living with, he's not taking care of you."

"No, no he isn't," Jeremy moans, aching. "Please, you take care of me."

11

Casey chuckles, tells him to take it easy. "We've got all afternoon, sweet boy."

"No, I've got to get back soon."

Teasing him again, taking his time, Casey continues to inspect the cock. Casey loves foreskin, and seldom gets to see any. "You shouldn't rush," he says.

But Jeremy has to rush it, at least he feels like he has to. He hikes his knees up farther as Casey's fingers start fucking his ass. Jeremy rocks his legs, holding his knees back with his hands now, loving each thrust of the long fingers in his ass. Jeremy grabs his cock, jerks it.

"That's it," Casey says. "Come on, let me see you come." And come he does, his ass going wild as Casey's fingers slam into him again and again.

At the end, another cry as Casey drops his head to clamp his mouth on Jeremy's spurting cock, Jeremy moaning as he drops his legs onto Casey's shoulders. He humps at Casey's mouth, coming down as Casey licks the cum on the insides of the foreskin. Casey wipes his mouth with his fingers, lifts himself up.

"Want another beer?"

Jeremy nods, watching Casey as he leaves the bed and walks out of the bedroom. He reaches down to touch his wet cock, still semi-hard.

Casey returns with two beers. "You got some problems at home, I take it."

Jeremy nods.

"He doesn't give you enough?"

"That's not it, really." He rolls over, hiding his cock.

Casey rolls him back, pulls his legs apart. "Come on, don't hide that sweet cock from me." His green eyes seem to glitter in the afternoon light as he gazes at Jeremy's cock. "God, I love an uncut cock."

Casey guzzles his beer, puts the bottle away and goes down on Jeremy again. Jeremy finishes his beer, watching Casey lick, kiss, and nibble at his cock.

Soon Jeremy is hard again, and he drops the beer to the floor. He moans, no longer caring about anything except the mouth on his cock, the twirling tongue teasing the exposed, sensitive head. There is nothing in the world like being wanted, he thinks, and he's wanted more than most. Gil loves him, sure, but too much sometimes. It all becomes too much sometimes, and he has to cruise, to go where he knows boys hang out. And that's what happened today, after he'd had lunch with his girlpal Blanche. He was strolling, window shopping, keeping his options open, and then he saw Casey. Casey was on his way into his apartment building, a bag of groceries giving him a bit of a problem as he opened the door. Jeremy went to him, helped him, and the connection was made. The offer of a beer was made. For a heavy moment Jeremy held himself motionless. He felt he was standing on a boundary that he could cross only once. And then in one decisive step he was over it. He followed Casey into the building....

Jeremy can't take much more of Casey's sucking, and tells him he has to get home. Jeremy leaves the bed and hurries to get dressed and leave. Casey tries to stop him, but Jeremy insists.

"I can't."

"All right, here's my number, call me. Okay?"

"Yes."

And Jeremy's out the door, trembling, feeling guilty.

In the evening, it's the same old routine with Gil. They eat, then Gil retreats to his study to go over papers he brought to the apartment in his bulging briefcase. Jeremy lies on the sofa watching a Dirty Harry movie, but he can't concentrate on it; he keeps thinking about Casey. The memories make him hot again, the thoughts of Casey sucking him, fucking him. He closes his eyes and brings himself to orgasm, then goes to bed.

Saturday evening, Valentine's Day, Gil takes Jeremy to their favorite cafe. Gil is kind and loving as they sit facing each other in a booth. "I love you," Gil says.

Jeremy smiles. They touch hands while they wait for the food.

Gil is in a hurry to eat dinner. He is up for sex tonight, Jeremy knows. He also knows that Gil will be in such a hurry to come, he'll get off within minutes and then roll off and fall fast asleep.

And this is how it happens, and Gil doesn't even realize Jeremy has not come. In the darkness, Jeremy stares at the ceiling.

Gil falls asleep, but Jeremy is restless.

After a while, Jeremy leaves the bed and walks into the bathroom to jack off, but he keeps thinking of Casey. He goes to the living room and dials the number. Casey answers. Jeremy wonders if he could see him.

Casey says, "Oh. Well, I was going out, but...." He pauses. Jeremy takes a deep breath. "C'mon over. Right away, okay?"

"Okay."

"I'll be waiting, sweet cock."

Within moments of arriving at Casey's, Jeremy is in bed with Casey. His head rests on the pillow, his ass in the air, his body totally vulnerable.

Kneeling behind him, Casey enters him, roughly, and starts fucking. "How does it feel, sweet cock?" Jeremy moans. His ass feels bruised, on fire. Gil has a thick cock and it always hurts afterward, and now Casey is in where Gil just left and the pain is dizzying, yet Jeremy says, "I love it."

Casey smiles, moves again, thrusting forcefully, slamming against Jeremy. The penetration is deep, total, and the fucking is done with a vigorousness that Jeremy has missed. He gets off being taken like this by another man, the force of a strong fuck, of a man stretching him wide open, making him beg for it.

As Casey continues, Jeremy jerks his own cock, secure now that this is right, this fucking outside his relationship with Gil. All he cares about now is the pleasure, the pleasure that comes from having someone so skilled satisfying Jeremy and himself. Suddenly Casey pulls out, barks, "Roll over, I wanna see your sweet cock."

Jeremy groans, dismayed. No one has ever loved his cock as much as Casey apparently does. Jeremy's cock quivers with excitement. Casey begins sucking it, making love to it. Jeremy shudders. What a thrill it is to be taken like this. This is what he needs, what Gil never gives him anymore, if, indeed, he ever did. Jeremy trembles, waiting, not knowing how long he will continue sucking before he starts fucking again. He weaves his hips from side to side, silently urging Casey to really fuck him!

Casey smiles, responds, slowly pushes his erection inside Jeremy's ass. He leans over Jeremy's body as he penetrates deep inside him. Jeremy whimpers as Casey grasps Jeremy's erection and jerks it while he fucks. Casey cries out, his cock spasming, a hot flood of cum into Jeremy's ass, an intense orgasm, and Casey continues thrusting. Jeremy groans with pleasure as Casey squeezes the cock, and finally Jeremy comes -hard, harder than he has in months.

Jeremy is still panting when Casey pulls out, rolls over on his side exhausted.

Jeremy takes Casey in his arms and kisses him, pressing into Casey's sweaty flesh. Casey cuddles against him, flushed and happy, his lips pressed against Jeremy's neck. "Such a sweet cock. Such a hot ass."

"I have to go," Jeremy says.

On the way out, Jeremy's eyes go to a huge arrangement of velvety burgundy roses in an elaborate vase on a low table in the hallway.

"Beautiful aren't they?" Casey says

"Yes, they are."

"You take 'em," Casey says.

"Oh, no."

"Please. I insist. I have to leave tomorrow and they'll all be dead by the time I get back. I want you to have them."

He takes the roses from the vase and goes to the kitchen. Jeremy stands in the doorway watching this beautiful, naked man as he lays them in a box in a layer of white tissue, then a layer of green, then cellophane, and finally a heavy candy-cane paper.

"From your lover?" Jeremy asks while he watches this operation.

"Yes. He's in California, and I'm joining him tomorrow for a week or so."

"He's a lucky man."

Casey's smile becomes pure spun sugar as he delivers the box to Jeremy's waiting arms. "And your lover's a lucky man, too." He chuckles. "And we're lucky to have found each other, sweet cock."

Jeremy nods.

Casey tells him to call him in a week or so, and kisses him goodnight, the long box crushed between them.

Gil looks around the bedroom and is startled to realize Jeremy has left him alone. At almost the same instant he experiences something far more startling: visions of two bodies on the bed, floating easily, timelessly, Jeremy being fucked by someone who is not Gil. He blinks, and the images vanish, leaving the bed darker, duller. He flicks the switch on the bedside lamp. The silence in the room is suddenly flat and harsh. He crosses to the window and stares down into the street. Traffic moves with eerie soundlessness on the avenue eight stories below. He crosses quickly to the bedroom door. He sniffs as he walks toward the entryway. A smell hangs in the air. It hasn't been there before. The smell is familiar. "Jeremy," he calls.

Finally he finds Jeremy in the kitchen, putting roses in a vase. He shoots him a questioning expression. "Where were you?"

Jeremy tries very hard to look as if he honestly can't imagine what the hell Gil is talking about.

"Out," Jeremy says, concentrating on the job at hand, then standing back, admiring the dozen beautiful roses.

Gil feels something constrict in his stomach. He rarely questions anything Jeremy does, and he almost never questions it in the tone of voice he uses now: "Where did you get those?"

"I found a shop open late. I'm sorry I forgot Valentine's Day."

Gil realizes this is hardly the moment to confront him, to ask point-blank if he has been fucking around, if his new admirer gave him roses after fucking the daylights out of him.

"It was an impulse," Jeremy says.

Gil isn't buying it. Gil senses a great empty space between him and his young lover, more space than there is in the entire room. But he knows if he presses Jeremy, he'll hate himself. "I didn't mean to question you."

"I'm glad," Jeremy says, kissing Gil on the cheek as he passes him on his way to the bedroom.

Gil follows him into the bedroom. Jeremy undresses, down to his Jockey shorts. He goes into the bathroom, and a moment later the shower patters like bullets against the curtain.

Gil sighs and gets into bed. He leaves the light on low. After two years, he has begun to feel more and more that he is losing Jeremy, and then Jeremy does something crazy like buying roses in the middle of the night.

Finally Jeremy comes out of the bathroom. He is glorious in his nudity, and Gil notices for the first time in a long time that Jeremy's visits to the gym are paying off: new muscles ridge his back, and his waist has gotten leaner. Jeremy climbs into bed. The springs bend under him, momentarily pulling him toward Gil. His eyes take a long swig of Gil, who is staring back at him. He blinks, draws in a slow, deep breath, then asks, "What is it?"

"You're sweet, you know. You're really sweet."

Jeremy chuckles, mostly to himself. "Yeah, I know."

PURE TEMPTATION
John Patrick

One night in early June, for one of the few times in Walter's life, he took delight in pure temptation. He first saw the flirty boy standing out in front of the bar, waiting for god-knows what. The boy seemed to be saying, Don't undress me with your eyes. You can only have me in my clothes. He was a blond, full-lipped, sleepy-eyed, heavy-lidded. His face had a dreamy innocence that Walter found absolutely captivating.

Walter didn't mind that the boy was just flirting with him, because through the tight wrap of the lad's clothing, Walter experienced the strange pleasure one can take in a body dressed for seduction. In Walter's mind, in those few moments they clung and touched more deeply than the naked ever can. A car pulled up and the boy got in and was gone.

The last time Walter had experienced anything like it, he found, to his great surprise, the object of his desire's obsessive craving for intimacy and for the most private of pleasures ran as high and strong as his, and seemed insatiable.

And now Walter wondered how he might have made out with this new temptation. He could not put the lad's image out of his mind. The impact of seeing him there, on the street, without meeting him again, continued to haunt him. But then it happened a second time. The boy appeared before Walter once again, by chance, out of nowhere, the experience of seeing this boy now became a more painful, almost unbearable test.

Walter had gone to the theater and the boy, small and lithe, shoved past him, clutching a Coke bottle and pressing his round, hard buttocks into his privates as Walter rose politely from his seat to let the boy and his older, well-dressed benefactor by.

At intermission, Walter saw the boy alone. He started to approach him, but then the benefactor suddenly appeared at the boy's arm, presenting another Coke.

Walter stood there, watching them. He noticed for the first time what eyes the boy had, as dark as any night has ever been. And he remembered that evening light when he first saw the boy. Walter had been going to leave weeks ago, but the light here in Los Angeles had kept him there. It had fascinated him, this light with no shadows that they have only in L.A., the city of angels.

And then he saw the boy. An angel, a dark, forbidding angel.

17

Walter watched them go back into the auditorium. He decided he could not follow them. He didn't care for the play; he just wanted to go back to his hotel. Out in the cool night air, Walter decided to put the top down and drive. Walter drove for over an hour and he was restless. He decided to stop in at Hunter's for a drink.

Johnny had been to the theater, and the john who had taken him said he was glad they had had sex before they went as he was too tired to do anything but sleep. Johnny said that was fine with him, and asked the john to let him out on Santa Monica Boulevard.

Now Johnny was ready to party. He went into Hunter's and found a stool at the bar. He waited impatiently for the barkeep. When he turned around, he saw another john, about forty, trim, dark hair, just watching him, across the bar. Johnny recognized the man. It was the same man who had stood out in front of this same bar a few nights ago and cruised him, and the same man who cruised him just a couple of hours ago at the theater. The man got up, came over to Johnny.

"Hi," Johnny said.

"Hi," Walter said, lifting one eyebrow.

Walter bought Johnny a drink. The iced Gold Tequila slid down Johnny's throat, and that exquisite salt-sour taste lingered in his mouth. While Walter told him everything he didn't like about the play, Johnny finished the drink, and sat in a state of pure bliss. The alcohol-induced drugged state eased away the tensions of the past few hours. The bartender returned and asked if Johnny wanted another. Walter nodded. Johnny smiled. "I'd love another."

Walter stroked Johnny's thigh. Johnny moved away and reached for his Margarita. Johnny needed another drink. "May I smoke?" Walter asked, and Johnny nodded. Walter lit a cigarette and inhaled deeply.

Johnny moved close again, and Walter's hand dropped to Johnny's groin. "See, you've put your hand on the problem," Johnny started to explain, his voice hush. "It runs in my family. My daddy also had the problem!"

Walter interrupted, "What are you talking about? What problem?"

Johnny sighed, "Well, I am... well, as you can see, I'm big for my age. For my size."

Walter squeezed the bulge. "I don't see that as a problem at all."

"It is, well, in certain situations."

"I think I understand, but that won't matter to me, you see."

"Oh?"

"I just like to watch."

"Oh."

Johnny liked it when they were quick about it. The way they would bear down, the way their mouths would open, they way they loved to drink it all in. Sometimes he would count, to count down. "Okay, now," he would say, and they would take his cum.

Then there were the guys who came, and didn't care if he did. And then there were the ones who never came at all.

"It doesn't matter," they would say. Sometimes they acted irritated if Johnny seemed not to care either, and then Johnny would say, "We can always try," and they would shrug their shoulders as if it really didn't matter, that it wasn't important.

But then Johnny would grab their pricks and say, "Trust me. It's my job."

Johnny knew Walter wanted more than to just watch him, but he went along with it. Back at Walter's hotel, the bedroom was decorated in pink. Johnny was astounded because he had expected something different; but it was all pink, the walls pink, the bedspread pink satin, the lamp shades of pink, and a pink bathroom. The effect was soothing; it made Johnny slow down, let his john take the lead for a change.

"May I undress you?" Johnny nodded. Just watch? Sure.

Walter removed Johnny's shirt and knelt to remove the boy's trousers and boots. Walter was thrilled. Having the boy relax and gradually become naked like this was a delightful treat. The closeness of the lad tantalized Walter and his excitement became intense as he imagined the boy fully naked, erect. Johnny remained passive, pliant, with a look of faint amusement as he watched Walter's shaking hands working to get his clothes off. Walter stopped to drink it all in. He sighed at the sight of the boy's magnificently delicate musculature. He nuzzled the bulge through Johnny's briefs, his hot breath tempting Johnny's prick with the promise of pleasure. He lingered, pulling aside the briefs, and sliding his tongue over the hardening prick, then he rose, his mouth moving upward over Johnny's stomach. He kissed, then sucked the waiting nipples, one after the other. Johnny slowly gyrated his hips as he fell backwards onto the bed.

Walter climbed over Johnny, his tongue snaking across Johnny's entire body. Johnny was panting hard as his desperation climbed. He wanted Walter to suck him. He had not come for the man who took him to the theater. He had not come all day, and Johnny needed to come at least twice a day. Walter tugged off Johnny's briefs, then got between his thighs. He took considerable time inspecting the massive organ. Such a cock would be a problem for some, Walter could see. It would even be a problem for Walter if Walter chose to take it up his ass, but that was not Walter's thing. Walter was a cocksucker, and this oblong, pink slab of meat was, without doubt, a cocksucker's dream come true. Walter commenced lapping at Johnny's cock, now swollen to nine inches in length, and Johnny could feel Walter's breath coming in short pants; Walter was becoming excited too. This was the only sign Johnny needed. He began gasping and groaning thrashing about. He was wild, craving more of this pleasure.

"You said you were only going to watch," Johnny moaned.

"It'll be all right I'll pay you more."

"Okay." Johnny lay back, satisfied, resplendent in his nakedness. He was so completely relaxed now he was almost asleep.

Walter sucked the huge organ into his mouth working his tongue up and down it. Johnny was soon moaning, and writhing on the bed, gasping and muttering "Suck it...." Johnny clutched at Walter's head, as the spasms overtook him. Walter pulled off the cock and the cum flowed over his hand.

"My god," Walter sighed as the cum just kept coming.

Finally, Johnny was done and he swung his legs around Walter's waist. "Fuck me," Johnny begged.

The idea stunned Walter. He had never imagined penetrating Johnny. It was enough to make him come. Even just watch him come. More than enough.

Yet, he rested his hands flat on the under-thigh and lifted Johnny up. Johnny's ass cheeks splayed open. Walter licked, then kissed the asshole, then rose to tear off his pants and briefs. His six-inch cock was dark, sleek, uncut. Fully hard, the foreskin disappeared, and the head was leaking pre-cum as he got back between Johnny's outstretched thighs.

Johnny looked at the prick. "Fuck me."

Walter agreed, brought the bottle of lube from the night table, and Johnny trembled as he watched Walter spread the lotion over his long fingers. Walter could feel the heat in the lad's face. Walter squeezed out another glob of lotion, and this time he painted Johnny's anus with it. Johnny groaned, his eyes closed as Walter's finger slowly pushed inside his lubricated ass. "You're so tight," Walter said. His finger stretched the tight ring, slowly sliding in and out. Johnny shuddered with pleasure. Yes, Walter thought, the boy does want this. He wants to be taken this way. Walter was gentle as he stretched the opening, whispering to Johnny, asking him if it's good, does he like it?

"Oh, yes."

Walter added a second finger, pushed the second finger inside the lad's ass, pushed both fingers deep inside the channel as Walter urged Johnny to open up to him. Johnny moaned as he did his best to remain open and loose to the invading fingers, gasping at intervals as the two fingers slid in and out of his ass. Walter was gentle and forceful at the same time, and Johnny's ass was now receptive, yielding, craving more. Johnny was obviously thrilled by it now, shuddering as Walter kissed his buttocks again.

Finally, Walter's cockhead pricked the ass lips. Johnny squirmed. Walter's action was slow, at first, but as his thrusts became more demanding, Johnny let himself go, matching Walter's pace, pushing hard into Walter. The sight of Johnny's delightful cock growing hard again, combined with the sensation of the penetration, made Walter tell Johnny how much he loved it. Walter loved all of it. He loved everything about Johnny.

"Come for me, man," Johnny begged as he jerked his hips back and forth, and his ass clutched at Walter's prick.

"Oh," Walter cried out, now over the edge, and his orgasm was fierce, his cum gushing into Johnny.

Johnny agreed to stay overnight. Walter said he wanted to feast on Johnny's prick once again, "After breakfast."

While the boy's nerves vibrated with happiness, he feasted on a sumptuous room service breakfast. Johnny never ate breakfast, so this was an unusual treat.

Stomach filled, freshly showered, with a moan of passion, Johnny threw himself onto the bed. He rolled his naked body from side to side, and then finally he settled on his back with his legs open. "I like what you do to me."

Walter smiled at Johnny. His eyes on Johnny's delectable boy-cunt, Walter quickly dropped his bathrobe.

Walter climbed onto the bed and immediately dropped his head to run his tongue over Johnny's hairless belly. Johnny moaned, raised his knees, and opened his thighs in a definite invitation. Walter's tongue left a wet trail of saliva as he slid his mouth down into Johnny's pubic bush. When he glanced up at Johnny's face, Walter found Johnny watching him, Johnny's blue eyes fixed on his mouth, Johnny waiting. Returning his attention to the huge, semi-hard prick directly under his chin, Walter extended his tongue for the first touch of the morning. Johnny groaned, raising his knees farther and holding them up with his hands.

Walter blew his warm breath on Johnny's open asshole, grazing the flesh with his mouth, teasing him. He fluttered his tongue along the outer lips, up and down, inside the channel. His own cock tingled as his tongue invaded Johnny. He slid his hands under Johnny's ass and he lifted the lower part of Johnny's body to feast on the asshole. Johnny had one of the biggest pricks Walter had ever seen, but he also possessed the most delectable anus Walter had ever encountered. Johnny groaned, his mouth open, his neck craned as he looked down to watch Walter's mouth take possession of his asshole. Walter wanted to fuck it again, to feel his cock slide in and out again. He admitted to Johnny that he had promised only to suck the prick, but Johnny said it was okay. "Whatever," Johnny said.

Walter lay on his back and wanted Johnny to climb over him and fuck himself with the massive hard-on. Johnny liked the idea, and climbed over Walter, straddled him, and then Walter took Johnny's buttocks in his hands and helped guide Johnny to his prick.

As the prick slid into Johnny, Walter wondered if Johnny understood how much he adored him. From the moment he saw him, Walter now told the boy, he was tempted by him.

As Walter's cock went in and out of Johnny's rectum, Johnny stroked himself, then his body suddenly jerked forward. Walter heard Johnny's heavy breathing, and when he looked up, he whimpered with lust at the sight of Johnny's cock gushing cum all over Walter's chest.

Johnny kept Walter in him; it seemed he fucked Walter's prick even harder after he had come. Johnny, Walter realized, certainly seemed more interested in giving him pleasure than anyone he'd ever met. Walter told Johnny how perfect his cock was, that it made him salivate. "Sure," Johnny said. He had heard it all so many times before, but he never grew tired of hearing it. He loved it when a man told him how pretty he was, how nice his cock was. But Walter went even beyond that, with all this praise of his asshole.

Now Johnny surprised Walter. He pulled off and, kneeling between Walter's thighs, he hoisted Walter's legs over his shoulders and got busy lubricating his renewed cock and then Walter's asshole.

"Oh, no," Walter gasped, but Johnny was already guiding the prick into Walter. Walter groaned as it went in. He closed his eyes and focused on the feel of it. A shudder passed through his body as the cock was shoved all the way in.

Walter heard Johnny whispering sweet words of encouragement. Johnny pulled out, applied more lube, making everything so deliciously slippery. Johnny began screwing it in and out slowly, playing with Walter's hard-on. When Walter cried out, Johnny started slamming his cock in to make Walter's orgasm more intense.

Johnny was preparing to leave the room. He noticed a book on the table and picked it up. Walter's picture was on the back of the jacket. "You wrote this, eh?"

"Every word," Walter said. "You may have it if you like."

Johnny smiled. "You know, if the way you make love is anything to go by then you must write some damn good stories."

"Thank you."

"Will you write about me?"

"Oh, yes. Now that I've seen all of your beauty, I will have to write about it. Not writing about it would be a sin. It would be like visiting Mount Everest and not writing about it."

It was all too much for Johnny to absorb, and he simply smiled, and, with Walter's book tucked under his arm, let himself out.

COMPANIONS IN ARMS
Tim Scully

"That isn't you, by chance, moving into this building?" asked Dhasan.

"As a matter of fact it is. How do you know?"

"I saw the name 'Scully' on one of the crates which came last week. It is sufficiently unusual for me to put two and two together and come up with the right answer."

I felt a bit annoyed. I had wanted to tell him myself and I hoped very much that he wouldn't put any more figures together. And, if he did, that he'd come up with the wrong answer.

"Can you afford it?" asked Neil from the sofa. "These places are expensive."

Trust a teenager to ask the question that everyone else would like to ask but doesn't like to!

"Actually I'm sharing it with a guy from work," I said.

Two pairs of ears pricked up.

"Oh yes," said Dhasan. "Who is he?"

"Chap called Danny Taylor."

"How old is he?" asked Neil.

"Oh. Twenty. Twenty-one. Something like that."

The exact figure was twenty and three months.

"And is he... er..." Neil persisted.

"Not at all. Definitely and categorically not. Danny is one hundred and one percent heterosexual so forget it," I said. "Anyway, you don't need anyone else. You've got Dhasan and me."

That afternoon we had both had him. All three of us were in that pleasantly drowsy state that seems to waft over you when you've had a really good session. I still had the taste of his spunk in my mouth. After giving him an hour to recharge, Dhasan had fucked his ass, allowing me, as he often did, to stay and watch. A more pleasant sight was hard to imagine – unless perhaps it was Danny Taylor.

"Tell us more," said Dhasan. "I like to know something about my neighbors."

There was quite a lot that I couldn't tell him and a lot I didn't want him to know.

Part of Defense Contract 1043 was moved to our factory. I'm sorry. That is all I can tell you. More than half the world's governments would love to get their hands or their eyes on any part of D 1043.

There were seven of them all told. Doctor this, doctor that, a few misters with more letters after their names than I've had hot dinners and Danny. The research people were housed in a small block on the outer perimeter. Our factory site used to be an airfield in the war. Danny, whose job was to keep a running audit on their expenses, was moved into my office. They couldn't find a desk for him so his computer had to go on a table they brought up from the canteen. I didn't mind at all. From my desk I had a wonderful view of two very long legs and a very substantial package at the top of them.

He was very, very, good looking. Tall, dark haired and with an attractive, smiling face. Needless to say, there was a non- stop procession of girls every day. "Danny, do you know how to change the cartridge in a bubble-jet printer?" "Danny, if you've got time can you come and look at the computer in our office? I think it may have a virus."

I was about to put my foot down on the grounds that they were disturbing my work when Danny did it for me. He explained that what he was doing was secret, went to see one of his bosses and a notice went up on our door that very day: 'NO ENTRY FOR UNAUTHORIZED PERSONS'.

"Where are you living, Danny?" I asked one day.

"In digs at the moment. Thirty-four Lewis Street."

"God! That can't be much fun."

"It isn't but it's all I could find. I've got a room and there aren't any bugs as far as I can tell. It's good enough for the moment."

"What do you do in the evenings?"

"Sod all. I stay in. I'm not that keen on getting mugged."

I suggested that perhaps he might like to go out for a drink. He was really keen so, that evening, with some trepidation I drove to Lewis Street. The usual party of teenage boys hung around on the corner. A drunk tottered out of an alley into the road, waved at the car and then collapsed. Empty fast food containers and drink cans swirled round in the breeze. I found number thirty-four. Few of the houses had numbers. You had to deduce from the last numbered house. I rang the bell.

"Who the fuck is that?" somebody shouted from inside. I opened the letter box and shouted "Visitor for Mr. Taylor!"

"Danny! Danny! Somebody for you. Come down and open the fucking door for Christ's sake!"

"Coming, Mrs. Anstey."

The door opened and Danny stepped out looking quite different. Light figure-hugging jeans and a red top set his build off to perfection.

"Phew," he said. "It's good to get out." The smell of boiling cabbage and dirty diapers drifted out of the door with him. I felt quite sick.

I took him to the 'George' which is a really nice pub about five miles out of town. It's on the river bank and, in the summer, it's really nice to sit in the garden and watch the swans glide by and listen to the conversation of the anglers.

Well, as you can imagine, there was a lot I wanted to find out. Three pints later I knew that he was keen on football and keeping fit and madly in love with a girl called Wendy who lived in his home town. He showed me her picture, which he carried in his wallet. She looked a nice enough girl.

Danny was obviously a non starter. There's always the chance with these people that the girl friend is imaginary but I didn't think so. But I did feel genuinely sorry for the guy. Lewis Street is the pits. He had to be got out of there fast and I had a small a very small apartment. It would serve as an interim measure. One of us could sleep in the lounge and the other in the bedroom. Sharing the bathroom was going to be a curse and we'd have to come to some arrangement about buying food and who was to do the cooking. I didn't see it as a long-term solution. Not then.

He was very grateful. He'd pay half the rent more if I wanted. I hadn't realized that D 1043 people were on a different salary scale from the rest of us. He actually liked cooking. He enjoyed shopping. His parents ran a big furniture store in the north of England and would send down anything we wanted. Things looked good.

Things looked even better a few days later. He was standing in our tiny entrance hall rummaging around in the airing cupboard for a towel before taking a shower, and he'd gotten undressed ready. I left the lounge to get a book and came face to butt with the nicest pair of ass cheeks I'd seen for a long time. There was loads of hair on his thighs but those big, marshmallow-soft globes were as smooth as a baby's. He swung round and I do mean 'swung'! It was enormous!

"Oh, hi," he said. "Do you want to use the bathroom? I'm sorry. I should have asked."

"No. No. You go ahead," I replied, unable to take my eyes off the luxuriant hair, his huge balls and, most of all, his monster cock. It was uncut and almost as thick as my wrist.

"I'm trying to find my towel," he said, turning again. As he reached up into the top shelf of the cupboard, his ass contracted beautifully and big dimples formed in the cheeks.

"Ah! Here it is," he said and, wrapping himself in it as if it were a sarong, he vanished into the bathroom. I went into my bedroom to recover my composure.

Wendy, I am sorry to say, proved to be very real indeed. She telephoned almost daily. He'd stand at the phone for ages. "That was Wendy," he'd say when he put the receiver down.

"I guessed as much. All right, is she?"

"Oh god, she's great!" and then he'd tell me practically everything she'd said.

The times I liked best were Thursday evenings. On Thursday evenings he went to his fitness club. He drove there and returned in the briefest, tightest athletic shorts you ever saw. I only caught a glimpse on his departure but Wendy, the silly cow, regularly forgot about the sports club.

"Oh hello, Tim. Is Danny at home?" and I'd tell her for the umpteenth time that he was at the fitness club.

"Can you get him to call me when he comes back?"

Those evenings were great! It didn't matter how interesting the program on TV was. I had to turn the sound off anyway so that he could hear. I just sat back and feasted my eyes on his legs and beautiful butt and delighted myself when I went to bed with fantasies of sliding the shorts down and screwing his ass whilst he kept talking to her.

"Yes, my darling. Oooh! Ah! Nothing my pet. I'll see you on Saturday. Oh, that feels so good!"

He went home every weekend to see her. Despite being so small, the place felt strangely empty without him. Not that it mattered much. I spent most of the weekend at Dhasan's place sucking Neil's delectable young cock or admiring Dhasan's skillful technique. Watching that enormous brown cock vanishing bit by bit into Neil's ass and listening to Neil gurgling as it went into him were enough to make me come. I never wanted to go home.

I was really fond of Dhasan. Sometimes when Neil had gone back to St. Bede's in time for the evening roll call, Dhasan and I would have a session together. Who, faced with a naked eighteen year Indonesian boy with a butt like a brown velvet cushion, and a long, thick, super-sensitive cock, would want to leave it and go home to what I had to suffer?

More often than not, I stayed as long as I could, hoping that, by the time I got home, Danny would have returned and have gone to bed. That was slightly dangerous. When we were back at work on Monday morning he always asked where I'd been. I didn't want him to know anything about Dhasan or Neil so had to lie and lies are so easily found out.

"I went to the cinema?"

"Oh, yes? What was on?"

"I went to the George."

"Was the band there or was it Saturday they were playing?"

Things with Wendy were not going well. I could tell that by the way he slammed the door when he got back.

"Good time?" I'd ask.

"Oh, okay. Yes," but I knew they weren't. He was perfectly all right again on Monday mornings at work but those silent Sunday evenings worried me.

And then, one Saturday afternoon, I was round at Dhasan's as usual. To 'make a pleasant change' as he put it, Dhasan had just fucked my ass whilst Neil sat in the armchair and watched, fondling his cock as he did so.

"I miss you during the week," said Dhasan after he'd withdrawn, leaving me feeling as if I'd been impaled on a post. "I wish you'd move in here with me. There's masses of room and you wouldn't have to pay any rent."

Before I met Danny, I'd have jumped at the chance. I said something about not wanting to leave Danny in the lurch.

"Is he a good fuck?" asked Neil. I was furious and said that, as I had told them both before, Danny wasn't like that. Dhasan took the heat out of the situation by getting out the sandwiches and cakes with which he regaled us on Saturdays. We sat munching them.

"How old did you say this Danny was?" Neil asked.

"Twenty," I said.

"Sounds good. Got a good body has he?" Neil asked. Dhasan raised an eyebrow.

"Well, he goes to a fitness club and he plays football. I suppose he has really," I replied. "I've never really thought about it." For lies, that one took some beating. I found myself thinking about Danny's body most of the day.

"I'd like to meet him some time," said Dhasan. "Why don't you bring him round?"

"He's busy in the week and he goes to see his girlfriend at weekends," I said.

"I'd soon make him forget her," said Neil. "A twenty-year- old with a good body.... Has he got a big cock?"

"No idea."

"I'll bet he has. Is he hairy?"

"I've never noticed. We sleep in separate rooms."

"If it was me, I'd steal a good look sometime. Like when he's going to have a bath or something," said Neil. Things were getting too close for comfort. I hoped I didn't show the embarrassment I felt. Fortunately, Dhasan changed the subject. We finished the sandwiches and cakes and, some time later, I got a mouthful of cream from our teenaged supplier and left for home, still feeling guilty and a bit resentful. To my amazement, Danny was there watching television.

"Hallo. What's happened?" I asked.

"Nothing."

"What are you doing here on a Saturday?" I persisted.

"It's as much my place as yours. I pay my half of the rent."

Something had obviously gone violently wrong. He didn't ask where I had been; just sat there watching some stupid cartoon.

"Put your coat on," I said. "We're going out for a drink."

"I'm not going anywhere."

"Yes you are. You need to talk to somebody."

"No I don't."

He argued the point but I think he could see that I was right. He put the coat on and followed me out of the door. We took my car and I drove to the George. We found a little alcove seat and I bought him a beer. He drank it without a word. Then he went up to bar and got me one and a beer and a whisky for himself.

"So... what's this about?" I asked.

"Nothing I can't handle."

"It's Wendy, isn't it?"

He sighed but said nothing. He didn't give himself time to say anything. He finished both drinks before my glass was half empty. I went up and got both glasses refilled.

"Thanks," he said.

I tried again. "Tell me about it," I said. He took a long gulp and began. He told me the whole story. I think he was pretty near to tears. He'd known Wendy since they were in school together. They'd been on holiday together a couple of times and he had done all those things girls expect their boyfriends to do when they're away. Then he'd got the job with our firm. He and Wendy had moved into a flat together which worked well at first but they started to get on each other's nerves. Hearing that the D 1043 team was due to move down south, he applied to join it. Just being with Wendy for weekends, he thought, would be the answer to their problem. It wasn't. He'd heard that weekend that Wendy was seeing somebody else. She'd admitted it even that she and the other guy fucked in the bed his parents had provided for them.

"I've had it up to here with women," he said and raised a hand to his eyes. Unfortunately the hand also held a glass of beer and he slopped it over his face.

I said all the usual things. 'Lots more fish in the sea'. He'd find Miss Right one day. It was better to find out now rather than later, etc. The fact is that I was beginning to wonder whether his bad luck might turn out to my advantage.

We finished our drinks. They called 'Time' and we stood up to go. I stayed upright. Danny fell down. I was amazed. I helped him to his feet. He brushed his jeans with the back of his hand. "Uneven floor," he explained. "Bloody dangerous."

The publican came up to us to ask which of us was driving home. I said I was and led my very unsteady companion out to the car. He fell asleep as soon as I was in it. I had to fix the seat belt for him and couldn't help noticing that he had a semi erection. I should, I thought, have taken him into the toilets first but home wasn't far away.

Praying that none of the neighbors would look out of their windows, I manhandled him out of the car and managed to drag him to the front door. He dribbled onto my wrist and, oddly, I didn't mind. It felt good to be helping somebody.

Once inside the flat I managed to get him onto the sofa. He murmured something about 'thanks' and 'good friend'.

I didn't want a pair of grubby trainers on the sofa so managed to get those off him. Then it occurred to me that, were he to stand up and try to undress, he was as likely as not to fall over and possibly hurt himself. Worse, he might easily be sick on the carpet. I brought out the bucket I use to clean the windows and then started to undo the buttons of his tank top. "Wharrya doin'?" he murmured.

"Getting you undressed."

"What for?"

"Well, you're in no state to do it for yourself."

To tell the truth, neither was I. My hands were trembling. Somehow or other God alone knows how I managed to get the top off and to pull his T-shirt up and over his arms. I'd never really had a close-up view of his torso before. He was magnificent. His arms were huge. Something to do with the fitness club, I guessed. The club was probably responsible for his well-developed pecs but the nipples were pure Danny. Big brown circles, each with a pert, upstanding pink nipple in the centre. I was dying to feel them, to tweak them to one side and watch the underlying muscle tighten, but I had work to do. The difficult bit.

He opened his eyes wide and muttered something as I fumbled with his belt and his fly.

"Lift your ass a bit," I said. He just lay there. I tried to pull them down and managed to expose about an inch of pubic hair.

"Lift your ass, Danny," I said.

"Whafor?"

"I can't get these off unless you do."

31

I put my hands under his butt and tried to lift him. All I managed to do was to compress the soft muscles. That was an utterly delightful feeling and my cock rose at once.

Danny seemed to get the message. He wriggled around. I got my fingers into his waistband and pulled. Jeans and undershorts slid down his legs together. I had a bit of trouble getting them over his feet but soon they were on the floor and my colleague was naked on my couch, semi conscious from having drunk too much and looking absolutely beautiful. His cock, thicker than I remembered it from the glimpse I'd had previously, lay across his thigh, giving me my first good look at his balls. They were the size of table tennis balls. Just looking at them made my mouth water.

"You ought to have a pee before you go to sleep, Danny," I said.

He frowned and screwed up his face as if he was trying to focus his eyes. I picked up the bucket, placed it on his thighs and, gingerly, reached for his cock. He grinned sheepishly. I am, as you know, not an expert in these matters but there was something about the feel of it that made me wonder if he really was as drunk as he was making out. I expected it to feel a bit like a piece of cold clay. Instead it felt warm and alive. With finger and thumb I maneuvered it over the edge of the bucket. It was sufficiently long to enable me to tilt the bucket without losing it but I held on just in case.

"Let it go," I said. A few drops ran down the side of the bucket and then a torrent. When he'd finished I gave it a shake. Was it my imagination or was it growing thicker? I didn't wait to find out. When you've got a job like mine, the last thing you want is a colleague who tells people at work that you're queer. Officially, the defense industry approves of the new anti-sexual- discrimination laws but just try to get a promotion if people know that you fancy cock.

I said, "Good night."

He didn't answer.

I emptied the bucket into the lavatory, washed it and went to bed.

At four o'clock in the morning, I woke up to find Danny sitting naked on the edge of my bed.

"I want to explain," he said, hanging his head in shame.

"Hey, there's nothing to explain. You're not the first person to get drunk after a row with his girlfriend. Forget it."

"No. It's not like that. I want to tell you."

"Not now, Danny. Tell me tomorrow at work."

"No. It's got to be now."

"Oh, okay, fair enough. Explain away."

"It's you."

"Me? What have I done?"

"Nothing. That's the problem. What I told you about Wendy wasn't the complete truth."

"What? Has she got two other boyfriends and not just one?"

"Just the one. But it's you."

"Danny, I don't even know the girl. I've never met her."

"I don't mean like that. I mean, I can't do it with Wendy any-more."

"What?"

"It's true. You see, I keep thinking about you."

"What?" I could hardly believe my ears. I swallowed hard. "You're shivering," I went on, rubbing his shoulder. "Come in here with me."

I, of course, was expecting him to refuse my invitation and tell me I'd got the wrong idea instead of which he slipped with remarkable agility between the sheets. The warmth of his body seemed to suffuse us both.

"You sure you don't mind?"

"No."

"You won't say anything at work, will you?"

"Of course not." I still wasn't quite sure what his intentions were and lay there with a beating heart. My cock didn't know either. It started to take an interest and then jumped into action. His hand had closed round it.

"God! You're so sexy!" he murmured.

I was about to say that he was even sexier than I had a hope of being but something held me back.

"You've gotta realize: I've never done anything like this before," he said. "Don't suppose you have either."

I said nothing. That hand felt really good. He took it away for an instant to feel under my balls. I lifted up a bit. I didn't want to appear too keen but it was only fair to allow him access. Sadly, he didn't seem to want it. His hand returned to my cock and started to wank it.

"You can do anything you like to me. Only if you want to, that is," he whispered.

I did. I wanted it very much. Tentatively, I reached towards him, touched his belly and slid my hand down through the dense thicket of bristly hairs. It wasn't difficult to find. More than eight beautiful inches of steel-hard cock never is. I clasped it between finger and thumb and gently retracted the foreskin. He sighed.

"Oh yeah!" he said. Encouraged, I reached down and played with his balls. They were so much bigger than mine and, dare I say, very appetizing. Would he let me? There was only one way to find out. I slung the quilt away. The room was just light enough for me to get a good look at him. He was absolutely beautiful. The smell of him was enough to send me into raptures, let alone the sight of that enormous cock pointing to the ceiling.

He smiled, showing a row of perfectly even teeth. "Do anything you want," he said. I lay alongside him and put my arms round his shoulders. He seemed to know what I wanted. I felt his breath on my face and then our lips touched. It was like being hit by an electric shock. His tongue slid into my mouth. There was no trace of the beer he'd been knocking back. Just a vaguely minty flavor. He's obviously been into the bathroom to clean his teeth. I hadn't but he didn't object as I pushed my tongue into his mouth. He sucked on it.

We must have lain like that for quite a long time and I don't know if he shuffled his body towards mine or whether I took the initiative. I know that we ended up pressing together and that his cock was between my thighs and mine was somewhere between his. Still kissing him, I reached down and put my hand round both of them. He liked that. He muttered something. I don't know what it was. Slowly, I wanked us both. I wanted it to last as long as possible. I knew there would be recriminations and a row in the morning and this would be the one and only chance. It had to be good.

"Go a bit faster," he whispered. I ignored him. I could feel his heart thumping in his chest. My finger touched the soft skin of his balls. I kissed him again and, as I did so, realized that I'd never kissed any of the others. I'd never wanted to. As far as I was concerned, Dhasan had a magnificent body, a big cock, and a nice ass. Neil had a very appetizing cock. Barry had a beautifully supple ass and was well equipped in front as well. Kissing them had never occurred to me. Danny was different; very different.

"Coming...." he said when our lips parted.

"Me too," I replied and clamped my mouth over his again. I felt the tremor run through him. He lunged farther forward, almost pushing me off the bed. It seemed to flood out of him, pouring all over my thighs, seeping between the cheeks of my ass and soaking my balls. He held me tight; so tight that I could hardly breathe.

"Oh God!" he gasped. "You're so...." and I came. It was the third time that weekend and, by rights, it should have been even less than the dribble I had produced when Dhasan fucked my ass. Instead you'd have thought I'd lived a life of abstinence for a year or more. Spurt after spurt soaked him, me and, unfortunately, the bed as well.

I'm used to someone saying "Hang on, I'll get a towel," and some sort of complimentary remark. Dhasan, for instance, would say, "You're a damn good fuck." Neil wasn't in the least interested in my ejaculations.

Once he'd shot his load in my mouth, that was it as far as he was concerned. He might say something like "You come a lot don't you?" as he handed me the towel. Barry enjoyed being fucked and asked when I'd next be in the area. None of them clung on to my heaving body as Danny did. It was a great feeling.

"Want me to go?" he whispered.

"Are you kidding?" I replied. So he stayed. We did just about everything that night or almost everything. I licked him clean and he did the same for me. I dozed off playing with his nipples and woke up again to find him licking my thighs. The sun was streaming through the window.

"Suppose I make some breakfast?" he said.

"You bloody dare," I replied. "All the breakfast I need is in these." I reached down and cupped them in my hand.

"Then you'd better do something about it, hadn't you?" he replied. He smiled broadly as he spread his legs apart. His cock hardened the moment my lips touched it. It tasted wonderful, as smooth and as sweet as the sugar plums my grandmother made for Christmas and quite as big. Slowly, I sucked in as much as I could, savoring the slightly different taste of the shaft. As if from a long way away, I heard him moaning. Holding the skin as firmly as I could between my lips, I moved my head up and down. The down strokes were the best. I sniffed the exquisite smell of his balls. He kicked his legs even further apart. I managed to get my hand under them and pushed a probing finger in. He gasped but made no move to deter me. A bit farther and I felt it. A tiny soft centre. I tickled it.

"Coming! I'm coming!" he gasped.

He didn't need to tell me! His ass cheeks clamped against my questing finger. He lifted himself up, almost choking me and then filled my mouth with jet after jet of his semen. Dhasan's tastes of curry. Neil's is nice but a bit insipid. Barry is flavorful but Danny was out of this world. It may sound stupid to say that it tasted healthy but it did. All that exercise had not only given him a superb body but a wonderful taste as well. I didn't want to swallow it and held it in my mouth for as long as possible.

Finally, I had to and looked down at his grinning face.

"Now it's your turn," he said.

And I was only too happy to oblige!

We spent all day in bed, licking, kissing, and sucking. I rolled over on top of him and fucked between his legs. That was great. Danny had muscles really gripped. I would have liked to have got into his ass but it was too much trouble to go and fetch the necessary stuff. Then he did the same to me. I don't think I was half as good as he was but, again, he came in torrents and kissed me afterwards.

We went out to the George again that evening. We had a meal and a couple of beers each. It was then that I had my brain-wave. I knew there was an apartment going for rent in Dhasan's block. With Danny's salary and mine we could afford it. He was all for the idea. I said we'd have to be careful Dhasan didn't find out Dhasan being so straight, he would be shocked and he was a good friend. We agreed to have two separate rooms but to use one, leaving the other looking as if it had been slept in. He said his parents would be glad to send down any furniture we wanted. As I was the eldest, the lease would have to be in my name so he said the furniture would be addressed to me.

"I can't wait to get the key," I said.

He smiled. "I've got a key of another sort," he said. "I'd like to see if it fits your keyhole."

"Well, drink up," I said. "Let's go home and try it. From what I've seen of it, it should fit just right."

It did.

It still does.

And mine fits his.

CUTE AS A BUTTON
Peter Eros

A deep layer of snow still crusted the shadowed part of the meadow, at the foot of the Yosemite Valley's soaring granite walls, making it easy to spot the gray coyote, sitting on his haunches, his nose pointed in the air, his high-pitched yip-yip-yipping echoing across the valley. It was mid-March and the morning air was unseasonably warm and humid. There wasn't any snow where I was. I crept into the sunlight and lay in the long grass. I watched.

On the far side of the meadow, a second coyote began to sing. For fifteen minutes or more they howled sometimes separately, often in unison while trotting closer and closer to each other. Finally they met, quickly took a couple of playful whirls in the snow and snuggled down together in the sun's rays. I felt very alone but the sun was warm and comforting. I'd already strapped my fleecy jacket to my back-pack. I stood and stripped off my tee.

"Turn around real slow," said a deep, mellow voice.

I did and was stunned to see a park ranger on horseback. Spare and tall in the saddle, he was impressive. His immaculate uniform fit like a second skin. His face was square-jawed, deep-tanned and handsome, the wide mouth full-lipped and inviting. His attitude was stern but there was a twinkle in the ebony eyes. I sprang a spontaneous hard-on. As I wasn't wearing underwear it must have been immediately obvious.

"Don't you know that the park is closed to the public, since the New Year's flooding? It's still dangerous around here. The bears are just coming out of hibernation. The animals think they won because the humans are all gone."

It was March, and I did know. I'd hitched a ride from LA on one of the trucks delivering building materials for the reconstruction work. Upset and disoriented, driven by both desire and fear, I'd stuck my thumb out determined to accept a ride from the first truck that stopped, regardless of destination. The driver was muscular and hairy, with an unruly beard and mustache. The sleeves had been ripped out of his checkered flannel shirt revealing tattooed biceps. His jeans were old and faded, the bottom button undone revealing a hint of hairy flesh. His bulge was prominent and inviting. At a truck stop outside Merced I sucked him off and he bought me breakfast, before dropping me a mile or so before the park entrance so I could skirt round through the woods.

The ranger was still regarding me.

"Are you alone?"

I nodded.

"What's your name?"

"Pao."

"What sort of a name is that?"

"Hmong. We're mountain people from Laos."

"Very handsome too. Nice bod!"

I blushed.

"You know, most of the camping areas were swept away in the flood and the lodges and restaurants are closed. Have you got some food?"

"Yes, sir," I lied, unless candy bars counted.

"Well now, what are we going to do with you? How old are you?"

"Eh, nineteen?" I made it sound as if I were seeking his approval to be so terribly young.

He smiled, dismounted and approached me. He pushed his hat back very deliberately and gripped my shoulders. He gazed very intently in my face as my knees turned to jelly, then kissed me full on the lips as his fingers pushed down the front of my jeans and caressed my upstanding tribute to his beauty. I gasped and his tongue took advantage, exploring my receptive aperture.

"Well, sad eyes, it looks like we've got something in need of urgent attention here, so I guess I'll just have to take you into custody."

He remounted, as I shrugged on my haversack, and he offered me the square-fingered strength of his hand to climb up. I clutched him around the waist, my erection snuggled neatly against his crack. He nodded in the direction of the coyotes.

"They've got the right idea, and they're both males."

I looked and sure enough they were humping.

We set off on a circuitous mountain trail past babbling streams, padding through mounds of damp pine needles and occasional patches of ice, breathing the nurturing aroma of pine, fir and cedar, till we reached the giant sequoias.

"These here are among the world's oldest living things. Some are 3500 years old."

Their red, rough-bark trunks thrust straight and tall like pillars in an ancient temple. I was in awe. It was how I imagined the immense, ancient forest in the mountain homeland of my people: a magical and mystical place. But the sun had not penetrated the chill shade of the trees. The front of my torso was warmed by contact with the ranger and my lower back by my pack but my shoulders and arms were cold. I shivered.

At a tiny isolated log cabin deep in the forest he told me to get down. I slid off awkwardly onto my rump on the hard ground. As I struggled out of my backpack he laughed, dismounted and tethered the horse, then offered me his hand. He pulled me up into his embrace and this time I was ready for him. I pushed my tongue into his mouth and explored the pearly teeth and solid tongue.

He gently disengaged, grinning broadly, and pushed open the door as he picked up my pack and pushed me into the cramped space, which contained a narrow bed, a pot-bellied stove, a tiny table, two chairs and a cupboard. It smelled of wood smoke and wool blanket. He kicked the door closed and placed my pack on the chair. He hung his hat on a hook, revealing his sleek black hair, pulled back in a plaited pig-tail, part of his Oglala Sioux inheritance, and pushed me down onto the bed. I didn't resist. Despite his firmness his expression was gentle and his smile reassuring.

He stood gazing down at me as he pulled a couple of condoms from his shirt pocket and tossed them onto the bed. Then he stripped first his shirt and tee, then his boots and trousers, then his boxers, draping his clothes neatly on the chair: enjoying my obvious admiration. His cock seemed to me enormous, stiff, curved and uncut, in a butthole of neatly trimmed black pubics. His scrotum was shaved and appeared to contain two good sized lemons. The almost hairless arms and shoulders, chest, abs, legs, thighs, butt and midriff were all impressive and obviously the product of much diligent work. He reached down to pull off my jeans as I flipped open my buttons and raised my butt.

His six-three, 230-pound frame enveloped me and pushed me into the thin mattress. I felt like I was melting into him, becoming part of him: erasing my own puny personality in something magnificent and wholly desirable. This was a fantasy come true, compared to my normal sordid and furtive jack-off and suck episodes with strangers in toilets, alleys and parks. I'd only been fucked once, by another kid from school a year before. His folks were out of town for the weekend and we serviced each other, imitating the pictures in a porno book he had picked up somewhere, overawed and ecstatic with the novelty of the sensations. But his dad was transferred to the East Coast the following month and we never got to do it again.

The Ranger cupped my face in his hands and looked into my eyes.

"My name's Cliff, sweet-lips, and you're the answer to my prayers. I haven't had any relief since Christmas, with no tourists around, so I hope you're ready for some real action."

"Yeah, please," I murmured. "But I haven't been fucked much, so go easy, okay? You're pretty big. I want it, but I don't know whether I can take it."

"Relax, Pao." He brushed my hair back from my forehead and then traced my lips with his fingers.

"We'll take it real slow and gentle, till you're used to it. If it hurts at all you let me know and I'll ease up. I want you to enjoy this as much as I know I will. You're just cute as a button."

Cliff slid down my body, kissing and nibbling my throat and then my nipples tonguing and chewing, lapping at the stiffening tips, sucking on one while teasing the other with his fingernails. I writhed and groaned with pleasure. It was a totally new and unexpected sensation. I surrendered my body and my will completely to his pleasure, sure that I had found my master; a man with no qualms about his sexuality, who would teach me how to cope proudly with my desires, dispelling the self-loathing and guilt inflicted by my macho family, who regarded me as diseased and untouchable.

The weight, the smell of him and the touch of his hot skin snapped my cock to throbbing attention. He slid lower, his tongue leaving a trail of saliva from the hollow below my pecs to my navel. Then he raised himself up and went at my crotch with a vengeance. My swelling glans throbbed as a drop of precum oozed through my slit. Cliff's tongue flicked out and lapped it up.

I shuddered. The head of my cock was sensitive. The feel of his skilled tongue rasping on my retracted foreskin set my balls in motion. Before I knew it I was jetting into his mouth, but he didn't pull away. His lips clamped around me and he sucked out my discharge as my hands fondled his bobbing scalp. My body arched and my abdomen contracted as my outflow pumped down his throat. He didn't relinquish me until I was spent. He licked his lips.

"Was that okay?"

"Oh, yeah! That was really cool. But I shouldn't have cum in your mouth."

"That's okay. I reckon I've got a sixth sense with this. You're clean, like me, babe. And we're just gettin' started."

Cliff knelt and hoisted my legs up over his shoulders. His face disappeared between my splayed thighs as he tongue-bathed beneath my scrotum, nibbling and sucking. His tongue probed my puckered and practically virgin rosette as his hands massaged my buttocks, yet another new sensation to totally dissolve all resistance. My asshole relaxed and Cliff's tongue entered me, probing deep.

As he ate my ass he clasped my cock in a spit-slicked hand and pumped me till I was straining once more on the verge of release. I was weeping with joy as my jism splattered over his hand, in his hair and the length of my body. Cliff moved in to lick up my cum, cleansing my satiated body. I pulled him down onto me kissing him voraciously, anxious to taste myself on his tongue, swabbing his mouth completely before lapping up the remaining drips of cum on his face and hair. I had never known such complete physical and emotional happiness. He could do with me whatever he wished. I was in love.

Cliff was rampant and ready. He positioned me astraddle his waist and lowered me so his prick prodded my primed pucker. He offered me a condom but I shook my head. If he was so trusting of me then I had to accord him equal respect. I grasped him firmly and pushed down slowly, easing his straining dick into my unpracticed aperture. He let me do the work, lying patiently beneath me, his hands resting encouragingly on my waist or soothingly caressing when I flinched. The pain was intense but I was determined. Finally my internal sphincter relaxed and the pain subsided.

Demonstrating an amazing suppleness, Cliff raised his legs, resting his ankles against my shoulders, and instructed me:

"Reach back and grasp the top of my thighs near my crotch, and pull me into you."

His feet slid down behind my back, pushing my torso forward so that I became a lever to lift his butt. At the same time he grasped my waist and pulled his head and shoulders up a little so he could suck my cock and fuck me at the same time. The feeling was extraordinary. It seemed as though his embedded cock had pushed through into my own so that we were truly one being.

Cliff's hips bucked against my ass with accelerating momentum, pounding my colon, which had engulfed his entire shaft. At the same time his lips vigorously suctioned the tip of my prick. My need had become greed. The slapping sound of his pelvis bouncing against my spread buttocks reverberated through my entire body as I slammed myself back onto him, my nuts drawn tight, ready to expel another load of love juice into the moist and hungry mouth.

As Cliff pumped his climax into my guts my balls erupted with a supernova of molten spunk. He kept pumping his cock against my prostate until my deluge had slowed to a dribble. His voracious mouth relinquished its hold on me with a satisfied smirk as his purged cock slid from anchor, reluctantly surrendered by my still-gripping anal muscles. It was as if they had found their purpose in life. The ecstatic fulfillment I had received overwhelmed all other senses. I wanted nothing else but more of the same. My colonic sense of loss when he withdrew pervaded my whole being.

Cliff enfolded me in his arms and sucked my mouth into his own, his tongue reaching for my tonsils. I opened my mouth wider, letting him explore me as I probed back, savoring the flavor of my discharge in his saliva. I felt totally enervated but exhilarated at the same time. My body tingled with gratitude and satisfaction as Cliff lay by my side and gazed into my eyes.

"I don't know where you came from Pao, or how you got here, but I thank whatever gods there are that I found you. You're the best sex I ever had. I think I've fallen in love with you. I know I don't want to lose you. How come you ended up in the States?"

"It's a long story. My father and uncles fought for America in the Vietnam War, but by the time the conflict ended they'd lost their homeland. They lived in refugee camps in Thailand for years. That's where I was born. We were finally allowed into America when I was eight years old. I went to school here. But now I've been disowned. I no longer exist, as far as my family and clan are concerned, because I refused to marry the girl picked out for me. I knew I was homosexual and I told them that no way was I going to screw up both our lives. I want to be loved by another guy. I have no desire to procreate. They threw me out. For them I am dead."

"Well, maybe I can find you a job here. That way we could stay together. Some parts of the park will be reopening soon but a lot of the former staff have found other jobs and won't be coming back. Would you like that?"

He was caressing my face and brushing back my hair. I reached out to him and he sucked my fingers into his mouth as I started to cry. I sobbed out my reply.

"Yeah, oh yeah! You've given me more joy than I've ever known. If I can work and live with you, I don't know what could possibly be better."

I curled into his embrace and drifted into a contented slumber.

I woke to the smell of cooking. My bare-ass chef had set-up a kerosene stove and the aroma of sizzling eggs and tomatoes blended with the steam from boiling vegetables. He glanced over his shoulder as I stirred.

"Hungry, hot lips?"

"Mmm!" I murmured contentedly.

That was six months ago. I'm now an associate in a souvenir shop by day and Cliff and I fuck our asses raw most nights. It's a full and satisfying life. I'm sure that most of the other rangers and staff know about our liaison but they're a pretty tolerant lot and no one has said anything derogatory to either of us. The only thing we have to be careful about at this time of year, late September, is cantankerous bears intent on their extreme, around-the-clock feeding, in preparation for the long, sleepful winter. They can be real ornery.

Cliff has coached me in a whole repertoire of sexual positions as well as forest lore. I've explored most of the park in his company and every inch of his magnificent body. He's given me books to read on Native American history and customs and has bought others to study my people's culture. As a result we've discovered that we have much more in common than just our sexual preferences. The steamy, hot intimacy of the sweat lodge, I've found, not only purifies your spirit, but it can also be a great prelude to sex.

The first time was after nightfall. It was as though the trees around us had suddenly disappeared. Night was everywhere. Insects sawed unseen. Cliff had chosen fifty or so rocks from the stream-bed, representing, he said, the grandmothers and grandfathers of the Earth. He placed them in a clean pit in the center of the lodge, or inipi as he calls it. While the rocks cooked we mended the willow frame, covered it with clean white canvas, tied on an outer covering of Native blankets and fixed an elk hide as the covering to the door.

Before we entered Cliff gave me my first lesson on how to endure the heat.

"Lie down if it becomes too intense, lift up the cover for a breath of air or simply leave. I can't say how long the ceremony will last or how hot the lodge will get. I don't have a thermometer, and it's over when it's over."

The ritual was divided into four rounds, each hotter than the last. Cliff used a pitchfork to carry more glowing rocks into the lodge for each round, while I used a forked branch to lay them into the pit. Cliff blessed them with sweet grass and cedar, then doused the rocks with water from a gourd dipper, sending mists of herb-scented steam throughout the pitch-black lodge.

At first the heat felt as though it was scorching my lungs, cutting off my air. But in time my body calmed. The heat seeped into sore muscles. Sweat streamed into my eyes and washed down the backs of my legs. The cleansing had begun. Cliff offered chanted prayers for our families, our ancestors, ourselves. His sacred pipe passed back and forth between us, the aromatic contents speeding me to euphoric mindlessness, as our wayward hands fondled each other's dick. After two hours we emerged from the heat and plunged into the icy stream. It was exhilarating.

43

We leapt from the water and ran to the cabin in the light of a full moon. After rubbing each other dry Cliff manipulated me into a new position. He lay me on the bed and got me to lift my legs back over my head so that my knees nestled either side of my head, my cock dangling above my own mouth. I was amazed that I could suck myself. Then, after greasing me well, he entered me from above, his ass-pounding assault forcing my own cock to tickle my insatiable palate.

Cliff started thrusting more strongly, bouncing wildly on my elevated butt, riding me harder than he'd ever done as I gobbled myself beneath him. I had been fucked enough that my anal muscles could now really open up for him, sucking Cliff into me. The days of having to be careful were over. He slid easily through my second sphincter. I wanted it all and could take it without trouble from any angle.

Late summer, after a week's coaching, Cliff required me to go into the forest for three nights and four days without food and water, dressed only in a native breech-cloth. He took me to a remote tract of woodland little frequented by tourists or workers. Despite the foraging techniques he'd taught me, and the extreme famishment that engulfed me the second day, I remained abstinent. During the fast, I rid myself of my anger and arrogance, and, Cliff says, brought out my inner child. I've been turned around.

At the end of the fourth day, as the sun disappeared and the moon bathed everything in its mystic glow, sexual need overwhelmed me. I'd bathed in a stream and felt clean and vibrant, but desperately lonely. Cliff had not come for me and I didn't know how to find my way back by the stars.

As a coyote yipped nearby I slipped through the trees to a clearing atop a little rise and faced the Luna traveler. Discarding my loincloth I took myself in hand and prayed to the moon for release. I lay on the ground and assumed self-sucking mode, my knees hugging my ears.

I didn't hear him but I felt his presence and glanced up as he overshadowed me. Dressed only in a coyote skin, the head framing his skull, Cliff ate my elevated ass, probing deeply with his tensile tongue before plunging his cock into my receptive passage. I cried out with sheer joy and the yipping coyote stopped a moment or two before resuming his anthem to the spirits of the night. The sharp smack of Cliff's belly slapping my buns echoed through the trees.

Cliff knew now that I was his. He rode me bottom-up, he rode me on my back with my feet ratcheting his spine, pulling him into me. He did me on my side, he screwed me with one leg raised, he fucked me in a shoulder-stand. He pulled me up into his strong embrace and entered me from below, my legs crossed behind his buttocks.

At first I was a willing rag doll, then an avid wildcat, then a screeching banshee, clawing him as my suction pump gripped him and my prostate quivered like a beaten drum skin.

As I felt Cliff's nuts shooting their load deep within me I thought my balls were coming out the head of my cock. I shot huge gobs of spunk between us, all over our chests and faces which Cliff scooped up with cupped hand and fed me as I gasped and trembled in ecstatic bliss.

Cliff's totem animal is the coyote and his Native name translates as Coyote Moon Challenger. He has renamed me Coyote Basking in the Sun, in honor of our first encounter, but he says he should have named me Coyote Who Fucks Like a Rabbit. But I don't think he has any complaints. I sure enough don't.

PERFECT STRANGERS
John Patrick

When Ben assured Stuart that he did not have to participate, but could simply add to the energy by being a voyeur, and that he would stick close to him or see to it he was comfortable if he were busy, Stuart said yes he'd go to the party a friend of Ben's was giving.

The "party" was held in an old warehouse. It was a large room, filled with heavy-beat but not intrusive music. Pools of light accentuated tables, slings, vertical and horizontal bars, whipping posts, or some bondage display a human form spread-eagled in suspension by ropes and clamps. In varying numbers and stages of undress, some twenty studs clustered around one piece of equipment or another, much like the stations in a medieval miracle play. On, in, or at each piece of equipment a single body, a bottom, would be the intense concern of one or more tops who sought to arouse him by whatever appropriate and creative means.

Stuart had to admit it was a smorgasbord of delight. All he had to do was choose a scene and watch, like a porn video come to life. All around them, bottoms were tortured exquisitely and usually an eternity later released extravagantly into sexual fulfillment.

Before long, Ben was pressing his body into Stuart's until his nipples were pressing against Stuart, erect and hard underneath his black T-shirt. Every time Stuart swayed and brushed against them, Ben moaned and arched him back. Every time Ben arched him back, Stuart pressed his thigh between his legs and rocked him back into him. Stuart's fingers found a tangle in his hair, wrapped around it. With every sharp tug, they ground against each other, private pain amid one man's voice after another. They fucked at each other during hard rocking songs, and caressed each other during slower country songs. Stuart wanted to cover every inch of Ben during one ballad that was so sweet it made him like country for the first time. He was shocked to find that he was tremendously excited aching with desire for Ben, long and hard and crazy. Just from dancing! He was wondering why he had waited so long to do this, to dance like this with Ben, when his voice took him back to the present. "I need you," Ben whispered sharply in his ear. As usual, those words sent an immediate message to Stuart's body, and Stuart was ready to lay him down right there, except that there wasn't any room. He heard the presence of other men around them now, several of them talking and none of them fucking, but they didn't care. It didn't matter that Stuart had never been there, didn't know anyone, and hadn't ever just fucked like a sex-starved lunatic in front of perfect strangers. It didn't matter that it was dark and uncomfortable this sensation was absolutely new. For once, control was just not part of the equation.

Nothing was on their minds but getting off. Ben opened his jeans after pulling off Stuart's. He grabbed onto Stuart's dick, and felt the warm slipperiness brought on by the precum. Stuart tried to grab for Ben's cock, and Ben let him. Ben moaned as Stuart straddled his body, and Ben leaned back against a wall, lowering his hips so Stuart could climb over him, fill himself with Ben's enormous prick. When Stuart settled with a hard slam, they both gasped, and their faces screwed up in mutual orgasm. Stuart didn't have time to reflect on how this was a first for such an event, he was too busy coming.

Ben's head snapped back. He didn't even feel the brick wall, he was so gone. He thrust up, deeper into Stuart, and wrapped his arms tightly around his waist, pulling him to him like the perfect sex-toy he was. It was violent and it was harsh, and every jerk of his body made Ben growl and Stuart scream. As Stuart panted and fought to catch his breath, he was conscious of several pairs of eyes glinting through the darkness, and knew that they had become the entertainment focus of the room. But Stuart didn't care. All he knew was that one series of spasms wasn't going to be enough for him. Ben turned awkwardly, keeping himself inside Stuart, and pressed him against the wall. Stuart started to slide down and, staying with him, Ben ended up on the floor, braced over him, while he moaned and gasped and started to whimper. Catching his legs, Ben pulled them up, his thighs now braced from Ben's hips up to his waist. His ass lifted off the floor, and Ben could see his asshole filled with his cock. The sight alone was enough to send Ben into yet another spiral of ecstasy.

"I'm not finished with you!" Ben snarled, pulling back to slam in again. Stuart's wails hit a new high note as Ben pumped, and the shifting position of his cock was just perfect for the a rhythmic fucking style that he was justly famous for, which would gave him some more time before another orgasm made them insane. Stuart tried to grab for Ben, and Ben caught his wrists and slammed them down against the floor. They fucked until Ben couldn't breathe anymore, until sweat matted his shirt to his back and the pool of slickness between them seemed like a thin layer of oil spread over their entire bodies. When he pulled out of Stuart's ass, Stuart screamed and clutched at the empty air, and Ben stood and watched him writhe in the final throes of an agonizing series of delirious shakes that almost, but not quite, got Ben horny again. Ben wiped himself off with his back-pocket hanky and tossed it to Stuart.

"Cool," said a voice from behind Ben.

"Way cool," said another. Amid a few snickers, they heard gentle clapping. Ben blushed, because of all the reactions he'd ever gotten for fucking, no one had ever applauded!

Ben helped Stuart up and held him. Stuart was trembling. Stuart had never had public sex before. Ben soothed Stuart with a reminder that the night wasn't over yet. But Stuart said he was not in the mood for any new adventures that night.

Back at the apartment, they were on the couch, and Ben was kissing Stuart, a sweet series of "let's-go-to-bed" kisses. Although Stuart started out feeling annoyed and snippy, having been fucked in front of perfect strangers, Stuart had to admit that his caresses were nice. Stuart was not used to having someone make these soft, romantic overtures to him. Even when he topped, he didn't like that. But for the first time, it seemed nice, it seemed right. Stuart let him unbutton his shirt, take his nipples into his mouth and then run his fingers down Stuart's back.

Ben moved onto the floor first, on his knees, and Stuart followed him, running his fingers through his hair for a change. Stuart began to kiss Ben's ass. He sucked on the skin. Ben moaned, determined to let Stuart play until he decided he'd like it better for Ben to take his usual role. Stuart hesitated from time to time, and Ben knew he was waiting for him to make his move. But the longer Ben delayed, the bolder Stuart got.

Soon, Ben was on his back not an odd position for him. In fact, it was one of his favorites, having a eager boy on top, bouncing up and down on his prick. But instead of telling him to get his cock up and into him and amuse him, Ben stayed silent, leaving it up to him. Stuart stripped off what remained of his clothes. Ben sighed when he saw Stuart's cock, a cock nearly as big as his own, hard and glistening, arching toward his belly. Then, slowly, Stuart mounted Ben and slid his cock into him. He slowly rocked on Ben, building until he was at a steady swaying movement that pleased him, instead of the rough staccato thrusts that Ben was famous for. Different, definitely different. But not without its charms. A bottom fucking a top. Stuart arched his back once, pushing up into Ben, and he leaned forward and caught Ben's wrists, as easily as Ben had caught his. Ben's eyes opened wide – this would normally be a moment where he would wrestle free, turn him over onto his back and hurt him until he apologized for such a possessive, dominant move. But instead Ben smiled and leaned back, surrendering. "Go ahead, you little slut," Ben taunted. "Take it. Take it deep."

"Fuck," Stuart snarled, this time in frustration, and then pushed himself up for better leverage. And while Ben infuriated him by smiling and keeping utterly still, Stuart rose and fell against Ben, harder and harder, until Ben could see and feel the familiar signs of his approaching orgasm. He grabbed Ben's cock and stroked it. When Ben started to pant, Stuart pushed up, turned his body sharply, and pulled out of him. Ben screamed and clutched at Stuart, but the loss of balance pushed him well out of reach of Stuart's drippy cock. His hands flew down to his cock, but Stuart caught them and held onto them, and laughed out loud as Ben's entire body shook and his cock throbbed in the shattering throes of orgasm interruptus. Stuart knew that sensation the start of the pulsing mingled with the swift fading of intensity, and the need for something more. And Stuart gave it to him, slamming back in. And Stuart kept on until Ben was wild with orgasm once again. This time, he let Ben come, and he came himself.

Wrapped in Ben's strong arms, Stuart realized he was tired of promiscuity, tired of desperate passion. He was tired of his violent anger and wished it was not a part of his life, of his personality. His heart yearned to be more gentle. And he needed Ben to make sense of an alienating world.

MY INITIATION
Barnabus Saul

You know me as your friendly pizza delivery boy. You can see me most any night on my black motor bike, the one with the heatproof compartment. You can see my leathers, black and red, more PV than leather, crash helmet. You can see my complexion, the color of my hair, my smile and the glint you hope to discern in my eyes when you take the boxes and hand over the money. You undress me with your eyes and examine my lean frame. A taut chest with small dark nipples, visible ribs; vulnerable. You assume my knob is frisky and my balls, sweating in leather, are low slung. You are aware of the intimate kiss of my arse without underwear on the leather seat of my bike. You experience a quickening in your prick as the obvious fantasies flit through your groin. Usually that's all there is. That's all you need to know.

I call with a largish order at a house on 17th. A house I always took to be flats, rented. There's a delay while the doorbell isn't answered. Then the door opens and it looks like the guy just got out of bed, barefoot, shirt pulled on and not properly tucked in, trousers hastily secured. I figure he's in bed with his girl who demanded a post-coital pizza. Watching television together. He had to get up. He's young enough, long blond hair and sunken cheeks, square chin. I can imagine him on the job, plenty of jab; his baggy pants do not conceal energetic hips.

I like hips like his; I notice in many porn films the American guys are lazy and lack energy, they pump back and forth keeping the torso rigid. But the French boys are something else. Their hips roll and swivel, spines coil and unwind, get it in really deep. I like to watch this happen; she is a lucky girl; I bet they wouldn't let me in to see the next performance? But there're twelve pizzas and that's a hell of a lot of pizza for two.

There isn't enough money. He shouts for Geoff or Jeff to bring some more; Jeff puts an arm round the door and waves notes. Jeff isn't wearing a shirt and my attention is drawn to an ample, square shoulder and the generous upholstery of a pectoral with an aroused cherry tit. Better still, I know Jeff. Jeff and I were at school together. I have seen Jeff naked under school showers.

Yes, it is Jeff right enough, he recognizes me and comes out from behind the door. He's still naked. The same dick bounces from his lower belly, the same chunky balls roll against the same muscled thighs. Has he been naked for three years? There are some guys who should be forbidden clothing, Jeff is an example. He is athletic, hard, smooth and already

51

fucking my eyeballs. A dark thread of hair describes a convex curve from his belly button broadening into the wispy forest of dark hair round his tool.

He yells my name and pulls me into the hall, tucking the extra notes into my leather pocket. He has been drinking quite a bit and is consequently relaxed and happy. It is very pleasant to be hugged by a naked and drunken man, to put your arms around him and find your hands on solid man flesh, nuzzle the powerful man scents at his neck. I recommend it.

When he stops hugging me I grin and tell him I am pleased to see him. It sounds inadequate. I have difficulty keeping my eyes from straying to his dick. It is relaxed but thick; it has already done service tonight and remains engorged while limp, awaiting the next call. A bright eye emerges from a crinkle of foreskin. As I say, it is a dick I have viewed before. A dick that has visited me often in my bedsit when my body has arched and I have gasped out loud, hoping the people in the next room are temporarily deaf or busy with their own pleasures.

Momentarily I wonder why would he be eating pizza naked with another guy? Proximity to his firm flesh and awareness of the warm aura radiating from his nakedness renders this a foolish question. I smile and follow my bone as, his arm around my shoulder, he leads me inside. He yells that the pizza's arrived and creates a stir. There must be a dozen naked guys in that room. I lead a sheltered life; I have never seen such a yardage of prong or so many loose nuts assembled in one place before. In showers boys shuffle and hide; mostly these guys are splayed out like goods in a supermarket. Please grope the merchandise. A TV pumps out hardcore. Lager tins litter the floor and full ones are stacked in a corner.

Jeff is being very tactile; his arms are still around me as he explains that this is boys' night. Lager, takeout and porn; no clothing allowed and no dares refused. It is more than an invitation. The guy who opened the door has shed his shirt and jeans and takes the last of the boxes from me. I don't know what to do with my hands anymore and would park them in my pockets. Jeff has found my bone. I take this as permission to bring all the ambitions of my school career to fulfillment and curl my fingers around his. The smell in that room of sweaty bouquets is intoxicating, 100% proof. The guy who is undressing me has no hair at all on his body; his groin is like fresh peach skin, his purse is costliest velvet. He has a way of removing my shirt that makes my nipples pulsate. I suppose I should be shy; I am not normally a naked person, but I tell myself in such company I should be embarrassed rather to be clothed, and I believe myself. My leathers slide down and as I topple to the floor they are removed above my head along with my boots in a tangle. I contribute my own leather and scrotum sweat smells to the heady miasma in the room.

Naked now, I wallow in the investigations of other naked males who have come to enjoy me. One squeezes a wedge of stringy cheese pizza in my mouth; someone else rubs a slice, warm and squelchy, over my balls and starts consuming it eagerly. There are fingers and tongues trying every crevice. I have always been ticklish; my uncle used to tickle me and gave me some of my earliest and most fondly remembered erections. The tongues at my navel now prove too much and I wriggle in a squealing heap along with more legs, arms, buttocks, balls and shafts than I am able to count. I am on a writhing bed of flesh and bones. I am able to lick pizza that has been smeared across the silken belly of the boy directly below me while my body is cradled on an undulating mass of buttocks. Heaven is made of this. I want nothing more. I am no intellectual. I finish the pizza and turn myself over.

My cock and balls leave one set of hands and mouths and are instantly seized by others. I find myself looking up in amazement at a beefy lad with a round belly and soft boobs who looms above me. His legs are astride my head and I am blessed with the full worm's eye view. His thighs are those of a sumo wrestler and his arse is well blessed with fat. He smiles down and I want to lick the baby softness of his double chins and sniff the scents of his neck. My mouth is open and I assume he is going to honor me with an insertion of his thick, stubby tool deep into my throat. But, better yet, he turns around and slowly squats. I gape transfixed as his thighs and buttocks slowly part, descending.

My face is clenched tightly in the ample folds of flesh that make his thighs and buttocks. I cannot breathe. I am lost, annihilated in the sweaty embrace of his widespread crack. It is like entering the tunnel of life and death. Will I ever emerge, and will the world still be the same?

The smells up here are mind boggling. Several guys are enjoying my own apparatus but I am barely aware of it. I think I have come several times, but I cannot be sure.

For an infinity it seems, his juicy rump rolls and grinds my face.

Finally I emerge gasping for air, only to take another session of my sumo wrestler riding my face.

He loses interest and flips me on top of his massive thighs, where I perceive my tongue is required to caress his ample purse. Simultaneously my rear has been lifted so I am on my knees and I am being rhythmically bumped by a lad who lacks length but has ample diameter.

Later, I will come to recognize everyone present by this simple contact.

When he is finished with me, Sumo pulls me again onto my back; he enjoys my wetting abilities and the rough damp stroking of my tongue. Again I am smothered by folds of prime juicy arse-steak.

This gives me an idea; it is a masterstroke. Into the fold of meat just to the right side of his pouting pussy I drive my teeth as hard as I can manage.

The effect is instantaneous. He screams out a barrage of swear words I am embarrassed to hear. It seems he is on the point of coming.

His beefy thighs kick out as he tries to stagger to his feet. He is thrashing about like a frenzied whale.

I lock my jaw like a dog and find myself lifted in the air still clamped to his buttock.

I don't let go.

He yells again and overbalances landing on his side with me on top. His rod is pumping uncontrollably, adding to the transport of ecstasy he must be undergoing. I can hear guys hooting and laughing at his predicament.

For a long time he suffers this agony and indignity, flailing and bellowing. His juices finally stop shooting and he stops trying to remove me by force, whimpering instead with the pain that my teeth are causing his rump, begging and pleading to be released.

I let him go and he just lies there, chubby, smooth and crying. His tits wobble gently in time with his sobs, making him look really sweet.

My prank is an instant hit with the guys. Someone tends to sumo's injury with a cold compress and we are both cheered and applauded.

Later, as I cuddle up to my gorgeous big sumo teddy bear, some of the guys ask if I would like to become a regular member of the boys' night gang. Would I? But when I have accepted the question arises of my initiation ceremony.

Sumo hugs me and his eyes glint.

THE SIDEKICK
Bert McKenzie

I begged my editor to pick someone else for the assignment, but he said everyone else was busy. Still, I had to try. Interviewing celebrities, and a popular TV show personality at that! I had planned to spend the weekend at the Pink Collar, where they were having a Mr. Leather contest. What a waste!

I'm the drama critic for the Sun. It's not the most glamorous of jobs but it pays pretty good and I get free theater tickets so I'm not complaining. It's just a job and something to do till my novel wins the Pulitzer. Meanwhile I have a small desk at the end of the city room and I get to do the occasional arts feature. But this feature was not one of my choosing.

"Rancor, the Dragonslayer" is one of the more popular TV shows in the syndication market, especially with the younger crowd, pre-teens through adolescents. The theme is simple enough: Rancor, a gorgeous, dark-haired man dressed in furry boots and a leather loincloth spends an hour each week fighting some fantasy character: a dragon, an evil wizard, a three- headed serpent and, in the process, manages to save one primitive culture after another. The show is usually picked up by some local station and aired just before the national anthem on Saturday night. Consequently I have only seen it once or twice. I'm usually cruising the bars on a Saturday, looking to get laid.

Unfortunately, this weekend my editor decided I would get the dubious honor of interviewing Rancor himself. Marcus Wainwright, the ex-body builder turned would-be actor was in town on some sort of promotional tour and I was assigned to interview him. Of all the stupid tasks I had to do for the paper, this had to be one of the worst.

So why did I put up such a fuss? Okay, I'll admit the few times I've seen the show I've been impressed. It's good for a laugh now and then. But the best part is that it does have a gorgeous main character who spends an hour each week dressed in only a skimpy loincloth. That makes it worth sitting through the ridiculously contrived adventure stories. But I am a serious writer, and how can I be taken seriously if I have to interview some uneducated clod who only spouts cliché dialogue and grunts on cue.

When I got to the hotel I found I was already vastly outnumbered. It seems every prepubescent girl this side of Springfield had decided to come and stage a demonstration. They all wanted a glimpse, a smile, an autographed picture, a chance to touch his loincloth and maybe reach underneath. Okay, so that last part was my wandering mind. I admit the guy is pretty hot. I flashed my credentials at security and was ushered into the elevator and up to the seventh floor.

Some fat, balding, Italian guy in a cheap suit greeted me in the sitting room of a large suite. He handed me a folder already filled with bios, background on the show and the actors and told me that Marcus would be right with me. I was then left alone to glance through the information. Typical press releases and publicity stuff. I didn't even need to meet this phony actor. I could write my article just from the information in the folder.

"Hi." I looked up and into the bluest eyes I had ever seen. They were in the face of Scott Sloan, the sidekick. Sloan was the only other regular in the series, the guy who was supposed to help Rancor in his adventures, and provide plot twists by occasionally getting captured, needing to be rescued, and adding a bit of comic relief now and then. Sloan was also one of the most beautiful men I had ever seen in the flesh. He was a little under six feet tall, with sandy blond hair, a round, likable face and a broad, white-toothed smile. His body, although not as pumped as the star's bodybuilder physique, was nothing to be embarrassed about, broad shoulders tapering down to a thin waist, and muscular legs packed into tight jeans. There was also a sizable bulge packed into those jeans as well.

"I know you're here to interview Marcus, but will I do instead?" he asked with an apologetic look on his face. "I'm sorry, but it looks like his manager wants him to rest before we do the local TV promo this afternoon."

I bristled at being brushed off so quickly. "My editor had this all arranged," I said as I stood up, preparing to leave. Actually I was grateful that I didn't have to go through with the interview.

"I know, and I'm sorry," the sidekick said. "It's just that ..." He looked nervously around. "Well, you know these stars." The man then laughed uncomfortably.

My anger began to subside, and I felt sorry for him, being put on the spot like that. "So you get to do the dirty work and send me on my way, Mr. Sloan?"

"Call me Scott," he said reaching out a hand. I shook it, noticing his firm grip. The man had incredibly long, almost delicate fingers. "I know they promised you an interview with Marcus, but really, I'd be glad to talk with you about the show if I can pinch hit for him."

Well, maybe this would give me a whole new perspective for my article. I sat down and pulled out my pad. "Okay, Scott. Tell me a little bit about the show." He began to give me all the press information I already had. He then launched into the official information on his partner. Apparently the sidekick had memorized his p.r. information well. Then I decided to take a different angle. "But what about you?"

"Me?" He had a shocked look on his face. "What do you want to know about me?"

"Well, you're the sidekick, and you're pretty popular in your own right. How do you feel to be working in Wainwright's shadow?"

He grinned another of those dazzling smiles. "I love Marcus. He's a great guy and we get along swell. There's no competition between us if that's what you're looking for."

"Wouldn't you like to be in a show of your own?"

"No. I'm right where I want to be. I live in the here and now. I don't plan for the future or dwell in the past."

I had to admit, this guy was good. He was almost too good, not giving me any dirt for my story. He was also giving me one hell of a bone in my slacks. Every time he smiled I just wanted to lean forward and kiss those lips, explore that mouth and those perfect teeth with my tongue. He seemed so genuine, not the typical Hollywood phony I expected to find.

"So what are your plans while here in our fair city?"

"We do that local TV station this afternoon, then we just hang around here until it's time to go tomorrow. This was supposed to be our vacation so they aren't pushing us much."

"You're just going to hang around the hotel suite tonight?" I asked. What a boring evening.

Again, that nervous look crept into Scott's eyes and he glanced toward the door to the rest of the suite. "Unfortunately the production company tries to keep a pretty tight rein on us. They think it might be too dangerous to go out in public. Crazy fans and all, you know."

I couldn't help myself. The words were out of my mouth before I knew what I said. "What a shitty way to spend a Saturday night. I'd love to show you around if you weren't cooped up in here."

Now that statement brought his biggest grin yet. Scott reached over and placed one of those delicate hands on my knee. "Well, if you're serious I could meet you in the back alley behind the hotel, say around 9:00."

"The back alley?"

Just then the fat Italian guy returned and ushered me out. But not before I again shook hands with Scott, and noticed him wink at me when his "nanny" wasn't looking.

At 9:00 I was leaning on the side of my car, looking up at the back side of the hotel. It was a tall, impressive edifice, built in the twenties with lots of fancy stone work, ledges, gargoyles and the like. But it was also the best hotel in our little Midwestern town. Then suddenly I spotted him, Scott Sloan, the sidekick. He was inching his way along a ledge on the seventh floor! I couldn't believe it. The man must be crazy!

As I watched in horror, knowing he would be killed, falling to his death practically at my feet, he jumped off the ledge, catching a stone gargoyle, then dropped down to another ledge, one floor below. Graceful as a cat, he scurried along the stone pathway, grabbed a flagpole, flipped over to a drain pipe and slid down three more floors. Then the man jumped onto a window ledge, reached down to where a fire escape hung and flipped onto it, walked down the stairs to the second floor, grabbed the counterweighted ladder and stepped off, allowing his body weight to bring the ladder gently down to street level. Scott stepped off in front of me, opened his hands in a theatrical pose and said, "Taa-daa."

"How did you ... I mean you could have been...."

"I used to be a circus acrobat. That's where they discovered me," he said with a laugh. "On the show I do all my own stunts and fight scenes. We're very low budget."

Only then did I notice what he was wearing. Scott was dressed in boots and leather pants, and a black leather vest that laced up, with no shirt beneath. It was one hot outfit and I was already beginning to get heated by the sight. His vest showed the tightly corded stomach I had seen on the TV show, but what was more obvious in person was the thin line of blond hair leading down between his pecs, around his navel and into those skin tight pants. The pants themselves had laces up the front over the fly, tied in a bow just below his navel.

"Am I dressed appropriately to go out exploring your town?" Scott asked with a grin.

"Well...." My voice squeaked in an octave above my natural register.

"If not I could always climb back up and change."

"No," I said, perhaps a bit too quickly. "We can go, um, to, um...."

"Well, how about someplace for a drink? Someplace where there won't be a ton of teenage girls. Maybe someplace dark and intimate."

"Get in," I growled, jerking the car door open. Once inside, I sped down the alley and out into the street. My mind was racing, not knowing where to take this handsome stud.

"Hey, that looks like a hot spot. I might fit right in." We had just turned down Main Street and there on the left was the Pink Collar. A number of men stood outside, dressed in their leather finest.

"I don't think you'd like that place," I said. How could I take this visiting actor and celebrity to a gay bar. For all I knew he might be totally straight.

"Why not?" he asked.

"Well, it's a gay bar."

"So what's wrong with that. Some of my best friends are gay." Okay, so he was an open-minded straight boy.

We pulled into a parking spot and hopped out. I wasn't oblivious to the stares that Scott drew as we walked up to the door. "Cover charge tonight," the man at the door grunted, then looked up and into Scott's smiling face. "Forget it, Mr. Sloan. Be our guest."

I was humiliated. He had been recognized. "Can I take my friend in with me?" he asked, putting a strong arm around my shoulders. The bouncer at the door didn't look too happy, but nodded.

Inside the bar was packed. We wormed our way to a table by the littler makeshift stage, and ordered a couple of beers. Then, as we tried to talk over the blaring music, the sound cut off, the lights changed, and a man stepped onto the stage carrying a microphone. He announced that tonight was the Mr. Leather contest, and invited anyone wanting to compete to step up. There were three men who climbed onto the stage. They were attractive enough, but none of them had the open good looks of my blond demi-god. "What do you think?" Scott asked as he nodded his head toward the stage.

"I think you should be up there," I replied.

"No, I meant, do you like any of 'em?"

"I still think you could win, hands down."

To my surprise, Scott drained his bottle, then climbed out of his chair and stepped up onto the stage. He was instantly greeted with whistles and applause.

The contest began and one by one the men stepped forward to do a brief routine. They danced a bit, flexed a bit, then stripped down to show their bodies. The first man only removed his vest to show his tits were pierced and attached to each other with a small gold chain. Number two took off his leather jacket and flexed his muscles to reveal tattoos of naked men on his back. The third contestant went a bit further and stripped off his chaps to stand before us in skin-tight leather shorts.

Now it was Scott's turn. I was really nervous. He hadn't prepared for this. What could he do? The music came up and he stepped forward into the spotlight, dancing and moving to the beat. He then unlaced the vest, slipped it off and stood bare chested, showing his incredible, muscular physique. He surprised the crowd by dropping down toward the floor and springing into a handstand, which popped the muscles out on his back. Next he kicked off his boots, then pulled the lacing at his crotch. My heart was in my mouth as I watched my fantasy man slip off his tight leather pants. He stood up, dressed only in a leather g-string. The full pouch of black leather was pushed forward, perched between thick, well developed thighs. He smiled and writhed to the beat of the music as the crowd went wild. Then he turned around, giving us a view of that perfect ass, the twin melons divided by the thin strand of black leather running up his ass crack. On his right cheek was a small tattoo of a red rose. Scott bent over, giving us a view of that delectable flower, then grabbed up his vest and turned to take a bow.

There was no question. The crowd response was overwhelming, and in a minute he was sitting back at my table with that wonderful smile, his hands holding the silver chalice that was given to him as a trophy. Photographers came forward, snapping his picture, and as they did, he reached out and pulled me up against his sweaty body so I would be in the shot. Then, while they snapped away, Scott turned and kissed me full on the mouth. I was in heaven.

After a few more beers he leaned forward and said, "Let's get out of here. It's a bit too close." I paid the tab and he slipped back into his pants and boots, but carried the vest. We managed to pull away from the crowd of men wanting his autograph, then dashed out the door and back to the car. "Well, what do you think? Did I fit in?" he asked.

"Yes, I'd say so," I replied. It occurred to me that this was all just an act. He was performing for the crowds. I just got caught up in it along with the rest of the on-lookers. "Where to now? Back to your hotel?"

Scott seemed depressed, dropping into silence. Then he looked at me with those intense, blue eyes. "I was thinking maybe we could go to your place. But if you'd rather not, I understand." I started up the car and drove like a demon to my apartment.

Once inside the door, he tossed his vest on the couch and grabbed me in a bone-crushing hug, pressing his hot, sweaty body against me and kissing me deeply, his tongue probing far into my mouth. When we broke the kiss, I staggered back, still dazed and confused. "I thought you said you weren't gay. Is this all just some kind of act?"

"I never said I wasn't gay. I said I had lots of gay friends. Most gay men do. Now are you just going to stand there, or are you going to get naked and make love to me?"

I quickly began to strip my clothes off, my cock already responding and swelling inside my underwear. But Scott just stood there, watching me. When I finally stood bare-assed naked in front of him, he smiled and kicked off his boots. "Come help me with these," he said and stood before me, waiting for my trembling hands. I slowly unlaced his fly and pulled down, sliding the tight leather pants to the floor. Then I reached up and pulled down on the g-string. His prick jumped to life, happy to be released from its confining leather prison. It was a beauty, eight inches of thick man-meat, capped by a shiny pink head just poking out of a wrinkled sleeve of skin.

My watering mouth couldn't wait, and I leaned forward, kissing it gently on the head. My lips were instantly rewarded with a thick dollop of sparkling precum. It tasted salty, whetting my appetite for more. Opening my lips, I pulled close and let the blond god sink his tool into my mouth. It filled me, pressing firmly on my tonsils and momentarily shutting off my air supply. But then he pulled back and I felt empty. In seconds I was again rewarded with that rock-hard shaft as Scott pushed into my mouth, picking up speed and beginning to fuck my face.

My tongue swirled around and around the shaft, darting under the foreskin to taste him, lapping up the generous flow of lube that oozed out of his piss hole. One of my hands gently cupped his balls, tickling and massaging them in their tight sack of skin while my other hand felt its way around to his ass, slipping my fingers between those firm cheeks and finding that hot, steaming pucker.

Scott groaned with pleasure and if anything, began to pump his dick into my face with more gusto. His hands cradled my head, those long fingers wrapping themselves in my brown curls as he fucked into me.

In seconds he let out an animal cry of passion and pressed me forward, flooding my mouth and throat with a hefty load of thick spunk. I swallowed as fast as I could, but his balls kept shooting more and more into me until it ran down my chin, dripping onto my chest.

We slowly fell apart, and I wiped my mouth with the back of my hand, savoring the last sensation of his fantastic load. "That was great," Scott said as he stared down at me, his blue eyes dazzling me. I knew he was a mildly famous actor and this was just a quick, physical escape for him. I didn't have any illusions or expect anything more. I slowly stood, stepping close, and he reached out to enfold me in his arms. For one blissful moment I felt a surge of love for this man. If only it wasn't just a quick bit of sex on the road.

"So, where's your bedroom?" he asked, holding me against his naked body.

I figured he wanted to use the john. "Through there," I said and pointed out the doorway to the other room.

Scott took my hand and pulled me after him, stepping into the dark bedroom. Then he stretched out on the bed, dragging me down on top of him. "I want you in the worst way," he whispered. "It's been ages since I had my ass fucked, and I want that big cock of yours inside me."

Not believing my ears, I instinctively reached for a condom on the night stand, opened the package and slipped it onto my still-hard dick.

Scott lifted his legs, pulling his knees up to his chest and forcing his ass cheeks apart. "Do it now!" he begged. "Shove that cock up inside me. I want to feel a real man fucking me."

I fell forward, my dick pressing against his tight hole. With a grunt of pleasure, I pressed forward and my cockhead slipped inside his ring. "Ahh," we both moaned in pleasure. That first moment when you slide inside is the best ... well, almost the best.

"Fuck me, stud. Fuck my tight ass. Pump me hard. Make me know what a real man feels like," he begged. I quickly obliged, pressing into him, sliding my hard seven inches deeper and deeper until my pubes were tight against his balls. Then I slowly pulled back, watching my cock reveal itself as it came out of his guts.

With a firm push, I rammed back in, making my hot television actor cry out in pleasure. He began to push back, meeting my thrusts, his ass milking my cock and driving me insane with pleasure. Faster and faster I fucked into him. We both began to groan and cry out.

In a frozen moment in time, my passion overwhelmed me and I climaxed, filling his ass with my cum as it pumped out into the latex bag inside him. At the same moment, Scott began to shoot again, his cock firing a hot blast of cum up onto my naked chest. Again and again he shot, splattering the two of us with white blotches of cream.

Slowly I slid out of his ass, pulled off the rubber and tossed it aside. Scott pulled me down onto his chest, gluing our bodies together with his cum. We fell asleep in each other's arms.

The next morning I awoke, alone in bed. I got up, threw on a robe, then stumbled out to find my TV star setting breakfast on the table. He was dressed in his leather outfit from the night before. "Hope you didn't mind," he said with that world- famous grin. "I was hungry and I figured you would be too. I raided your refrigerator."

We had just sat down to eat when there was a loud knocking at the door. I got up and opened it, and to my surprise there stood the fat, balding man from the hotel suite. "Figured you'd be here," he complained as he pushed past me and walked up to Scott. "It wasn't hard to figure out what was going on when I saw the papers." He had a morning edition of my paper in his hand. He threw it down on the table. There on the cover was a photo of Scott smiling at the camera, his arm around me, and the silver trophy in his other hand. The caption read, "TV star wins contest in local gay bar."

"This is gonna hurt your contract negotiations, you know," the man said. "Now come on. We got a plane to catch."

"I have to go," Scott said, his eyes looking downcast.

"I know. It's okay," I lied. "It was a lot of fun."

"Listen, can I call you when I get back home?" he asked.

"Sure," I nodded, but we both knew it was just something to say. He followed the fat man out of my apartment. I dashed to the balcony and saw them come out the main door and head for a black limousine parked at the curb. Scott looked back up at me and gave me a half wave. I figured that was the last I would see him.

The show really is pretty good once you get into it. Of course I don't ooh and aah over Rancor like you're supposed to. My eyes are on that blond sidekick, fighting along with him. Rancor may win the battle and get the girl, but I've had the sidekick, so I really know who won the trophy. Speaking of which, there's a silver chalice on my mantle, right beside the autographed picture that's signed "Love you." Shit, I may just take my vacation in Hollywood this year.

THE INTERN
Rick Jackson

When I accepted the offer to intern two days a week with an important San Francisco law firm, I knew the experience would open doors. As my classes at Stanford Law were winding down, I needed all the contacts I could get. I knew the internship would open plenty of doors. It did that along with a few windows I didn't even know were there.

My first two months were interesting and dull. I liked the idea of being involved in real cases for a change, but digging cites out of law books and databases could get pretty tame after eight or ten hours. I suppose, though, that I must have made an impression on someone because one of the junior associates picked me to help him hunt for a client's will.

Dave Williams, the associate, told me all about the problem on the drive down to the farm. Normally the firm keeps wills in the files, of course; but this guy was something of a character. To keep his name confidential, we'll call him Mac because every time I think of the guy, I think of Old MacDonald. As a hobby, he ran a dairy farm southeast of town; his money came from videotape production. The guy was only in his mid-40s and didn't expect to die, so he was in no hurry to bring the will into the office after he had signed it. Then he had that grotesque accident with his milking machine and his time ran out.

The heirs mostly nephews and nieces and several foundations were eager to start looting the estate, so we needed the will to probate. Our job was to ransack his farmhouse and find the will. Dave warned me that we would probably find all sorts of unusual things lying around because of his movie connections. When we got to the farm, Dave headed for Mac's office and sent me up to see whether I could strike pay dirt in his bedroom.

The place didn't look like a farmhouse; it was decorated more like the set of Frasier. His bedroom was something else entirely. I had walked all the way in before the impact hit me. Then I just had to stop and stare. Two walls and the ceiling were mirrored. One wall was papered with an enormous photograph of a man's sweaty chest with both hard nipples ready to let go a gleaming drop. The wall with the door was another huge photo, this time an artsy view of a man's firm tanned ass, all speckled over with golden sand. Even I could tell it was good photography, but it was oddly unsettling.

The books and photos I found as I sorted through the bookshelves and drawers disturbed me even more. One photo after another showed good-looking, well-built men beating off or dripping jism or doing each other up the ass. One whole drawer proved that the casting couch still lived. It was filled with pictures of Mac fucking his actors and models in every way I could imagine. Granted, I couldn't imagine very many just then, but Mac had been very, very inventive, indeed.

Many of the photos had close-ups of the actors' faces, twisted by pain or humiliation. The more I looked, though, the less sure I was about that. The eyes were clenched and the mouths strained in screams, but those faces glowed with a raw, elemental power I knew I would never understand. One photo after another riveted me. I couldn't tear my eyes away from those tributes to male beauty and the curious mix of agony and rapture I found there. More to the point, I didn't understand my own reaction.

When the guys at school had gotten all excited by dirty pictures, I was left unmoved and clueless about their reactions. These photos were somehow different. Thirty seconds after I came into the room, my dick was harder than it ever had been, and it stayed that way, throbbing and demanding to be let out for a run. Finally, I just couldn't take the strain of being cramped up any more and absentmindedly unzipped to stroke off.

I felt really strange I was lightheaded, my heart raced, and I had the oddest sensation in the pit of my stomach. I was too lost in spanking off and trying to find meaning in all those tormented eyes to hear Dave come in. I gather he stood looking at me for a while before he chuckled and made me jump halfway up my ass. He said, "I thought you might find those interesting, but let me help you with that."

Before I could even start to lie, Dave was kneeling before me and my rubbered dick was in his mouth. His lips made both my heads spin, but they were only the beginning. As his heavenly mouth slowly worked its way farther down my dick, his hands tore first at my clothes and then at his. I found myself lying on Mac's bed, looking up at a reflected image that was impossibly surreal: my naked body spread wide and humping upwards into Dave's tight, wet mouth. You would think that the rubber would have gotten in our way, but I felt every bump on his tongue as it tortured my head, every lash of his lips as my shank stretched tight, and every surging suck as he reached clear through to the bone.

His mouth was such a revelation that I didn't notice his hands, but the mirror showed me the no good they were up to. One was hidden under his face as it clenched and pulled at my tender nuts, but the other reached boldly up across my flesh and into my affections, caressing my hard belly and teaching my tits how fine a man can feel. That hand drifted along my flanks and across my pecs and then wandered like ravening Mongol hordes, aimlessly seeking adventure and conquest, yet leaving ruin and lamentation in their wake.

I watched my hands lay hold of Dave's head and ease it even farther down my dick until he ran out of face and I pressed my throbbing tool hard against the entrance to his throat. Even Dave's magical mouth was apparently bound by the laws of physics. No matter how hard I pushed down or humped up, I just couldn't work my way down his gullet. Tight as he was, Dave did his best to take care of me, and I have only one complaint: he couldn't keep his head pumping up and down my pounding dick forever.

How he knew when I was about to go all messy, I can't think; but he did and he lifted his head off my dick and let it slap up against my belly. In the next second, Dave was in my face, his lips tearing into mine as his tongue ripped deep along mine and took my breath away. I twisted slightly away from him to catch our reflection in the mirror, more out of wanton prurience than actually believing what was unfolding before my eyes.

I felt as if I were watching two other delicious creatures rolling about naked, their hard muscles rippling beneath eager hands. The men grinding their dicks together seemed too exotic to be Dave and me, but they were. I suddenly realized that I could be the man in all those pictures; I could experience what they felt. And with that realization, my dick swelled even more until it threatened to split in two. I made up my mind that I'd ask Dave to do me after he had finished showing me the rest of his tricks.

I don't know how Dave knew I was gay before I did, and I certainly have no clue how he decided I was a virgin. Maybe a good lawyer just has to read people well. He certainly knew how to read me, but I suppose with my dick fucking him in the belly, I was a large print edition. He moved from my mouth to rain kisses and nuzzles along my neck; but, when he reached my ear, he turned violent, drilling his tongue deep through my ear to lick my brain dry. My body heaved and bucked and shivered, but I was as powerless to shake his grip on my ear as I was to know where he was heading next.

When he had finished tonguing me as witless as a Carolina Republican, he licked his way south towards my tits. If his fingers had opened that particular window, the electric touch of his slick lips slurping up and down my swollen tit-stalks and what he did with the dangerous edge of his teeth would have shattered every pane in the Crystal Palace.

I couldn't take my eyes off our radiant reflections me humping upwards into his chest as he tore my tits towards a tort and him wriggling and clenching his firm, full ass. That hard butt looked every bit as powerful and empowering as the specimen plastered across Mac's bedroom wall only Dave's spectacle lacked the sand to bugger up the works.

Once my tits were toast, Dave started south again, but I shoved a foot into his crotch and pulled him back up so I could give him my pleading. I didn't even blush or stutter; I came out, wicked and wanton beyond belief, and just said, "Fuck me, Dave." I felt like a cross between HAL and one of those beautifully crazy boy-toys in the pictures, but Dave smiled and gave my belly a dig with his big dick by way of warning.

If I had hefted the thing first or tried to wrap my hand around it, even a dumb-assed virgin like me would probably have been more realistic about what to expect. I suppose maybe all virgins are dumb-assed, or they wouldn't be virgins.

Dave lifted my legs and put his monster bone against my hole. He had slathered handfuls of lube onto his rubber, but he didn't bother to take all day fingering me open. We were both in much too big a hurry for unnecessary details, and besides, given what he had, not even Paderewski's fingering technique would have saved my ass. He lingered for a moment, looking down at me looking up at him. Then he gave that foxy little smile he uses when he is feeling impish and planted his lips back onto mine.

Just as I started to suck his mouth tongueless, his pelvis pounded forward, reaming his rubbered dick through my ass and ripping my guts open. My head jerked away from his, but his tongue slammed back down my ear to confuse my brain into hoping I might survive. I couldn't think or talk or breathe, so I held on tight, grabbing Dave's back and pulling myself upwards as though he could save me from myself.

Even with the distraction, wave after blinding wave of agony flooded upwards from my mangled ass and, for the longest time, Dave just hung in there biding his time. I was just starting to breathe again when Dave yanked several inches of his monster dick out and put them back again the hard way. Again, I gasped and clutched against my tormenter's hard, naked body, but I did, somehow, survive.

Soon Dave was sliding in and out of my guts, ricocheting off my prostate, ramming his way into my pancreas, and generally having himself one very good time at my expense. The miracle was that as he used my body like a Disneyland ride. I wasn't having all that bad a time, either. Within two minutes tops, the pain had gradually transmuted to pleasure and my butthole was clenching down around Dave's dancing dick tightly enough to learn the steps. My hips once more humped upwards on their own, this time not digging my dick into Dave's lean belly, but cramming the savage width of his shank up through my guts.

Our bodies slammed together with thunderous claps of pelvis against butt as I gradually came to the realization that I was the one shouting out all the SHITs and OH, FU Ks. Dave kept himself busy breathing heavy and grunting each time his swollen knob grounded out up my ass. His hands held my shoulders tight from below so I didn't bounce forward however hard he fucked me and he fucked me plenty hard and deep and fast.

The feel of his lips on my ear and neck, the brutal ravaging of my virgin ass, the smell of sweat and man-musk, our sounds of animal lust, and the incredible feeling of surging fullness up my guts all spun together in a fearsome blending of images and fears, of dreams and destiny fulfilled until I slipped into that salacious stupor a lucky man can experience but once or twice in his lifetime. I lost track of details, but will remember until my final hour the way Dave's fierce fire of contentment burned out of control up my ass.

As I coasted and humped and slammed my way along Dave's dick, I became a man. I had thought myself a man for years; most boys of any age do. Only when he was breeding my butt, however, did I realize the full potential of a man's body and how to use it to fight my way towards perfection. One moment flowed inevitably, gloriously into the next as Dave banged my eager butt raw and then really let me have it.

I was shocked, sometime later, to discover we had only been at it about 25 minutes. The time between having my asshole ripped open and snapping back to full consciousness seemed at once an instant and an eternity. When I did snap back and found my bone still trapped between our rutting bodies, but gushing out more creamy marrow than any one mortal had a right to hold, all I felt was good. Dave must have agreed, because he lost his load just as I was running low.

His hands and teeth gripped my body harder, his hips humped dick deep up my ass in savage, rabbit-like strokes that only moved a couple of inches at a time, but slashed away towards glory until half-past forever.

By the time his nuts were drained and my ass had forgotten what boyhood felt like, Dave was ready to cuddle. Even before he tried to get all warm and lovey on me, I discovered another revelation: the dick up my ass when I had shot off not only felt fine, but it also kept my unit stiff and ready for more.

Dave's dick was no more out of my ass than I rolled him onto his back and reached down to lift his legs. He gave me that grin again and drew cocky, smart-assed parallels to Dr. Frankenstein, but once I was rubbered up afresh, he let my monster ravage his ass the way it deserved and it deserved every wicked, thick inch I had.

Two hours and four rubbers later, we were showering in Mac's Bauhaus Xanadu of porcelain and chrome when I thought to ask Dave whether he had found the will. He gave me a playful poke with his dick and guaranteed he had all the will I needed right where it counted. Mac's will had been in his office desk, right where he had expected. The only reason he had sent me up to search his bedroom was because he knew what I would find and hoped it would be more about myself than about Mac's taste in photography.

Much has been written of late about interns and sex with the boss. I'm totally against sex in the workplace unless I'm there and Dave is there and we both have the will.

THE FRESHMEN
Rick Jackson

Joey and I grew up next door to each other. We went camping as Boy Scouts and double dated later on. In fact, the high point of my youth happened just after we left high school when Joey and I borrowed his brother's pickup and took Jackie-Sue Peterson up to the lake to spend the long summer night tag-teaming her senseless. Even today, the image of Joey and me heaving away in the back of that pickup will get me hard in a flash. Jackie-Sue never could make up her mind which of us she liked better, but we didn't much care. I like to think that no single mortal man could satisfy her after we showed her what our big dicks could do.

Naturally the two of us went away to the same college, though we couldn't get into the same dorm. After our freshman year, students were allowed to move out of the dorms, so that summer session of '75, Joey and I found an apartment to share. Since he had a car and a pair of arms, I let him share the job of moving all my stuff.

The dorms back then didn't have elevators and I was on the eighth floor. Moving all my books and records and stereo gear was a major pain in the ass though I didn't really understand until later how much a pain it would be. The sweltering July heat didn't help. By the time our trailer was loaded, we had long since stripped to our jogging shorts, but were sweating like febrile field hands anyway.

In those innocent good old days, we 18 year-olds could drink. Joey and I trooped back up to my room one last time to down a couple of beers and cool off. We were sitting around with our second beers, talking of nothing in particular, when Joey's sweaty chest and shorts reminded me of our moonlit fuck with Jackie-Sue. I couldn't help getting hard, and Joey couldn't help noticing. I had just started to blush at not being able to corral my mustang, when the look on Joey's face changed my life forever.

His mouth was wide in a full, wry grin, but his eyes were haunted by a desperate, aching hunger I had never seen in him before. Those huge, soulful brown eyes rose slowly, almost worshipfully, from my crotch to visually rape my body before they remembered to hide the emotion that lurked, hidden and secret, in their depths.

We talked about something else for a while; I have long since forgotten about what. As our conversation rambled along, some subconscious corner of my mind was working overtime trying to analyze that look and more. Something was up, but I had no clue what it was.

71

Then the nickel dropped. Sitting there chatting with Joey, I realized for the first time how his body had changed. I didn't consider myself an expert in what made men look hot and sexy, but it was obvious even to me that the scrawny kid I had gone skinny-dipping with all those summers ago was gone forever.

Joey had filled out something fierce. His hairless pecs and six-pack abs were harder than the average Praxiteles', and the sweat drenching his body gave him a positively electric sheen. His face had strengthened, too. Joey's brow and jaw are as strong as any Mountie's, but his large mouth and full lips were deliciously sensual, even without the dimples he had in such abundance. The careless shock of sun-bleached straw cascading across his brow conspired to blend the strength of golden youth with the winsome eroticism of the archetypal farm boy.

I don't know how long I was woolgathering, but when I stopped staring and got back with the program, Joey was talking about how I didn't have to be sheepish about the occasional woodie. He said he hadn't been laid in so long that not even lashing the lizard was helping. All he could think about was getting off, but no matter what he did, he always needed more. He was waking up from wet dreams two or three times a night. If only there were something he could do.

Now, of course, I would have known where he was heading, but I was young and naive. After beating the bush for ten minutes, he finally came right out and asked if I could help him out. What he had in mind was kinky and would weird me out, but he needed it bad, and no one would ever know. When he came right out and asked me to whack him off, the whole idea was so gross and depraved and deliciously wicked that I thought my dick would explode on the spot.

I had never so much as thought about touching another guy's dick but Joey wasn't just another guy. He was closer to me than my snot-nosed punk of brother. Besides, he was right. It would look queer if someone saw us, but we knew we weren't perverts and that was all that counted. He suggested I get naked, too, so he could return the favor.

That night in the back of the pick-up, I hadn't bothered to look at Joey's stiff joint at least not consciously; but it was something awesome. Standing tall and half banging against his hard belly that sultry July afternoon, that incredible dick changed my life. I don't think I had ever thought of any dick but mine as being interesting, but with my first touch, I loved Joey's thick joint more than I understood.

My hands were shaking with the delicious anticipation of wickedness and clumsy because his joint was the wrong way round for beating off. The main surprises, though, were how soft the skin was and how alive and

72

throbbing it felt, more like some skittish woodland creature than my buddy's dirty dick. Joey's daddy hadn't had him cut so that was another wicked rush of discovery. I had seen untrimmed meat in the showers at school and so on, but Joey was my first chance to see how they really worked and what was connected to what.

I must have spent ten or fifteen minutes gliding his foreskin up and down across that glistening purple knob as Joey lay back and moaned like my best bitch. His balls hung heavy and low, but my free hand instinctively found them and hefted them high. Joey's crotch smelled like aged sweat and other nasty kinds of locker room filth but every whiff of that virile stench launched my pulse farther into overdrive.

His hips soon learned how to fuck upwards, lashing his way harder into my hand with every stroke. I looked up across the rippling muscles of his bare, sweaty torso at the rapture building on his familiar face and knew I was crossing a torrent on a very shaky bridge even if I was clueless what lay on the far bank.

Joey used my hand faster and harder with every stroke so that soon I was ripping his skin across his tender knob and thrashing clear down to slam my fist into his soft, golden curls. His lips moved to a newly discovered mantra "Yes. Yes. Yes. Yes" until his hips bucked high and he yelled out for me to stop. I had thought the whole idea was to get him to nut, but he said he was having too much fun just to blow. Instead, he would show me a thing or two.

I felt halfway goofy lying back to let Joey wrap his hand around my stiff dick but I also felt naughty and good. Soon, I felt even better. My crank didn't have the built-in knob-guard, but he did just fine for awhile. Then I warned him I was frictioning up and asked him to stop for a second so I could apply some spit to lube my love. The pervert did something which grossed me completely for about half a second: the crazy bastard stuck my big, nasty dick into his mouth.

Well, to be fair, he only stuck the head of my dick into his mouth. His face was too small to take any more than that without a struggle. I couldn't believe a guy would suck another guy's dick. Oh, sure, I'd heard wild stories and jokes about what gay guys did, but I'd also heard stories about trained gerbils and Elvis bagging groceries in Minnesota. Some stories make good entertainment, but nobody believes in them any more than in Santa Claus or the Tooth Fairy.

For the longest second of my life, I just did not trust my lying eyes. It was like having my tool start singing Tosca or catching a congressman telling the truth. Then, suddenly, my brain exploded with the hot, wet sensation of Joey's lips and tongue sliding across my knob and, later, his tight lips pounding up and down my shank as my head bounced off the back of his cock sucking throat.

He sucked my stiff dick better than any girl could firm, frisky strokes up and down as his hand played with my nuts and he Hoovered so hard I threatened to give up a nut. Of course, that's just what I did. I held out for two or three minutes, caught in a vortex of unfamiliar raptures and shattering taboos. By the time he was slamming his nose into my pubes, though, and his throat had taken control of my dick, I was primed to fire. Then I felt his fingers coast down across my asshole actually touching my shithole with his fingers while my dick throbbed down his throat!

There was no way I couldn't blow the nut of my young life down the perv's tight, hot throat. Fast as I was at splashing, though, it wasn't good enough for Joey. He cranked up his suction something fierce until he stopped waiting for me to spurt my jism deep and the crazy bastard was tearing the thick globs of jism up out of my balls like a starving jungle animal ripping apart his prey.

I had never felt never imagined anything akin to the savage rapture that wracked my very soul. As my guts churned to liquid and flared out through my screaming dick, all I could manage was screaming and holding tight to Joey's head as I fucked it full. I kept fucking and spurting and Joey kept bobbing and sucking until my balls ached. When, long after I had run dry, he finally gave up and eased his lips up and off my crank without losing a drop, I didn't know what to think.

When I saw the twisted perv licking a glob of my jism off his chops, it really hit me that he had taken a whole load of my slick, spermy spooge down his throat. I had already run into a lot of men who bragged they wouldn't do sloppy seconds because they weren't about to get another dude's spooge on their dicks and here Joey was EATING my stuff. I knew Joey was all right; he was my buddy but Jesus!

I just looked at him, wondering whether I was having a dream or stroke or what. Then he gave his dick a thwack with his hand that sent it bouncing up and then down hard against his belly, and he said, "Now you give it a try!"

Yeah, like I was going to stick his dick into my mouth and let him blow wads down my throat. There was zero chance of that in this lifetime. Still, he'd seemed to have a good time and his crank did smell exciting not good and certainly not clean, but wickedly interesting. I think what sold me at last was how Joey himself took the idea in stride as a possibility, almost as though men sucked his dick every other hour.

At least I could do something to help out, but I took things slow. At first I eased my face between his legs and sniffed his nuts. That same ambrosial scent of man-crotch seduced me into giving his scrote a quick flick of my tongue. Contrary to what I had expected, I didn't gag or puke. I had never tasted anything remotely similar, but it wasn't at all bad. It was wild and raw and salty, but somehow it didn't taste dirty.

I gave his balls a firmer lick and then kept going until I was sucking on Joey's `nads as though they were hard candies. Joey kept busy writhing around and hollering. I had no sooner sucked his nuts clean than the slippery slope made me wonder whether sucking the nasty head of his dick into my mouth was so outlandish after all. Once more, I used a quick taste of his knob, safely covered by his cocksock, to discover he tasted just fine. Then, slowly, relentlessly, I pried his `skin down, stretching it wide across his stinky knob, and followed it with my tongue.

What I had taken for nasty became my new definition of very nice, indeed. I wouldn't realize until much, much later that the taste of an uncut dick is man's oldest and truest aphrodisiac. That July afternoon, as I slowly sucked my buddy's shank to glory, I knew only that everything about it was perfect: the rapturous scent and taste, the hot throb against my tongue, the wet seal of my lips against his firm bone, the hard feel of his head nuzzled deep in my mouth, the grip of his fingers in my hair or his hands on my ears as he shoved up and down his surging shank, the feel of his nuts rising to press against my chin as his hips rolled upwards and drilled my gullet deeper.

Every sight and smell and taste and texture was so foreign that I had nothing to judge it by. I was lost, floating on a sea of churning sensuality with only one hard, throbbing log to keep me afloat. I gave myself up to Destiny and let myself scud across that heaving sea towards an unknown but immensely magical horizon. I knew only that even though I was lost, I had discovered myself at last.

Everything about Joey's naked body bred the ultimate in satisfaction. Now that I had learned how blissfully, soul-shatteringly, down-and-dirty fun fucking could be, I made up my mind that I was a man's man from that moment on.

Then Joey got all sloppy down my throat and I was too busy chugging cream to philosophize. When I finally pulled his saucy meat far enough up into my mouth to actually taste his bone's tangy marrow, I couldn't believe how many years I had wasted on burgers and ice-cream. Not only was Joey a hard, hunky source of savory protein, he was even free.

Later that afternoon he showed me other tricks when he licked my asshole raw and fucked me three times harder than we had done Jackie-Sue but by then I was beyond surprise. For the first time in my life, everything was new and exciting and I had a lifetime to learn it all. Joey and I are still practicing today, and you would think that after so many years together, he would have run out of randy revelations. He hasn't, though. If anything, the twisted bastard has grown even more cunning and unpredictable with experience, but I don't mind learning something new now and again. I'm as quick on the uptake as Joey is on the output. Nobody could ask for a better basis for a relationship than that.

THE NIGHT TAKES OVER
John Patrick

It is after midnight and I'm about to leave the bar, but I don't. I don't, because, all at once, the night takes over. From out of nowhere, out of the crowd there appears a young dancer. Transfixed, I watch the fleet glide of his body across the dance floor, finally coming to rest. Lithe and limber, his feet firmly anchored in wide shoes, now he begins to dance like a seducer of the first rank. There is a supple twisting of the head, slender articulate hands, coaxing nothings out of the air, giving shape to motion. The magic of chemistry refreshes me, brings a flush to my face. I must have him.

When he finally sits down on at the bar in the back, I move there and sit as close as I dare. The age gap yawns between us, but I feel violent and timid at the same time, utterly ageless.

He's mopping his face with his handkerchief and I offer to buy him a drink.

"I think you need one," I say.

He smiles. "You can't buy me a real drink, 'cause I'm under age."

"Oh." I should have known, since it's "Chicken Night," when they let the younger ones in.

"But I am thirsty," he says, stretching.

"What would you like?"

"Grapefruit juice."

When the bartender delivers two grapefruit juices, the dazzling dancer smiles.

We chat for a bit, and then he reveals, "I have to move out of my parents' house, but I'm too young to sign a lease."

"Tough," I commiserate.

We drink our juices in silence. The disc jockey spins "Electric Slide." His legs, stretched out for miles in front of him, are angling for action. His shoulders tense and his dark eyes flash. Everyone is moving in the same direction. He stands up straight in front of me.

"Let's boogie."

"I'm wearing the wrong shoes."

"Nonsense," he laughs. "Your shoes are fine. You're making excuses." His laugh has a nice, clear ring to it, bells at Christmas. He grabs both my hands firmly, irresistibly. "Come on, it's not often I get to dance with a guy so handsome."

77

I'm won over. With its amazing power, the music shakes the old man slack out of my body. I let the boy choreograph as much as he wants, and we enter a world of rhythm, silence and gesture, a world of our own. We close the place down.

We stop a block from his house. He has introduced himself as Gary. He lets me unzip his tight jeans. Now I would know whether he is for real or just a sexy twist on the Cinderella story, coming out at midnight instead of the other way around. Is it possible I am here, like a teenager, parked on a deserted street, kissing the bulge in the white briefs previously hidden under the denim? Is he really letting me do this? That yes is obviously the answer to that question gives me renewed energy. I prepare to pull the fabric back, expose his cock, but he pushes my hand away.

"I understand," he says in that smooth, firm voice. "You need it. But not tonight, not here." He zips up.

"No?"

"No. When is your next night off?"

"Tomorrow."

"Tomorrow night, go to the bookstore at midnight."

"Why the bookstore?"

"Because I tell you to go there. Because we do everything my way from now on."

A shiver of desire runs through me, at his order, at the words "from now on." At the knowledge that this is not going to be easy, and I desperately want it not to be easy. He turns, and I watch him as he begins walking toward home. Then he glances back, smiles. He returns to the window. "It'll be fine," he says.

And it is fine. Very fine. Gary knows the cashier at the bookstore so his age is no problem. "Come on, man. I have plans for you," Gary says, all business and concentration now. The obvious hunger in his eyes drives me to want to do anything he asks, anything at all just to see him satisfied, pleased. The bookstore feels surreal, the atmosphere fueled by the eerie music wafting through the dimly lit place, the scenes taking place all around. It is as if at any moment I might wake up and find it was all a dream. We get a buddy booth, and I finally expose his cock. It is long and tapering, uncut, as is mine, but bends curiously, kind of down and to the left side, and the head is bulbous and even nicked by what looks like a scar, as if maybe one or more previous cocksuckers had gotten carried away with the sucking of it.

I proceed to get carried away myself, and he says he hasn't come all day, that he held off, waiting until midnight, until I could take it. I eagerly open my mouth, and he teases me with his cock, edging close then pulling away. Letting me smell his cock, his balls. I look up at his face, pleading with my eyes, ashamed of how much I want to taste his cum, yet unable to control my body's burning desire to do so.

I open my mouth and start sucking, his balls in my hand, and he puts both hands on my head, slowing me down a little, keeping me steady, letting me know I am doing fine.

Then, with a tender arch of his back, he starts coming just moments after I get it completely down my throat. Now what he gives me is his cum. Pints? Gallons? Hard to say, but whatever the immense amount, I gulp and swallow and consume every last bit of it, letting it flow down my throat. His orgasm is short, doubled and tripled with a quick convulsion, so private, so disciplined that he made no cry, no whisper, no exhortation. Cum overflows my lips and splashes down onto the grimy floor of the buddy booth.

Wiping my mouth, chin, and face with my large, monogrammed handkerchief, I say, "That's quite something." I loved it, but he came too soon; I could have sucked that cock for hours. I try to hide my disappointment.

That smile again. "I told you it'd be fine," Gary says.

"More than fine," I say. Unfulfilled, I start teasing his smooth skin with my mouth and hands, feeling and tasting the succulent skin. In pulling his jeans down to expose his cock, I have exposed his asshole as well. I turn him around and begin to kiss his ass cheeks. His asshole is firm and tight and pink and clean. Could this be an asshole of many steamy fucks, mad fucks, quick fucks, fucks in strange places? Perhaps, but it is delicious nonetheless.

"Oh, yeah," sighs Gary as I shove my tongue between the cheeks.

I am stroking my cock. I carefully position myself over him.

As my cock glides in and out of his most tender and excited opening, sweat is pouring off me, and my eyes are fluttering with anticipation of orgasm. For me, this kid is the perfect thing to fuck: hot, tight, and eager. I fuck him harder and faster, feeling my climax starting to build. My cock is throbbing inside him when he, insistent, begins urging me to come. Almost there. Yes, almost. Coming, coming. Suddenly I hear a moan coming from next door. Obviously someone is watching through the glory hole. This startles me out of one fantasy, creates another. Gary obviously enjoys being on display. He enjoys every thrust, humping himself up and down on my cock. I explode with a spasming jerk that leaves me panting, wheezing, my legs trembling. Some of my cum squirts into his tender asshole before I can pull out.

Outside, he stops, turns, and smiles. Then he gets in his car and drives away, leaving me behind, alone in the night.

A GLOW IN THE NIGHT
Brian Chambers

The statue of the Union solider was still standing guard over the northwest corner of the square. I crossed from in front of Tom Hedrick's hardware store, waiting for a green and white Ford wagon to creep past. A farm couple, approximately a thousand years old, blinked and stared from the car. I didn't recognize them. They were in town, like half the other farmers in the county, for their big-time Saturday night. Their heads turned stiffly, like elves in the animated Christmas scenes that would appear in the window of Becker's jewelry store after Thanksgiving.

When I was a little kid, I had somehow become convinced that the statue's name was Jacob. He had always seemed sad to me, as though staring past the bank and the shoe store showed him something that hurt him inside. I stared up at him now, and for the first time I thought of the ordinary Civil War soldier as a person who had grown up in a town like this. As someone who had gone off to war when he was about my age.

It was inconceivable. My heart turned over in me as I thought of all the young men squatting around campfires in the soft early-autumn air. Late fireflies spangling the nights, perhaps the sullen murmur of distant artillery. God, what would it feel like? How could a man live with the fear in his belly, churning, cold, a constant, gnawing presence?

It was the final weekend of August, 1958. One week short of the first anniversary of that monumental moment when I had truly confronted and acknowledged to myself that I just plain didn't give a goddam about all the Debbies and Sandras and Bettys in the state. That I wouldn't get a hard-on if the whole Illini cheerleading squad were naked in front of me. That the most true and deep and intense yearnings I had ever felt were aroused by Sam, a halfback. Brad, from Chicago, with his cool grey eyes. The guy with the golden Elvis-hair laughing outside the Armory the day I visited Champaign the first time.

My first anniversary was coming up, and even in the bad nights I was still glad, still comforted, still happy to know that I had really truly finally realized and acknowledged the truth about myself. Not gay; I had never heard the word. Queer. I was a queer, and if that's the way it was, so be it. Not proud, but not ashamed. Just scared.

And, though I didn't know it, I was on the verge of taking the next giant step into gay adulthood. I was about to lose my cherry.

Yes, I was still a virgin. Still knotted in the stomach at the thought of how the hell a guy got from the aching fantasy to the sweet reality. And now, actually back in town for the first time in three years, I realized that I had left my resolve somewhere back along Highway 51. Driving through the cornfields, the seams in the concrete road beating rhythm under the Hudson's tires, it had seemed easy. I would go out to Coach Pete's house. I would catch him up on my life since we moved. I would tell him how much I loved being at the U of I.

And then I would just come out with it. Tell him that Donny Schlichter up in Champaign had said that the story of Coach Pete's wife being killed in a car wreck when they lived in Oklahoma was bullshit. That Coach wasn't married not because he was in mourning for his dead bride, but because he didn't like girls.

I would just come out with it. The conversation had been so easy in the car. Me hastening to tell Coach that I wasn't bringing it up to mock or frighten him...that I was bringing it up because that was how I felt too, and please, please, could he tell me what to do about it....

In the car it was easy. Natural. Just blurting it. Getting it out, and Coach Pete using that big voice of his softly. Telling me what I needed to know. Telling me how to get a man the way he used to tell me how to roll off and go back inside a trap block.

But now.... Now I couldn't even see myself driving to his house, much less talking to him. Much less telling him.

It's more than 35 years later, now. And I still can't believe how the Fates worked. There was a shuffle of feet. A big, solid shape in the dusk. Coach Pete.

Coach Pete himself. He nodded casually, stepped off the curb headed for Staufel's Cafe next to the shoe store. Then stopped, pivoted, his face lightened by a sudden smile. "Brian?" he said. "Is that you, boy? Is it really Brian Chambers, come back from the dead?" His hand was huge and dry and warm, and he wouldn't quit shaking my hand. His delight at seeing me was so obvious, so unfeigned, that it made me feel happy all over.

Jacob stood behind us, faithfully and stolidly looking over our heads as a high school coach picked up the threads with a defensive tackle and offensive guard who had moved away after his sophomore year. When I eagerly accepted Coach Pete's invitation to follow him out to his place on Waverly Road, I catty-cornered towards the bank and my car without a glance back at the stolid sentinel of my childhood.

It wasn't till I was following the blobbed redness of Coach's taillights along the gravel that I realized that I was excited by the prospect of being alone with Coach. In all the thinking and projecting and fantasizing I had done, I hadn't even thought of Coach as a man. A real man, but a man who if the story was true liked men.

Now I was thinking it. And now I had a hard-on.

My chest was tight as I pulled in behind Coach's green-on-green Rambler. His shape was dark against the fading light on the horizon. The silhouette emphasized the breadth of his shoulders, showed the familiar cock of his head. In a way it brought back the days of doing drills to his hoarse shouts. In another way it was something new. Brand new, and sexy as hell.

Those next moments, the Illinois sun pinking the sky, stars already dotting the dark canopy over the trees, will live inside me as a glowing bright spot for the rest of my life. Hell, it's already been more than 35 years, and that night under the sycamores and maples is still as bright and vivid a memory as I have.

We didn't even get indoors. I said something about the sunset, the strip of luminous sky along the corn-notched horizon. He put his arm over my shoulders, the way he would do on the sidelines when he was explaining something. And suddenly I was talking, blurting more wildly and less coherently than in my drive-time fantasy. There was an instant of surprise and confusion, the weight of his arm lifting as he thought I was objecting hysterically. And then there was the understanding, the peace, the flurry of emotion and motion that left me suddenly plastered full-length against my coach's solid body.

The first moments remain perhaps the most intensely wonderful experience in my life. I felt utterly safe. I felt as though I had come home and I don't mean to a particular small town in the cornfields. I felt as though all the turmoils and worries and fears of the year had been pointing straight to this moment in Coach's embrace...and that the press of those muscular arms made all the pain of the past three or four years worth it. More than worth it.

"This is what you've been dreaming of, isn't it Brian?" The voice was soft, softer even than I had imagined. His fingers were moving gently against my back as he held me to him. I could smell the clean laundry-soap smell of his blue cotton shirt, the faintest whiff of Old Spice.

I nodded. My chest was so tight I felt almost suffocated. I was happy, happier than I would have been with a state championship. His right hand petted the back of my head, the caress moving to the side of my neck. God, I was so happy!

And I was excited. The breathing warmth of Coach's big body was like a sexual blowtorch applied to my crotch. My cock and balls tingled with arousal. My cock was hard as a rock. As the embrace lengthened in duration, I could feel a quivering ripple through the body of my old mentor. His muscles tautened, his body gathered itself. I knew he was excited, too.

And then he moved his hips, thrusting against me with a subtle fuck-motion that made me dizzy. A rush of pleasure burst outwards from my guts, filling me, making me afraid for a wild second that I was going to climax right now, blow my wad prematurely.

I did. I came, my arms tightening so convulsively around Coach's torso that I heard the breath whistle from his lungs. I moaned rhythmically into the warm softness of his shirt as the pulsations of a huge orgasm throbbed through my body. My blood boiled as the ecstasy exploded in a torrent of hot juice that filled my briefs.

Coach knew it the instant I started to come. He murmured something soft and loving. The middle of his body moved against my spurting cock. I could feel the iron rod of his hard meat through our pants. His hard-on twitched in sympathy with the spasming explosions of my cum-shooting cock as I shuddered and gasped and moaned in the unutterable bliss of climaxing for the first time in my life in the arms of a big, a strong, a loving and beautiful man.

All the thousands of times I had jacked off, I had never felt anything so overwhelming and all-consuming as that orgasm. When it was over, I was left tingling with an afterglow that was almost as much a pleasure as an ordinary spurting release would have been.

"That's wonderful, Brian. I'm so glad." Coach's voice was such a caressing murmur that the words were almost inaudible. "You'll have some hard, mean, bad times, boy but you'll have a lot more times just like that." His arms tightened, pressing me against him as though he wanted to merge our very flesh. "You can't know what it means to me that you came back to me. That you let me be your first." I didn't explain how different my vision had been from the actuality. "Thank you, Brian. Thank you so much." He unwrapped his arms, took me by my shoulders, held us a foot apart. I looked up into the familiar face, the features little more than a blur now that dusk had deepened to night.

When his face moved towards me, my mouth responded instinctively. He kissed me so gently, so softly, so sweetly.... There was no tongue; it was lips against lips, and the current between us made my lips buzz as though I were kissing an electric wire.

"You tell me what you'd like," he said. "Tell me what you've thought of, what you've dreamed of. Let's make this first time for you something you'll never forget."

My head swirled, images tumbling and shuffling together with dizzying speed. "I'm not even sure," I said. "How would I know?" We chuckled together.

"Would you like to go inside? Take our time?" I nodded. He hugged me in the warm darkness again, then we went to his bed.

Coach's body was trim and solid; it didn't occur to me till later that he was only about 20 years older than I was, and that that made him still only around 40. I was hypnotized by his hard-on. I had seen hundreds of cocks in locker rooms, of course, but this was the first time in my life I had ever seen a hard cock, other than my own.

I could draw that hard slab of meat in perfect detail, even now, more than 35 years later. It stuck up at a sharp angle from the dark tangle of his pubic hair. His cock was a slightly flattened oval, veins crawling all over it like sexy detailing on an erotic sculpture. It looked huge, the base almost frightening in its immensity. His balls hung very low, huge orbs in a darkish, wrinkled sack.

And the head of his cock...God! I could draw that with my tongue! The knob capped the pillar of his hard cock like a helmet, the flesh swollen with his lust, and so filled with the hot blood of his arousal that it glowed like a living garnet. There was something massive and manly about the way his aroused manhood looked, and the effect on my nerves was so intense that it was debilitating. I felt weak-kneed.

My own cock was rigid as concrete, even though I had just come. I had never had such an experience before, and it was doubly exciting, somehow.

Coach Pete looked at my slim nakedness, smiling at my still-stiff cock. "Good boy," he said. "Not that I'm surprised." He caressed my face, pinched gently at my nipple, and then cupped my inexperienced manhood in his big hand. "Would you like to suck my cock? Or maybe you'd like to fuck me. Or me to fuck you. Tell me what you want, Brian. Tell me what would make this special."

I damned near burst into tears. He stroked my cheek again, kissed me briefly, gently.

"Would you fuck me?" I said. My voice quivered.

"It would be an honor." I will never forget those words. Never.

He put me on my hands and knees and lubed my asshole. My excitement was so vast that I was afraid I would black out. I pictured myself with Coach mounting me, thought of what I would look like with this big man pushing his hard cock up my ass. I whimpered with joy at the vision.

The knob of Coach's cock was warm against my asshole. I was scared, turned on, melting. "Just relax," he said. "Don't worry. You won't shit, and I won't hurt you." There was pressure. Pleasure shot through my whole body; my cock slapped against my stomach as a throb of pure excitement buzzed along my nerves. My asshole was suddenly hungry, all the nerves burning with desire. I moaned, my head dropping to the pillow. There was an instant of panic as I felt pressure on my butt like nothing I had ever experienced in my life, and then I felt the warm fullness of Coach's hard cock pressing gently into me.

I was no longer a virgin! I was losing my cherry to Coach Pete! The urge to weep with joy burned behind my eyes. The ecstasy of a fat cock burying itself full-length in my asshole burned behind my cock and balls.

"It really turned me on to have you come like that out there in the yard," Coach murmured. "I'm going to let myself come now without trying to hold back too much. Unless I miss my guess, you're going to want to come too. Don't worry if you don't get off while I'm fucking you. I want to suck a load out of your cock anyway."

He moved, humping slowly and gently in and out of my asshole. The friction was exquisite. I was breathless with arousal as my coach reamed my asshole with his big, hard cock. I felt an orgasm flaring up in my cock and balls, and I couldn't believe that I was really going to come again just minutes after blowing the biggest, most intense wad of my life.

My head was filled with the from-the-doorway vision of what we looked like, pale young man with a big, older man's cock pumping rhythmically in and out of his backside. The fires of bliss burned in the middle of my body, ignited all the other parts of me. I whimpered helplessly, and then Coach's fingers tightened on my hips and he gasped, "Oh, Brian! here it comes! oh, God, boy, I'm starting to come! Oh! Oh, God, yes! ooohhhhhh!" As the last sighing gasp escaped him, he shoved his cock all the way into my ass. I felt the twitching pulsations of his meat jerking in the depths of my asshole. I felt the spurting hotness of his juice gushing into my ass.

My own excitement boiled over again, and I started to spunk even before Coach was through squirting into me. The first pulse of my orgasm grabbed his cock, and told him what was happening. Even in the midst of his eruption, he reached around my hip and grabbed my cock. His fingers tightened, jerking me off. His cock moved in my ass. I nearly died, it felt so good. My sperm geysered onto the sheet, spotting everywhere, even splashing against my own ecstasy-twisted face.

"Well," Coach said when we were both through coming, "I didn't get to suck that load out of your virgin cock yet. But I guess I'll get my chance before the night's over."

He couldn't have been more right.

RIGHT ON TARGET
Jordan Nelson

Whap! The snowball caught me dead-on, knocking my wool cap askew. Served me right, I thought, for frolicking in the snow like a six-year-old instead of the 20-year-old I really am. I turned to catch the miscreant, imagining my attacker to be a small child in a ski jacket, having fun lobbing a well-aimed missile at a grown-up.

Imagine my surprise to see instead a tall, grinning brunet about my age, whose figure seemed trim, as much as his bundled-up condition allowed me to see, and whose sparkling green eyes told me he thought it was great fun to attack unsuspecting strangers from behind. My surprise at seeing that my attacker wasn't a kid was exceeded only by his surprise when I whirled and faced him.

"Oops!" he said. "You're not Larry."

"No. I'm not Larry; I'm Jordi. And who are you?"

"Are you going to tell the principal?" he teased. "Maybe I should give a false name?" Then, in seriousness and with a hand extended to shake for a truce, "I'm Adam." I accepted the proffered hand and shook. "You wanna take a shot at me? Would that make things even?"

I glanced over his shoulder to where two small boys were industriously rolling a huge mound of snow. "I'd rather we play cooperatively and build a snowman together," I said, jerking my thumb in the direction of the boys.

Adam threw back his head and roared. Then he followed my thumb to the tableau of the boys constructing their snowman and realized I meant it. He studied me a moment. "All right," he said. "I wouldn't mind playing with you." There was what sounded like a Significant Pause, and I debated whether I was reading into his words and his pause a meaning that he hadn't intended...or was Adam gay and interested?

Then Adam started rolling snow, and the moment passed. We worked together, building up a sweat despite the crisp weather. "Your snowball was right on target. Larry should thank me for taking the hit for him," I joked after a while. "Larry a friend of yours?"

"We've been buddies for years," Adam replied...too casually? This was getting more interesting by the minute.

When the snowman was finished small but complete, including rocks for eyes, a large rock for a nose, and a thin mouth made of small broken twigs we were both cold and tired. "Come back to my house for something refreshing, if you want," I offered. "I live a couple of blocks over that way." I pointed west of the park.

"Hey, I'd like that," Adam said decisively, and we trudged through the snow, out of the park, and down the few streets to my apartment.

"So what are you into?" I asked as we settled into the couch in my living room.

It was an open-ended question. He could've answered "I'm a lawyer," or "I collect football cards" or "I'm an exercise nut," or "My family." There were lots of ways to take the question. Instead, and to my delight, he answered, "I'm into men. Sexy men with good bodies and personalities to match. Like you."

"Well, then, we have something else in common besides both being kids at heart," I replied. "Say, would you be interested in seeing the rest of the apartment? You do understand the bedroom is all you haven't seen?"

"Very much so."

Which is how we wound up in the bedroom just seconds later, naked immediately after that, and flat on the bed in a fervent crotch-grind directly thereafter. It all happened so fast that I never even got a good look at Adam's equipment, but from the way it was digging into my belly, it was obviously sizable and eager and insistent. It felt as if his dick were trying to drill its way down to my asshole from a spot right above my pubic hairline.

My own dick was no shrinking violet either. As Adam's lips mashed fervently into mine, I thrust hard against his body, my seething tool burrowing into his taut body as if it were drilling for oil. His lips parted, his tongue insinuating itself into my mouth. I sucked it in avidly, my own tongue swirling around his as his probed into every recess in my oral cavern. It strained to reach as far toward my throat as it could.

As our mouths locked in erotic combat, my fingers sought out his nipples and tweaked them. The rubbery-feeling nipples grew firmer and stiffer as the eraser-like nubbins elongated in their eager response to my manipulations. I rubbed my thumbs over the tips of the mahogany buttons and felt the little bumps on them grow more pronounced under my stroking thumb-pads.

His Brillo-textured pubes coarsely ground into my belly-flesh as he shifted positions. Then he settled back into an alignment that meshed our pubic forests together, his dark brown hairs intertwining with my blond ones. Our dicks dueled as our mouths ground together in a fierce kiss.

Adam's hands locked onto my butt cheeks and pulled them toward him as if to merge our two bodies into one unit through sheer force. One hand slipped into my butt crack, and he ran a fingernail lightly up and down my ditch. Each time it trilled across my eager pucker, prickles of anticipation shot through me.

The nerves in my butt-pucker seemed connected to the nerves in my skin, causing gooseflesh to pop up all across my body as his stroking fingernail titillated the sensitized rim. Those nerves were connected to my dick, too. It inflated to astounding proportions as Adam's wicked thumbnail sneaked across my tender shithole.

Two can play at that game. Since my mouth was engaged in another prolonged, deep kiss, and I couldn't readily get to it to lube my finger with spit, I insinuated my hand between our two tightly pressed bodies with difficulty and located my seething dick, which was oozing viscous lube juice at a rapid rate. Running my index finger all around my dickhead, I coated my finger with lots of sticky lube and quickly withdrew it, heading south for Adam's ass.

My finger homed in on Adam's wrinkled doorway and proceeded to enter without knocking. I jabbed my finger at the entrance to his ass and found it tight and restrictive. But I persevered, wiggling my finger round in semi-circles as I pushed insistently inward. Quarter-inch by quarter-inch, I gained entrance to the humid interior of his tightly guarded rectum.

That was when Adam backed his mouth off mine so he'd have his teeth free to nibble at my nipples. My stubby nubbins toughened under his oral assault, his teeth grazing riotously across the landscape of my chest. He not only nipped at my brown protrusions, he pulled at my sparse sprinkling of chest hairs with his teeth, and each little tug made my dick throb insistently, as if to say, "Let's get on with the action."

So be it. I pulled free of his hard-working mouth and trailed my tongue down his chest, heading south at a leisurely pace. Though eager to reach his dick, I wanted to enjoy my trip down there. I trailed my tongue through his abundant chest forest, letting the hairs tickle my tongue as it moved through them. When I reached his softer belly-flesh, I took a deep breath and caught my first whiff of his groin-scent, an intoxicating mixture of musk and man-sweat that assailed my nostrils and inflamed my fuck-nerves.

I lingered in his belly-button, flicking in and out of it in little fuck-strokes that clearly implied what my dick wished to do to his body. I didn't know Adam's preferences anal or oral but I was eager to bury my stiff shaft into one or the other of his available openings.

I was also eager to swallow his hot poker and its thick outpouring. I'm very oral, and no encounter is complete for me until I've felt the man's dick dive deep in my mouth and discharge a boiling load of creamy cum down my gulping throat.

So I gave a last flick to his navel and continued downward toward the object I so craved. When I reached his sweat-infused pubes, strongly redolent of his erotic scent, I stopped to bury my nose in the fragrant forest. After gulping deep lungfuls of his sweaty-musky odor, not unclean yet very strong and heady, I finally found myself with my nose prodding his wrinkled sac.

I let my nose poke into the soft sac and mess around with the squishy contents. His full balls shifted around as my nose nuzzled into his ballsac. Then I extended my tongue and licked my way up the swollen bulk of his wrinkled sac to the base of his towering shaft.

When I reached the root of his dick, I paused once more to take a deep lungful of his essence. Then I tongued my way rapidly to the top, too eager to go slowly any longer. Reaching the peak, I dipped my tongue into his welling piss hole and savored the taste and texture of his pre-lube, mildly spicy, thick, and creamy. I stopped to reflect that if I kept this up, I was likely to come off without his ever touching me. Well, probably not really, but that's just how hot his taste and scent were making me.

Kissing his dickhead with pursed lips, I gradually opened my mouth wide to accommodate his mushroom head. At length my widespread lips had encompassed all of his considerable width. It was time to begin my slow descent. Tightening my lips around his pulsating tool, I created a moderate amount of suction as I began descending Adam's power tower.

Little by little that meaty throbber eased its way into my mouth till it filled most of it. Sucking harder, I was gratified to feel it swell within me, a rush of fresh blood making the already-stiff, already-swollen organ assume even more tensile strength and fullness. And now Adam took the reins and charged full-tilt into my more-than-willing mouth.

As Adam's dickhead knocked against my uvula, I purposefully relaxed my throat muscles to let the welcome marauder intrude into my throat. The girth of his dick was appreciable. Though I'd noticed his dick's length was very average, Adam's width became apparent when his dick lodged in the narrow channel at the back of my throat. It spread my throat walls wide, rubbing delightfully as it rampaged in and out.

The tender tissues in my throat were bathed with a lavish flow of pre-cum as Adam's dick scraped back and forth in my constricting passageway. I grappled with his body, pulling his thickly pelted belly against the top of my head. Adam groaned and began powering his fuck-tool in and out of my throat with ever faster strokes. Though I had barely begun sucking him, he was all worked up from the messing-around we'd done beforehand, and he was primed and ready to fire.

Or nearly so. I did my best to stave off his climax, placing my hands on his hips and trying to regulate his rhythm. As his hips tried to power his dick with huge, rapid lunges far down into my mouth, I tried to hold him at bay so he took shorter, slower strokes and didn't plunge quite so deeply. I wanted to enjoy sucking him for a while before his gusher ended the fun.

Outside the window, the wind picked up, rattling the window pane. I suspected the snowstorm they had predicted was setting in. Good! Maybe it would be too miserable out to walk home, and Adam would be stranded at my place for the weekend! I intensified my efforts to pleasure him. I wanted him to be eager to stay if the weather proved off-putting.

Right now, all he was eager for was to come. While half of me despaired that his dick was about to shoot off and withdraw from my mouth, half of me was eager for my turn. So I stopped fighting it and sucked harder, while increasing the speed with which my lips were moving up and down his shaft.

I gripped him tighter, bringing my tongue into play. My tongue did a little dance along the sides of his shaft as my lips travelled up and down that swollen, vein-ringed column of flesh. Whenever I reached the summit, I swirled my tongue across the tip and reveled in the spicy-funky taste of dick-drool that emanated from the piss-slit at a rapid rate. Putting a hand to his sac, I gently squeezed, encouraging his balls to give up their cargo.

They didn't need much encouragement. I think it was when I reached up with my left hand and pinched his stiff nipples that I pushed him over the edge, though. His body stiffened, and his hard-charging dick plunged farther down my throat than he had gone up till now.

I pulled back quickly so he wouldn't discharge his load down my throat where my taste buds would miss savoring the delicious flavor of fresh cum. Holding his dick in my mouth, I felt spurt after spurt of his thick jism coat my tongue. I absorbed as much of the taste as I could before the thick goo slid on down my throat and into oblivion.

When the last spurt had been wrung from his balls, Adam pulled out of my mouth and reversed on me, eagerly taking my dick into his mouth. My own dick was sloppy with its outpouring of sticky pre-cum. I'd been so wrapped up in my enjoyable task that I hadn't realized how much pre-cum I was putting out myself. Adam licked up every errant drop before settling in to suck me in earnest.

Clearly I was too hot to want foreplay; we'd kissed and fooled around enough already anyhow. It was time to get down to the serious business of draining my balls. Adam had a neat trick; he moved his head round in little twists, now clockwise and now counterclockwise, while his tongue swirled in the area under the flange of my dick. He did this while sucking and releasing, sucking and releasing, but all without moving his lips up and down on my dick.

It was a hellish kind of heaven, and finally, as good as it felt, I couldn't take any more. "Shit, man, suck me!" I begged, and Adam laughed wickedly but complied with my request. In purposeful swoops he dove rapidly down the length of my shaft, taking every inch of my considerable length (nine-and-a-half inches, if you want specs) into his mouth. Then he came slowly up the shaft till only my apple-like dickhead and nothing more was lodged in his mouth. He sucked very hard on that, then eased off the suction and rapidly swooped down again.

He repeated this oral tango about ten times, and I lost it. "Oh shit! Here it comes!" I warned him, emitting a strangled croak as my creamy semen flew up my dick shaft and splattered him at the back of his throat.

"Right on target. Now we're even for my hitting you earlier," he joked, referring to his earlier snowball.

I said, "You hit me with something cold and wet, though, and I hit you with something warm and tasty."

"Didn't I give you something warm and tasty?" he mock-complained.

"And you'll give me something more before the afternoon is over."

"I'd better leave now," he said, pointing out the window. I looked, for the first time since we'd entered the bedroom, and saw the flakes furiously swirling in the whipping wind.

"Unless you have plans for tomorrow, you'd better figure on spending the night here," I said.

Adam got up, went to the window, opened it, and scraped up some snow from the sill. "Yeah," he said. "I have plans for tomorrow. And they all involve your ass." Then he cupped his hand and formed a perfect snowball, which he let fly at me. It hit me square in the nose. Once again, he was right on target.

HE TOOK HIS SWEET TIME
John Patrick

I was on my way to the john. I had seen the stud with the trim, athletic build head in that direction and I was, truth be known, following him.

I entered the john and noticed he was there all right, and he had some kid on his knees before him. That quickly. The sound of the kid's mouth was loud. The kid gave a little sigh and shifted his weight, quickening his movement. The stud lifted his head slowly and he saw me standing there, watching. He did not turn away, did not stop the kid. He stared at me, blankly. The kid made another little moan, and the stud put his hands on top of his bobbing head, bunching up the curly black hair, gripping him, letting him know, letting me know, that he was about to come. I wanted to see the kid's face, see the cock he was enjoying so much. The stud shifted a bit so that I could at least see his cock moving in and out of the kid's mouth, the kid's hand around him, sliding him up and down in time with his mouth. There was a stiffening in his thighs and the kid worked faster for a moment or two, then the stud held the kid's head to him tightly. The kid began to slow down as the stud came.

I backed out of the room like a thief and ran up the stairs, looking over my shoulder.

I stayed at the bar for a few minutes, had another beer. The stud did not re-appear. When I took out a couple of singles for a tip, I noticed my hands were shaking.

Slowly I made my way to the door. Just then, I saw him again, looking refreshed, his long, sandy hair tousled, ambling toward me. He took his sweet time getting to where I had stopped, as if I was waiting for him, which, I suppose, I was.

"I shouldn't have invited you here," I said to him.

"Why not?"

I had lost my nerve. "I'm expecting someone."

"Yeah, me."

"No, no. I mean it. I forgot. I've got someone due any minute."

"You got something I could drink?"

"I guess. What do you want?"

"A beer, maybe. You got a beer?"

I got him a beer and he stood by the window drinking it quietly. He was still taking his sweet time. He hadn't given up. "Nice view," he said, looking out over the park.

"Yes," I said, admiring how his ass fit so perfectly into his jeans. The sight of it made up my mind for me. I had thought I would spend yet another night alone, jacking off to the memories of past loves. But now I no longer had to face that dull prospect. I stepped up to him, kissed him, pulling his head toward me, cupping his ears like shells. He unfastened my belt, unzipped my pants. Then he stepped away, and looked at me.

My back was to the window, and I leaned against it. My cock was hard, aching. He unbuttoned his jeans and reached inside and lifted his penis, raising one leg to find it, laying it in the fork of the seam. He was not circumcised and it looked the way all uncircumcised penises look to me, like the snake in the Garden of Eden. I wanted to suck it. I did not know how to stop wanting it so much.

He lifted my T-shirt off and moved his hands across my chest, pinching my nipples, then licking and sucking them. I could feel my prick grow even bigger.

Yet I pushed him away. He looked at me, astonished.

"I don't want to do this," I said.

He stepped back. He now had an erection. "Don't you like it?" He rubbed himself with one hand.

"Yes, I like it. I like it very much. But I don't want it."

I bent over to pick up my T-shirt. He put his hand on the back of my head, holding me down. He stepped over to me, his cock bobbing in my face.

"I didn't want to fuck you anyway," I heard him say. "Just suck it."

"No. Please, just let me go."

He loosened his grip, then dropped away. He went to the foyer and picked up his backpack. His sudden falling-away, his tentativeness, his loss of will, made me dislike him, and I realized that what I was disappointed. I wanted him to force me. That was the only way I could do it now, to be forced.

But he wasn't leaving after all. Now, he was only getting a condom. He thought that's what I wanted: to suck it with a condom on it. He came back, pulling the rubber over his cock. I sighed when I saw this. His cock was so big, so beautiful, and he had covered it with the latex. He flashed a wicked smile. I couldn't take my eyes off his cock. Then he stopped and stood before me, letting me absorb the full impact of his masculine beauty.

I turned away from him, spread my legs and gave him a clear view of what I hoped he wanted.

He put an arm around my waist, pulling me toward him so that my ass was high against him. He pulled my arms to him and took my two hands and placed them on my ass, and then with his hands on top of mine, he pulled me open, apart. He put my hands on his cock and allowed me to guide it in. With a low moan he entered me with such ease, such presumption, that I began to come the moment he was inside of me. He said, "That's right, that's right."

He let himself slide out of me, then he started again, prolonging my pleasure for another marvelous minute or two.

A PARTY FOR THREE
James Wilton

When he arrived, Greg was the third lad I had invited to live under my roof. I had picked him up in the local cruise bar where I had had such good luck over the years. Most of my guests are migrants who move to Florida hoping to live the good life and often engaging in hustling to make do until someone takes them in.

The other two left shortly after the new boy arrived and we were alone. Satisfying as Greg was, he was not quite as enthusiastic as I would have liked. He did all I requested but we grew apart as the weeks passed.

One Saturday evening we went out to my regular bar. The main reason was to visit with the friends I was likely to meet there and to give Greg a chance to party. I am never opposed to picking someone up but I was not hunting. As expected, I spent the evening catching up with my favorite bartender and several bar friends. Greg was off dancing with anyone willing to join him.

Later, he returned to my barstool. He was more physical than usual and I immediately suspected something. He whispered that he had a surprise for me. Not wanting to be rude to my friends, I made Greg wait. His impatience was obvious as he became more and more provocative with his contact. My friends and I all recognized his growing desperation as our mutual winks indicated. I figured that the longer I kept the kid waiting, the better for me. Once my chat with the guys was completed, I turned to Greg. He told me that he had found someone he wanted me to meet.

I followed him down the bar and caught the eye of a young man anxiously watching my arrival. He was a cute, youngish lad with shaggy blond bangs over his pale face. The baggy clothes hid his body but he clearly was not chubby. Greg introduced him as Dillon, a new arrival from the North. Dillon looked me in the eye and shook my hand firmly. His face glowed as he smiled and his eyes sparkled. Greg's wanton look made the whole situation clear: he was in lust with Dillon but knew the rules. No one living in my house tricks out. The only invitations come from me. Greg wanted this fellow but not enough to jeopardize his easy living conditions so he hoped to get me to ask the boy home for him.

Well, this was not going to be a difficult decision. Dillon was as cute as could be and seemed perfectly willing to become a third. Greg's longing guaranteed me a high-intensity session. I knew that the two boys together in the back seat would mean a passionate ride home with me left out. Dillon in the front seat would mean Greg leaning forward and enjoying the boy in front of him but I would miss the initial exploration. So, knowing that ardor denied is ardor enhanced, I put the new one in the back and kept Greg up front with me.

This was my turn to return his physical attention. A turned-on youngster can be a fun thing. His skin was so sensitive that my light touch on his thigh made Greg jump off the seat. As I trailed my fingers up, toward the crotch, my victim gasped in ecstasy. His basket contained one very hard erection. As I felt my way around this plaything, Greg pulled my hand away and warned me that he was too close to cumming. I laughed and complimented Dillon on his effect on Greg. My plaything decided that the safest way to keep me out of his privates was to play with mine. Without any complaints, I got diddled for the rest of the way. Cute Dillon just sat and was quietly sexy in the back seat.

Once home, the three of us headed directly to the master bedroom. This was my first chance to check out our new guest in the light. I sat back on the bed with Greg next to me and had Dillon stand up for our examination. I got the impression that Greg was eager to begin the action rather than submit his new find to my viewing. I had Dillon stand by the bed and show us what he had to offer. His face was as charming as it had appeared in the bar. He looked like a youngish example of a twenty-year-old, the age he claimed to be. Unfortunately, his baggy clothes still hid his assets so I had him stretch his shirt and pants across his chest, back, crotch, and ass. This showed that his body was well formed and tight. It also made him feel quite self-conscious. As Dillon began to show discomfort, Greg began to bristle and I enjoyed the situation all the more.

I had Greg stand up and put on a show for me. He stood behind Dillon and felt up the boy's chest as my eyes followed his hands. His touch defined the boy's upper body. It was surprisingly triangular for someone so young. His pecs were wide, matching his shoulders and his waist was quite narrow. Greg pinched the nipples for me and the three of us were pleased with the result: they perked up and stood out through the cotton fabric. Dillon's eyes rolled and he let out a gentle moan showing his pleasure.

I had him raise the T-shirt, then remove it so we had access to this adorable package. He was all he appeared to be. He was well muscled but not buffed. His skin was pale, not pasty. And, he had almost no body hair. There were wisps around the erect nipples and a surprisingly heavy trail from his navel to the waist of his pants. The removal of the shirt also exposed the front of his pants. There was an obvious erection within, tenting out the fabric. My guess was that he either wore boxers or no underwear. On closer look, there was a spot of moisture marking the tip of his cock.

Meanwhile, over his shoulder was a boy with the look of absolute bliss. He was finally getting his kicks from this kid he had found. That I was calling the shots and directing things toward my personal pleasure didn't bother Greg at all. He was thoroughly enjoying his tactile tour of this grand body. On my suggestion that he nibble on the boy's neck to get things even hotter, he jumped up and gave the blond's skin a velvety laving. This had the expected result and Dillon slouched back into his buddy's arms.

Greg was equally willing to continue with the next step. I had him open Dillon's slacks and peel them back. As I suspected and Greg enjoyed discovering, the boy had no underwear. As his pants were opened, that lovely line of hair descending from the navel widened into a brown bush. A little lower and the root of the dick came into view with the clear outline of an erection leaning to the left. I had Greg slow down and watched as the pants dropped slowly and caught his penis on their way down. At one point, the clothes caught as if hanging on a coat hook. Then the dropping slacks and the rising dick separated company and the tube of hard boy flesh snapped to attention as its covering dropped to the floor.

Dillon sighed with relief and Greg leaned over the blocking shoulder to see what he had uncovered. The sight made his eyes bulge and sparkle. The boy possessed a six-or seven-inch cock that stood out from his hard belly at a perfect forty-five degree angle. There wasn't a hint of a curve on the surprisingly thick member. I doubted that I could get my hand around that fire plug. Dillon had been so turned on by his treatment that the veins on his shaft were standing out and a thread of pre-cum seemed to stretch down to the pants on the floor. Below this beauty hung two balls proportional in size to the width, if not the length, of it. Their sack was surprisingly loose and low hanging considering the boy's state of arousal. The whole package was smooth, except for the ample bush above. I suspected that our friend shaved and it certainly added to the aesthetics.

As I was taking in this scene I looked up and caught Dillon's eye. He quickly looked down at his glorious equipment and then back up to my gaze. As he realized how much I was enjoying the view he sort of shrugged and then reddened as his eyes again dropped to his crotch. Seeing such a cutie blush melted my heart. I decided that it was Greg's turn to be the center of attention and give Dillon a break.

I had the boys switch positions and roles. I also had them turn to face one of my many full-length mirrors so that Dillon could watch the strip he was performing. As they walked, his dick barely bobbed, it was so stiff. When Greg stepped forward, his erection showed, too. His jeans were too tight to tent out but there was an obvious tube outlined on the diagonal across his lap. Once he was in place, I told Dillon to repeat the manipulation he had just experienced but to modify it to his heart's (and libido's) content.

As I watched, he raised Greg's hands to his neck and rested his own hands on the boy's hips as he perused him in the mirror. Dillon checked his subject up and down a number of times before zeroing in on his obvious erection. He lightly ran his fingers along the length of the shaft as if to be sure it wasn't a crease in the denim. This had an immediate effect on Greg, who moaned, rolled his eyes, and sagged at the knees. I was afraid that he might pop and I suspect that Dillon had the same idea because he quickly refocused his attention above the belt. He massaged the firm chest I had spent so much time enjoying. As expected, the nipples quickly grew and showed through the shirt. These gave Dillon a great toy. With a wicked grin on his face, he tweaked first one and then the other as he watched the effect on Greg, who thrust each pec forward to enhance the pleasure of each tit in turn. Finally, he broke the tension by laughing and pinching both firmly enough to bring a wince from Greg.

The break was short lived as Dillon pulled Greg's shirt out of his waistband and up over his head. He finished the task without looking since his attention was focused on the reflection of what he had uncovered. There was the lightly haired chest of my housemate. Dillon was fascinated by the pattern I had so enjoyed: a small patch on his upper chest fanning out to both nipples and then narrowing down to a line that only widened at the point of his navel. Dillon reached around and brushed his hands over this inviting fur. As he followed the definition to the tits he caused another spasm to pass through Greg's body.

Next, he followed the stripe past the navel and tried to trace it into the jeans. When he reached his maximum penetration, he withdrew and began to unfasten the Levi's. Just as he began to unzip them, he looked over his plaything and decided to check out the upper body once more before moving below the belt. His touch skimmed up, lightly passing the nipples, and paused over the exposed armpit hair. He reached out to the center of Greg's biceps, where he felt the nice definition just below the smooth skin. He gently pulled down on those bulging muscles as if to do a pull-up. His buddy responded by raising his arms as if in a lift. The result was a significant swelling of the upper body, much to Dillon's delight. The boys made eye contact as Dillon's expression acknowledged Greg's evident good conditioning and Greg smiled a response.

Another pause ended as Dillon's hands once again returned to unzip the fly and all three of us focused on the reflection of his hands in the mirror. With the heel of his hand intentionally pressing down the length of Greg's shaft, Dillon lowered the zipper in one gesture. As the denim spread out on either side of the open fly, the white briefs became exposed. I thought I caught a look of exasperation as Dillon realized that this presented one more impediment to his arrival at his goal. With a few deft yanks, he got the jeans below the hump of Greg's buns and sent the pants down, out of the way. There were the bright white briefs that prevented him from seeing the cock he had been seeking. Without the confining Levi's to encase the erection, Greg's dick tented out from the fabric. It was so excited that there were two precum spots darkening the whites: one over the spot the dick had occupied before the jeans were lowered and one in the center, just below the elastic, where the dripping crown now was.

Dillon reached below the shaft and lightly touched the bulging ball sack. As with the nipples, this contact caused Greg to gasp and try to double over in bliss. With one hand, Dillon pulled Greg's shoulders back as the other traced the rod to its moist head.

This action had the reverse reaction as Greg straightened up and tried to hump his dick into the hand so close to it. Dillon's impatience made him stop his play and reach for the elastic. The bulging dick below had already worked its way under the waistband and gave Dillon a gap on either side with which to grab the top of the briefs. He slid the underwear slowly down the length of that shaft.

As he reached the root, the body of the member was no longer confined and it popped out into the space in front of the boys. Both of them gave a sigh, Dillon out of satisfaction at finally completing his quest, and Greg out of relief at having his dick released. With a thrust, the briefs joined the jeans below the knees and Dillon got a view of Greg's crotch.

The boy's cocks were both inviting but quite opposite. Where Dillon's was average in length, Greg's was nearly nine inches long. Where Dillon's was thick, Greg's was slender. Where Dillon's was straight, Greg's had a pronounced upward curve. Below the dicks, though, they were very similar. Both possessed generous balls in ample sacks. Dillon ran his hands and gaze farther down to discover that where he had smooth thighs, Greg had hairy ones. These delighted Dillon, who ran his palms up and down the furry legs, causing his subject further and further arousal. By the time he realized the result of his actions, Greg's dick was bobbing and dripping profusely.

At this point, I'd had enough viewing and was ready to join in the fun. I had Greg finish undressing and had both boys stand in front of me, hands on hips. They retained their erections and offered me a sizable drop of precum to taste. As I licked up the ooze from each one, his dick jumped in response to the contact. Both also tried to push their dicks into my mouth to get the kind of release they craved.

Since I was already familiar with Greg, I focused on Dillon. The boy's thickness fascinated me and I tested my observation. Sure enough, I couldn't quite get my fingers around that shaft. My attempt caused the tool to stiffen even more and a flood of precum dribbled out for my further tasting. This time I ran the tip of my tongue down from the slit and tickled the underside of his dickhead. At that, the whole thing began throbbing and bobbing up and down. I ran my tongue along it and, with my hands free, I cupped both boys' balls and enjoyed the silky smoothness of the sacks. This added stimulation seemed to be too much for Dillon and he put his arm around Greg's shoulder and leaned on him for support. On a down swing of the cock, I trapped it with my lips and slid it into my mouth. It really was a strain to get my mouth all the way around that meat. I succeeded, but Dillon may have suffered some scraping from my teeth. He didn't complain and leaned toward me to get even farther into my mouth. It didn't take long to reach the back and such a broad penis was not going to be deep-throated. I gave him the best blow-job I was able to until I felt the balls in my hand begin to rise up in the sack as if they were about to blow. I backed off and eyed that slick beauty once again.

Then it was Greg's turn. His dick didn't cause a stretch but my nose was always far from his bush once he reached to back of my mouth. From my seated position, I wasn't going to be able to deep-throat him either but his moans let me know that he, too, was satisfied with my efforts. Again, rising balls signaled time to quit. Grabbing onto the two sets of balls I had been fondling, I pulled both of them down in front of me.

It was time for me to get some attention. They quickly stripped me naked and dove into my crotch. As Dillon began nibbling on my corona, Greg moved down to lave my balls, an action he knew I love. Dillon proved to be an excellent cocksucker as he slid down my length and then returned to tickle the underside of my crown. As hot as I already was, I couldn't take too much and called an end to this phase.

Wanting a chance to further my exploration of the new body at my disposal, I set Dillon to work giving Greg a blowjob. As the boy knelt over his work, his ass was open to my attention. I first licked the back of the exposed ballsac between his thighs. After a few laps, I continued my trail up between the legs and approached his rectum. I delayed my actual attack by making several rings around the pucker. I'm afraid that Greg lost the attention of his new friend, who froze mid-suck and waited for me to lick the bulls eye. Once I did, Dillon lurched back and tried to impale himself on my tongue. Instead, I widened my tongue and gave his whole anus a licking. With a moan of delight, he resumed his attention to the cock in his mouth. I backed off and wet my finger for a different kind of assault. I worked my digit into his tight ass as he wriggled in cooperation. Once I was all the way in, he bounced back on my hand as if to get more than I had. Clearly, Greg had found a versatile new plaything.

To complete the evening's entertainment, I decided to grace our newcomer with a three-way fuck. First, he was to prepare Greg to be the bottom. Dillon quickly explained that with his thickness, he found it best to loosen up his partners with some finger work before actually mounting them. It sounded fine to me as I leaned back to enjoy the view.

Dillon spread Greg's legs and knelt between them. Using some lubricant, he began by massaging the ass before actually entering. Meanwhile, he leaned forward and tickled Greg's dick and balls with his tongue. Clearly Greg was enjoying this and it relaxed him enough to make penetration quick and easy. First Dillon worked in one finger, then two and three. With some deft twisting of his hand, he created a wide opening in his partner's rectum. While he was concentrating on the action in front of him, I lubed my fingers and returned to his ass. For a while, we were both fingering the holes we were about to fuck.

Once Greg was satisfactorily opened, Dillon withdrew and lifted the boy's legs over his shoulders. He reached down to direct his dripping pole into its target but I brushed his hand away and took over that task myself. As he lowered himself toward Greg, I aimed his rammer at the greasy pucker. At the first contact, he paused and began a slow press. To distract Greg, Dillon bent down and deep kissed him. It seemed to work as I watched the head slowly pass through the sphincter. Using a rocking action, Dillon entered and exited a bit. Each time, more of his shaft disappeared until he was all the way in. During all this, I could hear Greg snorting as his body was stretched. Despite the discomfort he must have been feeling, his erection never sagged and actually dripped more as Dillon reached his maximum penetration. Pausing for only a moment to savor his accomplishment, Dillon began withdrawing until he was nearly out. As I watched the details closely, he reversed and plunged rather quickly to the depth of Greg's anus. At this we both heard the 'oomph' of someone getting the air knocked out of him. Back and forth, Dillon began the familiar rhythm of a fuck.

Craving my turn, I got up onto my knees between Dillon's thighs. For a moment, I waited, enjoying the view below me of a smooth, mounded young ass humping, a well-muscled back and broad shoulders rising above it. But, a moment was all I could take for I had to experience the pleasure I had just watched Dillon taking. With one hand on his ass to stop the action, I used the other to aim for his hole. Having already loosened his entrance, I wasn't too worried about taking my time and entered in one smooth lunge. As I ground my pubis into Dillon's buns, he arched his back. I leaned onto those inviting shoulders and grabbed him in a bear hug. I bounced myself against his back side before any withdrawal. Finally, I backed off and started to fuck this tight treasure.

After enjoying myself for a while, I pulled back most of the way and signaled Dillon to resume his fucking of Greg. Being in the middle, I let him set the pace. As he withdrew from his sheaf, I entered him. His forward thrust matched my pullback. There must be something innate about a sandwich-fuck because we slipped right into a perfect rhythm. As the sexual pressure began to build we both increased tempo simultaneously. Faster and faster we humped. Harder and deeper we pounded. Without any expressed signal, Dillon abruptly stopped and drove his plunger as deeply into Greg's ass as he could. His eruption came at the same time as mine and I, too, thrust forward to spill my seed as deep in his innards as I could. I could barely feel the contractions of his ass while he came because my orgasm was so strong and overwhelming.

When we were both finished, we both rested in breathless exhaustion. Once our pulses returned to the safe zone, the pile began untangling. First I enjoyed that sweet feeling of dismounting. As my dick popped out of Dillon, he whimpered a note of satisfaction. Then the procedure was repeated below me. In the throes of rutting, I had lost track of what was happening to Greg. It seemed a shame that he hadn't experienced the thrill we others had. As Dillon rolled off him, though, I saw hot cum smeared over his chest in testament to the hands-free orgasm he had experienced. The three of us were able to lie back and enjoy that gentle sleep.

The next morning saw a further cementing of our new, three-way relationship, which was to last several months.

Dillon was a welcome addition to our happy home since he brought a noticeable improvement in the level of Greg's enthusiasm in bed.

TEMPTATION
Sonny Torvig

I threw down the loaded brush and swore. Then I stepped well back from the canvas, and swore once more. I half closed my eyes to soften the dreadful clarity of my errors. It made no difference whatsoever. It was, even being generous, one shit painting. I sat down on the chair reserved for contemplation, and contemplated.

One week later I returned to the dry canvas and turned its face from the wall. In the bright light, and relatively fresh to my eye, it did not seem as dreadful as I had imagined. But however kind I might be to the finished work, it was not going to be good enough. I sighed, and took it back down from the easel. One week to go before my first exhibition and there was still a job to begin afresh. I had initially bluffed the number of canvases I was putting up for the show, and all the relevant information had now gone into the printed catalogue. I had no choice but to begin again, for there comes a time when no amount of remedial work will rescue a bad painting.

I placed a fresh canvas on the easel, and began. Soft charcoal lent gentle lines of definition to the hero destined to emerge. I glanced at the photographs taped to the top corner, and slowly created 'New Spartacus.'

He wasn't bad when the sketch was ready, but was still missing something. I stood back, I looked through my eyelashes, I sat opposite. It was definitely Spartacus in his last moments of imprisonment, hands bound behind him and the look of defiance carved into his face. But it wasn't alive, it lacked any passion for the subject!

I clumped down the stairs to the street, my stomach rumbling and my mind distracted. As the light had faded I had given in. I was either going to have to be content with putting a poor example of my art forward, or await a new day in the hope of fresh inspiration. It didn't look good from where I stood.

Wandering among the street cafes, sniffing at the many glorious smells, my stomach was hurting now, reminding me that I had neglected my own body during my attempts to draw another. I sat at my usual table on the edge of the square and cast an eye over the early evening customers. The beautiful people of the town out to be seen, frequenting the cheaper side of life. I snorted, and called Anton. He towered over me as I ordered some cheap and filling Pasta.

One day, when I had sold some work, I would have what the beautiful people had. If only the once. The house wine was light and refreshing, and

I spent more than I should. What the hell, I might be 'a name' by this time next week.

The cafe grew crowded and table space precious. So far my shabby clothes and cologne a la turpentine had kept intruders at bay, but inevitably I was asked to share as the evening wore on. He sat opposite, and ate in silence.

The scents of rich sauce and heavy wine were tugging at my senses as Anton silently poured my last coffee. The stranger looked up. I had noticed him eating at Antonio's before, always alone, always watching what went on around him. Perhaps, like me, he had an innate curiosity about people. "You are a painter?" He was soft-spoken, an air of playful curiosity in his tone. I nodded over my hot glass. "Oils by the smell. Nudes I would guess." Hazel eyes focused on mine, he raised one eyebrow.

I felt awkward, was I that transparent? "Yes, you are correct. I'm presently finishing work for my first exhibition." That felt good. "It' s on the subject of men's Heroes. But not nudes, I'm afraid, that subject was one I skipped at college. Life drawing is the hardest discipline, I think."

He smiled. His lips full and shining with wine. "Your exhibition is of glorious men, or of powerful women?"

What a strange question. "The first. Hector, Ulysses, Philip of Macedon, Spartacus." They all interest me.

He pushed his empty plate to one side. "All very athletic men, men who had courage. Men who never wanked or farted." That irked me. These heroes were my heroes, and I wasn't going to have them made fun of.

"The whole point of a hero is that he is above mortal man. Without that to strive towards, how are we to rise from the mire of pagan gratification?" His instant grin told me I had been deliberately baited, and I grew even more defensive as a result. "Look around you. How often does honor and integrity shine out round here?"

"You deny yourself half of your life, my friend. If you deny your primal drives, it must mean that you have some problem with them. There is a Fascist and a fucker in all of us."

I laughed, I had to. The wine and the warm evening had mellowed my need for loud defense. I lowered my voice. "OK, maybe I do. But I'd sooner strive than wallow."

"Oh I don't know. A little wallowing never did any harm." He sipped his glass, the deep ruby of the wine casting a glow of reflected light over his skin. "Are you ready for your exhibition?"

I wished he hadn't reminded me, and I seemed to deflate. "No. I've had to begin the last painting again. There is only one week to finish the work, and it's not going well." I looked up from my empty glass and shrugged. "It's Spartacus, he was a thorn in the Romans' side, and he's sure as hell one in mine."

"I would like to see your work, and know your name" He signaled Anton for his bill and drew out his wallet. "Do you mind?" He picked up my bill and waited.

I shrugged. There was no saying no to a free meal. "Do you want to know the name of the gallery?"

He shook his head. "Why not let me see your work now? There is no time like the present." I stepped back from my table to wait for him to join me. He placed a healthy tip beside his empty glass and moved out into the flow of the street. "My name is Jacques, in case you wondered." He held out a hand in confirmation. I shook it, and shrugged.

"People call me M ."

We walked in silence back to my shabby studio, creaking up the many stairs to reach the shadowy attic. The smells as I opened the door were so familiar and comforting, I still thrilled at that unmistakable perfume of creative effort. He breathed deeply of the heady mix of turps and oils, his hands on the hips of his well cut trousers. It was stuffy with the retained heat of the evening, and he immediately shrugged off his loose blouson, carefully placing it over the back of my contemplation chair. He turned.

"Now, let me see your work." He placed his hands in his pockets, and waited. I drew out the canvases from their protective lair and turned them all into the fading light, quietly marveling that I has done all this myself. I had not seen Hector for a good six months, and his proud pose lent me a fresh stirring of confidence. They all did as they looked at my guest, all of them proud and honorable men, their bodies carved and bathed in healthy Mediterranean sunshine. I felt quite proud as I stood back, forgetting where some of the more glaring errors had been committed, much time having elapsed. I joined my guest. "Well?"

He said nothing, but moved to examine each painting more closely. The time dragged by as he moved along the row of work, picking up the occasional piece and turning it to the windows. He. turned to face me. "Where is Spartacus?"

I moved over to the pile of canvases for cleaning and withdrew the dreadful hero, casually handed him the sad article, and waited.

"Underpaint, you do not use it. And you give no reflected light to the skin."

My skin prickled. This man knew what he was talking about. Just who was I sharing my unseen work with?

"You think those would improve things?"

He looked around the studio before he replied, moving to the deep windows to check the sun's direction. "I would like to see you again tomorrow, here, and I would like to show you how to raise your work from merely good, to the more heroic position of exceptional." He reached for his jacket. "I will be here at sun-up, and you will keep an open mind as to my teaching methods." I began to protest, feeling bulldozed. "Good, or exceptional. Which do you require, my friend?"

I had a great deal of trouble rising with the sun, and my first mug of cheap coffee hit me with a rush. I shook like a dog out of a river and padded about the big room in a pensive mood. The bucket of cold water I used to wash down my body made me wake up more than a trifle, and the cool of the morning made me dress more quickly than usual. I scrambled into some cleaner clothes in preparation, and tried to find a clean towel to scrub my hair dry. A nervous tension was beginning in my empty stomach as the light grew stronger. Had I time to go for a bag of fresh baguettes? Did I need to supply him with food?

All questions swept away as my guest breezed in only minutes later. He beckoned me to join him and left the room. I followed as he flew down the stairs, and staggered out to witness him opening the back doors of a van. "Here, help me take all this up to your studio. We will need everything with only a week to work in." I gaped. Stretched canvases, boxes of new and part-used paints, bags of tinned food and warm bread. He looked as if he were preparing for a siege! I pulled out the nearest bundle and began to follow his rapidly retreating figure.

"Just tell me. Why me? Why are you taking such an interest in my work?" I struggled to keep up with him as he vaulted the last couple of steps. He turned as he stepped inside my door.

"Because you have promise, and I invest in promise." I placed the heavy bag on the floor, carefully, and took some deep breaths.

"But what do you get out of it in return? Nobody, but nobody, does something for nothing these days."

"Well, if you are agreeable, I get a small percentage of your takings as the years progress. I have made a good living so far, and I don't think I'm backing a loser in this instance." He smiled and patted me on the shoulder. "I also get a great amount of pleasure watching someone reach something nearer their full potential. But that is more personal, and not quantifiable in cash terms." He was gone again. Jeez, but he was keen.

It took an hour to unload the van, and I was suffering from the shakes when we closed its doors for the last time. "Aren't you worn out?"

He slapped the van loudly and pulled out his keys. "No, and I haven't even started yet! I am going to park this somewhere safer than here, then I will be back. Is there anything you need more of that I might have missed?''

"Yeah, coffee. Loads of it. It looks like a long haul to the exhibition!"

I munched at some fresh bread as I unloaded the bags, marveling at the sheer amount of quality materials he had brought with him. He definitely knew his subject, judging by the variety of jars and phials I had never even heard of, never mind used. I was beginning to feel worried. Was I going to live up to all this confidence? My stomach rumbled some more. I fired up the primus under the battered old kettle and prepared fresh coffee. It had come to something when I considered electricity a luxury I could do without!

I stood at the grubby window and looked south into the morning, dawn's light beginning to kiss the lower roofs and caress its way down the warming walls. It would get almost unbearably hot in here as the sun reached its height, all this glass turning the studio into a greenhouse. I shrugged and sipped my coffee. No more dinnertime siestas for a while. I ran my fingers over my noisy belly, I was underweight. Ambition had a high price in personal cost, it seemed. The hiccoughs began, in response to the unusual breakfast of fresh bread, I supposed. I was normally careful to leave my shopping until just before closing, making the most of the end of the day throwaway prices. This fresh food was something new to my system! I could get used to it though, with some practice.

There was a thunder of feet as my sponsor raced up the stairway and into the studio. "Right, pour me a coffee, and let's get started." He turned and closed the door, turning the key. That made me curious, and I wasn't sure I liked being locked in.

"Why the locked door?"

He half turned as if not noticing what he had just done, "Oh that. That is to get the idea into your head that for the next week we are going to eat, sleep and breathe painting. No distractions and no visitors. I just hope you have a toilet in here!"

I had to laugh again, and pointed to the very primitive item tucked away in the eaves. "It is sufficient. I have a tap too, but no other modern amenities. It was the rock bottom rent that attracted me."

"Well, I'll make sure we don't live on cold food. You just concentrate on the art."

We shared the bread and coffee in silence, before he stood up with a rush. "Now, bodies." He pushed his hands deep into his pockets. "Why do you paint only men's?"

I had to think about that for a few moments before any reply came to mind. "I think it is because they are more interesting than the smooth curves of a woman. Plus, everyone paints women. I want to break that mold." I thought some more. "And all my heroes were men." It all seemed simple enough to me.

"Tell me, do you never try to work from life? I see so few sketch-books lying around?"

"No. Like I said, the subject scares me a little. Plus, I can't afford a model, but I try to make up for that by using photographs from old magazines."

He frowned, then turned to the window. I noted how the taut fabric closely defined his muscular body. No wonder he found stairways so little effort!

"Take your clothes off."

Now that one stopped me dead. "What? Why on earth do you want me to do that? It's me that should be learning some tricks of the trade, not wandering round starkers and feeling a real schmuck."

"I told you yesterday, you must keep an open mind regarding my teaching methods. If you insist on remaining clothed you will have to make do with merely being a 'good' painter, which is not why I am here."

He had me over a barrel with that one. I blushed wildly as I shrugged off my loose clothing, standing awkwardly in the middle of the floor. He walked around me and looked. Very intensely. He reached out and pinched my upper arm. I pulled away, but he shook his head and gripped my shoulder in warm fingers. I felt like a lab specimen as he poked and prodded at my body, at last stepping back and tilting his head to one side. "You are afraid of the body. We have some basic work to do before I begin sketching."

He moved closer, and cupped his hands beneath my buttocks, squeezing and rolling the muscle. I tightened up and winced at his intimacy. A hand ran around my waist and down the front of my left thigh. The strong fingers pressed against the soft inner skin and pressured me to spread my legs farther. He maneuvered me as if I were an artist's lay figure, turning me this way and that. He touched me, he stroked me, he pinched and poked me. He even slapped me lightly several times. I began to sense what he was aiming towards and as time rolled on, I grew more and more at home with my own body as an item of sculpture. As the day began to warm the room, he shed his own shirt and began to pose me, sketching loosely from around the room, moving in closer to catch a detail of light, half closing his eyes and sweeping at his large book studies. I grew accustomed to obeying his commands, moving more freely about the dais as he became totally absorbed in his work.

It was as the heat in the room grew to its most uncomfortable that he called a halt. "I need to let you rest a while before I set up the easel and create a more finished work." I was leafing through his book, turning my head in all directions to try and capture my body in the sweeping lines and staccato shadings. I was not to be seen, but the poetry in his line work was so free and uninhibited! I smiled as he handed me a bottle of cola, chilled in his cool-box.

"I look forward to seeing the result." I tilted my head back and took a deep draught of cool Coke, pressing the beaded bottle wet against my cheek. "This is excellent!" I looked over at him, and swallowed hard. He was carefully folding his remaining clothes over the back of my only chair, his bronzed back to me, those muscular cheeks now naked and in stilled motion. I looked away and tried to regain my lost composure.

"There is only one way to become comfortable with bodies, in my own experience" His voice came from close behind me, but I dared not turn. "You must become comfortable not just with your own body, but those of other men too." I felt the heat of him against the skin of my back and an instant tremor of tension rushed through me. "Now, let us get down to work."

I breathed out, having suddenly realized I was holding my breath, and returned to the dais. He moved in close and arranged me in the required pose. Only this time, something was different. I was being maneuvered by a naked man.

I suddenly wanted the floor to collapse beneath me as, against all my wishes, things began to stir in the undergrowth. With an inevitable rush of blood to my face I felt my cock gently growing to its full glory.

I tried to look unconcerned, but my embarrassment was as sharp as a knife. "Nice. But it's a bit like a yawn; you've set mine off now." He was laughing as my eyes fixed on his own growing cock, slowly uncurling from his thick black hair to stand pointing at my navel. I felt my face grow even hotter. "Hey, try and loosen up a little, this isn't unusual at all. We are both naked, it's all very new to you, and you're already acutely aware of your own body. Here." He stepped closer and stroked the length of my jutting cock. "It is nothing to worry about; it is just a part of your body."

He stepped up onto the small raised platform and took my hand in his. "Get used to it, you need to relax and get comfortable with naked flesh. Only then can you start to really create." He pulled my hand towards his own cock, my nerves screaming at me to escape. "Just take this in your hand for a short while. Come on, don't be shy." He curled my fingers around the warm silkiness of his skin. "Now just get used to how that feels for a while, absorb its warmth, the hardness beneath the soft skin. Draw back the skin and feel how different the head feels."

My heart was crashing drumbeats in my ears as I became more fully aware of what I was doing. Everything in me was crying out that I shouldn't be liking this, but beneath the protests I felt a surging excitement, a glorious celebration of the intimacy of our pose. I stroked him, felt the wiry curls at the base of his full length. Smeared my thumb over the wetted head of more slippery skin. He merely smiled at me and nodded. "It feels good, doesn't it? Nothing to be frightened of." He laughed out loud. "You should see your face, almost as if you expect it to go off like a gun in your hand."

I swallowed, hard. That was exactly what was turning my stomach to oil! He stopped his laughter, playfully squeezing my erection. "Come on, time to do some work before I get distracted." He turned and stepped down. I felt my shoulders relax.

He quickly walked away, and began to work on the naked canvas. Silence fell in the growing heat.

My mind was preoccupied with that last statement for the rest of the session, and it was still on my mind when we stopped for a coffee an hour later. I ached all over from maintaining the pose, and moved around to loosen myself up. I walked over to the easel and took a peek at the work. What a fucking mess! I could see that it was me who was there, but I was some unholy colors. The side of my face was livid green, the inside of my thigh a bruised blue, the length of my cock a very unhealthy russet. I frowned and surreptitiously looked over to the perpetrator of this ghastly explosion of color. I kept my thoughts about needing glasses to myself. The paints were not oils either. I touched the surface. Dry. That meant acrylics, and they were too fast drying for me! I couldn't afford to have paint drying on my brushes, or wasting canvasses with paint I could not wash off with a solvent. A nice luxury in my opinion. And the old masters definitely didn't use acrylics. No way.

"You look worried." He had been sitting in the contemplation chair, eyes half closed to appraise his progress. I felt very unsure about this. There was something about the charisma the man radiated that made me wonder if I was missing something vital.

"Aren't the colors a little wild?" I chanced a look in his direction. He didn't seem surprised at my criticism.

"Naturally, this is the earliest stage. Those are the colors beneath and above your skin, if you cared to look very closely. When I have filled out the flesh tones, the underpaint will still be faintly visible and give a truer definition to the body." He smiled at my doubtful glance. "You will see."

I returned to the dais, the merciless heat of the afternoon raising the levels of discomfort in the loft. I began to feel droplets of sweat running down my ribcage, my brow and scalp. On and on Jacques worked, actually spending very little time with his eyes on the canvas. I seemed to be the total focus of his labors. My muscles were beginning to shriek with the discomfort of holding the pose, and I tried to ease my rigid shoulders with a slight movement. He noticed instantly. "You must be in agony. Another break I think. Am I right?"

I nodded. It was with huge relief I clambered down, heading for the water bucket to wash myself down. Joy! The water was not cold by any means, but it was a damn sight cooler than the room. I had an idea born of desperation, and strode to the windows. With some care I managed to tape over one of the many cracked ones, and give it a sharp tap with a handy piece of timber. With even more care in my naked state, I removed the broken glass, and sighed in sheer pleasure as the afternoon's breeze played over my skin, cooling where water still remained. I heard sounds of approval, followed by splashing, and Jacques was beside me, one hot hand on my shoulder as he squatted in the window's gentle breeze. "Bliss, sheer bliss. That was a great idea." He left his hand on my shoulder. I stayed still.

"You're tight across your shoulders. Do you want some massage to loosen up a little?"

I nodded. Strong fingers gently caressed my tense muscles, moving back and forth between upper chest and shoulder blades. I felt comfortable with his touching, and smiled back at him.

"You should do that for a living."

"Oh, I did in a past lifetime. A parlor I later came to own, which gave me the money to start afresh. It was a long road from then to now, I can tell you." He kneaded my tension like bread. "What does Emcee stand for, by the way?"

I sensed a twinge in my groin even at the asking, and tried to reposition myself "It goes back to late school. I was nicknamed M, or massive, in the changing rooms. I leave you to work the rest out."

"I'm not surprised. Not surprised at all." A wet hand suddenly encircled my pulsing length, squeezing gently while massaging."

"Hey Jacques, you may have worked in a parlor, but that doesn't mean that every massage you give automatically necessitates a hand job!" I gripped his forearm to stop him.

"You don't like what I'm doing?"

What a stupid question! "Well, of course I do. Bloody hell, Jacques, I'm human. But I feel embarrassed." He continued to rhythmically squeeze my growing cock, even with my restraint, managing to draw back the foreskin. "Then it is time to grow out of that unhappy state!" Another hand slipped around my slim waist, and loosened my grip on his arm, warm breath on my neck teasing the downy hairs there. "Relax."

The rhythm grew more rapid, my cock now fully engorged, the tip glistening and moist with early warnings. His hot grip grew faster in its beat, nails digging into my groin as he grew more urgent in his breathing, teeth wet against my shoulder as he gently bit into skin and muscle. I groaned aloud as I felt the beginnings deep within, leaning my head back and allowing my weight to fall against him. He growled in anticipation as I began to rhythmically pump my groin into his hands, and with teeth-gritted frenzy I felt my hot jets of cum launch out and seek flight. My own grip dug into his arms as I shuddered down from the blazing heights of intense release. I was panting and sweating again.

The warm breeze through the window was some relief against my inflamed desires, but the sudden wanting that flooded through my every pore was intoxicating. I took a very deep breath, and rose unsteadily to my feet. Jacques was instantly on his way back to the easel, and my sudden sense of being deserted caught me unawares. I studied his body more closely, the tension across his shoulders as he picked brushes up, the more pronounced definition of one buttock as he leant across. I groaned inaudibly, and returned to the dais.

The time came when, after a good deal of frowning, Jacques sat back in the contemplating chair and nodded. "You must look closely at the work, not just at the surface but what the painter has done beneath." I wandered across and looked at the finished article. There I stood, as proud and defiant as Spartacus himself. I went over to my own painting and placed it beside his. I certainly had some learning to do!

I stood beside the chair and, with a new courage, gripped Jacques' shoulder. "You are an excellent painter, Jacques. I am amazed I have not seen your work before!"

He patted my hand. "Oh, I can copy well enough in this kind of work, but I have no original ideas to boast. My pleasure comes in the gardening of new talents. That is my skill." He rose from the chair, the impression left by the wooden slats marking his back and thighs. "What do you like to do when you have finished a painting?"

I had to consider for several moments before anything sprang to mind. "If I was satisfied with the piece I might treat myself to a glass of good cognac." I moved my own canvas back to the reject pile. "What about you?"

Warm hands were suddenly at my waist. "What I like the most is to make love." I felt his heat, sensed his gentle question. Hands slipped forward, their heat on my abdomen awakening my every sense. I placed my open palms over the back of his hands and slowly pushed them downward. A jutting cock slipped between my thighs as he pressed into an embrace, lush hairs tickling against my ass cheeks. His chin rested on my shoulder as fingers caressed my swelling cock. "When I say make love, I mean it. I like to make love to my students a lot, but most of all I like the last lesson, when they make love to me."

My throbbing abundance reared to rampant as his meaning sank in. I became acutely aware of the rigid length between my thighs. Very slowly he positioned me facing him, all the while keeping one hand or other fondling my aching flesh.

Our eyes met in an understanding, and I wrapped my arms around him, drawing him into a first kiss. His lips were full and soft against mine, his hot tongue slipping between us. I stroked his gorgeous cheeks, fingers tracing the path made by beads of sweat into the moist crevice between.

I felt gloriously at home with this tenderness, so fresh and honest. I traced fingertips around to his jutting cock, teasing the softness of the skin, rolling back the tender tip, to reveal a gloriously full head. He took my face between his hands and murmured, "Go down, go down and take my length into your sweet wet mouth. Taste a man, and let me anoint your face."

I moaned, out from my hidden depths rushed all the pent-up longings of my past, and with a trembling breath I opened my mouth wide, drawing in Jacques' eager hot flesh. Hard, salty, pulsing. I whimpered in excitement as back and forth I slipped; noises of wet slithering further animating my enthusiasm. I licked, I sucked, I lapped like a cow on a salt block. I moaned in sheer delight.

Jacques' hips were twitching beneath my hands, as I ran open fingered across his abdomen, feeling the muscle there tensing beneath my palms. I withdrew from his cock, catching my breath before licking my way beneath its twitching and over his soft ballsac. I lapped at the damp skin, nuzzled into the lush heat of his crotch. With great care I sucked one large sphere into my hot mouth and rolled it around in me. Like I'd released a ripe plum, it popped from my mouth, only to be replaced with its twin. His balls were wet against my cheek as I bit the soft skin of his inner thigh, licking the sweat away.

Hands drew me back to desperately impale me on his wild cock. I sucked then with a vengeance, fiercely as his moans grew more heated. I gripped his arse with bared nails as, with a roar of explosive force, he gushed his heat down my throat.

The amount he pumped into my mouth and over my face astounded me, never seeming to end. Hot ooze dribbled down my cheeks and chin, my lips wet and splashed with cum. I lapped him in, tasting his essence like a wine, licking the shining length of his cock clean, smearing him over my face with the softening flesh. I was in heaven.

115

It was without haste that the entire reason for Jacques' being there reasserted itself, and with a great deal of regret I untangled myself from our sticky embrace and refreshed myself with the bucket. Standing on the thick towel, I glanced over to him, already preparing for what was to be my tuition. I would have been quite happy to have continued with the present learning curve, but nagging thoughts of my first big chance reasserted themselves.

"Right, my friend. To begin with I want you to get used to having a model. I don't want to see anything like finished work. Remember those first loose drawings I began with. That's what I'm after. It will relax your movement around the paper, and give your eye time to catch important points." He smiled at my flushed cheeks. "I also want you to practice making me pose. I want to hear you instructing me into a different pose every few minutes. Never linger at this stage."

And that was it. He leapt up onto the dais, and waited. I gathered my charcoal up, and looked. In fact I spent the next hour mostly looking. It grew to be more fun than work, as I instructed Jacques into all manner of odd poses, keeping him on the move as frequently as possible. In fact, towards the end of the hour I began to put him into purely lewd positions, ending the session with one of mostly his buttocks, as he bent away from me to hold his ankles. I spent longer on that drawing, lingering on the sight of his pouting hole, my cock murmuring its desire to fill that hot and delicious avenue as soon as possible.

Jacques went throughout the sheets strewn over the floor and said nothing. Until he came to the last. He stood for a long time and considered the piece. "You really enjoyed that one, didn't you!" I nodded with a playful grin. "Well, that is exactly what we are looking for. You focused on something you really wanted, I presume?

Again I felt a grin spreading across my face. "Obviously. Well you can have it, eventually, when the work is done."

He patted my own backside on the way past. "But until that time, this is mine for the asking." A sharp thrill of expectancy shuddered through me, and ran to earth in my swelling cock. I gritted my teeth, and turned my attention to the next session.

It was as the evening light cast long shadows in the studio that I eventually put my charcoal down, rubbing my eyes in exhaustion. Jacques was himself a little subdued. He climbed slowly down from the dais and sat for a few minutes in the chair. "Time for food I think, and more liquid." I raised a hopeful eyebrow. "No, water. In this heat we need to keep up our intake. There is a way to go yet." He clambered up, and padded over to the bags.

Between us we put together a simple meal of fresh fruit and vegetables, bread and water on the side. I leaned back on my warm bed and closed my eyes. "I'm shattered!" I felt him sit beside me, his warmth radiating through my skin.

"It's been a hard day for you. All this new experience, and work too." A hand pressed lightly against my belly. "We'll both be fine in the morning. And if we are to make the most of the light, we'd better call it a day now."

For the first time ever, at the hour I would normally be out on the streets of Paris, I was sound asleep, lying on my bed with another man, a man who had begun to open my eyes. I woke occasionally just to remind myself that this was really happening to me. Like a fairytale come true he was there still, bathed in the pale light of the moon. I smiled, and went to sleep happy.

All too soon the first hint of daylight began to illuminate the cool room. and I shivered slightly in the cold before sun-up. A warm arm slipped across my waist, open palm spreading over my lower belly. Fingers closed gently around my morning glory, and squeezed the circumference of the base. My cock twitched harder. "Shall we warm up before we make a start?" His other hand slipped low down my back, fingers stroking my cheeks, pressing against my tight rosebud. I felt his heat slide closer, the hard tip of him suddenly pressing between me. As Jacques squirmed closer to me the heated length of him pressed between my virgin cheeks and hairs tickled against the base of my back. "I like to make love in the mornings too. It clears the head."

I wriggled against his pressing, the sensation of being wanted like this new to me. I tried to turn around to face him, wanting to kiss him, to caress the hair around his dark nipples. He embraced me the tighter, making me remain. I felt him reach back, sensed he was preparing himself, smelt a slightly sweet scent.

The full, slippery length of his throbbing flesh slithered between my cheeks, and with a new excitement, I reached back to part myself wider, inviting him into my heated embrace. Pulsing cock began to rhythmically press against my reluctant defense, its presence inflaming my curiosity. I tried to relax, but it was only the relentless nuzzling that eventually overcame my resistance. Very, very slowly a wetted cockhead stole into me, like a thief in the night. I held my breath as its swollen luxuriance throbbed in my tight, wet heat. Jacques was waiting; I could sense his restraint while I grew accustomed to my submission.

He tightened his hold, and as I yielded further the enormousness of his hot shaft welled up inside me. I groaned in dread that the feelings of being stretched beyond capacity might grow worse, but Jacques remained still while I grew more accustomed to his invasion. I began to squeeze and relax around his firm heat, his low grunts of appreciation spurring me on.

With great care I eased away from him, the relief making me sigh. Only his cockhead remained when I reversed my direction, and with sudden courage thrust myself back. Slippery with potency his great cock surged into my depths, only this time Jacques himself was growing more ardent. Nails raked my belly as he urged me onto my back; once again my guts were allowed to recover as he slithered free.

Very quickly Jacques had my heels locked over the back of his neck, and once again his fiery cockhead nuzzled against my no-longer-virgin hole. I closed my eyes and held my breath, as with a wonderful inevitability I was penetrated by his hard and insistent cock. Jacques ground deep into me, swiveling his hips as he heaved deeper. Again and again he almost withdrew his zealous throbbing, before wet and slippery sounds signaled his return. I shuddered with intoxication, my heart reaching out to this gorgeous man.

Our rutting became more and more frenzied as the rhythm increased. I dug my fingers deep into his shoulders as the ecstasy and pain grew to a crescendo, and with a moaning of surprise and release I felt the entire contents of my sizzling balls jetting out to bombard my chest with hot cum. His eyes tight shut, Jacques shuddered deep inside me, his abdomen tight as a board, and, with a long drawn out intake of breath, he drove into me with slow and intense thrusts. I could feel his ecstasy filling my guts, hot and searching, his cock gushing its offering into the very core of my being. I tightened around him, my ass muscles sucking him dry, clinging to his lust.

We slipped wet into a morning embrace, smearing over each other. Our hot mouths drank of cum, sweat and saliva as we lapped, sucking and licking in thoughtless rapture.

Very gradually we subsided into each other's arms, the day ahead of no concern. Warmth began to infuse the attic as the rising sun teased color into the sky. I could have made love to him for hours.

Sadly it was not to be, for all too soon Jacques leapt up from the wrecked bed. "Come on, we have things to do." I reached up to him and shook my head.

"No, can't we just stay a while longer? I want more!"

He put a cool foot on my sticky chest and rubbed. "No chance. We have a lot of work to do."

My heart sank. I did manage to persuade him into letting me washing him down, and both my swelling cock and I basked in the serving. His skin was warm beneath the cold water as I rubbed eagerly exploring fingers over him, rolling his ass cheeks in my palms, slipping his soft foreskin back to wet the smooth head so coy beneath. I couldn't resist just popping him into my mouth for a few moments, his thickening length slowly filling me with its succulence. He placed a palm on my forehead and gently pushed me back. "Wait! Not so fast. You can have your pudding, but only when you've finished the main course!" He stepped back. "Not that I wasn't tempted to postpone our work until later!" He turned his back, and strode to the chair.

Much to my confusion he began to dress. "I thought that door was staying locked?" I was awash with feelings about Jacques leaving me on my own, ones I didn't want to get used to. Feelings new to me. "Where are you going?" I tried to sound matter-of-fact. I wasn't sure it had worked. Jacques gave me a questioning look. Perhaps honesty was the best policy. "This feels strange to me, but it's a feeling I like. Like a lot. I've always preferred my own company, but suddenly I don't want you to leave." Then again, perhaps it wasn't.

He stayed still for a few moments, shirt hanging across his shoulder, tight arse dragging my eyes downward. "Don't do this Emcee, it will ruin your work to be so distracted." He looked concerned. "Don't forget that once your work has improved I will leave to find another student. We are together for this week or so. After that, who knows?" He stepped back to me, running his warm fingers down my cheek. "Enjoy our time while we have it. Forget what will happen afterwards, if you can."

I felt like a skyscraper had collapsed inside me. You know those films where the foundations are blown out by charges and the whole structure collapses so symmetrically? Rubble crashed into the pit of my stomach. I tried to lighten up in order to please him, realizing that I had to be different for him to stay. Perhaps if I made myself sufficiently memorable he would reconsider leaving. I shrugged my shoulders. "OK, how long are you going to be, and do I need to make breakfast while you're gone?"

"No, I am just going to get us a model. That way I can watch you work. I can't teach you if I'm stuck on the dais, let's be honest." He was dressed and at the door. "I'll be back with a Spartacus." The key turned in the lock as he left. The metallic clacking of the old lock made me shudder, a small shock of excitement thrilling my loins to reaction. I closed my fingers around my warm and eager length, hanging on to the future of those few more nights with Jacques.

I was dressed and trying to make some progress with a fresh idea, sheets of sketches littering the floor, when the door sounded Jacques' return. I turned as casually as I could manage, to be confronted by one huge son of a bitch. He grinned, and punched my shoulder playfully. At least I'd like to think it was playfully; it would certainly be classed as violence in any other company. I grimaced. He chuckled. "You need to eat more. I am Sorrel. Jacques and I work together a lot. Can I see your work?" His eyes rested on the canvases. I stepped aside.

"Over in the comer, those are samples of how I used to work."

Jacques looked over to me with a wry smile. "You have made your mind up?"

I looked over my shoulder to where Sorrel was bent over my canvases and nodded. "I think I owe it to myself to gain an education while it's on offer." I saw his face lighten, in relief? "I've a new idea for the 'Spartacus' already, there are some sketches here." I drew out the one nearest my intentions. Jacques frowned.

"Why naked, and why would a man about to be executed, very slowly, have a hard-on?

"Well." I struggled for explanation. "His captors would not care how he went to his death, but by being naked he was proclaiming his status, still the warrior, strong in his defeat." I was getting into this new image now. "The erection is another statement of no surrender, even in the face of death he can be virile, a figure of undaunted manhood." How on earth could I say that I was merely thinking of Jacques as I made the sketches.

Jacques was still frowning. "I think it best to give no reasons. Those could, perhaps, be read as rather adolescent. But, the painting will certainly be the one to gain notoriety, which is always worth a great deal to someone new. We will pursue the idea further.''

Sorrel returned from his perusal. "You have great promise Emcee. Now, let us get to work." And with that he began to shrug off his garments. I swallowed hard as what was revealed was a big man in more ways than one! He hitched up his balls after their imprisonment, and stepped onto the dais. I looked across at Jacques, who was also stripping. "Are you posing too?" I felt stirring in my tatty jeans as he stood in the morning sunshine. He shook his head.

"No, and you need to join us. The same rules apply as yesterday, only today will be easier for you; the first steps were taken into this new world then." He patted my ass on his way back to Sorrel. He stood beside the dais and beckoned me over. "Come on, you will have to get used to being close to Sorrel too. We are all in this together now." He patted the hard belly close to his cheek. I imagined it close to mine. Only not the cheeks of my face!

I really tried to give the impression that I did this every day of the week, shrugging off my kit and gathering my sketch pad. I looked up at the towering Sorrel and felt suddenly in the presence of great power. Like a Greek god he smiled down at me from his higher vantage, the scents of him deep and dark to my senses. Jacques was stroking his hip with too much affection for comfort. In a strange desperation, I reached up to Sorrel's hanging cock, and sucked him slowly into my hungry mouth.

He was big and warm in me, his pulse gradually swelling him to fill then overfill my mouth. I drew back for breath, eyes locked on his as I eased back, his skin shining with my saliva. I wasn't just hungry, I was ravenous!

Jacques gripped my jutting enthusiasm and squeezed. "Don't forget, no pudding until after the main course. Now, get the easel set up, pose Sorrel, and make a start." He gripped my shoulders and propelled me away from the new Spartacus.

It was the hardest days work I have ever done! Jacques stood over my shoulder most of the time, sounds of approval or counsel, an occasional pointing to areas I needed to reconsider. On and on, the tension mounting. How Sorrel managed to remain in the bound pose as long as he did I failed to grasp, but grasping was on my mind for most of the time. The heat grew stifling as the day advanced, and inevitably there came a point where none of us could continue. We sponged each other down with the now-warm water in the bucket, and took turns sitting close to the broken window in the breeze.

Sorrel spoke in a deep, quiet tone as he turned to me, his hand stroking the length of my thigh: "Jacques is a hard master, but I have seen many of his finds go on to great things. You will learn a great deal from him." He winked. "In more than just the field of your art." His chuckle reminded me of the magnificent Paul Robeson.

I felt brave, and stroked the tight muscles of his shoulders and back, sensing him relax under my fingers. I made love to that broad back, absorbing his silky heat through my pores. The last thing I wanted was to pick up a brush again. He rested his cheek on the back of my hand as I squeezed his shoulder to rise. Jacques was clucking again, pacing about in agitation.

All day the work continued, sketching, studying the colors beneath the obvious bronze of the skin, losing my inhibitions regarding wild underpaint. It dawned on me that in trying to go for a finished product from the very start I was rushing past the essential deeper visions of what lay beneath someone's facade. By the time the sun was beginning to sink the canvas looked terrible, and in days past I would have taken out a bottle of solvent to erase the horror. Today I was content to await developments.

The painting absorbed my immediate attention, but it was my imagination that had me wandering around behind an almost permanently jutting cock. The level of discomfort was intoxicating.

I breathed in the scents of Sorrel and Jacques at every opportunity, I paced close by in order to sense their radiant body heat, I grew more ambitious in my brushing past or against them. My whole being was aroused.

"What would you like me to bring in for our meal, Emcee?"

The question distracted me from my daydreaming. I looked vaguely at Jacques, and shrugged. "At this moment I'm so hungry I could eat a horse!" Sorrel chuckled. "As long as there's a lot of it I will eat anything you put in front of me." I watched as he quickly dressed and preened himself, taking up a bag as he headed for the door. Without another word Jacques left, the keys rattling in the lock before we heard his footsteps descend to the real world.

Instantly Sorrel was moving, stepping down off the dais while he eased his tensed muscles. He strode over to view the day's efforts, but made no comment. I watched him closely as he stood by the easel, catching his eye as he glanced over. "How do you come to know Jacques?" I grasped any question that came to mind, just to hear that voice. The tension between us was almost visible suddenly, my imagination running wild now that we were alone.

"We go back a long way, worked the same club when we first met. I worked on stage and Jacques in the recreation rooms. When he took over the place and began to make a winner out of it he offered me a partnership. Since then I have always had business links with Jacques, and I am his chosen model for new talent." He stepped over to me, soft cock gently brushing each thigh as it swung beneath the thick bush of hair. "But that isn't what you wanted to ask me is it, Emcee? You wanted to say something like...." Sorrel stood over me, his hot hand on my shoulder now. "You wanted to say that we should have sex. You have wanted to say it all afternoon. I could sense it between us. It is visible in your work so far." His luxuriant length was now swelling; soon it was twitching. It was glorious!

It was nuzzling now against my cheek, its throbbing pulse matching my own pounding heartbeat. I reached up to cup Sorrel's smooth buns, and gingerly drew his hot, moist cockhead into my naive mouth. I wasn't ready for the rush of Sorrel's enthusiasm as my wet clasping lips and tongue sucked him in. I gagged as he seized my head, forcing me into his wiry curls, my throat crammed with too much hot cock. I gagged and drew back, but the power of Sorrel's attraction drew me on. I wanted to taste him, swallow every drop he had to give me. I ached for him to show me all he knew.

I noisily gorged on his succulence, saliva and pre-cum dribbling down my chin as he slithered into me once more. My brow clung to his sweating belly with each beat of the blow job, the slapping noises only inflaming me further. Sorrel was groaning now, his nails digging into my shoulders, his thighs trembling beneath my clasping fingers. On and on I pounded over him, faster and faster his breathing. I knew he could not be far off and drew back, able to lick his cockhead whilst keeping him inside me. I rocked my head back and forth as I sensed the beginning, the shaft twitched and trembled between my wet lips, his movements beginning to jerk and stiffen.

Then at last Sorrel was coming. Hot cum exploded out of him and shot down my throat, splashed against my teeth, ran slowly down my lips and chin. I drew away and closed eager fingers around him, another jet splattering over my face. And another. I was wet and dripping with him, sucking his glistening abundance back into my mouth, sucking out his last offering, gently biting his flesh as he relaxed, softening inside me. I lapped my tongue over and around his softening cock, its heat filling my mouth with a comforting suffusion.

Reluctantly I let him slide from between my lips, the wet flesh slapping against his thigh. Sorrel bowed, his lips hot and dry against mine. His tongue wet and seeking as it eased between my teeth, wrestled inside my slippery mouth. His tongue was as ravenous as I as he licked his own cum off my face, the hot lapping over my eyes and nose an excitement in itself. I hugged his huge physique, like a big, soft toy that was mine. Like the big soft toy I had never had.

For the next few days I worked continually on two paintings. During the days Sorrel joined Jacques and me. And in the evenings, when the light had gone, he would leave.

Jacques and I ate, talked, and best of all, he made love to me. More and more I became saturated with the present, forgetting the days to come other than the promise that I could have his sweet arse when work was over. I gorged myself on his cum, I ached with his fucking, I basked in his affection. My work grew less stilted as I became more and more at ease with the continual presence of naked flesh. The touching became second nature, the sex at day's end a release of pent-up desire. The whole world could remain outside for these few days. Inside there was only passion. For paint, for sex, for food and wine. I was sublimely happy.

I found myself working late in the night, sitting alone in the moonlight and drawing Jacques as he slept, cavern black charcoal crumbling in my fingers as I caught the fall of cold light on his form. Those sketches I put out of sight, for I wanted my own piece of Jacques to keep once he had left. I felt a growing dread of that coming event, a nagging jealousy that he would move on to another, that I was merely one of many. It ate time away, gnawing at me like a toothache.

It was with a sinking heart that I looked to Sorrel on the last day. Jacques had left to bring back the evening's supplies, and one of the paintings was nagging at me. I stood a long time just looking from the canvas to Sorrel, a growing feeling of completion warming me somewhere inside. I placed the dry brush into a jar and stood back.

"You are satisfied, my dear, sweet Emcee?"

Sorrel's deep tone made me smile. I nodded back. He climbed down off the dais and came to study the work. There was silence between us for a long time.

"You must mark this piece as sold."

I looked to his face in question. "You think that will help the other works go?"

His arms were around me now as he leant his chin on my shoulder, his heat against my back. "No, sweet Emcee. No, I will give you whatever price you wish to ask for this work. You have created one of the best pieces I have ever seen from any of Jacques' interesting young finds." He kissed my neck and squeezed me close to him. I felt his breath on my skin. "You wanted me in every brush stroke. Your desire was behind each detail. Ah, yes, my sweet boy, I want to own the work of someone who feels that way about me."

I turned in his arms and began to feel a swelling in my throat. "Oh Sorrel, I do. I really do." I leant my brow on his hot and shining shoulder. "Jacques will go tomorrow, and he will take you with him to his next protégé. He will make love to them, bring them to their best work, capture something of their hearts, and then leave. And I will miss you both."

"And if I were to tell you that I do not want to go?" Sorrel's large hands were stroking my back, low to the curve of my cheeks. I squeezed his waist.

"I would continue to adore you, to paint you." I looked into his dark eyes. They never left mine.

"Would you draw moonlight sketches of me too?" He looked a little hurt as his voice grew quiet.

I stroked his cheek, cupped his chin in my palms. "Sorrel, I would create an altar to your beauty, right here, in this room and in my art."

Very suddenly we were in the powerful grip of something wild and unchecked. The wanting rushed to my hands, clutching and clawing at Sorrel's taut ass cheeks. His nails were dragged across my shoulders as our tongues penetrated and writhed against each other. Breath was instantly panting, hot excitement against necks and earlobes. I ached to fuck and be fucked, in any order, both at the same time. My desire was to revel in excess. Tear, bite, devour and inflame.

Sorrel was arching back, his large and dark nipples wet with my sucking. I felt them swell between my teeth, heard his sharp intake of breath as I bit down. His bunched fists punched into my shoulders as down I snaked, nipping and licking the flesh before me. His rigid cock slapped against my neck, its sleek heat and moist head pressing against my cheek as I lapped at his balls. Fingers raked back through my hair as I drew him into me at last. Filling me to slippery capacity once more. I banged my face against his sweaty belly as, again and again, I urged down the glistening length of his cock to nuzzle into his thick curls, his length throbbing against my tongue.

I ran eager fingers up to tease his pouting hole, wetting my thumb between my spasms of lustful hunger. He moaned as I slipped into him, his heat and the tight grip around the base of my thumb spurred my own cock to rise, rampant and wet. I sucked and I licked, I drew back his skin and ran my hot tongue over the wet and shining head. The musky smells of his sex aroused, filled my nostrils, transmitting heated feverish messages to my groin. I wanted to have control over my big man, and drew away as I began to sense his beginnings. Sorrel groaned aloud and came to his knees before me, our kisses more demanding now, biting and scratching, drawing shallow pain into the fray.

Inevitably we ended our passioned wrestling toward orgasm on my mattress, only this time I had Sorrel pinned beneath me. I pushed his wrists down into the soft pillows and bit his neck. He writhed beneath me, but remained. Again I lapped and nuzzled my way to his magnetic cock.

Its wet heat was rushing deep into my throat as even then Sorrel moaned out an exclamation. Jerking his hips off the mattress I felt his cock tremble inside my hungry mouth, the first explosive rush of hot cum bursting out to fill me up. I drew back to swallow, another gusher forcing me to let ooze run from between my lips, down my chin, down his wet, glistening flesh to black and curling hair. Sorrel roared out his release into me, pounding upward to drive his seed as far into me as he could. I drank of his excess, I reveled in its thick creaminess, wiped my wet hand over my face to smear him over my skin, licked my palm of his salty taste.

My own cock was screaming out for its own needs to be tended, and taking my courage into both hands I hoisted Sorrel's legs up before me. He closed his eyes and locked his ankles behind my neck. I reached for the tube on the floor and blindly squeezed cool gel over myself, its chill striking my thighs and belly as I ground into Sorrel. He reached down and parted his cheeks, and slipped my cockhead along the full length of his slick, deliciously inviting ass crack.

The pucker of his ring beckoned me in, and the wet heat as I slipped my first inch into him had me gasping for air. I had not imagined this could make me feel so damn good. His muscles tightened around me as deeper and deeper I sank into him, a slow smile crossing his lips as I swelled and impaled him. There came a second tightening of muscle and at last my belly ground into his cheeks. I urged myself that last little way, to be as far inside Sorrel as I could physically manage. He groaned and murmured. "Huge cock! I love it."

He squeezed deep, almost sucking me. I slithered out slowly, cooler air brushing my moistened skin, my belly slippery against the back of his hot thighs. He opened his eyes to watch my face, my mouth open in a gasp of ecstasy. He raised an eyebrow, fingernails dug into my back. I surged into Sorrel again, and again. His teeth bared, he gripped me tightly, urging me to fuck him. It took little encouragement to become frenzied in my assault on his arse, slamming against his wetted skin with inflaming slappings. He was panting now, his eyes no longer focused, tongue between his teeth as I tore away all my last reserves and arched deep into his sucking heat.

Higher and higher I rose, eyes tight shut and moans unheard as at last I felt the heat rushing from inside me. Nothing on earth could have held me back then, as with an intensity that had me crying out, head thrown back like a wolf in the night, I lost control. My white-hot cum gushed into Sorrel, his own cries coming through a distance to my ears. With spasmodic jerks I thrust my seed as deeply as possible, nails raking at unseen flesh, unaware of how fiercely Sorrel was bucking into me, drawing every drop of my essence from me.

It was with a shaking and quivering that I eventually slipped from Sorrel's embrace, sliding down to lie on his heaving chest, my cheek on his shoulder. His arms were around my waist, hands stroking my sweating back. I smelled nothing but sweat and cum, the undercurrent of Sorrel's own scent deep in its presence. He crooned soothing nothings, gently kissed my brow. For such a big man he seemed almost childlike in his affection. Sweat stuck us together, sweat and cum. This was indeed happiness of a new order. I could almost have cried, so right did the moment seem, so complete. In the turn of a page I had become full, Sorrel the one to bring me to new pastures. From this moment on I could get over Jacques, learn to move on to grass that was greener, and longer.

- – -

What I hadn't quite accounted for was the chemistry when Jacques breezed back into the stifling attic, throwing off his light clothes as he came to join us on the bed. He seemed ebullient and full of sparkle as he sat beside me, arm snaking around my waist. "So Emcee, have you finished do you think? I see you have added no more to one of the paintings." His eyebrows raised in question. "And I can smell the evidence of a good time had by both."

I felt my ears grow hot, but could not respond to his last comment. "It seemed wrong to try to improve it any further when I came to begin. I think it's that one I shall put in the gallery." I found myself studying Jacques closely, judging his reaction. He merely passed me a warm croissant and a slice of cheese.

Sorrel placed a hand on my back. "I have bought the painting already, Jacques. It is the best I have seen of all our ventures." The two shared a look that I could not read, momentarily feeling a stranger in their midst.

We ate in silence, looking across to the easel bearing Spartacus. I felt compelled to say something but could find no words to suit. I sighed, and reached down to hold them both. "I appreciate...." I gently stroked the silky abundance of their visibly awakening cocks. Closing my grip around them, I stroked a slow rhythm as flesh grew large and rigid in my hands. I momentarily released them and spun around to face the two, catching up the rhythm with growing enthusiasm. Sorrel groaned and lay back, his moist length jutting eagerly to the roof. Jacques closed his eyes and moved closer to his supine friend, leaning back to join Sorrel flat out on the mattress.

I was hard myself now, eager to anoint myself with their joint offerings at the altar of desire. I felt their twitching and bucking as my insistence grew. I leant first one way then the other, bobbing my hungry mouth over them, wetting and tasting the flushed skin beneath the rolled the foreskin back.. Sorrel was panting now, his arm around Jacques' shoulders. Both lay with their eyes closed and lips parted. My muscles ached, my senses tingled, and at last the moment came. With panting encouragement they writhed and twitched beneath my enthusiasm. I angled them closer, turning my mouth from one to the other. They were both leaning toward each other, cocks almost touching as I prepared for the rush.

It came. And how. With joint ecstasy the two cocks exploded over me. I rubbed, I sucked, I licked and I smeared. I worked them dry of cum, had them panting and moaning in delirious relief as I slowed to enjoying their copious endowments. I was wet and dripping, rubbing them into my very skin. The strong smells of sex filled my senses, the strong taste of that sex only making me even more hungry.

I felt strangely in control. Taking a position at Jacques's feet, I eased apart his thighs and drew them up, working my way to him, my hard and hungry cock jerking in anticipation. He murmured in delight as little by little I eased my lustful heat inside him. He was tight and hot around my length as slowly but surely I slipped inside him. He rhythmically swayed his hips as I felt his muscle tighten around the base of my cock, my flesh being massaged inside his hot arse. This was what I had been aching for all week, to drive my lust deep into his perfect hole. All reserves and restraints seemed to slip from my shoulders, the rush of possession lending furious energy to my loins.

Making love to Jacques was overcome by a primal desire to fuck him, hard. My belly slapped against the back of his thighs as faster and faster I banged into him. Eyes tightly shut I clawed and tensed every fiber of my body to focus on the intense sensations in my cock and balls, every ripple of flesh, every slip of wet skin against hard sex, every squeeze of muscle around the base of my immersed cock, the wet heat as I crammed as deep into Jacques as physically possible.

We were both panting heavily, sweat trickling between us to ease the friction of hair against sensitive skin. Jacques' nails dug deep into my shoulders as he sensed my coming at last. His own cock was slapping against his belly, rigid and flushed with thrusting anticipation. I seized it to mimic our rhythm, thrashing away in a frenzied need to feel him come in my hand. My whole abdomen felt to be on the verge of bursting, as with a trembling intensity the convulsions driving hot cum deep into Jacques' butt overwhelmed me. The wet slapping grew dim in my ears as my rhythm disintegrated into jerking ecstasy. Simultaneously, the throbbing cock between my fingers sent hot fluid jetting out over his belly.

Shuddering with a rush of exhaustion I slithered from Jacques' wet hole, and succumbed to his chest. Our hot bodies squashed cum between us, making our tender embrace slippery and sensual. For those minutes I had been completely unaware of Sorrel's presence, but as I lay my head on Jacques' shoulder I caught his eye. In that split second I knew the difference between infatuation and loving passion.

I kissed Jacques deep, my feelings slightly detached from him already. In my heart I knew that I was no more than an investment and a conquest. My eyes fixed on Sorrel,' and the flicker of distraction there. I had loved Sorrel, and suddenly I felt incomplete. I wanted it all today, I wanted Sorrel. I wanted Sorrel to make love to me. Instantly.

Easing myself to my feet I stroked Jacques' sated skin absent mindedly, looking for the gel as I crossed to Sorrel. He welcomed me with open arms, stiff cock rigid with desire. With loving care I smoothed the cool gel over his entire length, turning it into a glistening, slippery weapon of lust.

Squatting slowly over his loins, I reached down and touched the cool tip of him to my anxious hole. He was big, and I was not confident. The first inch of him slipped against the resisting muscle, resisting entry despite my wanting. I held to my gentle pressure, and slowly but surely felt the muscle yield. Warm fingers closed about my still-soft cock, gently teasing back the foreskin in slow rhythm.

My eyes fixed on Sorrel's eyes, I eased myself down over him. He held perfectly still as I let myself grow accustomed to his filling and swelling my hole. It ached fiercely; it consumed my attention. I felt his pulse in my very depths, tried to work my muscles around him. Hands flat on his chest I looked down. My ass cheeks were still some way off his hips, but already I felt I could take no more of him. I looked up again to see him smile at my dilemma.

I wanted him, wanted to feel all of his cock swallowed by my hole, but I was afraid of that last measure. I bit my lip as one warm hand stroked my cheek, and sat back.

As my weight drove him into what felt like my stomach I had to whimper, eyes tightly shut against the pain gushing through me.

I eased away from the intensity, but perversely I felt I was giving in. Once more I slipped back down his abundant length, this time watching Sorrel for his own pleasure.

I noticed that as I slipped over him his eyes shut in ecstasy as I drew away they opened. I became more used to the flashes of pain as my ass ground down onto Sorrel's hips, the feelings coursing through my veins rich and powerful.

I had really become complete, this was what I was made for. The rhythm grew to a steady tempo as I experimented with how deep I sucked Sorrel into me.

This was turning into a joyful celebration of our joining. Our eyes were fixed on each other, smiles of agreement and attainment on wet lips. I bent forward to kiss him, letting his bucking hips fill me to his own rhythm.

He drove faster and deeper, sending my face hard against his, his kisses becoming wilder and more needy. The intensity of pleasure and pain grew to both extremes as our breathing turned to panting. I felt a sharp slap across my ass as Jacques joined the moment.

"Fuck him, Sorrel! Oh, yes, give it to him...!"

The blows were sharp and distracted me from my inner pain. I was able to pound down over Sorrel's cock, sucking him into me. Harder and harder the exertions became, the moaning and panting louder and less guarded.

At last, with a long moan of intensity, Sorrel pumped me full. Again and again I felt hot fluids erupt into my guts. I writhed and twisted, wringing every last drop of him into me. Arms encircled my waist, and I leaned back against Jacques.

"And now we are one." The low voice in my ear was one of temptation. I could have wanted this every day of my life. But I knew the speaker of those words would not. I looked to Sorrel, and we understood each other.

Whatever the future might hold for my painting, I was his. For he was my muse, my god of desire, my lover.

NIGHT SEMINAR
Edmund Miller

I'm not sure whether he noticed me noticing him first or I noticed him noticing me. But I do know that it was from quite a distance across the room. We were in San Francisco, at a meeting of the Modern Language Association. This group is the professional organization of college teachers of English and (modern) foreign languages. A session on "Phallicism in Rock Lyrics" was just detumescing, and our eyes met across the room.

Now, when I say that our eyes met across the room, I ought to give outsiders a sense of the scope of an M.L.A. Convention. When it is held in a little company town like Washington, it attracts twelve thousand people. In San Francisco it can draw seventeen thousand. The meeting on "Phallicism in Rock Lyrics" was one of over five hundred such meetings. Meetings on "Dull Stuff Written by Obscure People a Long Time Ago" attract two hundred and fifty people or so. "Phallicism in Rock Lyrics" had sucked in considerably more. It was being held in a ballroom large enough to accommodate the maneuvers of the Sixth Fleet. And the ballroom was full. A lot of the members of the Modern Language Association teach in small towns at conservative institutions, and the annual trip to the Convention is a chance to let their hair down not by dropping water balloons out windows, but by thinking about literature any old dangerous way they want to and not just when it is filtered through the comma splices in their students' papers.

I was up on the dais blowing their minds in the first big public presentation of my career. My paper "Drunk and Disorderly: The Differential Weight of LSD and Alcohol in the Erotic Images of Jim Morrison" had gone over well. And I was basking in the glow. I had given papers at little conventions before and even one the previous year at a much smaller M.L.A. session. But the bigness of this crowd was exciting me turning me into a size queen at last.

As the adulation died down along with the bulge ballooning out the pleats in my trousers, he started to sidle toward me. When he got to the dais, he looked me in the eye, the crotch, the eye and told me how much he liked my paper and how well he thought it illustrated his theory of the sexual obsessions of modern pop culture. Still in the throes of my presentation high, I had not immediately squinted at his name badge, the accepted M.L.A. greeting. But the possessive reference to His Theory suggested he might be somebody. He was obviously distinguished and pretty nicely preserved inside the straight line of his suit (we let our hair down, but we dress up more than we do for class).

I focused my eyes on his name badge just as he was introducing himself. "Oh, yes, I know who you are. I'm a great fan of your book on The Dismemberment of Uranus," I said. "In fact, I...."

"Oh, have you read that old thing? Yes, I guess it did bring me a certain fame at the beginning of my career, but I'm doing very different things now. Of course, I was multicultural before it became all the rage, but you have to keep finding new things. I suppose you want to know what I'm working on now."

I had been checking out his high multicultural cheekbones during these observations and moving over to the edge of the stage so that I could sit with my crotch right in his face. "Well," I began, ready to score some points, "I have, in fact, read your big new book Horses and Whores in the Spaghetti Western, but I thought you'd be interested in the fact that I found Uranus very helpful in my disser ..."

"Yes, thank you, I guess I really did hit on some salient points that just needed to be made in that book." By this point he had his elbow up against my thigh, which I flexed a little. He admired my hair and told me about how hard it had been to find a publisher for his first book.

"Yes, I know. I've been trying to..."

He told me how much he was excited by being around fresh young scholars at the Convention and told me that this was the first time in ten years that his department had hired anyone new.

"Yes," I said, "in fact, tomorrow morning I have an inter...."

He wondered how I found a chance to work out as I obviously did with the horrible teaching loads young people always had to carry. He said he assumed that I must be pretty well fixed where I was and regretted the fact because this replacement position in his department was right up my alley in popular culture. He offered to put in a good word for me if I ever needed a recommendation.

"Thanks," I said: "that might be very useful because, you see, I actually am being   "

He rubbed me on the leg and said he had suddenly remembered a poem about Morrison that I just had to hear. Then he recited the poem:

Awash
Dickery-Daiquiri
James Douglas Morrison,
Straining for artistry,
Took to the brew
After his music's ly-

Surgic acidity
Chemo-poetically
Broke him on through.

He laughed and laughed and slapped me on the thigh. But he never did let me say anything. So I invited him back to my room.

In the elevator he continued talking, not only to me but to various people we encountered getting on and off all the way up. He did not introduce me to anyone. In the hallway, I tried once more to tell him about the next day, but he interrupted to compliment me on the poise I had shown in the presentation, which was quite remarkable compared to his at his first M.L.A. presentation. He told me the names of all the other panelists on that occasion, all big name people even then. He told me how much they had liked his paper and how they had reassured him that, despite his butterflies, his delivery had been completely calm.

As I retrieved the card key from the door to my room, he flipped on the light switch and began an anecdote about the decor in the Cairo Hilton, where he had once inadvertently let a snake into his room.

I turned off the light, and suddenly his talk went out. We could still see quite clearly by the night lights of the city. I kissed him, but just when he had adjusted to the turn of events and started to kiss me back, I pushed him away. We took off our shoes in silence. I loosened my tie and looped it around his neck, pulling him down on to the bed. He was still taking off his jacket as I tossed my shirt up into the air so that it billowed down over him like a snowfall. He disrupted the virgin snow by scrambling up to take his pants off. When he looked up again, I was standing naked in the window light, raising my arms over my head to show that the smooth, even color of my skin extended even to my armpits. I sniffed at my armpit while hefting my cock a bit to get it fluffed out to maximum advantage.

His mouth dropped open as if he was going to speak. I quickly moved over to him and gave his trousers a yank where they had become twisted around his ankles. He fell back on the bed with a thud. He might have been trying to say something, but he was not being coherent at all. I climbed up over him so that my big cock dragged up across his body. His mid-thigh contoured shorts were all twisted out of shape. I knee-walked over his body until I was astride his neck. I let the stark white head of my cock bounce against the gulping of his Adam's apple. I ran my hands down the muscles of my own thighs, pressing my thumbs into the ridges of muscle to create hard bulges.

He scrambled up under me on the bed so that he could hold my cock in his two hands, play with it, knead it, watch it grow. But I took it out of his hands, slapped it against his face a few times, and then bent over, slipping it into his mouth with a single smooth stroke. I heard a muffled groan as he opened up under me. He tried hard to suck back and forth, but he could hardly move in the position he was in. After a minute or two of this, I turned around, pivoting on my cock, which was still lodged deep in his throat. Not pulling back at all, I left him gasping, massaging the sides of my cock with the contractions of his throat. I pulled his legs up and straightened him out on the bed, drawing back on my cock for a moment to let him breathe. Then I pulled back a foot or so on my cock and began sluicing it slowly back and forth in his mouth. Slick with his juice, I moved it back and forth in a smooth, easy rhythm.

He began to get used to what he was doing and reached up to cup my ass. As he pulled my ass cheeks apart, I winked at him with my asshole. He started sucking harder, feeding me deep into his throat with his hand.

I reached down to smooth and tidy his shorts, wrenching them around straight and tucking his cock back in where it was just peeking out above the elastic.

I pulled out of his mouth and sat back on his face, pulling my ass cheeks apart with my hands so that he could get his tongue deep inside. I opened up easily and then clamped tight suddenly, holding him there. I think he wet himself at that moment. He scrambled up on the bed, his tongue still clamped in my ass, and poked a finger about the edge of the hole, trying to loosen me up and set himself free. I hung on.

Kneeling behind me now, working his tongue and finger together, he was talking to me at last. I had not quite decided to let him in, but he was getting me excited enough to start wondering whether I could lead him to where I kept the rubbers without breaking stride if the need should arise. Then with his free hand he reached between my legs to heft my cock. He pulled it back between my legs and I fell gently forward on to the bed with my ass in the air. I let go of his tongue, but only so that he could take my cock back into his mouth. He began licking slowly along the edge. It was throbbing. It wanted to fuck, to get back inside something tight and deep, like his mouth. When it was all slick again, he pulled it back to full length, stretching it back where it hung loosely away from my body despite the rigid weight of the thing.

Then he twisted my cock around in his hand, coaxing it along with his tongue the whole time. Before I quite knew what was happening, he thrust it up into my own asshole. It was wrenching to get the tip in, but then suddenly the shaft shot in after the tip, and all at once I had eight or ten inches up myself. I shot off, and he began poking his finger in along the edge of my cock until both his hands were drenched in goo.

The next morning, I could not sleep and was up by 7:00. I went to an early session I was not particularly interested in to distract myself and then just at 10:00 found myself knocking on the door of suite 1429 in the Hilton. A smallish man with pepper and salt hair opened the door almost immediately and ushered me in saying, "You must be Mr. Farquhar. We've spoken on the phone. Please come in and sit down. Let me introduce you to the other members of the committee, at least those who are here at the moment. This is Fatima ten Dick. She's our senior Shakespearean."

"Harrumph," she said, not offering her hand.

Somewhat taken aback, I could hardly get out an "I'm so glad to meet you."

"And this is Sister Bernardine. She handles the Poetry Center."

"How nice to meet you, Young Man!" she exploded. "Would you care for a cookie?"

Too stunned by the change of pace to say anything, I did manage to decline by shaking my head.

"How about some coffee? Tea? Coke? Water?"

It crossed my mind that I was already too nervous for coke but that smoking some tea might be just the thing to calm me down. Luckily, I realized what she meant and managed to stammer out "No. No, thank you. Thank you very much. Nothing for me" before embarrassing myself irretrievably.

"I see that you have an article forthcoming on Beowulf as a popular epic. Of course it would be fraudulent for someone to write on such a topic without fluency in Old English. Recite the opening lines of Beowulf." This was Fatima ten Dick again. "I have the text here for comparison. Begin."

"What?" I said, somewhat dazed.

"What about a macaroon?" said Sister Bernardine all in a breathless rush.

"Whatever are you doing?" asked the chairman, addressing ten Dick. Then we all tried to speak at once but stopped suddenly. After the brief moment of silence, the chairman continued, "What I think we ought to remember, Fat, is that this is a job interview and not a doctoral oral."

"What I suppose you'll be saying next is that it's perfectly O.K. for a candidate to forget everything he or she knows once he or she has his or her degree in his or her hand!"

"I'm afraid I'm really not prepared to go much ... ."

"How about some milk? It's really here for the coffee, but I think there's enough with one more interview today. Oh, look: hot chocolate!"

Sister Bernardine's raptures over the hot chocolate were interrupted by an imperious pounding on the door, which the chairman leapt up to answer.

As the door swung open and thudded against the wall, I heard a familiar voice in full throttle saying, "And why are you just standing there? The job candidates will be arriving soon. Get me some tea, will you, Sister Bernardine? Lemon, if you have it and half a packet of sugar. And I hope it's not too hot. Oh, and some of those cookies too. Shove over, Fat. Leave room for somebody else. Where are those resumes? Nobody ever shows me any-...." It was then that our eyes once again met across a room. And, somewhat improbably, he began choking on a cookie. I squirmed a bit in my seat. His mouth resumed normal operations after a moment or two, and the interview resumed.

COUSINS RUNNING WILD
J.P. Williams

One summer several years ago, I spent a wonderful week at Uncle Leo's farm. It was there that I first met my three cousins, Kerry, Kirk, and Kevin. They seemed like grown men although they were teenagers.

Kevin, with red hair and freckles, was my least favorite of the cousins. He would mess my hair up, rubbing the top of my head vigorously like his fist was holding a large cigarette he was putting out on my head. Kirk used to do an Indian burn on my arm he was the sadistic one but he'd always let me do one on him, which was nearly impossible since my fingers didn't reach around his massive forearms well enough to cause much harm. Then there was Kerry. Kerry was the handsome one. He didn't even look like a Martin. He had olive skin, whereas the others were pale. He had a dark, hairy body and luminous blue eyes. Kerry played this game with me where he'd wrestle me and make me sit on his lap against my will. The smell of his skin and the feeling of his hairy arms wrapped around me would make me giggle and grab him tighter, burying my nose in his shirt, face pressed up against his hard stomach.

One morning I was sitting on a rock at the side of the pond watching Kerry get out of the water after his morning swim. His floppy wet briefs clung to his genitals, which were clearly outlined and looked enormous to me. "Whadda ya lookin' at?" he asked me, smiling out of the corner of his mouth, revealing white straight teeth.

"You got hair on your chest already" I said, as I pointed to the beginnings of a substantial hair pattern that ran from his navel to his neck.

"Oh, I thought you wuz lookin' at somethin' else there for a minute," he said with a grin. He was soon staring into my eyes until I finally had to look away, or be trapped by the intensity of his accusing stare. He came up behind me, still wet from the pond, and held me in a bear hug, saying, "You just wait a few years and I'll have somethin' else to show ya besides the hair on my chest."

I could feel him press his crotch against me. I struggled to free myself from his grasp. I slammed my rear back, ramming into him hard.

"Watch out you little devil, you'll crush my nuts!" he hollered as he jumped back, finally letting go of me.

I ran, giggling, with him chasing me up the hill, threatening to beat my butt.

A couple of years passed and I didn't see Kerry once during all that time. Instead of vacationing at Uncle Leo's, we rented a place on Clear

Lake, a finger lake, closer to our home in Sacramento, and closer to the nursing home where my grandmother, on my father's side, was kept.

Then one summer the Martin clan staged a family reunion at Uncle Leo's farm and invited us to stay over for a while. Kevin and Kirk were working in Santa Rosa and only came out to the farm on weekends. Kerry had just graduated from State College at Davis, where he studied math and was planning to go on to engineering school in San Francisco on a sports scholarship. He was the star gymnast at school and my uncle would send us clippings from the local paper in Davis. I kept all the clippings in a scrapbook. I would pull the book out at night, when everyone was asleep, and fantasize about doing things, sexy things, with my handsome cousin. Kerry was the man of my dreams. I often had wet dreams about sucking Kerry's big hairy dick or being fucked by him, hard and long. I wanted to be just like him.

I tried out for gymnastics but was lousy at it so I took up track instead. At the end of my junior year, I'd won a sectional competition in the mile but was only 14th in the state finals. My coach said with my long, lean body I should take up running distances, and kept telling me I would make a terrific cross-country runner, or even marathoner, that is if I weren't so damn lazy. I thought about trying to work into longer distances during the summer and switch to cross-country in my senior year. Heck I didn't have anything better to do except jack off.

My cousins Kirk and Kevin were wild, running around with any girl who would have them, and were often getting into trouble, getting drunk and wrecking their cars and things. I was happy they weren't there to greet us when we drove up on Monday. I wanted a chance to be alone with Kerry. I wondered if he would even remember me, as I stiffly embraced my aunt and uncle and peered at him out of the corner of my eye.

Uncle Leo, who had put on about 20 pounds in the gut, put his arm around Kerry's shoulder and said, "Kerry is our good boy, he does his college work and is going to become an engineer he don't get in trouble messin' 'round with girls like his no-good brothers."

I laughed out loud and felt less awkward as I watched Kerry's face turn beet red. There he was, standing next to his father, squirming, and as handsome as hell. His eyes looked like they'd become even bluer, and a shadow of a thick beard covered his face. Above the collar of his faded maroon T-shirt, DAVIS written on it in big white letters, stood a tuft of his abundant, dark chest hair. I wanted to run up to him and have him wrestle with me like he did when I was younger. I would have loved to bounce in his lap and bury my face in his ... well maybe a little lower than his stomach but instead found myself extending my hand sheepishly.

Still trying to recover from the embarrassment of his father's comment, he grabbed my hand and shook it a little too vigorously. "I hear you're a runner," Kerry said to me. "Well, maybe we can run together in the mornings I have to do it to stay in shape for gymnasts you know," he said, smiling the same crooked engaging smile he had years ago.

"Great," I said nonchalantly, trying to contain my enthusiasm for the idea.

"We can go for a swim afterward to cool down," he said. I remembered his morning swims; my cock jerked in my shorts at the memory, and I reveled in the idea of seeing him once more dripping wet climbing from the pond.

Kerry and I were put out on the back porch to sleep that first night on a trundle bed. I got settled on the lower half, looking up at the beams in the roof to avoid being caught staring at what I really longed to see Kerry taking off his shorts and shirt. As he crawled in beside me Kerry said, "This isn't too fuckin' comfortable, is it?" laughing slightly.

It shocked me to hear him say "fuckin'" but I liked the way it sounded. "It's a bitch, but what-a-ya gonna do?" I whispered back.

He laughed and said, "Where'd you learn to talk like that, boy? I'm gonna tell your mama you said 'bitch'"

"Oh yeah, fuckin' gym boy, I'm gonna tell your fuckin' father you said fuckin'," I whispered gritting my teeth and trying to sound as tough as possible.

He laughed and grabbed me in a playful headlock and spat, "You little fucker, I'll fuckin' beat the fucking shit out of you if you fuckin' tell my fuckin' father anything."

I could feel his warm hairy skin on mine, and his familiar scent swept over me. Something warm and fleshy bumped against me through his underwear. As I bit his hairy armpit to make him let go I swear I could feel the bulge in his shorts start to grow as it poked into my thigh.

Damn, he smelled and tasted so good; my dick sprang up hard as a rock. Just then we heard my aunt call, "Is everything all right out there, boys?" and in a lower tone my uncle said, "I hope they are getting along okay."

Relaxing his grip on my head Kerry said, "We'd better get some sleep if we're going to run at six o'clock." Hesitating for a moment, as if he really didn't want to, he turned over, rolling back onto his side of the bed.

We tried to pretend we were sleeping. I listened to his breathing and could tell he, like me, was having a hard time falling asleep. My dick was so hard, I wanted to reach over and feel if Kerry was having the same problem. I hoped he did.

In the morning we slipped on our shorts and headed out for our run, stride for stride, first along the shore of the pond, and then into the fields that led onto a farm road. Kerry wore an athletic shirt and his chest hair stuck out all over. His legs were hairy too and he had on a pair of deep maroon shorts that said DAVIS over the left leg. We chatted a little while we ran, mostly about school, but after a while, I started to push the pace, and after a few miles I noticed his breathing become labored. Conversation had stopped altogether. As we headed back into a field surrounded by trees, Kerry started muttering and finally stopped, and stooped over in exhaustion, panting like a dog.

"Okay...okay you little bastard, so you can run a helluva lot faster than I can!"

I stood there, barely sweating; I couldn't help but laugh.

"You little shit, you're not so big that I can 't paddle the fuckin' shit out of that cute little bottom of yours," he said still panting like a dog. And in a calmer voice he ordered, "Come here you little shit." His breathing still coming hard.

As I got near him, I could see that sweat was pouring off his face, soaking his shirt. "What's wrong old man, can't keep up?"

He grabbed my legs and tackled me; we both fell to the soft turf and rolled around like a couple of schoolboys.

After struggling for a little while, thrashing around in the long grass, I let him pin me. He sat on my stomach; we were both panting, and his strong hands held my arms to the ground. Our eyes met and his look of anger and hurt pride turned to something else as he loosened his hold on me. His breath, like an intoxicating wave of purest desire swept over me. The look in his eyes, the smell of his clean fresh sweat, had me throwing caution to the wind. I put my hand behind his neck and drew his mouth to mine. We kissed long, and hard, quenching a longing deep inside; filling an emptiness that we never knew existed. I could feel the bulge in his shorts grow as we crushed our bodies together.

He drew away gently, a goofy look on his face, and said in a voice rough with passion, "If you ever tell anybody, I'll kill you."

I said simply: "I want you, Kerry! I want you bad. I've wanted you ever since that day when I was ten years old and watched you come out of the pond after your swim. My heart about burst seeing you standing there in all your glory."

We quickly ripped off our shirts, shorts and jock straps leaving us naked as the day we were born. My eyes drank in his handsome looks as we came together, rubbing all over each other's naked body. I ran my fingers through his thick chest hair, as I started licking him all over, burying my nose in his underarms and stroking my hands down his ridged stomach and around to his firm ass. I lowered my head to his beautiful, very thick cock, the large purple head straining toward me, glistening with precum.

Sliding down his sweat-slicked body, licking my way down his ripped abs, I took his cock into my eager mouth, cradling his cum-heavy balls in my palm. He stroked my hair and repeated my name over and over as I sucked like a baby, nursing on his bloated dickhead. I gradually slid down his shaft until my nose was buried in his musky pubes. I couldn't believe I actually had Kerry's dick wedged deep in my throat! I had wanted this to happen for so long a time and finally it was happening! I was incredibly happy at last!

Kerry wet his middle finger and gently worked it up my ass. "I want you, baby," he said as if in a trance. "I gotta get inside of you."

"I don't know. It might hurt."

"Oh, god, I've been hot for that ass of yours since we were kids."

Flipping me onto my back, he gently raised my legs, sliding them over his shoulders. Kissing my eyes, nose, lips, chin, then licking his way down my smooth chest, he stopped to gently suck one, then the other of my very sensitive nipples swirling his tongue around, around my sensitive nubs, sending hot sparks to my overload brain. He licked back and forth between them, and then down my tightly packed abs, licking and slurping out my bellybutton making me squirm with delight.

I writhed in ecstasy as he licked down the crease in my groin, sending hot jolts of passion to my loins. He then licked past my cock, taking my hairless balls into his mouth. He sloshed them around, making them dance on his tongue for an eternity, sending shivers up and down my spine. Just when I thought I would explode, he released them with a pop, cooling them with his breath, making them contract in their stretched, out sack.

He continued to lick lower along my perineum, gently nibbling his way to my tightly puckered boy-hole. The first touch of his tongue to my burning asshole sent electric shocks throughout my tight young body. I never dreamed anything could feel so good. He swirled his tongue around and around driving me crazy. I could feel my hole spasm around his tongue, trying to pull it in deeper.

He began a monologue that was very exciting to me: "Oh Joey, you taste so hot and sweet." Then, "I can feel you opening up for me." And, "You are so tight and hot in there."

"Oh God, fuck me! Fuck my virgin ass now!" I cried as he pressed his cockhead against my virgin asshole. I was insane with lust and wanted him to fuck me more than I'd ever wanted anything before. I pushed back, taking him to the hilt in one quick trust.

Now he began a new monologue: "Whoa cuz." "Oh yeah!" "God, you really wanted that big old dick of mine, and wanted it bad!" And, finally: "You okay?" he asked, holding me still as he bottomed out, his pubes grinding into my balls.

He stayed still for a while, until he could feel me relax, getting used to the feel of him embedded deep inside me, filling me to the brink with his pulsating ramrod. He bent down and buried his tongue in my mouth as he started to slide in and out of my hole; just an inch or two at first, then building speed.

It hurt a little in the beginning, but soon he was riding smoothly, all the way in and out until just the head remained trapped within my rim, then ramming me deep, all the while our mouths sucking hungrily at each other.

My cock stood straight up, causing his ripped abs to rub against the sensitive nerves in my dickhead on every stroke up my no-longer-virgin ass. The feeling was fantastic, and I came all too fast, coming hard as he rammed against something deep inside me. Every time his cock bounced off that button sparks shot through my veins and I saw stars and fireworks. My whole body was on fire! My cum flew everywhere, splashing off his tight stomach and hairy chest, raining down upon my smooth torso, face and neck.

Kerry's fucking grew more and more frenzied. He was like a lion in deep rut. Kerry's breathing became ragged as he was approaching orgasm, all the tendons in his body tight as a guitar string, driving for his climax. His fierce pounding of my tortured ass was bringing me closer to my second orgasm in just a few minutes.

Kerry's eyes rolled up in his head; every muscle in his body went taut, as he let out a roar from somewhere deep inside. He came hard, burying his expanding cock deep inside me, pounding me into the turf, jamming hard against the magic node I didn't know existed before today.

I could feel jet after jet of his scalding love juice splatter against my passion button. I came again from the sheer force of his orgasm, my cum splashing off his ridged torso and spraying down on my gleaming chest.

Kerry bent down and licked the slimy cum off of my chest, licking down my body to take my still hard cock into his mouth. I could not believe how incredible the sensation was, having my ass stuffed and my dick licked at the same time. I thought getting sucked was good, then getting fucked was better, but this WOW! His dick never left my ass as he eagerly sucked on my dick.

At that moment I was so glad he was a gymnast as he took me into his throat. Only someone as flexible as Kerry could do what he was doing. His dick was bouncing off my prostate with every bob of his head. He was quickly bringing me to another hard come. As I came it felt like my soul was being sucked out of my body. I thought I would pass out from the intense joy. I couldn't believe it, I came a third time in just moments, and I was still hard and so was he.

We lay in the grass, panting, kissing and touching, his dick still lodged deep in its new home. As I started to come back to earth, I felt transformed. I had feelings of ecstasy that I'd never even dreamed I could feel. I wished I could stay locked in Kerry's embrace forever. Kerry held and petted me gently for a long time, gently kissing my forehead from time to time and hugging me tight.

Kerry leaned up, his now limp dick slipping from my ass. "Hey, kiddo, we better get back before they send a posse out after us."

I hated the idea of letting him go. "But I don't wanna. Can't we just lie here forever?"

"I know what you mean, but we gotta."

Kerry pulled me up and we put on our clothes. We turned toward each other and stood looking into each other's eyes, my hands in his, saying nothing. I somehow felt a little sad, knowing that we could never have this first time again, as we headed toward the house. I looked over at Kerry and that feeling was replaced by the sheer joy of being in love for the first time.

That summer proved to be the best in my entire life. My parents went back to Sacramento and I spent the whole summer with Kerry. We pitched a tent in the woods a good distance from the farm and slept on the same air mattress, holding each other all night long. I loved falling asleep with his dick buried deep inside, and waking up with him still hard inside me. I would slowly rotate my hips, gently pulling him toward consciousness and a slow good morning fuck.

His running got better and my fucking improved to a point where I often demanded to be on top. When the summer finally drew to a close, we parted cheerfully for show, but were screaming with pain inside. He went to San Francisco for graduate school and I went back to begin my senior year of high school in Sacramento.

Kerry wrote to me every week about his classes, the gymnastics team, some of his friends. He also wrote nearly a page of encoded writing, in a code to which he gave me the key. In one letter he wrote: "The taste of your ass and cum in my mouth is always on my mind. I feel as though my dick will incinerate and my balls burst if I can't have you here beside me, beneath me, on top of me, me inside you, you inside me, every night."

During my senior year, I ran long distances, trying to keep myself from going crazy thinking about Kerry. Even when I was running, I'd pretend each step was bringing me closer to Kerry. I think that is how I won All State that year, thinking every step was bringing closer to having his tight, hairy body wrapped around me, fucking me hard, holding me tight.

I applied to only one college and thank God I was accepted. The family was delighted that I was attending the same school as Kerry. They felt at ease knowing they had my big cousin watching over me. They even paid for us to get an apartment together. We were in heaven.

HIS MAGICAL BODY
James Lincoln

"Damn, it's like a million degrees out." Jamie Hewson spoke without looking up as if I'd always been there. I opened the gate and pushed my bike up alongside his house, leaning it against faded clapboards. He was right; the sun blared down on us like some kind of psychological warfare.

"Just what are you doing?" I asked.

He was sitting on his sagging front steps studying his bare foot with the kind of absorption only kids exhibit. Hell, his tongue was even poking out of the corner of his mouth in concentration. After a moment he let go of his leg, flipped his blond bangs out of his eyes, and flashed a goofy, endearing grin. "Chigger bite. Itches like a motherfucker."

"Jesus," I said, cutting my eyes to the screen door. The front door was wide open and you could hear the television playing. "Like sands in an hourglass, these are the days of our lives...." Jamie waved his mother's proximity off as if shooing a pesky fly. "Screw her; she's deaf as a bat."

"You mean blind as a bat."

"Nah, she can see fine; can't hear for shit, though."

I rolled my eyes and threw my hands up in supplication to the gods who made my best friend so dense at times. But his momentary lapses into the moronic were somehow adorable ... as was his sharp nose and preternaturally red lips and ash-blond hair and his graceful yet ill-proportioned frame and sexy mischievous grin that flashed from time to time for reasons only he knew.

"I don't want you to think I'm gay or anything." I had once said to Jamie. "But...."

The two of us fell quiet now, listening to the sounds of our neighborhood on a summer's Friday afternoon. We could hear the ice cream truck playing the old song "Turkey in the Straw" on some distant street, and far away someone was cutting their lawn. Above the sun continued its slow burn across the inverted bowl of sky.

"We oughtta go swimming," Jamie said. My mind flashed on him in a tight-fitting bathing suit, an eidetic image that overwhelmed me. I could see the bulge at the crotch of his swimsuit no, not just an amorphous protuberance but a discernable shape, a definite outline. "Don't know anyone with a pool," I finally said.

"True," he replied.

I pulled at my T-shirt, unsticking it from my chest, shaking some air in. Jamie followed suit, then lifted his shirt to wipe perspiration off his forehead. I got a good look at his middle. A smooth white swath of skin, a cute little navel. He brought the shirt down, smeared with dirt now, and covered himself up again.

"I like you," I had said, trying to put into my eyes all of the tenderness I felt. "You're pretty cool, too," he responded, punching my arm. Then he skipped ahead to kick a crushed soda can across the pavement. Stupid.

"Look," I said now, "you wanna go to Tony's Market and get sodas?"

Jamie shrugged and nodded. "Lemme tell my mom." He stuffed his socked foot into a worn sneaker, knotted his laces, then stood up and poked his head inside the house.

My eyes went down his back to his bottom. I swallowed thickly then turned away, ashamed. "Dale and I are goin' to Tony's Market!" Jamie hollered.

"What dear?" A grating, screeching voice over the monotone utterances of television people.

"Dale and I. Are going. To Tony's," Jamie repeated, as if it was the hardest thing in the world to do.

"Is Tony's mother home?" his mom asked.

We laughed and shook our heads at each other. "Yeah, Mom," Jamie said, grinning right at me. His teeth were white and perfect. "

"Well then, have a good time." She'd dismissed us. He let the screen door slap shut, hasp jangling. Then we headed toward the foot-path through the woods, which would ultimately spit us out near the market.

"Funny," I said as we hit our stride. "Parents can be psychos or perverts or whatever, but you can't go visit a friend unless they're home."

"To supervise," Jamie said, mouth full of sarcasm.

"Right. To supervise." We both beamed at each other, sharing a moment, and for a split second I almost reached over and put my arm around his shoulders and gave him a hug. It scared me how close I came. I was so drawn to him literally pulled toward his wicked coolness that I found it took effort just to walk parallel like two friends might. The two of us wandered through the neighborhood, a tony little upper-middle-class section of town known as Oak Gardens. We went over to Bradford Avenue and worked down Kirby Drive, past the Cotters, who had one of those wooden big-assed women bending over in the garden.

"Yeah, I'd fuck her," Jamie had once said out of the blue. I nearly swallowed my gum at the time. Then I got a semi-hard just picturing him trying it with the lawn-art.

Now we were coming up on where the asphalt disappeared at a Dead End sign and the woods started, a constellation of thick maples and elms shouldering themselves off into infinity. "Hey," I said, stopping in front of the last house on the street before the woods began, a small two-story house hunkering down at the end of a long stretch of freshly cut grass. There was a sticker on the front door: a rainbow flag.

"That's the Skyler house?" Jamie asked.

I nodded.

"That's where you saw...?"

Again I nodded. The two of us stood there, hushed. Somewhere far off a crow cawed a couple of times. The lawn mower had either stopped or was out of ear-shot. I started to say something and smacked my lips in preparation but Jamie suddenly took off toward the gap in the trees.

"C'mon," he said. "I'll race you to Tony's." My friend disappeared into the woods, hair tousling with each bound. I looked back at the Skyler house once more, remembering what I'd seen and what I'd tried to tell Jamie about. He had put up his hands early on and said, "I don't want to know anymore." That had hurt. I frowned and then took off after him.

Jamie had stopped to push down his sock and scratch his bite, which let me catch up. When we finally got to Tony's Market we picked up some sodas Jamie got a can of Jolt and some Lay's potato chips, me a bottled Coke and then we wound past the old church on Allendale, picking our way through brambles until we got to Blind Creek. We held our sundries over our heads as we thrashed through tall grass like we were on safari. There was a small concrete foot-bridge over a bloated section of brook and we climbed up on top, legs dangling over the edge. This was known affectionately as The Bridge, as just about everything else in our lives was dubbed with a capital letter. The Building, for instance an old crumbling structure at the dump where we'd throw rocks through its windows until Mr. Creepy and his three-legged dog Hobo chased us off. Or The Tree, a massive weeping willow that we could climb up into and never be seen. Then there was The Marsh, or The Cave (which really wasn't a cave at all, but a hollow in some bushes), or The Hill, which we'd shoot down in Flexible Flyers come winter. Life was so simple then. And yet, at other times, more complex than ever.

Now, as we sat on The Bridge, Jamie cleaned out the rim of his cola with his already-dirty shirt and opened it. I watched the way his Adam's apple bobbed in and out as he gulped down the soda. The brown water was about twelve feet below us, shallow enough to see the rocky bottom, and still. A couple of deformed ducks with bulbous knots on their heads lolled about in a peculiarly random fashion.

For a long while we just stared at the malformed ducks, listening to birds in the trees and hearing the cars go by in the distance. Jamie was absently scratching at his chigger bite. I opened my bottle of soda and looked at the cap to see if I'd won anything. It was just a plain old bottle cap with nothing printed in it. I wasn't even a loser.

"Hey, there's a Ruffles in here," Jamie suddenly said with the force of revelation. He held up a potato chip from his Lay's bag."See. It's got the lines "

"Ridges."

"I should send it in. Get some free coupons or something."

"Why?" I asked. "They put a Ruffles in with your Lay's. Big whoop."

"It's very traumatic," Jamie grinned.

Then he ate the mysterious chip. For a while the conversation spun around urban legends about animals and fingers and other arcane items found in food items and the grand steps various companies went to buy the silence of the putative victim.

Finally Jamie upended his potato chip bag into Blind Creek with a shake. The dregs fell into the water. The ugly ducks with their cancerous knobs came over and pecked at them with little interest, leaving some to bloat into white pulpy things.

Silence. A pregnant pause, I think they say. I tingled all over, knowing something was about to unfold. Finally Jamie leaned nearer but kept looking off into the middle-distance, like he was speaking off-the-cuff, nonchalantly.

"So, tell me again about Skyler."

I went on to tell him again about the time some other kids and I were playing "Ghost in the Graveyard" late one summer night. I was the Ghost. The farthest we could go east was that Dead End sign I told you about. I hid in Skyler's backyard, listening to the others count to "midnight." Then they went into the "graveyard" looking for me, fanning out through the prescribed playing field of Oak Gardens. That's when I heard the garage door rumbling open at Skyler's house. Then, a moment later, the light came on in his den. I could see through the sliding-glass doors. It was like a what do you call those things they made us make for science class diorama. Or a little play, just for me.

I'd seen Skyler before. He was a tall guy with a mustache and short-cropped, jet black hair. Muscular, too. He came in with another guy I'd never seen, about the same size and build, only he didn't have a mustache and his hair was blond and longish. Skyler was holding the other guy's hand, pulling him through the den, on out of view, but the other guy suddenly stopped and pulled Skyler back to him and then pressed his mouth up against Skyler's. The two clung to each other tightly, lips to lips, trying to pull themselves into as tight as space as possibly as if trying to pull themselves inside each other. Skyler's hands went down the blond guy's back, cupped his rear, squeezed, pulled him tighter still.

So I resumed my little narration: "Then, before I knew what was happening, the blond kid had sunk to his knees and had freed Skyler's enormous dick from his pants. The blond stroked the dick up and down quickly and then impaled his head on the massive tool. I bet I wouldn't be able to get my whole fist around it, let alone get my lips past the head. I snuck a little closer to see. It was like a magic trick of some kind, a sword-swallower. I saw that massive length of meat disappear into the blond's mouth when it had nowhere to go except maybe down into his throat. I was fascinated. I moved even closer still. And then, suddenly, Ghost in the graveyard! Some kid had spotted me from the side of Skyler's yard. Skyler and the blond looked up and stared right at me through the glass door. For a minute I stood there frozen. Then I bolted. I even passed the kid running back to base. Didn't tag him, just kept running. That's what happened."

He didn't interrupt this time. He had listened to it all, continuing to look off into space. I could see through his shorts a lump poking against the material. For a second I couldn't catch my breath. My own dick hardened, throbbed.

It was like a film breaking in the middle. He stood abruptly and turned from me to hide his growth. "Hey, I gotta get back," he said. The sun was flattening, turning red on horizon.

"Jamie "

"C'mon, it's almost dark."

I followed him back through the tall grass whispering at our legs. We were both quiet. You could hear the rising and falling whir of cicadas in the trees. The light went fast in the woods. Everything turned blue-gray. The sun vanished completely. Jamie stopped and sat on a felled tree covered in moss to push down his sock and scratch furiously at his bite. He grimaced as he did. Intense. Something told me he was irritated by more than just that one itch. Something also told me he was stalling, trying to work something out in his head.

It was twilight. That magic time when you can hear other kids playing, delighted cries, exuberant squeals, growing louder in proportion to the fading light. When everything echoes. When you hear barking dogs in the distance, always the distance, never nearby.

I felt exhilarated by the coming darkness.

"Jamie?" His shoulders were slumped now, one foot up on the log with his sock pushed down to expose the puckered bite mark. But his scratching hand had gone limp and was dangling between his legs and he was looking off into space. In the blue-dark his hair had turned almost white and his pale skin seemed to glow. He shook his head to himself. He looked like he might be crying. I sat beside him carefully. He tensed for a moment. Just a flinch. "Jamie, are you okay?"

He turned to me. He was so close. I could even feel his breath on my face, subtle, short, hot puffs. His eyes were wet, his lips soft and angular. "I'm okay," he said, trying to flash a smile.

It didn't work. I looked down at his leg. The chigger bite. I touched it gently, feeling his cool magic skin.

"Dale," he said. It came out in a whisper.

I moved my fingertips up his smooth leg. Curvaceous. His flesh was cool to the touch, like marble, but silky, like velvet. I ran my hand up his calf, to his knee, over its crest, then down. He squirmed a little, arched his back, seemed to groan. My hand hesitated. Silence. No cicadas. No dogs barking. Just a heavy, heavy stillness. I moved in to him, letting my hand go across his middle to his opposite hip and pull him a little closer to me, turning him slightly on the log.

"Kiss me," he said, so softly I hardly heard it. A tear squeezed out his right eye and trickled slowly down his cheek. I leaned toward him and pressed my lips against his, closing my eyes and tilting my head slightly. Our tongues found each other. I'd say there were fireworks because that's what you are supposed to say, only it seemed just the opposite, instead a series of quiet implosions, pulling us to one moment in time and space. I withdrew after a bit and smiled. He grinned.

"Wanna get naked?" I asked conspiratorially. He couldn't form the acknowledging words so he nodded like a puppy. Then Jamie and I both grabbed our shirts and pulled them over our heads in one deft motion. His white chest glowed in the semi-dark, pale and smooth. Even in the frail light I could see his cock pushing against his shorts, straining to get out. I ignored it for now, sliding my hands down his legs until I reached his socks and shoes and pulled them off. The chigger bite was the one visible blemish on otherwise unblemished flesh. I leaned over and kissed it, then licked my way up his legs in fits and starts. Jamie climbed down off the log and sat on the ground, leaning against it. He made soft purring sounds. My tongue worked up to his right inner thigh he sucked in air through his teeth and tensed and then I went back down to his other leg and started at his foot, working my way back up.

Now my hands sought out his dick, grabbing hold of it through his shorts. He shuddered at that. "Suck," he managed. He may have said "me" but I didn't hear it. There was an edge of pain in his voice, his desire well aware of its opposite dread that of never being realized. I nodded and pulled his shorts down him, Jamie moving his hips beneath me. The shorts ended up somewhere behind in the brambles with our shirts. Freed now, his penis rose up to be sucked on. Instinctively I went for it. I wasn't copying Skyler's friend I knew what to do even though I'd never done it before. My hands wrapped around the tool and I moved them lightly up and down until his stiffness was complete. I was in awe of its slight upward curve and distinct head. "Oh God, Dale...."

I leaned forward and applied my eager lips, kissing him right on the cockhead. Jamie moaned. A large bubble of pre-cum welled up from his piss hole and glistened in the twilight. I leaned down and licked it off him the way one might brush a piece of food from a lover's cheek. The hole glistened again, more pre-cum oozing out. Now I squeezed around his base with my right hand and nestled my head into his crotch. My tongue came out and tested him with its tip. Then I licked up the shaft toward his glans, with long, flat-tongued cat-licks.

Jamie alternated between squeezing his eyes shut and opening them wide so he could see me giving head, as if to confirm it was really happening to him. His body spasmed. "Oh my God," he said. I laughed, loving it. I licked some more up his shaft, those full swipes, sloppy and wet. My tongue slipped up and moved around the corona. Then I slid my hand up his shaft and held him just under the bulging cockhead and pressed his dick back against his abdomen toward his navel, turning my head sideways, really getting in there to work the curve of his shaft and his vein with my tongue. This went on forever. Finally I backed away and let my hand slip down halfway and pulled his dick toward my face so it was looking me square in the eye. I moved forward and licked around the hole in circular motions that drove him crazy. By now his whole dick was covered in a glistening sheen of spit and pre-ejaculate. I felt it throbbing in my fist as I went down on him, wrapping my narrow lips around his dick and making a tight circle with them, keeping my teeth back, sliding down his shaft until its head pressed tightly against the back of my throat. I pulled back, unprepared for the gagging.

Then I closed my eyes, relaxed, breathed through my nose, and went down on him again, letting his dick burrow deep past my tonsils and into my throat. I worked my muscles on his cockhead and Jamie threw his head back against the ground and squirmed underneath me, unable to control himself. His bare feet were thrashing in dry leaves, toes wriggling, his hips moving up and down as I sucked on him.

A part of me was afraid he'd draw attention to us there in our secluded spot in the woods and another part of me didn't care. All I could think of was siphoning his cum into my throat. My hand pumped him up and down, a nice, steady stroke, trying to force him to explode in my mouth.

"Wait, wait," Jamie said, pushing my head back.

I resisted at first, obsessed with getting his wad, but he scooted back away from me. A slack thread of precum connected my zealous lips and his cock for a moment before it split in the air. Now thin ropes of shiny clear fluid were slinking out of his dick onto the leaves below.

"I don't want to come just yet," he said in a pitiful panic. "I want to "

I don't know what made me do it. He seemed so vulnerable then. I reached back over, grabbed his dick hard and popped it back into my mouth.

"Oh my God!"

I pumped his dick in a fisted hand and sucked on it with hollowed-out cheeks. Concentrating, I took some of him down. No problem. He slipped right in. Breathing furiously through my nose, smelling Jamie's magic scent, I forced more past that hitch in my throat, then all of him. He cried out. Jamie grabbed my head with both hands. I let him use my mouth as an asshole and he fucked me hard. His nimble fingers caressed my hair, pulling me closer and closer along his shaft until my nose was in his short blond pubic hair. He arched his back, his legs went weak, he bucked violently. "Oh fuck! Yes!"

I felt it erupt. Tried to swallow it all to swallow him, to swallow Jamie's magic. Some slipped out but I got buckets full down my throat. It squirted in me in thick waves and he squeezed his ass tight and shoved himself upwards with each load. I milked him until there was no more left. He slackened, shuddered, and then it was over. Jamie lay back on the ground like a rag doll. He face was as relaxed as I had ever seen it, making me realize how much subtle strain there usually was.

"Anything I can do for you?" he asked after a while, stroking my hair gently, looking at me dreamily.

"You've just done it," I said; I had come, too. Then I added with a sly but knowing grin, "But maybe later."

A honey-colored moon hung low on the horizon as we walked home together. This time, for once, I didn't have to work at keeping a parallel tread with the equivalent of a movie seat between us. I walked right up alongside him, arm over his shoulders, touching, finally, his marvelously magical body.

PRISONER OF LUST
Dan Veen

The suspect moves through the store premises, from hardware to toys then on to appliances. Suspect is the cutest shoplifter I've had all week. He's a handsome devil. Six feet tall, easy. Athletic build. A clear-skinned redhead (no freckles), green eyes. High school basketball All-Stars, I'd guess. This deluxe body saunters aimlessly through the aisles; he wears loose-fitting jeans and a T-shirt with sleeves rolled up in a '50s style.

He loiters near the boys underwear department my favorite department.

He pretends to be an aficionado of under things. He fingers the crotches of fabrics, stress-testing them for their ability to support his sizable box.

He rifles the white briefs, the boxers, the jockstraps. For his crime, suspect selects a simple but sexy lavender thong, the kind that rides all the way up into the butt crack, the kind you wear only when you know someone will be seeing you in them.

With a magician's sleight-of-hand, the perpetrator palms the lavender article and darts it into the crotch of his jeans.

That's when I clap the cuffs on him, just like they taught us in Rent-a-Cop School.

"Let go of me, you fucking pig asshole!"

He resists arrest all the way to the dressing rooms. Just tussling with him develops a regulation-size boner in my uniform.

"You bastard! You sonofabitch! Fucking pig!"

He names me every name in the name book. Hearing obscenities spew from his arrogant fresh face turns me on.

It won't matter how much he fusses. The mall is closing. The lights turn off. Me and my juvenile perp will be left alone here in the dressing room all night. Romantic, isn't it?

I shove him chest-first against the dressing room wall. Love hurts.

"You just take it easy, buddy boy," I breathe threats into his ear, "till I decide what I'll do with you."

First I frisk him my favorite form of foreplay. I take special care groping around his groin area. He could be packing a concealed weapon.

"What's this, a gun?"

"Ow! Leggo my fuckin' dick!"

I goose him around the crack of his butt. Yum. My hand rests unapologetically upon his crotch. I size it up. There's a hefty mound of malleable meat there. Hmm.

"You getting your jollies, pervert?"

"Yeah." I mush his pretty-boy face against the wall. "Matter of fact I am, kiddo. Punks like you are the best perks of this job."

Getting 'em there is half the fun. I like to taunt and humiliate 'em. The better to fuck 'em with.

I pull out his wallet. Plenty of money there for what he stole.

"Why, Christopher McKinley, Jr. According to your ID, you're just a baby! A mere child!"

"I didn't steal nothing. You can't arrest me. You're not a real cop." Christopher's trying to sweet-talk me.

"Hey, Christopher, baby, chill out." I pinch his cheeky cheek, like a doting uncle. Then I pinch both his ass cheeks to provoke him. "I am a trained officer of the law. Would I be guilty of any misconduct? Now drop trou, boy, or I'll have to strip-search you myself."

"You can kiss my ass. I don't have to submit to any of this bullshit. I know my rights. You can kiss my ass!"

I think I'm in love.

"All in good time, junior." I slap his ass instead. "We've got all night. Of course maybe you've got something to be ashamed of down there. Maybe you're less than a man in the cock-and-balls department."

That riles his butch-ismo.

"Bull-fuckin'-shit! I'll fuckin' show you who's a fuckin' man!" Christopher starts to pull his pants down, as eager to show me now like a kid playing doctor behind the garage.

With his handcuffed hands, Christopher fumbles at the front of his pants

The pants bunch down at his feet. The T-shirt exposes a smooth Christopher midriff with a fine pelvis dovetailing into a pair of white cotton briefs hugged with elastic.

Hammocked cozily in the white pouch of his briefs, like Grade A eggs in an egg cozy, are Christopher McKinley Jr.'s family fucking jewels. And what a family! A respectable fine upstanding family. The snug fabric firmly outlines the large sausage served between those eggs.

"Mmm. Christopher. You've got a dandy pair of everything, don't you? Even your knees are damn cute."

His naked knees twitch like my mere mention of Christopher's knees tickles them.

Christopher stands there before me, my self-conscious prisoner. His thick thighs are goose bumpy. He has the long-muscled, tanned legs of an athlete. These young legs have run track, jumped hurdles, vaulted poles pinned lotsa pussy. Many a cheerleader has sacrificed her virginity between those twin pillars.

"Very nice, Christopher. You're a fine young man with a fine young cock. Fuckable. Suckable. Edible. Shame to keep it cooped up in those shorts all the time. That sweet bulge is begging for release, isn't it? Yeah, you've got the kind of cock that's meant for the sporting life. It needs to run wild and free. It's got to romp and play and stick its head into whatever cracks and crannies it pleases, right?" I goad Christopher. I stare right at his crotch, like a snake charmer. "Now strip the rest."

"Well okay. But don't try anything."

"On the contrary, Christopher, I intend to try everything."

Christopher blushes. He slowly peels his shorts past his knees, down to his ankles, bending over as he goes, giving me a glimpse of his muscled dorsals, the fine spine, the dimples in his pelvis. His butt halves moon up behind him with a halo of peach fuzz.

When he ripples back to his full height, Christopher is flushed with embarrassment at exposing his floppy private flesh-parts to my scrutiny.

My oh my. I whistle appreciatively.

"Christopher, you must be the envy of the entire locker room."

Christopher's dick is too nervous to be aroused much, but there's no place it can hide. It's naked and vulnerable in the fluorescent light of the dressing room. You can see the wide helmet of the kid's dick encased by its foreskin.

Christopher's billiard-ball-size balls are beautiful as well. They hang lower now, no longer slung in his shorts. His balls look like they hurt. They are loaded down with the heavy cream of overproduced junior spunk. They glow like red-hot coals beneath his thatch of chestnut pubic hair.

Poor kid doesn't know what to say. My adoration for Christopher's cock is frank and blunt. No sidelong hopeful glances in the shower for me. Life is short, cocks are long, and great cocks like Christopher's should be worshipped like the Roman pagans did in shrines.

"And what do we have here, Christopher? Why, whaddyaknow, it's those skimpy purple briefs you lifted. Well, here's all the evidence I need to send you to J-A-I-L."

I hold it to my nose, inhaling Christopher's spoor, enjoying.

"A night in jail oughta teach a pretty young man like you a thing or two about the ways of the world."

"Oh no. Please don't send me off to jail, uh, sir. If I go to jail, they'll call my mom." (Christopher is suddenly so rattled that his dick bounces like a puppet as he speaks. He's no longer the arrogant punk I arrested.) "I'll do anything for you, man. Take all my money. Mom'll kick me out of the house. She'll cut off my allowance. She won't pay my tuition!"

"Shoulda thought about that before you swiped this."

I almost feel sorry for Christopher, standing there naked and helpless.

"I stole it for one of my girlfriends. She's kind of, well, kinky. She wanted me to wear it to bed with her. She insisted I steal it. She likes me to cum in it, and then she sucks it out. My parents are going to be gone this weekend. We were planning a party."

"You must really like this girl to steal something for her."

"Not especially. She just lets me do her whenever I want."

"Do what, Christopher?"

"You know." He stammers and murmurs like a little boy now. "Fuck her."

Christopher and I both look down at the gorgeous dick that Christopher fucks his girlfriend with. We watch it swell.

"Does she like you to fuck her with it, Christopher?"

"She's a fuckin' nympho. I just show her this dick and she practically turns cartwheels, begging me to screw her all over the house. She's cock-crazy. She says it's the biggest thing she's ever felt inside her. We fuck on my parents' waterbed. She likes to bounce up and down on it my dick, that is. I have to keep telling her it's not made out of rubber. She likes me to put it up her pussy. She sits on my dick and does some school cheers while I fuck her."

I'd be doing cheers, too, with a dick like Christopher's dorking me. Go team.

Christopher's impressive boner swells more and balloons out over his balls. His soft foreskin begins to skin back now. His damp pink dickhead peeps out. I've never seen one that big on a kid so young.

"You must be proud of a pussy-pounder like that."

"She can't get enough of it." Christopher shrugs, patting it. "She keeps trying to suck me off, but she can't fit the whole thing in here mouth. We're working on it, though."

"Amateurs. Would you like me to suck on it some?" I offer. Some?

Christopher is standing there, the light dawning on him as his dick rises. His dick loves the blowjob idea. The head of his meat pops out from his foreskin with a wet-sticky sound like masking tape peeling off.

"Your meathead wants to be sucked all right, Christopher. A stiff dick is the best lie detector in the world. That dick just isn't getting the mouth-action it deserves."

"Well. It is getting kinda hard. Do you think you can suck it better than a girl?"

"Girl schmirl. Guys know what guys like, Christopher. I'll seal my mouth around that meat till you pop and drop. I'll do a sperm count on my tongue just gimme a sample. Son, I've got a bona fide cocksucker's wide load mouth that'll tickle your ivory better'n any bimbo."

"Well, okay."

I open my mouth and my heart for Christopher. I loosened my jaw for maximum penetration.

"That's it, Christopher, come for poppa."

Christopher knows exactly what to do. He shuffles over. Young Christopher's dick props its bobbing head on the threshold of my lips. My tongue greets it. I French Christopher's juicy pee hole and make him shiver. "Ah!" I hear Christopher sigh above me and he thrusts.

Drops of warm Christopher pre-cum drool out upon my tongue. I kiss the boy's meaty head, envelop it with my lips. His dick looks giant as it waves up beneath my nose. I scrub my chin stubble against Christopher's cockhead. The heated poker rubs my jaw line. The crescent curve of his meat warms my cheek.

"What would your mommy say, naughty Christopher?" I whisper into his inflamed crotch. "Tell me to suck it, Christopher."

"Now suck it. Suck me off, cocksucker." He says, summoning his gumption, liking the nasty talk. "Suck, sucker. I want to see you suck my cock like you said you could."

His lip stick barges down my gullet. It's a challenge to swallow. My hands are helping all they can. They reach around to knead his butt cheeks. I splay each cheek apart, pulling his crotch into my face an inch at a time. His dick mashes my tongue as it fills my throat.

"Oh god! You are some sucker...." Christopher rocks his crotch above me. His handcuffed hands touch my head respectfully, suggestively. He's eager to push his dick to the back of my throat. But he doesn't know how far he can command me. Little does he know that I'm pure fuck putty. "Take all that meat, cocksucker, cumsucker. I've got a load, man, a load. It's gonna fill your mouth. You're a terrific peter eater."

I slurp his meat shaft loudly, to thank him for the compliment. Christopher dicks farther down my moist gullet. My throat muscles ripple the veins of his cock.

"Hey, that tickles!" He snorts nervously above me, holding my ears. Christopher's hot for his suck job now. I have this young boy fucking my mouth in a slow sawing motion that just gets faster. Each nudge moves the cockhead farther down my throat. His hips gyrate toward me now. He's helpless to stop. He has his own dumb mouth open now as he looks down on me, concentrating on fucking my face.

"Shit! My balls are busting!" He heaves. Christopher's dick and Christopher's balls are about to shoot me some of Christopher's hot young cum wad.

His ass nibbles on my finger, clamping down on it, so tight I'm already thinking what a fine tight butt this would be to fuck.

"Suck it out, man! I'm gonna shoot! Suck it all out!"

Christopher's dick is on the quivering, cum-pumping brink all right.

But I hold off, and give his steel-stiff dick a fulltime lick job.

I paint his cock with spit, plying the bristle brush of my tongue to scrub the blunt end of his cock. He struggles with his cuffs. He strains to cum. But I stick my tongue right in the hole, corking up his cum that wants to shoot so badly out of his fuck meat.

"Suck it, dammit! I've just got to come! I've gotta... I've gotta shoot it off!"

He's dishing his dick into my mouth, trying to pop that dickhead back inside my mouth for the final strokes that will make him shoot.

The boy is panting now, begging to be sucked. Christopher's mouth meat can't stand to be out of my hot glory hole another second.

Nunh huh. I shake my head, glossing my lips with his pre-goo as I do so. No dice. Not yet. No fucking way.

Poor horny handcuffed Christopher rages while I make him watch me do a slow striptease. I slowly strip off my cop's uniform.

At first Christopher won't look. But he's too worked up. His dick too jammed with jism. Curiosity gets the best of him. Christopher has to look. Just his looks make me moan.

He envies the dark, manly hairs on my chest, that vee down to my crotch. My wolf pelt coats my entire body. Christopher has probably never seen a man's body like mine.

He likes what he sees. He can't believe a full-grown man could desire to strip himself naked in front of him. Christopher blushes head to toe, but that makes me enjoy strip-teasing Christopher and his cock even more.

"Anybody ever suck your tits, Christopher?" I ask, licking my chops like a wolf about to eat a lamb.

Christopher says hun-unh. I lift Christopher's T-shirt. I help myself to Christopher's clean, white, smooth-muscled chest.

"Most girls don't know how to do that," Christopher sighs.

He says it tickles when my chin stubble scrapes his tender nipples. They already stand up hard.

"Yeah. Most women ignore men's tits when they fuck. They don't know how good it can feel to a man, too, to work the tits."

I feed on Christopher's pink tits, tongue-teasing them, nursing both sides with my hands and mouth, massaging his chest-muscles.

I move up into Christopher's armpits. Ah, the smell and taste of that salty junior man sweat. Christopher rotates his shoulders so that I have better access to them. Christopher's chest heaves in response to each lick.

Our dicks kiss. Christopher's dick starts to prod my balls, rubbing them back and forth beneath the shaft of my own dick.

It pushes farther, petting me between my legs. It slides between my thighs so that I'm riding it like a hobby horse. I tighten my legs up over it, squeezing the wide meat inserted there. I mover my butt along it, letting the hairs between my feather-tickle his cock.

"Oh god," Christopher moans while I dry-hump his cock. I kiss Christopher's offered-up throat and bite his ears. His shoulders struggle with the cuffs. If I were to release him now, Christopher couldn't help but keep up this fuck. Christopher is a self-conscious actor, not knowing what to do with his hands.

I kiss him and at first he's a little put off. But I squeeze his cock some more between my thighs. Christopher's baby-pink tongue ransacks my mouth, kidnaps my tongue, and takes it hostage into his own mouth. Better.

My young fuck monster is ready.

Now he knows nothing but fucking. He's in a fuck fever, fuck heaven. Christopher's balls are aching for eruption. He'd fuck a porcupine now.

"Ohhh, please!"

I have pulled away. His dick stands alone in mid-air, untouched. He's even anxious to bite my pecs. But I won't let him.

His dick is already well-lubed. The dickhead looks like one of those roll-on deodorants.

My ass is hot, fine and fuckable.

I cock it obscenely toward Christopher.

"Christopher. Tell me you want to fuck me. Say you want to fuck me. Say you want to fuck me up the ass, Christopher."

"Ohh, god. I " He waggles toward me.

"Say it." I back up to him, hiking my hindquarters.

Christopher's dick brushes through the slot of my ass cheeks. I allow it to slide through the valley of my ass, top to bottom, from lumbar to inner thigh.

"Let me, please! Oh god, I'm so fucking horny!" Christopher pants to put his dick up into me. He thrusts rabidly, ferociously, blindly.

"Say it. Tell me, Christopher. Tell me how hard it is. Tell me how bad you want it." I pull away from Christopher's cock, bad as I want it. I want even more to hear Christopher say it. Virgin words from Christopher's virginal lips.

"Let me fuck your ass! Please! My dick's so hard it's busting! Please let me fuck that hairy fucking ass!"

"I thought you'd never ask." Christopher's roll-on dick is mine, all mine, now. I scoot up on tiptoe and spread my hams so Christopher can see what he's getting into.

Christopher's cockhead mushes the ring of my ass as he tries to bury his bone. He fumble fucks me for a second. He's a virgin all over again, since the poor thing can't guide it with his hands. He gains leverage. He gets his target. And I get mine. Pops in to the notch.

The head of Christopher's dick is in. All my ass juices welcome it. I grab my own dick and start to jerk it, all the while coaxing my ass to open wide and take the rest of Christopher's Big Beautiful Bone!

He slides it in, whimpering and breathing along the way at the sensation of my tight ass clinging and hugging his fuck meat. God, but Christopher's cock is so damn wide, I can't help but go bowlegged from the penetration.

When his dick is pushed in all the way, I reach back, clamp Christopher's ass cheeks to press his cock into me more. He doesn't budge. Just having Christopher's meat in me makes my balls pump and my dick drool.

I drop to my knees, taking Christopher with me. Then I prop myself on my elbows, ordering him to fuck me harder. Hell, I'm still the boss.

It's difficult for him at first. Christopher's handcuffs rattle while he tries to gain momentum. He straddles my ass and paddles my butt cheeks like they were bongos. He rears back as best he can. He struggles to get the speed he wants, can't get the friction his dick craves. Then gravity makes his butt plugging cock plunge back into me.

I reach through my legs and grab Christopher's balls, yanking and stretching them.

My sweet. Christopher-fucked asshole is cum-drunk. I could twirl his cock around in my ass like a drum majorette's baton.

"Keep fucking me! I'm com-m-m-ming!" I yell up to the young man bumping his big beautiful ugly into my hole.

He's blathering a fuck chant up above me. His balls are on fire.

His cock tunnels through my guts. I can see his balls flap against mine. My dick seethes with fuck juice. All my cum barges out of my cock tube. I pull my cork and it spews.

My own cum lobs out on my face. I spray the tiles with jetting jizz. Christopher's dishing dick slops his cum into my bucket seat.

Finally Christopher collapses on top of me, his tool torqued into my dick-drilled ass. We both lie on the floor, recovering, young Christopher's dick throbbing in me like a second heart.

We fuck several more times that night, running naked through the darkened department store! In front of a wall of glowing televisions in Home Entertainment I take the time to give Christopher's dick the blowjob it deserves. He can't get enough of that great, deep pussy feeling in the back of his throat! The pull and the plunge. My rippling palate and the sanding tongue work Christopher's balls.

"Oh shit, I'm coming! I'm shooting right in that fucking hot fucking mouth!" Christopher squirms and drills and squirms and his ass slaps against the floor.

Cum dams up in my throat. Yummy Christopher cum washes around in my cheeks. I don't let a bit of his young bubbly cum escape. I can't bear to waste a drop of it.

For good measure I give Christopher a hickey on his neck that will be a deep purple passion mark by tomorrow. Christopher's buddies will rib him about it. They will ask him about it. I wonder what he will tell them? Christopher even thanks me as I dress him up to go. I'm not sure for what. The fuck? Broadening his horizons? Letting him go free?

We stand together in the empty street lamped parking lot of the shopping mall.

Christopher tries kissing me, but he isn't sure if that's what two men should be doing in public. I give young Christopher my mouth, tongue and all. I start to uncuff him to let my favorite prisoner go free. But he stops me.

"No. Leave them on," Christopher surprises me. He checks out the lump in the pants of my uniform. Young Christopher is suddenly brave with lust. "Let's go back to my parents' house. They're away for the weekend. They've got a waterbed. I can't wait to try it out with you."

I say yes, let's.

Now I'm beginning to wonder: who caught who?

161

I THINK I'M GAY
Jack Ricardo

I'm eighteen and I've been fuckin' girls since I can't remember when, but about a week ago I started wondering if I'm really a gay boy. Now I know that sounds kinda stupid, but it's true. What happened was, I was in this dance club I usually go to pick up girls and I got a little drunk. When the joint closed, this guy asked me if I wanted to share a six-pack in his pickup. No reason not to. Then before I knew it, I was getting a blowjob. Now, I had my cock sucked before, but always by chicks. A guy? Never. I tell you though, he was one good cocksucker. Heck, I came twice in a hour and went to bed one happy man.

I thought about that blowjob a lot, and I mean a lot. I even jerked off at night thinking about that guy doing me. That's when I got to wondering if I'm queer. And I wanted to find out. There were no gay bars in town I knew about, but I remembered seeing ads in our local newspaper about MEN SEEKING MEN. I answered one. The ad read, "MAS ULINE man seeking masculine man for safe times. GWM, 20 yo, five-eight, 135 lbs, crew-cut blond hair. AD#3954." I called the number and left a message on the telephone at the newspaper. I said, "Hi, my name's Matt. I think I might be queer. Give me a call." And I left my number.

A guy named Jason telephoned me the next day. He laughed because he thought my message was strange. Maybe it was, I guess. I laughed too. He asked me why I thought I was queer. And I told him about the great blowjob a guy gave me. A couple of hours later we were sitting in McDonald's drinking coffee. He wasn't a bad looking guy, I guess. With his crew-cut head, he looked almost like a Marine recruit. He told me my long blond hair was a turn-on and he said I had a swimmer's body. I was embarrassed. I followed him to his apartment.

Once we got to his place, he asked me what was so great about the blowjob I got from that guy.

I shrugged and said, "He was just one fine cock blower, that's all. But to tell you the truth, it was the best suck job I ever had. And something else too. It was kinda funny maybe. I mean, he wasn't some swishy fag, he was real manly. Like you. And I really liked seeing this macho guy's head bobbing up and down on my cock. I don't know why. Maybe it's cause he loved swinging on my dick so much. I mean, he just blew my cock like crazy and didn't let up until I was shooting my load down his throat."

My cock was starting to wake up just telling Jason about that beautiful blowjob. I was on the couch and he was sitting on the other side of the room. He asked me, "Did he suck your ass too?" And he started playing with his cock through his jeans.

"Heck, no," I told him. "You crazy? I wasn't even naked. He just unzipped my fly and took my cock out and started blowing." I was playing with myself now too, pulling on my cock through my jeans. "Man, when he swallowed my cock all the way down to my belly, I damn near crashed through the roof of his pickup. He was just so darn...."

"Did you feel his cock?" he asked.

"Heck, no. I just sat back and spread my legs and let him blow away. But he did take his cock out and jerked off while he blew me. When I came in his mouth he was just jerking his cock like mad, and he came too, on the floor of his pickup, and...."

Jason tugged on his cock and grunted. "Hell, let's get comfortable." And he stripped down to his underwear. One hard cock was outlined through the pouch of his briefs. He started mauling it. I mauled my own cock and stripped down to my shorts. I was standing in the middle of the living room with my stiff cock poking the front of my briefs. "You a good cock blower?" I asked him, rounding a fist around the shaft of my rod and grabbing the pouch of my nuts.

He laughed and said, "Try me."

"No, you try me," I said, stuck my hand in the fly of my shorts and whipped out my cock.

His eyes lit up like two bright light bulbs, and he grinned. "Bring it over here."

He didn't have to say anything else. I padded over, told him to, "Blow me," slapped my cock over his lips, and he started lapping his warm, wet tongue all around my dickhead. He was like a hungry lap dog, looking up at me with those big brown eyes of his while he slurped on my dickhead. I was getting warm all over. Warm, hell. I started sweating. Man, that crew-cut looked so great going down on my cock. And I was so damn pleased he was doing it.

"Great," I said, shooting my hips out to stuff my cock down his throat. It didn't get stuffed. He said, "Let's go in the bedroom." And he was panting when he said it.

No argument from me. I could hardly control my breathing either. We left our shorts on the floor. Jason lay down on the bed, spread his legs, grabbed his cock and said, "You really wanna find out if you're queer?" He was waving his cock at me like it was a red flag and I was a bull. "You wanna know, you gotta blow," he said.

I said, "Yeah," but not too loud. In fact, I almost whispered it. My stomach did a flip-flop. Jason squeezed the shaft of his cock and his dickhead became bigger than it already was, and redder, and started dribbling spit out of the piss hole. I took a deep breath and stood there like a dumb fool, just holding onto my hard cock and looking at his. Jason was still waving it at me. His balls were a big pile of hairy bags and hard nuts mashed on the mattress between his legs and settling right down the crack of his ass. He looked manly as hell but I felt like my feet were stuck in cement. I hefted my balls in one hand and pulled my cock with the other, like some horny dope. I didn't know what to do.

"If you don't suck this cock," Jason said, "you'll probably never know if you're queer or not." He spit in his hand and slid his wet fingers down the shaft of his cock and hunched up his ass. His rod was all shiny and his cockhead was shining like a star. He was sneering at me and teasing me.

He was right and I knew if I didn't go for that cock right now I never would. But I guess I was still a little scared. I mean, wouldn't you be too, if you never blew a cock before? But I wasn't gonna back out. I'm no chicken. I wanted to know if I was queer, so it was now or never.

I knelt on the bed between his legs. Jason lifted his arms to the back of his head. I could smell his underarms. His clipped hair was bristling like the Marine he probably was. His hard cock flopped back on his belly and was resting on his cock hairs just waiting for me to blow it. "Go on," he said, quietly, "or you ain't got a hair on your ass."

Well, I got a little mad then, cause I know I got more than one hair on my ass. Okay, I told myself, if you're gonna blow cock, blow it! And I did. I kept one hand on my cock and reached down to wrap my fingers around his. Christ, the damn thing leaped as soon as I touched it. And it was damn hot, like a red hot rod of steel. Shit, I nearly creamed my own cock just hanging onto his. What a fucking rock hard cock that macho Marine had. I couldn't hardly believe it. That's when I started knowing what that cocksucker in his pickup liked so much. Man, I never felt anything like it before, not even my own cock. Jason's cock was stiff and strong and...I squeezed it until more shiny juice leaked out of the piss hole and I wondered what it tasted like. Some juice spit out of my piss hole too, making my nuts flare up. I wiped the slime off my piss hole with one finger and licked it. I liked it. I wiped some slime off his piss hole and licked it too. And I liked it too. Better than my own.

"Oh, yeah, that's it," he said, shifting his hips up and down and making my fist fuck his cock. "Go down on me, Matt. Lick my dickhead. Let's see how queer you are. Blow me." His voice was so soft yet so deep and so goddam sexy and so fucking studly, I would have done anything he said. I kept my fist wrapped around his shaft and bent over and stuck out my tongue and got my first taste of cockhead and nearly swooned in my socks even though I wasn't wearing any socks. He moaned like a pussy cat in heat.

I liked him moaning while I was flicking my tongue over his salty cockhead. I wasn't even taking the whole rubbery thing in my mouth yet, but a fire was lit inside me like a blazing furnace. My chest felt so full that my brain was dizzy. I was hot all over, inside and out. I started licking his dickhead all around, trailing my tongue over the rim, slipping it up the path to the piss hole, then even gliding my tongue all over the veiny shaft, licking that stiff rod like it was the best friend a guy ever had. It started trembling and that made me more excited. I couldn't believe I was licking a man's cock but I didn't want to stop. I got so lost at slapping my tongue all over his rod I didn't know where my tongue was going. It was just flapping around like crazy and I was following it. And it tapped his balls. And, Christ, that got to me. His balls smelled sweaty and the fine hairs on his nuts tickled my tongue and sent more sparks to my brain. My chest was burning up. Jason must have been in that same fire too cause he moaned louder and ground his ass into the mattress and put his hands on my head to pull my hair and maybe cram his cock down my throat.

That's when I sat up, just to catch my breath. I wanted to tell him how great I was feeling, how he was such a great guy to let me do his dick, but I couldn't even talk I was breathing so hard. And, get this, I hadn't even sucked his cock yet! Not really. I had only licked it! But I wanted to blow it real bad. And damn, right at that second, I knew damn well I was a queer! I was a cocksucker, for God's sake! Hell, my cock was twitching with so much pleasure and my balls were aching with so much juice, I couldn't not be queer!

I must have looked like a dummy sitting on my heels and grinning like a loon and looking at Jason's cock and pulling on my cock and thinking about how I much I wanted to blow him. Then suddenly Jason sat up and somehow pushed me around and I was lying down on my back now and he was kneeling between my legs. "Relax," he was saying. "Take it easy, kid." My chest was heaving in and out like I had just lifted a thousand pounds. I was holding onto my cock and my balls and my mind was spinning into the ceiling.

Jason wrapped his fingers around my wrists and lifted my arms over my head and bent his whole body over me. When his rod brushed against mine, I shivered with heat. My insides were quaking. He leaned down and kissed me on the lips.

Heck, I was more than amazed, I was damn flabbergasted. I hadn't counted on that. Blowing a man's cock, yeah. I wanted to see if I could do it. But kissing a man? No way. But I sure didn't stop him; it felt too good and I wanted to eat him alive. Jason stopped himself when he pulled his face from mine and said, so softly, so sure, so damn manly, "There's more to being queer than sucking cock." And he slid up to sit on my chest, still holding my hands above my head. The stink under my arms and under his arms drifted to my nose and smelled like great fucking mountain men. And the bare cheeks of his ass settling on my bare chest was so sensational I wanted to tell him so, I wanted to....

He scooted up some more until his balls brushed over my mouth. I nearly died with gladness. Those nuts of his were big and they were hairy, and they felt like globs of pure molten gold. And they smelled better than his smelly armpits and I thought nothing could smell better than them. I opened my mouth and licked his nuts. Jason groaned. I groaned louder, even though the baggy flesh of his balls was flopping on my lips, almost like those balls were kissing me while I was kissing them. Then he started waving his balls back and forth over my mouth while I flicked out at them with my tongue, tasting the sweat and swallowing the sweat and loving the sweat and then reaching up and even sucking one of his nuts into my mouth. My mind damn near tore loose at the brain as the delicious chunk of one of his nuts filled my mouth and I gobbled it down, then gobbled both down. My mouth was full of Jason's hairy nuts and his manly smell was making me so weak and wonderful I could have died happy at that moment. I think I started growling and know I was struggling with my arms. But not to get away. I just wanted to grab him, to fucking love him, to swallow him.

Jason's body was shaking with as much feeling as mine, but he kept his hands clamped on mine and rammed his hips forward. His balls were pulled from my mouth but they immediately smothered my nose. I have never ever sniffed something so delicious as those sagging, soppy balls. I craned my head to lick them again, to swallow them again. I strained my neck, lifting it, wanting those balls again to fill my mouth so bad. I was lapping at them, licking them. And then, POW, all of a sudden I wasn't licking balls. I was licking Jason's asshole.

And, get this, I didn't even care! Christ, that tiny little asshole of his was hairy and wrinkled and smelled of rank sweat and I started flicking my tongue at his hole, stretching my neck for all it was worth, my arms too, and my muscles until I grunted loud as hell and broke his hold and grabbed his hips and pulled the cheeks of his bare ass apart until I was able to snake my tongue directly into his smelly asshole. I fuckin' melted at the taste of the juicy and soft and tender inside of his ass. It felt like I was eating melting ice cream and the creamiest pie I ever tasted, and I wanted more. I wanted to get lost in his fucking asshole, to drown myself in that beautiful fucking ass of Jason's.

Jason was sitting on my face, groaning, quivering, shaking his ass, mumbling at me to, "Eat that fuckin' asshole, kid ... oh yeah, eat that fuckin' hole! Eat me out, kid ... yeah, yeah, yeah...."

I held onto his hips for dear life, gnawed at his ass, strained my tongue to kingdom come until Jason was grunting and groaning and ramming his ass down on my face and I knew he was shooting off cause his asshole was breathing in and out like mad and my tongue was stuck deep up in his smooth asshole and getting strangled by the muscles of his asshole and my own cock went fucking wild cause it was shooting off all by its lonesome, without me even jacking it and without any lips around it. I yelled into Jason's asshole, and held onto it, and grunted into it, and chewed it, and groaned into it, and I swallowed his fucking asshole whole and slammed my hips to the ceiling and gushed my cum all over my belly while Jason's cum was splattering above my head and dribbling over my hair and my face.

Jason flopped backwards and lay there between my legs. His feet held my head. His ass was lying on my cum-slicked cock. My eyes were closed, my chest was still heaving, I was in deep space and easing off into some dream with his cum leaking all over my face.

From somewhere in the room a voice echoed in my dream. "Now do you think you're queer?" Jason asked. I just knew he was grinning that manly Marine grin of his again.

"No," I told him. I grinned to myself. "I know it."

THE TANTALIZERS
Leo Cardini

By the time I reach the end of the abandoned West Village pier with the useless No Trespassing sign, I'm feeling so damn horny I know once I take off all my clothes I'll either have to shoot a load or sunbathe with a hard-on.

But then I always get a little turned on whenever I stroll past the tantalizing assortment of Manhattan men naked on their towels on the south side of the pier. Soaking up the rays in the buff, they present such a cum-churning display of beefcake in the raw, and of manly endowments adorned with cock rings, piercings and the skill of the razor, that they torture my dick and inflame my imagination.

And then today there's also the thought of what I've got stuffed away in my knapsack, the constant recollection of it working on my easily-stimulated, nearly nine-incher until it flops around in my shorts in a semi-hard, show-off state.

I spread out my towel, peel off my clothes and begin rubbing suntan oil all over my body, secretly proud of the results of my rigorous workout routine as I massage the oil into the smooth-shaven contours of my gym-sculpted chest and tight, flat abs. Teasing myself, I save my crotch for last, first rubbing the lotion into my pubic bush, or what's left of it since I'd just trimmed it that morning down to about a quarter-inch. Then my nuts, large and loose in my carefully shaved ballsac. And finally, I wrap my greased-up fist around my thick, cut dick and stroke it up and down, the sensation of cock-stimulation spreading throughout my body.

No one is nearby (not that it really matters here in the Village), so I lie back with my legs spread apart and continue slow-stroking my dick. Then, when I can resist it no longer, I reach into my knapsack with my free hand and rummage about for the bottle of poppers I found this morning in a small, dusty head shop somewhere south of Christopher Street with a handmade going-out-of-business sign.

What the fuck's so special about a bottle of poppers? Well, these aren't just any poppers. In their distinctive dark-brown glass container, square at the base and gradually transforming itself two-thirds up into a smaller, circular, screw-cap top, its label simply announces: "Brown Bottle Poppers, made in Onacock, Virginia."

So if you're as young as I am, you're probably thinking, "Big deal. Never heard of them."

Well, I might be in my early twenties, but my Uncle Mike's twice my age, though you might not believe it to look at him. He's lived in the Village since college (I'm apartment-sitting for him this summer) and whenever he talks about Village life during that golden age of promiscuity known as the seventies, he holds me spellbound as he recalls a thousand and one cum-drippy adventures in sex clubs like the Mineshaft, sleaze spots like the Anvil and bathhouses like the St. Marks. And one of the things he always seems to remember fondly are Brown Bottle Poppers, a semi-underground product that were very popular at the time.

I find the glass container deep in my knapsack and there's a spark of connection between my fingers touching the bottle and my fist stroking my dick

I pull out the bottle, abandon my dick and raise myself up onto my right elbow to unscrew the cap. I expect they'll be totally ineffective after all these years and what I'll really be inhaling is simply a whiff of the past, my active imagination kicking in to coax the cum of out my dick with thoughts of my Uncle Mike and the Village he knew when he was my age.

But I hardly have the cap off when I'm startled by a pint-sized tornado whooshing out of the bottle with such force it almost leaps out of my hand. As I stare in amazement, the tornado becomes a boy no, make that a very young man, I think who lands gracefully on his feet in front of me. He's a broad-chested hunk with twinkling blue eyes, close-cropped blond hair and a boyish, handsome face lit up with an eager smile. As short as he's well-built, his magnificent torso's absolutely hairless down to his navel. Looking up at him from my blanket, I can't help but notice the narrow line of hair that descends from it into his blond pubic bush, and his thick, rubbery, smooth-shafted dick with an oversized cockhead that stares down at me from over the outthrust of his two large nuts in his pink, furrowed ballsac.

He rubs his eyes, flings out his arms into a wake-up stretch, and then, noticing me, says, "Man, do you ever have a big dick! So what year is this?"

I manage to mumble out a response and he says, "You mean, I've been stuck in that damn bottle for something like twenty years? And all because of a little innocent mischief! I mean, I only wanted to liven things up. By the way, my name's Gene. Gene...genie? Get it?"

But before I can get in another word, he continues with, "So thanks for letting me out, and yes, you do get three wishes. But forget about wealth and power. I'm Reformed, which means all you'll get from me are sensual pleasures beyond your wildest expectations. The thing is, once you shoot your load, that's the end of a wish. So, wish number one. What'll it be?"

"I think I need a little time to "

"Well, I don't mean to rush you, but it has been twenty years, and..."

He's tugged his dick into a full-fledged hard-on, which he now releases. It leaps into the air, settling into an up-pointing position, eight or so inches of beautiful meat drooling pre-cum like it's going out of style.

"Well, see what I mean?"

I'm thinking maybe he wouldn't be so impatient if I deep throat his dick and suck him off, when, looking down the pier with one hand shading his eyes, he says, "Now that's why I've always liked the Village so much!"

I turn my head to follow his gaze and, as if the moment wasn't unreal enough, I could swear I see my Uncle Mike approach us dressed in a thin white tank top and 501 cutoffs straining against the over-sized bulge in his crotch. Of course, it isn't him I realize a second later. But his hair's as dark and wavy, though longer and parted in the middle, and his chest as classically proportioned, his face as ruggedly handsome, and...oh, God is he hot! Just the kind of man I'd....

"Well?" Gene prompts me, "Your first wish?"

"That guy?" I say, pointing.

"Yeah. Couldn't you just lick the socks off his feet?"

"You can have his socks. I just wish I could get in his pants."

"Oh, I like the way your mind works!"

Suddenly Gene's dressed in denim shorts and a tight white tee shirt.

"Though I did see him first, you know."

A gold ring appears in his left ear.

"Hmm," he comments, frowning critically, staring out into space. Two rings join the one already there and a pink triangle tattoo flashes into view nearby on his upper arm.

I feel an onrush of lightheadedness, and his words grow distant as he says, "So meet me here tomorrow and I'll give you your second wish."

And as he heads down the pier with a springy step, I think of calling him back for help since I think I'm about to faint. My vision fades and flickers, the pier begins to spin, gravity deserts me...

...and though I can hardly believe it, I realize somehow I've been evicted from my body and resettled in the pants of this man's who's not my Uncle Mike. I mean, in them, like I've actually been transformed into the faded blue denim wearing dangerously thin, clinging to him for dear life.

Every step he takes is a fresh thrill as I feel the constant back and forth reposition of his cock and balls rubbing against me. His nuts are as large as eggs, though there's plenty of room for them in his loose, clean-shaven ballsac. His long, brownish dick shaft is thick and veiny, and not as easily maneuverable as his balls, and his huge, perfectly-formed cockhead's noticeably sensitive to my touch as it insistently struggles to burrow its way down my left leg hole.

And then in the rear his beautiful butt, smooth as silk and hard as rock, presses out against me, offering no resistance as I creep up into his crack to that most delectable, inaccessible region where a pink, puckered manhole ringed with moist, sweaty hair seems to lure me in, encouraging my efforts.

So, in as many minutes I've learned two things. One, be careful what you wish for, since some genie just might come along and take you literally. And two, if you ever get a wish or three to yourself, you could do a lot worse than wanting to be some guy's cutoffs, especially if he's one hung hunk who, if I can judge by the half-hard state of his dick, is every bit as horny as I am.

If I were still in my human form, I'd be arrested for feeling him up like this in public, but I'm not, and so I take full advantage of the opportunity to rub and grope, wallowing in my pleasure. I glean the lustful thoughts though the eyes of so many of the men we pass, and I feel a childish delight in knowing I have what they want as the two of us make our way towards...well, where are we going?

He travels east to Fifth Avenue, then north up to 12th Street, then east again to Third Ave, where he heads north for half a block. Suddenly he steps into the rightmost entrance of a wall of smoky-windowed doors with no sign announcing what's beyond them and pulls out a ten dollar bill from his right sweat sock, where he's stashed his money and his keys, to pay the cashier.

Now, in case you've never been there though you look like the kind of dude who has the Jewel is this little old theater with maybe two hundred seats that since the seventies has specialized in gay porn. But what makes it so popular is its basement, a temple to sleazy sex. You have to know to go down into the tiny lower level lobby with the two men's room and open the unmarked door to the left of them. Then you're in the basement proper where everything's painted black, a dark, red lit paradise where the middle third's two aisles of thirty or so small cubicles, each one measuring no more than a yard wide and one to three yards deep, most with a bench built into the wall opposite their doors.

The rules of the Jewel are simple: no public sex, play safe, and before you get it on with someone inside one of the cubicles, lock the door behind you.

172

I can't tell you how many blissful hours I've spent lost in lust inside the Jewel. But never like this! Disregarding the Jewel's prime directive, I feel him up with no sense of shame as the men posing in cubicles and the men cruising the aisles check him out.

Several times he stops outside doorways, considering the man within as he runs his hand across the growing bulge that presses out against me, making me hotter and hornier with each stroke of his palm.

He passes by the first several men after pausing to consider them. The next says, "Hiya Jesse, how ya doin'?" He smiles, responds with, "Hey Leo," and moves on. But now he stops at yet another open-door booth, clearly interested in its occupant seated on the bench inside and leaning forward with his forearms resting on his thighs. Shirtless and in cutoffs, he's a bit on the short side, but he's also beautifully built, with blond hair, arresting eyes and a come-hither smile.

He motions my master to enter, and as we step inside I realize it's Gene!

Now this isn't fair! He grants me a wish, and then he co-opts it! But hey, why make a fuss, huh? I mean, I've never been one to pass up a threesome with two hot dudes.

As Jesse locks the door behind us, Gene deftly unbuttons and lowers his own shorts down to his ankles while slipping off the bench onto his spread-apart knees. Resting his butt on his heels, he exhibits his pale, smooth, up-curving dick center-stage in the vee of his crotch. Commanding my attention with its constant twitching, I notice it looks longer and fatter than before.

Once the door's locked, Gene goes crazy with lust, twenty years of pent-up desire flooding out all at once. He buries his head in the fabric of my crotch, squeezes Jesse's ass cheeks, and commences licking the lengthening cock inside me. In seconds, his noisy, drawn-out slurps soak me through and through, plastering Jesse's dick against me, thrilling me to the very marrow of my fibers.

In the rear, Gene's fingers dig into the warm, unyielding butt flesh as they inch towards his hole, forcing me up there right along with them.

Still licking away as if his life depended on it, his restless fingers move around to the front of me, passing over my topmost button, quickly undoing the rest. Pulling his face out of my crotch, he reaches in my open fly, struggling to maneuver out Jesse's stiff, rigidly uncooperative dick that, once freed from my embrace, sticks straight up in front of Gene's face, his huge, mushroom-shaped cockhead rising magnificently above my top button, throbbing with impatience as Gene reaches in again to coax out his two huge nuts that finally flop down ripe and heavy in the open air.

"Mmm," Gene purrs, slow stroking his dick as he stares at Jesse's long, thick masterpiece of rugged beauty oozing a generous supply of pre-cum.

Gene reaches up to fondle Jesse's balls, his knuckles brushing against me. As he lovingly fingers them, Jesse stretches upwards, pulling off his tank top, the visual assault of his manly perfection overwhelming me as his flat abs, his well-defined chest, his hard-nubbed nipples, and finally his moist, hairy underarms come into view.

I guess it affects Gene in the same way because suddenly he's all motion again, shifting into high gear as he greedily licks Jesse's balls, getting them nice and wet all over again and then carefully sucking them into his mouth, his chin pressing against me. With his mouth full of nuts, he abandons his cock stroking to reach up and play with Jesse's nipples, gripping them firmly between thumbs and forefingers, twisting, squeezing and tugging, which Jesse responds to with an outthrust of his chest and a deep, baritone moan.

Gene releases Jesse's nuts and, with hardly a pause deep throats his dick. But he tries for too much too soon and gags, dismounting slightly, relaxing his gagging muscles and trying again. This time he manages to slide his lips all the way to its base with such ease I wonder if there isn't a little genie magic at play, and it passes through my mind that maybe my next wish will be for gagging reflexes with a turn-off switch for whenever a big dick comes my way.

When Jesse eases a resistant Gene off his dick and pulls him up onto his feet, Gene's cock rises with him, pressing against me between Jesse's legs, rock hard with practically no give to it. Gene grinds his hips against Jesse's and his cockhead burrows it way up between Jesse's legs, warm and pulsing in the snug space, inching its way towards his hole. Up above, I hear Jesse moaning, his husky voice thick with lust as Gene tongue-teases his nipples and then tugs on them with his teeth, his hands returning to Jesse's ass cheeks to steady himself.

Soon he drops to his knees again. Looking up at Jesse with pleading eyes, he says, "Oh man, if you only knew how long it's been since I've had a guy's dick in my mouth...."

"Meaning you want to suck me off, huh?"

"Yeah. Is that okay?"

Jesse responds by pushing Gene back onto his dick, holding him there with both hands

"Hell, I came here looking for a good blowjob, so...."

He forces Gene all the way down on his dick. Gene willingly deep throats him, wildly stroking his own dick with one hand while tugging on his nuts with the other as he commences working his tight lips up and down Jesse's cock with greedy enthusiasm.

Jesse hitches his thumbs in my front pockets and settles into it, looking down at Gene, wedding the sight of Gene's cock- worship to the sensation. As Gene's suck strokes grow more energetic, he begins to moan again as he tenses his ass cheeks, imprisoning me between them in the back as his nuts press against me in front, the overflow of Gene's cock sucking spit dribbling down onto me.

Listen, I've been on both ends of a blowjob, and I'm really not certain which side I like more. But I do know I've never enjoyed a good suck off more than this one!

The cubicle grows warm and humid with the passion of the activity and soon my every fiber's saturated with the sweet feeling of approaching orgasm. Jesse's moans modulate into a throaty wail and even Gene manages guttural sounds of pleasure, stroking his own dick with an ever-increasing motion.

And then it happens. Jesse roars and I'm sure the entire basement knows he's sending what sounds like an endless outpouring of cum down Gene's throat, setting off Gene, who explodes with jet after jet of cum landing hot and sticky in my crotch.

And as a tidal wave of orgasm washes through me, suffusing me with an all-pervading pleasure, the room begins to spin, a heady mix of cocks and cum and nuts and nipples and black-painted walls and red lit chests. And I ride the orgasm into heights and depths of pleasure more intense than anything I've ever experienced before...

...waking with a feeling of satisfied exhaustion, the warm rays of the sun kindly caressing me, and I pull myself up onto my elbows to see my softening dick slip off my right thigh down between my legs, leaving behind a hefty deposit of cum.

Sunning on the pier again the next day, by the time noon rolls around I'm beginning to wonder if I'll ever see Gene again, when I hear his voice beside me.

"So, was he everything you hoped he'd be?" he asks, shucking his clothes as I squint up at him.

"You should know. You were there," I say, sitting up.

"Yeah," he replies with a mischievous grin. "Mind if I borrow some of your lotion?"

"Go ahead. Except when I said I wanted to get in his pants, I didn't mean literally."

"Oh?"

"It's an expression. I didn't want to get in his pants. I wanted to get inside his pants."

"Oh? Well, that's hot too, I guess. But you've gotta admit it's not half as imaginative as what I thought you meant."

"So do I get a new first wish?"

"You Manhattanites are all so fucking greedy! I give you one, frankly, fantastically hot wish, and all you can do is cry 'but it's not the one I asked for!'"

"Well, it wasn't."

"But did you enjoy it?"

"Yeah," I reply, the recollection of it drawing my hand into my crotch to stroke myself.

"I thought so. Here," he says kneeling between my legs and brushing my hand away. "Let me put some lotion on that for you. And what you found inside his pants...was that satisfactory?"

"Like you don't know."

"And did you come?" he asks fisting the lotion along my stiffening dick.

"Did I ever! Oh, that feels good!"

"Then you've used up a wish. It's just that it wasn't exactly the wish you asked for, that's all. But anyhow, as much as I'd like to help you shoot your load," he says releasing my throbbing dick, "it's time to talk about your next wish."

"You fucking cock tease!"

"I know."

I'm almost horny enough to wish he'd finish what he'd just begun, but I catch myself and ask, "How about the same wish? Just get it right this time."

"Your wish, as they say..." His voice begins to fade and the pier begins to spin. "...is my...."

...I'm in a small, cool room in nothing but a pair of 501 cutoffs I know aren't mine. A narrow, white-sheeted bed takes up half the room, leaving barely enough space for a built-in ledge at its head, and a door at its foot.

I think I've been transported to the West Side Club, one of the few remaining bathhouses in Manhattan. Looking up and seeing that the walls of the room end short of the ceiling, where a large fan lazily rotates, I know I am. In fact, the graffiti on the back of the door reminds me I've had this room myself on occasion.

But why am I here? And alone.

I look around for clues. There's a watch and packets of condoms and lubricant on the nightstand, and under it a pair of sneakers and socks and a tee shirt. And that's it. No pants.

But of course! Because I'm wearing them!

I wanted to get in Jesse's pants, and that's where I am! Goddamn that Gene!

There's no towel or room key, which means he must be cruising around. How do I explain I'm in his room and in his pants when he gets back? And how am I ever going to make my way back to Uncle Mike's apartment without my keys or a stitch of clothing of my own?

I stand there frozen, unsuccessfully willing myself into action, when the knob turns, the door opens, and in steps Jesse, a towel tied around his waist.

"What the...?"

"Uh, sorry! I thought it was my room. Guess you left the door unlocked. I was just leaving."

"Wearing my cutoffs?"

"Well...you see...uh...just when I realized this wasn't my room I recognized them from the attendant showing you to your room when you first came in. And I just couldn't resist trying them on. I mean, it was like my dick just had to feel where yours just was...."

I give my crotch a tug, and I become aware of a leather cock ring from out of nowhere, warm and snug-fitting, prompting my dick to press down and out against his cutoffs.

"And then once I had them on and felt the denim creeping up into my ass...."

I turn around, lift one foot up onto the bed, thrusting my butt towards him, and run my hand along my ass crack.

"Well...uh...."

I twist my head around to face him, locking eyes with an astonished Jesse. My hole's itching, my dick's throbbing, and an involuntary moan escapes me.

He pushes my hand away, and slides one of his own between my butt cheeks, prompting another moan.

My cockhead slips out of his left leg hole and I become acutely aware of a warm pulsing where the cock ring embraces my stiffening dick and sensitive balls, like a living creature lusting after me.

"Mmm," I hear Gene's voice purr in my head, and realize that's no ordinary cock ring down there, but the little fucker is out to co-opt my wish again.

Jesse's hand has strayed down along the length of my cock shaft. When his fingertips reach the tender flesh below my piss slit, I begin to drool pre-cum like never before. Gene's doing, no doubt.

"Jesus, you're big!" Jesse says. "Turn around."

And as I lift my leg off the bed to face him, he sits down on the edge of it, carefully undoing his cutoffs and sliding them down until my liberated, cum-drippy dick jumps up in front of his face, repeatedly flexing in response to Gene's massaging embrace.

Jesse's magnificent cock pushes back his towel, upstanding in its stiffness, and he begins to stroke it as he leans forward into my crotch to lap up all the pre-cum streaming down the underside of my dick.

Then he wraps his lips around my cockhead and tongue-teases the hell out of my piss slit. Accelerating his own cock strokes, he slides his tight lips down my shaft, taking it nice and slow until his upper lip connects with Gene. He contracts his throat around my cockhead and Gene continues to fondle me, the two of them making me feel so damn good in no time I'm seconds away from orgasm.

Somehow I summon up the willpower to plant my hands on Jesse's head and lift him off.

"Have it your way," he says, sounding like I've offended him. "Besides, I'd rather fuck you anyhow. But gimme some head first."

I kick off his shorts and lower myself onto my knees between his legs, pulling them wide apart. He slides forward and his huge nuts slip off the bed, heavy-hanging in his loose, smooth skin ballsac. Above them, his thick, towering erection rises up between his muscular thighs against the backdrop of his black pubic bush and tight abs, the underside of his cockhead obstructing my view of his navel.

I grab his balls, drawing his dick forward to lick my way up his rugged shaft, tongue teasing his piss slit, forcing his cock to repeatedly flex out of control. And then I go down on him, losing myself in the act of swallowing up his big, hard dick until nothing else in the universe exists. But then he pushes me off, clutches his ballsac and forces his nuts out towards me.

"Lick 'em," he commands.

And as I suck them into my mouth and tongue them for all my life he reaches over to the ledge, grabs a sealed condom, rips it open and slides it down onto his dick

Once he's protected, he eases me off his nuts, helps me up and turns me around. Following his lead I lift my left leg onto the bed and lean forward, balancing myself with my hands extended head-high, one pressing against the door, and the other against the adjoining wall opposite the bed.

As Gene continues to make love to the base of my cock with throat-like contractions, my drooling dick thrashes around unobstructed in the open air. Suddenly, Jesse takes me by surprise by the force of his enthusiasm as he pulls my ass cheeks wide apart and goes hog wild eating me out, burying his face in my ass crack and plunging his tongue up my butthole with such force I have to push against the walls with all my might to keep from falling forward.

Then Jesse pulls his face out of my ass. While he reaches for a couple of packets of lube, tearing them open and greasing up his dick and my ass, Gene never lets me forget his presence, my breathing growing deep and labored in response to his intense lovemaking.

"Hope you like getting fucked good and hard," Jesse menaces unconvincingly with his hands on my hips as he presses his cockhead against my hungry hole. "Cause you owe me trying to steal my fuckin' cutoffs!"

"Just go slow at first, okay?" I whisper, pretending apprehension, my constantly clenching ass lips exposing me for the liar that I am.

He slips his dickhead in and I moan, giving into the exquisite sensation of this welcomed intrusion. The first few inches of his cock shaft follow and I close my eyes to fully appreciate it as I open up to him. Then, tightening his hands on my hips, he slides in the rest, filling me up, the pleasure so intense I need to shake my head back and forth to work off the excess.

Once he's all the way inside he hits my special spot, connecting with Gene, unaware he's part of a threesome with me in the middle. Then, after slowly pulling out, he begins to fuck me with an even-paced rhythm that gradually accelerates, each dick plunge uniting with Gene's caresses, causing my cock to spasm and drool like it's never done before, my pre-cum dancing in the air in long, thin strands.

The sensations increase until I feel like I'm drowning in a tidal wave of sensuality.

"Teach you...to steal into my room...." Jesse utters breathlessly through his exertions, his words mingling with my moans as he fucks the living daylight out of me. "...take my pants...oh, fuck!...such a hot little ass!...oh!...make you pay!...ah!...ah!"

And then, with one plunge more powerful than the rest, he roars like a lion and the first explosion of cum shoots out his dick, collaborating with Gene's efforts, forcing my own over-swollen dick to shoot a load that flings me into ecstatic abandon as I thrash my head from side to side and scream like my life depended on it, overcome by the sensation of orgasm that networks throughout my body as fireworks explode against my eyelids, until one final dick probe, one final Genestroke, one final shot of cum blinds me in a burst of pure bright light....

...and I awake spent and breathless, lying on my towel in the early afternoon sun with so much cum on me I look like I've just been the centerpiece of one hell of a hot circle jerk.

The next day, lying on my stomach with my legs spread apart and my cock and balls pushed down between them for maximum sun exposure, an oily hand sliding between my ass cheeks rouses me from the light sleep I'd drifted into.

"So how was he?"

I open my eyes, twisting my head towards the voice to see Gene kneeling beside me naked and erect with my bottle of lotion in his free hand.

"You should know. You were there. Again."

"Yeah," he says with that irresistible grin of his, kneading my balls under the pretext of rubbing the oil into them.

"Can't I ever get a wish to myself, without you butting in?"

Oh, I wish I hadn't said that! I mean, I only just met him two days ago, but I'm really getting to like him.

"Sorry," he says, deeply hurt. "I just wanted to be around you, that's all."

I turn over, sitting on my butt, the tell-tale hard-on he's given me slapping up against my belly.

"And I like having you around. A lot. But I'll tell you one thing. Your English sucks. When I said I wanted to get in Jesse's pants, all I meant is I wanted to have sex with him."

"So why didn't you say so in the first place?"

"I did!"

"No you didn't! You said you wanted to get in his pants! And I did just that for you. Twice, in fact! Excuse me for giving you a little more credit than wanting to waste you wishes on plain old sex, especially when you could've gotten that all by yourself. I mean with a body like yours " He runs his hand across my chest and my dick jumps. "And a face like that...."

Looking longingly into my eyes, he raises his hand to stroke my cheek, prompting a surge of affection to well up in my chest.

"Aaaahhhhh...."

He pauses and then leans forwards, tenderly kissing me on the lips.

Oh, yeah. He's definitely the kind of genie I could fall for.

"What do you say, Gene, to the two of us starting all over again. No fantastic wishes, no genie magic; just you and me."

"You mean that? You could like me for just being me?"

Words fail me and all I can do is nod.

180

"Well," he finally says, "all I can say is I sure got my wish."

Then that devilish grin of his steals over his face and with eyes a-twinkle he says, "But you've still got one wish to go. You want to get in Jesse's pants? I'll get you in Jesse's pants."

I'm about to protest that all I want is him when he stops me with, "Trust me on this. Your wish is my...."

The familiar faintness and spinning overtakes me and I find myself enclosed in darkness. Warm, firm flesh presses in on three sides. Where there isn't flesh, there's denim, snug against me. I feel hornier than I've ever felt in my life.

From above, I hear, "Haven't I met you before?"

It's Jesse's voice, the sound of it rumbling through me.

"Maybe. I try to get around," I hear Gene reply just as far above me as I feel a caressing pressure against me, causing me to swell with desire.

The tent-like wall of denim struggles against the assault of an outside force and then gradually parts as if ripped open. Huge fingers reach in, carefully maneuvering me out into the open air. I instantly recognize we're hidden away in a secluded section of the Ramble, an overgrown area of Central Park where men go to have sex with each other in the bushes.

Gene, lowering himself onto his knees, whispers to me through Jesse's moistening piss slit, "Oh, baby. I'm going to make love to you like you've never been made love to before!"

THREE FOR THE ROAD: MORE CARNIVAL NIGHTS
P. K. Warren

"Give me a boy whose face and hand
Are rough with dust and circus-sand
Whose ruddy flesh exhales the scent
Of health without embellishment;
Sweet to my sense is such a youth,
Whose charms have all the charm of truth."
– Strato

Like many boys, I ran away from home to join the circus. I never made it to The Greatest Show on Earth, but I did get to Sleeman's Travelling Carnival and Shows. Strictly second-rate, but I had to start somewhere. Besides, I liked the sleaziness of Sleeman's and I stayed with them for four years.

Travelling with Sleeman's Carnival and Shows had its up's and downs. Well, more downs than ups I should say, because the show seemed to be cursed with bad luck. And when trouble hit the show, it hit hard and would last a few days or weeks. More than not I went around with my fingers crossed at times, my legs, too and prayed it would keep mishaps at bay. Guess I wasn't praying hard enough the week they canned Jed, or, as he was known, Animal.

In the spring of 1982, I was starting my third year with Sleeman's when my boss, Bob, came to wake me one morning with news of having a new worker to take under my wing and show the ropes. My trailer roommate, the slime that he was, slipped out the door as my temper jumped fifty degrees. "No fuckin' way, Bob! Not now or ever again!" I yelled. "Find yourself some other sucker to handle your dirty work!"

"Oh, come on, Phil," Bob pleaded. "Have a cup of coffee first and wake up."

"I am awake and the answer's still, no!" I said, sitting on the edge of my bed. I walked to the kitchen table and sat down in my briefs as Bob poured us each a mug of coffee. From one town to the next, when we were set up, Bob's first stop each morning was at my trailer because I'd bought myself an automatic coffee maker.

That morning I wasn't in any mood to hear about new workers joining on. "Green help" we called them and more than not, if they weren't dangerous, they were a pain in the ass. The majority of them only lasted a week or two before running back home to mother; a couple would remain a month; and if we were lucky maybe one would last the whole season.

"He says he's worked for other shows," Bob was saying. "So I doubt there's any green left in him. Besides, you're the best one I've got that can make 'em or break 'em in a day's time."

"And it'll be one of those days that I get my ass killed by a green. No thanks, partner." By then I'd had my hands and fingers cut and pinched, hammers and wrenches falling within inches of my head to last me a life time all thanks to breaking in green-as-grass helpers.

"You always make a good pot of coffee," Bob said.

No matter how much I argued, Bob always won. "Bob, don't snowball me. What in hell did the garbage men drop off this time?"

"He talks a good story, but there's only one way to back it up and I came to the best man for the job."

"You know, Bob, if I didn't like you so much I'd tell you to go screw yourself."

"Wouldn't be your first or last time."

"One day it just might be, shoving all the green on me. So when do I meet our new star?"

"Right now," he said and got up to open the door. "Jed, c'mon in."

I half expected another flea-bitten, road-rat to come through the door. Boy, was I ever wrong! When Jed stepped inside the trailer I jest not, I nearly shit myself. Six-foot-two, straight blond hair to the shoulders, built and blue eyes was more than I could handle so early in the morning. Standing up I would've been weak in the knees. Sitting there in just my briefs, I suddenly felt like hiding under the table. Worse yet, when Jed and I shook hands he grasped my fingers more than my palm you know, like you would shake hands with a lady but even so, my hand felt small in his. Most of his face was hidden under a beard (which in most cases was a turn-off for me), but he kept it groomed and the mustache sharply trimmed. Broad shoulders, narrow waist, packed into tight fitted t-shirt and jeans I could easily overlook the fur on his face!

Luckily, Bob offered and poured some coffee for Jed, who sat across from me at the table, because if I had gotten up to do the same there would have been no way of hiding the erection tenting the front of my briefs.

Once Bob had informed me of the day's work planned he told Jed to hang out with me and then left. Jed and I talked a while longer about his past experience and then, I informed him of the rules we had to follow: no drinking while on duty; no non-show people on the lot before or after business hours; showers and clean clothes before we opened; no nudity of any sort during business hours.

"What about sleeping conditions?" Jed asked.

"Like any show, we don't have enough trailers to house everyone, so you make the best of it till a slot opens."

"How long of a waiting list is there anyhow?"

"Honestly, there isn't one. It's usually left up to the senior of each one who decides which one gets the next open bed."

"In other words, kiss ass until you get lucky."

"That's about the run of it."

"You got room for one more?"

"I only wish," I said, and meant every word. "My present trailer-mate is a real slime-bag. But once you get into a slot, you're there to stay until you leave the show of your own will or get fired."

"Mind if I ask what your position is?"

"Boy, is that a loaded question."

"I mean job-wise."

"Starting my third season with Sleeman's, hovering just below being a foreman."

"Not bad for a young kid; you must know the business inside and out by now."

"More than I thought I ever would, but I'll fill you in as the day goes on. Right now I'd better get dressed, or Bob'll have my ass on a fire."

"I'll wait for ya outside," Jed said and left.

I was almost tempted into telling Jed he could stay, but just as well. My cock sprang up to slap my stomach as I stripped off my briefs, before getting into the shower. With Jed around my friend had a mind of its own so I had to stroke the stiffness out of him.

After dressing and joining Jed outside, I realized I should have jacked off twice because my dick was quickly rising again. More than half the day I worked with a bulge in my jeans and pinched my nuts more than a few times, due to a lack of expansion room. Fact was, once Jed and I got to work I really got the chance to check him out. He didn't show much up front, but I've yet to find a small package that hasn't held some eye-popping surprises, but it was the ass that kept my dick jumping; every time he bent over that big bubble butt just swallowed the seam of his denim, practically screaming to keep it covered and contained. Half wishing his jeans lost the battle, I would've been on my knees in a flash!

Unfortunately, I wasn't to be that lucky. But I did find a new friend in Jed. We also had a lot in common, only he was straight and I was pretending to be so. And I made sure that side of me was kept in the dark by heading off the few on the show that did know about me. Not that anyone knowing had caused me many problems, I just found it better, day-to-day, keeping that knowing number at a low minimum. I was lucky in forcing my roomie into a corner because I gave Jed free use of the shower and invited him in for meals, when I felt like cooking, so the slime-bag spent less and less time in the trailer. Not that Jed hating his guts had anything to do with it, mind you, but by mid-July fate dealt me a royal flush, when the slime-bag got his sorry ass fired.

By then I'd gone through half a dozen trailer-mates and wasn't anxious to get a replacement any time too soon. As far as Bob was concerned I could keep the trailer to myself, but we both knew when I got my shit together Jed would be the next likely candidate to move in. But it would take two weeks, with Jed practically on his knees begging, before I relented and let him move in. And that first night was living hell for me!

First order of business was to brief him on the trailer rules: that we had equal responsibility for having the trailer ready for transport and set-up from one town to the next, shared the expense of cooking gas and electric, and washed the exterior when needed. Not that I had to worry, but another rule was he could not fuck any local sluts in the trailer, which Jed frowned upon. My own rules were that he shared the cleaning, showered and did his laundry regularly. "I don't live like a pig and I expect the same from you." I said.

"Hell, Phil, that's the least ya need to worry about with me."

"Let's hope so."

We stayed up half the night partying before turning in. Jed would be sleeping in the bunk above my bed. Anyway. I took a quick shower and got into bed as Jed showered. When he come out of the bathroom all he had on was a towel cinched around his hips and my cock was ready to rip through my briefs under the covers. Man, what a sight! Massive chest, powerful legs and arms, flat, ripped abs a true hunk of prime beef! From the bulge pushing out the towel, my guess about him packing a lot and showing little had been right. I could just decipher the shaft of his cock and the crown of the head before he turned off the light. When my eyes finally adjusted to the sudden darkness there was just enough light coming in through the window by my bed that I got a good shadowy look at his big cock and balls, to reach the bunk he had to step up on my bed and hoist himself up, and as he was doing so the towel fell to the floor. Momentarily, all his goodies, hips to toes, were suspended within hand's reach before he made it up into bed.

I think I audibly gasped, "Ja-ll...."

"Did I wake you, Phil?" he asked.

"No."

"I think we'll have to find a stool or something so I'm not stepping on your bed all the time."

"It doesn't bother me. You gonna be all right up there?"

"Without a doubt. Phil?"

"What?"

"I haven't said it yet, but, thanks for letting me move in."

Things went on as usual for a couple of months. Jed liked sleeping in the nude and hanging around the trailer in his briefs, and now and again I'd get a glimpse of his bare assets as he got into bed or left the bathroom after a shower. The least I went around in was my briefs or a towel securely around my waist, nothing short of torture. All Jed need to do was touch me and he could have bent me to his will and use. The most it got the was a mountain of teasing once he realized what my secret passion was.

It all started when Bob and I left on a two-day business trip. Early that morning I had put fresh sheets on my bed, because it was Jed's turn to do the laundry. I also made him promise not to bring a girl in while I was gone. By then I was keeping an eye out for him once or twice a month.

When Bob and I got back to the show Jed was still out on the prowl. I took a shower and went to turn in, only to find a very pleasant surprise waiting for me. No, it wasn't Jed, but close enough. Naturally whenever he bedded a local slut he used my bed, so the standing rule was that he changed the sheets upon finishing. He'd kept his promise of not fucking in my bed, but, I came home to find "someone" had been sleeping in my bed! And left his intoxicating musk lingering upon the sheets and pillow.

Before Jed returned I pulled the covers up over my head, worked three fingers up my ass and stroked off to an explosive, glorious finish, all the while deep-breathing Jed's heavy musk. (All right, go ahead, call me a pig! I deserve it. I also wanted Jed to fuck me silly but was too scared, in fear of rejection, to make the first move.)

The following morning, Bob stopped in as usual and announced we could have the days to ourselves until we opened for business. I offered to make breakfast but Bob declined and soon left. So I went to the task of making some for myself, while also knowing the smell of food would bring Jed running. As soon as things got going in the frying pan Jed's voice came from the bedroom. "Got enough for two?" he asked.

"Hurry up, or you'll be left licking the plate!" Jed's feet hit the floor with a "thump" and he dashed to park his ass at the table, naked as the day he was born.

"Jed?!" I yelled in surprise.

"What?!"

"I was only kidding. The least you could've done was taken time to pull on your shorts."

"When it comes to food and women I don't kid around, and it's not like you haven't seen me nude before. I've caught you looking!"

"Now, that's bullshit!"

"The only thing that's 'bullshit' around here, is you. And I'm not as dumb as you want to believe I am. I know more than you think."

"So just what is it you think you know?"

"It didn't take much to add two and two. You're a good-looking guy and half the girls on the lot would jump your bones, but you never give any of them the chance."

"Have you taken a close look at half of them?"

"All right, I know what you mean, but that doesn't explain why ya don't at least have a pretty one for a steady. If you're not hanging out with the guys, you're working all the time. Then after I moved in and started catching all the looks you thought you were sneaking, the rest of the pieces fell into place."

Yeah, Jed wise to me. "So what did it all add up to?"

"You're a fag under cover. But don't take that the wrong way; it doesn't bother me any and it don't make you are a bad person." After a pause he smiled and added, "Now, are ya gonna put something on a plate or let all that food burn up?"

Like I said, there was a mountain of teasing to follow. So much, in fact, that during the next town-jump we made Jed bought himself a jock strap to hang around the trailer in, or he'd go without once he drew all the curtains closed. Eventually he started with the touchy-feely crap and I'd easily cool his heels by saying that if he wasn't serious then, "don't start whatcha don't intend on finishing." Then one day it all came to an abrupt end.

In early September Jed sneaked a local slut back to the trailer during business hours, never taking the time to find me in order to be the lookout, and ended up getting caught with his pants down. Naturally, he blamed me, but at the time I was on the other end of the fairgrounds having dinner. But truth be known, had he just stuffed a sock in her mouth then all her hysterical yammerings would not have brought on all the attention he ended up with.

That first night alone in the trailer I slept in Jed's bunk and ended up crying myself to sleep. By the third week of October I was going crazy living alone and took the risk of hooking up with a deaf boy in a small North Carolina town, and for four nights in a row it was nothing short of magic nor shy of heavenly bliss.

When we reached our next destination there was a noticeable spring back in my steps. At least for a couple of days, before another spell of bad luck fell on our heads.

During one of our town-jumps the owner of Sleeman's hired a local trucker, which was the wrong thing to do without a thorough background check. The guy lost control of the rig going down a steep hill, one that he should not have been on in the first place, and jumped out of the cab before it swept the side of a house and destroyed a garage with two cars in it. At one point the ride trailer was ripped free, had rolled down an embankment, scattering the many parts of the ride over three back yards. Come to find out the driver had his license revoked two weeks before. And guess who they put in charge of the clean-up: me, the newest foreman! Man, I was ready to chew nails and spit nickels! After driving all night towing equipment to the next lot, I was sleep walking and half dead on my feet. But that was only the start of my troubles.

During assembly at the next location the floor of the bumper cars dropped with a "bang," sending a plume of dust fifty feet in the air. No one was hurt or killed, fortunately. The next catastrophe came during tear-down when they placed the lowering cable wrong on the Ferris wheel and collapsed a set of spokes with half the wheel still in the air.

I was packing up another ride when Bob came to get me, and I was more than ready to tear a few heads off because all the trouble with the equipment was on account of having far too many "green helpers," and hot shot wannabe's. "Who you got in mind that can handle the wheel without anyone getting killed?" Bob asked.

"Just you and me, asshole, because nobody else on this fuckin' show knows what the hell they're doing! I'm getting fed up with this shit!" I yelled.

"C'mon, I know how you feel, but I'm serious. We gotta get the damn thing down, so we can get the generators to the next spot, and I want to follow them with our trailers."

"Just leave my trailer where it sits...."

"You'll never get it in later."

"Then I'll park the damn thing on the road. Leave me the tractor with the small unit, change the wheel over to it, and I'll see ya at the next lot whenever."

"I've sent word down to winter quarters to send up another truck, so when it reaches us I'll send it back to pick your trailer up. So who do you want for a crew?"

I gave Bob four names and told him to "do whatever" with the crew who screwed up the wheel in the first place. It took us eight hours to lower the rest of the ride to its trailer. By then the sun had been up for a good four and I must have drunk close to five pots of coffee through the night. When the wheel was ready to go I held it up long enough so I could at least get a hot shower. One of the guys offered to unhook the electric and water lines to my trailer and got it ready to leave whenever the extra truck arrived. He even offered to stay behind with me, which I'm sure could have led to other things, but I sent the four of them down the road with the ride.

It couldn't have been more than an hour later that a knock came at the door of the trailer. When I opened the door I was greeted with, "Hi ya, honey. Heard you were waiting to get picked up!"

"What in hell are you doing here?!" I asked in surprise. It was one of our past workers, Sherry, who had left the show when she got word her father had died. "I'd thought you'd left for good."

"Hell, no! After putting up with my mother for a month that bitch, I split down to winter quarters. I've been down there getting things ready the past two months, waiting for you guys to pull in, then Bob called needing a truck and, well, here I am again. Did ya miss me?"

"You know better 'n to ask that...." Yeah, I had missed her. She had been my left-hand man around the show, could swing iron with the best of us, and my evil, little show-sister who couldn't make up her mind what she liked more cock or pussy. I was about to ask her what had become of her last girlfriend, when I nearly fell on my ass with a sudden lurch of the trailer. "What the fuck?!"

"Oh, that's just Animal hookin' ya up to the truck," Sherry said.

"Who in hell's Animal?"

"My asshole of a boyfriend," she said, then yelled towards the truck, "You stupid fuck! Next time tell somebody when you're gonna hitch up!"

A male's voice answered with: "Do your talking on the road, I wanna get the hell out of here."

Suddenly, it was if a block of ice filled my stomach. The voice sounded familiar. Can't be, I told myself, as he's been gone for months and you're just wishing. But before I could jump out the door, to look for myself, Sherry moved to come inside.

"You about ready to roll?" she asked as I stepped further inside.

"Just need to pack the coffee maker."

"Well get with it, before ants-in-his-pants gets really bitchy." I went about doing so as she kept talking. "Now, Phil. You know I love you and all, but I gotta set a few things straight."

"Such as...?"

"Well, for starters, Animal doesn't know about that other half of me and I haven't swung that way since we met. So, what he doesn't know or finds out from you can't hurt 'im any."

"I hear yah, zip the lips."

"Yeah. Another problem might be you."

"Meaning?"

"Well, not to hurt your feelings, but keep your fuckin' hands off him."

"Oh come now, give me a break."

"No, I mean it. And you'll know what I'm talking about when you meet 'im."

From outside came, "Come on, you two, let's get rollin'!"

That voice again made me feel dizzy, even more so when the trailer dipped to the side the door was on and Sherry's boyfriend stepped through it. My heart skipped a few beats and I plopped down into the table seat for fear of falling on my face. It was Animal. Or rather, Jed!

"Phil, are you all right?" Sherry asked.

"I think he's just seen a ghost, Sherry," Jed said and added, "Long time no see, buddy."

Deep down I wanted to leap into Jed's arms. Had Sherry not been there, I would have. But all I was able to do at the time was say, "Same here, Jed."

"You two know one another?" Sherry asked looking from Jed to me and back.

"Yeah, Phil and I were trailer-mates for a while, until I screwed up and got shipped down to our winter quarters."

Jed and I weren't really able to talk until we arrived at the next lot, when Sherry went off in search of Bob. During the drive there I had picked up on enough vibes from Jed that I should watch what I said with Sherry around, because there was a lot he hadn't told her about himself. And he even apologized for blaming me when he got caught and canned.

That same week Bob decided it was time he sent his trailer ahead of us down to our winter quarters, and trailer-mate with me. Which I really didn't mind, because it was like old times: my first year with Sleeman's I lived with Bob in his trailer until his wife and kids came out on the road for the summer months. We were also nearing the end of another season, and as we moved closer to it, the places where we set the show up were getting smaller and smaller by the week so having less to tow from one spot to the next saved money. Anyway, Bob moved his things in but it took another two weeks before his trailer made it to Florida. The guy who was supposed to tow it for him kept coming up with excuses not to, so I finally convinced Bob into doing it himself and taking three days to spend Thanksgiving with his family. You can say Bob and I had a better than normal employer-employee relationship, but that's another story.

Bob knew full well that Sherry, Jed and I were the best of friends, just as I knew of his dislike of them. So the morning he left with his trailer, and on account of his personal things being in mine, being the boss too, he left stern orders that neither Sherry nor Jed was allowed in the trailer for any reason. And I had every intention of following that law. Well, at least my intentions were good. How did I know Mother Nature would work against me?

Later that day, it started raining and then it was as if Hoover Dam had burst over our heads. At times it rained so hard you couldn't see two feet in front of you and the lot quickly turned into one giant bowl of slop. I was praying they wouldn't open the show. But they did. An hour or so before opening the rain stopped, customers began arriving and we had some heavy business for a while, until a severe thunderstorm moved in upon us. And I hated working in that type of weather, on or near a ride, because you never knew (and wouldn't) when, "Zzzzzap!" you're history.

It wasn't until around 10:30 that Sleeman finally closed us down, after I pointed out the clear fact for the second time that there were no people on the lot but his own and we were washed out for the day. When I left the office trailer Jed and Sherry were waiting outside, huddling under a split-open garbage bag, like a couple of drowned rats. They wanted me to join them at the show's hospitality tent.

I was about the only semi-dry person in the tent, having worn my rain poncho most of the day. But as usual, everyone there was light and cheery aside from being soaked through to the bone. Jed and I sat in on a few hands of cards, while Sherry did our service as waitress, and the time just flew past. It had also started raining heavily again, and a miniature river flowed through the tent. By around one in the morning I was feeling my drinks and made mention of turning in shortly. The three of us were standing off to one side and Sherry insisted on another round before I left and as she went to get our drinks, Jed stepped closer to bend my ear. "Think you could put us up for the night, buddy. Where we sleep everything we got is soaked through," he said.

"Bob'll kill me if I let you in the trailer. I really can't."

"Come on, man. I wouldn't be asking if there was one dry place around, but there ain't none. We just need a dry place to sleep a few hours, please?"

I knew I should have kicked myself, but Jed's little-boy pleading hit me where I lived. "All right, but the both of you are out before ten," I said. Next thing I knew Jed was grabbing me in a bear hug. Then he kissed me on the neck. Thank God I pushed him off me when I did, because I saw Sherry returning with our drinks. But there was one close-call I didn't miss.

Walking to my trailer I wasn't paying much attention to my steps. Right beside it was a hole for a new phone pole and, with all the rain we got, the area was one big puddle. Taking for granted I was clear of it, I found where that hole was. One minute I was walking between Jed and Sherry and the next, my head was at their feet with the poncho spread out around my head. Yeah, Sherry nearly pissed her pants over my little funny as Jed picked me up out of that hole like a rag doll.

Inside the trailer Sherry dashed for the bathroom, while Jed and I converted the kitchen table into a bed with my sleeping bag and an extra blanket. Then there was a sudden wave of shyness, because no one would undress until the lights were out. I was in bed only a few minutes when the seas started rolling, and it wasn't due to the amount of drink I'd had that night. Jed was fucking Sherry hard enough to rock the trailer. I lay there in my bed with the desire to join them, or at least try to, but the farthest I got was to sit up and jerk off while watching them. A couple of times Jed stopped and looked towards the bedroom, and I froze each time praying he couldn't see me in the darkness, which he couldn't.

Yes, I wanted more than anything to be in Sherry's place with Jed above me, but I stood my ground. But just the thought of it being so and watching Jed's ass rise and fall with every thrust into her, was enough to set my balls boiling so I was ready to cum my ass off in seconds. When I got too close I released my throbbing cock to cool off and started again, holding off long enough until I saw Jed was filling her up and I came right along with him, right into my hand.

It was just after nine in the morning when I woke up to the smell of coffee. I managed to push up on an elbow, my head pounding, to glance into the kitchen to find Sherry pulling my poncho over her head. She saw I was up and came back to my bed to say that I had nothing in the refrigerator. "So I thought I'd run down to the store for a few things to go with the coffee," she said in a hushed voice. "You don't mind, do you?"

"No, not at all, just as long as you're not hanging out here all day. If word gets back to Bob my ass is grass."

"He'll never know about it."

"For my sake I hope not. Where's Jed?"

"He's still sleeping after last night, you know?"

"Yeah, I know."

"We didn't keep you up, did we?"

"I was out the second my head hit the pillow." Which was a lie. "You need some extra money?"

"I should have enough, but it's my treat for you letting us stay the night. I shouldn't be gone more than a half hour see you then."

I lay back down for a while before Jed stirred and got up to use the bathroom. So I got up myself and pulled on a fresh pair of briefs, before heading to the coffee pot.

As I was passing the bathroom door Jed was on his way out, almost knocking me over. He grabbed me by the arm to steady me. "Sorry 'bout that," he said, standing in all his naked glory. "Me being here's like old time."

"Sort of, but not quite the same."

He released my arm. "What's the matter, you don't like me anymore?"

"It's nothing like that, I just have a headache after last night. Sherry left to pick up some things for breakfast. You have coffee yet?"

"That's what I got up for."

"Well, before you do anything I suggest you pull your pants on. It wouldn't look all that good if she walked in to see you naked in front of me."

"To hell with what she would think. Who cares?"

"I do, because she's also my friend."

"Party pooper," he said, reaching for his soggy jeans. "Seeing me nude never bothered you before."

"A lot has changed between then and now."

"Yeah, you've become a prick."

"And you've become the boyfriend to a friend of mine, in case you've forgotten." I filled two mugs with coffee then started the task of converting their temporary bed back into a table. As I was doing so Jed locked his arms around me from behind. "Jed, let me go!" I struggled to get free but he increased his hold on me.

"Did you get off on the show last night?"

"No, I did not! Now, let go of me!"

"Bullshit! I couldn't see you but I knew you were watching. Why do you think I kept stopping and looking up?"

"I don't care...."

"The hell you don't. I kept stopping thinking you would come and join in, that's why."

"I couldn't do that to Sherry."

"She would've loved it, taking both of us on, and was willing to do it. I even asked her if she would be into it and she said yes."

"Jed, why are you telling me this?"

"Because I wanted you to join in last night, you stupid fuck, for me!"

"Jed, don't do this to me. You don't want me."

"Like hell I don't!" he said and spun me around to face him. Forcing my chin up with a hand so I'd look at him, he added, "I'm only using Sherry as a way to reach you, and last night, by not coming to join in you really fucked my head up."

194

"Fuck you, you bastard!"

"I know you don't mean that, but I should've fucked you a long time ago."

"You had your chance back then, but this is now and you're with Sherry. So forget it!"

"I can't forget it. Now that I'm back on the show, every time I see you, I'm reminded I was too stupid to jump your ass back then. Why do you think I kept teasing you so much and practically begged you to let me move in, for that matter?"

"All that's history, in the past, so leave it where it lies."

"You don't know what you're saying."

"The fuck I don't! You're the one who's talkin' shit."

"Then I guess I'll have to prove it to you," he said, before his lips were pressed to mine.

I tried pushing him off me but the more I struggled, the more his kiss deepened and the stronger he held on to me. When his tongue pushed past my teeth and entered my mouth, my emotional reserve crumbled. Twisting my head to one side, to separate our mouths, I sobbed: "Oh God, Jed, don't do this to me now!"

My head was in a tailspin. Things were moving entirely too fast. There were so many things stacked against the prospect of starting, let alone maintaining, a deeper relationship with Jed, Bob was sharing the trailer with me, Sherry would kill me in cold blood because to have Jed meant to have him completely in my life and shared intimately with no one else. And what was going to happen when the show finally moved into winter-quarters at the close of the season? I was holding onto the counter to steady myself as tears left my eyes, trembling head to foot, trying to contain the sobs that pained my throat. Jed's arms came around me from behind, pressing himself along my back as they closed tighter around me. "Come on, Phil, don't fight it. You want me just as much as I want you," he said with his mouth at my right ear. He rubbed the fat tube of his denim-covered cock into the crack of my ass and began nibbling on my neck. My cock fully extended to its maximum eight inches and felt as if ready to split trapped between me and the counter with Jed's additional weight pressing from behind.

"Jed, stop it! We can't do this! Sherry's likely to walk in any moment, and then what?"

He released me and went to the curtained window. "Shit!" he said, letting the curtain fall back into place. "She's almost to the door."

"See what I mean? Start converting the table," I said, and moved towards the back of the trailer to fetch my jeans. But Jed grabbed my arm and held a clenched fist to my chin.

"One word to Sherry ... I'm warnin' you," he seethed.

They finally left around noon. By then my nerves were at their fragile ends, pretending nothing was amiss in front of Sherry. I barely said anything to Jed the whole time, and he was pissed. On his was out the door all he said was, "I'll see you later."

I didn't encounter Jed until I was making my rounds giving dinner breaks to the crew. Normally, I'd have broken with Jed after Sherry, but that night I left him for last. Coming off his ride he had one word for me, "Prick!" When he finally returned, five minutes late, he asked if we could talk. I just stepped around him and went about my business. After we closed for the night I made the mistake of going to the hospitality tent for a stiff drink. A few minutes behind me Jed and Sherry walked in. I chatted with her, while Jed went to the bar for their drinks. When he joined us, I downed the rest of my drink and left.

It was around two in the morning when I concluded the day's bookkeeping and had just put things away when a knock came at the door. Such early knocks meant trouble. I opened the door and there stood Jed, stinking drunk on his feet with a can of beer in one hand. Agitated, I said, "What do you want?"

"You're treatin' me like shit, Phil," he slurred, followed by a sloppy swig of beer more of it soaking his beard than ending up in his mouth. "And I don't like it one bit."

"Jed. You're drunk and crazy. Go to bed."

"Yeah, maybe I am. So fuckin' what?" Then he added, "But I ain't going to bed."

"Then go away and leave me alone."

"C'mon, man, I just wanna talk."

"We can talk all you want later."

"I wanna talk now. Can I come in?"

"No, you can't."

"Why not?"

"It's late, I'm tired and you're drunk. Just go to bed and we'll talk all ya want later, okay?"

"No, it's not okay! I wanna talk now!" he said loudly and threw his beer away. "And I ain't leavin' till you let me in, dammit!"

Jed glanced to the ground, then left and right, then up at me. "Are ya gonna let me in so's we can talk?"

"No."

"Then I'll just make ya let me in," he said and started pulling up his T-shirt.

"Jed, you stop it. You're not coming in, and I mean it!"

He said nothing until he stood bare-chested and bare-footed, with both hands at the waist front of his jeans. "You gonna let me in?"

I didn't respond.

"Suit yourself," he said and in seconds he undid and pushed his jeans down to his ankles.

I jumped out the door and shoved him before he stood up. He landed on his ass and sprawled on the ground. "You stupid fuck, I'll have your ass fired for this!" I yelled, not caring who heard me.

Jed kicked out of his jeans and got to his feet, naked as the day he was born. "I don't care! If you don't let me in I'm gonna streak through the lot and the center of town, and when I'm arrested it'll be your fault!"

"Bullshit!" was the wrong thing to say to him. Nothing like aggravating things further!

Jed turned and ran towards the midway. For half a second I stalled then took off in a dead run after him. I zipped out from behind the Glass House to find Jed leaning back against the fence with elbows resting on top, just standing there cool as a cucumber. "Hi, how ya doin'?" was all he got out before my fist connected with his solar plexus, knocking the wind out of him and dropping him to his knees clutching his stomach. He recovered quickly, tackled me at the legs, and I went sprawling on to my ass with Jed on top of me. I punched him in the face and he backed off, then he let fly at me and I thought for sure he'd broken my jaw. "I was only kidding, you stupid fuck!" he seethed at me.

Stupefied, I lay there slowly working my jaw with a hand until the shock faded. Twisting onto my stomach I crawled out from under him, and the heel of my foot swiped his balls.

"Shit!" he gasped, clutching the injury as I got to my feet.

"If you'd just take no for an answer, none of this shit would be happening, you asshole!" Turning, I headed back to the trailer.

As I got to the door someone called out asking if I was all right. I said I was. Only one other trailer was near me, within fifty yards, and the lights went out in it after my response. I cursed Jed under my breath for bringing on the unwanted attention. It was then that he ambled around the side of the trailer as I collected his discarded clothes. "Phil?"

"Shut up, and get your ass inside!" I seethed and followed him inside carrying his clothes. "I don't want or need any more trouble out of you."

Pulling the door closed behind me, I threw his clothes at him as he sat down in the seat at the table. My boot caught him in the head and his arm came up in delayed reaction. After the damage had been done, he swept the rest of his things onto the floor and sat with his arms folded on the table.

I wanted to kick the shit out of him, but I was no match for him in size or physical strength. Besides, the last thing I needed was to explain to Bob how his trailer got trashed.

I started the coffee maker and went to the bathroom for a wet washcloth, because I'd split Jed's lower lip. As he tended his lip I removed the coffee pot from its hot-plate and set a mug in its place. When it was full I set it in front of Jed. "When you finish that, get dressed and get the hell out of here."

Looking up to me he said, "I just wanted to talk. Can't you at least give me that?"

I sat down across from him with my own coffee. "So talk already. We've got all fuckin' night."

After a moment to collect his thoughts he started with, "I meant what I said before, before Sherry got back here."

"And did you hear a word I said?"

"I did, but I thought things between us would pick up from where they'd been left off...." And he carried on and on about how he couldn't stop thinking about me after he was shipped to winter-quarters (when I had thought he'd been fired and not laid off), and then meeting Sherry and hearing all about me through her, who he liked a lot, but didn't love.

"...I know I'm a rotten bastard for using her like I am, and I was about ready to look for work elsewhere; then Bob called needing that truck and I was the only one around. So I came out thinking...well...now I'm kicking myself in the head because I didn't have enough balls, back then, to really tell ya how I felt about ya.

"I also know that I teased the hell out of you but, at first, it was just fun and games to break up the time. I mean, your being gay never bothered me because I've had other gay friends. Then all that teasing got to me and I had to ask myself just where it was leading me. Anyway. Down in winter-quarters I met a local guy, one thing led to another, and it just happened. Or rather, I wanted it to. And it was nice, but, it wasn't right."

"Why not?"

"Because the whole time we was doing it, I was thinkin' he was you. And, now, you're acting as though you can't stand the sight of me and hate my guts."

As he stared down into his coffee, moments slipped past until I finally broke the eerie, dead silence.

"Jed, I never said I hated you."

"The way you act towards me says otherwise."

"Well how else am I suppose to act with all the shit you've been dumping on me, and doing especially tonight?"

"After the stunt I've pulled tonight, no different than you've been acting like," he said with an impish smirk, which brought pain to his damaged lip. "Damn, I never knew you could hit so hard."

"There's a lot you don't know about me. But piss me off enough, you find out some of those things the hard way."

"As I've already learned," he said, dabbing his lip with the washcloth.

"Yeah, well, play with fire you get burned. I'm lucky to have any teeth left in my mouth."

"Guess we should stop playing around before we end up killing each other."

"You want more coffee?"

"Yeah, but I need to use the can first."

"Help yourself." A moment later Jed called from the bathroom. "Hey, you think I'll need a stitch in this mess?"

Going to the door where Jed was bent at the waist as he examined his lip in the mirror over the sink, my breath caught in my throat at the view. There it was, his big, glorious bubble-butt, the one and the same , that had kept me with a hard-on most of the day when we first met. Only this time there wasn't any denim hiding its beauty. My dick started twitching in my jeans but I knew it was simply too dangerous. "Come on, let me have a look," I said.

Jed turned to face me and I took the washcloth to dab the cut on his lip. With my thumbs on either side I gently spread the cut to see how deep it really was. Jed yowled like a little boy. "Hey, that hurts!"

"Oh, grow up. It's just a surface cut and you'll live till the next one comes along. I'll get you a piece of ice to hold on it."

"I just hope the next time it isn't you again."

"Keep fuckin' around and it just might be." I went back to sit at the table ahead of Jed and instead of sitting across from me, he slid into the same side with me. Pushed into the corner I said, "Jed, drink your coffee, get dressed and get out of here. Now go sit on the other side!"

"I'm just sittin' here." Too close for my comfort. "But I'm not leaving till we finish this talk."

"So get on with it. But I'm warnin' you, any funny stuff and I'll knock your fuckin' block off!"

"Why won't you give me a chance?" Jed asked, turning in the seat to better face me, which also brought his cock out into view.

"Because it won't work."

"And why not?"

"Because I know it won't."

"You're not answering the question."

"All right, it won't work because you haven't totally made up your mind about which you're going to be, and your being with Sherry, even using her for the time, is proof of that. Another reason is, if I do give in I don't want a once-in-a-while fling. Now do you understand?"

"I think I do, but what exactly are you saying?"

"Shit, Jed, are you really that dumb? You weren't the only one lackin' the balls at making the first move when the opportunity was at our feet. I was scared you'd reject me, so I left well enough alone. Then you got caught fuckin' around, blamed me for your stupidity, and then you were gone." Tears rolled down my cheeks by then. "This trailer folded in around me and I got crazy enough to break some rules myself, because I was so lonely. I missed you more than I could admit. A whole lotta shit happened since then and now you're back wanting to pick up as if nothing's happened, and it's all the same again. And it isn't!" I thumbed my eyes clear before adding, "I wouldn't have shared you with anyone back then, and I doubt I can do it now."

"So eventually it has to be all or nothing?"

"My point exactly."

Jed got up and pulled his jeans on with his back to me. When he picked up the T-shirt I glanced up with a notion of telling him to stay, but let it float away. With one arm in the shirt, Jed stopped and glanced over his shoulder a moment, then pulled it off, flung it aside as he turned toward me. I thought he'd break my arm as he grabbed it and pulled me to my feet and into his powerful arms and embrace. "This night's only started," Jed said, as his mouth came to mine.

Weakly, I put up a small struggle, as if attempting to push him away. But Jed wasn't about to be persuaded, nor did I want him to be. He pushed back with greater strength until I was walking backwards towards the bedroom. Feebly I kept up an ounce of resistance. Jed thwarted by picking me up off the floor. Feet dangling, he carried me to the bed and pushed me down upon it. I raised up on both elbows and he stopped me there with an extended arm and pointing finger. "Move another inch and I'll knock your block off!" he said sternly. At least he didn't say fuckin' block.

As Jed lowered his jeans, his aroused cock sprang up and slapped his lower stomach with an audible "Thwack." I'd felt it rubbing against my ass earlier that same day, knew he was packing something extremely large and stiff. But even feels provesto be misleading, especially in Jed's case. Words fail on how to go about describing the sight before me, but I'll try. The weight of his cock and length kept it from rising higher than forty-five degrees off his body; it bobbed and swayed with his every heartbeat, thick as a baby's arm, fat, neatly cut, easily topping nine-inches in length, with a head that was larger than the shaft about the size of a baby's fist. I laid there gaping, excited yet fearful at the same time; it was easily the biggest damn cock I'd ever seen!

"What's the matter, Phil, ain't you ever seen another guy's dick before?" Jed asked, obviously immensely proud of his equipment.

"Well, yeah, but, shit! Nothing of your size."

"Don't worry, I won't let it hurt you."

"No, you're gonna kill me with that thing!" And I wasn't kidding.

Jed gave a chuckle and then proceeded to strip me down. He parted my knees, stood between them, then with his hands on either side of me, lowered himself till just our cocks were touching. A quiver raked my body as if jolted with electric shocks. He rubbed our cocks together while supporting his weight on his hands, then glanced up with a smile and asked if I liked what he was doing.

I reached up and pulled him down on top of me. "Jed, this is no time to be teasing or fuckin' around."

Jed kissed me passionately. My arms went around him to draw him as close as possible. He pushed his knees up under mine and he half-dragged me farther up on the bed so he could stretch out full-length on top of me.

I sucked his tongue when it entered my mouth, so intensely that he pulled away. "Damn! First ya bust my lip open and now, you wanna suck the tongue right out of my mouth."

"If I do, I might change my mind."

"Well, at least slow down and take it easy."

Jed pecked me on the lips before moving to my neck. Aside from the little kisses, nips and licks, that beard of his was tickling the hell out of me.

By the time he reached my left nipple, which he sucked and gnawed to rawness, and moved to the other, to leave it in similar condition, I was jumping and thrashing with every swipe of his whiskers. When I protested about more nipple torture, Jed just moved directly down to my throbbing cock and swallowed me in one lunge. It happened so swiftly and completely that I sat up in surprise, but he was having none of that and pushed me back down on the bed.

Sucking like a hungry calf at its mother's tit, Jed had me teetering on the edge of blasting off in under a minute. "Jed, I'm gonna cum if you don't let up!" I warned. He swallowed me to the balls and stopped moving, then flexed his tongue along my cum tube as he slowly, nerve-shatteringly, sucked and raised his head up and off my sensitive cockhead with a sucking pop. The sensations were so intense that when my cock slapped down on my belly I nearly went over the edge, which is where Jed kept me, on that sharp pain-and-pleasure edge of almost coming, yet not quite there, for what seemed like hours.

As I fought against the urge to come, Jed didn't waste a precious second in allowing me to cool off too quickly. He grabbed me behind the knees and hoisted them up and over my chest. I held my knees to my chest, and lunged his face into the crack of my ass. "Oh, fuck!" I gasped and used my hands to pull away from him.

"And where do ya think you're goin'?" Jed asked with his hairy chin resting on top of my asshole. He folded his arms over the backs of my thighs and hugged my lower back to his chest, as he sat on the bed and pushed his feet out up my sides to lock his heels over my shoulders. In effect, he had me pinned with no place to go without bringing him with me. Looking down at me between my calves, he smirked devilishly, dipped his chin and pressed his lips to my anus.

I've been rimmed plenty of times but nothing compared to how and what Jed did to me. He started poking my hole with just the tip of his tongue as if fucking with a miniature dick, and it felt good. "Do me, Jed! Eat my ass!" I said, while caressing his thighs and opening up to his swirling tongue.

Jed raised his head from my ass long enough to move his feet to the insides of my legs, heels still at my shoulders but my legs to the outside of his. Moving his hands to my ass he spread my hole open with his fingertips, then thrust his tongue as far up me as he could like trying to dig the meat out of a stubborn clam. With his tongue in me, he sealed his lips around my anus and sucked the crinkles of the ass lip smooth and into his mouth. He started turning his head this way and that and that damn beard came into full play. The more he stroked and brushed me with it, the more sensitive my ass became. After a few minutes it was as though every nerve ending suddenly move into my ass and I was being driven crazy, thrashing my head side to side, gasping and moaning, until I couldn't stand it anymore.

I reached up and took hold of his head with my hands, and pushed with my thumbs at his cheeks to raise his mouth off my ass. "Jed, stop! I can't take anymore!"

"What's the matter?"

"You know damn well what the matter is you're driving me fuckin' crazy!"

He took hold of my throbbing cock and I swatted him off. "Don't!" I said.

"Why not?" he asked with a crooked grin.

"Because ya got me so fuckin' hot and bothered I'm ready to bust, that's why!"

Jed lowered his mouth to my balls, moving them around in their sac with his light kissing and tongue before drawing one and then the other into his mouth, closing his lips around the sac and pulling until the tension/pain on my balls became too much to handle. Then he started working his hairy chin over my abused and super-sensitive hole. I grabbed him by the ears in frustration, and pulled until he finally caught on and moved up between my legs. "All right, let go of my ears! It's not like I don't know what I'm doing to you!" he hollered. Then kissed me.

He rose up on his hands. "Sorry I lost my head, but with an ass that tastes as good as yours I just can't get enough it goes right to my head."

"You're not gonna have one if you don't stop when I tell you to! You're driving me nuts!" He started moving towards my hips and I took hold of his head. "Oh, no you don't! You get back up here and stay a while longer."

"Oh, c'mon, you can handle a little more. Please? And I promise to stop when you say so."

"All right. But if you don't stop when I say so, I'll be spending the rest of my life in a nuthouse." Giving in to him was my demise. Well, not exactly, but it sure came close.

Foggy-headed me thought Jed was just going to eat a little more ass. Stupid me! That pig went right back to where I interrupted him and, damn him, wouldn't stop nor let up until I was crying and pleading. The least he needed to do was blow over my ass, never mind the lips, tongue and sinful beard, to practically have me coming apart at the seams. When he finally stopped of his own will a long rasp of breath left my lungs, along with every ounce of energy. Like a rag doll, I was washed out and putty in his hands. "Jed! You're killing me!" I yelled.

"I'm not gonna stop until you beg me," he said, and rubbed his beard into my ass.

"All right!" I jumped and thrashed. "Please! No more! Please, Jed, no more!"

"Not good enough." And he again attacked my ass.

I grabbed fistfuls of blond hair and yanked to get him to stop, but he just fought to keep his mouth glued to my hole and growled from deep in his throat. It was then I realized how he got the name of Animal, because it was exactly how he was carrying on. "Jed!" I screamed.

He raised he head from my ass. "What?"

By then I was drenched in sweat from the strain and struggle of trying to make him stop his maddening torture. Panting like an overworked horse, I screamed, "Jed! Please! Stop it!"

"Then say it," he said, coming up for air, only to park his hairy chin on top of my super-sensed hole.

"Jeeesus!" I gasped. "Stop it! I've been saying so all along, but you won't listen!"

"You're not saying what I wanna hear."

"Then what in hell am I suppose to say?!"

"Never mind," he said. And then attacked me again.

To say the least, by then, I wasn't in any shape to be thinking logically. All my circuits were being shorted out by a relentless beast. My entire ass, hips to hole, was on fire and I couldn't think straight if my life depended on it. And then, suddenly, there was a little glimmer of focus and the doorbell rang!

"Jed!" I screamed as his teeth raked my ass lips.

"Now what is it? If you don't stop yelling so much the whole town will hear ya."

"Fuck the town! Now get up here and fuck me!"

"What was that?"

"Jed, I need you! Please, do it. Do it now!"

"That's what I've been waitin' ta hear," he said and kissed my anal lips once more, before moving up between my trembling legs.

With my knees at his shoulders, Jed slowly bent me double until he touched my chest. Holding my head with his hands, Jed used his legs and hips to position the head of his massive cock at my spit-drenched, bloated hole. At the first touch I violently trembled, head-to-foot, in both fear and need, fear that he would rip me to shreds going in and need, because I wanted him in me so badly.

Passionately we kissed as he applied the slightest pressure, the sphincter yielded, expanded, and stretched to welcome his large cockhead. Pain and pressure slowly built, increased, as the anal ring resisted, unaccustomed to anything so imposing. Then, suddenly, the crown of Jed's baby-fist cockhead broke through the barrier, the sphincter snapped tightly closed around the neck, and stars danced behind my closed eyelids, as pain ripped through my middle like a bolt of white lightening. Jed was in me!

As I sucked air through my teeth, my hands flew to his hips to halt further passage. "Oh, God!" I said in a gasping howl. "Jed, don't move! I can't do this!"

"Easy, baby," he soothed and closed his arms tighter around me. "You've got me and I won't move."

I kept pushing at his hip until he took hold of my hands and brought them up back behind my head, holding them to the mattress with laced fingers. "Jed, don't! You're gonna kill me with that thing!"

"No, I'm not! You can do it." He kissed me a while, then asked, "You don't want me?"

"No...I mean, yes...I don't know! I need more than just spit and even then, you're likely to rip my asshole out!"

"I have no intentions of doing that, and I'm not pulling out. You just relax...."

Jed soothed me enough with his words, caresses, and kisses that I was able to slip into a state of limbo.

He took his time and stopped when the pain became too intense. Pushing in and withdrawing little by little, wetting the shaft of his prick, he began filling me up, taxing my limits.

I felt as though I were taking on a telephone pole; there seemed to be no end to the long shaft of his cock. I thought I would split in half when he reached a depth, better than halfway in, that my colon gripped him tightly and he could not move in or out. He settled his weight down on top of me like a comforting, warm blanket as we kissed and cuddled until I could relax. But I couldn't.

My lips were becoming raw and Jed's beard chafed my face, the colon-grip upon him all built to frustration. Jed was in me. No doubt about that. I had him, but I really didn't have him completely. I grabbed hold of his ass, dug my fingers into his cheeks, and forced the rest of him into me. The pain was like nothing I'd felt before, but I had Jed in me with his balls pressed to my lower spine. "Are you crazy?!" Jed gasped in surprise.

I'd been ripped before and I knew I was then, because the discomfort ebbed to a dull ache quickly. I would be sore for days, even weeks, but I didn't care. "I wanted you, now I've got you, down to the balls," I said with a smile, and tears blurring my vision.

Jed withdrew a little and thrust back in with a slap of his hips on my ass. If he hadn't been holding on I would've flown right through the wall of the trailer. He was so far up me the head of his cock could have fucked my throat, or at least that's how it seemed at the time. Then Jed withdrew till the head threatened to pop free, and I could've cried with an overwhelming sense of emptiness. He slowly pushed back in, filling the void.

Jed shuddered. "Damn, you're tight! You sure ya done this before?"

"Not with you, but that ain't no pussy down there."

"No kidding! I don't know if I can hold off much longer – I'm almost there."

"Then do it, Jed. Fuck me!"

"Baby, are you in for trouble!"

Jed pushed up on his hands and jerked his long hair to one side of his head, drew his knees up the bed a bit and asked if I was ready. I pulled and pinched his nipples in response, and he growled from deep in his throat. And then he started.

A few slow and easy strokes in and out increased with speed, ever increasing, until he was fucking me fast, deep, and furiously. Jed was wild. I was being driven wild as he turned my insides out. He was an animal blinded by beastly carnal need to pounce, to penetrate, to pulverize, to fuck in triumphant freedom!

I cried, thrashed, screamed, and yelled beneath his sweaty bulk. Filled and emptied, only to be filled again as his hips pounded my ass with audible sound. My fingers clawed and raked the flesh of the beast above me. I gnashed my teeth and pushed with every ounce of might to no avail. I bore down to force him out by contracting my anus, but his spear was sharp and sure of any and all resistance. Pain and pleasure became one with a burning heat within me and burst in a fireball.

Jed threw his head back and howled from his very being as the hot liquid embrace of his cock tightened and relaxed with each plunge and withdrawal. Pulling and sucking at the pain in his balls until they relinquished, and let their fire flow.

He thrust into me to the balls once, twice, and then a third time so painfully deep I could fight no more. I gave up the battle, gave myself completely. And the release was complete. Jed thrust in a last time and I came without being touched. My cock jerked and spurted a long rope of cum that jetted onto my cheek. Jed stabbed my depth again, my cock spurted, and a line of white struck my right nipple. With each additional plunge of Jed's cock, he forced, pumped, the jism out of me as he flooded my ass with his.

Jed pushed in and moved my knees from his shoulders to his hips, before coming down to lie on top of me, heated, sweaty, and spent. With my legs and arms locked around him we lay still and content until our rasping breaths leveled off and returned to normal.

Jed moved his head to one shoulder, turning his face into my neck. "Are you all right?" he asked.

"Sheesh!" I sighed.

"Well, now I know you're at least alive."

"Barely."

I moved slightly to deepen the comfort of being so content. "Am I too heavy for ya?" Jed asked.

"Not at all. You just stay right where you are." I wiggled my butt. "God, don't you ever go soft?"

"Not when it's this good. Want me to pull out to give you a break?"

"Don't you dare! You do, I'll knock your block off!"

"You trying to tell me something?"

"Do I need to put it in words, after all the hell you've put me through to get this far?"

"It'll take a while. Are you up to it?"

"Jed?"

"What?"

"When that beast goes to sleep, then you can pull out...."

When Jed ran out of gas and passed out beside me, he had cum four times and fucked me in every position we could get into, on and off the bed. I had come twice myself, and the second was more glorious and volcanic than the first.

Before passing out from exhaustion, Jed bent nearly double to suck me to orgasm as his fourth and final load jetted into my cum-saturated bowels.

I woke a short time later to the smell of burning coffee. Any longer and I really would have had an unexplainable mess on my hands. I bolted from the bed to the kitchen and shut the hot plate off on the coffee maker. What little had been left in the pot evaporated in the course of about five hours of my being fucked silly by Jed.

When the pot was cool enough to be washed out I set the maker up for a fresh brew. Jed came ambling in to plop down at the table and pulled me onto his lap. "Why'd you leave in such a hurry?" he asked, kissing my shoulder.

"Another minute and we would've had a fire on my hands. Can't ya still smell it?"

He sniffed the air, then my neck and shoulder, hugging me back against his chest. "Smells like hot coffee, and hot sex a few hours ago. Everything all right?"

"I saved the pot, but, I can't say much about myself. I feel like ya dropped a ride on me."

"Like my dick's not gonna be sore for a month?"

"Nor my ass."

Jed pushed back with his right foot to lean against the windowed wall, bringing his left foot up on the seat before drawing me back to lean against his chest. With his arms around me from behind we waited for the coffee to finish brewing.

I was falling back to sleep when Jed said, "Our mornings should've been like this all along."

"Don't start with that shit now," I said. The coffee was ready and I got up feeling like one giant sore. "God, what time is it?"

"Right there on the coffee maker, silly."

It showed nine-thirty, but I'd unplugged it for a while, so it had to be closer to ten. Still not in logical thought patterns, I glanced to my wrist. "It's a quarter of ten."

"Thanksgiving morning," Jed added.

"And you already stuffed your turkey last night," I said, setting a mug near Jed. Sitting down across from him, I went on, "I've gotta get dressed and call Bob around noon, so by the latest, eleven, you're showered, dressed, and out of here."

"And if I don't leave?"

"Then one of your bosses, who does have the ability to fire you, will order you to. Do I make myself clear?"

"You haven't got the heart. Or was last night like fucking my way up the corporate ladder?"

My hand swung out and slapped his face (very soap-opera like). "You bastard!"

I got up and started for the bedroom, when Jed came charging up from behind. In a push-and-shove tackle I landed on the bed face-down with Jed straddling my legs. "Jed! Don't!" I howled, pushing up on my hands. He pulled them out from under me and my head hit the mattress, as he thrust his full length into my sore and battered ass. "Jed! Stop!" I sobbed under him.

He thrust in and out, sucked and bit the backs of my neck and shoulders, until he lay spent and panting on my back. "Get off me, and get out, you bastard!" I seethed.

Moments passed and then, Jed started crying. "I'm sorry, Phil, I didn't mean to hurt you!" he sobbed. It was then that I lost it myself and cried, too.

Eventually we both showered and dressed separately, and I called Bob at home shortly after noon. It was an hour or so later that Sherry, Jed and I went into town for Thanksgiving dinner at one of the taverns. It wasn't anything like home cooking, but I called my family just as they were all sitting down to the holiday feast.

Later that night we were just stalling before closing the show because a handful of people were still on the lot. I was walking around with Sleeman's son, when he stopped to talk with Jed. I left the two alone and, Sherry working the ride next to Jed's, chatted with her until they were done. "When are we closing?" she asked.

"Shortly. You got plans?"

"Yeah, I'm going to bed, After last night my head is pounding like a drum."

"Too much to drink?"

"No more than three, but some fucker spiked the last one."

Jed, no doubt, I thought. "You gonna be all right?"

"You know me. Knock me down, I come back for more. At least I know Jed went prowling all night after he got me to bed."

"No problems, are there?" I asked, fingering the collar of my turtle-neck up a bit more to hide all of Jed's marks.

"Oh, hell no. Every once in a while he needs to get away, you know? And have a good time. He never got back 'till late this morning, and he looked worse than I felt."

"And it doesn't bother you?"

"I don't own him, and I'd rather have 'im go prowl then get tensed up and take his shit out on me. So how was it?"

"Meaning?"

"Just before we went into town this afternoon, a little bird told me about a fight on the midway last night between you and a naked Jed."

"Sherry...." I managed, before she cut in.

"No, I'm not mad at you. When we were still down in winter quarters, on a night he went to prowl, I saw him get into the car of a known local closet case. Jed never got back till late the next day, so I have a good assumption of what went on. But don't you dare tell 'im I know about that, nor that I know he spent the night with you. And that shirt you put on today doesn't fool me for a minute. You still look like you were attacked by a known animal."

"So what happens now?"

"We just go about as usual, and keep things under our lids. Chuck's coming, so watch what ya say. Hi, Kitten. When we gonna close this dump?" she asked Chuck as he joined us.

Kitten was another pet name for the boss' son. A month shy of his eighteenth birthday, cute as a bug's ear, with a desire of his own to keep hidden. Which is another story.

Bob was due back late the following morning with a surprise of some sort for me. He wouldn't say what it was when we talked but knowing him, that could be anything from rotten eggs to more green help. Anyway, I had to clean up and air the trailer that night, so I got to the task right after we closed and slept soundly.

I woke up shortly before noon. I realized I was beaten and bruised, inside and out. My body felt like I hadn't moved a muscle in a month. Eventually I dragged myself out of bed and showered while the pot of coffee brewed.

I'd slipped into jeans and just sat down with my first mug of the day when the door popped open and Bob walked in.

"Glad ya made it back," I said.

"You won't be," he answered, and I went flying into the wall from being punched in the arm.

"Whatthehell?!" I yelled, holding my injured arm.

"What the fuck did I tell ya before I left?!" Bob seethed at me, thoroughly pissed. "You had those two deadbeats in here, didn't ya!"

It was good to know I worked on a show with such nice people. Some dirt-bag had seen and snitched first chance he or she got.

"Bob, I suppose who told ya forgot to mention that it was a night not fit for man or beast to be out in. It rained like hell all day and they got washed out and wet to the ass, so I just let 'em sleep one night."

"So what? When I tell you follow, or do anything, you do so to the max. This is the first and last time you go against my words, or you'll get thirty times as much as ya just got. Do I make myself clear?"

"Yes," I said, on the verge of bursting into tears.

Just to shed some light on the "better than normal employer-employee relationship" I had with Bob: Practically around the clock, day after day, Bob and I lived under one another's feet except for a month or two every season. Under those conditions it only takes a short time for a bond to develop, and for me that went beyond just being friends. Bob, to me, was my best friend, big brother, and the father I should have had, all rolled into one. By then it had even gotten to the point of me calling him "Dad" when his daughters were on the road, because it was the surest way of getting his attention; heck, I even called his wife "Mom" for the same reasons. Anyway. That morning when Bob hit me, or rather punched, the effect was like a house of cards falling. The physical damage always recovered. The emotional damage was an entirely different matter.

Yeah, Bob was pissed at me but good. Being good-hearted and sweet by nature isn't always the best person to be, but I wouldn't have let my own dog sleep outside on a night such as the one in question.

At any rate, Bob's little surprise for me was waiting outside the gate. It was another ride that Sleeman had bought from another show called the "Zipper!" And I use to hate flies until I found out what lurked behind them! And now I had just opened a can of worms to make it harder to explain the mess before me, back then.

The "Zipper" ride stood in the air about ninety-feet when assembled, and it looked like, well, a giant cock pin wheel, double-headed, with a chain saw blade along the perimeter. The free-spinning passenger cars were suspended from the perimeter chain, and, well, when the whole thing got moving you were in for one hell of a ride.

But the "Zipper" parked in front of me was on its trailer with all kinds of extra shit hanging off it, tree limbs, clumps of earth and grass, maybe even cow shit and a bird's nest too. Yup. Somewhere along the road someone had rolled it. Jed stepped up alongside me and said, "Holy shit!" And that was only putting it mildly.

I glanced at Bob and he gave me a big shit-eating grin. Taking a last look, I turned and started for the trailer, before Bob grabbed my arm.

"No fuckin' way, Bob. Not this time!" I said as I pulled my arm free.

"But we got it for you!'

"Then take it back for a refund. I don't want it!"

"The sale was final so you're stuck with it."

"It doesn't look too bad," Jed put in.

I could have kicked Jed in his shins, then dragged him into town for glasses. That ride, even racked on its trailer, looked like a giant, broken erector set, plain and simple. By then I was getting a headache just looking at it, and the work it would need in repair, made my stomach roll especially after hearing the surprising plans Bob had in store for me.

Sleeman wanted that ride fixed and running within six months, if not sooner. Being so close to the end of our season, Bob wanted me to drive the ride down to our Florida winter quarters right after we set up in the next town. Now that wasn't so bad. My two-month vacation would start the twenty-first of December, so the deal offered me nearly three weeks of sun and sand before heading home to New York, for the holidays. The bulk of the work I had to do, or so I thought, was to have the "Zipper" stripped down, so to speak, to its infrastructure before the rest of the show came in off the road. Then Bob lowered the rest of the boom on my head.

"I'm sendin' Jed down with you, so you'll have things ready to go when we pull in."

Yeah, when trouble hit Sleeman's Carnival and Shows, and in my case too, it hit hard!

Our destination was Hillsborough Bay, east of Tampa and north of Ruskin. Jed and I never left the next town the show set up in until well after midnight because the ride-trailer was un-insured at the time. Fortunately Jed left me alone by crawling into the sleeper for a long nap, so I could shake the willies of pulling that bent and twisted mess behind me. With just an ounce of luck the trailer frame had survived the roll, but it was the beast mounted on top it that made the first few miles really spooky. I wasn't set on breaking any speed records, however, that damn ride rattled and shook, pissed and moaned like an old whore at every turn and bump in the road.

To say the least I was a nervous wreck until I got on 95 South, and got the old feeling back of being "Queen of the Road!" By then I had worked all day, driven half the previous night moving the show, and hadn't had a shower or sleep in over twenty-four hours. I also needed to take a wicked piss so, nature needing dire attention, I pulled into the truck stop at Jacksonville.

While the rig was being fueled, I hit the john as Jed went to wait in the coffee shop and order us an early breakfast with plenty of coffee for me. Afterward, we got our gear from the truck and headed for the showers.

I was about to enter one shower stall, and Jed another, when he grabbed hold of an arm and pulled me in behind him. Even that late at night we weren't the only ones thinking about personal hygiene. I yanked out of his grasp a bit too hard and went flying into the wall opposite the stall. "You're crazy," I told him, and seeing other movement glanced to my left. Just as Jed pulled me back into the stall with him, another trucker walked by and whispered, "Enjoy," before Jed closed the door. "Relax," Jed said, "we're just gonna save water."

Yeah, right! We would have saved more water showering separately.

Putting it mildly, showering with Jed was really nice. We stripped down and got into the shower and washed one another with the curtain open, until the whispering trucker popped his head above the partition in the stall next door. Jed noticed him first when coming up for air from my ass. "Do you mind," he said, "this is a private party." Then he snapped the curtain closed.

What our showering amounted to was getting clean with a lot of foreplay tossed in for good measure. Just before Jed was going to stake his present claim, that incorrigible trucker from next door decided to reach over the partition and inch the curtain aside with his fingers. Jed was livid, to say the least, and I had all I could do to dissuade him from punching that guy's lights out. It was fun while it lasted.

With an irritated and horny Jed sulking in the sleeper, we left Jacksonville and a short time later picked up I-75 South. I had just pulled into the flow of traffic, what little there was of it, when Jed decided to crawl up front and keep me company, just as naked as the day he was born. "What in hell are you doing?" I yelled. "Are you totally crazy?"

"I'm totally bored back there and nobody will see me, except you," he said with a mischievous smirk. "So relax and enjoy the ride."

It's a miracle we didn't get killed that night. Jed sat as close as he could and started screwing around. He took my right hand off the wheel and brought it to his blood-engorged cock. I thought it was just going to be a nice jerk-off session, when Jed freed my stiff cock from my jeans, but I soon found out he had other ideas as well.

After my shirt came off I raised my butt up off the seat enough so Jed could get my jeans down to my thighs. Sitting down again, he pushed them down past my knees to tangle around my feet. I was about to tell him I'd have trouble if the need arose to shift gears except Jed was a mile ahead of me. He lowered his head between me and the wheel and swallowed my cock right to the balls in one complete lunge, cutting my words off with a gasping breath. As his head began to rise and fall, his hot mouth stroking my every inch, he reached down and pulled the lace-tie of my boots free. As my left foot came free of boot and jeans, I changed feet on the accelerator pedal until Jed freed my right foot. All but for socks, I was as naked as Jed. I spread my knees wide and just let Jed go to town on me.

It didn't take long for him to have me hanging on the edge. He pulled off and left me hanging to cool down, before going down to my balls. I pulled the tie from his pony-tail and his damp, long hair fell about his head and tickled my thighs like tiny feathers. Caressing his back and shoulders was the easy part of reciprocate, but I wanted to do more for him and attempted to reach down between his legs in search of his fat cock. I grasped the head by leaning to my right. I found it wet and slippery and the pre-cum oozed from it.

To make it easier on me, as well as move things along, Jed knelt and laid his leaky monster on my thigh. Then he stood up, bent at the waist, and, back pressed to the roof of the cab, he brought it to my lips. It wasn't the best way to drive, watching the road from the corner of my left eye, but I wanted as much of him in my mouth as I could handle, which had been about half in prior attempts because the head was just too massive for my throat.

As if matters could get any crazier, driving a tractor trailer while sucking dick, they surely did when another rig began to pass us.

I popped Jed out of my mouth with a glance to the side mirror and told him to get in the sleeper, before the cab came even with us. Jed wouldn't move, caring not in the least who in that rig saw anything. Just as the cab drew parallel to us, Jed reached down through the wheel and turned our interior light on. Next thing we hear is the air-horn from the other truck. I glanced to my left just as the interior light came on. That other trucker wasn't bad-looking, either. Late thirties, dark hair and mustache, and an open button-front shirt showing a thick mat of a well-developed chest. Wouldn't you know, what I could see, he was stroking a rather large cock of his own.

It was times such as this I became angry with Sleeman for not putting CBs in his trucks, because encounters like that, especially during the night, occurred more often than most would let on about. Anyway we rode side-by-side for about ten minutes until the other driver dropped his load, turned his light out, and sped down the road ahead of us.

Jed turned our light out and was ready for more than giving shows down the highway. He was also getting tired of standing. By then I was ready to stop on the shoulder and finish things up in the sleeper, but Jed had something else in mind.

Sitting on the edge of the seat, Jed adjusted it down and back as far as it would go. Parking his butt on top of the seat-back, he threaded his left leg between me and the door as he sat down behind me. Jed hugged me from behind, drew me back into the seat with him, then toyed with me, leaving my nipple as his right hand slid down between my legs.

Crazy, and stupid too, but it felt so good! Ten miles north of Tampa, Jed raised my hips and my seat became his hips, with his massive meat stuffed up my ass. The truck bounced along the road and he counteracted with his strong hands on my hips, fucking me deep with the last few inches.

As I left I-75, to pick up Route 4, I took the ramp slow and easy. By then I could not hold off any longer. Jed's stroking hand took me over the edge and I blasted my load all over our legs and the floor below. A short drive later the ramp of the second exit was taken at a slow crawl so we would be stopped by the traffic light. With one foot on the breaks, Jed pushed me up on the steering wheel and fucked the hell out of me. When he finally came I thought I would go flying through the windshield, out over the nose of the rig and be back on Route 4. He pulled back with just his cockhead in me. I felt his cock jerk before he slammed home and growled like a bear as the first, second, and third spasms shot his hot cum deep within me.

Finally spent, Jed drew me down into the seat with him, his cock still hard up my cum-filled ass. The light changed to green, the third time I believe, and we rode to the hamlet of our winter quarters.

Eventually Jed softened enough to pop from my sloppy hole; then we pulled over before reaching the road to Sleeman's lot. We got dressed and pulled up to the gate a short time later. It was like coming home again, because, in housecoat and slippers, Bob's wife came from the house to greet us. She treated me like one of her own.

A lot of people tend to say and believe that travelling with a carnival or circus is a very unstable life. I usually keep my mouth shut because, frankly, they don't know what the hell they are talking about. Sure, we move from town to town by the week or month through each year. But there is always the sense of home. In my case, as well as many others, you don't need a bloodline to have family on the road because everyone looks out for his co-worker brother and sister. Bob and his wife, without the actual paperwork, had adopted me, so it wasn't like I went without parental guidance and care.

After chatting with my mom and getting my keys for the lot, she let me know that I wouldn't like what I saw. "Bob parked his trailer in the thicket for you and there's four flea-bags out back. Now that you're here, I wash my hands of the whole mess," she said.

No, I did not like what I saw!

The Sleeman lot was divided into four sections: From the road to the gate stood the house, a house trailer and spare road office. Beyond the gate was a small field with ample room to park thirty-plus trailers in three parallel rows. Beyond this front field was a stand of trees and heavy undergrowth the width of the lot and roughly fifty-yards deep. The driveway curved right, then left through the thicket before opening up to the extreme back of the lot, where all the rides were parked and worked on when Sleeman's Carnival was off the road. The thicket divided the lot in half with enough clearing in the middle to park one camper.

When I stopped the rig at the back of the lot I was so upset that I didn't know which to be, a crying mess or overheated pressure-cooker. Trailers were parked haphazardly in the front field, and the back field looked no better than a junk yard. And had the rest of the show been coming in behind me there was just no room for them to park in. The only thing that looked in order was Bob's trailer nestled within the thicket, however, a few low-hanging branches over the drive would need removing.

Shutting the rig down, and not having said two words, Jed asked, "What's wrong?"

"I thought you were down here getting things ready for the off-season."

"I was, until Bob called for that truck."

"Well, I've got news for ya, this place looks like a shit-hole!"

By the time I got to my living-quarters, Bob's trailer, I was near dead on my feet. After getting out of the rig Jed and I walked through the lot for a closer look at the entire mess. The light side of the bad coin was the lawns hadn't been cut in over a month. The dark side, trailers and equipment we had scattered from there to hell and back.

The sun was just inching above the horizon as we stood by the "Zipper" trailer, again, and just the sight of the crew's quarters, a long, narrow building divided into eight closet-size bedrooms, made my stomach roll. There was trash scattered all around, and the building was in dire need of repairs and paint.

When Jed returned with his duffle bag from the rig, and I followed him into his room, I practically ran back outside. "Now what's the matter?" Jed asked, coming out behind me.

"A pig wouldn't live in a hole like that, and I'll be damned if we sleep in there!" I seethed.

"Quiet, or you'll wake the others!" he said through clenched teeth. "I know it's a little mess, but, it's not too bad. And I don't need the others knowing my business, big mouth."

"Well, excuse me!"

"Are you coming in or not?"

"Not, and I want that room cleaned up, today."

"You pulling rank on me?" he asked, crossing his arms at his chest and giving me a mean look.

I turned and walked to the rig to get my things from it, ready to cry. Jed walked up and asked, "Are we going to your place?" When I didn't answer he grabbed my arm. "Don't shut me out, Phil, not now."

"Jed," I said, turning to face him, "I'm not shutting you out. I'm just really tired and not ready to deal with this shithole, and the last I need is any shit out of you about pulling rank."

"All right, I didn't mean it. The bottom line is that you're still one of the bosses."

"I want you to work with me, not against me."

"You've got that, so what do you want?"

"First, I want you to find out who else is here...."

I wanted Jed and the others to be at my trailer by noon, or they could all, except Jed, pack their shit and head down the road. I needed a working crew to clean up that lot and have it ready for when the rest of the show pulled in off the road, and not a bunch of lay-abouts. And the task would start that afternoon, from the road to the thicket.

Jed promised we would have at least that much done before nightfall. But I had strong doubts about even putting a dent in half that much. What trailers were there needed to be towed to the back ten of 'em to attack the knee-high grass, while a tree and other fallen limbs were cut up and carted away. Then the trailers would have to be towed back to the front field and parked properly.

When I told Jed not to make any promises against great odds, he bet me it would be done in time, If Jed won I was his for the following week at any time of day or night and wherever opportunity lay. If I won, Jed was mine for the week with one additional item to sweeten the pot. It took him a while, moaning and groaning, but we shook hands to seal the deal.

Jed and the others were on time and waiting when I stepped out of the trailer. Three of the workers I knew from the road but the fourth guy, a so-called friend of Sleeman's, was a newcomer. When I informed them all of what work would be done that afternoon, and in the subsequent days, the new guy, Bryan, spoke up with, "Who died and left you boss?"

In so many words Jed set him straight: "You give Phil a hard time," Jed warned, "and I'll kick your ass before he fires ya!"

My age, at the time, worked against my being respected as a foremen. Taking work orders from a 22-year-old, with only three years of road experience, rubs a guy the wrong way when he's worked the road twice or four times as long. But those who worked with me knew I wasn't big in the head about things, unless they pissed me off, because I was a hands-on foreman. And my hands got just as dirty as theirs.

The six of us worked our asses off until "Mom" came out and put an end to the noise. Just as well, though, because there wasn't any outdoor lighting.

Back at my trailer I told the guys that I wanted a clean crew during off-hours, and, "Come first light we start work on that shit-house you're living in. I'm not having a bunch of pigs living and running around this place."

"When do we get a chance to do laundry?" Bryan asked.

"In an hour. If you want a ride, meet me at the pick-up," I said. Jed and I needed to do our own and were going to have dinner at the cozy Italian place next to the Laundromat in town.

I'd opened the invitation to the other three as well, but an hour later, only Bryan showed up. He sat between Jed and me for the drive.

While Jed and Bryan finished loading the washers needed, I went to get us a table and order a pizza and beer dinner for the three of us. Bryan joined me as the waiter left with my order and sat across from me, with his back to the door. Jed had just walked in and was in hearing distance when Bryan asked me, "What in hell's eating at Jed?"

"You got somethin' to ask, you ask me!" Jed said irritably, sitting down to my right.

"You don't have to bite my head off with your first words since we left the lot! Sheesh!"

"I just don't feel like talking. Is that all right by you?"

"Sulking about it won't change things, Jed," I said.

"I'm not sulking. I just feel like ... well, like a plucked chicken. A naked one."

"You gotta take your clothes off to be naked, Jed, or plucked," Bryan put in, to Jed's dislike.

"You're none of the above," I quickly put in, before Jed could seethe at Bryan. "And stop being a sore loser. You look good."

"Loser?" Bryan asked in surprise.

"All I needed was ten more minutes."

217

To change a flat tire on one of the trailers, and park it back in the front field. Yeah, Jed lost the bet, because half the downed tree still lay where it had fallen, too. So there sat Jed, a beardless one at that, looking positively gorgeous. And I couldn't wait to get him back to the trailer and pull the tie out of his ponytail. I'd told him he could leave the mustache and a good thing, too. He looked ten years younger, but that beard had hidden a pimply baby face. Without the mustache and his long hair, he could have passed as a beautiful girl.

"C'mon on, Jed," I said. "The reason so many people are staring at you is 'cause they'd love to fuck your brains out!" Upon my saying that, a noticeable blush colored Jed's cheeks, as well as Bryan's.

"Honest, Jed. You shouldn't be sore over losing your beard, you look better without it," Bryan added, before glancing down at his plate.

"You wouldn't look so bad yourself if you got rid of that wire on your chin, either," I said.

Bryan was Jed's opposite: Not as tall or as built, but his hair was long and black, with long lashes to enhance his hazel eyes. And he acted differently there in the restaurant, not the rough, tough person I had first met and the sudden change sparked my curiosity.

Jed had gotten to know little about Bryan in under two weeks, before he was called back out on the road with the extra truck. What he did know was that Bryan seemed to be friendly enough towards him and the others, but generally was quiet and stayed to himself in the off-hours.

When Bryan went to use the bathroom I slid my right hand onto Jed's thigh under the table, hidden under the table cloth. Jed glanced at me in surprise.

"Don't get me started," he said under his breath.

"Relax, Jed, no one can see under the table. What do you think Bryan's story is?"

"Whatcha mean by that?"

"Suddenly a different person off the lot, commenting on your looks, and sneaking glances at you. Don't tell me you haven't noticed?"

"All right, so he's acting like you did the first few months we shared that trailer, so what? Now, c'mon, take your hand off my leg before he comes back or I'm not gonna be able to stand up."

"When and where, any time, I recall the bet was."

"Please, Phil, not around the kid."

I slid my hand up to his crotch. "It's kinda late, now," I said, feeling the long, fat tube of his cock swelling under his jeans. "But if my guess is right, Bryan might enjoy a better look at you."

Bryan returned and we left for the Laundromat shortly after. On the way I caught Bryan glancing at Jed's noticeable erection in his pants. As soon as our wash was dry, I stopped at the local store for a couple of six-packs. I invited Bryan in for a few beers. My plan was to have a few beers and smoke a joint and see how far things went. I also told Jed he would be spending the night, no matter what happened, and to remove his shirt and boots. Just to get Jed started, I pulled his fly down to find he had put on underwear for a change. "The jeans too, Jed, since you've got other cover on."

"Come on, Phil, don't push your luck with him."

"Let me worry about that, but don't fool yourself into believing no one will figure it out if we're gonna continue as we have been."

"I just don't want any trouble from the others, and the less they know the better."

"There won't be any, because they know you can beat the tar out of them. And if Bryan doesn't go for the bait, then it's his loss. Now off with those jeans."

Bryan knocked a few minutes later. I half expected him not to show; taking his clothes back to his room provided him a viable excuse for not coming back. As Jed stood at the kitchen counter, rolling a joint clad in just briefs, I went to answer Bryan's knock. What I wasn't expecting was a new Bryan to step inside. In the time he left our company he had shaved off what little beard he had been able to grow. But he was more surprised than I was upon seeing Jed stripped down to nearly nothing. Of course he blushed, which was always a good sign, before his eyes returned to mine. "You didn't need to shave," I was saying as Bryan sat across from me at the table.

"Earlier you said I might look better if I did, and I thought Jed wouldn't feel so bad about losing his, so I lost my beard, what little I could grow."

"Well, you do look better than before. Why anyone wants a beard in Florida is beyond me."

Playing his part, Jed opened beers and sat down next to me, then added, "Welcome to the Clean Chin Club, Bry'," and shook hands with him, and his face deepened in color.

Conversation was light: "Where froms" and "Why on the roads" as my right hand raised havoc on Jed's thigh under the table. When our cans were empty I knew Jed was uncomfortable over getting up for the second round his briefs barely containing his bloated cock so it was as good a time as any to fire up the joint and pass it around. And you can always explain away the crazy happenings which tend to occur as a result of being stoned. When the joint became too small to safely hold, the buzz taking a stronger hold, I asked Jed to get up and roll another "and fetch us fresh beers while you're at it."

The moment arrived and, sure enough, Bryan's eyes darted immediately to Jed's. It cleared the table. There was a noticeable jump of surprise before he quickly glanced up at Jed and to me, looking as if he had fallen asleep in the sun.

"So what repairs does your room need?" I asked Bryan to break the tension he obviously felt.

"Well, ah, I'm in number one, next to the shower, and all the dampness is trashing the wall."

"That shower needs to be stripped and re-built," Jed said, standing at the edge of the table opening our beers, with the head of his cock stretching the waist of his briefs away from his body. "They just slapped it together and now the floorboards and walls are about rotted through."

"Anything else, Bryan?" I asked as Jed finally sat down beside me and lit the next joint.

"The door sticks and what's left of the old shade is stapled to the window."

"I told him to take another room, when he joined up, because one use to be old fat-ass's." A former employee who weighed close to three-hundred pounds and who was fired after someone discovered a small hole in the wall of the shower.

"It was the best one available at the time."

With no doubt the best view available, I thought, finding a half-ass patch job of a particular hole in the wall. "I have an expense allowance for lot repairs and other things, and we start work on that shit-hole tomorrow, so I want you and Jed to make a list of what needs to be done to your rooms. I know there's enough paint in the tool shed to do the whole building inside and out; agree on a color and I'll pick up a gallon, because white's the going shade."

Under the table my left knee was between Bryan's when he moved in his seat to get comfortable, coming into contact with me. After he settled down I relaxed the muscles of my leg and came into contact with his inner right thigh. He did pull away as I increased the pressure.

Eventually Jed got up to use the bathroom and upon hearing the door close behind him, Bryan asked, "Are you and Jed...well...I don't know how to put it."

"Better than friends?" I offered.

"Yeah."

"We keep each other company. Does that bother you?"

"I guess if it did, I wouldn't be here."

"Sounds like you've done more than guess about things. Am I right?"

"Well, the most I've done is thought about it, but that's all."

"That's how things get started and then, you just go and do it."

"Well, that's easier said than done, because just the thought scares me."

"When there's a glimmer of interest, there's always going to be some amount of fear involved, no matter what we do in life, of the possibilities we might be capable of doing as well as fear of the unknown. So you have every right in the world to be scared."

"You make it sound so easy."

"It's never easy the first time, or any time you meet someone new."

"Were you scared with Jed?"

"Yeah, and at times he still scares the hell out of me. But putting myself in your shoes, I've been there, done all of that and I'm still doing it. All you really need is the right opportunity to change thoughts into reality," I said and got up to roll another joint.

When I gave Bryan the joint to light, he said: "I wouldn't know the first thing to do, not that I have much to offer."

"You just relax as best you can and let it happen. And it doesn't matter what you do and don't have, it's how you use what you've got."

"I doubt I'd be any good at it."

"There's only one way to find that out," I said, pulling my T-shirt off. "Are you game for sleeping here tonight?"

"I guess so."

"The choice is yours, and the answer to the question is yes or no."

"Yes, but what do I do?"

"Relax, let yourself go, and enjoy the party," I said, as Jed came out of the bathroom.

For his first time in deeper waters, I thought Bryan doubted himself more than he should have. Naturally he was unsure and timid, scared too, but I did not rush him into doing anything. We started on our third beers and smoked a fourth joint, before moving to the bedroom, where Jed and I removed Bryan's clothes.

By the time he stood nude as we were, Bryan was trembling with sexual heat. As each piece of clothing was removed, each section of his body was caressed, kissed and licked before moving on to the next. And he had more to offer than he gave himself credit for. When his jeans and underwear were removed, his cock protruded proud and erect with the head bobbing around seven inches before him on the end of a veiny, fat stalk.

Down on my knees I took him down my throat in one slow, tongue-swirling plunge until my nose was buried within his pubic patch and pressing his ample balls back between his legs with my chin. He gasped in a high pitched whimper and rose up on the balls of his feet, grabbing my shoulders with his hands for balance, as Jed spread the cheeks of his firm, round ass and sent his tongue in search of the bundle of nerve endings buried within.

Bryan had no place to go but up, between the sucking mouth on his cock and the tongue invading his ass. He tried raising one leg in an attempt to pull away from the new, intense sensations of being serviced front and back but only succeeded in opening himself up farther to the onslaught. When my hands came to his chest and the fingers sought and found his protruding nipples.

I began pulling and kneading those hard little points, sending shockwaves of pain/pleasure coursing throughout his body. He gasped and moaned, twitched and trembled, grabbed my head and fistfuls of hair as he catapulted up and over the sharp edge of release. He thrust the head of his cock deeply down my throat, held me fast by the hair, and cried out with the first jump of his spasming lance sending one, then two, and a third rocketing shot of his cum down my gullet.

Jed made sucking sounds as Bryan's anus clenched and relaxed around his probing tongue, as we pressed and massaged Bryan's balls between our chins. I pushed Bryan back by the hips and locked my lips around the cockhead until his climax ebbed and the last drop of his bitter-sweet essence coated my tongue. I probed the piss slit hoping for more, then tongued him out of my mouth, before gently pushing him towards the bed, where he collapsed, panting and spent.

Jed pulled me to him and pressed his mouth to mine, thrusting his tongue into me for a taste of Bryan within my mouth. What little remained I gave up willingly, having had most of Bryan's cum jetted down to my stomach. Pulling away and in a husky, lust-filled voice, Jed said, "I want you," and bent me over the bed between Bryan's legs.

With his face between my ass cheeks and his tongue creating havoc in my hole, Jed pushed me farther up on the bed until I laid on top of Bryan. We embraced but he turned his head to one side when I attempted to kiss him on the lips, so I kissed his cheek and chin until he turned his head again, presumably to ask me to stop, and I pressed my lips to his. He resisted at first but timidly gave in, and my tongue entered his mouth. He relaxed his jaw and began kissing back with little sucks on my tongue.

Jed's tongue left my ass and then he pulled Bryan's stiffening cock up between my legs, with the head at my asshole. His tongue returned and then left, only to return again, knowing he was eating ass and sucking dick one after the other and back.

I knew what Jed was up to when his hands took hold of my hips and began pulling me back, yet pushing Bryan's cockhead against my spit-wet and bloated anus. Bryan looked up at me with lust filled eyes and began passionately kissing as Jed tongued him into my ass. With a hand at my lower back, Jed pushed me down and Bryan's cockhead shot past the sphincter.

My mouth left Bryan's as a stab of pain shot through me, and I yelped when he thrust up with his hips.

"Easy!" I hissed. "That's not pussy you're poking back there!"

"I'm sorry, but Jed pulled my balls."

I was about to criticize Jed for being rough with Bryan's first time, but he pulled me up and back by the shoulders, forcing Bryan up my channel all the way, and clamped his lips over mine, stifling my protest of complaint and surprise. The fingers of his right hand found my left nipple and he began pinching and pulling it painfully. I grabbed both his hand and ponytail with my hands to get him to stop, but he curled his other arm around my head and kissed me harder. The pain of my tit and lips mashed against my teeth overwhelmed the one of my ass.

When I stopped fighting, Jed wrapped his arms around me and raised me up a little, then lowered me again, moving Bryan's hard cock in and out of my ass. "Take it, baby!" Jed said when his mouth left mine. "Take that cock up your ass and get it ready for me." He lowered me to Bryan's hips and moved behind me and straddled Bryan's legs together, before rising me a few inches again. I pulled the tie out of his hair as he said, "Use your hips, Bry', and fuck that pussy on your cock. Get those knees up and the feet up under your arms ... yeah, like that! Now get your little boy-butt where ya want it. I'll hold 'im and you stretch that ass for me...."

Before long I was lying down on Bryan's thighs with my arms around Jed's middle, holding on as Jed fucked my throat and fucked back onto Bryan's cock, with him pushing me back towards Jed by the hips. Jed was sucking my cock until Bryan gasped, "I'm gonna come!"

"Cream that ass!" Jed said, letting my prick slap back and down on my stomach. "Do it! Fuck your nuts up his ass and I'll fuck 'em deeper when I get in there, with your juice slicking my pole. Come, Bry'! Bust your nuts!"

Jed thrust down my throat and held me down on Bryan's spasming cock, as he moaned and howled jets of hot cum up my ass.

Before Bryan could recover from the throes of climax, Jed pulled me off their cocks with fire left in their wake. My head reeled as Jed flipped me down on the bed on my back, raised my legs to his shoulders, and thrust his full length up me with Bryan's jism for lube.

Poor Bryan nearly got trampled in the process and rolled away as the slap of Jed's hips against my ass filled the room. Kneeling not far from my head he watched in amazement as Jed pounded the hell out of me, his long, golden hair framing his face, swaying this way and that with his sawing hips and forceful, powerful lunges.

Then Jed thrust all the way in and stopped, drew his knees up under my back, and held my thighs to his chest as he sat back on his heels. He hooked Bryan behind the head with a hand and drew him in to kiss. "Don't quit on us now, Bryan. This party ain't over by a long shot," Jed said. "You a man, Bryan."

"Yeah!"

"Get your big dick in Phil's mouth and make 'im clean it off for ya! Yeah, that's it, " Jed said.

As Bryan fed me his cock, Jed pulled him in for another kiss. Then I heard him say, "And men can suck nipple on a woman or a man...Yeah, like that...Oh, boy! ...Get that tit, Bry, you know how it's done...Get Phil's knees up under your arms...All right, bro, now watch this action.''

Jed moved in and out of my aching ass, letting Bryan watch as the massive shaft of his cock fucked my hole. Then I felt a hand on my sex engorged cock.

"Com' on, Bryan, you watched me do it and I'm a man so you can do it, too...!"

It seemed like time stood still; then Jed started pumping my hole when warmth surrounded the head of my cock, then a few inches of shaft.

Jed soothed Bryan with encouraging words as he took more and more of my cock into his mouth. When the head touched the back of his throat his stomach spasmed as he gagged and pulled off a little, Jed telling him he was doing great for his first time and he could handle more with enough practice. To let him know just how good it felt I pulled down on Bryan's hips, drawing his cock deeper down my throat.

Bryan caught on quickly. He fucked my throat and sucked about half my dick with ease, as Jed resumed fucking my ass right in front of his face. It was like hours slid past, fucking and sucking like a well-oiled machine, until the three of us fell over the edge of sexual bliss and came. Jed blasted his load up my ass right about when Bryan fucked another load in my mouth and down my throat. He only flinched when I came and kept sucking until I was dry.

With Jed curled into my left side, and Bryan my right, the three of us slipped into a deep, dreamy sleep.

- — -

By the end of that first week back in winter quarters, the three of us Jed, Bryan, and I were the devil dogs of the lot, the lot was cleaned up and ready for the rest of the show to come in off the road, the crew-shower was stripped and re-built, Jed and Bryan's rooms had been gutted and redone and we were slowly refurbishing the other rooms and the building itself as we started stripping down the "Zipper" the trailer and that of each other's jeans.

Bryan's induction into the adventures and pleasures of male-to-male sex proved to be his turning point in life. In the days that followed he became more relax, and sociable towards the rest of the crew though never flamboyant, unless in private with Jed and myself. And even then he was more so, just one of the boys, at ease with a newfound freedom, willing to explore uncharted waters, and always seeking answers to his many questions.

It wasn't a threesome every night, but there were enough. Then the show came off the road in the middle of the second week and our rompings were limited to either Jed's or Bryan's room, because Bob did not want either of them near his trailer for anything not that it stopped me from sneaking Jed in late at night when all windows were dark at the house.

The night prior to the start of my vacation, after spending hours sexual bliss and cuddling contentedly in bed, Jed asked if I planned to return for a fourth season with Sleeman's. "So far I haven't got any plans of doing otherwise. But I would like a better reason for coming back."

"All or nothing," he said flatly.

My spirits dropped and I was contemplating sending him back to his room, when he hugged me closer. "Then I guess you'd better tell Bob you'll be needing our own trailer next season."

"You mean that?"

"I'll be here when you get back...Now what're ya doing?"

"Shut up, and love me, you animal!"

My vacation was cut short when Bob called me at home on the morning of January 6, 1983. During the off-season they would contract some of their rides and other attractions with other shows, until the start of their annual season in February. Sleeman had booked a small unit for two weeks in Fort Myers and he was swamped with preparing things for the road and mending the mangled Zipper.

"We want you to manage the unit and crew for us," Bob was saying. "We need you down here, now. I know you can handle it, or I wouldn't be askin'."

"If I didn't love you so much, I'd tell you to go screw yourself. When do you need me?"

"No later than tomorrow night...."

My head reeled with sudden shock, however, I just packed like a madman and Bob picked me up at the airport that night. Back on the lot, everything was waiting to roll with my personal camper head of the pending convoy, half the reason I agreed to return so early. The other half of the agreement was that Jed would be my foreman. I asked him where Jed was and Bob handed me an envelope. My name was scrawled on the envelope and inside was a letter from Jed:

Dear Phil, The most I can hope for is that, within your loving hear, you can forgive me for not being there when you come back. You haven't been gone two days and already I'm falling apart without you. Bryan has tried to help, but it's not the same as having you here. He isn't you. I know he means well and suggested I head home for the holiday, so that's what I'm gonna do. I'm going home and not coming back, because my place is with my wife and kids. I feel like a no-balls coward not telling you this before or in person, but don't ever doubt my love. I do love you and always will! My name isn't Jed, it's Glenn, and there's a lot of other things I should have told you about me but I've hurt you enough as is which is the last thing I ever wanted to do.

I'll never forget you, Phil, never! Maybe if things don't work out back home I'll be back, or catch up with you somewhere out on the road. Please look after our little brother, Bryan. All my love, Jed (Animal, Glenn).

"What's that all about?" Bob asked as I shoved the envelope and letter in my pocket.

"Never mind," I said, fighting back the urge to cry. "Is Bryan on my crew?"

"We're sending you down with experienced guys, not green."

"This is one green I can handle and have him broken in for the road. He's coming with me. Or else."

"Or else what?"

"I'm flying back home, tonight."

"All right, you've got him. I've got another green if you want him."

"Who?"

"Chuck Sleeman," Bob answered. "Seems the old man wants him to get his hands dirty."

I smirked. "And he will...."

- The first installment of P.K.'s tales of life on the road appeared in "Boys of the Night".

HIS SWEET ASS
Kevin Bantan

"You like it, don't you, faggot? Fat dick up your ass. A beer- can-sized dick stuffed in your sweet ass. You know you love it. You know you would have begged me for it, if I wasn't horny enough to do your pussy. Yeah, you would have been on your knees, looking up at me with those brown, puppy dog eyes, begging. Kissing my fat bulge, like it was your god you were praying to. Yeah, that's what your kind does. Feels good, huh? Ready for my jizz to mark you, faggot? Ha, ha. Ready or not, faggot. Ready...or...oh, God."

I sighed. I could do better. I knew it. I was tempted to blame my morning run of bad prose on the tacos I'd had for dinner last night, but that would have been like blaming the ocean for ships sinking.

I looked out the window. My heart leapt. It was that too-cute white boy walking his little dog. Every day or so I would see him with his blond, mongrel pet. Dark straight hair and eyebrows. Equally dark eyes. Brown? Black? I sighed again. Considering that the neighborhood was so close to Moravian College, he could probably be a student. That would make him legal, at least. And he lived nearby. And he had a habit of walking down the alley on which my tiny efficiency apartment was located over a garage. My garret. Ha, ha, as the fucker said.

Awesome cheekbones, too, I noticed, as he turned to look at the dog sniffing the neighbor's grass. The morning sun hitting his angular face cast shadows on it. Dog walker, thy name is gorgeous. Oh, sure, Kevin, wax bad poetically, too, while you're at it. I kept looking at the young man, who was now showing me hemispheres that could have become a globe, were they stitched together. I sighed. I wondered what kind of ploy I could use to entice him into my cramped living space. The etching ruse wouldn't work. I didn't have etchings, anyway. A couple of nice watercolors, though. "Hi, there. My name's Kevin, and I'd like your opinion on the placement of a watercolor I just purchased. Oh, you're a chemical engineering major? No sweat. Philistines are allowed to darken my threshold." Yeah, that one's a sure winner, Bantan.

He was moving toward the bend in the alley. Goodbye, beautiful. And your little dog, too. God, how derivative can you get? Maybe it was the tacos. He disappeared from sight. Another opportunity wasted. And wasting time was exactly what I was doing, sitting there, writing trash.

I decided that I might as well get the food shopping done. That, at least, would be productive. Maybe. I tied the black patent leather combat boots covering my lower legs and jeans. Gee, what a rebel, he said to himself. The jeans were a nicely faded blue, my long T-shirt and ball cap, black. And as I walked into the Shop Rite, the customer service rep would announce, "Ladies and gentlemen, now entering the store is Bethlehem's only black punk! He's also a newly-failed writer." Hmmm. Maybe I'd shop at the Giant, instead.

I went looking for my keys. Once I found them, I started another search for my store list. Which was on the refrigerator, where it always was. I wondered how I could be so scatter-brained, but I didn't trust myself to answer the question. I checked for my keys again. Did failed writers become obsessive-compulsives, too? Next my face would probably break out with acne. I could just hear that tidbit announced over the Shop Rite intercom.

I locked the door, then tried it to make sure that it was. Stop that, Kevin! Just stop it! I walked down the wooden stairs to the sidewalk between the house next door and the garage. My car was parked across the alley, next to Moravian's baseball field. "Hey, little boy, care to shag some balls?" I chuckled. That wasn't a bad line. Maybe.

So it was that I had a smile on my face, when I saw the blur in front of me as I stepped out into the alley and collided hard with something. The force of the impact laid me flat on my back, stunned. Then I was being licked. Licked? Oh, a dog. I covered my face, defensively.

"You okay?" a voice asked. Ah, the something I got bowled over by. Yeah, I'm fine. I always just lie in alleys, pretending that I'm doing a disaster drill. Except that the rescue squads never show up, damn them.

"I have no clue." What a succinctly honest answer. Never had a clue, never would, except that I was only now admitting it.

"I smacked into you pretty hard."

"No kidding."

Then he was hovering over me. I wanted to shout, "I've died and gone to heaven!" when I saw who it was.

"Do you realize that you're bleeding?" I asked. He touched his forehead and felt the wetness there.

"Now I do. Do you think anything's broken?" My heart, if you walk away.

"I doubt it. A Mack truck didn't hit me. Although you look pretty well built." Had I actually said that? "And you did lay me out." As opposed to laying me, unfortunately.

"Sorry. Muffy picked that moment to spy a rabbit and take off."

"Lucky me." Muffy?

"Here, let me help you up."

He did and brushed me off. That was nice. I wanted to brush him off, but I didn't know if he had fallen. Probably not, the way he was built. But that didn't adequately describe the solidly muscled physique. I wanted an excuse to keep talking to him, but I couldn't think of one. Until he touched his head again.

"I think we should take care of that head wound." When in doubt, overdramatize, that's my motto!

"It'll be okay. It's just a scratch."

"Scratches can get infected. I live on the second floor here. Let's at least get a bandage on it."

"Okay. Lead the way. Here, Muffy."

What kind of a boy would name his dog Muffy? Answer: a gay boy! That probability cheered me. So did the fact that he was coming up to my etchingless garret. I led him through the Spartan kitchen, past the desk holding my computer and printer, around the corner to the bed.

"Why don't you sit there. I'll get the first aid kit." He hesitated. He was right to be suspicious, if he was, because there was a wing chair available. "It'll be easier for me to clean and dress the cut," I said as convincingly as I could.

"Oh. Sure." Maybe straight boys did name their dogs Muffy, after all, I was thinking, because this guy wasn't striking me as gay, given his reaction to the prospect of sitting on the bed.

I returned with a bottle of rubbing alcohol, a cotton ball, and a Rite Aid sheer strip. What color did you expect me to have? 'Flesh'? I sat down next to him. He seemed to be nervous. I uncapped the bottle and tipped some alcohol onto the cotton.

"This will only hurt a little. What are you so nervous for? I'm not going to attack you."

"Sorry. Owww."

"Did it hurt that much?"

He looked at me sheepishly. "No. Despite how I'm built, I tend to be a wimp where pain's concerned."

I chuckled politely and looked across the room to see my tall engineer boots sitting next to the desk, right where I'd taken them off last night. Oh, no. If he saw them, he'd think I was into S/M. Well, I was only into it a little bit. As in a little bondage and discipline, but not pain.

"I'm not into pain, trust me."

"Why did you say that?" Because it's a known fact that failed young writers also go into non-sequitur senility very quickly.

"In case you saw my boots," I said, pointing.

"Oh, I see. They're way cool."

"Really? Thanks."

"Do you wear them in or out?"

"Out, like these," I said, lifting my left leg. "I guess I have a boot fetish." I also have a boy fetish, but the straight boy was not going to drag that out of me.

"Cool. I like boots."

"Let me get the bandage on. At least it's not bleeding much now."

I did a little more disinfecting with the cotton ball before securing the bandage onto his forehead. I felt bad about the fact that his great face had been marred, because up close he was absolutely stunning. And he had big, brown, puppy dog eyes.

"By the way, my name's Matthew." Matthew and Muffy. Picture it.

"I'm Kevin." We shook hands. Nice, firm grip.

"Good to know you. Hell of a way to meet, though."

"Sure was. So, are you a student?"

"Yes. A grad student at Moravian. Are you a student, too?"

"No, I'm afraid I'm long past that."

"You can't be serious."

"Completely. I'm blessed with good genes, though."

"They are nice. You wear them well, too."

"Thanks. I meant the other kind."

"I know." He laughed. It had a nice sound to it, especially coming out past even, white teeth. "So, what do you use the computer for?"

"I'm a writer." Well, I was when I still knew what a declarative sentence was.

"What do you write?"

"Gay erotica." It was out of my mouth before I realized it. It was the damned senility kicking in. Fortunately my skin was dark enough that he wouldn't see the blush. He wouldn't anyway. Even as my face colored further, he was fleeing down the alley.

Except that he wasn't. He was still sitting next to me, and little Muffy was asleep at his feet. How touching. So, why hadn't he fled?

"So, do you write from your personal experiences?" His lips formed a sly smile.

"Sadly, no. I don't date much. There don't seem to be a lot of white guys in the Lehigh Valley, who are into black guys." Even figuratively.

"But it would take only one, right?"

"Right. Especially if he was an Adonis like you."

"Likewise. I'll take that as the come-on line."

With that he leaned into my face and pressed his lips against mine. I pressed back with the fullness of my heritage. His lips weren't as ample, but he sure knew how to use them. And his tongue, which was dueling with mine in happiness. Our arms went around each other as Muffy lay oblivious to the lust raging not far above her little head. Or his.

He came off my mouth and looked at me from under the heavy lids of arousal.

"I can hardly believe this. Sitting here kissing a certified Adonis. Man, I'm glad I got a dog." Even if its name was Muffy, girlfriend. I yanked up on his T-shirt.

"I frequently see you walking her and kept trying to figure out an excuse to meet you. And I did, thanks to Muffy."

"Yeah, only she's a he." Figured. He undid my jeans, as I did the same to him. However sexy it was to undress each other, it was less efficient than shedding one's own clothes. So that's what I suggested. I was out of my boots, socks, jeans and shirt in about a minute. Matthew was disrobed in short order, too.

Oh, the sight of him. His body was splendidly defined, but not in a muscle-bound way. Still his muscles rippled and his tanned skin was smooth. We embraced and kissed again. His skin was soft and a delight to caress. He felt the same way about mine and said so. After all, I wasn't that much older than he was.

We ended up on the bed with him on top of me. We talked about what we liked to do as our bodies pressed excitedly together. It seemed that we were compatible, although Matthew said that he hadn't been fucked much. We decided that he would do the honors. "I want to suck you first, though. I love to suck cock. Man this is beautiful, Kevin. And so dark. It's almost ebony. Like Stanley's. My high school sweetheart. He was light-skinned, but his cock was dark brown."

With that he drew my mushroom into his mouth and slowly took in the rest of me. He sure must have liked to suck on boys, because he was doing a great job of making me hard. And even when I was erect, he managed to fit all of me into his mouth and throat. I wondered how big Stanley had been. I watched the beautiful face move up and down on my shiny pole and questioned if it were really happening. Maybe I'd blacked out before I left the apartment. No, the sensations that Matthew was making my shaft experience were all too real. So much so that I had to stop him.

Curiously, he was erect, too, simply from blowing me. A cocksucker of the first order. I reached into the top drawer of the nightstand and snagged a condom and lube tube. He scooched up my body, his maleness waving happily, as if he were Muffy expecting to get a treat for having been extra good. I sheathed his pulsing member slowly, enjoying the hardness, the aliveness of his cock, which looked as if it were nearly as long as mine. It was thicker, for sure. "Yes, sir, a real beer can."

"Huh?"

"Bad writing. Ignore me."

He leaned down and kissed me. "I think not."

I slathered KY over his latex-covered erection, keeping it interested in me. When I had him glistening, he kneed down my body, and I reared back to make myself vulnerable to my stunning lover. Matthew positioned himself and nudged his glans into me. I swallowed it obediently. He took hold of my ankles and spread them. I liked that touch, being kind of into submission sometimes. I inhaled as his length and girth invaded me, stretching my muscles.

The fullness felt good, once he was in me for a minute or so. He moved easily and deliberately, sliding about halfway out each time. I don't exactly know what it is, but I think that a guy's abdomen looks so sexy when he's fucking me like that. And Matthew's rippling muscles made him only that much more alluring. I love it, too, when guys watch themselves fuck. I don't think it's an ego thing. I do it, too, and I suppose it's a kind of satisfaction that we're intimately connected with another male, giving and receiving pleasure from the act. Besides, it does look erotic as hell to see my cock moving in and out of a guy. Maybe it's a power thing, too.

"You feel great, Kevin."

"So do you." Muffy snorted in his sleep. Shut up, Muffy. Who asked you?

"God, you're beautiful." He let go of my ankles to lean forward and kiss me.

When Matthew straightened up, I planted my wide feet on his pectorals and played with his nipples with the first two toes of each foot.

"I love having my nipples played with. But I've never had them done by toes before."

"I'm an erotic writer, remember?"

"You're erotic, period. That's all I need to know."

"You sweet talker."

"You sweet ass," he said and chuckled.

As he humped me, he played with my legs, which felt especially good. His hands were surprisingly soft, and the sleek on sleek contact made me tingle and squirm. He finally stopped driving my right leg crazy in order to take my dormant ebony sex into his hand. His fingers teased it lightly, causing more squirming. His masturbatory action was almost sadistic in its molestation, the pleasure bordering on agony. But I was rock hard as a result, I admit. He praised its beauty again as he continued to caress it with achingly good results.

"Stanley's head was lighter than his shaft, but yours is uniformly dusky."

"Hershey's Special Dark cock and balls with milk chocolate body."

"Yeah, you sure are a rich chocolate color."

"That was my nickname in college. Chocolate. Choc, for short. One of my classmates gave it to me after he held a Hershey bar up to my skin, and it matched."

"Cool. Where'd you go to school?"

"UCLA."

"No kidding. I'm impressed."

"Why? Moravian's a good school."

"Yeah, but it's not UCLA."

"Maybe that's good."

"You think?" No clue, again, but I didn't say it.

He had stopped fucking me while we talked. Now he started in earnest, grunting from the enjoyable exertion. I love a man at work. He had relinquished my needy penis, so I took his place and stroked myself in time to the pummeling in my gut. Mister Special Dark didn't need much encouragement, as wired as the nerves were from Matthew's exquisite torture. I looked at the beauty rutting in me as I coaxed myself the last few strokes to orgasm. Matthew was sweating and panting. "Oh, Christ!" I cried and watched my boy cream arc from my slit onto my body. My partner evidently found it an irresistible sight, because seconds later he said, "Oh, man, Kevin. Oh, God." I felt him swell and lose himself in me.

We were lying side by side in bed, the storm of hedonism having passed without awakening little Muffy.

"I need to ask you this. Why in the world did you name your dog Muffy?"

"Because I read somewhere that having a cute dog was a good way to meet women. I wondered if I might meet guys that way. So I gave him a gay-sounding name, hoping it would click with the right portion of the population."

"Good idea. But Muffy?"

"I call him George otherwise."

"Oh."

"Kevin? Can we get together again?"

"As soon as we've recovered, hunk."

"Sorry. I can't stay. I have a one o'clock class."

"I see."

"No, really. I want to see you again. I do. I can't believe my good fortune in meeting you."

"How about dinner tonight?"

"I have a six o'clock, but then I'm free. Sounds great. Okay if I bring George?"

George was almost as bad as Muffy, I thought, as I drove out to the Shop Rite on Linden Street. I walked in ready for the clerk's rude comments. I was going to scream at her, "Well, at least I have a boyfriend!" I knew that was derivative from one of the Airplane movies. I didn't care. I had made love with one of the most beautiful men I'd ever seen in my life. I also didn't care that I was writing crap or that I was senile. The heavy soles and heels of my patent leather boots thumped confidently down the aisles, as I chose items for dinner.

Matthew showed up at about seven-ten without George. He was with a neighbor woman, who loved his company, he said.

"As Muffy or George?"

"George. She's a lesbian." He accepted the glass of white wine offered. And the kiss. I could hardly believe my good fortune, when I studied his dark, angelic countenance. It seemed that Matthew couldn't, either, from his frequent touches and kisses. Life was strangely great all of a sudden.

He enjoyed dinner, which was simple but tasty. We ate it sitting in the only two chairs available; the wing and desk chairs, our plates and glasses sharing a small, squat trunk. My new boyfriend called my apartment cozy, but he was being kind in the extreme.

Supper was enhanced for Matthew because I was wearing my engineer boots. He commented on how sexy they looked as much as how good the food was. He was also curious about my non-existent sex life.

"I can't believe that as beautiful as you are, you don't have guys eating out of your hand."

"I just don't seem to have luck with men." I didn't add that I was a three-time loser. The two men I've loved most in my life were murdered; Kinga in D.C. and Jamal in L.A.. And my own high school sweetheart was forced to have a sex change by his sister. I moved here to get away from the memories. I had enjoyed growing up here and decided to resettle here after Jam was gunned down.

"I'm sorry, Kevin."

I shrugged. "It happens, but it's made me circumspect about relationships."

"That's understandable."

"Hey, cheer up, Matthew. You turn me inside out, so there's hope for me yet. Just keep focusing your gonads on the boots."

He did and asked me to put them back on after we'd undressed. I was happy to oblige. Accents can add exciting touches to lovemaking. And I always felt sexy being booted.

He insisted on worshipping me orally again, once we were on the bed. He settled himself between my legs, and I rested my calves on his back, which he told me he liked. I lay back and focused on the sensations my nerves were telegraphing to my brain from the ministrations of Matthew's hot mouth. Mercifully, thoughts of premature deaths vanished under the assault of lips, tongue and saliva. I sighed in pleasure as he took me higher and higher. I got to the point where I was ready to let him suck me to orgasm. However, he sensed that I was getting close and stopped immediately.

"Man, that was great!"

"Thanks, but I didn't want you to lose it. I really want this glorious cock inside me," he said, holding my erection firmly.

We kissed some more, while my sodden sex dried out. Then Matthew sucked on my dark nipples, easily raising them to bold relief.

"Are you sure you weren't a vacuum cleaner in a previous life."

"Automatic pool cleaner," he said and attacked my belly button next, lapping at it as if his dog had given him a few pointers.

When he was satisfied that I was ready to accept the condom, he covered me with an almost devout attitude. He lay down and I diddled him with a lube-covered finger. He felt tight, but he managed to relax the longer I finger fucked him. Of course by that time I was soft again, but more lube and digital stimulation brought it rising back to life. "If I hurt you at all, let me know."

"Don't worry. Owww."

"I haven't done anything yet, asshole."

"I was practicing. Seriously, I want you in me more than I've ever wanted anything in bed."

"Except for sucking my cock."

"All right, second most thing I've ever wanted."

I eased into him slowly, feeling his sphincter clamping down on me in protest over the insult my girth was causing it. "Breathe, Matthew." He did, and that helped me to slide it all the way in. "Okay?" He smiled and nodded. I spread his legs and held down his thighs in a show of power. I bent to kiss him as I moved easily in him now. He accepted my tongue and sucked on it like a teat. He was playing the passive role so well that I couldn't resist.

"You like it, don't you faggot?"

"Oh, yes, sir."

"Big fat dick up your sweet ass."

"It's huge, sir."

"Beer can-sized dick , eh?"

"Sir...ahhhh." He shot three white volleys of pure boy. With that I came, too. Hmmm. Maybe sometimes bad writing could produce good results. And sweet ass.

PASSION ON AND OFF THE ROAD
John Patrick

"...The new sensation of motoring went to Proust's head as it did to Henry James's," A. L. Rowse said in Homosexuals in History, "and a young motorist went to his heart. 'His black rubber cape and the hooded helmet which enclosed the fullness of his young, beardless face, made him resemble a pilgrim or, rather, a nun of speed.'

"Proust did not immediately fall in love with this young addict of speed. A year or two later he met him again and was struck by the extraordinary ripening of his natural intelligence. 'He was an extraordinary person, and possessed the greatest intellectual gifts I have ever known,' Proust said; and to Gide: 'His delicious intelligence so marvelously incompatible with his station in life, which I discovered with amazement, added nothing to my affection for him, except that I enjoyed making him aware of it.' Evidently this discovery was an excitement in itself to a sophisticated intellectual; it added further pleasure to contact with the young man to aid in developing his mind. This is perhaps the best aspect of such relations, certainly a beneficent result. Proust took him into his service, and fell in love with him. The words of Albertine may well have been Agostinelli's: 'Without you I should still be stupid. You have opened a world of ideas to me that I never dreamed of, and whatever I've become I owe to you alone.' Proust had said: 'May the steering-wheel of my young mechanic remain forever the symbol of his talent, rather than the prefiguration of his martyrdom!' But fate lay in wait for them both. Proust was a generous master, but his love was possessive, like his insatiable need for self-assurance.

"In time Agostinelli felt cooped-up in the Paris apartment, and went out on night-adventures of his own, while the master worked at his book through the night. Agostinelli was as keen on women as he was on speed; both were elements in the attraction he had for Proust, but the one created jealousy as the other created anxiety. At last Agostinelli could resist his demon no longer and determined to learn to fly and to escape from confinement.

"It was Proust's generosity that enabled him to achieve this. He fled to the south of France to a flying school, made rapid progress, and on a solo flight, too soon, plunged into the sea. Thus ended the great love of Proust's life. Nothing but what is good is known of this brave young mechanic, as intrepid as he was intelligent. Proust said that he 'wrote wonderful letters....'"

We often imagine sex with a mechanic would be rough trade at its best. "One of the most sexually exciting and mysterious times I had when I first started hanging out with sexual outlaws," Chris Wittke reminisced in Drummer, "was 'rough trade.' I didn't know what it meant, but it sure captured my imagination. I had heard hustlers described as 'trade,' and I assumed the meaning of the word was self-evident: the hustlers sold their bodies for cash. I assumed 'rough trade' was just a variation on that theme, it probably applied to the meaner looking guys who were a little rough around the edges, but available for a fee. And that was true, but it was only part of the story. Like so many multi-faceted phrases in the English language, 'rough trade' can have other meanings as well.

"I learned another meaning when I discovered a steam bath in a blue-collar working class neighborhood in a blue-collar working class town not too far from where I live. The steam bath wasn't a bathhouse, in the gay sense of that phrase. There was no constantly blaring disco music, or mirrors everywhere, or private rooms or open sex. This steam bath was a place where off-duty cops and regular guys from the local Italian and Polish and Latino communities could unwind in the sauna or the steam room, but what I knew in my heart was that wherever there's a place in which men are told it's okay to feel comfortable with their dicks out in front of other guys who also have their dicks out, a good percentage of them want to get sucked off. I visited this steam room regularly for months. hoping to somehow 'break the code' and tap into what I imagined to be a rough trade 'homosex' underground.

"And after about six months of making myself a regular at the place it finally happened. One of the biggest loudmouths of the regulars who was always talking about football and chicks and his bitch of a wife and what a pain in the ass it was to be a cop on third shift, found himself alone with me in the very foggy steam room.

"After several minutes of staring straight ahead so as not to call attention to myself for fear of giving away my hidden agenda, Officer Loudmouth stood up to stretch his muscles. He let his towel drop and turned around to reveal his cock at half mast. 'This heat gets me up,' he grunted.

"'Yeah,' I said, non-committally.

"He startled me by moving so quickly in my direction, my heart seemed to skip a beat. He grabbed the back of my head and forced his dick down my throat. Maybe forced is the wrong word, since it was something I wanted desperately. The only thing he said to me as he took advantage of my skill and desire was 'I thought so.' He held me firmly and took me roughly but it wasn't much different from the jocular roughhousing I saw him do with his friends at the steam room many times in the past. And I wondered if any of them had sucked his cock before? And I wondered, as he fucked my face with a growing intensity, what it felt like to him to know that in spite of the times he had mentioned chicks and his bitch of a wife and how hard it is to be a provider nowadays in front of me, I now knew a deeper truth about him.

"That was the day I learned the best meaning of the phrase 'rough trade.' You trade a bit of your time and he trades a big chunk of his identity. It's easy to figure out the winner in that scenario."

HELL ON WHEELS
John Patrick

"Hell is the place where someone
yearns for what will kill him."
– Dante's Inferno

"Hey, faggot!" The voice came louder and Billy turned on the corner where he had been leaning against the wall, looking available. Billy did not respond.

"Hey, you deaf, faggot?"

Billy looked to see three studs in an old, black Cadillac Fleetwood were on the corner behind him. He shook his head and looked away. Ignore them, that was the best course.

"Hey, faggot, can't you see we talkin' to ya?" the voice came again. Billy looked. It was the guy in front, at the wheel. Handsome, in an ugly way, with dreadlocks, and a smile like the Cheshire cat in the Disney version of Alice in Wonderland. "You too much of a faggot to talk to two brothers, man? You too much of a cock-suck? Huh, faggot?"

Billy braced himself. These three needed a little education. He ambled toward the car. Upright, Billy was six feet tall, and his muscles made his walk, even in a shambling roll, menacing. He leaned onto the car, dropping his hands across the roof, noisily. "Anything I can do for you boys?" he said with the smile he always turned on a john in a Cadillac.

"Yeah," the stud in the front seat growled, "you can suck on this for me, faggot."

Billy looked down into the front seat to see the man at the wheel had pulled his cock from his jeans. It was the ugliest, biggest black dick Billy had ever laid eyes on. Downright obscene. Billy was fascinated.

"You want it, fag?"

"Looks interesting."

"Okay, get into the back seat, fag," he went on. "We got some plans for you."

Why not? Billy asked himself. He wasn't doing any business tonight anyway, and this might just be fun. He had long harbored a kidnapping fantasy, one of the few he hadn't lived out. And if they killed him, well, so be it. "Life is short," was Billy's motto.

As they drove along, the lithe, light-skinned dude in the back seat drew Billy's head into his lap. Billy soon had the thick black dick unleashed from the captivity of the dude's jeans. The man who had

241

originally talked to Billy turned around in his seat to get a view of the action. He had a dirty grin over his face. "You like Jet's cock?" he asked.

Billy ignored him, preferring to fill his mouth with the cock. Jet began to push his cock into Billy's throat, holding Billy's head still. "Yeah, Bobby, you gotta have some of this," Jet was soon telling his friend in the front seat, whose crazed eyes had not left the spectacle of the face-fucking of Billy.

"We'll get there soon enough." Bobby turned to the driver: "Turn here, Bo. We'll go down to the park."

Bo abruptly turned the car and they sailed into the park. Jet had stopped face-fucking Billy and let the young prostitute do his thing. While Bo parked under a chestnut tree, Jet was coming, his jism spilling out on Billy's cheek. "Oh, man," Jet mumbled, over and over. "This kid sure can suck dick."

Bobby opened the car's rear door and stood waiting. "You ready to suck me?" Bobby asked Billy. The black man pulled his zipper down and he let out that huge cock, free of underwear. It was semi-hard and Bobby wagged it at Billy. "Well, you ready for me?"

Jet pushed Billy away and shook the last drops of cum out of his still half-erect dick.

Billy fell across the wide seat, putting his face in position to view Bobby's cock up-close. Bobby wasted no time; he grabbed Billy's head and shoved his crotch toward Billy's mouth. Soon unable to breathe, Billy found no other option but to relax and let the cock slide in, deep in the warmth of his mouth and to breathe through his nose. "Good, little white boy punk, now suck it, suck that big dick. Make it come, just like you did Jet's."

Billy sucked. He gave it his best shot, a fifty-dollar blowjob at least. Through closed eyes, he heard car doors opening and closing. He grunted as he felt a hand at his ass. Soon his pants were being pulled down and fingers were exploring his anus. Spit was applied and one finger, then two were inserted. He groaned. Moments later, a hand was parting his cheeks for something much bigger than the fingers that had been massaging him. Then a cockhead was being pressed with incredible force against his ass-ring. Bobby pushed his cock deep in Billy's throat and he groaned, and a second later the cock at his ass shoved and was in too, past his ring and deep inside him. Billy was being fucked at both ends by big black dicks. A first time for everything, he said to himself.

The black cock in his asshole suddenly slipped from the opening on a backstroke. It was Bo who was now whispering softly in his ear, "Just relax, faggot. Just relax. Let it in."

Billy swallowed hard as Bo slid back in. Just then, Bobby's cock was going off inside his throat and Billy pulled back, but not before a load of jism was left on his tongue. Bobby let go of Billy's head as he backed away and Billy spat the jism on the floor of the Cadillac. While Bo fucked Billy, Jet came around and took Bobby's place. He lifted Billy's head up and forced it onto his semi-hard cock. "Yeah, suck it again, pretty boy."

Billy opened his mouth and Jet brought the head of his cock to Billy's lips. Billy kissed it and Jet began to slap the cock against Billy's cheeks, again and again. Billy moaned.

Before long, Billy was reduced to a trembling mass, a tormented soul pleading helplessly, moaning only for the stud not to stop fucking him.

Billy had brought his hand to his own cock and was obviously caught up in the throes of his on-rushing orgasm. His ass muscles clenched tightly on the burrowing cock and squeezed; his hips rose, strained up to take all of Bo and, with exquisite timing, Bo stabbed his stiff prick in to the hilt and came. Billy's straining limbs went rigid, every fiber of his body tightened and he screeched through tightly clenched teeth. Then a tremendous convulsion shook him and he flailed about wildly on the seat cushion.

Billy was still trembling when he was rolled over onto his back and his legs were pushed wide apart to fully expose his ass, dripping with cum. Jet was back inside the car, easing his cock into Billy's aching anus. The other two had climbed into the front seat. Jet took Billy in his arms and began kissing him full on the mouth as his cock slid all the way in.

"Hey, Jet," Bobby said, turning to look at the lovers, "you wanna take that one home?"

Jet didn't respond; the answer was obvious.

And now, Billy knew as he kissed Jet back with equal passion, he was being kidnapped for real.

EXTRA BODY WORK
David Henry

On a sultry August night, Frank and I, co-owners of the Zorro Brothers' Auto Service, were working on our prized possession a 1957 Mercedes Benz 300SL "Gullwing." We bought it last summer at a little-publicized, sparsely attended estate sale. It had been in terrible shape, which was probably why we'd been the only ones to recognize its true value. We've worked on it ever since.

The care we lavished on the "Gullwing" was the same that we lavished on our business. After six years, ours was the most successful auto repair service in the area. You see, we knew when we moved here to Lincoln, a progressive college town, we'd be successful because students in progressive college towns tend to own awful cars that are constantly in need of repair. There's also an endless supply of young men to look at and give excellent service to.

Frank and I liked to know right off the bat which of the guys who come in with their cars would be, shall I say, amenable to our services of a more priapic nature. So we've decorated our office with pictures of hot guys built like brick shithouses, who are in various stages of undress. Cocks and asses of different sizes and hues of the rainbow made an exhibit that would rival any at the Metropolitan Museum in sheer beauty. So what if they drove away or scared some guys? There were plenty others who were interested in some extra body work.

We've had a good thing going, Frank and I, for a long time now, ever since we met in juvenile hall. It was a racially divided place, but even though I'm black and Frank's white, we found a common bond in the love of cock and ass. That first taste of a thick, uncut dick had me hooked for life. Frank has told me that he loves the feel of my rock-hard cock splitting his ass cheeks apart, probing his chute, and then pounding into him like there was no tomorrow. And, to top it off, he shoots a truly magnificent load!

Anyway, we were working on the car and I was having a hell of a time trying to concentrate. Although we've been together now for 18 years, we still found each other irresistible, so we had made a pact: no sex before a certain amount of work was done; otherwise nothing would get done. Storing up my sexual energy made my cock strain against my boxers like water stopped up by a dam. I was sweaty. Frank was sweaty and I knew he was hard as a rock, which made me sweat more. I wanted to take off my T-shirt, but I knew that my bare chest would be too distracting for

245

Frank. He might lunge at me or something. I closed my eyes thinking about his hard shaft rubbing between my ass cheeks and his fingers encircling my balls, alternately squeezing and caressing them. I thought about my pre-cum dribbling onto his fingers and his hand working its way to a slow, steady jack while his throbbing, hot member eased itself of its own accord into my love canal. I thought of his tongue snaking its way across the nape of my neck, his hot breath on my neck. The socket wrench slipped from my hand and landed on the garage floor with a loud clink.

"Hey. You all right?" Frank asked. He looked across the engine at me, concerned.

I picked up the wrench. "Sure. just lost my grip there."

"We're almost done. We can knock off early tonight." He winked.

I winked back and reapplied myself to my work. A few minutes later we were done. There came a knock at the door. Frank looked at me as if he were wondering if we were expecting someone. I shrugged. He moved to answer the door.

Standing there was a young man in his early twenties, wearing sandals, gym shorts, and a Zorro Brothers' T-shirt. The Zorro Brothers t-shirt is black with a white Z emblazoned on it. It's very popular and helped us pay for the "Gullwing."

The young man said, "I saw your light on and I thought I'd just stop in. "

"We're closed," Frank said. I could tell he was taking in the kid's good looks and muscular body. I wondered how big the kid's basket was.

"The last time I had my car in, you guys mentioned something about extra body work. I didn't think anything of it until I talked to some friends of mine who've been satisfied with the extra body work they've gotten here," the kid said.

"What's your name?" I asked, stepping closer as Frank shut the door behind the kid.

"Alan."

"You think highly of your friends' opinions, Alan?" Frank asked. From behind, he put his hands on Alan's shoulders and kneaded them.

"Sure."

I let my fingertips graze Alan's arms and he took a deep breath. "From the looks of your amazing v-shaped torso I'd say you're a gymnast," I said. I began running my hands over his chest.

"Yeah. How'd you guess?" Alan had closed his eyes and had begun the heavy breathing of the sexually aroused.

"I've encountered your kind before. Your chest is bulging, Alan."

"Yeah, this shirt's bursting at the seams," Frank said. With that, we grabbed at Alan's shirt and ripped it off. Alan was only momentarily surprised.

Frank encircled Alan's waist with his right arm, while he tilted Alan's sweaty head back and browsed his neck, ear, and cheek with his tongue, leaving a glistening wetness in its wake. For the time being, I just watched my lover work Alan over. Frank's index finger played in and around Alan's belly button and it felt like he was playing with mine. I swallowed Alan whole with my eyes his washboard stomach, his smooth chest, his thick neck. I caressed my hot rod through my sweat pants and I grasped one of his pink nipples between thumb and forefinger and kneaded it. Frank bit his ear lobe and then plunged his tongue into his ear as far as it would go. The way the kid was fidgeting and moaning, you'd think he'd never had this kind of attention before. Well, maybe he hadn't.

I glanced down at Alan's crotch and saw that his pole was tenting out his gym shorts. "Why, Frank. He's giving us a salute." Then I leaned forward and began a tongue assault on the nipple I'd been kneading. It was good enough to eat, so I nibbled, too.

Frank reached down into Alan's gym shorts to caress the kid's hot and hard prick. His fingertips brushed the very tip of the kid's body. My hand was still rubbing my crotch. The pre-cum was getting my boxers wet. Knowing that the same thing was happening with Frank made me hotter. We got the same idea at the same time, Frank and I. I dropped to my knees and then we yanked Alan's shorts and underpants down. The kid's eight-inch, stout, pinkish pole snapped to attention, curving ever so slightly to the left. The hair at its base was a wavy light brown.

"You like?" Alan asked.

"We like," Frank and I said.

My lover rubbed and squeezed the kid's egg-shaped balls. I licked at the very tip with my tongue before taking the entire shaft into my mouth, releasing it and then licking my way up and down it. Alan yelped.

Frank said in almost a whisper, "He's got a pretty mouth, hasn't he? Fuck it, Alan. Fuck his mouth until your dick or his lips fall off, whichever comes first." He moved back and forth against the kid's body, which made Alan sway back and forth, too. His dick, dripping precum, moved in and out of my mouth, gently at first.

"I'm going to get you ready for me, boy," Frank said. I sucked harder because I knew that meant he was going to prime the kid with his fingers as he always did with me before he'd fuck me into oblivion. First, he'd stick his index finger into the kid's hole, then the second finger, then a third until the kid would start squealing.

"You like that, boy?" Frank asked.

247

The kid squealed in response. I'd have squealed, too, if my mouth hadn't been full of Alan's cock, which, miraculously, seemed to get bigger and harder the more I sucked on it. I looked up and saw Frank biting Alan's neck, leaving bluish-purplish marks. I knew they must hurt, but the kid didn't tell him to stop.

"Goddam, this butt was just made for fuckin'," Frank said.

"I'm gonna blow my load any second," Alan announced.

I re-focused my attention on the dick in my mouth and clasped his butt cheeks. I felt his legs tremble, his thighs shudder. I took my mouth off his throbbing tool a millisecond before it erupted and caught his creamy man milk in my hand as he cried out, "God help me! Oh my God!"

I stood up, satisfied that I had helped him to that sterling moment of melodrama. I offered him my hand and said, "Lap it up."

He licked my hand clean like a man starved. His legs gave way and he would have collapsed had Frank not held him up.

"We're not through yet," my lover cooed and made Alan bend over. I held onto him while Frank pulled down his work pants. I gasped at the sight of his nine and a half inches of thick, hard man meat. Alan was about to get a real treat. Frank took a tube of jelly out of his work shirt pocket and squeezed some into the kid's love canal. He replaced the tube and then, from the same pocket, took out a rubber. I opened the wrapping, threw it onto the floor, and then rolled it onto his cock. He grasped Alan's hips and then guided his stud plug into the kid's hot butt.

Frank said, "He's got a great hole, man."

I was breathing pretty heavily now, watching his dong disappear. "Yeah," was all I could say.

"Just fuck me," the kid said. "Please!"

As Frank started to slowly pump in and out of the kid's anal passage, I said, "I'm gonna give you something constructive to do, baby." I stepped out of my sweatpants and boxers. I was pleased to see Alan looking suitably awed at my massive member. It loomed in front of his face long and heavy, all nine and three-quarters inches of it. "C'mon, baby. Take as much of it as you want, all of it if you can."

The kid's mouth was like a vacuum pump, he sucked the thing in so hard. I told him not to choke himself, but I had nothing to worry about. The kid was a master at the sucking trade. He tongued all up and down my shaft, paying special attention to the veins that bulged out. He sucked just the tip, drawing more pre-cum out. Then he took it all in his mouth in one gulp.

When the tip of my cock bumped the back of his throat, it sent chills and thrills through me. Man, I loved getting sucked.

Minutes passed and the garage no longer smelled of oil and grime, but of sex and sweat. Fucking the kid's face reminded me of the first time I'd fucked Frank's face, what a rush it gave both of us. I wanted to be inside of my lover. I wanted to pump in and out of him like a piston in a fine-tuned engine. The sight of Frank picking up speed in Alan's ass and the sounds of his grunting and Alan's slurping and moaning over my cock made my cum-packed balls shrink into a tight wad that hugged the root of my prong. Frank and I looked into each other's eyes.

He said, "Man, this boy's no amateur. His fuckin' ass just grabs at my cock."

"No work for you, huh?" I said.

"Shit, no."

Frank bore down and began to thump harder. I could tell that with each journey his cock made into Alan's ass, his cock got closer to the kid's belly. The thoughts of past encounters and this present one flooded my mind and I couldn't hold back the explosion any longer. I felt my hard meat burst into an intense, red-hot flame. I yanked my rod out of Alan's mouth so I could shoot my curdled cream all over his face. All six shots landed on his cheeks, his chin, forehead, nose, in his mouth, and in his hair. Then I saw Frank shove his cock home, throw his head back, and roar. He was coming like crazy.

"Keep going," Alan pleaded. He reached down between his legs and began beating his meat.

Frank continued pounding his dick wrench into him. His eyes were locked on me as I slumped against the "Gullwing." Alan howled and emptied his dipstick again. His milky liquid splattered onto the garage floor. Frank pulled his cock out with a pop. He pushed a weak-kneed Alan over to me. As he walked toward us, he carefully pulled off the rubber, which was now filled with his juice. He dumped the rubber's contents onto the kid's bare, sweaty chest. Then we licked him clean. I knew Frank was as hungry for me as I was for him.

We left Alan sprawled against the car. I walked over to a chair and sat down. Frank, standing in front of me, reached down and milked my dick as if it were a cow's udder. Soon it became harder and bigger again. I felt like I was drugged, really high. Frank's cock still stood erect, smeared with cum, and delectable. He positioned his ass over my piston and slowly sat on it, taking it all into him. God, I loved invading him. He held firmly onto my shoulders, his head tilted back and eyes closed as he wiggled to make sure I was completely inside him. He began to plunge his asshole up and down on my dark, hard shaft. His pecker was plastered to his belly by a blob of cum. His balls bounced nicely on my hairless belly. My dick rammed into Frank to the tip and then back to the base, up and down, over and over. I didn't want it to end.

Frank's voice was hoarse when he said, "Fuck me, man. Fuck my ass good. I love it when you fuck my ass." He bucked his hips faster and faster. His knob welled up and white cum exploded from the tip, some of it finding its way onto my belly.

I couldn't stand it anymore, so I shot a load into Frank, whose pucker squeezed more juice from my throbbing fuck wrench. Some of my cream overflowed from Frank's bunghole and slithered down between my legs. Then my monster escaped from Frank's hole. He sank onto my lap and we sat like that, entwined on the chair, for a few silent moments. Finally, Alan, whom I'd forgotten about, said, "Hey, when you guys get your car fixed up, will you take me for a ride?"

Neither of us answered at first. Then Frank said, "No way, boy."

"Why not?" Alan demanded.

"Because, baby," I said, "it's only built for two."

The kid pulled his shorts back on and said, "Can I have a new T-shirt at least?"

"They're in the box by the door," Frank said.

Alan went to the box, picked one out, and put it on. "Thanks. My friends were right. They said you do some wicked extra body work and you really do!"

Chuckling, he left, leaving Frank and me alone again. We kissed deeply, our tongues probing the warm wetness of each other's mouth. Memories of our lives together and thoughts of the future more extra body work, more young men, more of each other made us take hold of each other's spark plugs. We started working a slow jack, our hands making squishy noises because of the cum on our cocks. More extra body work. Well, we deserved it.

A CRUDE DELIVERY
Corbin Chezner

Brock opened the bottom drawer of his desk and plucked out a whiskey bottle and shot glass. He seldom drank on the job, but after what the company had put him through today, he figured why the hell not? He poured the glass full and tossed down the brown liquid. As the liquor settled warm in his stomach, Brock sank back against his office chair and sighed. He looked up at the clock. 8:15 p.m. The Tulsa shipment was 15 minutes late already. He hoped it wasn't a sign of more trouble.

Today hadn't been as bad as he'd expected. Most of the truckers had been surprisingly understanding about the situation. Too shocked to react, he figured. Who'd ever dream, for God's sake, that someone would build a fueling station without a damn turnaround? He'd never be able to fathom how the company's engineers could have fucked up like this. Never! If he'd had his way, the new Corpus Christi refinery annex wouldn't have opened until they got the turnaround road built. But headquarters hadn't asked him, of course. No, those big-shots in Houston weren't about to ask him anything. Never mind that, as fueling supervisor, he was closest to the problem. One thing was for sure: the oil company wasn't about to lose even one day's precious production time. Not when they had Brock to take all the heat from irate truckers. He poured himself another drink and tossed it down. Combat pay. That's what he deserved.

At the crest of a hill 20 miles north of Corpus Christi, a fog bank suddenly drifted across the highway. "Damn!" Jake let off the accelerator and slammed the 18-wheeler into a lower gear. "I should have known we'd run into this down here."

"Think we'll make it in time?" his apprentice relief driver asked. Jake looked over at the young blond. Damn, Timmy was a good-lookin' son of a bitch. Too good lookin' to be drivin' a fuckin' truck. Jake had a mind to whack Timmy upside the head, but he didn't. Timmy was half Jake's age and eager to learn. Too damn eager. It made him nervous.

"What's the time?" Jake barked, raking blond hair away from his forehead.

Timmy glanced at his watch. "8:15 already." He met Jake's gaze wide-eyed. "We're past due, ain't we?" He blinked yellow lashes across aquamarine eyes.

"We still got time." Jake clamped down on the toothpick he kept in his mouth. The elements had been against them this trip. First the rainstorm in the Texas Hill Country. Now this. Maybe he'd been a fool to

251

take on the company's challenge. But the money had been more than Jake could resist. The company had offered a big bonus enough to cover Timmy's meager wages with a nice windfall left for him. All they had to do was deliver this load of crude oil and be back in Tulsa within 20 hours. At the moment it looked damn near impossible. Yet, if things began to fall into place now...

Jake took a deep breath and crossed his fingers.

So far, Timmy had been, well, cooperative, at least. Suddenly, Jake's balls began to tingle again. The tingling began every time Jake thought about the power he had over Timmy. It had continued off and on all the way from Tulsa.

Timmy must have felt the pressure too. If Jake gave him a poor report, he could crimp the little dude's career. For a while, at least. Damn, things had changed! Jake had come into the business the old way. He'd sucked the right dick, and found a trucker who had agreed to hire him as an apprentice. Not that the ones coming up now didn't suck dick! He smirked to himself. Difference was, nowadays the dick-sucking started in truck driving school. That's what Jake suspected, anyhow.

"Never been to Corpus," Timmy said suddenly.

"Yeah? Well, you won't see much of it tonight." Jake slammed the rig into a lower gear and pulled into an exit lane. "Nice town, though."

"How long will it take to unload?"

"Damn well better take no more 'n half an hour." Jake scratched his balls and looked over at him. "You need to whack off or something, better hurry it up." Timmy heard the chuckle erupt from his mouth, and then he felt his dick pulse. Damn! He had to get a grip on himself. He glanced sidelong at the trucker. He was one hot motherfucker, this Jake. Hot, like he'd always thought truckers ought to be. Timmy had been mesmerized by Jake's crotch all the way from Tulsa. The trucker had to have big balls and dick both. He had to, the way he filled out those Levis! Timmy admired Jake's powerful build, too. His shoulders were broader than half the cab, it seemed. His big arms were damn strong.

The whole trip, Timmy had been in awe of the way the trucker handled the rig. The way he'd grip the 18-wheeler's steering wheel like a vise. Timmy tried not to, but now and then he'd look down at his own slight 21-year-old build, afraid he couldn't measure up.

A tall, lean dude with a black beard stopped them at the gate. The name Brock was stenciled on the pocket of his blue work shirt. He held a clipboard in front of him and looked up at the cab. "Tulsa?" Jake nodded. "What's the chances of gettin' us outta here in half an hour?" As he gazed down at the good-looking stranger, Jake's dick pulsed again. "Got problems, I'm afraid," Brock said, shaking his head dourly. The black-haired dude grimaced and studied the pavement for a moment then met Jake's gaze again. "How so?"

"Two ahead of you, for one thing." Brock pointed toward the storage tanks.

"Damn!" Jake slammed his hand against the steering wheel. Then he looked back toward the storage tanks. Studying them for a few moments, he asked, "Where's the damn turnaround?" Brock fidgeted and looked away. "Ain't none."

"Excuse me?"

"Ain't' no turnaround. You'll have to back out to the highway when you're through."

"I must be hearin' wrong." Jake shook his head, as if to loosen cobwebs. He looked over at Timmy and then back at the bearded stranger, Brock.

"You heard right," Brock said, grimacing again, "This annex was built without a turnaround road."

"What the fuck?"

"Might as well come inside. Have a slug of whiskey."

"We're due back in Tulsa by 6 a.m. !"

"Won't do you no good to lose your cool. C'mon inside. Shoot the shit for a while." Jake pounded his fists into the steering wheel again. "Damn! Motherfucker! Piss, shit, fuck!" Finally, he sighed and rested his head against the steering wheel for a moment. "Go on inside, Timmy," he said finally. "I'll handle the unloading."

Inside the office, Brock introduced himself to Timmy. Jesus! Brock was as hot as Jake, Timmy thought. But hot in a way that was different. Timmy's queer friends in Tulsa thought him weird when he let on that he preferred older dudes of, say, 35 or 40. "Lookin' for a daddy?" they'd tease. He didn't bother trying to explain to them that, in his opinion, a man didn't come into his own until he was 35 or so.

What could he say? In his mind, a man looked...well, manlier once he'd reached that age. Pretty young men were a dime a dozen and left his dick limp. Rugged men turned him on. When he shook hands with Brock, Timmy's dick pulsed again like it had been doing with Jake. He averted his eyes. Could the dude tell?

Brock walked over to a desk and brought out the whiskey bottle and two shot glasses. He slammed the glasses against the top of the desk and poured both full. He handed one to Timmy. "Here. This'll warm up your gut for the trip back." He tossed down his own drink.

Timmy wasn't used to the hard stuff. But he didn't want to let on. His dick pulsed again, and that made him nervous. He arched his head toward the ceiling and gulped down the liquor. Within seconds, his stomach was on fire. He tried not to, but finally he had to cough. Brock laughed.

As the liquor spread to his stomach, Timmy grew to like the warm glow it gave him. The lean, bearded fueling supervisor leaned toward Timmy, probing the blond with his brown eyes. "Damn if the burn of whiskey don't make my dick hard!" Laughing, he grasped his cock for emphasis. The dick outlined through Brock' s denim uniform confirmed Timmy's suspicions. The cock was long and thick, a fine fit for the dude's physique. "A young stud like you must get horny on the road." Fondling his crotch again, Brock's gaze met his. A wicked grin spread across his face. He had Timmy pegged, and Timmy knew it. Timmy fidgeted and looked toward the doorway. Brock snickered. "Worried about your boss?"

"Wel..." Timmy fidgeted, leaning on one foot and then the other. A thin sweat broke on his forehead. "You mean to tell me he ain't been in your pants yet?"

"Huh?" Timmy was wringing his hands now. "He's...Jake is married." Brock arched his head toward the ceiling and roared with laughter. "Hell, that don't mean nothin'." The next thing Timmy knew his jeans were down at his ankles and Brock had him bent over the desk. The older dude leaned against him, probing his hard cock between Timmy's legs. Timmy was on fire. Suddenly, Brock's tongue slithered inside his ear, and a wave of pleasure shot through Timmy's body as Brock tickled his neck with his black beard. Timmy heard himself moan, and Brock spat in his own hand and stuck his index finger into Timmy's ass.

Timmy couldn't quite believe it when he heard himself begging: "Give me your cock. Please!"

At that, Brock spat on his dick and he continued loosening Timmy's hole with his finger. Finally, he directed his fiery pole inside. Timmy flinched and gasped as Brock's cock stabbed at his insides. Brock held his dick steady, giving Timmy time to adjust. Timmy steadied himself by grasping the edges of the desk. Brock leaned forward again and thrust his tongue inside Timmy's ear.

"Oh, man! Fuck me!" Timmy pleaded. "Fuck the livin' shit outta me!"

Finally, Timmy gasped again as his sphincter capitulated to Brock's big dick. Brock pushed all the way in. The tip of Brock's cock massaged Timmy's prostate, and once again Timmy gasped, this time with pleasure. He was floating in space now, higher than he'd been in a long time. He could only moan and mutter. "Do it! More!"

"You're gonna get all my cock now, little dude," Brock managed breathlessly. He dug his fingers into Timmy's waist and increased his thrusts. Brock plunged his throbbing pole all the way in until his pubic hair tickled Timmy's butt. "Oh, yeah, you got it all now."

Then he retreated until the head of his cock kissed the fiery opening to Timmy's hole. He hesitated so he could hear Timmy beg for more.

"Don't stop, man," Timmy heard himself plead. "Please, don't stop."

That turned Brock on even more. He started again, faster and harder now. In and out. Out and in. Long, experienced, manly thrusts.

Timmy thrashed his face against the top of the desk. Finally, Brock arched his back and squeezed Timmy's waist tight. He gasped, "Oh, mother-fuck!" as he jerked his hot load of cum deep inside Timmy's quivering hole.

An instant later, Timmy gave in, too. He slammed his own load against the side of the metal desk, where it dripped onto the floor. Timmy and Brock wiped themselves clean with paper towels from the bathroom. A couple of minutes later, Jake stomped in, still seething from his bad run of luck. As Jake and Brock sat filling out the paperwork for the delivery, Timmy looked on, worried that his boss might be on to them. Several times Timmy thought he saw Jake's nostrils flare, like he could smell cum or something. Timmy decided he'd play innocent, no matter what.

Finally, Jake asked him to go unhook the truck from the storage tank so they could start the trip back.

Jake kept watching Timmy out of the corner of his eye. Or that's the way it seemed to Timmy, anyhow. Finally, around 1 a.m. Jake pulled the rig off the interstate into a rest stop.

"Pit stop?" Timmy asked sleepily.

"I need to piss," Jake said. "And then I have some other business to take care of."

"What?" Jake looked over at Timmy. "Before we get back to Tulsa, I gotta have me a taste of that young prick of yours."

Timmy started to say something, but he stopped himself. What could he say? More room would have been nice, but Jake and Timmy made do in the 18-wheeler's sleeping quarters.

The way Jake hesitated when he went down on Timmy made the young blond think Jake had never sucked dick before. But it didn't take Jake long to get into sucking. After a while, Timmy pulled Jake's head away from his cock and went down on the trucker himself. Jake pulled Timmy's head to the base of his cock; he leaned against the corner of the cab and moaned. After a spell, he muttered, "I want your cock."

Timmy thought Jake wanted to 69, but when Timmy started to maneuver into that position, Jake stopped him. "No, not that. I want your cock inside me."

Hearing the married hunk wanted to be fucked startled Timmy but it also made the young dude's dick rock hard. Timmy could fuck or be fucked it didn't make a whole lot of difference to him. For sure, nobody had to ask Timmy twice.

It took Jake time to adjust to a dick up his butt, but once he did he went wild. He pulled his meaty legs tight against his brawny upper torso, planting the soles of his feet against the ceiling of the cab. "Give me your cock, dude," he hissed. "Push your meat all the way in me."

Timmy complied willingly, plowing the full length of his eight-inch cock into Jake's spasming butthole. When he was as deep inside Jake's hole as he could go, Timmy hesitated for a moment.

Jake dug his fingers into Timmy back and begged for more. "Fuck me harder! Faster!" Timmy resumed thrusting then. All the way in. Then out again. Faster. Harder. Jake thrashed underneath his young relief driver. "Give it to me, Timmy. Feed me your cum."

Finally, Timmy lunged hard as he could into Jake, so forceful that his cock exploded inside the truck driver's ass. He arched his head back and hissed, "Motherfuck!" Then Jake let loose, squirting a load of thick cream that landed like lumps of white gravy across his beefy upper torso.

"You gonna give me a good write-up?" Timmy asked Jake as they pulled into the truck yard early that morning. "Depends." "What do you mean?"

"You take on as my relief driver permanent, you get the best damn write up you could ask for. Otherwise, well...."

He looked over at Timmy and smiled wryly.

Timmy shrugged and returned the smile. "Fine with me."

About the Editor

JOHN PATRICK was a prolific, prize-winning author of fiction and non-fiction. One of his short stories, "The Well," was honored by PEN American Center as one of the best of 1987. His novels and anthologies, as well as his non-fiction works, including Legends and The Best of the Superstars series, continue to gain him new fans every day. One of his most famous short stories appears in the Badboy collection Southern Comfort and another appears in the collection The Mammoth Book of Gay Short Stories.

A divorced father of two, the author was a longtime member of the American Booksellers Association, the Publishing Triangle, the Florida Publishers' Association, American Civil Liberties Union, and the Adult Video Association. He lived in Florida, where he passed away on October 31, 2001.

ng any underwear. "Excuse me," I said, having a hard time looking
ed by that bulge in his crotch, "but don't I know you?" "Maybe," l
of te   bout a m
Ray   God, you
er?   in?" he a
"Lik   s stronges
ody   e on Gree
he l   I ever sa
to t   any ideas
:ing   ne same
:oul   ery long t
rac   ne swell.
with   e in store
go c   behind s
ee u   in public
" he   went to the
cy.   grabbed a
d. I
rac   t, so firm
:, ha
1 m   bing dick
g, I   n cock, be
ound of unzipping filled the small space. I don't know who's hand
before I knew it, I had his rod in my hand, and mine was in his. "
do?" he asked, his tone challenging. I knew exactly, and sank to r